Love in Los Angeles

Starling, Book 1
Doves, Book 2
Phoenix, Book 3

By Racheline Maltese and Erin McRae

Avian30
New York, New York
2018

Avian30
New York, New York
ISBN: 978-1-946192-10-3
www.Avian30.com

Starling by Erin McRae and Racheline Maltese
Previously published by Torquere Press, 2014 and Avian30, 2017

Doves by Erin McRae and Racheline Maltese
Previously published by Torquere Press, 2015 and Avian30, 2017

Phoenix by Erin McRae and Racheline Maltese
Previously published by Torquere Press, 2015 and Avian30, 2017

First Avian30 Printing: November 2018
Printed in the USA

Starling

Love in Los Angeles Book 1

1

After yet another fight with his boyfriend about work-life balance, Paul Marion Keane gets to the small suite of offices that belongs to the writing team of hit TV show *The Fourth Estate*. At seven thirty the lights are still off.

Between the fight with Craig and a stack of notes to go through on an episode that isn't even his, Paul is grateful for the time alone. He's got a pitch for a plotline to work on too, but suspects it will wind up relegated to a C-plot.

He punches the lights on, drops his bag on his desk, and walks into the kitchenette for a cup of terrible coffee. At which point his already unpleasant morning becomes ridiculous. Their intern Nick and some unidentified boy are making out against the counter in front of the damn coffee machine.

Paul reaches around them to grab a mug out of the cabinet. "Seriously, what the fuck?"

Nick unsuctions himself from his companion and turns around sheepishly. He's trying to shield the other guy, but he's taller than Nick so it's not very effective. The other guy is also startling in appearance: Red hair, dramatically freckled face, and ridiculously plump lips. Paul can't help but focus on him despite Nick's fidgeting.

"We didn't think anyone would be here," Nick says.

"Obviously." Paul shoves into their space to grab the carafe out of the coffee maker. "When you get caught making out with someone at work, apologize first."

Nick backs up nervously, but the other guy slides down the counter as if this absurd turn of events is merely mildly interesting.

"Also, start the coffee if you're the first one in." Paul isn't sure what to do. His emotional spoons are low and yelling seems like the best choice. "Don't you have homes, either of you?"

"He didn't want his roommates to know," Mr. Unidentified says. He blinks at Paul mildly.

"And who are you?" Paul asks.

"Production assistant."

"Right," Paul turns the sink on to fill the carafe. "Should have known from the hideous cargo shorts. Do you have a name?"

Unperturbed by the insult to his wardrobe, he grins. "Alex."

"Nice to meet you," Paul says grudgingly, but doesn't extend a hand. Under the circumstances there's only so much courtesy he can muster. "Nick, go do something useful." Despite everything, Paul can't help but smile when Nick reaches for Alex's hand and give a little squeeze before bolting.

Alex hoists himself up to perch on the counter. "I'm sorry he's —"

"A giant fucking closet case and completely dysfunctional?" Paul pours the water into the coffeemaker and shoves the carafe back in with more force than necessary. He hopes the anger hides how intensely pathetic he feels today. "Yes, thank you, and welcome to Hollywood."

"I've been here for two years," Alex notes.

"Whatever."

"Bad morning?"

Paul cocks his head to the side and considers the question. First Craig stormed out this morning and now these two? He's reminded of his mother's insistence that he's the luckiest man she knows–not good lucky or bad lucky, just *weird* lucky.

"Strange morning, as far as it's your business," he finally replies.

Alex blinks back at him.

"Piece of advice: Don't screw idiots who aren't out and have your next tryst in a different department, okay?"

Alex nods. "Yeah. No problem." He slides down from the counter. "Although, that's two," he says as he saunters out. "Hope your day gets better."

Paul shakes his head and laughs. "Yeah, you too."

When Alex is gone, Paul sighs. He has no energy for this, and Nick is an idiot with whom he should probably go have a heartfelt and sympathetic conversation.

◆

Despite the aborted morning makeout, Alex's day doesn't get truly weird until after the cast and crew of *The Fourth Estate* break for lunch. The assistant director tells him to pop over to wardrobe when he's done.

"The hell?" Alex asks around a mouthful of chicken and rice.

"It's another paycheck," Gary says in lieu of explaining.

Alex swallows. "Awesome. Explain." Too many pranks happen on sets for him not to want the full story.

"We've got a line that references a specific type. Because we occasionally work with morons, the background selection is inadequate, and you're today's lucky winner."

Alex sets down his fork. "Neat. How big's the check?"

◆

Alex only becomes clear on what he's gotten into when he gets back to set in skintight jeans and a shirt he would never wear. His buddies on the crew start ribbing him immediately. They only eventually shut up because there's work to be done. But the hundred extra bucks to do a cross and react to one of the principals reacting to him is hard to argue with no matter how many times he'd almost gotten his balls caught in the zipper back in wardrobe.

The backstage spirit that permeates *The Fourth Estate's* narrative isn't that different from the atmosphere that permeates Alex's working life behind the scenes of the show. The dramas of a ruthless, dysfunctional, crack team of reporters differ only in degree from the bullshit of a set for a highly rated nighttime TV drama. The problem isn't even *Fourth*; it's that L.A. people work long hours, are casually cruel, and relentlessly judgmental.

No one tells him is that the line meant to reference him is *Who's the twink?* Alex isn't supposed to engage with the line so the words aren't supposed to matter to him. But when Liam (who plays James, a former field reporter turned anchor) tosses it to Natalie (Marjani, James's co-anchor, ex-lover, and frequent rival) after the cross, Alex can't help but retort. Because *not likely*.

He realizes his mistake immediately but waits until they call cut before he puts a hand to his mouth to apologize. He's been on sets long enough to know better. "Sorry, sorry, I know...I'm sorry –"

"No." A voice drawls the word loudly from somewhere behind the monitors.

The objection belongs to Victor, their showrunner. Alex wants to fall through the floor. Among other things, he would really like this day's double paycheck situation not to end in no paychecks.

"I am so –"

"Shhhhhhh." The shushing sound reminds Alex of a snake. "Keep doing exactly what you're doing," Victor says.

They reset the scene and go again. This time, when Alex retorts, Liam – James – breaks off from the cross to get in his face. They start bantering. Alex has always had a retort for everything, and there's no reason for that to change now that there's a camera on him.

Alex isn't sure if Liam's words are angry or flirtatious – or quite how in character any of this is – but Liam's attentive blue eyes keep him anchored in the strange moment. In Alex's peripheral vision Victor holds up his hand and makes a looping motion. *Keep going.* Alex doesn't know if it's meant for him or Liam or the camera operator. He keeps talking.

They do several takes. Alex keeps wondering if this is what happens when you're dead: Your life, exactly as you've always known it, turned on its ear and set in endless repetition.

Between the third take and what's apparently going to be a fourth, Victor points to him and suggests he join him in his office when he's done.

Alex nods. You don't say no to Victor Salcido Santillan. Ever.

Even when you really, really want to. Although, in this moment, Alex is not sure he does. He's just been effectively given a line. Or several. And that could mean far more than a hundred bucks. It could mean this month's rent, although only because he lives in a shithole apartment with a roommate. But he still thinks he might be in trouble.

"We're going again," Gary shouts as Alex rubs his sweaty palms all over the pants the wardrobe department provided.

Everyone resets as Victor walks away. As he goes, he calls out fondly to Alex over his shoulder, "Don't ever wear cargo shorts again".

Alex stands there feeling lost and cursed.

"It's okay," Liam says, with a glance towards the departing Victor. "Everything's going to be great."

♦

At midnight Alex finally pulls his car into the little parking lot behind his apartment building. He takes one last moment for himself, wrapping his hands around the steering wheel and taking a deep breath before he gets out.

There's a flight of stairs, narrow and poorly lit, that leads up to the apartment. Alex fumbles for a moment to find the right keys to unlock the multiple latches on the door. Inside, all is the same as ever – ratty couch, rattier chair, milk crate coffee table, and his roommate curled up in pajamas.

"What happened to you?" she demands when he shoves the door closed behind him and drops his keys back in his bag. "You look terrible."

"Thanks, Gem." Alex closes his eyes and wishes for more time to let the bizarre events of the day settle in. "Why are you still awake?"

"You didn't answer your phone. I was worried."

Alex opens his eyes and looks at her. "You waited up for me?" Her concern is still something he's getting used to. Back home in high school in Indiana, Alex came and went as he pleased.

Gemma is perched on their lumpy, faded couch. She's wearing her grey pajamas covered in angry clouds and her chin-length black hair is pulled back into two uneven pigtails. Her laptop is open in front of her.

"Don't you have an audition tomorrow morning?" Alex asks.

"It got cancelled." She turns her attention back to her computer. Her voice is the dangerous kind of controlled. Alex asks nothing more, lest he walk further into that minefield.

"Which you would have known if you'd picked up your phone," she goes on. "Where were you?"

Alex digs his phone out to check the alerts. Sure enough – three missed calls, including one from Nick, though that can wait. "I was at work."

"Until midnight?"

"Do you not pay attention to anything I do?" Crew days are long. Longer than actor days, which Gemma should know. Sure, Alex is usually done much earlier than this, but erratic hours are hardly unexpected in either of their lives.

"You look like shit," Gemma says bluntly.

"It's been a long day, okay?"

"Take your shoes off. There are leftovers in the fridge if you're hungry." She turns her attention back to her laptop.

"Thanks, Mom," Alex mutters on his way to the kitchen.

"I heard that!" Gemma yells. Alex hums to himself as he crouches in front of the fridge to examine the leftover options.

"Work was weird," Alex says when he's finally seated across from her in their ratty armchair, a plate on his lap. The paint on the wall behind Gemma is chipping. The lamp beside her, that they picked up from the curb one trash day, makes the cracks stand out more visibly than they do in the daytime.

"What happened?" Gemma shuts the laptop, hugs it to her chest, and waits for him to find words to answer.

Alex is grateful. He's spent plenty of time training her to be quiet when he needs her to be. "Do you want to go out to dinner this weekend?" he asks. Bribery seems like the safest tactic to hand.

She looks skeptical. "A roommate date?"

"Totally. We can get tacos. Or sushi! Or anything you want."

"Alex," she says warily. "I know you like to do the cagey thing when stuff's happening, but can you talk to me?"

He looks at her over a mouthful of warmed-up rice and tries to be the picture of innocence. "Mmm?"

"What's going on?"

He swallows. "I was an idiot at work and instead of firing me Victor offered me a part." The words come too quick, but they're terrifying.

"A part in what?" She frowns.

"*Fourth Estate.*"

Her mouth opens a little. "But you're a P.A," Gemma says slowly.

"Yes."

"You're not an actor."

"No."

"How did that happen?"

Alex sets his plate down on the milk crate stack passing for a coffee table, crosses his legs and curls up into the chair. He can hardly explain any of this to himself. None of it feels real yet, and there's a frightening ominousness to this kind of unknown.

"I told you," he finally says. "Weird fucking day."

"What kind of part?" Gemma demands. "None of this is making any sense. Like at all."

"I don't know." That, in fact, is a lie. But if he tells Gemma about the series of stepping stones Victor put in front of him – including a chance to be a principal in the magic world where it all works out and he comes back next year – he's both afraid that he'll jinx it and that Gemma will murder him in his sleep. "They're still working out the details."

"Are you going to do it?"

"I don't know."

"What!" Gemma shrieks.

Alex jumps. He's used to her volume but the explosions still catch him off guard.

"What do you mean you don't know?!"

He stretches a leg out and curls his toes against the edge of the milk crates. "I'm a P.A."

"Who just got offered a part on a major network's Thursday night anchor!"

"Yes."

"Why would you say no?"

Alex thunks his head against the back of the chair. "God, Gemma, do you really want the list?"

"*Yes.*"

"It's long," he warns.

"I've got all night. It's not like there's anywhere I have to be tomorrow."

Beyond his own reasonable fear and unreasonable guilt, Alex feels genuine sorrow for her. Auditions may be a dime a dozen in this city, but it can take thousands of them for any one person to reach their dreams. "I'm sorry," he says sincerely.

"It's not your fault."

Alex knows that's a hard kindness for her to offer, but Gemma is an extraordinarily good friend even if, or perhaps because, they met on the internet. They've been in this together ever since they moved to L.A. after high school graduation with little more than their love of stories. But Gemma is the one who wants to be a star. Alex has always wanted to make movie magic, but he's never wanted to be it.

Their apartment is the worst sort of shithole, but it has locks that work and a landlord who doesn't care that they're still occasionally, if increasingly rarely, unemployed kids. Compared to the welfare cheese of his upbringing, it's at least an adventure.

Gemma, as is her narrative destiny, has a waitressing gig and is registered as a nonunion extra at Central Casting. Alex signed up for the city's film and TV internship program as soon as he got here. It had cost him nothing and also paid him nothing, but there was a real job on the other side of it. As a P.A. he's been hired, or not, on a day-to-day basis since. It's not secure, but then, nothing for him ever has been.

"I don't even know if this is going to happen," he finally says. "There are a lot of factors in play. If I even start this process the rest of the crew is going to hate me. I'm not sure the cast is going to be thrilled either. You should have seen the look Natalie gave me. And even if it was going to happen for sure, I did not come to Hollywood to be in front of the cameras. I don't know if I can do this."

Good things like this don't just get handed to him. Anything Alex has, he's gotten because he decided he wanted it, figured out how to get it, and then put in whatever work was required to secure it. He trusts the results of his own efforts; he doesn't trust other people. A prize that comes with risks he hasn't even begun to calculate could be all sorts of dangerous. And Alex hasn't survived by not calculating his risks.

"Obviously you can, if they offered you this."

"I don't know if I want to," Alex says slowly for what feels like the thousandth time. He doesn't know how to explain his innate reluctance to someone who wants so badly what he's been handed. "They didn't pull me because of what I can do. They pulled me because I look like a twink."

"You are a twink."

"I'm not –"

"You are skinny, vaguely hairless, and young."

"Gemma," Alex protests. She may not be wrong, but getting slapped with labels she knows mostly from gay porn is completely awful. Where Alex comes from, getting labelled like that gets people beat up. Or worse.

Gemma is unconcerned with his discomfort. "Seriously, though. What happened?"

Alex stabs his fork into his rice. "They needed a certain type in background for James to rag on. Apparently even the fucking T-shirt and clipboard do not save me from resembling that particular type."

Gemma considers that for a moment. "Okay, I get that's not a typical reason to have something good happen to you, but do you know what it's like being *Gemma Hyong* in this town?"

Alex shakes his head.

"It closes a lot of doors."

"You had an audition last week," Alex says, trying to be encouraging.

"Yeah, to be a sex trafficking victim. Again. And I didn't get it, again, because my tits are too small. The doors that open for me are horrible. But they're still doors. Other people walk through them all the time."

"Yeah," Alex says cautiously. "Not like this."

"Right, explain to me how being called a twink turns into a part?"

Alex sighs. If he'd kept his mouth shut, he could have avoided this whole thing. "It pissed me off, the line. So I said something back, on camera, and Liam decided it was a great time to test my improv skills."

"What did you say?"

Alex scowls. "I don't know, Gemma. Tune in and find out while I hide under my bed with the tequila. Jesus." He tucks his knees up as close to his chest.

"Sorry," she says, although she doesn't sound like she remotely means it. "But I still don't understand."

"Victor called me up to his office after for a very long, very scary chat. He liked the moment, thought there was room for a new character on the show, and thinks, maybe – since he couldn't take his eyes off me and neither could anyone else – that it should be me."

Gemma is silent for a whole five seconds at that. "Alex, that's incredible."

"Victor is crazy."

"Victor is legendarily crazy," she corrects. She reels off Victor's back catalogue of shows in syndication along with their associated network battles from when they were in production. "But he's the best. And the people he writes are so real. You can't say no. Like, fame and money and I hate you, but art," Gemma finishes softly.

Alex mostly ignores her. Listening is way too scary right now. "What if I want to say no?"

"You don't want to."

"You don't know that!"

"Alex, you can't say no. You'll be a star! You'll be able to afford your rent! You can get cuter jeans!"

"My jeans are fine," he snaps. Saying yes for such reasons seems inherently dreadful, even if the prospect of reliably making rent is appealing.

"Your jeans are atrocious. You can get a car that works! You're Marilyn Monroe, you don't say no."

Alex sets his plate down on the milk crate. He's not hungry anymore. "Marilyn Monroe is dead."

"AND FAMOUS. DEAD AND FAMOUS, ALEX, YOU DON'T SAY NO."

Alex laughs. Gemma is actively absurd, but she's also a little frightening right now.

"I'm thinking about it," he finally says, because he is, even if not for any of the reasons Gemma is telling him to. But for all his hesitation, his instincts are telling him to do this. Alex trusts his instincts, even if he doesn't know what's going to come of all this. Besides, she's not going to stop being scary unless he assures her he's already working towards yes.

2

The house is dark when Paul pulls into the driveway. Craig's car isn't in the garage.

"Hello?" he calls when he gets in the door. There's no response, and he doesn't know whether he should have expected one. Todd, his white and tabby hodgepodge of a cat, comes trotting down the stairs and rubs against his legs. But there's no excited bark from Beau or greeting, however grudging, shouted from Craig.

Paul flicks on the lights as he makes his way to the kitchen. Todd follows, mewing piteously at his heels as if everything in the world is terrible and it's all Paul's fault. The cat isn't wrong.

There's a note on the counter written on the notepad they use for grocery lists. Craig's handwriting is neat.

I'm staying at Tara's tonight. I'll come back to get my stuff while you're at work. So pretty much anytime this week. Don't call.

P.S. Beau's with me. Good luck with the damn cat.

Paul reads the note twice, then balls it up and throws it across the room. It's not a remotely satisfying gesture.

Todd yowls his displeasure at being ignored. Paul sighs as the house settles with a creak around him. His boyfriend left and took his dog. It's an awful country song.

Paul fills Todd's food bowl and changes his water. He leaves his bag on the counter before he heads upstairs. He's not sure if he can sleep alone in the bed tonight, but he's perfectly sure he can cry in the shower.

◆

By the morning, Paul's grief is less about Craig – things had been messed up between them for a while and his schedule was probably the least of it – and more about the eerie quiet of the house. Being single has always leant him an unsettling feeling of isolation. It's stupid and unhealthy, but Paul loves being in love, and now it's down to him and the cat. Todd is awesome, but he's always been a mercenary sort of cat, more interested in food than laps.

"Maybe I can learn something from you, buddy," he says, patting the animal's side as he puts his bowl down.

Todd meows happily, and Paul zones out on watching him eat for a minute. He does this thing where he squeezes his eyes shut as he crunches his food that Paul finds stupidly adorable.

He sighs. His life is suffocating, and he can't imagine it's going to get better anytime soon.

◆

Paul knows he's right when he gets to work and finds Alex sitting on his desk, a most Los Angeles sort of changeling. Somehow, he's not surprised, even though there's little interesting or appealing about the office itself. Like all the other backstage spaces for *Fourth*, and indeed the rest of Hollywood, it's drab and involves a lot of fluorescent light and dingy white walls in need of a good scrubbing. The once-expensive but now decrepit and mismatched ergonomic chairs don't make it any cheerier.

"No sign of Nick?" Paul drops his things down like Alex isn't there. Maybe he's not. Maybe he's simply a ghost of yesterday's disasters.

Alex levers himself off the desk and follows Paul into the kitchenette. "I'm not here for Nick."

"I sure hope you aren't here for me, because let me tell you, I am some bad company right now."

"I'm hiding from Victor."

"Oh. Well. Aren't we all?" Paul says amiably as he rummages around in the tiny refrigerator for some juice that isn't the wrong type of furry. He doesn't mean it. He likes Victor more than most of his crew does. Paul doesn't mind the demands he makes of the people he's deemed worthy of his attention. Even the extent to which Victor tends to interfere with those people's lives doesn't really bother him anymore.

Alex leans against the doorframe but doesn't say anything.

"Why're you dressed up?" Paul asks. Not that he knows Alex's personal style choices, but cargo shorts and nerd T-shirts are the uniform of the P.A. unless it's cold enough for flannel. Certainly, it's what Alex was wearing yesterday. But today he's in tight, dark green cords with a long-sleeved and very fitted gray V-neck. "Are you about to quit?"

Paul watches Alex ponder the question. He looks pained.

"I don't know."

Paul gives up on the contents of the fridge and shoves the door closed with his hip before leaning back against it. "What is your deal?"

Alex ignores the question. "If you were offered an opportunity to do something you never wanted to do but maybe only because you never knew you could, and it would change your life – like in ways everyone fantasizes about but no one can really imagine – would you do it? Even if the offer was because of something stupid?"

"I'm going to go with yes. Granted, I don't know you or what the hell you're talking about, and my partner walked out on me yesterday and took the dog, so I might not be your best source of advice right now."

Alex's eyes widen comically. "Oh wow, your day did not get

better."

Paul surprises himself with his own laughter. "No. No, it really didn't. Although that mess started before you cursed me with your well-wishes, so don't get cocky." He pauses. "What about yours?"

Alex shakes his head, and that startled look returns. Paul knows he's an asshole for finding it appealing.

"I don't know yet," Alex says. Then, having seemingly found whatever he was looking for, he's out the door.

Uncertain what to do in the face of that abruptness, Paul yells after him. "I'll give your regards to Nick!"

Alex doesn't respond.

◆

Alex's life becomes frightening and disorienting. That, it seems, is how fairytales work.

There are meetings and more meetings, screen tests, and all manner of awkward conversations. These mostly involve people Alex had been happy to avoid in what he's now starting to think of as his former life as a P.A.

Victor offers him a temporary gig in the production offices to shelter him from the worst of trying to do his usual job in the sea of interruptions and vanity the process becomes. When Alex says no, that he'll deal with whatever shit he gets from the crew for his sudden and possibly imminent change in circumstance, Victor nods with satisfaction. Alex suspects he has passed a test he didn't know he was taking.

He changes his clothes in the studio bathroom between work and meetings. It's a practicality but also deeply strange. Every time he walks back out the door he feels different than when he walked in.

Alex wonders if this process is supposed to teach him how to act.

◆

"We're adding a character," Victor tells Paul late one night when the writers' room is otherwise empty. Everyone else apparently has some semblance of a life. "That P.A. we pulled from the background shot. Alex Cook. Now Zach Reagan, junior reporter. New kid on the team. Young, but smart and hungry."

"Yeah?" Paul looks up from his notes. There have been rumblings, but coming from Victor like this means opportunity. It also explains some things about Alex, who Paul's been seeing around more and more in less and less explicable circumstances. No wonder his eyes are always so wide.

"Yeah," Victor confirms, but his tone is mocking. "And he's not going to be minor. So, if you want to pitch something that's not cleanup on everyone else, this is your chance, because I'm going to make you fix the rest of the cycle."

"Okay." Paul takes a breath and has ideas already. "Thank you." This is a vote of confidence and a reward for years of doing the shit work.

"You should know," Victor says, in the thoughtful voice that means he's plotting something. "He looks like a delicate little thing, but he's very much not."

"Zach?" Paul asks. "Or Alex?"

Victor just smiles. "Show me what you've got on Monday."

◆

Paul comes up with his first pitch over a weekend alone in the house, in sweatpants with the stereo cranked up. Todd protests the throbbing bass with narrowed eyes every time Paul paces in front of his chair.

On Monday Victor looks at what he has and tells him to make it happen.

Paul practically careens out of Victor's office to track Alex down wherever he might be skulking about the studios this time.

"Walk with me," he says when he's found him in an empty office, flipping through some papers. He's wanted to do that since he fell in love with *The West Wing* as a kid.

Alex gathers up his papers and goes with Paul. He's quiet, but Paul isn't surprised. In each of their strange and brief interactions Alex has used surprisingly few words while being a surprisingly massive presence.

Paul leads them through the maze of corridors, picking a route where they're unlikely to run into other writers. Or Victor. He watches the way Alex moves beside him, to understand his body and his secrets and where he hides his tension. "Victor decided it's my job to figure out who he thinks you are when you're Zach," he says eventually. "So I need you to talk to me, about anything, I don't care what. I just need to understand the rhythm of your voice."

"I don't have the job yet," Alex says.

"Victor asked me to rebuild the rest of the season around the introduction of your character." Paul feels sick as he says it. He doesn't know if he has permission to reveal this secret, even to its subject. He also doesn't know why Victor made him the messenger.

Alex doesn't react to the news. "Zach isn't me," he eventually says.

"Really? It wasn't you who was pissed off at one very choice word?"

"Can we consider that overlap aberrant?" Alex asks.

"No," Paul says thoughtfully.

"Why not?"

"Because you're twenty, don't like to talk, and tossed the word *aberrant* at me."

"So?"

"So that's interesting."

Alex makes a noise under his breath that sounds faintly like a cat hissing. "You're as bad as Victor."

Paul smiles. "Thanks for the compliment, but no. Talk to me?" He tells himself the query is about research and not his own growing interest. Or that outside of Victor the only person he's talked to in days is his cat.

"About what?" Alex looks surprised but not annoyed at Paul's persistence, which is a relief. Scaring the kid off wouldn't do anyone any favors.

"Seen any good TV lately?"

Alex stops walking to stare at him. Paul stamps down his own excitement at the attention.

Alex's eyes, a brown so dark they're almost black, fix on Paul's face. "You're an asshole."

"So are you."

Alex laughs, sudden and sharp. After a beat, he shakes his head. "I have to go."

As he walks down the corridor he gives Paul a look over his shoulder, part wary, part challenge. Paul takes a deep breath and reminds himself firmly not to be an idiot, lest he go after Alex the way he so badly wants to. He suspects the impulse is self-destructive. Any interest in Alex on his part is inappropriate. Just because he wants a challenge doesn't mean he should inflict that desire on anyone else.

Stars have to make the first move. That's how Hollywood works. Paul makes his way back to his office. At least he has a better sense of who and what Zach can be now.

3

Alex signs the papers. He tries to read all of them first and fails, not because it's hard, but because it's boring. He worries a little bit for his soul as he scratches a pen, not fine enough for the occasion, over page after page of agreements. Victor looms from behind his desk. A network executive stand at his side. When it's all over, they both shake his hand.

As far as the union is concerned he's J. Alex Cook. There was already an Alex Cook and an Alexander Cook, and the thought of being called Jasper, as his mother named him, in *TV Guide* is more absurd than he can reasonably handle.

Work begins immediately.

Six weeks later, in the first week of September, the episode with the unintentional repartee airs. Gemma watches it and cackles loudly enough for Alex to hear from his bedroom, where he's got headphones jammed on while he goes over his lines for the next day.

Three weeks after that, Zach gets his first plot. From there everything goes crazy.

Somehow, it all harks back to that first line from Liam. The fans who always wanted James to be gay suddenly have someone for him to be gay with, which is infuriating. The actual point of that moment was that James is an asshole who doesn't view other people as real. But now that corner of the world wants a romance.

The ridiculousness manages to spread to the rest of the audience in part because Liam plays it up on his social media in a way that leads to the appallingly offensive #WhosTheTwink hashtag. Gemma sends him the link, and Alex makes the mistake of looking at it between scenes at work. He proceeds to flip out until Victor, who seems to be everywhere these days, asks him why he cares.

"You're gay, you're young, and you're beautiful, Alex. Why does this bother you?"

"Other than the fact that the straight internet is tweeting it 'til it trends?" Alex snaps.

"Yes."

"I'm smarter than that," Alex tells him. "And I'm from Indiana."

He's grateful that Victor takes that for the answer it is. The thought of trying to articulate it further is painful.

♦

As they wrap a few days later, Victor beckons Alex over with a crooked finger and invites him up to his office.

No matter how many times Alex has seen the inside of this space over the last few weeks, he can't feel at ease here. He stays standing as Victor settles himself behind his desk, sitting only when Victor gestures for Alex to take the chair across from him.

The office is intimidating by design. Unlike the functional shabbiness of the space Paul shares with the other writers, Victor's office is sleek and pristine. The walls are white, and the glass shelves built into them glitter in the light. The shelves themselves are full of the awards Victor and his shows have won. The desk, in contrast, is a glossy black, solid and sharp-edged like the shelves. Scattered across its surface is the detritus of the day-to-day business of running his empire: Scripts, a laptop, two tablets, a voice recorder, and a notebook. No technology is beyond or beneath him.

"How are you?" Victor asks. Victor is no less intimidating than his office, surely also by design. He's not tall or particularly muscular, but he's solidly built. His skin is a warm golden brown, his hair jet black. Alex doesn't find him attractive, but that's because Victor exists beyond such questions. His charisma is overwhelming and more than slightly frightening. He commands attention simply by doing nothing so much as sitting behind a desk. Alex shakes his head. "People keep asking me that. But I'm pretty sure they don't want the answers."

"Because they're being disingenuous or because the answer is terrible?"

Alex's smile is all teeth. Something about Victor makes him profoundly aware of his canines. "Yes."

"I can assure you," Victor says. "I don't ask questions I don't care about the answer to."

Alex collects his thoughts. Victor waits. He'll wait for any answer he wants for as long as he has to.

Alex is surprised he doesn't fear Victor more. Everyone else seems to. But while the focused attention of other men has always felt like danger, with Victor he is, he thinks, safe. And if not, at least he's protected from anyone outside the room. Alex knows to take a bargain when he sees it.

"I'm in over my head. And I'm lonely," he says.

He hadn't meant to say that second part. But that's what Victor does: force everyone he encounters to confession.

Alex understands why his buddies on crew are either awkward or awful with him and he should have expected the volume of people in the audience who hate Zach vociferously. The faux enthusiasm from people who are now his cast mates is harder. If Gemma isn't jealous, he can't understand why they are. Then again, they don't know Gemma. Before he can manage any of that aloud, Victor speaks again.

"Did you think it wouldn't be lonely?"

Alex blinks at him slowly. He can play the waiting game too.

Victor picks up a paper clip from the surface of the desk and uses his thumb to pry it open. "Weren't you lonely in Indiana?"

Alex isn't sure if the fidget is supposed to convey boredom or what Victor likes to do to other people. "I was all sorts of things in Indiana."

"I'm sure." Victor's voice isn't sharp, but he's definitely scolding. "Now. Let's talk about all the sorts of things you should and shouldn't be here."

"Like what?" Alex asks warily.

"Like don't be the twenty year old star that gets caught having a drink at a bar. Don't do drugs, either, but you're not the type. Don't fuck fans, prostitutes, or anyone who will blackmail you. Don't get your heart broken, because no one here has any time for that, and don't –"

"I *know* all that," Alex snaps.

"Do you?" Victor raises his eyebrows in a mockery of innocence. "You'd be the first of many."

"I'm not an idiot."

Victor leans forward over the desk. "You don't even know what you are."

"And you do?"

"I know what you can become. And I have no interest investing time in something that's going to blow itself up."

"Has that happened before?" Alex isn't sure what he thinks of Victor calling him a thing. He is, however, sure he wants to know whether Victor has a habit of breaking his new toys.

"You're from Indiana, what do you think?"

Alex doesn't want to talk about Indiana. He also doesn't want to rise to the bait. Victor hasn't said *don't fight*, but he's pretty sure punching his showrunner is off the list of things that are allowed to him. "Fine. Any suggestions on what the hell I should do?"

"You need a team. Lawyer, accountant, agent, manager, publicist. I trust you're smart enough I won't have to explain why. And," Victor looks Alex over with an appraising eye, like he's a statue the man is considering adding to his collection. "A personal trainer."

"Fuck you."

"No?" Victor purses his lips as if in delight that Alex is pushing back.

Alex wonders why people don't hate the man more than they already do. "Why are you like this?" he blurts.

"Because I enjoy it, and it's useful." Without dropping Alex's gaze, Victor twists the paper clip until it snaps.

◆

Victor gives Alex a list of names and phone numbers. When Alex asks if his own team should be so blatantly comprised of people with loyalties that lie elsewhere, Victor smiles his shark smile and says to consider it a starting place.

Alex goes to Liam the next day. This new life of his is at least somewhat Liam's fault, and he's never seen him be cruel to anyone, only at times clumsily unaware of other people's boundaries. Alex is by far the baby of the cast, and Liam has the fewest years on him of any of them, allowing Alex to feel a little less like a kid who needs handholding.

Liam is surprisingly helpful. His dark curls bounce as he nods thoughtfully. He understands the problem immediately, although he seems unduly amused by it. But a few days later he gets Alex a list of names that don't represent a conflict of interest with anyone else on the show.

Putting his script aside between takes, Alex drops into his director's chair and scans over the names, not that he recognizes any of them. "How did you come up with this?"

"I know a lot of people. All of whom are too nice to me."

◆

Margaret, the woman Alex settles on as his manager because she seems as judgmental as he is, tells him to lock down his Facebook. He doesn't use it because he doesn't like anyone from high school enough to keep in touch, but locking it does at least put an end to the friend requests from people he doesn't know.

Alex looks forward to their first full business meeting. No one recognizes him as he takes the elevator up to her office in the nondescript Beverly Hills office building. Margaret's office is decorated in mint green and white, with a plush couch against one wall and framed abstract prints in pastel colors. The effect is soothing – nothing like Victor's stark office – and very Los Angeles.

He sits in the chair across from her. Margaret asks, as she chews on the end of a ballpoint pen, if the green cords are the only nice pair of pants he owns.

"I have the same pair in gray," he tells her.

She frowns. Margaret's a tall woman with rich brown skin. Her hair is twisted into innumerable braids and wrapped, crown-like, around her head. Alex has never cared much about his appearance, but he is very aware that Margaret is a hundred times more elegant than he could ever hope to be.

"We need to do something about that." She shuffles some papers on her desk as if she's flipping through some sort of new celebrity checklist. "Next up. You can't get caught having a beer – you're still only twenty – and you can't get caught having a fling."

"Yeah, I know. Victor already told me."

"Did he? Good."

Alex wonders how many more lectures on these subjects he's going to get from people who should have no place to tell him what to do. "I don't like people and I don't have any free time."

Margaret gives him a skeptical look. "You live in L.A."

"My entire social life revolves around hanging out with my roommate and talking about the sort of hot boys neither of us will ever have a chance to get near."

"I don't believe you." Margaret twirls her pen across her fingers. Alex finds it far less unsettling than Victor's paperclip.

"Why not?"

"I can't speak for your roommate, but you're one of the hot boys now. Also, you need to move."

Alex is outraged. "Why?"

Margaret glances down at his paperwork. "Because you live in a shitty part of Little Armenia, and there's no reason to do a job this hard if you can't live somewhere wonderful. You'll also probably want some security soon."

He takes a deep breath. Then a second. He's gotten so used to his crappy apartment and his routine with Gemma. Even now that he's filming regularly for a big deal TV show, he never considered that the job would necessitate a change to his home.

"You should probably let your roommate know."

"I'll bring her with me," Alex blurts. The decision as snap as it is absolute, although he can see by the flicker across Margaret's face that maybe it shouldn't be.

"Is she going to be your girlfriend?" Her voice is full of judgment.

"I – no…I…oh God. No," Alex stammers. He's not going to be in the closet and he certainly wouldn't admit that he would consider using Gemma that way if he were. His heart starts to race. While he knows this isn't quite a panic attack, he has the suspicion one might be waving to him from across the street.

◆

The panic attack arrives when Shawna, a grip who works on a show two stages down from *Fourth* and who he's been friends with for years, insists they go out dancing. Alex isn't sure if it's to celebrate or let off some steam, but the idea of *do this now while you still can* is definitely clear.

Normally Alex would flatly refuse. He doesn't like other people, and he's really not into having other people's bodies near his. But if this is the last time he'll be able to do anything like this, he'd be a fool to say no. He can spend the night drinking soft drinks and being Shawna's wingman.

But it's already too late for anything so simple. Within an hour of getting there, a man dances up close to Alex and slips his arm around his waist. While Alex is pondering whether Victor would approve, the guy calls him *Zach*. It's way too uncomfortable and invasive. Alex tries to bolt but the guy grabs his arm and pulls him back in until their bodies are flush against each other. The man's breath is hot on his neck.

Alex is lithe and clever and strong enough to handle himself – he wrestled in high school and men bigger than him should never, ever grab him in ways he doesn't want to be grabbed – but his arm is at a bad angle and all he can hear is Victor's voice in his head that he *can't*.

Alex can't get angry; he can't throw a punch; he can't even shove his way free. He can't, he realizes, decide he doesn't want this man touching him and do anything about it any more than he could have decided he wanted him for five minutes and done anything about that either.

The horror freezes him in place. Shawna has to rescue him by stomping a spike heel into the guy's foot. She grabs Alex's hand and runs them out into the breezy and too bright L.A. night.

4

The first time Paul sees Alex act he understands what it is about him that fascinates Victor. There's something about Alex – and therefore Zach – that makes him seem like he's never been owned, not by a job, a religion, or an ideology, and certainly not by a person or a relationship. That's so unlike most people that it makes him irresistible as puzzle to solve or a toy to own. Paul's not unaware of the irony, but he's also not immune to Alex's pull.

Now that everything is official, he aches to write for Alex, to solve with his words the mystery of who he will be as a performer. The work makes everything else in his life a little less awful, even when writer's block keeps him up too late. Paul's alone. His own projects outside of *Fourth* aren't getting any traction. Craig still has his dog. But the ring of Alex's voice when he speaks as Zach makes the words come a little easier.

While Zach isn't his and Paul's not the only one writing for him, he feels possessive of the character. He can't write a scene for him without remembering the clever, fearless kid he once chased out of the writers' room for making out with their intern.

◆

There are a lot of things Zach does that Alex would never in a million years do. Some are little things, like how he dresses. Some are bigger things. Like voluntarily visiting a prison to interview inmates.

Alex thinks he's going to be fine until he gets to set and finds a reasonable replica of a prison visiting room. The fluorescent lights, metal chairs, phones, and Plexiglas panes are all too spot-on for his comfort. But there's no way to say that or show that he's ill at ease. Not without raising questions Alex doesn't want to answer about his sister and Indiana and weekends spent driving to Putnamville with his mom until he finally refused to go anymore. He takes a breath the way he used to on those not-long-enough-ago trips and braces himself.

When he has the mechanics of the scene and the equipment of filmmaking to focus on, he's fine. It's during the frequent stops and hurry-up-and-waits that the institutional setting starts to get to him. The minutes tick by with excruciating slowness. After three hours, Alex can't take it anymore.

"I'm sorry, I need a minute," he says when they're called back to start the next page. He needs to get out in the hallway at least and breathe something like fresh air.

"You just had a break, we don't have time to wait on you,"

someone from the crew snaps.

"Then make some," Alex snaps back. He knows he shouldn't even as he speaks. He is talent; it's not his job to make anyone else's more difficult. Lashing out is also a very good way to show exactly where his vulnerabilities lie. But he feels like he's suffocating, and his rational mind is not in control. He has his limits, no matter how often he gets the message that such things are, for him, not allowed: Because he's not a *real* actor and because America thinks it owns anything it can see on its TV screens.

Before the guy can say anything back – or Alex can dig himself any deeper – Victor is there. He doesn't look at Alex as he pulls the guy aside.

To tell him what, he doesn't know and is afraid to contemplate. Victor knows about his sister; there is no information about any of his people Victor doesn't feel entitled to. Despite his apparently uncontrollable little outburst, Alex doesn't want that information to spread further or get more attention than it already has. It's bad enough being the gay kid from Indiana. He doesn't also want to be the gay kid from Indiana whose currently incarcerated sister tried to stab him in the ramshackle kitchen of the ramshackle house they grew up in. Twice.

His mom only knows about one of those times. Victor had somehow gotten both out of him.

After Victor releases the guy – looking shaken and subdued, back to the crew – Alex expects Victor to round on him next. Victor does meet his eye. But instead of crooking his finger and telling Alex he had better come with him, he nods and moves along.

Somehow, Alex manages to get through the rest of the morning. Once they break for lunch he peels away from the group headed for catering. He needs some time alone and to be nowhere near anything that resembles an institutional setting.

He finds a nook behind a bunch of the set flats, out of the way and certainly out of sight to any casual passersby. He sits down with his back against the wall, puts in his headphones, and closes his eyes.

Five minutes later he's startled out of his solitude by a shadow. Someone has rounded the corner of the flats and is now looming above him. Alex opens his eyes, fully ready to snap again, only to find that it's Paul.

"It's you." Alex hopes he'll go away.

"It's me." Paul smiles and sits down on the floor next to him.

Alex pauses his music and looks sideways at the other man. He can't help but wonder if he's been sent by Victor and, if so, for what incredibly intrusive purpose.

"I need to talk to you," Paul says. "So I can write for you."

"Again?" Miserable and shaky as he might be right now, he

doesn't want to offend anyone else by being today's bad attitude bear.

"Mhmm."

"We already did that."

Paul smiles. "I know."

"Did you need something else?" Alex still doesn't get why Paul is here.

"It's been a while. I wanted a refresher."

Paul doesn't look like he's being deceitful, but still, Alex is twitchy and annoyed. "Why? If you need to watch me, you can stream the episodes now." It's an obnoxiously cocky thing to say, but it's true, and Alex would really prefer to be alone.

Paul frowns in thought. The gesture makes his forehead crease and his eyes look even kinder. He might be a writer but he's built like the guys Alex and Gemma still only talk about. He's fit, with pale skin a little tanned from the sun. His hair is blond and his gray eyes are completely intent on Alex.

"That's not remotely the same. You're more than some small talk and a collection of edits, no matter what marketing tells you. People change and grow all the time, show me how that works for you. Or, you know, be grumpy," Paul says with a shrug. "It's all data."

Alex doesn't quite know what to do with any of that, so he snarks something about clichés. Paul snarks right back, smiling the whole time. Like everything else for Alex lately, it's a dare, but it feels different – and better – than most of the others.

When Paul gets up five minutes later, Alex feels more like a real boy than he has in a while. Maybe he can resume this day from a place resembling neutral.

Also, Alex notes after Paul disappears around the corner that for a writer, Paul has a great ass.

◆

Gemma doesn't ask Alex if she can come visit the set, but Alex knows what such a visit would mean to her. Both because of her professional ambitions, and because of how much she loves *The Fourth Estate* and indeed all of Victor's work. Plus, Alex owes her. Not only for putting up with his surliness at home, but for her support and encouragement ever since they first met online and started talking about moving west. It's a small gesture to make in repayment, but it's what Alex can do right now.

Seeing the two parts of his life – one almost old, one still very new – interact is strange. He watches Liam and all his clichéd black Irish charisma shake Gemma's hand. His gaze is like the beam of a lighthouse, all focused on her. His smile is warm, and Gemma glows with the attention. Alex is good and doesn't roll his eyes when Liam winks at her. It's profoundly surreal.

He nods Gemma – and her incredibly loud yet surprisingly tasteful high heels – down a hallway in front of him. This may be his life now, but there's absolutely nothing about it that feels normal.

When *The Fourth Estate* first aired three years ago the critics had ignored it as an unexpectedly soapy backstage drama from Victor, from whom everyone expected something better. But it had claws and stars, so people watched it, even if just for the occasional partial nudity.

But somewhere towards the end of the second year, things on the show had shifted, and what had seemed disjointed and incoherent started to reveal itself as part of a much bigger plan. The audience realized its shallow, trashy drama was no more shallow and trashy than their own lives before the critics did. Now it's event television, pulling in everyone from teenyboppers to their grandparents.

Alex had watched it before he started P.A.ing for it. The glamour and thrill of working on a show – either as crew or as an actor – isn't what most of the audience assumes that it is, but it's still magic. The work of storytelling is incredibly satisfying, at least when he's not terrified he's going to fail. He'd forgotten that, these last few months. There had been so much to be frightened of. But now, seeing his work and his world through Gemma's eyes, he can feel his perspective start to shift. He *is* lucky to be here. Even if that luck comes with so many downsides.

As he and Gemma run into people, Alex makes introductions and Gemma holds her own, happily chatting about plots and arcs and relationships in a way that hews a surprisingly gracious line between fan and aspiring professional. He's proud. And grateful.

Alex is fascinated by watching Gemma get to see how the real people of the cast and crew intersect with the characters they all carry around with them. Some, like the irritatingly extroverted if friendly Liam, are far from their alter egos. His character James is reckless as hell, eagerly facilitating everyone else's inevitably awful choices. Marjani – Natalie's character – on the other hand, is almost as much of a diva as Natalie is. The only one of the cast Alex is sure he likes is Raphael, who plays the star member of their fictional journalism team. The character is a mess, but Raphael seems well-adjusted. At least for L.A.

Gemma floats through it all. When he walks her back to her car before the afternoon's shoot, she kisses his cheek.

"Thank you for a peek at the dream," she says.

♦

The network, Victor's people, and Margaret all try to start Alex off small with the media. Margaret assures him over and over that they're always going to say *no* a lot. That's not personal; it's not even about the fact that Alex has no idea what he's doing.

Instead, she says that the secret to success is to always leave everyone wanting more. Alex nods. He understands; it's obvious and in the very way *The Fourth Estate* is written and structured. No one but Victor could get away with doing that to an audience for over a year before they understood what they were watching.

Alex tries his best to follow Margaret's advice and Victor's example. He never mentions his family in interviews if he can help it, but there are two weeks where every gossip show is obsessed with the idea that he doesn't know his dad and that there's some drama involving his sister. On the days when how hard it is for him must seem obvious, Margaret asks Alex why he's doing this. He says that Gemma told him he's Marilyn Monroe and not allowed to say no.

"Sometimes, on TV, it's important to be less strange," is her only response. She doesn't even blink.

Alex laughs and crinkles up his eyes.

"That," she exclaims, "is your secret weapon."

◆

Alex's first TV interview that matters is a late show after the late show. Paul and Victor watch it together on the shitty first generation flat screen with the dodgy cable connection that lives in the writers' room. In television no one sleeps.

When the host finally asks Alex if he's gay, Alex giggles, squints, and smiles sly. "Is this something we didn't know?"

"America just fell in love with him," Victor breathes, leaning back in a chair with his feet on a desk, beer bottle halfway to his lips.

"America's not the only one." Paul murmurs. He's not sure if he means it as a jibe at Victor, who is notorious for his fascination with his stars – rumors have been going around about him and Liam forever – or his own personal moment of realization.

◆

In January Alex wins a People's Choice award for Best Newcomer.

Liam gives him a bright *Congratulations!* when Alex slides back into his seat at the awards show. As is usual from Liam, it's both sweet and excessive. Alex finds it faintly irritating. He has never believed in the myth of the perfectly kind and utterly humble star. The day-in and day-out of *The Fourth Estate* largely hasn't changed his mind. Liam is trying to be that guy all the time and Alex doesn't get it.

"You know, that category is new," Liam says, nodding at the trophy in Alex's hand as they leave together for the after party. Alex doesn't want to go, but Victor had sternly instructed him to be there and even Margaret had reminded him that he's contractually obligated to attend.

"Mmm?" Alex says vaguely. He never paid much attention to awards season as a civilian. He always cared more about the stories people told than the glamour of the red carpet. That's still true.

Liam nods. "It exists this year because of you."

"Oh?" That's a disturbing thought. Alex didn't come to L.A. to be an actor. For L.A. to be rewriting its rules for him seems a break in the order of the natural universe. Who knows what calamity could come from that.

"People – and advertisers – are hungry for you. And your Cinderella story."

It sounds like something Victor would say. Alex has another disturbing thought. How much time does Victor spend talking about him to Liam? To anyone?

He's going to demand more information on that subject from Liam but they step outside. There are fans staked out. The noise and the shouting and the flashes are overwhelming. He takes a deep breath and, along with Liam who loves shit like this, handles it as best he can. He signs a few things to be gracious, until a girl grabs his arm and pulls him way too close. Then the person next to her grabs him too, fingers digging into his shoulder. More hands reach out to him, landing on his sleeves and even in his hair. Alex feels like carrion being fought over. He doesn't hear what any of them are yelling, but disentangles himself as politely and quickly as he can. He seethes internally that his gratitude must extend to what no real person would be expected to bear.

When the Emmy nominations come out that summer, *Fourth* is up. One of the nods is for writing; it's not for an episode that has Paul's name on it, but Alex finds him the next morning to give him a high-five anyway.

5

Awards season, which seems to take up half the year, is tense and exhausting for everyone. The airing structure of *Fourth* may be quasi-groundbreaking, but one of the downsides of not shooting on a normal schedule is that major writing times overlap with days the rest of the industry takes off to party. It doesn't make any of them live quieter, more responsible lives. Combined with the last minute changes that are part and parcel of the very chaotic *Fourth Estate* beast, Paul can't wait for everything to calm down and go back to normal.

They win at the Emmys for Best Writing and Best Directing, although they miss Best Dramatic Series. Victor grumbles in a manner intended to be entertaining all through the celebration. Once the hangover from the celebrations wear off, Paul starts planning the real victory party.

He's almost not surprised when Alex is in the writers' room the morning Paul invites everyone over to his house the next weekend. Paul's seen him moving in and out of the different spaces at the studio when he's not on set. Like an unsettled cat, Alex seems to be trying them out for comfort. More and more, though, he's been landing here.

"Don't you have a trailer?" Paul asks as he squeezes by Alex and starts unpacking his laptop bag.

Alex is squinting at the massive bulletin board that takes up most of one wall. Cards scrawled with notes on character arcs and plot beats are thumbtacked to it. Alex must know it represents a map of his future. "Am I in the way?" he asks, not taking his eyes from the cards.

"Not yet," Paul says like the question is reasonable. No one complains about Alex regardless of where he lands. He's a star now, and no one complains about stars to their faces. "And I'm glad you're here. There's going to be a party next week, you should come."

"Another one?" Alex is already dressed as Zach for the day – at least, Paul feels safe assuming Alex would never choose an outfit that makes him look so delicate. The way Alex carries himself when he's off duty doesn't suit the pale blue shirt in an almost feminine cut, much less the scarf he has looped around his neck or the pants that might have been painted on for how tight they are. Not that Paul is looking.

"At my house and for fun," Paul reassures him. "Totally off the clock. No cameras and no official business. Work people, but what can you do? It's not like any of us have lives."

"I don't know." But when Alex bites at his lower lip just so and smiles, Paul knows he'll say yes. "You guys should celebrate your win. I wasn't a part of that."

"We were writing for you," Paul says. "You were it."

Alex turns to look at Paul over his shoulder. His lips part slightly in wonderment and he looks startled in a way Paul knows isn't a reaction to a simple compliment. "Okay."

♦

As people start to pile into his house, Paul realizes he's hosting this party not only because he can, but also because he must. When they had been together, Craig had always resented these events. No matter how many times Paul tried to explain the subtleties of becoming a team leader in the high-stress hothouse of a Hollywood writer's room, Craig was never willing to hear it.

Despite hosting a party to pull the team together being work for Paul, he wasn't lying to Alex. This isn't putting in face time for anyone else. But Paul has built his career – slow and steady will one day win the race – by taking Victor's benevolence and mentorship and trying to be the most diligent and loyal guy in Hollywood. He hasn't hopped from job to job. And, no matter how many times he's wanted to, he has never abandoned a gig or a crappy fix-it job on someone else's shitty script for a better opportunity.

If he's allowed Victor to always count on him in ways that make other people in the writers' room think he's weak and Craig think he isn't any good, Paul has done it because he knows that one day, Victor will pay that debt. The agreement between them is mostly unspoken and deals with Victor may smell faintly of sulphur, but Paul believes in his choices. He's been part of Victor's nearly inner circle for a long time. He trusts the man, such as it is, and the dividends are finally starting to come due. Paul being allowed to write for Zach is going to change everything.

Which means Paul has to hold up his end of the bargain more now than ever before. Victor isn't kind in a way other people easily understand. So keeping everyone human and happy has always been one of Paul's jobs.

Alex shows up later than Paul expects, apparently happy to nab a beer from the kitchen and drift through a party where he runs no risk of being the man of the hour. He's wearing a plain black T-shirt and jeans. When he slides out onto the small second floor balcony with the smokers he looks almost like what he once was – a random P.A. none of them had ever noticed before. But now, in a room full of people, no one can look at anyone else.

That magnetism a strange gift, one that Liam and Natalie both have as well. Everyone on the show possesses an eerie charisma of one form or another. Paul's always wondered what that's like; to trail such a wake or to expend whatever massive energy output it takes to dampen it. He assumes he'll never know. Having watched Alex wrestle with it in himself these last months makes him almost glad of it.

Alex's silhouette through the glass, the orange embers of cigarettes, and the lights of the city combine to tell too much of the story of L.A. It's a place for fallen things, Paul's family had warned him when he'd first come out here. He can't imagine what Alex's must have said.

He reaches for the door handle but thinks the better of it. Alex is a big boy and can get his bearings at a party without Paul's help. They'll find each other later, he's sure.

◆

The room is easy, no one is trying to impress, and Alex feels unexpectedly comfortable. He's aware of Paul's steady presence as he moves around the house and feels safe in the knowledge that no one here wants more of his time, attention, or body than he's willing to give. He doesn't have to be on, and that's a relief; other people are never easy. In that regard, he finds L.A. harder than Indiana. Alex is fairly certain everyone in this city is always auditioning or rehearsing, no matter what they do or what they aspire to.

Alex doesn't understand it. If L.A. teaches anyone anything, it's supposed to be the scope of dreams and the limits of opportunity. He transcended the limits of his own life, the one he was raised in, the day he got in his car and drove to L.A. For him possibility should have ended there. But everything that's happened in the last year is a new sort of vastness. What's happening to him now isn't supposed to happen to anyone.

He has another drink and, as the room watches him, he watches Paul.

◆

Alex finds him alone, eventually, in the kitchen, restocking the beer in the fridge.

"I'm glad you came," Paul tells him, offering him a cold bottle.

Alex takes it. "Thanks," he says, both for the drink and for Paul meaning it.

Paul regards him in silence for a moment. "How are you?"

"Here." He doesn't know any other way to articulate his current state of being in all its forms.

Paul laughs, loud and surprised like he sometimes does. Alex grins back at him. Paul's smile stays and his eyes meet Alex's and linger. Alex knows he's doing the stupid squinchy-eyed thing that so many people apparently find attractive. He turns his head away a little, not sure what he should be expecting or wanting out of tonight yet.

"Hey, no." Paul raises his hand and presses two fingertips, dry and warm, against Alex's temple. He turns Alex's head back until their eyes meet again. With a question in his eyes he drops his hand slowly, from Alex's face to his side. Alex knows it's to give him a chance to stop him if he wants.

He doesn't, and Paul's hand settles on his waist.

"Party's out there," he says and tips his head back towards the living room. "Want to go join?"

"Not really," Alex says. Not only because there are people out there. He'd much rather stay here – with Paul – and see what happens next. It's a new sort of thrill, not one he's used to at all. But it doesn't feel bad.

Paul smiles at him, delighted and maybe a little surprised. "Well then." His fingers tighten on Alex's waist and he draws Alex closer to him. There are fine striations of brown and blue in his gray eyes. As Alex watches, Paul's eyes dip to his mouth.

It's not an invitation Alex has any interest in saying no to. But before he can do anything about it, one of the grips appears in the kitchen doorway, laughing and saying something to someone over his shoulder. Alex jumps back; Paul lets his hand drop from Alex's waist. Alex appreciates it. There are witnesses to nearly everything Alex does now; whatever is starting with Paul, he'd rather not have an audience.

The grip doesn't seem to realize he's interrupted anything. Paul leans close again and whispers in Alex's ear, "Now do you want to go back out there?"

Alex nods. Paul takes his hand and leads him out of the kitchen. Alex hides his smile in his shoulder.

◆

Paul keeps a hold of Alex's hand until they're at the side of the room. There he tugs him a little closer, sliding his hand back around Alex's waist. He starts moving his hips to the beat.

"Really?" Alex cocks his head questioningly, though he doesn't step away. "We *just* almost got busted in your kitchen."

"Do you mind?"

Alex shakes his head, looking perhaps a little surprised at himself as he does.

"Then c'mon. I know you can," Paul tells him. He puts his other hand on Alex's waist too. No one who can control their face and body they way Alex does when he acts can't dance.

Alex smiles that small, dangerous smile of his and puts his hands on Paul's shoulders. "Okay."

Game on. Alex moves beautifully, easy and strong to the beat. Paul can feel the power of him under his hands, the physicality of his magnetism. It's extraordinary. Paul imagines this is why Alex doesn't like to speak; maybe he simply doesn't need to, his body a more faithful storyteller.

When Paul had invited Alex to this party, he'd entertained vague fantasies of getting to talk with him meaningfully and maybe making out with him in a corner. But Paul has been thinking about Alex as desirable and intriguing for so long that with him in his arms now Paul wants nothing more than to go big with that desire. He can't imagine a few kisses being enough.

Songs pass and they keep moving closer to each other until they're far too close. Paul hopes Alex knows he can do what he wants here; sure they're still being watched but it doesn't matter. This feels way too good, and Paul pulls them together until their thighs are brushing and his arms are snug around Alex's waist.

Their eyes keep catching in the dark. More than once Paul's gaze drops to Alex's mouth. Alex tightens his fingers on his side when it does, his eyes flickering between Paul's lips and his eyes. When the song shifts again to something heavy and slow their foreheads brush together. Alex's nose touches Paul's cheek.

They both hesitate, and Paul sways in a little before he steps back and asks, "Do you want another drink?"

"Sure," Alex says, breathless like the movies.

"I'll be right back." Paul finds his hand and squeezes it before threading his way back through the room.

◆

As the night goes on, the crowd thins out and Paul and Alex switch from beer to mixed drinks. It's one of those innocuous, unspoken things Gemma would define as a sign, and Alex is pretty sure is them egging each other on, step by tiny step. Whether that's towards oblivion or a hookup, he refuses to let himself be sure.

They drift apart and together over and over, never dancing again. Sometimes they stand too close, Paul whispering harmless conversation in his ear, and sometimes too far, Alex calling something sharp and funny across a room, not for the purpose of saying *I'm still watching you* but rather, *you're all I can see.*

Which is not good. Alex is smart enough to know that as cool and hot and seemingly lovely as Paul is, a lot of Alex's feeling towards him is likely rooted only in timing, or the fact that Paul never changed the way he spoke to Alex when his circumstances changed. Both magic and normal are sexy.

But his opportunities are far and few between in his new life of look but don't touch anything. Yes, maybe it would be awkward or dumb, but on some level he knows that Paul's just a writer. If things go wrong for some inexplicable reason, he's not someone with any authority over Alex, and he's not someone he has to see on a daily basis. There's no reason that a drunk and friendly grope could somehow cause more drama than everything that's happened to all of them in the last year.

If he has this opportunity, he's damn well taking it.

♦

Paul starts to tidy up at one. It's not as harsh as turning on the lights to kick everyone out, but it does the job. His hands are full of other people's beer bottles when Alex finds him again but says nothing. Paul asks him to stay, despite every instinct telling him that he has to let Alex run the show. But this is, after all, his house, and Alex can perhaps have no power over him if Paul doesn't invite him in first.

Alex nods, and for a moment says nothing. Then, "Do you want some help?"

Together, the task goes faster. When they're more or less done, Paul is happy to show the last stragglers out the door and note that Alex's is the only car remaining besides his. Paul smiles to himself. He won't have to deal with hungover colleagues coming to retrieve vehicles in the morning.

He turns around from the door to see Alex halfway up the stairs, a hand on each banister and with a smile far more shy than the rest of his choices suggest.

"Are you inviting me upstairs in my own house?" Paul laughs.

Alex backs up the flight, disappearing out of sight behind the wall when he gets there.

Paul bolts up the stairs after him, laughing again when he finds Alex still hidden behind the wall and biting his lip.

"What?" Paul asks,

"I'm an idiot," Alex says. "Which one's the bedroom?"

"The one with the cat," Paul murmurs. But instead of opening the door he closes the distance, savoring again the bare inch he has over Alex and rubbing their faces together until they slide into a kiss neither can be blamed for.

He snakes one arm around Alex's waist and hitches him closer, his other arm stretching out to fumble for the door.

It opens, and Todd darts out with a sharp meow and runs down the stairs.

"He has to stay in for parties," Paul says, breaking the kiss but still breathing right against Alex's mouth, "else he drinks all the beer."

Alex laughs, crinkles his eyes up, and this time doesn't look away.

Paul kisses him again, slides his hands up under Alex's shirt, and murmurs into his mouth, "Should have done this that first time I caught you with Nick."

Alex shivers. "But then what would have happened?"

"Everything." Paul turns them so he can back Alex into his bedroom and skims his hands up his sides until Alex takes the hint and gets his shirt off. "Fuck," Paul breathes at a body somewhat more built than he expects. He's wiry without being delicate and freckled *everywhere.* "You are beautiful."

"Don't," Alex says, but it's distracted and out of breath. Paul lets it go. Alex thanks him by grabbing his face and shoving his tongue in his mouth. Eventually he pulls back, worrying his teeth over Paul's bottom lip as he goes.

They pause briefly, looking at each other, taking stock of the moment and what's about to happen. Paul hurries to lose his shirt too.

"What do you want? What do you like?" he asks, fascinated by the prospect of being able to make Alex speak. But Alex doesn't answer, distracted by tracing his fingers up Paul's stomach and over his abs.

"Jesus," Alex says.

Paul doesn't say anything. It's nice to be appreciated but it's not like he works out for reasons of sanity and health.

Alex hums and scratches his nails across Paul's side.

Paul stills his hand, squeezing it in his own. "Get naked," he says. "Let me take you to bed already."

There's a moment where Alex falters. It's small, barely there, but Paul sees it, and it makes him doubt the assumptions he has about Alex's history. He does his best to brush past the doubt and the guilt it brings him. If nothing else, it can wait until tomorrow.

But then Alex is naked, in his bed, propped against the headboard, and saying something smart about Paul not moving fast enough to take either of them anywhere.

Alex takes himself in hand and jacks himself slowly. As Paul gets out of his jeans he tries to remember what it was to be that young and fearless and terrified.

He gives up, instead crawling onto his bed and licking a long stripe up the pale and freckled inside of Alex's left thigh. He holds eye contact with him as best he can and smiles when Alex shoves a hand into his hair.

When he doesn't drag Paul's mouth to his dick, Paul has to take a moment to remind himself of *twenty, famous and odd*, before saying, "Do you want to fuck my mouth?"

"God yes." Alex lets go of Paul's hair to go up on his knees.

Paul, in turn, slides onto the floor. His own knees will survive. He blinks up at Alex, coltish and powerful and strange above him.

"So, show me what you've got," Paul teases. That's enough for Alex to get his hand back in Paul's hair and feed his dick into his mouth.

Alex is gentle with it at first, but it doesn't seem to be out of caution. Paul does his best to work with Alex's rhythm and swirl his tongue around the head of his cock, as Alex is, quite obviously, uncertain and trying to read his reactions.

He puts a hand to Alex's hip to push him back briefly. "Whatever you do," he says, his lips wet with him now, "don't take your eyes off us." Paul dips his head back in, blinking up through his lashes at Alex, as he wraps his lips around the head of his dick and sucks hard.

♦

Alex cannot believe this is happening. But his own shock has become such a constant state of affairs he's starting wonder how severely his perception has been altered. If his fairytale has stunted him, though, he's grateful for it, especially if it'll mean he'll last a little longer because *oh God*. There is no way he's going to be able to keep his eyes open – right now, he's not convinced he's not going to tip over – and Paul's going to have to live with that.

At least that's what Alex thinks until Paul pinches the inside of his thigh sharply every time his eyes roll and flutter closed. He wants to be more outside of his own thoughts than he is, but Paul's not letting him.

"Too much," he eventually manages to choke out.

Paul pulls off. "Good." His fingers knead at Alex's ass and delve between his cheeks.

That's the point Alex decides he should probably freak out except for the fact that it feels spectacular, fantasy and reality colliding perfectly. Alex takes a deep breath and runs his hand through Paul's hair. One more sharp learning curve with no warning won't kill him. This one feels better than most, and Paul doesn't even push. Literally.

Eventually Paul drops his hands from Alex's ass and takes his cock back into his mouth. Alex smiles to himself and hardens his gaze. That's all about self-satisfaction until Paul's eyes go liquid, and, wow, that's a lot.

"Fuck, you have no idea, do you?" Paul pulls back enough to say.

Alex keens.

"Spoiled," Paul says, jacking him hard and sliding his other hand between his own legs.

"Yeah," is all Alex manages until his mouth becomes frozen open in pleasure in those few moments before he comes across Paul's face. His stomach muscles contract so hard with the force of it he suspects he'll be feeling it tomorrow.

When Alex falls onto his side on Paul's bed they're both a mess, Paul scrambles up to rub every inch of himself against Alex, and they kiss wet and messy, filthy and desperate. Somehow it's this moment, not when he came, that Alex feels like is the first time he's ever really understood sex. He sees his ability to form thoughts and judge circumstances for a brief instant before it leaves him.

Alex flips them, startling Paul. Alex cackles. "High school wrestling," he says before he slides down Paul's body, scraping teeth over muscle.

"Oh my God," Paul laughs.

The blowjob isn't expert, but Alex can't help but award himself points for enthusiasm. Paul doesn't seem to mind, either. He gasps when Alex moans around him and, when Alex's fingers stray up to Paul's nipples, his back arches off the bed with it.

♦

Alex and Paul lie together, tangled on their sides, foreheads touching. They stare at each other, and it feels magical and terrifying.

Alex's brain comes back online slowly, swimming up through the haze of pleasure. He wishes it wouldn't, even if there's a relief in taking himself back under control. He's cold and needs to pull up a blanket, put his shirt back on, or press closer into the heat of Paul's body. But he has no idea which of those options is appropriate. He's naked and in another man's bed, anxious with uncertainty and vulnerability. This is part of learning curve, but as much as Alex wants everything his life has to offer now, he has no idea how to move through this moment.

"Hey. Are you okay?" Paul's voice is gentle and low. He gropes between them on the mattress for Alex's hand.

Alex is more than okay, though he doesn't have the words for what, exactly, he is right now. He opens his fingers so Paul can interlace his.

♦

Paul smiles. Watching Alex blink in his bed, heavy-eyed, strong-limbed and – for once – relaxed, feels like a privilege. Instinct and Alex's eyes tell him this is a rare moment and, as with all rare and fragile things, care should be taken and gratitude given.

Alex fidgets with Paul's hands. When he finds the ridge of scar at his wrist, his eyebrows pull in a little, and he presses his thumb hard against it. His fingers go searching for its twin on Paul's other arm. "Where did you get these?"

Paul is not remotely prepared to answer that question, and the shock of it throws him. He doesn't think of them that often.

"Where do you think?" He lets the South Carolina come through in his voice more than it usually does. Alex's eyes flick up to his face. He doesn't look contrite, merely surprised. Paul should be offended; the rudeness of the question in any circumstance aside, it's the worst pillow talk he's ever encountered.

Instead, he's fascinated. It's almost an act of vulnerability for Alex to touch Paul's wrists like this after putting himself in Paul's hands; to admit, in such a bald attempt to right the scales, how badly tipped they'd been.

Paul wants to keep doing this – pillow talk, sleeping together, spending time with each other – to see all the ways Alex will find to shock him and all the ways he can keep Alex in his hands.

When Alex says nothing and the silence stretches out, Paul kisses him again.

♦

Alex begins to feel the first stirrings of claustrophobia. It's not an unfamiliar feeling – it comes in crowds and at events and sometimes from being in front of the camera – but here he has no defenses against it, not with the additional vulnerabilities of being naked and in Paul's bed.

He pulls back and sits up. "Where's your bathroom?"

Paul points over his shoulder at the door.

"No identifying animals?"

Paul shakes his head. "Not this time."

In the bathroom, Alex blinks against the brightness. He adds the fan for the blissful wash of white noise. It doesn't shut up his brain the way being with Paul had, but it at least makes it harder to concentrate on the roil of thoughts that has started up again.

He washes his face because he needs to and because he feels like he should do something other than hide in here while he collects himself. When that doesn't take long enough, he fidgets with his hair, which is a predictable, glorious mess. He breathes deeply until he feels sure of the limits of his own skin again.

Once he feels stable he runs a washcloth under warm water for Paul. His face is even more of a mess, not that he seems to care. Which is hot in its own way.

When Alex returns to the bedroom, Paul is lying on his side under the covers with his arm crooked under his head. "Stay the night?" he asks.

Alex reaches the bed and remembers that he knows how to be brave, because he wants this too. "I would have anyway," he says and tosses Paul the washcloth.

"Thanks," he says with a surprised breath. After he's scrubbed his face he adds, "Just wanted to be sure."

Alex slides under the blankets and into Paul's warm and welcoming arms. For the first time since his arrival in Los Angeles, he's sure he's made the right choice.

6

Paul wakes up first. Alex's face in sleep is lovely; younger than it looks when he's awake, relaxed and at ease except for the way his brow furrows when Paul disentangles their limbs. As much as he would love to stay in bed with him, Paul remembers his brief flight the night before and wants to give him whatever space he'll need when he wakes up.

He leaves the bedroom door cracked open and goes downstairs to tackle the last of the cleanup from the party. Todd is sprawled blissfully in a puddle of midmorning sunshine, and Paul stops on his way to the dishwasher to rub his belly with a foot.

Most of the mess left in the kitchen is dealt with by the time he hears movement from the bedroom. He takes a last private moment to smile to himself before the footsteps start down the stairs.

He turns around to see Alex hovering at the bottom of the flight, one hand on the railing.

"Good morning," Paul says. Alex bites his lip before he smiles. He's in his clothes from last night but still barefoot. It's absolutely adorable.

"Hi," Alex says. He sounds almost shy again.

"How did you sleep?"

"Are you always so polite to your guests?" Alex asks as he leaves his perch by the stairs and comes into the kitchen.

"Southern hospitality," he says with a shrug. "Do you want anything to eat?"

"No. Thanks." Alex steps into his space and kisses him.

Paul expects a quick peck; instead, he gets pushed up against the counter with Alex's hands in Paul's hair and his tongue in his mouth. Alex swings so quickly between shyness and boldness that can't get a handle on what to expect from him. He's fascinated.

He grabs Alex's hips to hold him there. When Alex tries to pull away, he follows. Alex's eyes are unnervingly dark with the rest of him so fair. He blinks them open as he presses a last, soft kiss to Paul's mouth, and they catch and drink the sunlight in a way that makes Paul need to take a breath.

Alex asks, "Can I invite you to take a shower in your own bathroom too?"

Paul laughs and tightens his hands on Alex's hips. "Yeah. *Yes.*"

◆

Paul's body is glorious – lean but thoroughly muscled, with good abs and strong thighs. Alex savors the opportunity to get his hands on it again, this time in the light and under soap and water. He marvels at himself as he does. He's never spent time with someone like this before. Never had anyone he wanted to spend time with. Or anyone he trusted.

Paul washes his back for him. Alex closes his eyes and rests his forehead against the cool tile while Paul's hands, firm and sure, knead their way across his skin. His brain is still churning, wanting to analyze every one of Paul's movements and find the correct response, but it quiets as Paul keeps touching him.

Alex feels lazy, heavy with the heat and with arousal, but eventually he pushes Paul out of the way and rinses the last of the shampoo out of his hair before reaching for the tap.

"I should get going," he says regretfully and shoots Paul a smile when he pouts.

Paul presses his fingers to Alex's naked side before grabbing towels for them both.

"Thanks," Alex says, as he starts scrubbing out his hair.

"Anytime." Paul kisses him again before wrapping himself in his own towel and disappearing into the bedroom.

Alex feels satisfied with himself as he gets dressed. The lessons Margaret and Victor both repeat to him of storytelling and fame – leave everyone wanting more – apply to real life, too.

Paul teases him at the door when Alex worries about having to go out in last night's clothes and then offers to lend him something. Alex makes a face at him and turns him down. Leaving Paul's house wearing Paul's clothes would leave even less doubt as to what he's done.

Paul holds Alex around the waist. "Can I call you?"

Alex doesn't know what to say, but Paul seems determined to wait him out as Alex flicks his eyes over his face. The answer is obviously yes, but Alex feels paralyzed at the idea. Other people learn this part of the process in high school, but he's never dated anyone and doesn't know what happens next. Eventually he nods.

They trade numbers, and Alex has his hand on the doorknob ready to go when Paul catches him for one last kiss.

If Alex puts his dumb victory playlist on and sings along as he drives home, there's no one around to judge.

Gemma is worried and loud when he gets back to their apartment, even though he texted her the night before. She wants to know *who* and if it was a good idea with the *you know...and all* because she can almost never bring herself to say the word *fame* without whispering. Mostly, she doesn't even do that.

She also wants to know *what*, in a blow-by-blow (and, oh, how accurate that request is) way, until Alex retreats into the shower again to get space from her. He feels ridiculous, he only just got out of the shower at Paul's and is hardly dry from that. But desperate times and all that. He's fairly sure that, unlike his bedroom, she won't barge into the bathroom.

He stares at the dingy and cracked tiling of the shower stall where a splash of plum memorializes one of Gemma's more unfortunate hair color experiments. He's going to have to look for a new place soon. It's way overdue, but he's used to this crappy little apartment; he's already had enough change for a lifetime.

Alex's assumptions about privacy prove wrong. Gemma does have the audacity to join him in the bathroom while he's under the water. He's glad their current shower curtain isn't clear like the last one, which mold and mildew destroyed; their apartment is inherently gross and he and Gemma are both terrible housekeepers.

Even with the shelter of the opaque curtain, Alex feels uncomfortable. He doesn't want her here as he checks his body for marks. Alex feels like there should be some, but there aren't. If she doesn't leave soon, he's not sure he can stop himself from talking to her about the roil in his head regarding last night.

"What are you doing in there? Your hair was wet when you came in," she demands.

He speaks as authoritatively as he can. "I will have this conversation with you later."

"Why not now? Is it because you need more private time?"

"I am late to brunch and in the shower, not trying to jerk off," Alex says sharply. Shawna had invited him earlier in the week, and if he doesn't get there soon she's going to want to know why he was delayed. Alex doesn't want to answer any questions about that at all.

He shuts the water off aggressively. "Tonight, okay? Sunday. HBO and all that?" He holds his breath as he waits for Gemma to retreat. Amazingly, she does.

7

Paul arrives early for weekly brunch with his friends. The house had felt too empty after Alex's departure. He tells himself to stop moping over him being gone. Getting used to having someone around after only one night is not going to lead anywhere good.

Besides, brunch brings with it friends, mimosas, and the prospect of his dog. Beau is still in Craig's possession, though it's been months since they last fought about him. Thank God for restaurants with outdoor patios.

When Paul gets there he crouches next to his chair to rub Beau's ears. He's carrying on a conversation half with Craig and half with Josh on the other side of the table when Shawna says, bright and excited, "My darling Alexander, you made it!"

"Yeah, sorry, couldn't find a parking spot."

Paul's heart jolts. That's Alex's voice and he's here, in one of the last places Paul would have expected to encounter him.

He gives Beau a last distracted pat between the ears and gets back up in his seat. Alex stares at him for an instant before he turns, obviously tense, to say something to Shawna.

Alex is no longer wearing the T-shirt he left Paul's house in. He's replaced it with a tight dark green V-neck. Sunglasses are shoved up on top of his head over a knit beanie that hides at least most of his distinctive hair. Paul wants nothing more than to get up from his chair and round the table and kiss him, but even if Alex weren't someone who gets an enormous amount of attention in public, they haven't talked about this. They haven't talked about anything. Whatever happens here needs to be Alex's call.

Since Alex looks even more startled than he usually does, his call is, apparently, to pretend last night didn't happen. Paul understands there are any number of good reasons for that. But he wishes they were at least sitting next to each other.

Shawna puts a hand on Alex's shoulder until he sits down. "Hey, so, I think you know most of these guys –"

"I'm Brian." He interrupts her because that's the kind of thing Brian does.

Paul watches as Alex turns to look at him, a faint frown creasing his eyebrows as he judges the weedy-looking guy with the obnoxious moustache. Paul approves of the reaction. Brian goes around the rest of the table introducing everyone. He ends with "and that's Paul, Craig, and Divorce Dog."

"Excuse me?" Alex asks.

"Honey, there have been custody battles waged over actual

children of actual marriages far less ugly." Brian says.

Alex's eyes go from Beau, whose ears have perked up in hope of a new friend, to Paul. Alex stills for an instant before he gives Paul a small, sweet smile.

"His name is Beau," Paul tells him, after a pointed look at Brian.

Alex leans out of his chair and offers the dog a hand to sniff. "Hi, Beau."

"If you had been subjected to their shrieking on the matter, he'd be Divorce Dog to you too," Josh supplies helpfully.

Paul laughs. So does Craig. Alex sits up again, smiles sharply, and focuses on his menu.

♦

Alex is grateful when the food finally arrives. It gives him something to concentrate on other than not doing what he wants to do, which is to share a private smile with Paul and nudge their feet together under the table.

If the damn dog (he's a really cute dog) is anything to go by, Craig is the same ex who walked out on Paul the same day Paul walked in on him and Nick; the day Alex's life changed forever. He can't help but take a moment to look over Craig appraisingly. Attractive, athletic, clearly a bit of a gym rat, and a couple years older than Paul if the lines on his sun-weathered face and the little bit of grey in his short black hair are anything to go by.

That they're all at brunch together the morning after he and Paul have hooked up is bizarre, spooky, and awkward. Alex isn't particularly superstitious, but he is starting to wonder what it is that Paul's doing to him – or what that one day over a year ago is doing to all of them.

As the conversation spins around him he feels increasingly out of place. Not because of what he does or how many people know his face. But because he's twenty and lives in a tiny apartment with a roommate he met obsessing on television shows via the internet. He still can't order a drink in public.

Alex vaguely remembers that Paul turned thirty – there'd been a party; any excuse for a party at work is taken – a few months back. The table laughs over his and Craig's 'divorce,' and someone else starts talking about a play date they had with their nephews and starts showing photos around. As Alex passes the phone with the pictures of two little toddlers along the table he feels miserably young.

Young and impermanent. Paul has history with Craig; however painful their breakup was, they have a dog and seem easy enough together now. Alex wonders if, like the story of his fame, his story with Paul will be about how he didn't exist and was never supposed to, and, one day, how he didn't anymore.

He's pulled out of his thoughts by someone yelling "cheese!" and laughing as they hand a phone to Paul, who starts typing on it. Twitter, or maybe Instagram, because someone else takes a picture of their plate and Paul is laughing about hashtags and *New mystery members of #TeamBrunch!*

Alex doesn't get caught in any of the pictures, for which he is grateful. It's hard enough to be in the world as it is. Margaret – with no small amount of exasperation – always assures him that he can go out for simple things like meals without the world ending. But it's hard to be stared at and interrupted on the street and harder still to be put on the internet he once loved so much too.

As the meal winds down Paul catches his eye more frequently. Alex doesn't know what to do, so he doesn't do anything.

In his car, he pulls his sunglasses down to see his phone over the top of them and texts Paul: *Sorry that was weird. It was good to see you.* The car starts to heat up as he waits for a reply. He turns the engine on to get the AC going.

What are the chances we both ended up at the same brunch?

Given Shawna, apparently pretty good, Alex texts back.

I didn't put her up to that.

I know.

Come over for dinner sometime this week? Paul asks.

Alex bites his lip to check his growing smile. *When?*

Friday?

◆

Monday morning Alex feels like he's dragging. He's not alone; the whole of *Fourth*'s crew seems slow and cranky. For Alex, though, it's not because he's tired, but because he's distracted. A weekend without alone time is not a weekend. And now he's back at work he both wants to run into Paul and wants some distance to collect his thoughts. They spent the night together and now have a dinner date; one more new thing in Alex's perpetually changing life.

Liam, meanwhile, is working his last nerve. He seems to think the solution to everyone's Monday blahs is to actively badger them between takes about how awesome their weekend must have been for them to feel this awful.

Alex gets what Liam is going for, even if he wishes Liam would take his enthusiasm somewhere else. Liam can grate, but he's also one of the people Alex feels easiest around, an unexpected outcome of the way they have to interact in front of the camera. But Alex doesn't want to tell anyone about hooking up with Paul, and he particularly doesn't want to tell Liam about it. Not only is he a gossip, he's casually graphic about anyone and everyone's sex lives regardless of his own involvement in them. Alex doesn't feel able to be casually graphic about his own sex life at this point.

Alex isn't actually sure he wants that to change, either. He likes having a secret that's actually, he hopes, a good thing. A delicious thing. A thing he wants more of. But it's so goddamn distracting. Which is bad. There's work to be done, and the cameras never miss distraction. What Alex needs to be thinking about isn't his relationship with Paul, but the relationship between his character on *Fourth*, Zach, and Liam's James.

"So I heard a thing," Liam says in between scenes. He bounces a little on the balls of his feet in front of Alex's chair, where Alex has his headphones on and is trying to refocus before the next material.

"What?"

Liam either doesn't hear the annoyance or chooses to ignore it. "Apparently someone had a very good time at the party on Saturday."

Alex gives him a glare that Liam pays not the least attention to. That's frustrating if unsurprising. For as good and expressive an actor as he is, Liam is often awful at picking up other people's body language. Alex is going to have to resort to chasing him off with words.

"There were a lot of people at the party. I'm sure somebody enjoyed it," he says.

"Were one of those somebodies?" Liam asks, scrubbing his hand through the back of his slightly too shaggy curls.

"What I do in private is not your business. Or anyone else's."

"Dude, hanging all over each other at a party with half the crew around is not private."

"Liam –" Alex starts. They have always had very different levels of comfort with aspects of their lives being made public. Alex wants to make very clear what is and is not acceptable for Liam to talk about Alex doing anywhere near a camera. Before he can get any more words out though, Liam's eyes light up.

"It wasn't just the dancing! You hooked up with him!"

Alex drops his head into his hands. How can Liam be so bad at social cues and yet pick up on *that*?

"Don't be like that! This is amazing! Paul is awesome! Alex! How was it?"

"How do you know it was Paul?" Alex hisses from between his fingers.

"I have sources."

Alex tips his head back and stares at the ceiling in lieu of committing murder. He wonders who talked and why. Given that half the crew had been there, the list of suspects – and motives – is discouragingly long.

"So how was it? Is he good?"

Alex snaps his head back down. "No!"

"No, it wasn't any good?" Liam's eyes are wide, concerned, and utterly insincere.

"No, I am not having this conversation with you!"

Liam pouts.

Alex laughs. "Do you think that's going to work?"

"One of these days, something's going to get you to crack. When was the last time you even got laid?"

Just then they get called back to start shooting again.

"Working now!" Alex sings. He kicks up from the chair to push past him.

Liam jogs after him. "We're not done with this."

"Find someone else to bother!"

8

When lunch comes, Liam decides to follow Alex's advice and find someone else to pester. *The Fourth Estate* shoots on the lot's least far-flung stage. It's easy enough for him to jog past the courtyard with the shitty coffee place and go poke around the boxy office building where *Fourth's* writers have been cruelly, yet conveniently, consigned.

He never gets there. Victor intercepts him, hooking elbows with Liam as their paths cross on the asphalt.

"And what are you doing?" Victor purrs as they walk.

Liam laughs. That voice is Victor's bored voice, and Liam – more or less like everyone else on *Fourth* – serves at the pleasure of his amusement.

"I was about to seek out some gossip, but apparently you've come to deliver instead?" he asks hopefully.

"Not likely. Does anyone know where you are?"

"Crew's on lunch. We're on lunch. And they totally have to lay track before the next shot. I have time." Liam's not supposed to stray so far from set in costume without a P.A. at hand to fetch him back, but if he can't help himself, he at least tries to choose his moments. He doesn't like disappointing Victor.

Victor doesn't agree. "Mmmmhmmm."

"Alex wanders off all over the place all the time."

"Liam, Alex is a cat," Victor says in a voice that's supposed to make Liam focus but is, in actuality, as interesting and distracting as nearly everything else. "He knows where and when his dinner is served. You, on the other hand, are a dog that chases squirrels in the neighbor's yard for days at a time."

"Ow. Ow! That is harsh." Liam laughs and presses his free hand to his heart.

"Would Carly tell me I'm wrong?"

"Fine." Liam concedes. His girlfriend and Victor agree on most things, especially those that regard him. "But you still want to know the thing I was on my way to find out about."

"Really? And what's that?" Victor's voice is gentle but Liam knows he has not yet succeeded in making his case.

"Alex and Paul."

Victor squints. "Alex and Paul what?"

"Sitting in a tree, K-I-S-S-I-N-G," Liam hisses with glee.

Victor stops dead, causing Liam to trip over his untied shoelaces. "Repeat that."

"Alex and Paul. Isn't that totally awesome?"

Victor stares at him.

"Is that not totally awesome?" Liam deflates a little.

"Who told you and who knows?"

"Alex confirmed it by yelling at me when I mentioned half the crew saw them hanging all over each other at Paul's on Saturday."

"Happy Monday to me," Victor murmurs. He disentangles himself from Liam and pats his cheek. "Be a good boy and eat lunch. I'm going to ruin someone's day."

◆

Paul's glad to stay back when everyone else in the writers' room goes to eat. He's been distracted all morning and the usual banter and grumbling of the office is getting on his nerves. With the place to himself, he can sit with his laptop on his thighs, his feet up on someone else's chair, and his mind on Alex.

Suddenly someone touches him. Paul jumps, but it's only Victor, lifting the headphones away from Paul's ears.

"Lunch time," he announces.

"Jesus, Victor." Paul puts his feet back on the ground, his heart pounding. "What's up?"

Victor drops the headphones unceremoniously onto a table. No apology for scaring the shit out of Paul is forthcoming. Paul's pretty sure Victor wouldn't even understand why there should be.

"Come with me," he says. Paul follows obediently as Victor sets out on the long way around to catering. Once the hallway is relatively clear Victor says, "So. You and Alex."

"How do you know about that?" Paul is surprised – although he probably shouldn't be – that word has already managed to reach Victor.

"Liam told me."

"Liam wasn't there."

"And?" Victor asks.

"Oh." Paul has long had – from multiple sources – more information on Victor's relationship with Liam than he wants. Paul has never been able to make sense of it. Victor's magnetism, he gets. And Liam is pretty and can be charming, when he wants something. But how they could possibly work together is baffling. Mostly, Paul tries not to think about too much.

"Oh. Yes. Exactly." Victor mocks; Victor always mocks. "Would you like to explain to me why you felt the need to take out your dysfunctional singlehood on Alex of all people? He's ten years younger than you."

Paul is affronted. Usually he's fine with Victor's encyclopedic knowledge of the one-night stands and personal debacles of his staff. But Victor's desire to comment on this suddenly strikes Paul as even less appropriate than the Liam thing.

"I didn't take anything out on him," Paul protests. "Alex is a big boy, he can handle himself."

"When it comes to this, I wish he didn't have a need to. Do not fuck with him."

Paul has dealt with Victor continuously for years, ever since he first hired him as an intern on a show now long gone but still much loved. Still, Paul feels a little thrill of animal fear at that particular tone. Not that he's inclined to give into it. Most things with Victor are a test anyway.

"It's not like that," he says easily. "It was good. It *is* good."

Victor looks skeptical. "This is not all in the past tense?"

"We've got a date on Friday."

"Do you now?"

"Yeah. He's coming over for dinner."

"You're serious right now." Victor sounds appalled.

Paul gives a little shrug and refrains from reminding Victor that he's known Alex a while. Or that it was Victor himself who assigned Alex to Paul. This isn't just a blowjob and a bucket of inappropriate workplace romance. Even if he is self-aware enough to know it's definitely all that too.

Victor narrows his eyes. "All right," he says finally. "This could be good."

Paul is amused, now that he's sure he's not getting shouted at, how everyone is always merely a character in Victor's world.

Victor goes on. "You're way more functional when you're not alone –"

"Thanks, Victor," Paul says. Because *really*.

"It's true; don't start. And I'd worry a lot less about Alex if he wasn't single."

"What are you worried about Alex for?"

"Many, many things." Victor nods to himself. "All right. But be careful of him. He has his own mind. And you front well, but we both know you were a mess long before Craig and you're still a mess now."

"Once again, *thank* you." There are days when Paul can't believe someone hasn't hauled off and hit Victor long ago. Despite the debt Paul owes him, this is one of them.

"I came to find you to yell at you, you know" Victor's voice gentles.

"I know," Paul says. "It was hard to miss."

"I feel like I should go yell at Alex instead."

"Are you going to?" Paul asks, some mixture of curious and cautious. He's not sure what Victor wants from Alex beyond better ratings. The possibilities are almost enough to make him worry.

"No. You know what you're getting into, or at least you should. And Alex...." Victor trails off before spreading his hands expansively. "Alex always lands on his feet."

By the time they get to catering, there's a bustle of people. Victor steps out of the flow just before the door. Paul stands aside with him.

"Did you know his birthday is on Thursday?" Victor asks.

Paul ducks his head, a show of self-consciousness for Victor's entertainment. "No, Victor, I didn't IMDB him." He had a while ago, back when Alex first started acting on *Fourth*, but Paul hadn't retained the birthday details. He's a little surprised that Alex is only turning twenty-one; he's far more sane and put together than Paul was a decade ago, although that may not be saying much.

Victor grabs his upper arm and squeezes it in approval, possession, and maybe even comfort. "You're terrible. Go eat. And tell him not to freak out about Liam."

♦

You didn't tell me your birthday was Thursday, Paul texts Alex later that afternoon as a way to open the topic.

He doesn't get a response for hours. *Keep forgetting, and I don't want it to be a thing.*

Actual convo for later? Paul tries.

I guess. It's not like I've never had tequila before.

If Friday's gonna be too hungover for you, just let me know.

No, Alex replies. *Looking forward.*

"Aren't you always," Paul murmurs before he sets his phone down and gets back to work.

9

The week between his hookup with Paul and their planned dinner date is long. Alex is working five full days in a row, which means he has very little time to do anything outside of work. The ten-hour turnaround he's guaranteed feels a lot shorter with each passing day. Besides work and sleep, he has a meeting and a few phone calls with Margaret. She's found a movie opportunity for him, if he's interested. Given how reluctantly he accepted the part on *Fourth*, he's surprised to find that he is. No TV show lasts forever, and whatever Alex is going to do with the rest of his life, he'd be foolish to limit his options.

Aside from work and meetings and planning, there's also Paul. Alex doesn't see him much on the lot but Paul texts him throughout the day and in the evening. He's never pushy or intrusive, but he is quietly insistent about his interest in Alex. It's yet another new experience to have someone other than Gemma to communicate with who is always willing if not eager to talk to him. Slowly and carefully, Alex lets himself enjoy it.

On Wednesday, Liam sheepishly admits that the gossip about Alex and Paul had made it to Victor…somehow. It's not hard to wring out of him that it was Liam himself who talked. Alex is thrilled when his reaction to that not-quite confession makes Liam feel guilty enough to not badger him for a record forty-eight hours.

Thursday they make a big deal of his birthday on set. There's cake and booze and more attention than Alex wants, but less than there could be. Besides, the thought is nice. Birthdays were never a big deal when he was a kid.

Paul is there, to say hi or Tweet semi-officially for the show as is his habit. Alex isn't sure which, but decides to enjoy it regardless. He laughs and poses for a picture for him after Liam puts a plate of cake in his hands and pushes him forward. Paul winks when he lowers the phone. Alex smiles back. Even if it's not entirely a secret at this point – Liam is definitely giving Alex knowing looks around Paul's shoulder – it's still fun.

Alex's mom calls while he's driving home. Traffic as usual is awful; the mess that is the L.A. highway system never ceases to amaze Alex or to piss him off. But today it means they get to talk for forty-five minutes before Alex pulls into his parking lot and has to think about going inside and dealing with dinner.

But even then he sits in his car in for another fifteen minutes while they finish catching each other up on everything going on in their lives. At least, almost everything. If Alex can't figure out how to talk about Paul with Gemma or Liam, he sure as hell doesn't know how to talk about him with his mom.

Eventually he says *I love you too* and hangs up. It takes him a couple of tries before the odd homesickness for a place he never liked subsides and he feels ready to go inside. Every thought of home is hard for him. He misses it and his mom, even as he doesn't miss growing up in Indiana at all.

10

Friday drags as Fridays do. Paul is tired but excited by the time he finally gets home. It's only been a week since he had Alex here, but it seems longer. He can't wait to see him again away from work. Alex is clearly, maybe even calculatedly, a compendium of stories that he might one day tell Paul, but only if Paul very, *very* lucky. Now that the weekend's here Paul doesn't just want him, he wants to earn those tales.

He turns on the iPod player in its dock on the counter. He hums along as he cooks, stopping from time to time to take a disgruntled Todd down from the counter when he gets too bold in exploring what's on the stove. He's in the middle of setting the table when his phone buzzes with a text. It's Alex saying he's almost there.

Paul sees his car pull in the drive from the window and meets him at the door. He leans against the frame and grins when Alex gives a little wave as he comes up the walk.

"Do you always wear that hat out?" he asks. Alex has on the slouchy brown knit beanie from brunch.

Alex lifts the strap of his messenger bag over his head and sets it down by the door. "Only when there are people. A fan made it for me."

Paul shuts the door. "You wear a hat a fan made you to hide from your fans?"

"She was very sweet."

"You are very strange." Paul raises a hand with a questioning look on his face. When Alex doesn't back away he tugs the hat off, smiling at the way the red strands spike up in every direction. "I like you better without it."

When Alex doesn't step away, Paul combs his fingers through his hair, smoothing out the worst of the tangles. Alex watches him with that stillness of his until Paul curls his fingers around the back of his head. Alex takes the hint and leans in to kiss him.

Alex deepens the kiss and digs his hands into Paul's hips. That's new, and Paul smiles against his mouth. When Alex breaks the kiss he doesn't pull back, but leans his forehead against Paul's shoulder. Paul, after a shocked second, realizes that Alex wants a hug. He wraps his arms around Alex's back and is rewarded with the feel of Alex's arms around his waist. Alex's hair is soft against his cheek.

They stay like that for Paul doesn't know how long. Then Alex's stomach growls.

Paul chuckles. Alex laughs sheepishly and disentangles himself.

♦

"I never had Thai until I got to L.A.," Alex says as Paul passes him a plate. "I still can't get my mom to go out to anything other than Italian or Mexican when she's here."

Paul reaches for the corkscrew and tries to mask his excitement over Alex volunteering information. "I suggested Mexican one time when my family was visiting. There was an uproar," Paul says.

"God bless America." Alex watches Paul's hands as he opens the wine. "Land of the free, home of the narrow hick palate."

"How long did it take you to try sushi?" Paul asks. It's been a long time since anything other than meat and mashed potatoes had seemed unfamiliar and intimidating. But sushi had been his own personal barometer of *Oh, I'm in a big city now* way back when.

Alex wrinkles his nose. "Embarrassingly long. Gemma finally made me, which…awesome. Unlike the kimchi she told me was coleslaw."

"It's effectively coleslaw," Paul points out.

"I like it now! But it was my first night in L.A. and I was not prepared. She's sort of a food menace. Day two was kale chips, for which I was also not prepared."

♦

"Since you're officially legal now," Paul says as he pours wine for them both. "Also, happy birthday."

"Thanks." Alex takes a tentative sip of the wine. He's not used to being served dinner like this, not by a man interested, apparently, in wooing him. Business dinners with expensive food and wines he can't pronounce are becoming somewhat of a norm for him. But this – sharing food in someone's house – is not. Alex's life jumped from one extreme to the other. In those moments where he lands in the middle – in what might be called *normal* – he has no idea what to do. It can't be harder than anything else he's dealt with in his life.

"Have anything fun planned?" Paul asks.

Alex plays with the stem of his glass. "I got six different offers from three different clubs wanting to host a party for me for free. Great publicity for them. Strange for me. So, no." Not that he'd had any interest in a big industry party. There aren't enough people he'd want to invite. Or enough that he'd trust to even consider drinking around. No, that list for now is limited to Gemma. And now Paul.

"Doesn't sound too festive." Paul sits down across from Alex and reaches for his napkin. Belatedly, Alex remembers he's supposed to put his on his lap.

"Home, Gemma, and nothing to do for a night is plenty festive." He's been looking forward to it all week. Almost as much as this date. Which he should probably let Paul know. Alex nudges Paul's foot gently under the table. "So is this."

Talking to other people is something that Alex has struggled with his entire life. In Indiana, there was no one – besides his mom – who he could talk *to*. He was too different and life was too hard. Then he'd discovered the world that existed on the internet, outside of the bounds of Paragon. He'd met Gemma and other people who were, more or less, like him. Or at least were not like the people he had grown up with and who he saw at school and work every day.

Moving to L.A. had opened the world to him all over again. He didn't have to be wary of everyone he passed on the street or saw in the store. Except then he'd become J. Alex Cook and he did. Now the internet isn't a refuge anymore either. He has work to distract himself with, and Gemma of course, but aside from her – and Liam's gregarious attempts at bonding – he doesn't really have friends.

And now here's Paul, who can carry on a conversation in a way that makes Alex want to talk. He's smart and thoughtful and asks Alex questions about himself and offers information about his own life in a way that makes it clear that he's interested in Alex, not in scoring some sort of celebrity points.

It's scary, but no more so than the night when they'd hooked up. Giving someone information about himself is a way of giving them power over him. But he trusts Paul. Has, for some reason, ever since Paul caught him making out with Nick back before everything changed.

They have more in common than Alex expected. For one, their families. Paul talks about his mom and his sister, but makes no mention of his dad. For another, they both have work commitments beyond being average L.A. workaholics.

There's *Fourth*, obviously. Paul talks about some original pilot scripts he's working on, but doesn't seem to want to dwell on that topic. When Alex mentions *Paradise Square*, Paul eagerly asks about it.

"Historical drama," Alex tells him. "Immigrants and poverty and gangs and disease in Five Points. It's going to be filming in New York this winter. What days I'm needed is still getting sorted, but I wanted to see what it was like doing something I asked to be in."

Paul smiles. "You're spoiled for choice, aren't you?"

"Terror of the fairytale," Alex says. He tips his glass, watching the wine slide over the surface of it.

"Disney or Grimm?"

Alex considers it. "Andersen," he says.

"I look forward to seeing you in it. You'll be beautiful."

"The princess is always beautiful," Alex says derisively.

"Not in your fairytale. In New York."

"Is there a difference?"

Paul takes some time to think the answer through. "New York is temporary."

Alex traces his fingers over Paul's. "So am I." He doesn't know how to explain that that's not about the fact that he's not going to live forever, but that he hasn't been alive for longer. There's hardly a moment with Paul that he doesn't feel young and impermanent. "And so is the story."

Paul flips his palm up and smiles when Alex laces their fingers together. "You're going to have a busy winter. We're working on something now that'll put you on the road too."

Alex looks up from their intertwined hands, curious.

"Exteriors in D.C. And then some stuff here, but out on location."

"What's that?"

"So you know the thing where Zach can speak Farsi and *really* wants a story?"

"I don't know, tell me more about my character," Alex says drily.

"He's going to get himself into Iran. Details TBD. But word on the street is you're going to be spending some time in the desert this winter."

Alex knows he should be excited. New York, then D.C., then whatever southwest desert they'll use. It's more travel than he's ever done before, and he feels embarrassed and awkward. He's been to New York City and doesn't love it – the buildings are too high, the streets are too dirty, and there are too many lights and too much media attention. D.C. is completely new to him and therefore intimidating. Whatever he'll be doing in the desert won't be as bad, but it's one more unknown on top of the rest. Holding it all in his head at once is hard. Alex knows he should be grateful for these opportunities, but what he really wants is six months in L.A. with time to get used to all the other new things in his life. Like moving. And Paul.

"Well then," Alex says, holding up a pale, freckled arm. "I recommend buying stock in sunblock."

◆

They talk so much that dinner takes forever. Eventually, though, they manage to push back from the table. Alex is keenly aware of the heaviness of the moment, even if it's clear that they both know what they want.

"Am I taking you to the couch or the bedroom?" Paul asks as he takes their plates to the sink.

"Bed." At least in bed, Alex won't have to think. For now he distracts himself by crouching down to pet Todd who's flopped on the floor and looking hopefully at him.

After a moment, Alex looks up to see Paul watching him, an unreadable expression on his face.

"Sorry." Alex stands, not sure if he's overstepped somehow.

Paul shakes his head. "Glad you're making friends. Let's bring the wine upstairs, too, okay?"

◆

They're quiet on the stairs, and Alex feels no less awkward when they get to Paul's bedroom. The room, now that he's letting himself look at it, doesn't give much away: pale yellow walls, dark blue comforter, white trim around the windows and doors. The airiness of it is all California, but it lacks the blunt excess of his costars' massive and ugly houses. He likes it. Even so, the contrast to his own apartment remains immense and fills Alex with a certain degree of shame over his choices. Alex thinks about the nights Paul spends alone. He's fascinated by the mystery of normal adult life.

Paul sets down the wine and glasses on the little table next to the armchair that resides in the corner of the bedroom. The silence stretches, snapping only when he finally takes a step toward Alex.

Alex closes the rest of the gap and kisses him hard, pressing against him. Paul slips his hands into the back pockets of Alex's jeans and kneads at his ass.

"Clothes," Alex mutters as he starts frantically trying to pull Paul out of his.

They break apart only for the logistics of it all. Getting socks and pants off is tricky, especially when they're both so eager to get to each other's skin that hands keep getting in the way.

Once they're both finally naked Alex pushes Paul into the armchair, which faces the bed and gives Alex a million ideas that range from sitting there getting a show to simply relaxing with a book while watching Paul sleep.

Right now, though, he wants his hands on Paul. He straddles Paul's lap, wine glass in hand, and offers him a sip.

"No," he says, when Paul tries to take the glass from him.

"All right. But you may regret this," Paul says with a wicked smile, before he lets Alex hold the glass to his lips again and tilt.

The second the glass is out of the way, Paul fists a hand into Alex's hair. He kisses him hard and, when his mouth opens, feeds him the wine he's let pool on his tongue.

Alex moans, hips grinding against Paul, and almost drops the glass.

Paul laughs, breaks the kiss, and catches it just in time.

"Do that again," Alex says breathlessly, wiping wine from his chin and loving the mess of it all.

"Sure, but I hold the glass."

By the time they've finished the wine, Paul has his arm tight around Alex's waist as he shifts and grinds over him. He whimpers softly into Paul's mouth.

Somehow, Alex feels drugged by less than half a bottle of wine and the miracle of Paul's kisses.

♦

Paul nips at Alex's lower lip. "You good?" he whispers. Alex is so damn lost to it. A frantic nod and a whimper before Alex wraps his hand tightly around Paul's dick is all he gets in response.

Paul lets his head fall back against the chair, drops the now-empty glass out of his hand onto the carpet, and lets Alex drive until Paul comes all over the both of them.

"Hold on to me," he says once he's caught his breath. Alex is still shifting, restless and desperate over him.

With an arm under Alex's ass and another across his back, Paul gets them to the bed, barely. It's only a few steps, and he is happy to leave Alex's ass hanging off the edge, his legs in the air. Paul kneels again – there's something about Alex that just does that to him – and this time licks over his hole.

Alex whines and twists.

"Okay?" Paul asks. They've been taking risks together that aren't entirely stupid, but aren't particularly responsible either.

"Don't talk, don't stop," Alex gasps.

For a moment, Paul only obeys the first command because Alex tortured, unable to stop moving and unable to get or give himself relief, is the hottest thing he has ever seen. His spent dick twitches in sympathy. He'll be jerking off to this all week.

"Come on, come *on*...."

"Patience," Paul breathes. The sound Alex makes is hopeless. Paul's body tries so hard to react to that it hurts. He presses an arm across the back of Alex's thighs, folding him in half, gets his other hand on his dick, and licks until Alex comes so hard he's pretty sure the neighbors hear it.

After, he somehow winds up pulling Alex down onto the floor and into his arms.

"What the fuck happened there?" Alex sounds dazed.

Paul laughs and quickly finds himself unable to stop from sheer delight.

Alex smiles and his eyes crinkle but he doesn't seem to have enough of himself together to laugh yet. He loops his arms around Paul's neck and slumps his head against his shoulder.

Paul wraps his arms tighter around his back. "You are unbelievable."

"Not just me," Alex says.

Paul laughs again and kisses the side of his neck. He strokes his back gently as Alex breathes into his shoulder.

"Everything okay there?" Paul finally asks, when a couple of minutes pass with Alex saying nothing at all, just growing steadily heavier in his arms. Paul's starting to get cold and his leg is a bit numb because it's tucked under the weight of both of them and they're *on the fucking floor*. Alex is warm against him, though, and Paul is happy to stay here as long as Alex needs them to.

"It's too much," Alex says into his skin. He sounds small and far away.

It's not a yes, and Paul goes still, afraid suddenly that maybe he has pushed Alex too far. The idea of letting go of him now or ever is devastating.

"Do you need to stop?" he asks, although there's nothing to stop right now except their strange cuddling in the possibly even stranger afterglow.

"No," Alex says and finally lifts his head to look at Paul, blinking like he's just becoming aware of where he is. "No, it's good." When he smiles, Paul relaxes. "I liked it," Alex adds. In another breath the smile turns wicked.

"Good," Paul says, relieved. "Because you have an amazing ass that deserves to be appreciated." He lets his hand drop below Alex's back and squeezes at it.

Alex giggles, before he blinks up at Paul through his lashes with a look that's so dangerous Paul groans.

Despite that moment of boldness, once they finally get themselves untangled enough to stand up, clean up, and stretch out on the bed for a nap, Alex stays pressed close to him. He's even quieter than usual as they lay side by side, their breaths syncing up almost immediately.

Paul rubs a thumb absently over Alex's hip until they both slip into a doze. He wonders, if Alex always lands on his feet, exactly how far he's falling right now.

When Paul wakes, it's to Alex hovering over him, happy and looking like he's about to get in trouble for something. Paul's first random thought, after *thank God* that he looks okay now, is that Alex's dark eyes are mesmerizing.

"How are you?" Paul lifts a hand to brush at Alex's cheek. His skin is so tempting.

"Hungry." Alex turns his head to kiss Paul's fingers, then sucks at the tips of them.

Paul presses his thumb to the corner of Alex's mouth. "Do you want to eat, or do you want to fuck again? Because if you keep doing that, your options are going to be limited."

Alex pulls away from Paul's hand with a last nip to his fingers. "Eat."

◆

They eat on the couch, passing the container of cold leftovers back and forth and gossiping about everyone they know on *Fourth*. They don't talk about what people on the show might be saying regarding them. Alex feels, in spite of the complications sex supposedly brings, like he's hanging out with Gemma. Being with Paul is easy and fun. But more than that, it's comfortable. Alex has never been completely at ease around anyone. But with Paul, he feels muscles that have been tight for years relax. And Paul seems to enjoy him, too. He's attentive and eager to listen to Alex, no matter what Alex is saying.

Alex doesn't know what time it is when he finally retrieves his bag from where he left it sitting by the door and follows Paul upstairs to fall back into bed again. They don't stop talking when Paul turns out the light. With Paul's voice quiet and intimate in the dark, Alex feels his universe expand.

In the morning Paul is still in bed when Alex wakes, though he's sitting up and has his tablet on his knees.

"Hey you," he says.

Alex mutters and pulls the blanket over his head and presses closer to his thigh. It's bright in the room.

Paul touches his hair gently. "Not a morning person?"

"It's Saturday," Alex complains. If days off are for anything they for getting caught up on sleep.

Paul chuckles. "You're welcome to stay in bed all day."

Alex battles internally over the offer. In the plus column is a day in bed with Paul, with nothing to do except share space and time and the very high likelihood of more sex. He's eager to get all of it for as long as he can. That said, he's starting to feel restless. He's too much in his own head even with Paul right here beside him. Alex worries this might be both too new and too much of a good thing. Perhaps there's a compromise to be reached. He pushes back the covers, sits up, and smiles into it when Paul leans in to finally kiss him good morning.

Paul sets his tablet aside. "Shower?"

"Not yet," Alex says. It's warm in the bedroom with the sunlight coming in, and he's still a bit sticky from last night, but getting up for a shower will mean the end of this extended and glorious date. Wary as he is, he's not ready to go just yet, so he pushes down the blankets and slides down the bed to settle between Paul's legs. Just because he's not willing to spend the day in bed together doesn't mean it can't start it on a high note.

They eat breakfast downstairs. Todd decides the new human is a sucker who will share the milk at the bottom of his cereal bowl. Alex and Paul talk about going to brunch with the crew tomorrow, and Alex and the cat reach a compromise: Todd gets the dregs of the milk, but with the bowl on the floor.

Alex asks quietly if he can come back later tonight, too.

"Stay here today, save yourself the trip," Paul offers.

Alex rubs Todd's ears and wonders how he used to get along with Beau. "I have some work I have to do," he says. The statement is only partly a lie. There's a call to his agent he needs to make, emails have been piling up that need answering, and he pretty much always has lines to learn and research reading to do. "Ask me again next week?"

"Will do."

When Alex is ready to leave Paul drags him into a kiss by the door. It takes effort not to let himself get lost in it. If he lets go completely he's not sure he'll ever leave, and he needs to.

As usual, Alex is a relieved to be alone in his car. Once he gets a few blocks away, he has to remind himself not to pull over to take a few deep breaths. L.A. cops are assholes, and he's way too recognizable. He knows he should head home; Gemma's probably going to be annoyed if he's out too long. But he wants some more space and time to himself first, so he drives down to the pier and parks in one of the awkward public lots off to the side of the highway that are always a little deserted because the tourists don't realize they're there.

He's been coming here a lot in the last year. The beach is one of the only places he doesn't get recognized. He looks like one more pretty kid in a stupid beanie nursing unlikely dreams in Santa Monica – no one notices and no one cares. He pays the muni meter, takes off his shoes, and sits cross-legged in the sand far enough from the water that no one gets within twenty feet of him.

The ocean is good for feeling small. Sometimes that's overwhelming, but today it feels grounding. One thing he wishes Victor had told him before his life blew up is that fame mostly will make you feel like less than you have ever been.

He wonders if fame, or the age difference, or his own lack of experience with other humans is what's making everything going on with Paul feel so good and so temporary. Alex is pretty sure Paul will show him things, and then he'll be gone into some real relationship, with a real adult who's a real person all the time; they'll even get another real dog. Todd probably misses having a dog around; Paul probably worries about that. Alex laughs to – and at – himself. He's already in deep if he's worried about the cat.

While he's stewing, Gemma calls to complain of boredom. Instead of telling her to fuck off, he convinces her to come meet him.

She shows up an hour later wearing cut-off jeans and a loose white shirt that ripples in the wind. She sits down silently in the sand next to him.

Alex surprises himself by saying, "I think it's time to start house hunting."

Because she's Gemma – and because they've talked about it faintly in the past – she starts listing her requirements before Alex has a chance to ask her if she wants to move with him. The presumption is annoying, but not unexpected.

Eventually, he makes her run up to the pier proper to get them beach fries and lemonades, because the one time he tried that since *Fourth* he got mobbed by a bunch of tourists. When she comes back, he asks her if she's ever had anal sex. He regrets the question the moment it passes his lips. He knows it's his own fault, but she manages to overshare, tell him nothing useful, and make several sets of unpleasant assumptions about his life in the process.

While Gemma babbles, Alex stares at the ocean from behind his sunglasses and eats his fries. When he can no longer avoid some sort of response to her monologue, he says, "So rimming's good; you should try that."

She tackles him into the sand, laughing, when he refuses to say anything more. Alex wonders if this is what college would have been like.

He feels sad when he has to get back in his car to follow her home. The drive is lonely, but once there he happily face-plants on his bed and takes a two-hour nap. When he gets up, he emails Margaret – his favorite source of advice on how to be an adult. *Having an attack of the grownups. I need to buy a house, and I need an assistant. Probably not in that order. Help?*

She drops him a note back from her phone reminding him he has a financial advisor he should talk to about the first, but that she'll see what she can do on the second. Alex looks around his room. He wonders if, when he and Gemma move out, he should leave a note in the crevice by the window jamb. He wants whoever the next tenant is to know that yes, there are cockroaches and the faucet drips, and the tiling in the kitchen is super ugly, but this place, small and terrible, may just treat them kindly.

11

Paul has work he should be doing, but he procrastinates for hours before he makes himself face it. When he eventually does, he sits with his laptop and his notes and tries not to be too aware of the spaces where Alex isn't, or the clock and how slowly it's moving. In the afternoon, when the space and the quiet finally get to be too much, he puts his iPod on and loses another hour running.

He showers again when he gets back and feels a pleasant burst of satisfaction when he sees Alex's toothbrush, forgotten or deliberately left, by the sink. Eventually he calls his sister, Sarah, but that turns out to be a mistake. She keeps asking him how his weekend is going, and he can't give her any detail without admitting he slept with J. Alex Cook. Sarah watches *The Fourth Estate* and knows who he is. Paul doesn't want to contemplate how awkwardly she might take this news.

When Alex finally texts to say that he's on his way over, Paul sends back an invitation for sushi.

Instead of a text in return, he gets a call.

"I can't go out for dinner."

"Why not?"

"Because I'm me, and people are assholes. I want to spend time with you, not have fans taking photographs or trying to touch me like I'm some good luck charm."

"You went for brunch," Paul reminds him He wonders how fucked up Alex – or Alex's life – is if he's balking at a late-night run for sushi.

"Strength in numbers and also gays," Alex says flatly. "I can't, Paul."

"It's a little place." He wants Alex in his home and his bed, of course, but he wants to be able to go out with him too. "You're allowed to go out and do things in the world."

"Most people disagree."

Alex's words make little sense and feel frightening. Sure, fans can be weird, but the house arrest mentality is unsettling and, Paul thinks, paranoid. "No one will bother you. Code of the native Angelino and all that," Paul says carefully. It's the truest of Los Angeles's theoretical and unwritten laws: No one ever bothers a star while they are eating.

He can practically hear Alex thinking about it. When the quiet drags on, he can't resist the urge to push. "Do you not have your hat?"

Alex laughs. "Okay. Fine."

◆

Alex has only been away from Paul for a few hours but, as he pulls into Paul's driveway, he feels like he's been gone a lot longer. Paul is waiting for him at the door, a dark silhouette against the cozy glow of light inside. He kisses Alex as soon as he steps across the threshold, warm and easy. Paul's mouth feels more familiar to Alex than two nights together would seem to allow.

"Ready to go?" Paul asks, when he finally pulls back, reaching up to straighten the beanie on Alex's head.

"If there are fans I'm blaming you."

At the restaurant while they wait for the hostess, Paul puts a hand on his back. All else being equal, Alex would quite like for him to keep it there. But they're in public and a gesture witnessed is a gesture that other people get to own. Alex doesn't want other people to have this part of him too. He steps away.

Paul gives him a look, confused and a little hurt.

"Sorry," Alex mutters. He's not sure how to explain himself in words. "I –"

"It's fine. I forgot," Paul puts his hands in his pockets with an apologetic smile. "Sorry."

Moments later a girl approaches. Phone already in hand, she asks for a picture. Alex says no to her, sweetly but without apology. He doesn't feel remotely guilty for it. Paul said he's allowed to have a normal night, so that's what he's going to try to do.

As the girl walks away – at least she was polite; some of them aren't – Paul murmurs, "I see what you mean."

"The internet's not going to like that," Alex observes.

"What's the internet going to care?" Paul asks.

Alex gives him a condescending look.

"Okay, why are you going to care that random people you don't know on the internet care?"

"Wait and see." Alex is slightly more amused at the potential headache ahead than he would be otherwise. At least he'll get to make the point to Paul. The other man may have a house and a cat and an ex who took his dog, but Alex has fame. Adulthood, apparently, does not automatically allow another person to understand the price he pays for living in the public eye.

♦

Alex says he doesn't want to wait around and get spotted again, so Paul suggests they get their sushi to go rather than bailing. Alex agrees, looking relieved and grateful. Paul wonders at that; it doesn't seem hard to be kind about whatever reservations Alex fairly has about being in the world. Paul is starting to recognize that there may be a learning curve here for the both of them.

In the car he hands Alex his iPod and tells him to pick the music. It works reasonably well to distract Alex from his funk. By the time they pull into Paul's street they're arguing over the merits of various shitty country-pop bands. Paul mocks Alex's selections while Alex cackles mercilessly at some of Paul's playlists.

The internet, it turns out, cares. Alex was apparently right. Paul should have known – he does after all tweet occasionally about the show and has interacted lightly with some of the fans. But engaging fans about his job on the internet is light years away from strangers on the internet caring deeply about who Alex is having dinner with. While Alex sets out plates and chopsticks Paul checks his own phone and is shocked to find hundreds of replies to Alex's little-used Twitter account.

Despite Alex's refusal, there is a picture. Taken from behind and with only a sliver of his profile showing but still, there's still no mistaking him. His distinctive beauty is his blessing and his curse.

What surprises Paul most, though, is that he's in the picture as well. The fans desperately want to know who is out on a Saturday night with J. Alex Cook.

I dunno! Whoever posted the picture – presumably the girl who asked Alex for a photo – has responded to several inquiries of varying degrees of intrusiveness. *Some guy. I think they were there together.*

Ohmygod is he there on a date? Does Alex have a boyfriend??

The conversation devolves quickly as someone shows up convinced, and apropos of nothing, that Alex is, in fact, involved with Liam and couldn't possibly be with any other random guy. After that, the whole mess of speculation and anger spins so far away from reality that Paul doesn't know how to process it now that it touches his own very real life.

Alex looks up from unpacking the food and sees Paul staring at his phone with a mix of bewilderment and horror. He asks, his voice mild, "Was I unspeakably rude to say no to a picture, or a cheating lying whore for not being with Liam?"

"I suppose I should have seen this coming." Paul admits. He doesn't know if he's supposed to apologize – for the internet or for the fan or for suggesting they go out in the first place – but Alex doesn't ask for anything. He clucks at Todd and nudges him away from where he's eyeing the takeout bag.

"And people wonder why I never tweet," Alex mumbles.

◆

Alex doesn't mention the Twitter explosion again. Still, Paul keeps rolling it over in the back of his mind while they eat and play Trials Evolution for a couple of hours, whooping and laughing whenever one of them finds a new and spectacular way to crash. Eventually, their laughter peters out.

Paul looks at Alex, leans against him, and says, simply, "Bed."

Upstairs they're domestic. Paul swaps contacts for glasses while Alex smooths on moisturizer.

"Rules of the game, huh?" Paul wraps his arms around Alex from behind. He dips his head to rest his chin on Alex's shoulder and looks at the image they make in the mirror. They look good together. Paul's mind is running ahead of the situation, surely, but he can't help but imagine them in pictures like this.

Alex smiles into the mirror. "Gemma's fault, actually."

"I'm starting to get the impression most things are."

"She's the loyalest friend I've ever had," Alex says tightly.

"How many people from high school are you friends with on Facebook?" Paul asks, even though he's just been given a pretty clear *do not go* signal.

"I don't use Facebook." Alex twists out of Paul's arms.

Paul wants to talk more about that, to explore explicitly how lonely Alex is even without worrying about getting photographed at restaurants and gossiped about on the internet. But Alex clearly doesn't. Paul leaves the subject alone for now. He follows Alex back to the bedroom and catches him in a kiss which turns to laughter as they fall onto the bed.

The sex is easy. Alex's responsiveness in bed draws Paul in and makes him want to stay here forever. When he looks at Paul down the length of his own body, Paul can't look away. He uses all the things he's learned from watching Alex – both at work and now in his home – to coax out reactions. Alex hides his secrets deep and well, but Paul wants to reveal them all and make Alex tell him everything he's not saying.

After, they press their foreheads together to stare at each other for far too long until Alex says, "You're not very attractive as a cyclops."

◆

In the morning, they drive to brunch together. Alex is nervous on the way over, but when Paul asks if he's okay he nods.

"I'm fine." In truth, he has any number of questions, none of which he knows how to ask. Are they going to brunch *together-together*, or as two people sharing a ride? Surely the group will know their arriving together isn't purely platonic or innocent, and maybe they should talk about that. But Alex doesn't know how to begin to ask the question without sounding like he's asking for some kind of declaration from Paul.

He probably should have thought this through better.

Conversation stops at their already mostly-populated table for twelve when they walk onto the patio together.

Brian twists around in his eternal seat at the head of their table. "Well, well, well."

"Hi Brian," Paul says benignly.

"Am I correct in assuming we're supposed to change our usual seating arrangements based on this development?"

"How do you know we didn't park at the same time?" Alex says at the same time Paul says, "We don't *have* usual seating arrangements."

Brian ignores Paul. "That you said that, for one," he tells Alex. "For another, that we all know Paul."

"Don't," Paul and Shawna snap simultaneously. That earns a few chuckles as seats get shifted around so that Paul can be in reach of both Alex and Beau.

Alex is glad to leave Brian to Paul and takes shelter in conversation with Shawna. He's still painfully aware of every time the larger conversation turns back to him and Paul. Every so often Paul squeezes his knee under the table when it happens, a little gesture of solidarity. Alex appreciates it, even though Paul touching him in public is risky, as last night at the sushi joint demonstrated so well.

Alex is more than aware of how often he's probably going to have to say no to what he is learning is Paul's propensity for public displays of affection. Paul touches everyone, all the time. Even innocently, Alex can mostly never have that. The mess of yesterday notwithstanding he still wants something for himself.

Eventually, somewhere in a side conversation Alex isn't paying attention to, someone must say something they shouldn't. Paul's voice goes sharp.

"Hey, I get that you're all being my awesome asshole friends, but can we maybe do that regarding someone less likely to wind up on TMZ or at least about someone we don't actually like?"

Alex turns his head to focus on Brian, who pulls back in his chair.

"Do we like Alex? I didn't know that had been decided." The obvious pleasure he's taking in making everyone uncomfortable shocks Alex. Before Alex can say something sharp that would likely necessitate a quick and awkward exit, Shawna balls up a used napkin and tosses it at Brian.

♦

"So you know what the oddest thing about that was?" Paul asks as Alex pulls out of the parking lot.

Alex considers his options. There are a lot of them. "Your creepy hipster friend literally twirling his moustache at me?"

Paul laughs. "No, but fair. Not being able to hold your hand."

Alex hadn't expected that. Paul's sweetness takes him by surprise. Not that he didn't know Paul can be sweet. But that Paul seems to want to keep being sweet to Alex.

"Thank you for not," Alex says, then frowns at himself. He does want Paul to know he appreciates whatever sacrifices of PDA he's is making on Alex's behalf. But that didn't come out right. "That felt weird for me too."

Paul's relieved breath is audible. Slowly, almost shyly, Alex reaches across the console and takes Paul's free hand where it lies in his lap.

Their plan was to go their separate ways after brunch. But when they get back to the house Paul has to look in on something in his email. While he gets that sorted, Alex gets out his tablet and curls up next to Paul on the couch. Soon Todd comes to join them, stretching out at their feet as they deal with the administrativa of their lives.

When the room loses the sunlight in the late afternoon, Paul turns to Alex and says, "Stay?"

"My call's at six," Alex warns.

"I'll live. And if you need to go to bed early –"

"For sleep?" Alex asks, all perfectly plausible and full-of-shit innocence.

When they do turn in, after catching up on the latest Sunday night prestige show over a pizza, Paul makes a point to suck marks into every part of Alex's body the camera will never see.

12

The morning is harsh. Paul considers getting up with Alex and going for a run, but gives up the idea for the thrill of Alex, dressed for the day, sitting on the edge of the bed and kissing him before he goes. It's warm and sexy and domestic. The two extra hours of sleep after Alex leaves, in a bed that smells of him, aren't bad either.

There's a writers' meeting first thing at work. Paul pitches an idea while Victor watches him with his fingers steepled in front of his mouth. The concept has nothing to do with Zach, but Paul had finished this outline sitting in bed Saturday morning watching Alex wake up beside him. There's a prickle at the back of his neck telling him that Victor, with his eye and memory for the personal affairs of his people, knows that.

His suspicions are borne out when, after the meeting, Victor beckons Paul to follow. Once they're in the kitchenette, Victor closes the door behind them. "I saw you were out with Alex this weekend."

"Yeah," Paul says, a little cautiously. He'd thought that Victor was okay with this. But maybe now that the situation is somewhat public knowledge he's going to get yelled at.

"And things are okay?" Victor asks sternly. Paul feels like he's being drilled by a cross between a doting parent and a hostile prosecutor.

"They are." Paul wonders where this all is going.

"I'm glad you got him out of the house. I'm assuming that was your idea?"

"Did everyone see that picture?" Paul asks. Is there any element of this thing with Alex that Victor won't take notice of?

"Get used to it or become hermits together." Which option Victor favors is obvious. He has never picked favorites to let them languish in the shadows, onscreen or off.

"He doesn't like the attention." Paul's not sure if he's defending Alex's choices, which seem so justified in the face of the bullshit that comes with his life, or lamenting them. Paul doesn't want to have to live like that himself.

"Alex wants a normal life so badly he's never going to get one," Victor says, "because he's never going to do anything except go to work and sit at home so the crazies can't get him. You're getting him out of his cave and his comfort zone. That's good."

"I don't know what to say to that," Paul doesn't know how to articulate the scope of the things he's starting to learn Alex is uncomfortable with. He is also uncertain about where those boundaries lie. As much as Victor's insight might be of some use, he very much does not want to risk touching on something Alex might not want him to share.

"You don't have to say anything. You're being good to him," Victor says smugly. "Is he being good for you?"

"He is."

"Good. Keep that up."

Paul nods. He feels strange with the weight of a promise made about Alex, but not to him. "I will."

♦

"I heard you were cheating on me again," Liam says at lunch.

Alex doesn't look up from his phone. Paul is texting him about his latest shitty Facebook game addiction. *I'm stuck on level 65. Tips??*

"When aren't I?" Alex chooses distraction over annoyance as he types back, *Better reflexes. And younger fingers.*

"You weren't this year at the Emmys when you sat next to me all night," Liam points out. The fans had an absolute field day with that one, and Liam hasn't yet gotten tired of teasing Alex about it.

"I didn't pick the seats," Alex says as his phone buzzes again with another text from Paul. *Are you volunteering your services?*

"But you gave me a hug!" Liam protests.

At work. As are you, Alex thumbs into his phone. "Because you hugged me and there were cameras. Slapping you would have been bad press. Also, Victor would have yelled."

"Ouch. Wounded," Liam says.

Alex ignores Liam's hand-to-heart melodrama to roll his eyes at the latest text from Paul. *It's lunchtime! And I'm stuck now!*

Alex hesitates only a moment. The fantasy of what might happen if he went and found Paul in person is nice, but it's only a fantasy. Even if he were brave enough to consider it, Alex can't imagine it would be possible to have a quickie on the lot and not get busted. He texts back *Patience.*

Paul's disappointed response comes almost instantly. Alex laughs to himself as he sticks his phone back in his pocket.

"Who are you texting?" Liam asks as if he can't guess perfectly well.

"Someone by the grace of whom I am not putting you in a headlock right now."

"Damn, that's some good sex if it's got you this chill."

"Am I?" Alex asks. He's never quite sure what to do with Liam and his persistent attempts at whatever friendship he's after.

"You're talking to me and haven't yelled yet?"

Alex considers how much energy he's willing to devote to being offended by Liam right now and decides not much. The return on investment is guaranteed to be low. "Do you ever stop talking?"

"Not when it gets me good details, no."

"What details are you getting?" Alex asks, exasperated.

"That you're having sex, that the sex is with Paul, and that the internet knows about it, which means that the gossip is, for once, based in fact."

"The internet knows nothing."

"It knows you got sushi with Paul. How is that place, by the way? I've been meaning to try it."

Alex kicks Liam's shin under the table. "How come every time you're out with someone the internet never decides you're a slut and a cheat?"

"Because I'm poly and the internet decided I was a slut and a cheat a long time ago. Not news anymore. Doesn't make it true – I mean, I am a slut, but…. They still know a lot more about me than they do about you. Downside to your air of mystery, J. Alex."

Alex suspects the real reasons are more gross than that. Liam is the handsome straight TV star heartthrob. The general public may not understand the consensual non-monogamy thing, but that's not Alex's problem. Being the pretty twink is.

"Please don't," he begs.

Liam perks up even more. "Hey, what does Paul call you in bed? He's a writer, he must be great with all sorts of words."

Alex can feel his face go scarlet. The memory of Paul's breathy, wrecked *Alex* in his ear right before he'd come Sunday night is remarkably effective at turning him on, no pet names required.

"What the fuck is wrong with you?" Alex demands.

Liam looks like he's just getting started. "Because Carly and I –"

Alex reaches across the table and claps a hand over Liam's mouth. "Stop! Stop talking! Now!"

Liam cracks up. After a horrified moment Alex registers the joke and drops his hand; he's still learning how to laugh at himself. He's still pissed about the maniac fans. Liam can shrug them off in a way Alex can't, but he's also good at distracting Alex, even if it's with his own ridiculousness.

◆

That week the official casting decisions for *Paradise Square* get announced and Alex's busy life gets a lot busier. There's press to do. The movie needs to start the cycle of advance hype and the general public wants more about how J. Alex Cook is going to play some historical, non-gay character. Margaret is a lifesaver of organization and efficiency, leaving Alex to do his job of taking calls and doing interviews as the wry, sharply charming young star he's expected to be.

In between conference calls he flips through his phone to look again at a picture Paul has sent of Todd curled up on a hoodie Alex left at his house. *Somebody misses you*, the accompanying text reads.

Alex replies with *Give him a pet for me ;)*. Later he has to delete the message thread that follows. The horrors of getting caught sexting are too terrible to contemplate.

The new project creates a nightmare of scheduling to work out. *Paradise* wants him to film in New York the same month *Fourth* wants him in D.C. By the time those negotiations are settled Alex feels like he – and not his time – is the commodity being haggled over.

When, tired and annoyed in between takes one day, he says as much to Liam, Liam asks him why he ever expected anything different.

The only involvement Alex has in his schedule is signing off on how few work-free days he's going to get over the holidays. He has a stab of regret about that. He'd been looking forward, in a vague sort of way, to spending a more or less 'normal' Christmas with Paul. Except, now that he thinks about it more, Paul is probably going to be out of town with his own family. So that hardly matters, he tells himself. Though there's a pang of regret about that too.

On the faintly bright side is the fact that Alex won't have enough time off to make going back to Indiana for Christmas worthwhile. He sends an awkward email to his mother. He doesn't think either of them are used to the idea that he's the kind of person who's spending Christmas in New York City and can easily afford to fly her out and pay for a hotel room for her. Her response is immediate and enthusiastic, though. So that's one thing to look forward to.

Otherwise, Alex isn't sanguine about the future. He finds it almost impossible to imagine leaving at the end of November and coming back at the end of January without finding Paul wrapped up with someone else. Someone real, whose hand he can hold. There's so much Paul wants, and Alex can offer him none of it. And while he trusts Paul – his loyalty seems beyond doubt – Alex knows how much he needs companionship, a partner in life as well as in his bed. Paul won't want to go two months without that just for Alex's sake, and Alex can't blame him.

When Paul calls later that night, Alex answers eagerly. If the expiration date of this thing is approaching, Alex wants to get as much out of this while he can.

<h1 style="text-align:center">13</h1>

Margaret finds Alex an assistant named Yancy Eckert. She's in her early thirties and is an actual professional, not another one of those barely organized recent L.A. arrivals doing the work for the money or the connections. Alex tells her point blank that he's glad they're not peers – not in age or circumstance – because it means they can be friends. He also asks her to remind him when stuff is going on he's supposed to go to her for help with, because of all the things he's done in L.A., having an assistant feels the most morally dubious. Certainly, it's the thing that would most puzzle and possibly upset his mother.

At least Paul approves, happily telling Alex it's about time. He confesses that he's teetered on the edge of hiring someone himself for years, what with the hours he works and the ambitions he has. Alex has to stop himself from offering him Yancy's services in response. He processes that for an evening of curious confusion with Gemma as she paints her nails a particularly off-putting shade of pale blue.

Of all the things of his that Gemma has always helped herself to, she makes no assumptions about Yancy's time or interest in picking up her dry-cleaning. Alex is puzzled enough to ask for an explanation, but Gemma brushes off the question, saying he'd understand if he were a girl.

♦

The next time Alex stays the weekend Paul watches him, amused, on Saturday afternoon as he pulls a notebook and a battered textbook out of his bag and cracks them open.

"What's that?" He squints at the cover, but can't make it out. It's in a non-Roman script.

"Farsi book."

"You're learning Farsi?" Paul isn't completely surprised. Studying is exactly the kind of thing that Alex, intellectual and inexperienced with acting, does. But he's still a little stunned. This is no small commitment of time or energy, and Alex has boundless reserves of neither.

Alex flips the book open to a dog-eared page. "Zach speaks it, so I need to – want to – at least a little. If he took it on at random, so can I. Especially if he's going to get his ass into Iran in the next couple of months."

"Why didn't you go to college?" Paul asks. It's a thought that's been worrying at him for months now, since before they started this thing. Alex is so sharp and takes such obvious pleasure in using his mind. Fairytale aside, what Paul knows of his path makes no sense to him.

"I didn't go to college because three weeks after high school graduation I got in my car and drove to L.A."

"But before that?"

Alex leans over to fish a pen out of his bag, then looks right up at Paul with a gaze that's loaded. "Don't think that just because you went to college and I didn't doesn't mean we're not both from some hick-ass towns in the middle nowhere."

"I know where I'm from." Paul doesn't know whether he should be offended or amused. He's only named the town that he grew up in, not told any stories about it. Paul wonders if Alex went ahead and researched that, too, or is making not entirely incorrect assumptions about Southern and gay. But Alex sounds upset, and this goes on the list of things Paul's going to have to pry out of him, someday, when Alex is ready.

"And where are your wrists from, Paul?" Alex singsongs under his breath.

Paul sighs. They haven't talked about that since their first night together. Paul's going to have to tell him eventually, but that isn't a conversation that needs to happen in a pissing contest of *my life was worse than yours*. Especially when he still doesn't know all – or even most – of Alex's story.

He lets it go for now. "What does your name look like in Farsi?"

Alex looks as wary as he does pleased.

"Like this," he says. He tears out a page of his notebook and starts to write. On the line below it, with a glance up at Paul that's a little bashful and incredibly gorgeous, he writes something else and spins the page around so Paul can see. "And this is yours."

♦

"You know Alex is going to be gone for, like, two months, right?"

Paul regards Liam over both the top of both his laptop and his glasses – it's been that sort of week – and is glad the office is empty aside from them. "Are you supposed to be here?" he asks. He knows Liam's situation with Victor gives him free reign of anything involving *Fourth*, but he also knows Victor has strong feelings about Liam's tendency to wander.

"Relax, I'm off the clock. Also, I know he was just in here, so spare the lecture."

Alex was in the building for a meeting and had stopped by to say hello. His appearance had been surprising and brief, and Paul is now trying to finish his work so he can go home and spend another weekend with him.

"Consider it spared," he says, wanting Liam to get to the damn point.

"Mhmmm. But yeah, he's –"

"I know what his schedule is, Liam," Paul says.

"Oh. Oh, Great. What are you going to do about it?"

"What do you mean?"

"He's going to be on location for a long time. And I know how gone you are over him, so. He's got a couple of days free in New York. Even if he didn't – you should go see him."

Paul sits back in his chair and flicks a pencil between his fingers. "You think that's a good idea? And you think you're the person who should be telling me it is?" Usually it's Carly who calls him out on his shit, if she believes there is shit to call him out on. Since it's highly unlikely she's subcontracted her advice giving to her ridiculous boyfriend, this particular brainstorm is all Liam's.

Liam shrugs eloquently. "Dude, if you don't, I don't want to deal with your pining."

"You also don't need to spend time in this room," Paul points out, although they do see each other socially often enough.

"Yeah. Well, or his, 'cause I have to put up with him in D.C., and comforting the lonely and lovelorn is not part of my job description."

"Really?" Paul says. He knows damn well that comforting the lonely and lovelorn is in fact one of Liam's many hat tricks. He points the pencil at Liam. "And is this part of your job description?"

Oddness of the messenger aside, Paul's thrilled at the idea. Those two months are approaching quickly. The idea of a separation that long has been daunting – too daunting for him to try to think about a solution other than enduring it. Miserable schedules are, if nothing else, the nature of their business. Paul is aware he's being more than a little pathetic considering that right now he and Alex have hardly been together for two months.

"Oh, no, man," Liam gushes. This is just 'cause you're awesome together."

"Thank you," Paul says cautiously, still not quite sure what Liam is up to. He may be sincere, of course, but he may be here at Victor's request or out of some misguided thing because of Carly, and wow, Paul's life is awkward. Alex may not know the half of it yet, but Liam sure as hell does.

"So, you'll think about it?"

"I am going to think about it a lot," Paul says. "Now get out of my office." Paul waves a hand at him and returns to his computer.

Liam laughs as he goes. "Not your office, Paul," he calls back. "Yet."

<h1 style="text-align:center">14</h1>

Houise hunting is peculiar.

Gemma gets mistaken regularly for Alex's assistant or girlfriend; sometimes both. Realtors speak down to him more than once. Alex is never sure if it's because he's so damn young, or if they assume that all actors are stupid.

He's deeply irritated by it, in part because of the truth in the assumptions. He has no real idea what he's doing. Having houses talked up to him as investments or party spaces isn't useful. What he needs is a place to live that's extravagant in terms of what he's come from, but not extravagant in terms of what he is.

When he tries to articulate this to Gemma it comes out as, "I don't care about hot tubs."

Gemma, in turn, informs him that she totally cares about hot tubs.

♦

Eighteen prospects later, Alex finally finds a house he's interested in. It's on a dead-end road, has some awesome outdoor space, a decent but not military grade security system, and a massive living room and open kitchen. There's a loft-like space at one end of the common area that contains another, smaller living space and a bedroom and bath that would be perfect for Gemma.

Aside from that, there's a proper – and separate – second floor with a master bedroom and bath. More importantly, he can afford it without freaking out. No matter that his financial advisor tells him he can easily go for seven figures, no fucking way. The thought gives Alex hives, even more than that he's looking at a house on foreclosure. He feels shady about it, as if he's betraying being from Indiana and poor.

He tells Paul as much that weekend, as he gets ready to start the process of buying the place on Monday. Paul answers carefully, and Alex can understand that. He considers how awkward a position he may have put Paul in by talking numbers. Paul may already own a house, but Alex makes way more than he does.

"So," Paul says as they make macaroni and cheese for lunch. "Want to know more about the onscreen adventures of Zach and James?"

"Do I?" Alex asks, dubious, as he cubes Velveeta.

"I suspect it's the kind of thing you might want preparation for."

"That doesn't make me feel better. But go ahead." If Paul wants to share it's probably a good idea to listen.

Paul takes a deep breath. "The long-awaited romance plot is about to begin," he says in a dramatic TV-announcer voice.

Alex's heart sinks, but he has to laugh at Paul's ridiculousness. Which maybe was part of the plan.

"That's going to be...fun." He's going to have to deal with the renewed enthusiasm of the fans, and, for that matter, Liam. Alex is continually appalled at the existence of his own public life. Liam, though, will flirt with furniture if it'll get him petted and cooed over by yet another talk show host or hostess delighted to be anything but impervious to his charms.

"Yeah," Paul agrees.

"I mean, I knew it was coming."

"The entire fan base and most of the TV-watching public outside the fan base knew it was coming."

Alex smiles ruefully. "Yeah. I'm going to assume you're not responsible for any of said romance plot?"

Paul shakes his head. "I write what Victor tells me to write. But none of this was my idea."

"I mean I guess it could be worse," Alex says, trying to put the best spin on it, for himself and for Paul who clearly feels bad about all this, his fault or no. "It makes sense within the story. And Liam and I have good chemistry together. Horrifying as that is." What he doesn't say is that even with his relatively limited data on the matter, he knows that the way he connected with Liam on camera is part of why Victor reordered the world for him.

Sometimes it's heartbreaking for Alex to know so much more about the future than his character does. Alex muses about it as Paul puts the macaroni and cheese in the oven and Alex starts washing dishes. It's one of the costs of table reads and understanding how made up stories work. Zach doesn't know it, but he's about to get played out of a story. Again. He's not as vicious as he likes to think he is, and because he's so focused on the little scandals – mismanagement of military contracts in D.C., who cares? – he's always missing the bigger story unfolding much closer to him.

James is starting to see it, but James is more worried about Zach at the moment than whether rival reporters' stories are all based in fact. Alex almost feels jealous, not of the circumstances or the people, but the clarity that a life written to forty-seven minutes plus commercials on a weekly basis necessarily provides.

Paul gently hip checks Alex aside so he can wash his hands at the sink. "Those can wait," he says of the dishes. He dries his hands on his jeans and wraps his arms around Alex's waist. "And we have half an hour 'til food is ready," he adds with a suggestive look.

Which isn't to say that Victor's creations don't still have ridiculous blinders on, Alex thinks as he follows Paul to the couch. Not just about the futility of their schemes – any plan that requires another person to do exactly what you expect is a bad plan – but about the gravitational pull they increasingly exert on each other.

15

Despite upcoming drama in the script, Monday morning Liam is as cheery and chipper as ever in between takes. Alex wants to kick him as he paces by his chair *again*, because his constant need to move is distracting as fuck.

"Stop," he says shortly when Liam circles him on his third time around a winding, circuitous, and strangely unwavering route.

Thankfully, he does. Less thankfully, he stops right in front of Alex.

"You're not in a good mood," Liam says carefully.

"Is that a statement or a question?"

"What's wrong?" Liam asks.

"Nothing's wrong," Alex says shortly.

"Bullshit. You've been glaring at me for like the last twenty minutes and I don't think I did anything wrong?"

Alex sighs. "It's not you," he admits, as fun as it would be to blame this day on Liam.

"Boy troubles?" Liam asks ridiculously.

"No," Alex lies. He doesn't want to discuss these things with Liam on set of all places. Things with Paul have been so good, but Alex can't stop looking at the calendar and counting down the days he has left. They're getting close to the middle of November, and the prospect of the end is starting to wear.

"You know you can talk to me if you want." Liam puts both hands on Alex's shoulders and squeezes affectionately. Which is as annoying as hell. Alex has gotten used to people's hands on him for the sake of getting him dressed and made up as Zach, but he still doesn't like to be touched in most moments. Like this one.

"Liam? Personal space," he snaps irritably.

"Oh. Sorry man." Liam shuffles back and looks sad.

Alex sighs, exasperated now. "Don't do that."

"What's that?"

"Look like a wounded puppy when I yell at you."

"I am sorry," Liam insists, but then bounces again, all concern apparently gone. Alex wonders how Carly puts up with him. He knows how incredibly unkind, not to mention unfair, it is to wonder if that's why she and Liam have the arrangements that they do.

◆

Paul does his research and talks to Victor – who is more than enthusiastic about the idea of him taking some time to be with Alex on his next adventures – and makes a good chunk of the necessary arrangements. He can be in New York the week before Christmas with Alex, and as he marks the dates on his phone he thinks about the new year and everything after that. He can't wait for any of it.

Now he just has to tell Alex it's going to happen.

16

"Let me get this straight," Gemma says, sitting cross-legged on Alex's bed. Alex is packing neatly for D.C. and New York and utterly randomly for staying with Paul over Thanksgiving because one is work and one isn't. "You're spending Thanksgiving with the guy you're convinced is going to dump you the second you leave town –"

"It's orphans' Thanksgiving; if we're actually dating he hasn't said so; and maybe, just *maybe*, I'm wrong about everything and we can all die happy."

"There's no need to be snippy," Gemma tells him. "Next, you're going on location for two months, but when you get back you'll hopefully sign some papers and then we'll own a house?"

Alex side-eyes her, even though he knows she's trying to provoke him. "Apart from the fact that I will own the house and you will be paying way-below-market rent for our new and improved lifestyle, yes."

"Cool," she says. "Should I assume I'll never see you anymore when you get back, too?"

"Well, if I'm wrong, since we'll have a nice house, I'll be able to invite him over." His tone is condescending, but he's too nervous to be able to fix it.

"I don't know, Alex." Gemma is perfectly capable of matching his tone. I think we'll have to have a talk about you having strange boys up in your room with the door closed."

"Not even." Alex frowns at his suitcase. "If I decide I need another pair of shoes can you FedEx them to me?"

"Right. Because there are no shopping opportunities in D.C. Or New York."

Alex doesn't respond to her, staring blankly at his suitcase instead. He feels overwhelmed and now embarrassed. He's still not sure he likes having a life where he can buy another pair of shoes just because he packed poorly. Everything in his life feels like excess now.

"Are you nervous?" Gemma asks.

"Terrified," Alex admits.

"Why?"

"Because I'm going to New York to prove to everyone I can do something I never wanted to do in the first place," he sighs.

"Do you like acting?" she asks. "You've never said."

♦

Paul has taken to leaving the door unlocked for Alex. When he walks in that night, the lights are all on, music is playing, and Paul meets him in the foyer to wrap him up in a kiss. It silences his fears, at least for now.

"Help me finish the grocery list," Paul whispers in his ear when they finally break apart.

Alex snorts. "Sexy."

Paul kisses him again, then drags him into the kitchen by the hand.

The evening feels like the first night of summer vacation as portrayed on screen and not in the reality of a poor part of Indiana. But tonight all responsibility is gone for now and all the world seems to offer to possibility and adventure. They sit at the kitchen table for hours, drinking spiked cider, checking recipes, and talking as they knock knees under the table. Alex keeps looking up from writing things down to see Paul looking at him with a soft expression. He always smiles back.

"Do you want me to go to the store with you tomorrow?" Alex asks.

Paul looks surprised. "Are you sure? You don't usually like doing things in public."

"If we go early enough there won't be anyone there," Alex explains. "Plus it's the day before Thanksgiving. All the fans are going to be too busy travelling to make my life stupid."

◆

They go up to bed soon after they eat dinner but don't sleep until late. Paul takes Alex out of his clothes and pushes him into the armchair. He spends a long time working him into incoherence and then desperation, licking over his cock and his balls and his hole until Alex finally grabs his hair and fucks his mouth.

Paul keeps waiting for Alex to ask for the things they haven't done yet. As much as Paul wants those things (and *fuck* he wants them badly), they need to be Alex's call. Alex doesn't ask, though, and so Paul doesn't push. It's not like he ever stops craving the things Alex does let him do.

After Alex comes, laughing through the breathlessness, he stands, pulls Paul to his feet and goes to his own knees, back straight and posture perfect on Paul's bedroom floor. Alex has no trouble holding eye contact now when he looks up at Paul through his lashes, his eyes strange and dark and his tongue wicked. This is a boy, Paul thinks – right before he comes with a particularly clever twist of Alex's hand – to whom it's dangerous to teach things. He never wants to stop.

In the morning Paul coaxes Alex out of bed with coffee and the temptation of a hot shower. Then they go shopping, Alex in his beanie and Paul with his list.

"I can't believe I forgot to get canned pumpkin earlier," Paul says as they wander the aisles. "They're completely out."

"It's the day before Thanksgiving. Of course they're out." Alex crouches down to check the very back of the shelf.

"Maybe if someone had been less distracting, I would have remembered earlier."

"So sorry," Alex says in a song-song.

"No, you're not." Paul savors this little bit of utter normalcy, grocery shopping with an Alex who is happy and relaxed. He still won't hold his hand, but he does take an almost childlike delight in running down the empty aisles with the cart. Paul is content.

♦

Back at the house they start cooking. Paul is charmed and delighted that he gets to teach Alex this too. It feels significant, letting Alex handle the recipe cards Paul's grandmother wrote out years ago. He's glad not to be caught out as he watches Alex squint over measuring spoons and the spice rack.

"Who all is going to be here?" Alex asks as he balefully regards a pecan pie crust he can't get to lie right in the pan.

Paul squints at the pot he's stirring as he counts off on his other hand. "Most of the brunch crew. Shawna. Brian." Paul chuckles when Alex makes a face. "Craig for sure. My damn dog. Josh might be coming, Liam and Carly –"

"Liam's coming? Why does no one tell me these things?"

"You work with him every day. I assumed he'd mentioned it." Paul says

"He never did. Doesn't he have somewhere else to go?"

"Why are you so freaked out?" Paul asks. Liam isn't Alex's favorite, but he surely likes him better than Brian. Alex's reaction seems out of proportion to the situation.

"He's exhausting," Alex says. "And he's going to have opinions."

"Well. Yes." Paul sets down the spoon and looks at Alex for a moment. "Okay. This is a story you should hear. Because it's hilarious and because you need to know it."

"...Okay," Alex says nervously.

"So, Carly's my ex-girlfriend."

Alex stares at him. "But you're gay." He hesitates. "That probably wasn't a useful thing to say."

Paul lets it go. "We met at UNC, she was a couple of years behind me and crewed some of my projects. When she moved out here we got in touch again and one thing led to another and –"

"You *dated* her?" Alex struggles to absorb that piece of information.

"Yeah. She wasn't like…I wasn't using her to hide anything, I guess is what's important. I mean, not from anyone else."

"Then – what – what were you doing?"

"I'm not unattracted to women," Paul says easily. "They just don't rock my world like men do." He turns around to see Alex staring at him and gives him a pointed look up and down in reply. "Case in point. Anyway, when we broke up, that was why, and Carly was the one who helped me figure that out. There was a lot of honesty in that breakup. And we're still close."

"You didn't know?" Alex's face is twisted with disbelief. "I knew I was gay in middle school! You were older than I am right now when you figured it out. What the hell is that?"

"South Carolina, Alex," Paul says gently as he can. "Small town – God, not even a town. Middle of nowhere. Old family. I mean, home is a run-down farm house. It used to be something grand, but. It's not a place where stuff like that gets talked about. I knew…something, at least. But being queer wasn't something it could be, and I liked girls enough, so it wasn't."

"I don't understand."

"Yes, you do." Paul touches his shoulder on his way to the cabinet for the salt. "Even if it wasn't exactly the same for you – and I still don't know what it was for you. But I was a good kid. I played sports, I got good grades. But by the time I got to high school things weren't good anymore. My grades dropped. I was pissed all the time. I started getting into fights. I got busted for drugs once. Just pot," he says at Alex's expression, as if that's the important thing to clarify in all of this. "Nobody could figure out what was wrong. *I* couldn't figure out what was wrong. But I got called names and got into more fights because my father was very clear that no son of his was going to be a sissy fag."

"Oh."

Paul measures out salt into the palm of his hand and shakes it into another pot. "I told my sister. Swore her to secrecy. She promised never to tell our parents, then told me to never, ever tell either. She wanted to protect me," he says. "And I'm still not sure she was wrong to. I can't imagine what would have happened if I'd been able to make myself come out while I was still living at home."

"What did happen?" Alex's voice is timid.

Paul says nothing. He knows he's going to have to tell this story eventually, but he's not there yet, despite his best efforts.

"This feels like a movie, and I don't like it. I want you to be happy."

Paul continues as if Alex hasn't said anything. The story is hard enough for him to tell without having to deal with someone else's reaction to it. "By the time I did, it almost didn't matter anymore. I know that's anticlimactic." He grimaces. "Mom and Dad separated my senior year of high school. Which was...awful for a whole lot of reasons. At least after that there wasn't anywhere to go but up. Not that it made it any easier to be honest to myself. College was good. Better, at least. Getting out of the house was good, even if my father wasn't living there anymore. Sometimes you just need to get out."

"I can imagine."

"No kidding." Paul lets the conversation hang there for a moment.

Any hopes Paul has that Alex is going to say something about how the hell he landed in L.A. vanish when Alex asks, "So you finally – what? After college and after Carly?"

"After Carly," Paul nods. "Most of that is to her credit. She spent a lot of that time teaching me that as good as maybe we were together, it wasn't good enough for me, and that I deserved better than that. She spent a lot of time keeping me out of the worst of my brain too. Wasn't fair to her, but I still appreciate it."

"Sounds like a fun time."

"I've had worse. By the time I finally did come out, I think exactly no one was surprised. Word made it back to my dad – of course – and he wanted to disown me. According to my sister, Mom called him and yelled at him for an hour, then told him she'd already disowned him instead, and he could continue to stay the fuck away."

Alex laughs, "You mom sounds awesome."

"She is. You'll get to meet her tomorrow. Her and my sister. We always Skype on Thanksgiving."

"Things are okay with them?" Alex asks. "Like, is that going to be weird?"

"Things are great. They'll just never be good with my father."

"I'm sorry." Alex goes to where Paul is standing at the stove. He wraps his arms around Paul's waist and presses his face into the back of his shoulder. "You didn't say anything about the scars."

Paul closes his hands around Alex's to silence him. It feels less peculiar and awful that he's mentioned the scars this time, but Paul still doesn't want to talk about them. "It is what it is," he says, while Alex holds him tighter. "I'm here now. And so are you." He turns around in Alex's arms. "What about you?"

Alex chuckles damply. "It's a lot to process," he says. He works his fingers in and out of one of Paul's belt loops.

"I know. Take your time. It's the past, it's not going anywhere."

"Deep," Alex says.

"Writer." Paul kisses Alex's forehead

"Wait," Alex says, grabbing his arm with a look of alarm on his face. "Awful question: How did Carly meet Liam?"

"Not through me, thank God. That incestuous plot point is completely random."

"Okay, good. Good. Does Liam know?"

"Oh, Liam knows," Paul says dryly. "Liam thinks it's hilarious."

"Of course he does," Alex mutters. "Liam's capacity for delight in the absurd is boundless when there's sex involved."

They're cheerful but quiet after that, focusing on the work of cooking. Paul appreciates it. The quiet gives him time to think about what it means that he's told that much of his story and that Alex seems so comfortable sharing space with him.

When Paul mentions the latter, Alex says, "I don't hate spending time with everyone. Gemma's great when she's not asking for details about my sex life. My mom, too."

"What about me?" Paul asks, fishing.

"And you," Alex's tone more serious than Paul expects. "You don't ask me to do anything other than exist. Which assumes that I actually do. You are exactly the opposite of everything else in my life right now."

♦

In the late afternoon, pies done, turkey brining, and several funny discussions about whether marshmallows go on candied yams or not, Paul insists they go out for salads and smoothies. "We're going to be eating starch for days," he says.

"You want to pregame a holiday event with health food," Alex deadpans.

"Yes?"

"Oh my God. I wish I could say no."

In the car they discuss workout habits and neuroses. Alex for once gives up on avoiding mention of his life to talk about the inappropriate interest fans take in his physical shape and what they conclude it means about his value as a person.

"God forbid I wear a T-shirt that doesn't fit," Alex gripes.

"At least a little bit of beer won't make anyone think you're pregnant. Carly's life? Actual hell."

When they get to the place, it's filled with rollerbladers and joggers eating outside at picnic tables with umbrellas. The atmosphere is all wrong in Alex's head for November, but that's why the world was built in L.A., he supposes. Weather-wise, at least, it's Camelot.

"Can I stay in the car while you grab the stuff to go?" Alex asks. Beautiful as the day is, there are plenty of people out there, and Alex doesn't feel like being spotted or photographed.

"Uh, no?" Paul replies. He says it so easily Alex knows it would be churlish to argue further.

They eat outside at one of the picnic tables. There's a nice breeze and the sky is bright, so Alex's beanie and shades look almost seasonal, rather than like the camouflage they are.

◆

Back at the house that evening, Alex makes Paul drill him on his Farsi, handing him a stack of handmade flashcards. They lie at opposite ends of the couch, legs tangled, as they chat about *Fourth* and the language and Zach, and what the hell the character is thinking in the material on the other side of D.C.

"No prison," Alex says.

"What?"

"I don't care if he gets captured or tied up and held for ransom or whatever, but don't put Zach in prison."

"Okayyy," Paul says cautiously. "You know that's not up to me, right?"

"Victor knows," Alex adds, trying to warn Paul off with a look. "At least, I told him."

To Alex's relief Paul nods and changes the subject to why Zach thinks he'll be able to pass anywhere in Iran undetected.

"Not like he's inconspicuous," Alex agrees, gesturing to his face and hair.

"Some people are too smart to be safe."

"That could be the tagline for this cycle, you know," Alex points out.

"Maybe we should change the name to *The Zach Show*," Paul suggests.

Alex laughs and kicks at him. The flashcards go flying, but neither of them move to deal with them. They stare dopily at each other until Todd decides to investigate the new toys.

◆

They leave the flashcards on the floor when they go to bed. Despite it being with intent, once they hit the soft surface of the mattress they realize how tired they are from a day mostly spent in a too-warm kitchen. Paul is the first to complain aloud, rolling his shoulders and giving Alex a look that is both hungry and pathetic.

Alex shoves at his shoulder. "Stomach," he says. When Paul complies he straddles him to knead at his shoulders.

"You are the best," Paul mumbles into his pillow.

"I have no idea what I'm doing."

"I don't care. You're naked and bringing about a cessation of pain."

Alex works in silence, hands slipping lower as his dick fills against Paul's ass. He can't help but bring his hips into it, thumbs dragging up the long and knotted muscles of Paul's back.

Paul moans.

"Like that?" Alex asks.

"You should fuck me."

"I should," Alex says, even as he knows he shouldn't. He wants to, and he can almost bear the thought of this weekend as a fabulous parting gift in his too-young-for-Paul life. But there's only so much loss he can recover from and still be able to throw himself into work Monday night when he'll be in D.C. and Paul will still be here. He also has no idea how to say no.

Paul can't see him though and blows right by any hesitation in his voice, telling him what it would be like, how tight he'd be for him and how big Alex would feel inside of him as he fucked into him.

"Yeah, just like that," Paul breathes when Alex can't help but snap his hips forward, cock pressed tight against his ass.

"You make me crazy," Alex says, knowing it's true in more ways than one.

"Good."

"Fucking back like I can't do the job myself," he says a little breathlessly, because clearly, rutting against Paul is exactly how he's getting off tonight.

Paul laughs with delight. "Then show me what you've got," he says. "Make sure everyone knows."

"I wish I could." Alex says as leans over to rummage in the bedside table for lube. He squeezes some sloppy over his dick and Paul's crack; it makes the slide even better.

But in the back of his mind, Alex knows everything else is about to be a mess.

17

They wake up late, drifting comfortably in the warmth of the blankets and each other before they have to get up and finish the rest of the meal prep. The prospect of two months away from home and from this – particularly after Paul's unfulfilled request last night – is starting to loom unpleasantly.

Alex gets dressed thoughtfully. He knows everyone who's going to be here and doesn't have to worry about good impressions. But he's here with Paul in an odd, undefined role somewhere between co-host and principal orphan. Even if he's not sure how he could, Alex doesn't want to screw it up.

"Oooh, soft," Paul mutters approvingly, when he wraps his hands around Alex's waist and smooths the fabric of the gray wool sweater down with his thumbs. He kisses Alex before he goes to check on the turkey. It feels like reassurance, and Alex is grateful.

People start to arrive in the early afternoon. The house has been such a refuge for Alex lately, and he can't quite get a handle on the noise and the babble of the group. Having Carly and Craig and Beau – who curls up on one corner of the couch like it's his old favorite spot, which it probably is – here makes everything more fraught. Alex can't help but look at them and think about the lives they had with Paul before Alex existed.

He wonders who will succeed him in this place once he's gone. In the middle of his musings Paul catches his eye across the room and beckons him with a tip of his head. Alex goes and Paul wraps an arm around him. He kisses the side of his forehead, an indulgence of public affection that Alex, here, can let stand, if only for the novelty of it.

When Paul murmurs "I'm glad you're here" into his ear, Alex can't help but be happy, whatever may come.

"Me too," he says.

♦

Alex accidentally winds up in a corner with Craig.

Alex feels like a deer caught in the headlights. Craig says, "Hi."

"Why are you here?" Alex asks. "I mean. Not *here*." He tries to backtrack and flails his eyes around the room in search of Paul or any other plausible escape. "I mean, why didn't you go home? Where are you from?"

"Hawaii," Craig tells him. "It's a long, overpriced way to fly just for a few days, so I usually stay here. Not *here*, here."

"Oh. Okay." Alex tries to ignore the obvious fact that Craig is mocking him.

Awkward quota of socializing fulfilled, Alex is more than ready to move on, but he has no idea how. At least in the midst of this mess he can take a moment to enjoy the fact that he's a couple of inches taller than Craig.

But before Craig can move off graciously instead and presumably award himself points for a minimal level of awkwardness with his ex's famous boyfriend, Alex blurts, "Why didn't you take the cat too?"

Craig starts laughing and can't seem to stop.

Alex feels too horrified to speak. Into his silence Craig says, "He doesn't like the beach."

♦

Getting the turkey out of the oven and onto the platter is nearly as awkward. It takes both Paul and Alex, a great deal of chaos, and Paul possibly burning his leg through his jeans on the pan. At least he swears a lot, but he waves Alex off when he offers to go fetch him a Band-Aid or something. But when they get it to the table, it looks beautiful, and Paul offers Alex the honors of carving the bird. Alex may never have had a father at home to know what the gesture means, but he knows it means something.

After dinner, Paul video calls South Carolina. Everyone gives the screen a wave, and Paul tugs Alex forward for a proper-if-via-internet introduction.

"This is Alex, Mom," Paul says over Alex's shoulder while Alex waves at a camera that has nothing to do with his job. Paul has her eyes, he notices. When she beams and waves back at him – he has her smile, too.

If Paul were Alex's boyfriend, this would be a significant moment: meeting his family. But Paul isn't his boyfriend. Still, it's almost easy to imagine how he could be. Especially once he meets not only Alex's mother and sister but his brother-in-law and his adorable baby nephew.

He knows Paul's sister Sarah watches the show, but she's not shy at all about calling him *honey* and asking him what side of the marshmallow-on-yams debate he's on. It all feels good. If Alex can somehow stick around in Paul's life until he returns from New York, maybe the boyfriend conversation is one he can think about having.

For now though, the prospect still feels so terrifying and so adult, that on top of everything else it's too much. After the excessive consumption of pie, Alex finds himself hovering between spaces, trying to escape the crowd in the living room. But like any good party, the kitchen is also full of people looking for alcohol and scavenging food.

He startles when Carly approaches him from behind, her fingertips playing at the inside of his arm.

"Not like what you grew up with, is it?" she asks.

Alex feels odd not knowing what to say to her when they've already met so many times. But now that he knows she dated Paul, he realizes she may well know things about him.

"Default question," he says. "It's not personal," she says. "It's odd for everybody. The only one here who grew up in L.A. is Brian."

Of course it's Brian, who is, as far as Alex can tell, not just mean but the absolute worst sort of hipster. Alex is fairly sure that Brian makes up random bands to say he's into just to be sure no one else has ever heard of them.

"Nothing's ever personal," Alex says.

"Everything's personal," she counters with a toss of her hair.

Alex squints at her. "Are you trying to figure out if I'm going to be a jerk about Paul being your ex?"

"Are you?" Her gray eyes squint back at him, a clear parody of his own distrust of her motives.

"Not really." Alex isn't sure how he would be a jerk to her even if he wanted to. "Definitely weird about always being the last to know,"

She laughs. "Fame will do that to you."

It's strange to Alex to hear the word so baldly. Gemma still whispers it, like *cancer*. He tells Carly that, and she laughs in delight, tossing her wavy dark hair back over her shoulder. She goes on to punctuate the rest of their conversation with inappropriate whispers of *like cancer* until Alex hurts from laughing.

Paul looks over at them and smiles. Alex blushes. When his words wind down to nothing, because the day is long and the people are many, Carly kindly squeezes his arm and tells him there's no shame in escaping upstairs to hide for a little while.

"Liam has to do that sometimes too."

18

After fifteen minutes and no Alex, Paul goes looking for him. He finds him on his side on the bed in the dim. Alex has one hand on Todd who, eyes closed and purring, is in a state of bliss in his party-exile.

"Hey," Paul says quietly as he sits down on the edge of the bed. Alex blinks before focusing on his face. He looks startled. It's still a look Paul finds incredibly appealing.

"Sorry for disappearing," Alex says.

"How are you doing?" Paul scratches behind Todd's ear, then rubs his thumb over the back of Alex's hand.

"Recharging. I'm okay."

"Do you need anything?"

Alex shakes his head.

"Stay up here as long as you need," Paul tells him. He loves having Alex next to him downstairs, but he knows Alex is strange with crowds. Paul wants to be able to give him the space he needs. "Text me if you need anything."

Alex smiles sideways at him. "Okay. I will."

Paul leans over to kiss him – gentle, sweet, and cautious – before he goes back downstairs.

At the bottom of the stairs, Paul finds Liam waiting for him.

"He cool?" Liam asks as he herds them into the kitchen and away from whatever football game most everyone is now not watching.

"General question or specific question?"

Liam laughs.

"It's a lot, I think," Paul says, squinting at Liam. They're friends, ostensibly, but they've never quite clicked. Paul knows that's less because the Carly situation is awkward and more because he and Liam just don't innately get each other, but it's still something he feels guilty about. No one should know as much intimate trivia as he does about Liam regarding someone who isn't a very close friend.

"All this luck and people think he must be designed for the results of it," Liam says. "He's really not though."

Liam trying to educate him regarding Alex feels strange, but the simple fact is that Liam has probably spent more time with Alex than anyone else – Gemma included – over the last year. Also Liam is famous, has been acting since he was a kid, and has perspective and insight on Alex's experiences that should not be ignored. Paul realizes he should probably stop trying to avoid the ever-increasing number of overlapping relationships in their mutual web of friendships and start counting them as useful. After all, Liam is the one who first suggested New York.

"Do we have you and Carly for the whole day or...?" Paul asks.

"We're due at Victor's at eight."

"Only Victor would make Thanksgiving a late-night poolside soiree." Paul isn't quite sure where Carly is and isn't tangled up with Victor and can't imagine asking. Each time he offers dry commentary about the situation in reluctant hope of finding out more, he gets nothing. Carly enjoys forcing him to ask for things directly, and Paul doesn't mind thwarting her from time to time.

Liam chuckles, but doesn't seem inclined to offer any further insight. It is, in its own way, rather sweet.

Ten minutes later Alex texts Paul from upstairs.

I'll be down soon, it reads simply. *Thank you.*

Paul knows he has a dopey look on his face as he texts with a boy in the same house with him. He doesn't really care.

"Is that him?" Liam asks.

Paul nods.

Liam gives Paul a thumbs-up and moves away. Paul wonders why Liam has chosen to appoint himself head cheerleader for Team Alex-and-Paul but decides not to question it. In the casually vicious place that Los Angeles can be, Paul is happy to take all the enthusiasm he can get.

When Alex finally reemerges, everyone is in the living room talking over the TV. Paul watches him as he comes down the stairs. His hand is wrapped tightly around the bannister like a declaration of belonging and his own right of place. Paul smiles. This house has a lot of history for him, and he loves the thought of how much of it Alex will eventually claim.

Alex takes the empty seat on the couch next to Paul and leans into his side. Paul wraps an arm around his shoulders. It's a profoundly normal moment, which is something Alex has said he's wanted badly and something Paul has done his best to give him. But moments like this are also rare and fleeting. Paul can't keep Alex next to him always.

The party goes late. Paul is relieved when everyone is gone and they can finally clean up, or at least start to. With just the two of them in an otherwise empty post-party house, Paul is reminded of the night they first hooked up. But tonight they don't fuck; once they get into bed they curl up around each other, tired and happy to do nothing more than fall asleep together.

◆

Friday is a day the world that needs nothing from them. Paul is thrilled for the break. They sleep too late and wake up just enough for sex. After Paul gets up to get a washcloth, Alex pulls him back into bed for another nap.

The day, when they face it, is mostly a haze of watching bad TV and eating turkey sandwiches. Alex drifts from his notes and books to his phone to Paul's side, tucked in and still. For some reason – maybe it's the quiet after yesterday's chaos – today feels more snug and domestic than the other weekends they've spent together. Paul feels like Alex belongs here more and more with every passing day.

In the evening Alex's quiet starts to worry Paul. It's more profound than usual, and something about his mood seems gloomy, even melancholy. When Paul, unsure of what he needs and unsure of how to get Alex to tell him, suggests they go to bed early, Alex acquiesces easily. Perhaps the anticipated separation anxiety is getting to both of them.

In bed, in the dark, Alex seems to come back to himself a little. They spend hours talking about nothing in particular. But by the time they doze off, Paul knows that Alex's favorite book as a child was *James and the Giant Peach* and that he grew up poorer than he likes to talk about.

Saturday, Alex says he needs space.

"Movie date?" Paul suggests when Alex tries to express that he needs to get out of the house.

Alex nods. "Two hours in the dark without having to talk to anyone sounds perfect."

That night in bed, Paul can't stop himself from telling Alex that he wants to fuck him, too.

Alex says, "Good thing for you that you are," with a laugh, even though Paul knows Alex knows that's not what he meant.

Alex is right of course, but to Paul it feels like a sea of things they should address even if they both lack the courage for it.

19

Alex fears the sex in the morning will be slow and thoughtful. He doesn't want this to feel like goodbye or just enough; he wants it to feel as good as it always has. But Paul seems happy to take cues and thankfully their last morning together in bed is fun and full of laughter.

They lie on the pillows catching their breath, heads together. Paul smiles when Alex laces their fingers together. Alex takes a moment to watch his face; the last chance he might ever have. At least from so close and intimate a perspective as this.

"Are you excited?" Paul asks.

Alex isn't sure. It feels churlish to say no. But he's not excited, not really. Especially not at the prospect of leaving Paul. "I will be, when I get there, I guess. But change is scary, I don't like planes, and there's a lot that could go wrong."

"With the planes?" Paul teases.

Alex shakes his head. "No. Not with the planes."

"Look, you're gonna be great. You're – "

Alex cuts him off. He doesn't need Paul's encouragement. Especially on the points he's not even worried about. "This is all new for me. I'm still working on not fucking it all up."

"You're good at new things," Paul says. He squeezes their twined hands. "I mean, you're good at this."

"This is new," Alex concedes.

"I mean, not that new – " Paul teases.

"Paul." Alex nudges at Paul's feet under the covers.

"And it's good, right?"

Alex feels his smile brighten despite his worries. "It's really good." He looks down at their clasped hands, then up at Paul again. He feels frighteningly vulnerable. "I'm going to miss you."

"I would tell you it's just a couple of months with Christmas smushed in the middle, but...." Paul takes a deep breath. Alex wonders where this is going. He has a strangely sinking feeling. "I was talking to Victor and Liam and we decided – "

"You decided?" Alex says dryly. Whatever he was expecting, this is clearly about to be some bonus WTF of epic proportion.

"We decided," Paul continues, "that maybe it would be a good idea if I came and visited you in New York."

Alex doesn't say anything for a long time. He knows the silence is ominous. "When were you going to tell me?" he finally asks, quietly, before adding, "Or, you know, ask me?"

"Before you left."

"Before I left?"

"I was nervous," Paul says carefully.

Alex goes still. "Nervous about what?"

"It's a big thing," Paul says.

"Did you think I'd say no?"

"Is this you saying no?" Paul's voice is conspicuously tight with worry.

"I'm not supposed to say no," Alex says, despite knowing that's not an answer at all. "But I need to be able to. You should have asked."

"I think this is me asking?"

"No, this is telling me something Victor and Liam apparently decided with you. One of those people is my boss."

"He's my boss too. And a friend."

"Yes, and he doesn't control how you wear your hair, when you eat, when you sleep – "

"Definitely when I sleep."

"You know what I mean."

"So I phrased it poorly."

"And sprung it on me when I'm about to leave and we can't discuss it because it was apparently never up for discussion." Alex sits up and flings the covers back.

"Hey, hey, hey." Paul sits up and grabs Alex's hands.

"Do not patronize me," Alex says. He modulates his voice carefully: Not petulant, wrathful. He doesn't yank away from Paul as he says it, though he wants to. "I have been going crazy all weekend, maybe for weeks, thinking that this was our last big hurrah, because I don't even know what we are. And I was prepared for that. I was ready to be grateful to you for this time and get drunk with my roommate, and then you had to go and do this!"

"Isn't this good news?" Paul asks.

"NOT WHEN YOU'RE MAKING ALL THE DECISIONS."

"What – what are you talking about?" Paul stammers in the silence that follows.

Alex's heart is racing and his palms are sweating. He'd trusted Paul, at least to understand how little control Alex has over anything in his life. How much he needs people in his private life to not make decisions for and about him, too.

"You came up with this and then got it cleared by Victor?" he demands. "And *Liam* – how the fuck does Liam come into this? Did you actually run it by him before you talked to me?"

"No," Paul says, clearly disoriented.

"What a relief."

◆

Alex grabs his jeans from where he'd tossed them last night as they were getting undressed together.

"How do you not know what we are?" Paul finally asks. Out of everything, that's the one that stings the most, somewhere over the hurt that Alex thought Paul would leave him.

"What are we, Paul?" Alex reaches for his shirt.

When Paul gets up on his knees on the bed and grabs his wrist, Alex stares at his hand until Paul lets go. "We're – " Paul starts, then hesitates. This feels like a moment where there are no right answers. Out of all the mistakes he's made, he should have asked Alex about this most of all.

"Nothing, apparently," Alex says, quiet again now and chillingly calm. He puts on the shirt.

Paul's mouth drops open. On some level he understands that Alex is terrified, has been terrified for days, if not weeks, if not possibly this entire year plus of his strange good fortune. It's all bursting out now, at Paul.

He tries to tell Alex as much, but all he gets for his trouble is Alex storming out of the bedroom.

Paul yanks on a pair of jeans and grabs a T-shirt out of his dresser.

"Would you stop acting like a child?" he calls down from the landing as he struggles into the shirt. He's furious.

"I don't see why I have to when you're treating me like one," Alex says.

"You are being ridiculous. This is seriously one of the craziest fights I've ever had."

"Speaking of other things you have an excellent track record with," Alex says loudly but not really to Paul as he joins him downstairs.

"Look," Paul says, "We are arguing in circles. You're pissed at me for not communicating with you about us and for making a hash of it when I tried. But you're yelling at me because you don't want this to be over while deciding it already is. Frankly, I'm fucking confused."

"You were the only person who didn't want anything from me and that I didn't owe anything to, forgive me for being upset."

"Well, there's an amazing summary of your problems with intimacy," Paul shoots back.

Alex gapes at him. "Are you writing an afterschool special? Is this really coming down to my owing it to you to take it up the ass?"

"Jesus Christ, that is not what I meant, but if you weren't so fucking terrified of – "

"No," Alex says. "You don't get to call me a coward. I have had my life pulled apart and put on display. I've had my body evaluated like fucking livestock so I could afford better jeans and stop my roommate from hating me forever because I got the big break she wanted. I have done everything in my fucking life, on my own, since I was eight. You do not get to take that from me because you're a melodramatic asshole who has decided I don't measure up to your happy fun times gay checklist."

Paul makes a noise of frustration.

"What?" Alex snaps.

Paul holds up a hand. He's trying to stop himself from making things worse.

"WHAT?" Alex repeats.

"Do you want to hear that I feel like slapping you right now so you'll shut up? That I want to hold you until you sob out whatever fucking misery has just surfaced in your head? Because neither of those impulses are appropriate or fair. So I'm going to go out for a run, get some air, and try to calm down. I suggest you do the same."

"I'm not a child."

"We've covered that," Paul snaps as he shoves his feet into the tennis shoes left by the door. "Prove it to me by still being here when I get back, and we'll hash this out. Because newsflash? While you were worried about me dumping you, I somehow skipped over *boyfriend* and went straight to *partner,* but I suppose you're probably pissed about that too."

Paul slams the door on his way out.

♦

Alex stares at the back of the door unable to make sense of what just happened.

He wants to yell, *You're fucking right I am* at Paul, because he's furious about one more decision Paul made about him that goes way beyond semantics.

He also wants to run after Paul and say *please don't leave me alone,* because the house is silent and empty in the sudden aftermath. It's frightening.

He wants to cry, and he wants to throw something, and none of those are adult responses, so he doesn't.

Alex walks back upstairs. When Todd meets him at the bedroom door and rubs against his legs, his eyes start to sting.

His suitcase is at the foot of the bed, open, half-empty, the clothes and contents scattered across the room and all over the house. He looks at the clock on the nightstand and tries to judge how much time he has before Paul gets back.

Then he starts packing.

He has to keep picking Todd up out of the suitcase.

"Hey, no," he says, when Todd tries to crawl in yet again. "You can't come, buddy. You don't want to be Divorce Cat." His voice echoes and small in the stillness of the house.

Once he gets his bag downstairs, he sees that his hat is still tossed over the back of the chair in the kitchen where he'd left it when they got in from the movie yesterday. Alex lets it stay.

And then he leaves.

◆

By the time Paul is done with his run, his head is clearer. He's now willing to admit that, for all of Alex's horrible fear and anxiety that had fueled the utter stupid of that fight, he's not blameless either.

He rounds the last corner before his street wishing they at least had more time to talk everything out before Alex has to leave for his flight.

When he gets to his house, Alex's car isn't in the driveway. When he goes inside, he calls out to him anyway, just in case it's some sort of awful, impish prank. But Alex isn't there and neither are his things, except for his beanie resting on the back of one of the kitchen chairs. If it's a sign, and Paul is sure it must be a sign, he has no damn idea what it means.

20

"**W**ow, man, you look like shit."

Alex makes an apologetic face to the woman at the desk who is trying to check him in to the hotel in D.C. as Liam bounces up to him. "So would you if you'd spent a cross country flight sobbing into your eye mask."

"Aww, you guys are so cute!"

Alex doesn't even have the energy to remind Liam of bystanders. At least Natalie and Raphael are in a different hotel. "We had a fight."

"Oh. Oh shit. Why?"

"Does the thing where you, Victor, and Paul made decisions for my life without consulting me ring any bells?"

Liam splutters. "Dude, that is not – "

"I've barely slept. Everything's crazy, and I'm pissed at you. Please go away?"

"Do you want to talk?"

"No, Liam. I do not want to talk. I want to drown myself in the bathtub, but a nap is going to have to do," he says as he collects his key card.

"I'm in 723 if you want to talk."

"Right." Alex walks away.

"What room are you in?" Liam shouts.

"Not one I'm going to holler across the lobby at you," Alex calls back without turning around. Fuck his life. And night shoots on top of it all.

◆

The last thing Alex wants to do is check his phone, but he's been off the grid since LAX and the task is unavoidable. Thankfully, everything in the handful of notifications can be ignored for now, but there's an email from Paul.

He stares at it for a good fifteen seconds, reading the subject line – simply, *Alex*, like he is the problem in this whole mess – over and over before he finally opens it.

It's many screens long, but the gist of it all is in the last sentence: *I adore you. I fucked up, and I'm sorry. Can we work this out?*

Six hours of misery on the plane was plenty of time for Alex to come down from his pitch of righteous anger and realize how awful and unfair he'd been. He fucked up, too, badly, and they do need to talk, but he hasn't slept and has only a few hours before he has to be at work.

Got to D.C. okay, he replies. *I know I was an asshole. I'm sorry. But I*

99

*didn't know we were together and I really didn't know we were married. I'm
21 and trying to do TV and a movie a long way from home. I can't do this
right now.*

Alex hits send, sets an alarm, and collapses onto the bed without
bothering to take his shoes off.

◆

He's woken, not by his alarm, but by a pounding on his door so
insistent he thinks for a moment the hotel is on fire. He takes a
moment to lie there and consider whether or not that would actually
be an awesome turn of events.

But when he gets out of bed and looks through the peephole, it's
just Liam.

"What do you want?" he asks as he opens the door. He feels
disgusting and has no bandwidth for whatever this is.

"We gotta talk, dude."

"Jesus Christ, if this is about Paul you've – "

"Noooooooo, it's not," Liam says, pushing his way into Alex's
room. "The timing's shit, and I'm sorry. I'm still willing to listen if
you wanna talk about it, but trust me, you're gonna be less pissed at
me about a whole set of other things if we have this conversation now
as opposed to later."

"Okaaaaay," Alex says, puzzled, as he lets the door slip closed.
He retreats into the bathroom to brush his teeth and splash water on
his face to prepare for whatever the hell is happening now.

Liam leans against the bathroom doorframe, ignoring Alex's glare
in his direction.

"I want to tell you this now before we have to shoot the stuff
tonight, because it's, you know, *stuff* and you deserve to know it, and
– "

"What is it, Liam?" Alex tosses down the towel and props himself
against the fake marble of the bathroom counter, folding his arms
over his chest.

"So, I'm bi."

Alex cracks up.

"Dude! Hey!" Liam looks affronted.

That makes Alex stop with a hand over his mouth. "You're
kidding. You are actually kidding."

Liam shoves his hands in his pockets and for once in his life says
nothing.

Alex lowers the hand over his mouth slowly. "You're not actually
kidding."

"Hey, man, don't stereotype."

"Liam!"

"Yeah?"

"What the actual fuck."

"I'm not in the closet. I mean – it's not a secret."

"Like fuck it isn't," Alex shoots back.

"It's complicated, okay!" Liam retorts.

"So explain it!"

"I'm trying!" Liam looks wounded. "You laughed in my face."

Alex cannot process any of this. "I'm not going to apologize for anything right now," he says carefully.

"Yeah, that's…yeah, that's probably cool. Anyway." Liam shuffles his feet and gives Alex a look Alex knows he practices. "I wanted to tell you before we had to shoot the kiss tonight."

"Thank you for the advance warning."

"You're – "

"No, seriously, Liam." Alex pushes past him out of the bathroom. "Why the fuck is it that I have no time to process anything because everyone in my life keeps waiting until the last minute to drop bombshells on me? On purpose?!"

"Dude, I'm sorry Paul – "

"Does Paul know about this?"

"What does that have to do with – "

"Does. He. Know?"

"Yes." Liam sits down cross-legged on the end of Alex's bed. "And if he didn't say anything it's 'cause he's a good guy, so don't be pissed at him for my choices, okay?"

Alex stares. "Please tell me you haven't slept with him."

"Nope."

"No you haven't or no you're not telling me?"

"No, I haven't," Liam says seriously.

"Okay."

"Okay?"

"Only about that," Alex clarifies. "I'm still pissed at you."

"You know this isn't about you, right?" Liam says in a manner that suggests he has a lot of practice pointing that out to people, whether true or not.

"And that's why you're telling me this and why the internet has spent the last year thinking we're dating."

"Look, I'm sorry about that. It's not fun for Carly and me either, but there's nothing – "

"*Bullshit.* You played that up every second you could. While saying you're straight. Who does that?"

"It's helped both of us," Liam says mildly.

"I'm the fucking twink. That's what helped you," Alex snaps, before cursing under his breath.

"Ego, ego," Liam teases in lieu of yelling back.

"You know what I mean." Alex deflates.

"Yeah. I do."

"So *why?*"

"I'm with Carly for one. For another, you wanna try explaining non-monogamy and/or bisexuality to *TV Guide*?"

"Alan Cumming," Alex replies.

"Great name, right?"

"Are you trying to get me to storm out of my own hotel room?"

"Look, it's not convenient or salient or easy. I've never lied about it. I've omitted, and I've dodged, but I have never lied about it. You can go back through every interview and check that."

"But, because it wasn't going to get you the cover of *People*, you didn't tell," Alex clarifies for him.

"Yeah," Liam says. "Like why would anyone not make that choice?"

Alex is horrified. "Do you want me to congratulate you?" He crosses his arms in front of his chest. He understands being in the closet – no matter what Liam says – but he's not going to cheer the man on for being mercenary.

"Come on, aren't there some things you want to keep out of the product?"

"Yes, and as the last twenty-four hours has demonstrated, I don't get to have any of them."

21

Paul gets Alex's reply as he's walking down the hallway to the writers' room. He nearly fumbles his phone as he tries to juggle it, his bag, and the door.

He's done reading the message by the time he gets to his desk but can't begin to think of a reply. Alex never does use very many words, but he is always devastatingly good at communicating himself.

Okay, he replies before shoving his phone back in his pocket. "Message received, darling," he mutters under his breath.

During lunch, Carly calls. Paul leaves his laptop open to where he's continuing to fail to fix a scene and walks out to the hallway.

"Does everyone know?" he asks. This information diffusion is even worse than when they'd first gotten together and a lot less happy. Paul hopes that Alex hasn't seen that there are paparazzi pictures of him from LAX on the internet. The internet, because Paul is morbidly curious enough to have checked, is in fact having an absolute field day trying to figure out why Alex looks so miserable.

That the prevailing assumption is that he finally broke up with the jackass he'd been dating instead of, or in addition to, Liam is a whole new level of horrible. And not only because they're not entirely wrong.

"Liam told me. He's worried."

"Oh."

"Are you okay, Paul?"

"I just had someone walk out on me last night for the second time in a year."

"Oh, honey."

Paul makes it to the courtyard, where he sits down on a bench and presses the phone hard against the side of his head. "Yeah."

"Do you want to come over sometime this week? Not to talk if you don't want to. Get you out of your space."

Paul thinks of his empty house, his own too-full mind, and the way Carly continues to try to help him be a functional man. "Yeah. But I know you're judging me."

"Sure, but I'm luring you in with my compassion first."

Paul puts back his head and squints against the brightness of the sky. "Why do you put up with any of us?"

"You and Liam, you mean?"

"And so many more."

"You two are my most special of special snowflakes," she says with a certain degree of weariness. Paul manages a smile anyway. "But this is what I do. I'm good at it, it's good for me, and you certainly need it."

◆

That afternoon, Victor breezes into the office and surveys his hardworking minions with satisfaction. Then his eyes land on Paul. "Is everything set for New York?"

"Come with me," Paul shoves away from the desk and stalks out of the room.

Victor follows Paul into the kitchenette. "Ooooh, drama," he drawls in the San Francisco gay accent that marks all their divides – from generational to experiential – in a way Paul finds particularly irksome in the moment.

This is not a conversation he wants to have. The subject matter is upsetting, Victor is unpredictable, and the whole matter feels like a test he doesn't know how to pass.

"New York isn't happening," he says. "I fucked up, and you let me do it. Alex may be overreacting but he isn't wrong, and I am way too used to you pulling all the strings to think how I made your friendly advice sound. You are some sort of fucked up, Victor."

"I told you to be careful of him," Victor says mildly. "And it's your life too."

"I'm aware of that," Paul snaps.

"Apparently not enough. And don't blame me for your sloppy sentence construction." Victor watches Paul intently, fascinated with how he's reacting. While Paul is used to this level of scrutiny, right now it feels more unsettling than it has in a long time.

"It would be a lot easier to feel like I wasn't one of your creations if you didn't keep treating me like one."

"You've always been a character in my story, Paul. You keep missing the point is all."

"Really? And what's that?"

"That no one cares about stories where no one ever says no and everyone always lives happily ever after."

◆

Alex is relieved to go through hair and makeup and let himself sink into the headspace of not quite existing. Sometimes he hates it, but right now he appreciates not having to worry about anything.

The sun sets earlier here and it's colder than he's gotten used to in L.A., especially with the wind off the tidal basin. It's one more strange and surreal thing in his strange and surreal life to be here in D.C. for a job he never planned on having. He never even came here when he was growing up, although he saw photos from school trips other people from better towns posted on the internet.

The Washington Monument is shorter than he thought it would

be.

Alex tells Liam that, while Liam fidgets with yet another random app on his smartphone. Then he says, "Don't even." He knows the next thing to come out of Liam's mouth is going to be a dick joke.

Liam is quiet for another moment, then puts his phone away. "You're freaking out."

Alex gives him a look and tries not to see the people who are starting to cluster around the edge of the area they've got closed off for filming. All this day needs to make it better is fans. "No, I'm not."

"Yes, you are. This isn't about the thing, is it?"

"It's not about the thing."

"You're a shit liar, Alex."

"It's not lying, it's acting," Alex says haughtily.

"...Dude, that's fucked up."

"I am reminding myself that I am a professional." Alex focuses not on Liam, but on the lights on the water. Beyond them, the majestic columns of the Jefferson rise above the skeletons of the cherry trees. "And in thirty seconds I will be right with you, but currently, yes, I'm freaking out."

Liam checks his watch.

"Oh my God, seriously?"

"Shhhhhh, twenty-five seconds left. Freak out wisely,"

Alex doesn't even think he's teasing so much as respecting the process. "It's not about the thing." Alex's life is too much of a mess for Liam's bisexuality to be the centerpiece of his day.

"Is it about you being here, doing this, and having no clue what your life is right now?"

Alex hugs his arms around himself. "That, and in about fifteen minutes I have to make out with you, on camera, which officially makes this the second weirdest day of my entire life."

"Hey, I only get second place?"

"The first-weirdest day was totally half your fault too."

"Whose fault was the other half?" Liam asks curiously.

Alex isn't sure what to say. He's never told anyone about the run-in with Paul the morning his life exploded. Besides, it's easier to blame Victor.

Liam taps his watch before grabbing Alex's shoulder. "Time's up. Let's go rock this."

◆

Halfway through the night, Alex realizes that Liam didn't decide to come out to him at an incredibly inconvenient time because he suddenly felt the need to absolve himself. Yes, the burden created by the audience's preoccupation with the sex lives of *Fourth's* stars is significant. But in the scene James has his hands in his pockets and is talking – quietly, earnestly, shyly – to Zach about truth and honesty. For once, nothing he's saying has to do with journalistic ethics or even the appalling lack of them.

"Everybody here's got a lie," he says. "I don't want to lie to you anymore."

As they reset the cameras for the sixth of what feels like twelve different angles on the damn kiss, Alex realizes Liam's giving a better performance because there's truth underlying it. He wanted Alex to know that and give more because of it too. The situation is humbling, and Alex isn't sure if he has more to learn about life or acting in the face of it.

♦

Back at the hotel Liam walks with Alex from the elevator to his room.

"I'm, like, just around the corner there," he says once Alex manages to get his key out and his door open. Then Liam hugs him tightly.

"Liam, what the fuck?" Alex tries to keep his door open but it's awkward with Liam affixed to him.

"Good job tonight," Liam says, muffled over Alex's shoulder.

Liam's sudden bursts of thoughtfulness and awareness of others are as surprising and unpredictable as his need to – inconveniently, at the moment – physically express his affection for the whole word.

"…Thank you," Alex says tiredly, finally hugging Liam back. The door clicks closed again. "You too."

"There you go." Liam unwraps himself from Alex, and looks him in the eye intently for a moment before patting his cheek. "You're gonna be okay, man."

Alex has to bite his lip. Unexpected sympathy is even worse than unexpected hugs. His eyes suddenly sting. "Okay."

"I'm down the hall if you want to talk."

"*Okay.*" He's amused more than otherwise, but still. "It has been a really long day. I'm going to go sleep, and then you can bug me more in the morning, yeah?"

"Cool!" Liam bounces away.

Alex rests his forehead against the door before he manages to get the key in the lock again. It's been the longest day.

22

S o there's this thing you do, that I don't get," Paul says, kicking his socked feet against Carly's. They're in her bed – Carly in pajamas and Paul in sweatpants and a ratty T-shirt that pass for the same – with beer and a bag of ranch-flavored chips, half-heartedly watching *Jaws*.

"Yeah?"

"Why do I always have an awesome time with you when I'm miserable?"

She shoves another handful of chips into her mouth. "Because I am awesome, and most of the time we spend together has involved you being miserable, which is what happens when you date girls you shouldn't be dating."

"I'm starting to think I maybe shouldn't be dating."

"Ya think?" Carly asks.

"Thanks."

"Look, I'm just saying you didn't magically stop being nuts when you realized you liked dick the mostest."

Paul cackles. Carly is the most awful and awesome of all his friends. Even with her long, wavy hair up in a messy, lopsided ponytail and the hideous yellow and pink pajamas that completely clash with her tawny skin, she looks amazing and slightly terrifying. He's very fond of her.

"So what's your call?" he asks. "Permanently broken or temporarily broken?"

"You and dating or you and Alex?"

"Me, mainly."

Carly ponders for a moment. "Mmmmm, thoroughly broken."

"This door number three thing you do is really annoying, by the way."

"But it works. You, on the other hand, do not work. You fall in love with every good fuck that comes your way and yet can't figure out that you're the common denominator enough to love yourself? As usual, my friend, you should be smarter than your bad crazy."

"And yet...." Paul steals a handful of chips.

"And yet. So what's the plan?"

"A vow of celibacy while I convince myself maybe he wasn't the one?"

"Wait, seriously?" she asks, sitting up and clicking pause on the shark.

Paul nods solemnly.

"That's not good. Like, you can talk all you want about not fucking around, but you're too much like Liam. Just monogamous.

You need someone in your bed like people need water."

Paul thunks his head back against the headboard. "No kidding."

"Why haven't you gotten blindingly drunk yet?" Carly asks.

"You mean why didn't I bring over something better than beer?"

"Yeah, this is entirely about my need for gin." Carly rolls her eyes. "You're such an asshole, answer the question."

"Because every night when I get home, I think I'm going to see his car in the driveway, or I'm going to wake up to him climbing into bed."

"Because you're delusional or because you think he wants to fix it too?"

"That's the problem," Paul says as the pause timer expires and the shark action recommences. "I can't tell."

23

When he wakes up on day two, Alex feels like a human being again. The crisis, at least for now, is past.

Zach and James kissed and the world didn't end. Alex, meanwhile, didn't combust from the horror of it. Or freeze at the feel of lips other than the ones he wants and doesn't get to have anymore. And all things considered, Liam was more decent about the whole thing than Alex expected.

Alex may not feel in control of his world, but he feels capable. The thought of going for a second day without disaster in a new city is appealing. So is a proper breakfast and a foray to a bookstore. Since they're shooting nights this week, he has his days to himself. In a city with an actual winter, Alex thinks he might even be able to remain unseen.

It doesn't work. He left his beanie at Paul's and there are fans loitering outside of the hotel. It's amazing to him what people think counts as inconspicuous. He has to offer to sign something for a girl and chitchat with her friends in order to convince them not to follow him. While he does, the Margaret in his head is telling him not to negotiate with terrorists. He winds up purchasing a new hat, acrylic and ill-fitting, from the first street vendor he sees.

D.C. isn't like L.A. at all. The buildings are shorter, and it's actually built for pedestrians. Although the spoke-and-wheel street layout complicates navigation, it's not hard to find a bookstore. Alex feels himself relax when he pushes open the door and is greeted with a burst of warmth and the smell of coffee.

He spends an hour browsing, picking up books at random and skimming through them. History, art, politics, literature, poetry, philosophy – he investigates them all. He hardly has time for leisure reading anymore, not with his life and his schedule. He misses it. When he was in Indiana, he never had the money for books and he'd soon exhausted what the public library had on offer. Even after three years in L.A. – one of them as a TV star – new books still feel like a delicious indulgent luxury.

The coffee shop is maybe half-full. The occupants look to be mostly local high school kids with laptops and textbooks, or sitting with their friends talking. Alex swallows down a stab of envy. How different his life would have been, if he'd been able to have bookstores and coffee shops and other kids like him growing up.

He should do this more often, he thinks as he finally makes a selection.

He spends the rest of the afternoon in his hotel room curled up with his book.

◆

Alex and Liam get driven in a car to location that night because no one trusts them to get to set in a city they don't know. Once they get there Liam spends as much time as he can on the edge of the shoot area, signing things for fans and smiling and waving into smart phones, while reminding everyone there will be no kissing on set tonight.

Of course, the fans have never believed Liam on this sort of point. Given what Alex and Liam filmed last night – not to mention the fact that Liam is bi – they suddenly look a hell of a lot smarter for their skepticism. Liam's repeated demurrals only seem to summon more of them. Alex considers joining Liam to see if his own overwhelming lack of enthusiasm will drive the spectators off. He decides to huddle by a heat lamp at crafty with some of the hair and makeup crew instead.

◆

"Hey, you want to get a drink after?" Liam asks, checking his watch when they call the last shot of the night.

"Everything's closed," Alex points out. It's almost three in the morning.

"I know a place."

Alex squints at him. There's a halfway decent chance Liam does know a place. But while Alex may be legal now, drinking at some illegal after-hours bar doesn't seem like the best plan in the *don't fuck up in public* sweepstakes.

"Is this place your hotel room?" Alex asks, somewhere between dubious and hopeful. Somehow, Liam's room would be the lesser of two evils. His life is damn surreal for having come to this.

"Dude. Minibar!"

◆

"This is your idea of a minibar?" Alex says when they walk in. The full-sized bottle of scotch on the dresser renders that something of an understatement.

Liam immediately snags the glass tumblers the hotel set next to a complimentary bottle of ridiculous mineral water. "Compared to the bar at home, yeah."

Alex watches Liam as he pours them both a drink and accepts his gratefully. He's been to Liam's house many times – almost exclusively for work-related parties – and considering he has a whole room full of manly leather furniture, books Alex is sure he doesn't read, and one hell of a bar set up, he can see his point.

They wind up lying on the bed, side-by-side and shoes still on. While Liam seems mesmerized with the rapidly dwindling contents of his glass, Alex balances his on his chest and stares at the ceiling while he talks about Paul – not what happened, but what it was.

"Anyone could see that," Liam says at one point, when Alex finally says the L-word.

"I didn't know that's what it felt like," Alex says.

"Like what?"

"Abject terror."

Liam laughs. Alex swats at him, knocking scotch all over them both. Alex curses and bolts upright to try to deal with it, but Liam puts out a hand for him to stay put.

"It's a hotel, so it'll get dealt with when we call for them to deal with it. It's also alcohol, so it will evaporate quickly, and neither of us is wearing anything nice enough to care about."

"This is not a life I'm used to," Alex says distantly. Liam is peculiar, and the idea of other people at his service is still a philosophical problem for him.

"Go bring us the bottle then. You'll feel better."

"Now I know why Carly refuses to live with you," Alex mutters as he fetches the bottle and restores their drinks.

"You ever let Paul see your place?"

"No."

"Then don't judge my housekeeping in a hotel when I'm trying to get drunk."

Alex arranges himself cross-legged on the bed. He stares at Liam, who always seems to be trying too hard. "Sometimes I can't figure out if you're the happiest guy I know or the saddest."

"Yes," Liam says, clinking glasses with him. "You think you're the only one who finds this life lonely regardless of who you're in it with?"

"Yes?"

"No. We're a species made to do this to people, not to have it done to us. No one will ever understand what it's like to be you. If you can remember that, you'll be less pissed all the time and less of a shit to the people you date."

"Er, thanks?"

"No problem."

"Sometimes I hate you."

"I know. Is that getting better or worse in the last forty-eight hours?"

Alex laughs and drains his glass. In this quiet late-night dark Liam is beautiful. Alex wonders if all the usual chaos of his body language and intrusiveness is meant to dull that. Being beautiful in Hollywood is so dangerous; maybe Liam knows that as well as him.

"I'll let you know," he says

He finds it odd that Liam should feel suddenly so much more like a peer. They've always been acutely different. That, combined with the age difference, has largely made it seem like Liam is cool and Alex just isn't. The reality is far more complex.

Liam is a hot mess of secrets that Victor is somehow forcing him to confess on TV. That's strange and a little bit ugly. Alex realizes he can feel victimized and exposed by his fame all he wants, but his life may always be more his own than Liam's ever will by the simple virtue of being out and not wanting to sell every single secret he has.

"I've misjudged you," Alex finally says.

"Yeah?"

"It's not a compliment." Alex lies down, and Liam flops down next to him. Alex supposes scotch and a king-sized bed and four in the morning will do that to anyone.

Liam chortles. "I like you."

Alex turns his head in what feels like movie magic slowmo to see Liam's blue eyes blinking back at him. He's not surprised at all, because Alex *knows* stories. Even if he's crap at predicting how they end, in the last year he's gotten very good at understanding how they begin.

"Yeah?" Liam is staring at him, and the whole thing feels loaded and odd.

Alex nods.

Liam kisses him.

He tastes like scotch and doesn't kiss like James. In Alex's altered state it feels easy. Liam doesn't kiss like James and it doesn't seem like a bad idea. This can't cost Alex any more than losing Paul had done.

"This is a really bad idea," Liam says against his lips.

Alex wonders why. He's single. Liam is poly. He laughs into Liam's mouth and has one terrible moment where he remembers the wine in Paul's. Maybe Liam is right.

"You don't give a remote shit, do you?" Liam asks.

Alex shakes his head, sits up, and toes off his shoes. "Now you get to prove to me you're not a liar."

"You don't actually think that," Liam says.

"I don't. But you would if it were useful," he says as he pulls his T-shirt up over his head.

"Christ, you're direct."

"Someone has to be." As with Paul, now that Alex knows he can have this, he wants to take it. And with Liam at least he knows where he stands.

"Fine," Liam says. He sits up, sets his glass down decisively on the night table. "I let you fuck me and we consider the matter of my truthfulness closed."

"I think it's already closed." Alex wrinkles up his face up at Liam's ridiculousness.

"Okay. But fuck me anyway?" Liam sounds exasperated. "Because I want you to and I'm drunk, very cute, only slightly pathetic, and asking nicely."

Alex runs a nervous hand through his hair.

Liam stares at him in until some sort of realization kicks in. "What? You don't top?"

"Think harder." Alex tries to squash the impulse to be defensive.

"Oh shit, you've never done this before." Liam scrambles to his knees and reaches for Alex. "We're going to have so much fun!"

Making out with Liam is hot and messy and fun. Alex figures out a bunch of small and specific things that get him going fast. It's good for Alex's ego, knowing to breathe just so against Liam's ear or to tell him how very good he is. It's even better for his confidence to not only have control, but to know what to do with it. He can thank Paul for that, though he tries not to dwell too long on the thought.

They get naked fast, mainly because Alex is already halfway there. Of the many things Liam is, a tease is apparently not one of them.

"God, I love that you take up so much more space than me," Liam says. Alex pins him to the bed and bites at his neck hard. He hasn't spent much time thinking about the fact that he's taller and broader than Liam, though it's obvious now.

"Twink my ass," Alex murmurs. Liam cracks up and slaps his in response.

Alex's laugh cuts off in a gasp.

"Oh really," Liam says.

"Apparently," Alex says and returns to biting across Liam's throat and shoulders and chest.

"You tell me when you want to add that to the to-do list."

Alex doesn't know what to say and doesn't want to think about it right now, so he bites harder.

When they have to pause for Liam to dig condoms and lube out of his bag, he realizes how glad he is that they are both drunk and hilarious and chatty. Alex is nervous.

He doesn't think of himself as a virgin, didn't even before Paul, and yet here he is in this absurd situation with TV star Liam Campbell's rather stunning ass staring him more or less in the face. His brain insists that this is a momentous occasion. As dumb as that is, Alex is fairly sure it's not the wrongest thought he's ever had.

Liam tosses the supplies on the bed. "It's just sex. And a little bit of technology. Relax," he says with a kiss so easy and intimate it takes Alex aback.

It's nothing, however, compared to Liam taking his hand and showing Alex how to finger him. It's weird and a little stupid, and they both giggle through it until Liam goes breathless. Alex can't remember the last time he's felt as glad to be as young as he is. The sounds Liam makes as Alex pushes one of his legs back so he can get deeper make his dick twitch.

"God, I could spend hours sucking at your thighs," he murmurs into skin.

"No one's stopping you."

Liam helps him with the condom. Alex isn't sure if that's sexy or not, but it's a great distraction now that his brain has started up with the momentous occasion nonsense again.

"You're going to stop thinking the second you're inside me," Liam says. "And then I'm going to give you too much direction, and you'll get pissed off and pound me into the mattress. Trust me, it's gonna be great."

Liam isn't wrong, despite leaving out the part where he's insanely tight and the slow push into him is some of the most exquisite torture Alex has ever experienced. Liam's on his knees, ass in the air, shoulders down on the bed and hands folded under his face as it happens. At first it's too much for Alex to look at him as he sinks inside, but then it's too much not to.

When Liam starts sucking on his fingers, Alex swears and pulls them away, replacing them with his own. "You need all the dick, don't you?"

Liam nods frantically, and Alex huffs out something of a laugh as he pistons his hips in earnest. Whatever this is about – and Alex can't think enough to even try to figure it out right now – it's no longer about who they are when they're wearing clothes or making words. While there's nothing at all surprising about Liam being needy and vulnerable in this way, Alex knows the signs of secrets by now. They make his heart go tender.

Liam comes first, frantically pumping his own cock and still sucking on Alex's fingers. Despite the relief Alex sees roll through him, Liam barely pauses in fucking back hard onto Alex's cock, spitting out his fingers and urging him on, a litany of *come on, come on, come on.*

Alex cuffs him lightly on the back of the head then digs his wet fingers into his hair. "Impatient asshole," he grits out fondly before he spills into the condom.

24

Alex is grateful, relaxed and still turning the whole thing over in his brain. But mostly, he is content.

"So what did you think? Awesome?" Liam asks as he takes the lead in getting them cleaned up. Alex can even recognize that Liam isn't fishing for compliments. He just wants to know he's done the right thing in showing someone something new.

He closes his eyes and lets himself drift a little. "Awesome."

"Good," Liam says softly. He climbs back into bed and drapes an arm, a leg, and half his body on top of Alex.

"I fuck you, and you cuddle me," Alex murmurs sleepily. "Is that how this works?"

He's making fun, but Alex is relieved for Liam's warm weight over him. Putting words together coherently is still taking some effort. He's not as broken as he was the first time Paul took him apart and then had to hold him until he put himself back together, but he's still a little fractured. It seems to be happening in slow motion this time.

"Alex," Liam says, aggrieved. "Cuddling is the best part of fucking."

Alex pushes some of Liam's curls out of his own face when Liam turns his head up to look at him. "Oh, is it now?"

"Mhmmmm." Liam works a hand under Alex's side to wrap around him. "Don't tell me this this is new too."

"No. Would you stop wiggling? No. I just, I don't know," Alex says, not able to articulate his warring feelings of comfort and claustrophobia to Liam any better than he could for Paul.

"Should I move? I can move. I'm not a dick. Not like that, anyway."

"Hey. What kind of teacher are you? Don't give up on me that easy." Alex gives him a tentative smile. Movement or words of any sort are an effort, but not an unpleasant one. For months Alex thought Paul was the only person he liked to have push his boundaries. Now there's Liam too. Maybe he just enjoys having his boundaries pushed – even when that's uncomfortable – more than he thought.

Liam smiles back and wriggles closer. "That means you're staying the night, right?"

"Presumptuous," Alex says.

"Dude, that ship sailed, like, an hour ago."

"Someone's going to notice."

"Naw. Do you have any idea how many guys I've passed out drunk with before?"

"That's encouraging." Alex considers asking for more data on the subject but decides against it. If he needs to know something, Liam will tell him. Whether he wants to know or not.

"No one's going to notice. Or care. Like, I can check the hall for you if you want, but it's five in the morning and your room is a long way away."

"Not that far," Alex protests, even though he doesn't really want to leave. Liam feels good stretched over him. With this to focus on, the memory of the fight with Paul is fading even further away.

Liam hums. Alex doesn't say anything else but also doesn't make a move to get up. Eventually,

"It's okay if you don't want to sleep alone."

"I know."

"That's new too, isn't it?"

"Be quiet and go to sleep." Alex is running out of energy to keep the conversation going. The sound of Liam breathing is soothing and his body is warm and lulling. Almost all Alex wants right now is to fall asleep.

"Okay." Liam helps get the covers up over both of them and wraps himself around Alex once again. "Sweet dreams."

"You, too." Alex wonders what there is to dream of when the world is temporarily perfect.

◆

When they wake up early in the afternoon, Alex does make Liam check the hall for him before he darts back to his room to turn into a human being who should be having regrets. But he can't bring himself to. He's tired – probably overtired, really. He hasn't slept enough in days. But after he takes a shower he wants food more than he wants more sleep.

His positive attitude lasts until he gets downstairs, because something about Liam reading *The Wall Street Journal* over what probably, since they're shooting nights, counts as breakfast, makes him want to punch people.

"Is that an affectation or is that for real?" Alex asks as he sits down at Liam's table in the hotel restaurant without invitation.

"I like to pretend I know what's going on with my investments." Liam doesn't look up from the newsprint as he sips his coffee. "Want the *Post*?"

Alex snags the paper without comment. There's something about working on a show about fake news that has made him compulsive about keeping up with real news. Reading, however, is difficult; Liam keeps kicking his chair.

Then the fish heads make everything worse.

"What the fuck is that?" Alex asks when Liam's food arrives.

"Japanese breakfast."

"There are fish heads."

"Yes. They come with the fish."

"Do you know how often you make me wonder if I'm hallucinating?"

"Under recent circumstances that sounds suspiciously like a compliment," Liam says, still focused on his paper. It may be *The Wall Street Journal*, but Liam is reading the style section.

"Why did you order that?"

"Because it's good, and I haven't been to Japan since before the show started, and because I like it."

Alex rocks back a little at that. Liam isn't being a dick; Alex is. "What's Japan like?" he asks. "And why did you go?"

Liam lowers the paper almost suspiciously. But then, as the waitress comes to take Alex's order, he starts to tell him about a childhood Alex finds unimaginable: Early fame, deeply involved parents, and money not just for necessities, but for breakfasts anywhere in the world. Liam speaks joyfully of his travels, but with a blithe tone that Alex knows he could too easily take as cruel.

At the end of a long story about the street numbering system in Tokyo, a porn shop, and elegant gothic lolita fashion trends, Liam says, "So I just figured out a thing about you."

"What's that?"

"You're Eve."

"Pardon?" Alex is too sure he's heard wrong to even begin find his way to pissed.

"Way more interested in knowledge than consequences," Liam toys with an unused fork. "And way more intentional about it than everyone thinks."

Alex scrapes his own fork across his plate with a horrific sound, then stabs fitfully at his hash browns. Liam is astute and Alex feels seen against his will. But the oddness of the comment – and of Liam – leaves him feeling fond. "We can be friends now," he mumbles.

Liam barks with laughter. "Victory is mine."

"Don't get overexcited. You called me a chick and my memory is long."

"And that ain't all," Liam says, sliding one of the spare forks into his pocket.

Alex wants to ask what he's planning to do with it – it's better than acknowledging the dick innuendo – but decides against it, since the answer will probably make sense to Liam and absolutely no one else.

25

Alex expects being in D.C. to get easier as the days go by, but it doesn't. If anything, it gets harder. He still misses Paul desperately. Liam is being surprisingly lovely but he by himself isn't enough to absorb all the loneliness of the city.

The material they're shooting doesn't make things easier. It's all heavy and intense, and while acting is just work, the mood on-camera follows Alex off of it.

For Zach, everything is falling apart. Alex can relate uncomfortably well to his character's sense of loss even if the subject is different. More frighteningly, Alex can also relate to Zach's terrible sense of victory as he lays out to James plans he knows he shouldn't be so eager to make.

"I'm going to Iran," Zach says.

James looks horrified. He asks "Why?" with an intensity that comes either from his field experience or the personal investment James has come to have in Zach. Zach gets his concern, but doesn't back down, explaining as best he can why this is exactly what he needs to be doing. The situation and Zach's language skills James knows. Zach's passion to do right with them in a sea of the cynical and selfish, James is hearing, on some level, for the first time.

That moment of discovery is thrilling and bittersweet for both Alex and Liam to play.

They're filming in front of the Capitol, and Liam's sitting on the curb of the Reflecting Pool while Alex stands so their eye lines can be all mismatched.

"My ass is freezing," Liam complains in between takes.

Alex gives an overdramatic sigh. Liam is fishing for comments about his ass and possibly for offers to warm it up. Alex has absolutely no desire to go there while other people are around.

It's a good break from being in Zach's headspace, though, because Zach is anxious and afraid of James's reaction, whether it be anger or an attempt to stop him.

What Liam-as-James does eventually say, over and over again as they line up all the shots is, "It's my job to tell you not to. But what do you need?"

It feels like a reminder of how promises can be terrible things.

♦

By the time they wrap for the night they're both eager to get back inside a warm building. At the hotel they cross the lobby together, chattering and exchanging glances without touching.

Once the elevator doors close behind them, Alex crowds Liam into the corner. "God, I can't wait to get you upstairs." In bed, Alex won't have to think.

Liam stops him before the inevitable kiss, although barely.

"Hey, careful," he points up at the ceiling. "Security cams."

Alex blanches and reels back.

"Hey, hey, hey." Liam laughs and doesn't let him pull completely away. "They don't have sound."

"Oh," Alex says.

Liam laughs again. "So you should stop touching me, but definitely not stop talking. Seriously. How are you so paranoid and yet so bad at this?"

"It's new," Alex snaps.

"Mm, yes," Liam hums. "Let's go make it less new."

♦

"Three things," Liam says when Alex follows him into his hotel room.

"Yeah?"

"One, it's your job to tell me what you want. I don't want to assume or not assume when that's me, and I don't want you to assume or not assume that I always say yes, even though I mostly say yes."

"Text messaging is the better part of valor?" Alex teases.

"Something like that. Two, you bit the shit outta my neck."

"You loved it," Alex breathes, pushing into Liam's space a little, even as his hands on Alex's hips hold him slightly at bay.

"I did, and I have an awful reputation, so no one is ever going to think twice as to how such a thing might have happened. But you should still be aware."

"Yeah, okay," Alex nods. "What's the third thing?"

"Is there anything you don't want to do with me?"

"That sounds an awful lot like thing one."

Liam pulls Alex to him. "Sure, but it still stands."

♦

Later, when Alex is on his back and biting at the heel of his hand to muffle the sound because Liam has two fingers pressed up inside of him, he finally understands what Liam had meant earlier.

He comes like that, Liam's mouth on his cock.

Liam asks him questions afterward, too many, because Alex's brain is not online. But they're all yes or no, one or the other. Eventually, Alex manages to convey that yes it was good, that he's a little bit cold, and that he would like a glass of water.

While Liam fidgets, probably in vain, with the room's thermostat, he explains that while Alex doesn't need to be able to articulate what's going on in the moment for him during sex he really should learn how to identify and articulate it after the fact. Sure two data points is not a trend, but Liam is getting the picture. Alex didn't even know a picture was there.

"So I, or anyone, can know what you need," he says. "And you're totally not weird, that's a great place you get off to. I do it too sometimes and I love it, it's pretty much the only time my head ever feels quiet."

Alex smiles and doesn't even make a joke about how Liam so rarely shuts up. After what they've done together Alex believes him.

"And it's cool you like to hang out," Liam goes on, making a gesture that, Alex assumes, is meant to encompass the way Alex is still stretched out on the bed. "I just kinda need to do stuff for people or cuddlewhore after is all."

Alex snorts with quiet laughter. He has no idea what they're doing.

26

Victor is home, in his den, reading a book when his cell phone rings. He's not surprised it's Liam, although he is surprised by the hour. Even in L.A. it's late. With the D.C. team shooting nights, he's not sure when or if Liam is sleeping.

The second Victor picks up, Liam is already babbling. "Okay, so, I know you're gonna yell. But if I don't tell you you're gonna hear it somewhere else, like from Alex or when I'm drunk, and it's going to be a lot worse for me if you do."

"An auspicious start." Victor sets his book aside so he can focus on Liam. "What did you do, and why is Alex involved?"

"See, okay, I hooked up with him."

Victor squints at the bookshelves that line the walls of the room, full to bursting with books and DVD cases. He can't cow Liam into being less of an idiot with a glare like he could if Liam were there in person, but he can express his displeasure at the furniture.

"Hooked up with whom," he coaxes, for clarification. He's unconcerned that it sounds more than a little menacing.

"With Alex," Liam repeats.

"You did what?"

"Alex and me."

"You did *what?*" Victor doesn't often yell. He doesn't often need to. It's much easier to intimidate people with quiet. But Liam's caught him completely off-guard, and he's concerned.

"Dude! We didn't fuck on the National Mall. This isn't, like, stupid – "

"Yes it is stupid!! Jesus Christ, Liam, what kind of a fucking idiot are you?" Victor feels bad about the cruelty of the words the moment he speaks them, but he's appalled.

"Why is it stupid?" Liam's voice is distant. He's probably pulled the phone away from his ear.

"Other than the fact that you felt the need to call and confess to me, which probably ranks it pretty high on the list of idiotic things you have done?"

"Well, yeah."

"Does Carly know?" Victor is well-acquainted with the nature of their arrangements. If Liam is calling him, he wants to make damn sure he hasn't fucked up with someone even more important.

"Victor, seriously." Liam sounds subdued but not defensive. If experience is anything to go by, that means that this is for real. And if it is, it means Liam's done everything right, according to his understanding of his contract with life. Heaven help everyone. "You're pissed. Which, you know, not surprised. But I probably

122

deserve to know exactly why."

"Is this going to happen again?"

"Yes. That's why I called."

"And Alex is okay?"

"Alex is fine, Victor." Liam's patience, on the rare occasions he chooses to be patient, is maddening. "Why is it dumb?"

"Alex is in D.C. right now, with you, and headed to New York next week – even if that's not one of my projects – because I pulled him out from behind a clipboard and dropped him in front of the camera."

"Yeah?"

"None of what I've done to him is anything he wanted for himself."

"No," Liam says. "He's doing pretty okay, though."

"And he just ended a very promising relationship with Paul because the three of us were making decisions about his life. According to Paul according to Alex, at least."

"Yeah, I got that lecture, too. He's not totally wrong, you know."

Victor breezes past that one; he's already told Paul everything he needed to about that, and Paul's feelings and Victor's miscalculations have nothing to do with Liam now. "And now you've hooked up with him. It's not that I don't trust you, and at least you're only five years older than him – "

"It's just that you don't trust me," Liam teases.

"No," Victor says. He doesn't trust Liam's judgement, and there's a significant difference. "The fairytale comes with costs, and I don't want this, of all things, to be one of them."

"Victor! You're worried about us." Despite everything, Victor has to smile at the glee in Liam's voice. If only more people understood his feelings more often.

"I was not built to deal with you mere mortals," he mutters.

Liam's laugh is delighted. "Careful, someone might figure out that you're human after all."

"Perish the thought."

"Alex is gonna be okay, you know."

"Alex will always be okay," Victor says firmly. "I made sure of it."

"Then why are you worried?"

"Because my favorite people are the ones who surprise me, and I adore you all."

27

Paul goes for a run before work. The sun is coming up, the streets are quiet, and it's almost peaceful.

He wishes he at least had Beau to run with, and wonders if it's worth thinking about getting another dog. He's been pining about dog jogging for over a year. But Todd is territorial and doesn't need the attention a dog would, so maybe it's best things stay as they are.

On the corner he gets flagged down by one of his neighbors, a grandfatherly man named Tom. Paul stops to say hello; Tom is the opposite of the stereotypical Los Angeles experience in so many ways and has always been amusing to interact with.

They exchange pleasantries in a way that's reflex, but Paul now recognizes as a struggle. The human impulse to tell the truth when asked how he's doing is something clearly not entirely trained out of either of them.

"I've been worse," Paul says when it's his turn. He makes himself smile, even though the fact that he's even out here indicates he's also been much, much better. Staying fit is one thing, but the pace and distances he's pushing himself for aren't healthy and he knows it. But then, that's the point.

"That's good, that's good. Got plans for the holiday?"

Paul's lost track of so much time in the last few months that, even with Thanksgiving being days ago, it's hard to believe that Christmas is a few weeks away. "Yeah. Going back home for a week. Are your kids coming out this year?"

"Yep," Tom nods. "The grandkids too. It'll be a whole swarm. If I don't see you before, be sure to have a good holiday."

Paul picks his earbuds up again. "You too. Say hi to your wife for me."

"Will do, son. Enjoy your run."

Paul still needs to cancel all his reservations regarding New York.

◆

Driving to brunch on Sunday without Alex in the car next to him is lonely, but Paul's been stuck in the house all weekend working. If he doesn't get out and interact with actual human beings he fears for the future integrity of his soul.

He misses Alex's shitty country pop music.

At the restaurant there's another seat reshuffle. He winds up with

Craig and Beau on one side of him and Shawna on the other. Shawna spends the meal kicking Brian under the table whenever he starts to opine on something snarky and not at all amusing.

"What are you doing this afternoon?" Craig asks him as the meal is winding down.

"Nothing scheduled. Why?" Paul asks, because *moping over my latest ex* isn't an appropriate answer when the second-to-last ex is asking.

"Beau and I have a date at the park with a Frisbee. If you want to get out of the house, we'd love to have you."

Whether Craig is inexplicably hitting on Paul or taking pity on him, it's still a more appealing idea than going back home alone.

"Sure."

♦

The park they go to isn't the same one they used to frequent when it was Paul and Craig driving to brunch together before spending the afternoon hiking somewhere or other. There's still plenty of sun and green space, and Beau is ecstatic to run after the Frisbee as many times as they want to throw it.

Hanging out with Craig is easy, familiar, and even fun. By the end of the afternoon they're sitting side-by-side on the bench of a picnic table, getting caught up on work and families and gossiping about their friends. Beau sits at their feet and gnaws a stick he'd decided to fetch back instead of the Frisbee on his last run. If Paul lets himself think about what might happen next, it doesn't seem like a bad idea.

They get tacos for dinner without anyone having to worry about getting spotted by overenthusiastic fans. Paul is the one who suggests watching a movie together, and Craig offers his apartment.

They don't finish the movie.

They make out and jerk each other off on the couch without even bothering to hit the pause button. Paul feels vaguely guilty that his self-imposed celibacy lasted only exactly as long as he had avoided temptation. But it feels too good to lose himself in a familiar body and hands that know him.

If Paul closes his eyes he can almost fool himself into thinking Craig feels like Alex. The fantasy isn't fair to anyone, but it's there.

They curl up together on the couch while they catch their breath. Craig's apartment is smaller than Paul's house, but the leather couch and the modernist art hanging above the TV feels so much more like L.A. success.

"Want to stay the night?" Craig asks.

Paul does at least pull himself together enough to say "No. Not this time, at least," because there's dumb and then there's moronic.

"You know where to find me," Craig says.

Alone at home, even with Todd curled up at the foot of the bed snoring softly and adorably, Paul wishes he'd stayed anyway.

♦

Paul and Craig's first dinner plans get scuttled when Paul gets caught at work. He's rejiggering a plot for the third time, because the guy who's supposed to be doing this has great ideas but sucks at execution under pressure. Paul has no idea why someone who hates the fast-paced high-stakes nature of the TV game would choose to be in this business in the first place.

He texts Craig from the parking lot to meet him at the house.

This time, they skip the pretense of the movie and go straight to bed.

♦

Paul wakes up in the morning with Craig asleep next to him, Todd blinking at him from the chair, and Beau curled up in the corner that had always been his. It's exactly the way things had been for years.

The room looks as though Alex never existed, and the whole thing was just a particularly elaborate dream. The thought should be an idle one, but once it's there Paul can't get rid of it. It scares the absolute shit out of him.

Carly, when he calls her about it later that day, is absolutely unsympathetic.

"You are adding tragedy to tragedy," she says bluntly. "Seriously, Craig?"

"Would you prefer someone random?"

"This shit with Craig will only end in tears. Again. I would prefer you to get your head out of your ass and not make this so much worse for everyone involved. You're not the only one breaking over this."

"How do you know that?"

"Liam," Carly says simply.

"What's Liam doing?"

"If you want information about a relationship between two adults you are going to have to talk to either of them yourself because that is not my story to tell."

"But Liam's telling you," Paul says snidely.

"Liam is my partner," Carly says pointedly. "And you, meanwhile, need to stop fucking settling."

"Well, I can't have what I want, can I?"

"You can have a lot more than you're getting. And I don't just mean in terms of fucks."

28

After the last of the overnight shoots, Liam dismisses their car and tells Alex they're going for a walk. Alex is dismayed, but Liam seems to have a plan. He heads off down the street, giving Alex the opportunity to follow. Alex goes. There's something compelling about the offer.

Liam smiles when Alex falls in beside him, then starts talking. He narrates less what they pass than what Liam says Alex should do if he can find the time.

"Everything is haunted," he says. "And most of it doesn't want you here."

"I'm not really a believer," Alex says.

"In what?" Liam counters.

"Monsters. Ghosts. Astrology. Magic." Or God or anything else requiring belief. Religion has always been physically dangerous to Alex, a closeted gay kid with no father in the worst town in Indiana. Too many people, if they'd known what he was, would have felt the need to 'fix' him. Usually with violence and all in the name of God. It hasn't left Alex with particularly nice feelings about belief. And the rest of it – magic, monsters, or anything else – might not have hurt Alex, but they were never around to help, either. Alex keeps his faith confined to himself.

"Wow. You really haven't been paying attention."

Alex frowns but doesn't ask what Liam means. He's not sure he wants to know. And Liam's beliefs, whatever they are, at least seem benign.

They walk the length of the reflecting pool. The water shimmers in the light of the streetlamps, and ducks mutter sleepily to each other. This late, there's no one else around.

The reflecting pool is so long the Lincoln Memorial nearly takes Alex by surprise, transforming suddenly from a pale form in the distance to a massive construction of marble shining softly in the moonlight.

"Go on up," Liam tells him, when Alex hesitates at the bottom of all those steps.

"Aren't you coming?"

Liam shakes his head. "Take some time alone with it. Everyone should." Then he disappears from view.

Alex almost panics. He is outside, at night and all alone, and it's not a feeling he's had since he left Indiana. First L.A. – and then fame – made it impossible for him to be alone. This is a gift he's been given, but all it does it make him want to text Paul, so he can have it too.

He takes a selfie, joyous, awkward, blurry and poorly lit in the dark. With all the time he spends on camera for his job, and dodging the cameras of strangers, Alex doesn't take his own picture much. But this one feels important. He wants it to exist, and, what's more, he wants to share it. He sends it to Paul with a note that just says *Thank you.*

Alex hopes he'll understand that he means for the gift of a whole city that, at least for a moment, has no people in it. Alex is only here because of the stories Paul writes for him.

Half an hour passes before Liam rejoins Alex, reappearing out of the dark as suddenly as he'd disappeared. It scares the shit out of Alex.

"Don't *do* that," he scolds, clutching his heart and learning against a pillar for dramatic effect. He's been spending too much time with Liam.

"Sorry," Liam says easily.

By mutual and silent consent they walk around to the back of the monument and sit there on the wide stone ledge facing the river. Liam pulls out a flask and they pass it back and forth as they sit staring out at Virginia. Liam, without prompting and for no reason Alex can fathom, tells him about the real story behind *The Exorcist* in excruciatingly weird detail until Alex feels sore and miserable with five a.m. cold.

"I'm gonna go back," he says, standing and stretching. "Sleep for a few hours. Try to forget all the creepy shit you've told me."

"And then?" Liam asks, his agenda unclear.

"Then," Alex says, handing him his second room key, "you're going to come wake me up. Make it good."

"Cool." Liam takes the key with a wink and twirls it in his fingers.

lex jogs off with a wave to find a cab before the city wakes up, and Liam pulls out his phone, thumbing through to his entries for Carly. There's a decent chance she'll still be awake, and he's glad. Good times and hard work without her by his side to share in the adventure just don't make sense any more. Alex, too, is a hefty responsibility, and she's the only one he can talk it through with. For all Victor's voyeurism, there are some details he never wants.

When he gets to Alex's room, the heat's been turned up too high. The drapes are pulled closed against the winter sun that's finally starting to rise, but the desk lamp in the corner is on, bathing the room in a soft yellow light. Alex is asleep on his stomach, naked, a sheet barely covering him.

He's beautiful, not that Liam doesn't already know that, but he's tempted to let Alex sleep. None of them ever get enough rest. Night shoots and being on the road make it worse. But Alex had asked for something very specific, even if he hadn't done so very specifically. The few agreements that exist between them boil down simply to a requirement that they take each other at their word. Liam tries to do that with everyone because then he is not responsible for their shit. But it's even more important with someone as unique and reticent as Alex.

He sets his bag down, toes off his shoes, and shrugs off his outerwear. He considers doing it noisily to wake Alex up, but he's pretty sure that's not what's wanted. When he's down to his briefs, he puts a hand on Alex's shoulder and kisses the side of his face. Alex's eyes flicker open. Liam is rewarded with a bright smile and a mumbled greeting as Alex rolls over onto his back and stretches like a cat.

Liam knows it's much permission as he's going to get until Alex is a little more awake.

"Drift as much as you want," he murmurs as he strokes his hands up and down Alex's sides. They're both already half hard.

Alex may be out of it, but he's definitely with him, humming happily as Liam drags his lips over his body. He digs his fingers tightly into Liam's hair to pull his head up and demand a kiss. Then he whines at Liam about his not being naked.

Eventually, Alex gets on his stomach with Liam half on top of him working two fingers into him as Alex ruts against the bed. He's clearly both turned on and frustrated as hell, chanting *more, more, more* at Liam.

"I can't read your mind," Liam says tight against his ear. "What do you need?"

But the only reply he gets is more frustrated, beautiful neediness. It's hot, but it's also just this side of awkward. On the list of people Liam does not need to risk making the wrong guess with, Alex is surely near the top. Or, he thinks darkly of the lecture from Victor, every single entry.

"Do you want my cock, baby?"

Alex nods frantically. Liam has to close his eyes against it for a second lest he wind up coming right then and there from the combined force of friction and fantasy.

"Where?" he barely manages to ask.

"Oh my God, Liam, where do you think?" Alex finally says in a burst of frustration.

Liam cracks up. "I want to hear you say it."

"Why?" Alex whines.

"Because it's great material for the spank bank?" Liam offers.

It's Alex's turn to laugh. After that, they're both a little more awake and a little more able to talk about it. Alex isn't being symbolic or any sort of fucked up about it, although Liam can tell he might be if he weren't so hot for it. Still, it seems like a good thing and a happy want and Liam's turned on and honored and amused to be the guy who gets to go there first.

Alex has to open the condom for him – he uses his teeth – because Liam's hands are already stupidly slick with lube. After that, they manage to keep the fumbling to a minimum, even if their lack of sleep makes up for sobriety.

Alex tenses up as soon as Liam starts pressing into him, and Liam has to talk him through it, distracting and praising and reassuring him millimeter by millimeter.

"Holy fuck," Alex finally manages once Liam is all the way in.

"Good? Bad? Indifferent?" Alex is like a vise, and Liam needs some guidance before he just takes what he wants.

"Move," Alex demands.

"I fucking love you right now," Liam says, the chuckle reverberating between and across their bodies.

It's clumsy at first, Alex hissing in uncertainty as both of them shift their hips to look for the angle that works. Then everything catches just right and *more* and *move* shift to a constant stream of *yes*, Alex jerking himself off frantically, even as he grabs at his balls to try to stave off the inevitable.

Liam's hand joins his, and then it's a litany in Alex's ear about how tight and heavy his balls are and how ready he must be, and how he needs to hold on for just a little bit longer, just until he can't anymore.

Eventually, Alex comes with a shocked-sounding moan.

Liam pulls out and strips off the condom. When he comes over Alex's back, it's with a gasp and a whimper.

◆

"That was good," Alex says, into the soft warm space that smells like Liam and sex.

Liam rubs his back. "There you go."

Alex finds it less scary – and easier – to stay down in the place where he can't process yet or even make words. Which is good, because if he tried to fight this right now he's sure he'd fly apart entirely. So he clings to Liam and lets himself sink.

It's a little bit terrifying.

◆

Twenty minutes later, Alex jerks awake in Liam's arms. For a moment he doesn't know what city he's in, or who he's with. Slowly his awareness of his body filters back in and so does the rest of the morning. He rolls out of Liam's grasp.

Liam turns over to face him. "Are you okay"

Alex scrubs his hands over his face. "I'm good," he says at random. "Just...be normal for a minute, okay?"

Liam plumps his pillow fastidiously then flops back down on it. "Normal for me, or normal for what you like dealing with?" Liam

"I still can't tell if you're the most generous asshole I know or...."

"The most asshole asshole you know?"

Alex wonders if he'll ever understand Liam's contradictions. "Yeah, that'll do."

"You can kick me out you know, if you want space for real."

Liam seems sincere in a way Alex can't quite fathom. "I'm still deciding."

"What do I have to do to earn my keep?" Liam gives him a ridiculous look that's both hopeful and suggestive.

Alex laughs. "Do not make another pass at me right now."

"What about scurrilous gossip? Does scurrilous gossip work?"

"I don't know. Depends on the gossip."

"How about me and Victor?"

"What about you and Victor."

"Me. And. Victor."

Alex would smack Liam for being so condescending, but he's busy trying to get his head around what he's just been told. He's tempted to laugh in Liam's face and call him a liar. But since last time he did that led to being bed with him right now, Alex figures he's probably better off taking this one at face value.

Still. He has to say something. "That's a giant case of what the fuck."

Liam nods.

"You know what people would say about that," Alex adds.

"You asking?"

"Yeah. Yeah, I guess I am."

"It's not a deal," Liam says defensively. "It's not, like, the casting couch."

"Okay. What the hell is it then?"

"Complicated. But also not. Like, we have date nights once a week."

"You promised me gossip and I can't decide if this is way too much or not enough."

Liam sighs heavily. "Look, Victor's a lot less interested in sex than control. We get each other, it's cool. Trust me, however you think it works, it doesn't. He's not my boyfriend or anything."

"You have date nights at his house once a week but you're not boyfriends."

"We are what we are. And we both know where we stand with each other. Also what even is your logic, you were over at Paul's way more than that."

"I have no idea how to process any of this," Alex says sharply. He very much does not want to bring Paul into whatever bizarre story time is going on right now.

"Hell of a week, huh?"

"Fuck you."

Liam cackles. "So...are you worried you're next or are you jealous?" he teases.

Alex laughs nervously. He doesn't know what to say. Victor is fascinated with him. None of them could deny that.

"Dude, I mean, you're beautiful. If that was what you wanted, Victor would find a way to give it to you, but you really don't. And that's a good thing."

Alex narrows his eyes. Liam is giving him vast swathes of information, but he can't make the pieces form into any coherent whole. "Why's that?"

"Because you don't need him. We both know you're not one of his little lost lambs."

"What then?" Alex fires back. "Am I one of yours?"

"Yeah," Liam says simply. "For now."

Alex doesn't say anything in response. As offended as he should be, *lost* and, in a way, *innocent*, have certainly been apt words for the last couple of weeks. But Liam's ongoing info dump has only added to his disorientation. For all the things he was asked and told before fame became his life, over a year later he still feels like he signed a contract made of constantly shifting words, ominously permanent and never read.

"Why are you telling me this?" he finally asks.

"One, Victor is important to me. Two, you should know how surprising you are. Three, you keep complaining that everyone is keeping you out of the loop. Now you're in the loop."

30

Paul blinks awake in the grey light of early morning. The buzzing of his alarm had woken him, but now that he's up he's not sure how he'd been able to sleep. Parrots are sitting in the tree outside, cackling up a storm.

All chance of even five more useful minutes of sleep gone, Paul rolls over to check his phone for any early morning work emergencies. Craig grumbles something sleepily at him. The familiarity is disconcerting, even if Craig isn't awake enough yet to articulate an unhappy comment about Paul's work habits.

There are no emails declaring that the world is ending via script problems, deadline issues, or another war between Victor and the studio, for which Paul is grateful. There is a picture from Alex that Paul clicks open a little warily. But he smiles when he sees Alex, flanked by D.C.'s seemingly ubiquitous marble columns, smiling up at him from the screen.

Paul locks his phone, not because he feels guilty for the thrill that Alex has given him this, but because he doesn't want to get caught.

Downstairs in the kitchen, waiting for the coffee to brew with Craig still asleep upstairs, Paul opens the picture again to stare at it more. He has no idea why Alex sent it, but Paul is glad to have it. Alex looks easy and happy. At least it's proof that Alex is real.

On his way out the door he finally replies, *You're welcome*. Even if he's not sure what he's being thanked for, he's grateful to have given Alex something.

31

New York is cold and dark and tall.

Alex arrives at night; His life no longer has any recognizable cycles to the days. He spends the car ride to the hotel looking out the windows and wishing he were anywhere else. This city is never easy for him. As often as he's been here since, the lights and the skyline and the noise always evoke for him the first time he came here, when his life was an unrecognizable whirlwind of fairytale insanity. When *Fourth* had sent him to New York for that initial round of press, he'd never even been on a plane before.

That in a couple of days he's going to start something completely new – a movie, with all the attendant glamour – makes it all that much more intense.

Alone in his hotel room, Alex turns off the lights and lies on the bed and looks out at the night. He feels small and not in a good way. Liam will be in New York in another couple of days, visiting friends and family over his own break from *Fourth*, but he's not here now. If he were, Alex would go find him and undoubtedly spend the night with him. Who he really wants, though, is Paul. Alex has been fucking Liam for the last few weeks, but it's still Paul he longs for and Paul who feels the most familiar.

It's not that late in L.A. Alex pulls out his phone.

◆

Paul's just gotten home from a long and frankly awful day at work when his phone rings. He glances at it to assure himself he can let whatever panicky writer it is go to voicemail. Seeing the name on the screen gives him almost an electric shock.

"Alex?" Paul answers. Surprised is an understatement; even with the picture Alex is the last person he expected to hear from. At least Craig isn't staying over tonight.

When Alex doesn't say anything right away, Paul says "Hello? Alex? Are you okay?"

"Tell me about your first night in L.A.," Alex finally says. It's the first time Paul has heard his voice in weeks.

"What?"

"It's home, and it's you. New York is really hard right now."

Paul isn't sure what is going on or how much stock and hope he should place in Alex's use of the word *home*. He's completely taken aback, both by Alex's unexpected call and by his question.

He also has no idea what he's supposed to do, so he does as he's told.

He sits on the loveseat by the window in the living room and looks out at the quiet street while he tells Alex about the day he'd spent moving into his first apartment here.

"I think it was as shitty as you say yours is, and my roommate was quirkier than Gemma."

Alex chuckles softly.

Paul goes on to tell him about how he'd fallen asleep that first night on his bed, just a mattress on the floor at that point. "I couldn't find where I'd packed my sheets. And then I woke up in the middle of night because the pipes were clanking. That stopped, finally, but then the streetlight outside was too bright and the crappy strip blinds were no help at all."

"I hung towels over the windows for the first couple weeks," Alex offers.

It's one of the few specific mentions Alex has ever made of his own apartment, and Paul is wary of asking for more no matter how much he still wants all of Alex's stories.

"Yeah. See, that makes sense. I went running."

"In the middle of the night?"

"My instincts for self-preservation have never been the best."

Alex asks more questions, and Paul tells him more of the story. After every question and every answer the silences get longer. Eventually, Paul watches three minutes tick by on his watch without either of them saying anything.

Finally Paul says, his voice is soft and close as if Alex were right here on the couch with him, "What time's your call tomorrow?"

"Seven."

"I'll let you get to sleep, then."

"Okay." Alex doesn't add anything else. Another thirty seconds pass before he says, his voice barely a breath, "Good night."

The line clicks silent.

Paul has no idea what the hell just happened and is sure he's never going to tell anyone about it.

◆

On the *Fourth* lot, the office starts to feel devoid of human life without the manic bustle of filming and as people take off for the holidays. The dingy hallways look even sadder than usual, and the sets and soundstages are quiet and empty.

Paul misses Alex at home and at work, where Alex never appears anywhere he shouldn't anymore. Paul can't figure out the midnight phone call and after a while he stops trying. If nothing else he's grateful for another sign that Alex was real.

A quiet office and no crises to fix means more time for his own projects. Victor finds Paul at his desk late one night with his laptop open and glasses on, working not on *Fourth* but on a pilot. For once Victor doesn't even stop to say or ask Paul anything, just nods from the doorway and moves on.

Paul leans his cheek on his fist and scrolls back through the pages he's written. At least he's doing something right.

<h1 align="center">32</h1>

Alex finds that filming *Paradise Square* is a little different from doing TV, but the essentials are the same. The familiarity of the routine is good, because it's the only thing he's used to right now. He's got a different character, and after the terror of the first few days – he can act, yes, but he's only ever acted Zach – he starts to think that this might be something he can do. It's a challenge, but a good one. He's making progress towards proving himself.

New York, however, remains hard.

The fans have found his hotel again. It's almost impossible to move around outside without them noticing and trying to follow. He thinks about sneaking out one morning before they or the city at large wakes up. He wants to walk everywhere. It's not a safe option for him and the schedule leaves no time, yet still he wishes. New York is so unlike L.A. – gritty, dark, and above all *cold*. But there's a freedom here too, that of anonymity and the promise L.A. once offered him: A new life, far from whatever troubled him in the past. But that's out of reach, at least for Alex. Fame has laid its claim; he'll never be able to reinvent himself again.

He's glad when Liam arrives in town.

Assuming nothing, Alex texts him on his way back to his hotel from set that evening. *I want to see you tonight.*

His phone buzzes while he's walking into the lobby. *Come out with us. I'll make it worth it after.*

Who's us? And I'm not bargaining with you for sex.

I'm bargaining for your time. Just wear your damn hat.

Us turns out to be a group of Liam's friends from high school, including his childhood best friend, Charles, and a bunch of film school geeks, all of whom think they're going to be the next Tarantino. Alex meets up with the group for dinner, and then they embark on a bar crawl.

As a whole, the group is almost as loud and obnoxious as Liam is, and, on the surface, are even less to Alex's taste. Yet, none of them give a shit about who he is when he's not a guy in jeans and a beanie, even if Charles watches Alex closely in a way that screams Liam-related backstory.

Alex stares back with an intensity he knows is almost confrontational. He thinks he finally understands why Liam's worked so hard to be as charming and charismatic as he is, if Charles — possessed of deep brown skin and a classical dancer's body – is what he's been competing with since he was a kid. Somehow, though, the observation only helps Alex look at Liam with a level of fondness that is probably unwise.

They're in a dive bar with red walls and too many Christmas lights, all of them grimy with being up year round, when Liam polls the group on what the word for a male starlet should be. When everyone but Alex gets distracted by a discussion of which it-girls they would, and would not, do, Liam tells him he's decided it's *starling*. They are, he notes, an invasive species.

◆

Liam and Alex end up back at Liam's parents' Brooklyn brownstone. Without any good reason to be in the same hotel anymore, Alex's accommodations are out of the question. Even with the separate garden entrance and no sign of Liam's parents, Alex worries this choice isn't any wiser.

"Don't they know Carly?" he hisses as they make their way down the hall to Liam's old room.

"Sure. They know a lot of things. It's cool."

Everything about Liam's life represents a different sort of discretion than when Alex told Paul not to hold his hand. He's trying to understand, but even right here, with his hand in Liam's, the gulf between their lives and their fears seems insurmountable.

Any worries about closets and secrets or the immense, persistent loneliness of New York are burned away once Liam shuts the door of his room behind them. He leads Alex to the bed.

They get naked, and Liam digs his fingers into Alex's bare hips. Liam makes it so easy for Alex to let go of everything. He closes his eyes and lets himself drift as Liam prepares him, then sinks down onto Liam with the same steady concentration and ruthless determination he does everything with.

"Holy shit," Liam gasps, as Alex starts to move. "You learned a new trick."

Alex shifts to brace his weight right on his thighs. "Practice makes perfect."

"Bullshit. You've never practiced a thing in your life."

"Yeah," Alex says and leans down to brace his weight on his elbows and bite at Liam's mouth. "But I still get better."

"Fuck yes, you do," Liam pants and grabs the back of his head to yank him into the kiss.

◆

Over the next few days Alex settles into a rhythm of work, Liam, and not sleeping particularly well.

Spending nights at Liam's parents' house is the best. Even if it's more lavish than anywhere he grew up, it's a home, and he's honored and touched by Liam's trust in inviting him in and letting him stay.

Alex loves his work, if not the spaces in between. Wrapping himself up in Liam, not only his body but his kindness and tenderness, makes things a little easier.

♦

"So you want to tell me what you're doing, wasting all your time in New York with me?"

Alex tenses at the question. They've gotten naked and into bed; this is not what he was expecting. It's been two weeks since he first went home with Liam, and they've spent almost every night together with no need of discussion.

He tries to ignore Liam's words now and reaches for him instead, but Liam bats his hand away. Alex isn't sure if he's supposed to be hurt, embarrassed or amused, but he does pull back a little.

Liam speaks again. "There's a whole city out there full of guys prettier – and probably less annoying to you – than me. So what gives?"

Even with the self-deprecation, Liam's charisma is still stunning. "I told you I changed my mind about you," Alex says, knowing he sounds like he's acting.

"Mmmmm, yeah, I know." Liam plays with Alex's hair. "I'm trying to figure out how much."

Alex rolls onto his back and stares at the ceiling. Glow-in-the-dark stars are stuck to it from, presumably, when Liam was a kid. But they've left the light on, so Alex can only see their outlines.

"Fuck," he says to himself. Liam has always been able to see through him. When Alex first met him that was a nuisance. Then it became a comfort – Liam was one less person Alex had to explain himself to. Now it's a threat. He can't hide from Liam.

Liam says nothing, but continues to pet his arm.

"This is the thing where I have to tell you the truth because of one of your stupid lists of things, isn't it?" Alex says, still not looking at him. He could evade and avoid, but it wouldn't work. Not for long enough. And it wouldn't change what both of them know.

"It would help."

"Should I go?"

"No. Talk."

"But I don't talk, Liam."

"You do to me."

"Because you're annoying and won't shut up." That's not exactly why. But what else can Alex say?

Liam grabs his hand and squeezes.

"This is so good," Alex says, anguish bubbling up with the words. He doesn't understand why everything – even his respite from other pains – has to be so hard.

"It really is. The best, even." Liam brings Alex's hand up to his mouth to kiss. "But I can't be for you the way you want right now."

"Carly."

"Not Carly. Not really. Although, yes." Liam shifts and turns to Alex. Having the man's full attention, which is so often so scattered, on him is strange. "Look, you're not the only one people are hard for. Like, *love* – awesome. But don't fall for me. 'Cause I can't, okay? I love you, and I don't work that way, and you're just being fucked up over Paul anyway. So…okay?"

"You're not making sense."

"You've understood every word I've said." Liam's eyes dart between Alex's, like he's making sure he's paying attention. "And you're an asshole for making me say them without confessing first."

"You're still holding my hand."

"So?"

For a long time, Alex says nothing. When he finally turns his head to look at Liam, Liam is looking at their hands. He asks to stay.

"Yes, yes, totally, thank God." Liam sounds as buoyant as ever. "You're an idiot," he adds. He grabs the back of Alex's head and kisses him hard.

It's surprising and funny before it shifts into something else, slow and strange and difficult.

Liam rolls on top of him, tells him he's going to fuck him, and takes forever getting to it. Normally, Alex likes this sort of thing. With Liam, he usually banters through it; with Paul, he begged. But this here and now feels like Liam memorizing him, mourning him. Alex knows he'll soon do the same in return.

But it's hard to believe or behave as if it's truly the end. After *Fourth's* winter break is over, they'll be back to being paid to kiss each other as two men who don't even exist.

Right now, this is the most of Liam Alex is ever going to have. In a moment whatever they've been doing with each other is going to be more than it's ever been before. After that they will become less forever. It's an awful feeling.

When Liam finally pushes into him, Alex is on his back, folded in half. He's never been fucked like this before. The angle's insane, and the claustrophobia of the position is only working for him because everything else is such a mess. His throat is tight with tears and he's not even hard.

It feels good anyway. Arousal, as he's used to understanding it, creeps up on him eventually.

Liam's face above him is beautiful, shuttered and pained. He's clearly trying to make this last. When his eyes open, it startles Alex badly. He tries to push his head further back into the pillow to get some space from the other man's gaze.

But there's no space to get. Liam whispers "No," in his ear softly when Alex closes his eyes.

So he does as he's told. This is a gift, and Alex knows enough to take it on the terms it's being offered.

Liam says, "I promise you I'll miss this," and shoves his hands, grabbing sharp and tight, into his hair.

Alex comes.

Liam lets him close his eyes then as he works towards his own orgasm. His panting in Alex's ear sounds not quite like exertion, but the soothing noises made toward children and wounded animals.

Other than dealing with the condom, Liam doesn't even bother to clean them up after. He pulls Alex close, tangles their legs, and presses their foreheads together. Alex is reminded of Paul, and that's when he breaks.

Liam takes his hand again and kisses his palm.

◆

When Alex wakes up the next morning he finds Liam on his side, dressed now and watching him. When he sees he's awake, Liam squeezes his hand and silently slides out of the bed.

There are very few other options, and none of them are good. Alex drags on his clothes and follows him upstairs where the deep silence of the morning is suddenly broken by Liam's mom. Her unexpected presence in the kitchen may be the strangest thing to happen to Alex all month.

She greets them both with hugs and with pancakes. Surrealism, apparently, comes with chocolate chips. Alex says *yes, please* to orange juice and wonders how many broken hearts she's nursed for Liam in mornings-after through the years.

He doesn't feel heartbroken, though, not exactly, as he pours syrup and listens to their friendly chatter. Heartbreak was walking out of Paul's house. This is something else, something profound and deeply aching.

His relationship with Liam only ever had a name as it was ending, and maybe even only because it was ending. Alex is still not sure what that name even *is*. This doesn't feel like anything he thought it would except for the grief that he's holding, precious and odd.

But then, Paul never felt like anything Alex expected either. That was different than this, but maybe part of the point. All Alex is sure about right now is that of everything Liam has taught him, the least important has been the mechanics.

Liam and his mom don't require much from him in the way of conversation, and Alex is glad for the chance to simply sit with his thoughts. There will be more of that, later, when he's well and truly alone. For now it's enough to be here, where it's warm and home-feeling, and watch out the windows as the snow start to fall.

33

The night after Liam breaks up with him, Alex goes out with some of the cast and crew of *Paradise*. He's never socialized this way before, never wanted to, but his options are limited to going out or staying in his hotel room alone and moping over both Paul and Liam.

Alex is tired of feeling sorry for himself. He's never been one to wallow in his pain; he likes to take action to solve his problems. And if a bar in Tribeca has never been his particular poison, well, he's been trying a lot of new things lately.

There's a guy there, a friend of somebody in the cast, who stares at Alex from the moment Alex walks in. For the first half of the night, Alex avoids the looks. Nobody looked at him like that before his life changed, and now it feels like everyone does. Alex never trusts the sincerity of it. People like to look at the things TV shows them, but it doesn't mean they're truly interested. Alex has also never known how to look back.

Paul never stared at Alex that way, not in a manner that was about assumed possession. Neither did Liam. But now Alex doesn't get to have either of them. A hookup with a guy he hasn't known for at least a year was unthinkable a few months ago. Now, it feels like the inevitable outcome of the math of misery and strategy.

The next time the guy tries to catch his eye, Alex lets him.

He knows people are watching them when they leave the party. He doesn't have the energy to care.

In the hotel room – not Alex's – Alex tells him exactly what he wants, closes his eyes, and gets it.

The next night it's somebody else. The night after that isn't much different.

Busy now he sends Liam when his phone buzzes halfway through the fifth evening, or maybe the sixth.

Is he someone I know?

Who says it's only been one?

Alex wonders if Liam is simply incapable of letting go of people no matter how the relationship changes.

♦

When Alex gets off work the next day, there's another text from Liam. *We need to talk.*

I thought we already did that, Alex types back.

Come by the house tonight.

No.

We're having this conversation. I really don't think you want to have it at your hotel.

Alex knows Liam is going to call him on his recent extracurricular activities. He also knows that isn't going to be about them getting back together. Why Liam feels the need to intervene in Alex's promiscuity when Liam is just as wide-ranging in his habits, Alex doesn't know. But for all Liam is baffling and often irritating, he never pushes Alex in any way Alex doesn't like. For that, Alex types back, somewhere between angry and meek, *Fine.*

◆

They end up in Liam's parents' tiny backyard, bundled in their coats, in ass-numbing patio chairs.

"All right," Liam says. "You want to tell me what you've been up to the past few nights?"

"It's none of your business," Alex says shortly.

"Dude. We're friends. You said so!"

"So?" Just because Alex agreed to come here doesn't mean he's going to make it easy on Liam. Too much of this moment is his fault.

"So I care, and you tell me this shit."

"No, I don't." Alex understands everyone rewrites the past. And while he accepts that he might have an overly romanticized version of what happened between him and Liam, he is one hundred percent sure it didn't involve any of the confessions Liam now seems sure he made.

"You did when it was Paul."

"No, I didn't." Alex protests.

"Yeah, you did. You just didn't realize it."

"That makes this better how?" Maybe Liam isn't wrong. Maybe he really did worm himself into Alex's life not just as a lover, but as a confidante. Alex doesn't like the idea that he revealed himself to Liam without knowing it, but he supposes that's what sex does. At least the advice – and encouragement – Liam has always given in response hasn't steered him wrong yet.

Liam kicks his shoe against the edge of a loose flagstone. It's an oddly soothing rhythm. "I want to hear you tell me what you think you're doing. Because you don't know your own power, and that's fine when it's just you being neurotic about fame, and it can also be really fucking hot – "

"Thank you?"

" – but right now you're fucking around with random dudes, and I have no idea what that's about."

Alex tips his head to the side and studies the patterns the shadows of the bare tree branches make against the fence. "You told me to find shinier toys in New York."

"I did. And now you're playing with rusty cans."

"They're not utter strangers, they're industry – "

"And in the closet."

" – and it's not going to wind up on the internet."

Liam blows out a tense breath. "This is not about the internet. You and I? This? This is fucked up, but we have trust. What the hell do you have with these people? Mutually assured destruction?"

"Apparently the closet has advantages for both of us," Alex snaps. "Also, what the fuck? You sleep around."

"Alex."

Alex turns toward him. Liam gives him an absolutely devastating look and counts off on his fingers. "One. I fuck friends. And your choices are your choices but I'm careful."

"Which is why you sucked my dick without a condom or a conversation?"

"Yeah. So. I get to make mistakes too. Also, you keep complaining that everyone talks about you without you present. Where do you think that stops exactly?"

Alex stares. He'd never even considered the possibility that Paul would talk about their time in bed together with anyone. Much less Liam, or anyone who would talk to Liam. Carly, maybe?

"Sorry?" Liam offers.

"Who do I yell at first?" Alex says to the universe at large. Suddenly everything that's happened seems small and funny and terrible.

"Can we get back to that? I was counting."

"Uh...." Alex will never understand the things Liam chooses to care about from moment to moment.

"Two." Liam holds up another finger. "I have watched you from the beginning of this. I know you. You deal with your shit by making shit harder for yourself. And that can be awesome. That's how you get better. But, three." He holds up a third. "You're not fucking around with random people to learn something new about yourself. You're fucking around to make shit hard for yourself, because it makes you miserable. You think you should be miserable, because you're not getting what you actually want. That's fucked up. Because, four – " Liam holds up a fourth finger before pointing his whole hand at Alex accusingly, " – if you keep this up in the direction I think you're going, you're going to wind up chasing the kind of destruction that isn't about being on the cover of *Us*."

"What are you talking about?" Alex asks. He's never seen Liam look this serious.

"Look, I know you grew up in a tiny town in the middle of

nowhere and there's all sorts of history that seems really abstract to you. But you can't sit here in New York City and ask me that question."

"Don't you think that's kind of alarmist? Especially now." Alex asks faintly through his own dawning horror.

"I'm not sleeping with you now, and I know how to be careful. Also, that's kind of the point. Alarms are for before the house burns down."

Alex sits very still, doesn't look at Liam, and doesn't say anything. He's pissed at Liam, but he's also self-aware enough to know that's because Liam's right. Alex is embarrassed and ashamed. His fingertips prickle, cold, maybe, but also perhaps the tingle of adrenaline at whatever near miss he's had.

"Look. Alex. You scare the absolute shit out of me– "

"I get it," Alex says tightly.

"You do?"

"Yeah."

"Okay," Liam says, still kicking the flagstone. "Are you pissed at me?"

"Yeah." Alex folds his arms over his chest. He wishes Liam would hug him. Among other things, he's cold. But he needs to sit with this by himself for a while.

"I figured. It's cool."

Alex laughs, tense and a little watery. "This has been the weirdest fucking week."

34

In his mother's kitchen in South Carolina, Paul is on drying duty. His sister Sarah is washing and hands him wet and still slightly soapy, dishes. Mike, Paul's brother-in-law, is upstairs putting the baby down for a nap. His mom sits at the kitchen table fidgeting with a pack of cigarettes. Eventually she'll go outside onto the verandah to have what she'll swear is just one but is always two.

In his pocket, Paul's phone rings. The chime makes Paul jump, and he almost drops a dish trying to fish his phone out of his pocket. The call is unlikely to be important, but L.A. has long trained him never to ignore what could be an opportunity. Sometimes he's not even wrong.

A glance at the caller ID surprises him. "Alex?" he says, fumbling the phone to his ear.

Alex, if it is indeed him and not a misdial, doesn't say anything.

"Let me step outside," Paul adds when he sees his mother and sister exchanging meaningful and somewhat smug looks.

Alex still doesn't say anything.

Paul turns off the light by the front door so moths don't keep flying at his head. "Are you still there?" He doesn't mean to sound annoyed, but what other options are there?

"Yeah," Alex says.

"Are you – "

"In New York."

"I was going to say okay."

"That's annoying," Alex says, more directly than Paul is used to.

"I'm sorry."

"I've had a really fucked up week."

"Yeah?" Paul asks, hoping for any sort of story that will help him understand. Alex has so often been all sharp edges and dark spaces.

"Yeah."

"Is *Paradise* okay?" He doubts work is the problem, but Paul suspects it's the safest thing to ask about.

"That's great, actually. Turns out I can act." Alex giggles. "I died yesterday."

"...What?"

"My character," Alex says. That should have been obvious; Paul wonders what it is about Alex that makes it not. "Death scenes are fun."

The conversation, like so many he's had with Alex, is nothing like normal. Paul realizes, too late now, that very little with him ever will be.

"...Okay," he finally says. "I don't know why you're calling, and

I don't know what to say to you."

Alex is being marginally less frightening than the last time he called out of the blue, even if no less strange. That, as well as whatever he and Craig are trying to do, makes Paul feel a little bit bolder, as if he can survive all possible answers, even though he's not sure that's true.

"So," Alex takes a loud breath like he's going to explain but then stays silent, having apparently thought the better of it.

"Alex."

"Liam and I had a thing," he blurts. "And then he dumped me. At his parents' house. With some advice I sort of intentionally took in a really stupid way, so he spent last night yelling at me for my bad choices and wow, you were right about closeted guys. I don't mean Liam, by the way, and I'm sort of freaked out, and I hate New York. My life got taken away from me eighteen months ago and was given back to me changed. My mom gets here tomorrow too, and I just…hi. I didn't know who else to call."

The words tumble out of Alex like a flood. It's a lot to take in. There are several items Paul desperately wants more information about from the Liam thing, which stings, to the demise of it, which honestly has him a little bit worried.

"What do you need me to do?" he asks.

"I'm not having a crisis." Alex sighs. "Just stay on the line."

"Okay," Paul says. "Okay. Do you want to talk about any of it?"

"Not really. Not now. Not yet."

"Right." Paul feels a little guilty for how bitchy he sounds, but Christ, *Liam*? "Tell me about your first night in New York then," he says, flipping the tables on Alex after their last late-night call. "Not this time, I mean. The first time." Paul still knows so little about Alex's life before they got involved. Even now, when he has no claim on Alex's stories or his time, he wants more. Also, Alex called him.

Alex laughs weakly. "I'd never been in a hotel before. Other than the motels on the drive out to L.A., I mean. The windows were too big."

Paul sits down on the steps and settles in to listen.

35

Alex's mom arrives the afternoon before Christmas Eve. For the first couple of hours it's bizarre. This is not Alex's city, he hardly knows what his life is, and being with his mother makes him feel vividly like who he was before. He tries to see himself through her eyes but doesn't know what to make of himself.

They haven't seen each other since last Christmas when Alex flew her out to L.A. Despite the time they spend on the phone together, they're both unsure around each other for the first few hours. Alex feels embarrassed by the hotel room he got for her, which is possibly bigger and definitely nicer than the trailer he grew up in. Laura is either mirroring his discomfort or likewise doesn't quite know what to do when confronted with her strange son in a strange new city.

They make awkward small talk about her flight and the traffic from the airport while she unpacks her suitcase. Alex, finally desperate to get out of a room where he feels – wrongly, he knows – that neither of them belong, asks if she wants to get a drink.

"It's two in the afternoon," Laura says reproachfully, but her eyes shine with mischief and delight.

"It's even earlier in L.A."

"Oh, I have missed you, Alex," she exclaims and hugs him tight.

In the hotel bar downstairs they both get a beer and sit in a corner at a high-top table for two. Now that they both have something to do, the silence is less awkward. They spent a lot of evenings like this when Alex was in high school – not sitting in hotel bars, of course; such places didn't exist in Paragon except on TV. But on the nights when neither of them had to work, they'd sit on the back steps of the trailer, each nursing a beer. Sometimes they talked, sometimes they didn't. Those evenings, peaceful and with a comforting sense of solidarity between them, are some of the few memories Alex has of Indiana that aren't awful.

For several minutes they both sit in contemplative silence. Alex wonders if his mom is remembering the same things he is.

Laura finally says, "Are you seeing anyone?"

Alex looks up at her sharply, not offended, but surprised. She's never asked him anything of the sort before. That she's asking now is either an indication that he's not a child in her eyes anymore, or a reassurance that he can tell her about all the things he never talked about when he was growing up.

He wishes he had a simpler, happier answer for her. "No. Yes. I mean. I don't know. It got messed up." He doesn't even know if he means Paul or Liam.

She frowns at that and asks a couple of vague questions Alex

151

doesn't know how to answer. She's clearly trying to suss out if the problem was Alex's inexperience or Alex's gay and famous life. He in no way feels comfortable telling her that the answer is obviously both.

Not that that's anything new. He didn't even come out to his mom until five minutes before he got into his shitty Dodge Neon to leave Indiana forever. In retrospect, he is sure his mother always knew. Now, he feels more than a little ashamed of his cowardice. This, however, is not that. Rather, he doesn't want her to worry any more than he wants to let the air touch the recent disasters of his heart. They feel as embarrassing as they do sacred.

When she asks if he's happy in the face of so much unsaid, he confesses that he hates New York. It isn't much of a confession until he tells her why, and then her face goes gentle. He's never told her he was scared, not once, not even when this life was beginning.

♦

They have tickets, thanks to the connections Alex now has, to midnight mass at St. Patrick's. Religion was never an issue with his mom growing up, which was one of the mercies of his childhood. But this is a different kind of thing, ritual and community for the sake of it and an opportunity he's supposed to take simply because he can. Even though it would probably mean more to someone else who has less ability to access it.

For all those reasons, he hadn't been sure if it was a good idea to go. But Margaret and his mother had cooed about it over the phone. Once they're there he's glad they did, if only for the warm bustle of the crowd on a cold night and the enchanted look on his mother's face.

Alex can't wear his hat but he's also not the most interesting figure in this particular crowd, filled with local politicians and celebrities way more famous than he. The cathedral and its patrons make him feel small, like the beach does.

They muddle through the service – they're not Catholic, only theoretically Methodist, but when getting them the tickets Margaret had insisted that was a trivial detail. The service is showy, and if his mom were more religious she'd probably be uncomfortable with it. As it is, Alex finds the pomp and ceremony fascinating. And after a month of playing an Irish Catholic immigrant to the city on film, there's something to be said for seeing the rituals up close and personal.

He spares a thought to wonder if Liam is here too, somewhere in the crowd. Liam hadn't mentioned it, but they haven't spoken since that night in Liam's parents' backyard. But Liam is Catholic – Alex knows from one of his bizarre rambles about 16th century saints and canonization laws – and certainly would be more at ease here. He wonders what Liam would think about his own attendance. Probably nothing more than that it was good Alex was having yet another new experience, and one very unlikely to get him into any sort of trouble at that.

When they are asked to exchange the sign of peace with those around them, Alex laughs at his mother's delight in strangers and finds a certain relief that no one's eyes flicker over him in any way that marks him out from the actually faithful. Between the actor thing and the ever so gay thing, he had been slightly worried.

They emerge from the overheated church into the snapping cold outside to the peal of bells and the sky dark beyond the glow of the city. Looking up, Alex realizes that it is, in fact, Christmas. He threads his arm through his mom's as they walk and feels at peace.

They cross the street to Rockefeller Center, which is crowded with tourists when and the people spilling out of the Cathedral. After half an hour, the crowds ebb, and it becomes as quiet as New York ever does.

Alex buys them both hotdogs and sodas at a cart, and they sit on one of the benches that line the walkway down to the viewing area for the skating rink. In the midst of the lights and noise of the city, his mother's presence, from the lines on her face to the way she brushes her hair out of her eyes, feels familiar and comforting.

"I'm buying a house," Alex says without looking at his her when they've been quiet for too long. "We should talk about what to do about yours."

"What's that supposed to mean?" she asks.

"It means I have money I don't even know how to spend, and Indiana is cheap. I've been too freaked out by everything to solve my own housing crisis much less do right by you. But…I don't know. Just tell me what needs doing, and we'll get it done. Or, I mean, if you want to move. Just. You know. Merry Christmas or something." He hunches his shoulders almost up to his ears, awkward and embarrassed all over again.

"Alex."

He's glad she doesn't manage anything more. The Midwest is good for that. The whole conversation is hitting a raw place he doesn't want to think about. Sitting here, he feels like the sheepish, sullen, and occasionally funny teenager he was not all that long ago. "Don't worry about it," he says. "I forgot to go shopping."

36

Liam greets Carly at the door with a wild hug and an enthusiastic kiss, then grabs her hand and drags her into the room. New Year's with Liam's family – all generations of it, all packed into a reconstructed black box theatre on 42nd Street – is a must for the holidays and completely worth flying out for.

When she finally finds Alex she wraps him in a hug too and rocks a little until he finally relaxes and hugs her back. It's good to see him; she's been more than a little worried about him. She didn't sign up to take care of Alex on top of everyone else in her life, but sharing advice won't cost her anything and he could use it.

"Hi, Carly," he says, his voice drily amused, when she lets him go.

"Hello, Alex."

"…That's not a good voice."

"Come with me," she says and hooks an arm through his elbow. She has an agenda and nothing to gain by delaying.

She drags him to the back of the room, where it's darker and quieter and there's less chance of an audience. None of this needs one, and Alex has always functioned better outside a crowd.

"Okay, real talk time," she says.

"Yes?" Alex looks a little scared.

For a moment, Carly feels bad for him. Alex has nothing to fear from her, but he doesn't seem to know that, and she doesn't have the energy to explain it. "So, the genius thing where you called Paul about Liam? Total asshole move. I mean, I am sorry you were messed up about that, because Liam really does adore you. You guys are good now, right?"

"I thought that's what you were going to yell at me for."

Carly waves that off. "Oh, no, honey. I'm glad you had a good time." She loves Liam's affectionate heart that wants to care for all the world, and she's glad whenever he finds someone who makes him happy. "I am going to yell at you about Paul, though, because he's fucking Craig again which is more bullshit than you thinking Liam should be your boyfriend – "

"I didn't – "

"Rounding up! Let me finish, then you can talk." Men need to stop talking over her when she is, as usual, the only adult on deck. "Look. We are all fucked up, but we also all adore you. And you're being fucking nuts and also an asshole, so you should decide what you're doing so you have a plan when Paul is done with his self-injury routine."

Alex's eyes go a little wide. It's the exact opposite of the cute squinty thing he does when he smiles.

"Oh, sweetie," Carly grabs his hand to squeeze it. She wonders how much Paul has told him, but he's a smart kid in any case. "Paul's fine. He's just stupid. But please, figure out what you're doing with him."

"He's back with Craig?" Alex asks.

"Total bullshit," she says firmly. She squeezes his hand again before she drops it. "Which is why you need to figure your shit out. Now come on, baby boy, you need a drink."

◆

A drink he gets, more than one, because the showdown with Carly, no matter how harmless, was sort of scary, and the Craig information is additionally unpleasant at best.

The family atmosphere – and the fact that he's now apparently part of that family – is excessive. Within a couple of hours he feels like he's being passed around the room, not as J. Alex Cook, actor, but as Carly's friend, Liam's coworker, and *I heard you had Kathleen's pancakes the other day*. Alex wonder if the whole planet knows what that's a euphemism for.

Charles is there, as well as the rest of the crew Liam dragged him out drinking with on their first night in New York. He nods across the room to Alex at one point and only says hello much later. Alex is glad he's not more drunk when it happens; this time he might have asked him if he's fucked Liam too.

Alex also notices two girls he's seen random tabloid gossip about Liam hooking up with at various points. Carly seems super chummy with one of them but slightly and unkindly amused towards the other. He kind of wants that story, if only because it has nothing to do with him.

Liam comes to check on him periodically between stints at bartending, but it's nothing more than playing the good host. Alex appreciates the opportunity to be just like everyone else, introversion and recent excursions by his dick aside.

At eight, as platters of food are set out, there's an announcement that they are all now officially locked in, as the street has been closed for emergency vehicle traffic only.

When Alex finds himself in a conversation with Liam's father that's probably only awkward in his head, he winds up blurting something about how they should throw one of these shindigs in the event of zombie apocalypse. Luckily, Liam's father laughs, probably because no matter how awkward Alex is being, it'll never live up to Liam's weird.

Fifteen minutes before midnight, Liam wraps an arm around

Alex's waist and tells him to be by the doors by five to twelve. When he asks why, Liam says, "Trust me."

Two minutes before the ball drops, Liam leads Carly, Charles, the two girls, and Alex outside into an empty 42nd Street, just east of Times Square.

"Look up," he whispers in Alex's ear.

The ball, all lasers and glitter, is right there and the massive and miserable crowds are at least fifty feet away.

"Oh my God."

"Right?!" Liam says smugly as the countdown from sixty starts.

By the time they get to thirty, Carly has an arm around Alex's waist, and Liam's half climbing on his back. Alex doesn't have eyes for any of them. All he can do is watch the spectacle.

"One day, I am going to host this thing," Liam whispers into his ear at twenty, jerking his chin towards one of the many stages covered with celebrities and cameras.

At ten, Alex wonders what it says about a city that it marks a new year with a fall, but he shakes it off to shout the last numbers with the rest of them.

Midnight comes, and Liam kisses Carly, long and wet. Alex keeps staring at the ball, as if making sure it won't fall any further, through buildings and concrete. He only tears his gaze away when Liam grabs his face and kisses him too. Alex laughs at the hint of tongue.

When he gets through the line of them – because Liam kisses everyone with varying degrees of enthusiasm – he pulls out his phone to text someone. As Carly catches his eye, Alex does the same: Gemma, because it's a decent thing to do, and he loves her. Paul, because the truth is that he is Alex's wish for the new year.

♦

Paul is kissing Craig, the sound of the crowd in Times Square a roar from the TV, when his phone vibrates in his pocket. He knows it's Alex.

It takes him a moment to disentangle himself from Craig and from the rest of the group crowded around Brian's living room. Out in the hallway he checks the text. It is, in fact, from Alex. All it says is *Happy New Year*, but even with everything that is fraught between them it makes Paul smile.

Happy New Year to you, too, he sends back. *Hope you have magic.*

He stares at the screen for another few seconds to watch the message send and wonders what Alex is up to tonight. Can he ask? Does he even want to know the answer?

Before he can decide, a reply comes back. *I already do.* And then, a picture: An empty street in front of the crowd and the air full of confetti. *Wish you could see it.*

Paul melts a little. He thumbs back *It looked pretty cool on TV.*

"Paul?"

Paul looks up from the phone to see Craig leaning in from the doorway.

"I was wondering where you went." He looks at the phone in Paul's hands but doesn't ask.

"I'll be right there," Paul says. Craig nods but doesn't move from the doorway, so he has time to see but not reply to Alex's next text. *Carly says hi, by the way,* God knows what that might mean.

They trade sporadic messages over the course of the next three hours. Craig doesn't look thrilled whenever he sees Paul with his phone out, but doesn't say anything.

At actual midnight Craig has his hand on Paul's hip as he kisses him again. Paul's phone buzzes in his pocket, and he knows Craig can feel it.

He's not judicious and doesn't move away from Craig as he checks the text. *Happy *real* new year,* Alex has sent. *Magic to you, too, but beware.*

Of what?

Paul doesn't get to see Alex's answer, because Craig grabs his hand and gives him a look that's a little pissed, which is probably fair. Alex is going to have to wait. Paul hates that, but he also believes he will. There's still some thread connecting him and Alex, and it's not going to snap tonight.

Paul's out on the back porch, escaping the loud and getting-too-drunk crowd, when he finally checks his phone again.

Do I really need to tell you?

37

After the holidays, the return to life at *Fourth* is a slow trickle, with production and writers filtering in a couple of weeks before the actors are back on set. Paul's one of the first there simply because he's in town, and it's become increasingly easier for him to write – whether for the show or his own projects – in the office.

Outside of his own house, Paul is less haunted by an Alex that was his and less dogged by a Craig who is trying to get him to be a better boyfriend this time around. Even after over a year's intermission, the habits of his work and his inability to negotiate with Craig about them successfully seem to remain.

He's the only one there one afternoon when Victor strolls in and spins a chair around to sit in front of his desk.

Paul looks at him over the top of his laptop. He hits save but doesn't say anything. He also doesn't stop typing. Victor hasn't even said hello yet.

"So," Victor finally says, crossing an ankle over his knee. "You're here. Liam's back in town, and Alex is going to be back in a few weeks. Are there going to be explosions?"

"Which particular set of circumstances are you referring to?"

"Whichever one is going to end in pyrotechnics."

"Liam and I?" Paul is sure that Victor knows at least part of that story. If it involved anyone else it would be reasonable to assume its conclusion would end, not just in vicious gossip, but somebody taking a swing at someone.

"Is that the one?" Victor asks mildly.

Paul isn't fooled. This isn't Victor in search of entertainment. This is Victor desperately concerned and checking in on his people. He's rarely so obvious about it, but he's seen it before regarding Liam, and, increasingly, Alex. Paul wonders what he's come to, that he's now on Victor's Needs Care list.

Paul looks at his computer screen. The cursor flashing at the end of a sentence is easier to endure than the other man's stare. "I don't know."

"I'm very aware," Victor says carefully, "that none of you are exactly okay at the moment, and that you and Liam have never been as close as would be convenient."

Paul isn't sure how to take that.

"I'm not thrilled about that," Victor adds into the silence.

Paul snaps his laptop shut. He is done with taking advice, or instruction, or whatever it is from Victor. "Yes, because I planned for Alex to walk out on me and then fuck Liam because he was pissed at me for conspiring with the two of you. Nobody's thrilled, Victor. Sometimes that happens, and I have to tell you, it would be a lot easier to be an adult about this if you weren't so sure none of us are up to the task. Just so you know, I heard about Liam from Alex, which was a pretty damn adult thing for him to do even if I don't understand the why about any of it."

"If it helps, I had rather considerable words with Liam about it."

"That's your business," Paul says.

"Why do you always shut down when – "

"Because you're my friend and my mentor and my boss, and I did not volunteer to hold Liam's secrets, especially when they are continuously provided to me without his consent or mine. It's a pain in my ass, and more unwelcome today than usual."

"Would you rather I said I was worried about you?" Victor asks.

"It would at least be relevant, so yes."

"Fine, I am worried about you. And I don't understand your choices."

"And what choices are those?"

"You've been working on my projects for how long now? Seven years?"

"Eight." Paul has no idea how this conversation has suddenly shifted into a discussion of his career.

"Eight years. I know you have ambition, but you've never even tried to move on. Add in Alex and Craig and whoever else – you can yell at me about being in control of your own destiny all you want, but you're trying to serve too many masters and not one of them is yourself."

"I have a plan," Paul says more than a little defensively.

"It's not working for you," Victor says.

"It was starting to."

"Then what is it you're so damn afraid of?"

Paul laughs sharply. "You, Alex. Everyone keeps telling me be careful what I wish for. And I wish for a lot. But I am also surrounded by the costs of success. I don't ever want to be you."

"Paul," Victor says reprovingly. "None of us here are fucked up because of success. That's the fun icing on the cake. I am the way I am because this is the way I am. Just because my life would not make you happy, does not mean it makes me unhappy. Quite the contrary. You should know better."

"Who's unhappy?"

Paul turns towards the voice.

There, in the doorway of the writers' room, Liam lounges. Paul has no idea how long he's been standing there. He assumes not very – Liam isn't known for quiet or still – but it's hard to be sure.

They all stare at each other for a moment.

"How is he?" Paul asks Liam.

"I'm going to assume you mean that in the least pornographic way possible."

Liam is exhausting, but Paul makes a gesture for him to continue.

"Better than he was, I think."

Paul nods. "Okay. Good." There's a part of him that can't stop picturing Liam and Alex together now. He wants to believe Alex never connected with Liam the way he did with Paul, but that's probably not true. Certainly, it's not fair and not his business.

"How are you?" Victor asks Liam pointedly.

"It's been a month," Liam says wearily. "How's Paul?" he asks back.

"Right here," Paul says sharply. He's less than amused with whatever double act is playing out in front of him. "And I've been better."

"Alex is totally fucked up over you," Liam informs him, like Paul wants that information in front of Victor. Or from Liam at all.

"Is that supposed to be comforting? I don't want him to be fucked up. I want him to be happy." Paul means it, but he also wishes the situation was less of a mess for all of them.

"With you," Liam says.

Paul shakes his head. "I'm in a relationship."

"Give him some time."

Paul doesn't know if Liam means Craig or Alex and has no interest in asking. He sighs heavily.

Victor, done with this drama, tosses his keys to Liam. "Go wait in my office. I'll cook you dinner."

Liam beams, gives a little salute, and is gone.

Victor puts a hand Paul's shoulder as he stands. "You need to stop being so nice about your desires."

"You have no idea." Victor underestimates him. Because there was nothing nice and everything glorious about the way he and Alex devoured each other. And, unless he can get it together and make it work, there probably isn't anything nice – in an entirely different way – about what he's doing to Craig either.

38

By the weekend Paul attempts to put all thoughts of Alex and Liam – and Alex *and* Liam, because that image is vivid and pretty and awful and odd – out of his head. He and Craig have beach plans.

It's overcast out when they wake up – late, because they've both been working a lot and sleep and sex are good – and nowhere near the forecast eighty. The beach is one of their good places, though, and they've been looking forward to this all week, so they go anyway.

They park in their usual lot and Craig frowns when Paul pulls a sweatshirt on over his T-shirt. Skin may be awesome but the wind is off the water and it's January. It's cold. Beau, no longer Divorce Dog, is thrilled to be out of the house and trots happily alongside them as they walk hand-in-hand above the surf line.

For long stretches of beach they're alone. It's wonderful, though, despite the gray, to walk and let their shoulders bump together, as they banter and laugh about utterly stupid shit. A string of breakups and actual divorces split up their social group early on in their relationship. In the isolating aftermath they'd learned to be very good company for each other. Carly always used to say they were boring, but sometimes Paul looks at her life, and this mess he's coming out of with Alex, and thinks boring is great.

When the afternoon starts to close in they build a fire on the beach and sit tucked close next to each other. Craig runs back to the car for a blanket when the temperature drops again. Beau naps next to them, twitching his ears whenever the fire pops.

They fall quiet eventually. With his head on Craig's shoulder Paul looks out at the water through the translucent tongues of flame. The water is grey and choppy, but the fire is warm, and the rush of the surf is soothing. Eventually, he drifts off.

He wakes a little while later. The sky is a shade darker, and the fire is a little lower.

Craig presses a kiss to the top of his head. "Hey baby, how're you doing?"

Paul assesses. He's a little cold, a little stiff, and getting hungry. This part of the day is just about over, but he doesn't want to go yet. "Really good."

Craig hums, "Good." He settles his arm more snugly around Paul's back. Beau yawns and nestles his head back down on his paws to drowse.

39

When everyone returns to *Paradise Square*, Alex feels better than he has in a long time. Everyone's rested from the break, and shooting outside in sub-freezing weather feels slightly more tolerable than it did before.

For whatever reason, everyone is treating him less like an interloper now. As much as he doesn't want to admit it to himself, that's probably because he's spending less time running off to Liam, who returned to L.A. late on New Year's Day with Carly in tow. He's also no longer fucking people's friends he met at the few cast gatherings he went to just before the holidays.

Press for *Fourth* is looms, which is slightly terrifying. Doing print interviews during the hurry up and wait on set is one thing. Doing the big morning shows with the screaming fans outside and the insipid banter inside is something else. Especially when all they want him to do is talk about kissing Liam. Some days it seems no one gives a shit about Zach and James – or TV shows having actual plots – at all.

Meanwhile, photos of his mother and him after midnight mass have emerged, and there's a dark sort of hilarity to being seen eating a hotdog quite so all over the internet. It's absurd enough to be funny, and if his fans are going to be intrusive, at least they are also cooing over his mom.

But on the whole things are fine – or at least more fine – than they've been in a long while. So when one of the A.D.s throws a fit at the extras and his walkie into a pile of suspiciously colored snow, it's awful and yet hilarious in just the right kind of way.

The day brings back memories of the horror stories he and Paul had delighted each other with about everything that could and did go wrong in the day-to-day of their existences. So when he's back in his room that evening, he leaves his Farsi notes on the nightstand and pulls out his phone.

◆

Paul's at home on the couch, Todd snoring softly from the chair in the corner, when his phone rings. A glance at the caller ID shows that it's Alex. After the few calls Paul has gotten from him over the past month Paul is less surprised as he's been before, but he is worried. Alex calling hasn't meant anything good for him yet.

"Hey," he says. "Are you – " Remembering Alex's admonishment, he cuts himself off. "How are you?"

Craig's won the miserable schedule sweepstakes this week so

Paul has the house to himself, a fact for which he is grateful as he closes his laptop and braces himself for whatever insane adventure Alex has had this time.

"Hi, Paul," Alex says, like his name is enough of an answer. Then he dives into his story.

He's not broken or lost or upset, which are all good things but throw Paul badly. If he's meant to mend or soothe, he can try that and make sense of it. But Alex is laughing, and the only thing Paul can do to that is lose himself in the happiness of the sound.

"I miss you," Paul says softly when the story winds up. He doesn't mean to, because then they're going to have to talk about things, and that's probably unlikely to end well. But every fiber of his being wishes he were in the same room with Alex right now.

There's a long silence as Alex doesn't reply. Paul has to force himself not to fill up the space with apology or nervous chatter.

"I know about Craig," eventually comes his response.

"Carly?" Paul asks.

"Carly," Alex confirms. Then, "I miss you too."

♦

Alex should stop calling, but Paul keeps answering the phone. Whether that's because he wants him or wants him back – or thinks they can be one more version of the strange friends they've been since they first met – Alex has no idea. But he can feel himself being a little nuts, because when it comes to Paul he is a being of pure want. It's new in its way, a sort of desire and longing only made possible by too many disasters and his recent education less at Liam's hands than at his heart.

They talk about none of it, however. Not the fight, not Liam, and certainly not Craig. They don't say *I miss you* again, they just talk, mostly about nothing in particular while Alex tries to wind down from his days on set. It's oddly domestic. When they don't connect by phone, because Craig is over or Alex has been spending social time with some of the *Paradise Square* crew, they text.

The times Paul doesn't reply right away, when Craig's asked him to put the phone away or they're otherwise busy, make Alex antsy. He still has bad days, and while it makes things better when he can look forward to calling Paul at night, their unspoken *do not go* list gets in the way.

He can't say why when he's exhausted or heartsick or feeling fucked up or confused about everything, and Paul doesn't try to pry it out of him. It makes Alex snappish and sullen because as much as he wants Paul, he needs him to be his rock. But Alex can't have that. The absence of it and the reasons for it make him crazy.

◆

Paul should stop answering the phone. But he can't bring himself to. Alex's pull on him is as magnetic as it's ever been, even when he's three thousand miles away and continued contact is an extremely bad idea.

As eager as he is for Alex always, he's not always successful at reigning in his own temper and snappishness when Alex gets reticent and bitchy. But the nights when Alex isn't happy and doesn't get pissed and doesn't *talk* – when he's just a distant breath on the other end of the line – are the worst. Sometimes Paul hangs up at the end of a call wondering if he'll get another. Somehow, he always does.

The night the phone rings around two a.m., Paul is grateful Craig is a sound sleeper, and he slips out of bed with a kiss to his shoulder. While Alex often calls late, it's usually not excessive and Paul learned long before Alex not to ignore middle-of-the-night calls.

When he answers, Alex immediately starts in on a story. He's not babbling. The story is precise and well formulated, like he thought about how he was going to tell it in the cab back to his hotel. Even so, Paul can tell he's drunk and trying to extend the moment through the pleasure of an audience.

"So why didn't you go home with him?" Paul eventually asks, amused, after Alex has run out of glowing adjectives for the very cute and very flirty boy at whatever party he's been at.

"Because I am trying to make better choices."

"Like staying out until five a.m. and calling me in the middle of the night?"

"I said better, Paul. Not good."

Paul laughs at that. Alex is in no condition for the alternative. "What would you have done to him?" he asks, before he can think the better of it.

"Maybe I wanted to be done to."

"Well, that's precise and informative," Paul says carefully.

"What? Maybe I just wanted some head."

"I know you, Alex. You wouldn't be that coy about wanting your dick sucked," Paul says.

"Yeah. Okay…. Look. Repertoires expand, okay?"

Paul laughs and shakes his head. Alex's economy and choice of words always surprises him. "Tell me about it," he says in the wrong tone for it to be meant as a phrase of agreement.

Shockingly, Alex does. He goes on and on about how tight this guy's jeans were and how much he wanted everyone to leave so he could say *stay right there, honey* and sit on his dick. Eventually Paul finds he has to ask the obvious question.

"Have you?" he asks.

"Have I what?"

"Alex – "

"Your breath is ragged. Are you touching yourself?" Alex says.

Paul can't tell if his tone deflection or indictment. "I am trying not to. My *boyfriend* is upstairs," he hisses.

"Yes," Alex shoots back.

"Yes, what?"

"Yes I had Liam's cock in me and I miss it." Alex pops each word.

"You're more drunk or more vicious than I realized," Paul tells him.

"Maybe I'm just learning how to say things," Alex retorts. "Or maybe, I'm finally figuring out how to want things."

"Do you always do everything in the wrong order?"

"I don't know. Do you always go from zero to married in your relationships? Or do you stop short of that and just have really sketchy interactions with your crazy exes who are totally not over you?"

Paul has no idea if Alex means Craig or himself. He's afraid to ask.

"Go back to the boy," Paul says. That's safe compared to everything else.

"Man," Alex says pointedly. "More hung than me. Can we take a minute to celebrate skinny jeans?"

"We can until I have to get them off someone," Paul says.

"I didn't know you didn't approve of my clothing choices."

"I don't think I approve of clothing on you at all."

The way Alex's breath punches out of him in response is shockingly hot. It also encourages Paul to keep going, like he's as drunk as this very dangerous creature he can't seem to let go of.

"Would you like that?" he asks. "The world where either of us has enough days off for me to keep you naked all the time?"

"It sounds terrifying," Alex says.

"Why?"

"Because you overwhelm me. Because you're asking me if I'd like to not have to think or speak or do anything but suck your cock. How am I supposed to give any answer to that other than yes?"

It's not the most Alex has ever said to him in a sexual context, but it might be the most coherent thing Alex has ever said to him in a sexual context. All Paul can grapple with right now though is that little whine creeping into Alex's voice, the one that begs and pleads and always tells Paul it's all too much even as Alex asks for more.

"Are you touching yourself?" Paul asks.

"No."

"Well, maybe you should be."

"Fuck," Alex says. "I don't have enough hands."

Paul can tell when he's dropped his phone onto his hotel bed and is fumbling with his clothes.

"I told you skinny jeans suck," he says when Alex returns.

"Say something useful," Alex demands.

This time Paul can't stop the laugh, and he smiles when he hears Alex chuckle in sheepish reply.

"So we're going to make this real simple," Paul says as he wanders into the kitchen to put even more distance between what he's doing and what he should be doing. "In part because you need to go to sleep, and I need to not get busted."

"Yeah?"

"Yeah. You jerk off, and when I say stop, stop."

"Paul – "

"Did you think I was going to stop teasing you?"

"No," Alex says once and then again. It sounds like relief.

Paul doesn't come — he wants this to be all about Alex — but by the end of the call he's relieved too. Climbing back into bed beside Craig he feels no guilt, just the exquisite torture of Alex's breathless whine still ringing in his ear. But they'd acknowledged every one of their red lines only by storming recklessly past them.

Alex doesn't call the next night, and Paul is glad because he has no idea what he's meant to say.

When days stretch out into a week without any word at all, Paul wonders if Alex had gotten out of him the last hurrah he'd been looking for since November and really is gone now. It's a dark thought, and may be unfair to both of them, but neither of them have ever been fair to each other, or themselves, in any of this.

40

Filming in New York is starting to wrap up, which means both even more press for *Fourth*, and the looming prospect of returning to home. L.A., City of Angels and also Paul, and Craig, and the whole giant mess that Alex was happy to pretend was a little less real than he knows it is so long as he was attached to it only via a phone line.

The seeming unreality of it is nothing like an excuse for not calling now, though, as much as Alex might want it to be. As many times as Alex thinks about it, and as much as he wants to, in the end he doesn't reach for the phone again. There's nothing he can say that he would mean.

The interviewers (the less professional ones, at least) and the internet still want to know about him and Liam. The newest pet idea – there aren't any credible rumors, but fans like to spin bullshit – is that they somehow hate each other.

Spend five minutes with him, Alex wants to say, with an overwhelming fondness. *You'd want to strangle him too.*

When he gets asked, the third or fourth time, about how well everyone in the cast gets along, with the unspoken but obvious subtext of *how do you and Liam get along?* he's tired enough and annoyed enough to put on his sly smile.

"Oh, everybody's great friends. Yeah, Liam and I did New Year's together here in New York. It was amazing."

The internet goes insane.

That's bad enough as it is. The fact that Alex has only his own stupidity and impatience to blame for handing that line to the maniacs makes it worse. But New Year's was a good night, and he could maybe have shrugged it off, if it weren't for the pictures.

I wasn't sure if I should post these, the captions online read. *But after what Alex said about Liam, it's not like they're hiding anything ;)*

It's not pictures from New York. They're from D.C. The shimmer of the reflecting pool and the stabbing column of the Monument glow behind two figures that are unmistakably the two of them.

None of the hyperventilating fan girls and boys on the internet know it, but he and Liam were on their way to the Lincoln Memorial that night. The more-than-grain of truth in all the suppositions about what they were up to that are also so fucking far from the truth is – after everything – heartbreaking.

In a way, Alex is glad to have the pictures, creepy and fucked up as that is. They are his only souvenir of something he still doesn't know how to classify. *Relationship* is far too tight a box now that it's over. *Affair* seems too open. But what Alex does know, even from this short distance, is that he was happy during what were also probably some of the worst weeks of his adult life. It makes him furious that people have decided to intrude on that.

Margaret gives him grief over the interview. Not because it was bad, but because he wasn't in control of himself to have offered up that tidbit of information – not that she knows the full story of it either. Liam sends him a few texts that Alex suspects are at least intended to be annoying.

Eventually he gets Liam to shut up with, *New Year's really was great* and *Paul and I had phone sex.*

When Liam doesn't have a response beyond *Cool!* Alex knows he's probably making more of a mess of everything than anyone wants to deal with.

That night, he lets himself be dragged to a party at Soho House by a couple of the wardrobe girls on *Paradise.* The second he's there, it feels like the worst choice ever. He just wants to talk to his friends, not hang out with their friends of friends of friends who desperately need to feel like they're getting their $900 per month's worth in celebrity hobnobbing. The whole winter rooftop with heat lamps thing is also more ridiculous than Alex can stand.

A drink doesn't make it better, and he feels good about his decision to leave until he tells his companions and actually goes. There are paparazzi outside – not just for him, never just for him, thank God – and they're loud, shouting for his attention. On one hand, it's less creepy, because unlike the fans with smartphones sneaking pictures of him, he knows they're there. On the other, it's harder to remain calm and firm in his need to treat them as invisible.

When one of them grabs his arm, it becomes impossible. A flash goes off too close to his face. He's physically unbalanced by resisting the unwelcome hand he can't yank away from without looking like the worst sort of asshole (not that he doesn't already by virtue of the venue). Someone is shouting a question at him about Liam.

"We were with his girlfriend," Alex replies to the question he's only half-heard about New Year's. "His parents were around too. Opposite of scandal!"

He tugs away from the hand on his arm and somehow finds his way into a cab, despite the spots from the flash still going off in front of his eyes. It takes a moment for him to even remember to give the driver an address.

As the car finally starts moving, he slumps against the door. None of that is anything that hasn't happened to him before, and while he never likes it, right now he feels shaken by the clamor far more than he usually does. The detached place he can usually fall back into when the world is too much isn't there. He doesn't understand how there can be real people these things happen to any more than he understands how he can be one of them.

Somehow he gets back to his room, where he shuts the city out behind the drapes and flicks on all the lights. It's still not enough for comfort, and in spite of the bucket of bad ideas it probably is, it's easy to reach for his phone for what he knows will be.

Paul has always picked up. He does tonight, too.

He sounds wary, at first, until Alex starts talking. Then he sounds worried. Alex tells him everything – the poorly calculated interview, the photos, the party, the paparazzi and how his most tender secrets are somehow currency.

"I wanted to hit them," he confesses.

He closes his eyes with a different sort of relief entirely when Paul responds, strangely gentle, "Wouldn't anyone?"

"I want to come home." Alex hates himself for how pathetic it sounds.

Paul hums, and it's soothing. "You will be soon."

"I know," Alex says. It's a little sad. But then he keeps talking.

♦

Paul listens with as much shock as concern; this isn't banter or ill-advised innuendo. This is Alex scared and broken again in ways Paul's only just coming to understand. At first he keeps an eye on the clock; he and Craig have plans tonight and honest to God he's trying. But Alex needs him, and Paul needs more than anything to be here for him. So at one point, dangerously close to the line when cancelling is going to become standing up, he interrupts Alex and says he's got to do something.

"I promise I'll call you right back. Just stay by the phone."

There's a rustle that he's pretty sure is Alex nodding. His heart aches for him. So do his hands.

He gets Craig's voicemail; he's probably in the car already. Paul should probably feel worse about that then he does.

"Hey," he says, when Alex answers on the first ring. "Back now. I'm yours all night."

Alex says, "Good."

♦

In the morning, Paul has a text from Craig which, given the voicemail, not to mention everything else, is probably fair: *I think we need to talk.*

They meet for dinner at the same sushi restaurant Paul had first been spotted at with Alex. It's Craig's suggestion and Paul can't tell him no without telling him why. There's so much writing on the wall already that there's absolutely no point in adding any more.

"So, about last night," Craig begins, once they've gotten their drinks.

"I'm sorry," Paul says. He is, though not in a way that's useful.

"No, it's – " Craig stops himself and shakes his head. "It was Alex, wasn't it?"

Paul nods, once. "Yeah. It was."

Craig looks at his glass and bites his top lip in the way Paul remembers falling in love with, when they'd first been together. He looks up at Paul. "I don't think this is going to work."

"I – " Paul starts, but stops at Craig's resigned look.

"I'm glad we tried again," Craig says. He doesn't sound angry. Just so tired. "I always would have wondered, otherwise."

Paul nods. He doesn't trust his voice right now. "Me too," he says. He's not sure if it's true, but he owes Craig the kindness.

"I'm sorry I took Beau."

The laugh, watery and sharp, bursts out of Paul before he realizes it's going to. He presses his closed hand to his mouth and looks over Craig's shoulder at a spot on the wall until he's sure he can look at Craig and hold himself together at the same time. As inevitable as this outcome probably is, he really had tried. If any number of things had been different, he and Craig still could have been very good together. He's mourning the loss already.

"I'm sorry I'm an asshole," is what he finally says when he's sure looking at Craig isn't going to crack him a little.

Craig smiles, but it's strained. "Only when you try to be."

Paul isn't sure if he means about the sorry or the asshole; he's pretty sure Craig's right about both.

They finish the meal talking about small, quiet things. They split the check, hug goodbye in the parking lot, and go their separate ways.

In his car, Paul sits with his phone balanced on the steering wheel as he types a message to Carly. *Free tonight? I need to get blindingly drunk right now.*

41

The flight back to L.A. is almost nothing like the flight out to D.C, for which Alex is infinitely grateful. He's glad to spend it sleeping, instead of trying not to cry. But while he's definitely less miserable, Alex feels just as uncertain.

As the plane circles LAX on its descent, Alex braces for the moment the wheels hit the tarmac. It's his least favorite part of flying; it feels so close to a crash.

The plane lands safely, though, and as it taxis to the gate Alex turns his phone back on and scrolls through the notifications. Emails from Margaret; a late exhortation from Gemma to have a good flight and call her when he lands; and a text from Carly.

Paul and Craig are done, it reads. *Got a plan?*

What the fuck am I supposed to do with that information? he types back, stunned, as the jet way rolls out to meet the plane.

The reply comes back sooner than he expects as he waits for the people ahead of him to shuffle down the aisle. *Whatever you want. That's the point.*

When he wheels his suitcase into what is still, for a few more days, their shitty apartment, Gemma's on the couch with a giant bowl of popcorn. The fact that it's all like he never left is faintly irritating. He's changed; the world hasn't; and now he's expected to sit down and eat popcorn.

"Hey, stranger," Gemma says as he takes off his jacket.

"Hey."

"I know you were making a movie and all, but way to keep in touch."

"Gem...." Alex starts guiltily. He's barely contacted Gemma at all since he left over a month ago, which makes him the worst of roommates and friends. But he could hardly talk about what he was doing with the people he was doing it *with*. Explaining things to a third party was beyond his capacity.

Something in Alex's tone makes Gemma sit up straight and pats the seat next to her. "Oh my God, what happened, and tell me everything." Interpersonal drama is for Gemma what certain high frequencies are for dogs.

"Um." Alex sits down next to her cautiously. "This is all like...like you can't tell anyone ever. I know I tell you to keep secrets all the time, and I'm sure you don't and that whoever you tell is trustworthy or at least batshit crazy enough that no one would believe them if they talked, but this is like orders of magnitude, okay?"

She frowns. "What did you do?"

"Liam."

She squeals and kicks her feet so that the popcorn spills everywhere.

"Okay, the sudden feeling I have that you've been reading porn about me and a colleague on the internet is extremely uncomfortable."

"He's so charming," she whines.

"Not really," he says dryly. "I mean, yes. But not the person you think he is."

"Obviously."

"Look, you can't tell. And not just for my sake. He's in the closet, the thing with Carly is very real and very serious, she knows, it's all fine, but not for the world, okay?"

While she agrees to keep the secret, Alex makes her swear again and again to silence in the course of a conversation that covers about eighty percent of the madness. After Gemma's curiosity and his own need to tell someone outside of that mess about it has been satiated, the conversation culminates in a planning session regarding the impending move. If everything goes as expected, closing is happening the day after next.

"You seem different," she says, when they get to the end.

"I'm a beautiful person who goes to beautiful parties with beautiful people now," he says sharply although only a tiny bit unkindly. He tries to pick some of the spilled popcorn out of the couch. "What's your story?" he asks.

"I'm the girl who used to want to be famous," she says. She doesn't even sound like she's lying.

◆

Moving does not go smoothly, not that they had any right to expect it to. The paperwork is fine, and signing the final dotted lines is a lot less scary than it seemed when Alex was first planning this. But there are boxes everywhere, first at the old apartment and then at the new house, which is open and echoing and bare. By the end of moving day Alex is sore and cranky and exhausted and feels homesick for their old place.

"This feels like a museum," he says, sitting cross-legged on the rug in what will probably be the living room.

"It needs furniture," Gemma says, lips pursed and hands on her hips as she surveys the space thoughtfully.

Alex groans and flops onto his back on the floor.

◆

That night in his new bedroom, Alex lies staring at the ceiling for far too long. This is a moment, and maybe after all the other moments he's had recently, this one should feel less by comparison. It doesn't.

He pulls out his phone to reread the text from Carly, then scrolls to Paul's name in his contacts. Now that there's no reason he shouldn't call and nothing stopping him from getting in his car and driving to Paul's house, doing any of that feels impossible.

The idea of being with Paul again had been lovely as a fantasy and an abstraction. Here, in unfamiliar surroundings in a familiar place it's too easy to remember all the things that had gone wrong.

But with Gemma down in the loft instead on the other side of the wall Alex is lonely in the vast expanse of his new house. He's never been any good at backing down from challenges anyway. He hits the call button.

"Alex?" Paul always answers with his name. Some things, at least, don't change.

"Hi," Alex says. "It's my first night in the new house. I feel like I should tell you a story."

"That sounds dangerous," Paul says.

Alex laughs. The assessment is certainly fair. "The movers weren't hot, and I didn't fuck any of them. Also, why do I hurt all over when I hired people?"

"I broke up with Craig," is Paul's incredibly not helpful answer.

"I know."

"Carly?" Paul asks.

"It would be nice for once to get some of this news from you," Alex says mildly even as he's aware that maybe Paul doesn't owe him anything anymore.

"I think you need to blame other people for that," Paul says cautiously. "Time and place. And it only just happened."

"Was it because of me?"

"Yes. No. I mean, yeah, but Craig and I have always had plenty of issues before I knew you existed. So...whatever makes you feel better."

"I'm willing to feel guilty about Thanksgiving. I'm not willing to feel guilty about Craig. Believe it or not, I'm trying to be an adult here," Alex says.

"What do you want me to say, Alex?"

"I want you to stop babying me. 'Whatever makes me feel better,' what the fuck?"

"You may be trying, but you have none of your shit together," Paul says wearily.

"Thank you," Alex says sharply.

"It's got nothing to do with your age. It's your life," Paul continues. "It's insane."

"I appreciate the vote of confidence."

"This from the guy who spent so much time at my house because it felt normal."

"So what if I did?"

"Alex," Paul says, his voice placating. "I'm not...." He stops and starts again. "I'm just saying. Your life is strange and hard. It would be strange and hard for anyone. But there are resources. You know there are people you could talk to."

"You mean therapy."

"I mean – yeah. Yes. I do," he says firmly.

"Paul?"

"Yeah?"

"What happened to your wrists?" Alex says. Paul may have a valid point, but Alex is so not the only one of them who is screwed up.

"What does that have to do with this?"

"My life is fucked up, but I never tried to make myself disappear."

There's silence for two terrible seconds. Paul snaps, "Why did *no one* notice you until Victor picked you up and dropped you in front of a camera? Now they've seen you, and they can't look away."

"Victor's a wizard."

"He didn't create you, Alex."

There's silence for a moment. Alex says softly, "Somebody noticed me before Victor did."

"What are you talking about?"

"You did."

"Well, arguably, Nick did then," Paul says.

"No. Not the way you did."

"And what way was that?"

Alex takes a breath. "Like I wasn't invisible. Like I wasn't an interchangeable part of the L.A. monster."

"Alex – "

"You still do. My invisibility's just different now, is all. Paul," he says. "And maybe you're not wrong. But you're fucked up too, and I can't be the kind of adult you need me to be. Not now. Not when you can't be single for seven whole days in a row."

"What does that mean?"

"It means it's my first night in a house I bought, my room is full of boxes, and I go back to work tomorrow, which means I'm going into the desert," Alex says, annoyed but also a little proud of what he's managed to accomplish.

"That's not a helpful answer, although I'm sure that's the point," Paul snaps. "What are we doing?" he asks, more softly.

"Me? I'm working on being twenty-one and not being late to work. What are you doing?"

Paul snorts. "Yeah. Okay. Fair, I guess. You should get some sleep."

Alex sighs. "Okay, Paul? New rule. You don't ask me what we're doing 'til you can get your head around me setting my own bedtime."

♦

The sun's not even up when the van comes to take him to location. There're some guys from the crew too, and Alex is fine with that. He doesn't want a car, and he doesn't want a hotel closer to the site. He just wants his own bed as much as he can have it and a few hours passed out in the back row of seats when he can't.

The weather out at Kelso is variable in the extreme – cold as fuck when they get there with a rapid climb to uncomfortable heat during the late morning – but Alex likes the labor and ordeal of it. It's a welcome change from all the parts of his life that are supposed to be easy and aren't.

Other than having strangers constantly reapply his sunblock between takes, the desert is mostly good. Even the absence of familiar faces helps a little bit. The idea of being at the lot with Paul or Liam isn't awful, but he can't say he minds putting that reunion off for a little while longer.

The desert is also beautiful. The sky is massive and endless, and as much as Alex does love the work, he wishes he had time alone on the dunes, watching the sun come up without anyone else around. He takes some amazing pictures that he emails to his mom.

<h1 style="text-align:center">42</h1>

Alex hasn't been to brunch in weeks, so there's no particular reason to miss him more this Sunday than all the previous ones. Paul goes anyway, even if he's glad Alex is most likely sleeping off a long week in the comfort of his own home not that far away.

Paul ends up talking to Shawna, who it transpires has been in much closer contact with Alex since he hit the desert. Paul is genuinely trying to figure out where he's been misstepping. Maybe part of treating Alex like an adult is to get his head around the fact that he has plenty of relationships that aren't mediated by him. Or Victor.

Paul probably won't ever not feel a little protective of Alex, but Shawna's frank assumption of Alex's ferociousness as they talk about the work he's doing is a little chagrining. Alex may be more broken than the rest of the world knows, but maybe the rest of the world also knows a little more about how strong he is than Paul does.

At home, Paul works on being single. It's easier to let go of Craig than he might have expected. Some of that is because Paul hasn't managed to let go of Alex at all, which brings its own guilt, but Paul is grateful for at least one loss that doesn't sting any more.

Paul starts working out again and this time paces himself, running around the neighborhood without pushing himself too hard or trying to constantly make life painful for himself.

When he gets back from his runs he makes dinner and then spends the evenings on the couch or on his bed or at the kitchen table writing with just Todd for company. The house still feels empty, but at least it's not unbearable anymore.

That said, the other downsides to being alone make themselves evident quickly as well. But it's not all bad; one night, he jerks off not to memory or fantasy of Craig or Alex or anyone else he's ever been with, but to straight-up porn. Paul realizes it's kind of awesome to get off and have it not be about anyone else for a change.

♦

Back on the lot, filming carries on with everyone else. Paul keeps an eye on social media and is amused by fan speculation about what a film crew for a show ostensibly set in D.C. is doing out in the desert. The fans know Alex is there too, which leads to other speculation Paul finds a lot less amusing.

The fans who assume Liam and Alex are dating are as dedicated in that belief now as they were before Christmas, and they're taking that theory to some strange conclusions. For instance, they assume that Liam is driving out to the desert every evening to visit Alex, which makes no sense whatsoever on any number of levels. Liam's on the lot and is spending at least half the time he's not working irritating Paul.

Late one evening he looks up from his desk in the writers' room to see Liam hanging in the doorway.

"Working. Out!" Paul snaps without bothering to make any inquiry as to what Liam wants. He's in no mood for conversation, and Liam usually responds best to simple and direct. But Liam doesn't leave.

"Hey, man, just wondering..." Liam swings a little on the doorframe. "Have you heard from him?"

"Yes," Paul says shortly. There have been a few texts back and forth since the phone call the night Alex got back to town. Paul braces himself for further questioning, but none is forthcoming.

Liam nods with satisfaction, and Paul wonders what the other man knows that he doesn't. Before he can work up the patience to ask, Liam turns on his heel and is gone.

43

Alex finally reaches that familiarity with Kelso that he can forget the trailers and equipment and everyone else and focus on the dunes and the mountains beyond them. The eight-year-old in him who spent summer wandering through woods and fields is endlessly fascinated by the sand, rocks and shifting shadows on the dunes. He desperately wants to explore.

Today at least, the rest of the crew doesn't share his calm or his joy. No one's been sleeping enough, things keep going wrong with the equipment, and tempers pop and simmer. None of it is helped by the heat, which skyrockets as the morning wears on.

Even Alex starts to feel shitty as he sweats through his costume and his sunblock in record time. By midmorning he's fighting a headache. The glare of the sun off the sand does not help with that. When he stands up from the crouch where Zach's been bent over some of his equipment the blood rushes disconcertingly out of his head.

Lunch makes him nauseated, and the headache doesn't get better. Eventually he throws up. He pushes aside the flutter of concern from the both the director and the safety monitor to insist that he's fine, that he can keep going, that people have worked through worse before. It's not untrue.

He goes back to do the take again and wishes his mouth was less dry. Even the thought of water makes his stomach unhappy. He also wishes the breeze was doing more to keep him cool.

◆

With two units shooting this week, it's less that Liam has more free time, and more that the *Fourth* schedule has been a little bit more flexible to accommodate everyone else's other interests. While most of the cast is either sleeping in or whining at their agents about wanting more, more, more – as if they have the time or stamina for it – Liam's doing a brunch for an arts education charity. There are fans outside, but then there always are, especially at stuff like this that easily features half a dozen people someone cares about.

Carly has begged off. Doing sound editing on commercials is generally way more nine-to-five than his job, and she's always been insistent about keeping it that way. Another random charity lunch decorating his arm isn't worth the later hours to her. Liam can understand that; he's always been more than happy to do whatever is necessary to make sure she gets the space for the life and career she wants. He feels honored that he gets to be a part of that.

Besides, as of two days ago she has an engagement ring on her finger and they haven't told anyone outside of their most immediate circle. Her attending an event with him without announcing it first would instigate a media feeding frenzy that is unlikely to be pleasant. And while Liam's usual impulse with anything that makes him happy is to share – Carly saying yes has made him happier than anything else ever – he's enjoying these few days of having their engagement belong just to them.

After the lunch, since he's not in any rush and the fans are pretty much the only people who don't find him too excitable, Liam stops to chat. He finds it strange when people want him to talk to their smartphones as opposed to them.

There are lots of awkward questions which generally fall into three categories: *Marry me, marry Alex*, and inappropriate requests for various forms of physical contact. While Liam has no objection to physical contact in principle, getting involved with fans is a bad idea. And given what happened between him and Alex, all those questions cut a little too close to the bone.

Somehow, in one of those awful moments when all the questions hit at once, Liam manages to get everyone to shut up for half a second. Later, he'll wonder if this was the gift of big hand gestures or simple bad luck.

"Three things, which should cover all the questions," he says into the nearest cellphone camera. "One, Alex is a dear and awesome friend and that's it. Don't badger him about it, 'cause it pisses him off, and I hate when he's mad at me. Two, but yes, I also like boys – no, no, no shut up and let me finish – I am only telling you this because, three, Carly and I got engaged two days ago. And she likes me better when I'm not asking her to keep my secrets."

With that Liam smiles smugly, waves, and tells everyone to have a beautiful day, before getting into the waiting car. It only takes about five minutes before he starts wondering if that was one of his really bad ideas that's going to cause Victor to yell. Then he realizes he should probably call his publicist. Ten seconds later, as he's still trying to figure out the appropriate chain of next events, his phone starts ringing and doesn't stop.

♦

The day on set is fairly quiet. Between meetings Victor is in his office going over plans for *Fourth's* next cycle when his phone goes off. The voice on the other end of the line is concerned, and after a few sharp questions Victor asks several more, all worried.

It's the A.D. on location in Kelso. Alex collapsed during filming, and is being taken to the hospital now. Heat stroke, is the unconfirmed verdict. His temperature had been far too high and he wasn't sweating. Whatever the case, his condition is definitely not anything to be fucked around with and is scary as hell for everyone involved.

Victor knows he'll react later – the thought of anything happening to any of his people is devastating. The thought of it being Alex, who never even asked for this life, is worse. But an emotional response now would be self-indulgent; too many people are relying on him. There's delegation to do, because a principal getting rushed to the hospital from set disrupts everything. There's insurance to deal with, because even if today is all they lose in filming time that's still a day gone. And there are calls to be made. Alex's emergency contact is his mother.

Victor calls her himself, because fuck policy. She takes the news that her son is hospitalized with the sort of calm crisis management that tells Victor as much about Alex as it does about her. Victor lets her know what's going on as best he can and gives her the contact information for the hospital. There's press to yell at too. Somehow this has gotten out instantly – Victor wonders darkly if the EMTs are on Twitter – and no, heat stroke is not a euphemism for drugs or a nervous breakdown; it's fucking hot in the desert, and Alex has always pushed himself hard.

When everything that needs to be dealt with immediately has been dealt with, Victor heads downstairs to the writers' room. Word spreads fast and he wants to get to Paul before anyone else does. Paul deserves to know what's going on, but Victor also knows he's going to want to do something stupid about it, and he would prefer to head that off.

While he's en route, his phone goes off again. His heart lurches badly at the ring. He answers, expecting a possibly awful update on Alex. Instead, his assistant informs him that Liam has chosen this day and hour to suddenly come out of the closet and that it's all over Twitter.

It is some magic of Alex, Victor thinks, that everything he touches seems to explode all at once.

His instructions to his assistant are simple: Get Liam on the phone, be gentle with him, tell him to expect a call from Victor in fifteen minutes and do *nothing* in the meantime.

"Tell him I'm not pissed," Victor says before he hangs up. Worried, yes; this wasn't planned, and he wants to make sure Liam is okay. But angry? Not in the least. Liam finding his own way is his favorite thing in the world.

When he gets to the writer's room and shares the news, he nearly has to staple Paul to his chair to keep him from going to the hospital to be with Alex.

"Why can't I go?" Paul sounds closer to anger about it than Victor has ever heard him about anything.

"Alex is fine," Victor tells him firmly. "He's stable; he's recovering; and he needs rest. You are not restful. I will take the blame for you not being there if he's pissed, and I will keep you updated myself, but you are to stay here, and then you are not to get into your car tonight except to go home. Do you understand me?"

Paul blanches a little at the word *stable*. Victor can't blame him. It's supposed to be a good word, but all it does is remind people how anyone it gets applied to very recently wasn't.

Victor puts a hand on Paul's arm. "He's going to be fine."

Paul nods rapidly. This is why Victor has to stay calm. If he isn't calm, he can't force his people to be.

"Stay by your phone," Victor tells him, already on his way out the door. "I'll call you as soon as I can."

♦

Victor waits to go to the hospital until that evening. As much as his impulse is to get to Alex first, there's not much he can do but get in the way. Once he knows he's no longer packed in ice, he heads to the set first to see how people are and talk to the A.D. and the safety captain. On top of everything else they'll have to deal with the union, and Victor wants to make sure no one was pushing Alex but Alex before that particular headache begins.

At one point he finds himself yelling at everyone for being afraid of him before he thanks them for being so damn excellent at doing everything right in a terrible situation. Before he goes, he exhorts everyone to check the internet at their earliest possible convenience, so they can know just how bizarre this day has been. It's not quite gallows humor, since everything is going to be okay, but it's close.

Alex is asleep when Victor gets to his room at the hospital. He looks like shit and fragile in a way that he usually doesn't. Then again, everyone looks like shit when they're in a hospital bed, and there's something to be said for situation normal.

Eventually, after Victor stares at him for fifteen minutes, Alex's eyelids flutter open.

"Could you feel me staring at you?" Victor asks.

Alex huffs a sound that might be a laugh but might be pain. Victor takes it as invitation to pull a chair over to the bed and sit down.

"Are you pissed?" Alex asks. He doesn't sound scared so much as faintly amused.

"No. We have good insurance. And you're not dead. If I'm pissed, it's only a little at myself."

"Then why are you here?" Alex asks.

181

"Because someone should be, and I already told Paul no. Also Liam."

"Why?"

"Because this one is my job. I gave you this life, and if you ever need help because of it, I have to be the first and last person in line to provide it. Also because Paul is still working on seeing you as an adult, and I know Liam drives you bugfuck."

Alex laughs, but it's weak and scratchy. "I feel bad about that."

"Don't. In either case." Victor reaches towards Alex briefly, but pulls back before touching him. "Are you up to talking for a little bit?"

Alex nods, and as much as his eyes don't quite want to focus or stay open – Victor knows that's the muscle relaxants to stop the shivering that went with the ice – there's a hint of trepidation there now.

"Good. So, there's some other stuff going on, that I'd rather you know about sooner than later."

"Okay?" Alex says.

"Liam came out today."

"What?" Alex tries to sit up, but his muscles won't support him. Victor does touch him then – he grabs Alex's shoulders, gently, and presses him back to the bed.

"To the entire internet via a random fan's smartphone. Don't worry, he's implicated exactly no one but Carly, to whom he is now engaged, by the way."

"Tell me I'm hallucinating."

"Would that make it better?" Victor asks. He's always been fond of Alex, but never so much as now.

"No, but…that's an insane choice."

"A little bit, yes."

"What was he thinking?"

"That he wants to be a good man. Can you imagine how I feel?" Victor feels as exhausted as Alex looks. The admission is nothing Alex could be expecting, so he makes his voice quiet, kind, and private.

"I can't answer that," Alex says.

"I know you know," Victor says, enjoying confirming, in the midst of all this, what are probably some of Alex's worst fears.

"Proud," Alex says.

Victor smiles. Alex, his best student, has found the only possible answer. He puts a hand to Alex's hair and leans forward in his chair to kiss him on the forehead. "And that's why I'm not pissed at you."

<h1 style="text-align:center">44</h1>

Once Alex has slept for approximately a year he feels less like death. As a bonus, they finally let him have his phone back. There are more or less a million things on it to check, and he's bored enough to tackle at least the important ones first. He happily takes the excuse of heat stroke and hospital to ignore the rest.

He calls his mom and spends a blissful twenty minutes being chatted to; it's exactly the comfort that he wants right now.

Gemma, worried, offers to come visit.

He texts back, *Thanks, but I'm exhausted. And completely fine. I'll see you on Thursday.* Talking on the phone is one thing, but he's not up to people yet. He's being kept for observation another night because apparently one of the perks of fame is more hospital food.

Liam he texts too. *Congrats on the engagement. And everything else.* Alex means it. Deeply. But that doesn't mean it doesn't also hurt on multiple fronts, not that these things have happened, but that he has, once again, been the last to know.

Paul, he calls.

"Hi," he says, a little sheepishly, when Paul picks up.

"Jesus fucking Christ, Alex," Paul breathes.

"Yeah. Hi." Alex grins at the ceiling.

"How are you doing?"

"To be honest, I feel terrible. But they tell me that's normal."

Alex can hear Paul shoo Todd off his chair so he can sit down. "Should you be doing anything other than resting?"

"I'm bored."

"So am I, but I also want you to get better."

"I notice you're not telling me to sleep."

"I also notice you told me you feel like shit and why, but we can talk later," Paul says softly. "Look, Alex, the longer I stay on the line the more likely I am to say things I really shouldn't say, especially not over the phone. And I want to come see you, but Victor would kill me."

"Okay," Alex says easily. He recognizes that they're stepping into a dance with each other again. A little more cautiously than the first time, to be sure, but with no less intensity. "I get it. I just wanted to say hi."

"I'm glad you did."

♦

After he's made his phone calls, Alex has little to occupy him other than social media. He knows he should avoid it, since it's never given him anything but a headache even before he was in the hospital, but he can't look away from the train wreck of *Fourth* fandom as it unfolds. Liam has come out and has gotten engaged, to a woman no less; and Alex almost died. The internet has devolved into incoherent key mashing and internecine conspiracy theories. Also, a lot of people are angry.

Very, *very* angry. Angry at Liam for lying for so long while also being off the market. Angry at Carly Amadahy, alleged beard, for existing. Angry at *The Fourth Estate* and Victor for putting Alex at risk. And then angry at Alex and Liam by turns for upstaging each other with their ridiculously well-synchronized media crises. That part is nearly funny, except for how it's somewhat true. Everyone's PR teams are furious.

Predictably, the media the next day is a mess. Alex's publicist issues a statement for him. Victor issues statements about everything for everyone. Liam does a ridiculously lovely daytime talk show interview: Focused and kind and as straightforward as he can be on the burdens his choices have placed on others.

Alex watches it all from his hospital bed. The interview goes a long way towards easing whatever regrets he's been nursing about his affair with Liam, no matter how complicated it remains in his head. He doesn't like the idea of feeling so vulnerable to someone he's so not fucking ever again.

♦

Alex gets discharged at noon the next day and is relieved when only a few paparazzi are outside the hospital. Gemma, bless her, is there to pick him up and does not immediately throw herself at him in a rib-crushing hug, for which he is grateful.

"I need a Big Mac or I'm going to die," he says as soon as he's waved to the photogs before sliding into Gemma's car. Hospital food is horrific and he finally feels like he wants to eat again besides.

She cackles and throws his hat at him.

He spends the rest of the day drinking Gatorade and sleeping off the last of the horrible either in his room or on the couch that they desperately need to replace. He finally snaps at Gemma to stop hovering the eighth time she checks in on him, and they both enjoy the quarter hour of bickering that follows. After, they look at furniture websites while leaning against each other companionably. Alex emails Yancy to ask how necessary it really is to see furniture in person before purchase.

Ultimately, in the absence of much else to do, and with a wealth of new data that makes him finally realize that he's not the only one who has ever found public life challenging, Alex also spends a lot of time thinking. He wants Paul, he has no doubt about that. But he also wants a life that he chose for himself, not one that he stumbled into by accident or magic. And if he's going to get it, he needs to start making some serious, thoughtful decisions.

The scope of what he's trying to achieve is frightening. The chance of failure is non-negligible. But Alex is determined.

45

For Paul, at work, everything is strange all over. The offices have to churn through all of the rescheduling necessary in the wake of a three-day delay in second unit filming. Not to mention the general insanity that Liam can't seem to stop trailing in his wake. Every time it feels like the world has adjusted, another country is heard from.

At one point a particularly odious televangelist escaped from the eighties suggests *The Fourth Estate* is forcibly turning its stars gay. Victor thinks it's hilarious, but Paul finds himself angry and unsettled. Liam, meanwhile, wants life to go back to normal. Paul feels a little bad for him. He clearly had no idea his admission would be this disruptive for this many people for more than twenty-four hours.

It's a relief when the weekend finally comes, and Paul skips his run to sleep obscenely late on Saturday. It's easier to stay in bed than get up and be tempted to do things. Like call Alex, or go visit him. They're working toward something, slowly but surely, and Paul can't get ahead of himself. If he does, he's afraid he'll break the spell and lose everything.

He only gets out of bed when hunger makes further sleep impossible. He's in the kitchen, trying to decide what to make for lunch that requires the least possible amount of effort, when there's a knock at the door.

"Wanna hear a story?" Alex says, when he opens it.

Paul stares at him. He's got a new hat on and his messenger bag slung over his shoulder. Paul realizes he's remembered every freckle on his face perfectly.

"I know the adult thing to do would have been to call, but I decided I didn't care," Alex says.

Paul knows he should be more measured but after the last few days he no longer cares. He takes Alex's face in his hands and kisses him as hard and with as much tongue as possible. Alex isn't startled at all and doesn't seem to care that they're doing this in Paul's open doorway in broad daylight. His feet aren't even over the threshold of the house, but on the concrete just outside.

Alex gasps as the kiss breaks only enough for Paul to turn his attention to mouthing at his jaw. He pushes Paul back slightly. "Can we fuck and then talk?"

"We should – "

"We should do a lot of things." Alex walks Paul backwards into the house. "But can we have this? No matter what happens?"

A month ago, or even a week ago, Paul would have told Alex he was being immature. That he was using sex to solve problems that were much bigger than he realized. But a lot has happened since then. From the sad, quiet closure of the final ending with Craig to Liam's public admission and Alex's scare in the desert, it seems like the most reasonable, elegant, and mature request in the world. They've earned this.

"Yeah." Paul stands aside and Alex slips past him, surreptitiously waving to the cat as they head upstairs.

The sex isn't as frantic or as complicated as it could be. Alex asks if he has condoms as opposed to rifling through his drawers. Paul's heart aches that he no longer feels completely at home in this room. He also doesn't help Paul undress or give Paul any chance to undress him. His whole attitude is almost clinical until he kicks aside his socks and finally looks at Paul.

They devour each other. Paul has never seen the Alex who backs him onto his bed before. He has all the power of his anger and the intensity of the gaze that he usually gives the camera. But Alex isn't unhappy and his eyes are only for Paul.

Alex sinks down onto his cock with a relieved little laugh. Paul chastises himself for assuming Alex's earlier murmur of "I'm going to fuck you now" had meant something else. Although that too is definitely on his to-do list, now that they can, apparently, have this again. The second Alex starts to move, that thought, and every other thought Paul has ever had, is gone.

Somewhere in the heat of it, when his hands are tight around Alex's hips helping to slam him down around his dick over and over, Paul asks, "Why are we so good at everything?"

"Because I'm awesome," Alex manages.

Paul is delighted by the teasing look he gets and by the loveliness of laughing again in bed with this boy who can be so funny but, with the rest of the world at least, is usually too sharp for joy.

"The thing is," he says, getting his hands under Alex's thighs and hitching his legs further up the bed, "So am I."

Alex keens.

Paul makes soothing noises at him even as he fucks up into him, Alex fists his hands hard into Paul's hair and stares him down. "Not here to be soothed," he says.

"Yeah?"

"Yeah," Alex says, punctuating the sentiment by biting at Paul's lower lip.

"Does that mean I get to fuck you into the mattress?"

"Break the fucking bed."

Paul damn well tries. He has wanted this, in this way, for so long. Alex being delighted and challenging is completely enchanting. Paul comes when Alex grabs his own dick with both hands and jerks himself.

"Jesus Christ, let go already," Paul growls as he starts to come back to himself. It's enough to do the trick.

♦

Alex grabs Paul's hand, pulls him down to lie facing him, and presses their foreheads together. For the first time since he got on the plane to fly to D.C., he feels like he can breathe. He knows that's largely endorphins talking; not all the time without Paul has been bad. Indeed, a lot of it was necessary. But the relief of being here in Paul's arms is overwhelming. There's no guarantee of this working in the long run, Alex knows enough to be sure of that, but he also knows enough now to savor this moment for what it is.

Paul tangles their fingers and kisses the back of Alex's hand. "I missed you."

"Yeah," Alex breathes. "I missed you too."

"So can I ask why?"

Alex twists onto his back, looks at the ceiling for a moment, then makes himself look back at Paul. They've come this far, and they need to have this conversation, but he's still buzzing with afterglow and wishes they could put it off just a little longer. But that's not the adult thing to do and he wants so badly to get it right this time. He doesn't say anything right away.

Paul squeezes his hand. "Hey," he says gently. "It's me."

"How do you do that?" Alex searches Paul's face.

"Do what?"

"Fuck me like that and then hold me. Like this," he says. It's not a question he could have asked – or an admission he could have made – three months ago. But all sorts of things feel possible now that didn't before.

Paul grins. "Because we're amazing at everything."

"It's been a long week," Alex says eventually, when the silence stretches out. Apparently Paul is willing to wait for an answer. Alex is grateful. "And yet somehow I ended up with a lot of time on my hands. After the desert, and then after Liam...."

"How did you hear about that, by the way?"

Alex rubs a thumb over the back of Paul's hand. "Victor showed up at the hospital. I was still really out of it. I woke up, and there he was hovering by my bed like the goddamn angel of death. It was slightly terrifying," he says sheepishly.

"Well, there's a way to get the news," Paul says.

"Yeah. He was...he was very human too in that moment. I can't imagine what that day was for him." Alex feels ill at ease talking about his new found – and likely temporary – empathy for Victor. He worries Paul will tease him about it, but the other man remains silent.

"Liam was very brave," Alex finally says. "And he did something he's never wanted to do because he wanted something else more. It made me think about what I could get, if I bent a little."

"Alex...."

"Shhhh, let me finish," Alex says gently, even as has to look away from Paul in order to be able to continue. "My life is messed up and it's never as much in my control as I need it to be. I'm twenty-one and new at everything. You noticed that. You didn't always react to that the way I wanted you to, but you weren't wrong."

He is lightened by the admission, but he still feels frightened of whatever comes next. Despite what he said to Paul on his doorstep, he doesn't want only this. He wants so much more.

"You've changed. Since you got back. And I don't mean the sex thing," Paul says, his voice quiet and close. "You clearly have a plan. And I never want to let you out of my sight again,"

Alex tries not to be smug, but the praise for his focus and Paul's need for him is everything he's wanted to hear since he stormed out of this house all those weeks ago. "You're not the same either," Alex says thoughtfully. "I've learned a lot."

"It's been a long winter," Paul says with a weariness Alex feels certain they've both earned. "I want you to know. I adore you, you drive me crazy, and if we're having the conversation I think we're having, you need to know how very high the stakes are. Because I can't do anything else. It's not in me."

Alex nods, letting the thought settle. "I know." He is overwhelmed by Paul's declarations, spoken and not, but, like much else with this man, so good. Still, Alex has no intention of letting this conversation linger only on his own wounds. "You have problems too, and I can't be the fix for them. You've been holding yourself back, and I have no idea why."

"Victor asked me the same thing, you know."

"Did he?" Alex asks, vindicated and amused.

"Yeah."

"What did you tell him?"

"That I was scared of turning into him."

Alex giggles. Victor is a laser. Paul is a softer light, still electronic but more diffuse. "I don't think that's possible."

"I'm scared of getting what I want." Paul says abruptly.

"Why?" Alex is baffled.

"Afraid of losing what I have, I guess."

Alex frowns. "You can't live like that, Paul."

"You are not, as you've so eloquently stated, the only one with problems. And I know you know that, but – I can't always be perfect for you. It's not fair to me for you expect it. But, fuck, I need you to talk to me."

"I'm learning how," Alex says seriously. He knows that logistics, not feelings, are the limiting factor here, and that he owes Paul all the effort he can give.

"I'm noticing."

Alex squeezes Paul's hand. "We're both fucked up. But I want you, and I want to make this work. I think that means I'm willing to be the adult I'm not ready to be, if you can be the ambitious adult I know you already are. Because I'm going to take over the world whether I want to or not, apparently."

"You want to," Paul says, matter-of-factly.

"I do. If I'm going to pay the price for this life, I am going to make it everything I can. But I need you to stand on your own two feet beside me for it or you're going to blame me, and that won't end well."

They talk for hours. Most of it's about identifying problems instead of solving them, but it's a start. They break only to order Thai food, which they eat in bed.

"I'm not normally this much of a slob," Paul says at one point after accidentally dropping noodles on the duvet. "But you inspire me."

Alex laughs.

"I can see doing this forever," Paul admits with his mouth full.

"You know I won't always be this young, right?" Alex can't wait until that's true, but he also knows his youth and presumed inexperience is part of his appeal to some of his fans and, probably, some of his friends. "Things won't always be new, and I won't always be the one with less experience."

"That makes you more appealing. Not less."

"Oh. Okay," Alex says softly when he can find his voice again.

"See, not quite as fucked up as you think," Paul says. "Now, can we talk about how I like people and you hate them? Because that's going to be a thing."

Alex thinks that's a not a particularly fair assessment of a real problem, but it breaks the ice on what Alex knows is a very necessary public/private discussion.

He watches curiously as Paul fumbles for words to explain why things Alex has already decided are trivial and impossible matter so desperately for him. "It's like asking me not to write," Paul says. "If I don't, I can't see."

Alex refrains from asking what happens if Paul can't see – whatever the answer, he is not ready to hear it. Instead agrees to have dinner with Paul once a week out in the world. He reserves the right, however, to wear one of his hats.

"Was I supposed to assume you were coming back, when you left it?" Paul asks.

"I don't know," Alex says. "Maybe I just knew I wasn't going to be safe without you anyway."

46

The first time Paul goes over to Alex's house is a momentous occasion of an unexpected sort. Paul's never seen Alex's old apartment, though he'd been curious enough about the place Alex spent the rest of his life. Alex always seemed embarrassed about the place. But when he calls Paul and invites him over to his house now he sounds eager and excited.

Paul spends the whole drive over wondering what Alex's space is like and how he'll fit into it.

When Alex answers the door, smiling shyly, Paul forgets about everything but him. When Alex pulls him across the threshold and kisses him before the door is even closed he laughs with astonishment.

Gemma is perched on a barstool in the kitchen looking like a particularly protective mother bird. Paul met Gemma back when Alex had taken her to visit the set, but once they had started hooking up Paul and Alex had been too wrapped up in each other to spend time with anyone's friends beyond those few awkward group brunches.

Paul turns on all of his charm for her, and is pleased to see her soften.

"He's dreamy," she hisses, not quietly at all, as she sweeps past them on the way to her part of the house. "Well done."

"Gemma!" Alex protests, his cheeks flaming with embarrassment. Gemma laughs at him.

"Are you saying I'm not dreamy?" Paul asks once she's gone.

Alex's cheeks are still scarlet. "I hate both of you."

Upstairs, Paul steps into Alex's room and instantly feels like he belongs there. He looks around for a moment, then realizes Alex is still hovering in the doorway. Paul gives him a confused look.

"What are you doing?" Paul asks.

"Looking at you in my space."

"Possessive." Paul chuckles and lures Alex in, snaking an arm around his waist.

Alex doesn't budge, but he does smile. "After all the time I've spent in yours, it seems fair."

"Thank you for letting me in." Paul presses forward to kiss him. Alex finally steps forward to meet him halfway.

Paul winds his arm around Alex's waist and pushes the door closed, swings him around and pushes Alex towards the bed.

They try to be quiet because Gemma is still in the house, but Paul doesn't hesitate to kneel in front of Alex to help him out of his jeans, before crawling up the bed to hover over him.

Alex reaches an arm over to fish condoms out of the bedside table.

"You know," he says, while he helps Paul with one. "I've never had a guy in my own bed before."

"...Really," Paul says. After so long, it feels ridiculous to get confirmation of old suspicions that don't even matter anymore.

"Mhmm." Alex pets a hand over Paul's hip. "So no pressure or anything."

They're both laughing when Paul finally pushes into him. But then they go quiet.

Paul leans his forehead against Alex's, and Alex loops his arms around Paul's neck to hold him close. They move careful and slow and breathy quiet with an intensity that is so exquisite Paul has to kiss Alex to cover the sound of their soft whimpers.

◆

Tangled up on their sides, in the strange too-much mood that settles over them once Alex crawls back under the covers from cleaning them up, Paul asks, "Is this what it was like with him?"

He knows he shouldn't. But Paul's self-destructive tendencies have always gotten the better of him at the worst possible moments.

Alex goes very still. "Paul. Are you really asking me this?"

"You fucked him when you wouldn't fuck me."

"I was fucking you," Alex says, a little sharply, though he doesn't pull his hand away.

"You know what I mean," Paul says.

"Yes, and you're being gross. My choice to have sex with someone didn't obligate me to make sure that person was you." Alex hesitates, then says slowly, "The thing with Liam – when it was offered – was lower stakes than you and I were. Or are."

"Did doing that make it higher stakes?" Paul knows he's lucky Alex hasn't started yelling at him. But he needs to know. Even if he shouldn't need to about any of this.

"No. No, that's not what made it higher stakes."

"Alex."

"Paul?"

Paul tries to smile, but it's strained. Sometimes it still feels like every time he thinks that Alex is going to talk to him, he stops abruptly. "Come on, give me something here."

"I don't know what to say to you. I feel like the things that will make you feel better aren't true."

"I should worry about it less than I am," Paul admits.

"Yes. You should." Alex squeezes his hand a little too tightly.

He's quiet for a long time, and Paul thinks that's all he's going to say. He is at least grateful that Alex isn't yelling when he finally speaks again, rubbing his thumb along the side of Paul's wrist.

"I know it's hard for you. God, it isn't easy for me. I'm still trying to learn how to talk about it." Alex takes a breath and flicks his eyes up to Paul's. He holds his gaze intently. "Most relevant to you," Alex says quietly, "it is a thing that is profoundly over. But I'm grateful for it. It was important to me. And it was important to him too, I think. I need you to respect that."

As heart wrenching as what Alex is – and is not – telling him is, there's a quiet certitude to it that somehow neutralizes his fear in a way nothing else has managed to yet. His words echo what Liam has said to him on the matter. Even if Paul doesn't know if he'll ever be able to understand exactly what happened between them, he knows something about the value of experiences as mementos.

47

Liam isn't sure if Alex is avoiding him in the days leading up to filming James and Zach's big reunion for actorly reasons or because there's going to be drama about their history and Paul's reaction to it. Liam refrains from working too hard to figure it out, only because there's not much he can do; their work schedules aren't meshing at all right now. The logistics of it alone are incredibly odd.

The set isn't closed because it's just a kiss, but people are quieter than usual, something which seems to come from Alex, who has dragged his chair into a corner and jammed his headphones into his ears. Even Liam can read the clear *do not approach* of Alex's body language, and it's not something that changes once they're in front of the director and the camera.

The moment they start rolling, as Alex's eyes meet his for the first time that day, he understands. This is the work, and sometimes, you have to use your fucked up life to get it done. Zach and James are never anything but right with each other, even when things are terrible and full of fear.

"The guy in my head is in love with the guy in your head," Alex says without ceremony when Liam drops down next to him at lunch.

"Awesome," Liam says. He can't imagine Alex wants to hear more: About how monogamy is a myth; about how everyone, not just actors, are a thousand different people; about how the best things in life always hurt just a little, and that's how you know they're real. Alex relies on him to be happy and blithe, and today, Liam can provide.

48

Of their many agreements over the next several weeks – Alex wonders sometimes if he should go to law school when the world changes again and he isn't famous anymore – doing things in the world with Paul is the hardest. The difficulty doesn't stem from Alex having issues. The fact is that Los Angeles is a legitimate pain in the ass. Fan interactions feel easier with Paul by his side, but also, his boyfriend has a hashtag. They don't even go to that sushi place that often, but as far as the world is concerned Paul is #sushiguy. No one finds this funnier than Carly.

The brunch crew, which Alex returns to tentatively, is also amused. Alex even smiles when Brian starts crowing about *stories of Paul's heterosexual past* the day after he makes the mistake of tweeting a picture of the whole group. It finds its way to the fans via somebody's ex's sister's kid's teenaged babysitter. The barrage of internet communications Alex receives in response runs the gamut from bizarre to hilarious, and they're made better by Paul's recitation of the greatest hits the following week.

A few days later, Margaret utters the dreaded words, *We need to talk*. Apparently Paul now merits his own strategy, or at least the discussion of one.

"I don't want to keep him secret," Alex says to her. "I just want to keep him mine."

Ultimately the plan amounts to little more than refusing media questions on the matter and strategically holding hands in public so that people get the message.

The whole thing makes Alex grind his teeth. He still, and probably always will, resent a public that thinks it has any right to any part of his story, but Paul's pleased for how the plan works out in his favor. Which helps. Alex doesn't want to take away Paul's ridiculous adolescent joy about finally being able to show the world he has a boyfriend. Besides, it's a thing he's wanted for a long time, too.

♦

In June they start talking about living together. It's way too soon; they've only been back together for six months. But they've gotten in the habit of negotiating their way through questions and potential obstacles. There seems to be no need to stop now. Plus they're bad at spending time apart even living across the city from each other. At least Alex now has a place Paul can come to, and after he gets used to having someone else in his space he can't let go of it.

196

Gemma is a complicating factor, but in the end she makes things easier. The conversation is a strange one. Alex sits on the chair across the living room from her like nothing in their life has changed, telling her what he and Paul had discussed the night before and asking if she'd consider it.

Finally Gemma asks, "You want to know if I mind moving to Paul's house so you can shack up with your boyfriend here and be disgustingly domestic together?"

"Pretty much."

Gemma frowns as she considers it. "Do I get the cat?"

"No. The cat comes with Paul."

More seriously, Gemma asks, "Are we going to have some official rent deal written on paper, or is this all going to be verbal so you can screw me over at some future point?"

"I really hope you know I would never screw you over." Alex knows he's often a shitty friend with a sharp tongue, but cruel he is not. Still, trying harder and being kinder will also need to be a part of his ongoing attempts to grow up.

"One *hopes*, but we should still make it official."

"That's fair." Compared to the papers he signed for *Fourth*, this will be easy.

Gemma squeals and launches herself at Alex. "Then of course! But you're helping me move."

"I'm not helping you do shit. We're hiring people. Hopefully people who are hot this time and that we can ogle."

"That totally counts as helping."

49

Paul sits at the Alex's kitchen island looking over the last details of the pilot pitch he's been working on forever. He started working on this pitch at the kitchen table of his old house, the one he used to share with Craig. Alex's house is bigger than that house was and newer. The kitchen is brighter, even with late afternoon shadows stretching over the backyard and into the canyon behind the house. Some of the appliances on the counters came with Paul. Some are new. Todd, who acceded to the change of habitation with the grudging acquiescence of a benign dictator, sits in front of the sliding door that leads out to the deck. His tail twitches as he watches a bird alight on the railing.

Alex sits on the other side of the kitchen island, his own laptop open in front of him. He's pretending to catch up on the news, but every time Paul looks up, Alex's eyes are fixed on him.

Finally Paul puts the binder-clipped packaged in his bag for tomorrow. Alex slides off his stool, kisses Paul fiercely, and takes him to bed.

In the morning, Paul goes to Victor.

"Can we talk?" Paul asks, standing in the doorway of Victor's office. Whenever he imagined this moment in the past, he thought he'd feel nervous. But this is a moment that's been a long time coming. He knows Victor's been waiting for him to do this. What's more, Paul wants this.

Victor waves him in.

"Okay." Paul lays out his timeline for an exit – he's committed to the current cycle and will definitely see it through – but after that…. Victor watches him through it all with hawk-eyed fascination.

"I've been loyal, and I've done my time." Paul pushes the treatment and pilot script across the desk at Victor. It's ballsy, to spell out the plan before Victor has even looked at his work. But this is the time to go all in. "And I've written this. So help me get a pilot ordered and get the hell out of here."

Victor sits back in his chair and regards Paul for a long moment. Then he smiles. "It's about time. Should I thank Alex for putting you up to this?"

"No. He just reminded me to get around to doing what I've been meaning to do all along. Not everyone has his luck. Not everyone wants it. So this is me asking."

"You didn't ask," Victor notes. "You told. But this is still me saying yes. We'l make it happen." He reaches for the package. "I'm proud of you, Paul. Both of you."

50

In July Alex finishes filming for the summer cycle of *Fourth*, and Paul finishes writing for it forever.

They don't have much time to relax, though. Paul's house needs to be packed up so Gemma can move in and Paul and Alex can finally, officially live together. The process takes longer than moving out of Alex's old apartment did. Paul had a life there for years before Alex was even in L.A. He owns furniture that deserves a fate other than burning.

"I'm going to miss this place," Paul says, looking around at his room that's been reduced to boxes and a disassembled bed frame. Afternoon light streams through the windows unfiltered by curtains and paints yellow rectangles on the floor. The room seems oddly smaller now, the way rooms do when they're empty and stripped of all the equipment of life they once held. Paul hasn't seen it like this since he first moved in, years ago. There will be other houses, of course, and hopefully with Alex, but this is the first one that Paul owned himself. The prospect of leaving is unavoidably bittersweet.

"Mm." Alex says from where he's sitting cross-legged on the floor, sorting screws. "You can always come back and visit." His shorts are dusty, and there's a smudge of dirt or grease or something on his cheek. He's impossibly beautiful.

"It won't be the same," Paul says. It comes out sadder than he means it to.

Alex looks up at him, his dark eyes squinted against the sunbeam inching its way over him. "What's it like? To leave a place you know you'll miss?"

Paul considers it. Not only the question, but the idea that, in Alex's mind at least, everywhere he goes is better and makes him happier than where he's been. His heart gives a little flutter of joy that he gets to be a part of Alex's better future.

"It hurts a little," Paul admits. "But not as much as it could."

"Why's that?"

Paul crosses to where he's sitting and crouches in front of him. When Alex gives him a confused look, Paul can't help but kiss him. "Because my favorite thing about it is coming with me."

Doves

Love in Los Angeles Book 2

1

Paul has asked him, more than once, if climbing feels like flying. "No," Alex always tells him. "It feels like being a very tiny bug on a very big rock. And a lot like almost falling."

"Please don't fall."

"The entire point is to not."

This high up it doesn't feel like bugs or falling. It feels like rock and his ropes and the wind in his hair, even if Paul will yell at him again for not wearing a helmet.

He slips, just a little, and his palm stings on stone. One more scrape for Zach, his character. Victor will be thrilled. For Alex, it's a reminder that he wasn't quite careful enough. For Victor, it's pain for one of his beautiful things, which, as a rule, he delights in. It's a mark of how long Alex has had this impossible life that Victor's inevitable reaction doesn't even seem that fucked up anymore.

When he gets back to the ground there will be a dozen things to worry about, from the *Fourth Estate* renewal that's taking longer than it should, to Paul's pilot that he's hoping anxiously for a pickup on, to the trip to South Carolina they're finally taking now that they both have time. But while Alex is up here, there's nothing to worry about except not falling. He happily puts all of his concentration into that and lets the rest of the world fade away.

On the descent, he startles a family of cliff swallows. Alex grins as they swoop away.

<h1 style="text-align:center">2</h1>

arry me?" Paul asks. Alex is at the bathroom sink brushing his teeth before bed.

"What?" Alex spits before he chokes on the toothpaste in horror. He meets Paul's eyes in the mirror.

"Marry me." Paul folds his arms over his chest. He's dressed for sleep, just in boxers, and his blonde hair is spiky from where he's been running his hands through it in frustration over a script all evening.

"Paul."

"Yes?"

"Nooooo."

Paul hides his disappointment well, but Alex is more horrified over the fact that Paul even asked the question than worried about his feelings. Paul laughs like it was all a joke and nudges Alex to the side so he can wash his face. Alex keeps staring at him. If he stares long enough, maybe Paul will explain whatever train of thought led them to this junction.

He doesn't disappoint. "Sorry," Paul says. He pats his face dry. "Momentarily overwhelmed by domestic bliss."

"Witty dialogue is not hiding the fact that you're crazy."

"I can only do my best."

They've been living together for almost a year now, and they've never talked about making their relationship legal. Alex doesn't see why they would. Paul's thirty-two, but Alex is only twenty-two. In a normal world, one in which Alex has never lived, he'd be finishing college this year. Instead he's the unexpected star of a hit TV drama, in a relationship with one of the show's writers. And he has no interest in carrying on this conversation further.

"You want to get un-overwhelmed and fuck me instead?" Alex asks.

"That's a sexy come-on."

"You asked me to marry you while I was brushing my teeth and we have a flight in eight hours. Go with it."

Paul laughs. "You're not too sore after your climb?"

"Sore, yes, 'too', no. Besides, I'm making you do all the work."

Paul swats Alex's ass as he walks past him out of the bathroom. Alex drops his toothbrush into the sink. When Paul does things like that he loses all ability to do anything but respond.

♦

Traveling with Paul is both more and less difficult than traveling on his own. Paul insulates him from everything invasive and unsettling about it, but they also draw attention when they're together. The world doesn't know Paul's face the way it knows Alex's...yet. Paul's been working hard to make himself a brand in preparation for what he hopes will be a long and successful run for *Winsome, AZ*, the show he's still waiting for the network's decision on. And while they don't do press about their relationship, it's no secret. Alone, Alex can be a guy who just sort of looks like J. Alex Cook. With Paul by his side, everyone knows exactly who they are.

In airports, people generally have the decency not to approach them. But the world is full of fans who are not as stealthy with their smartphone cameras as they would like to think; Alex has been considering starting a pinned map of airports from which blurry pictures of his sneakers have been posted.

He sits silently next to Paul as they wait for their plane to board. He has no interest in having yet another conversation that's going to be misheard and disseminated over the internet.

◆

On the plane, they're in coach, and Alex squeezes into his seat by the window as quickly as he can, pulling his beanie down until it covers his eyes. Paul smiles at the absurdity as he stows their carry-ons and takes the seat next to him. They'd bought the one on the aisle too, just to have a little more space and privacy, but there's no universe where Paul doesn't want to be pressed up against Alex as the plane takes off. When it leaves the ground, Alex twists in his seat so he can press his head into Paul's shoulder instead of against the window.

"Fuck, I'm in love with you," Paul whispers in his ear.

Alex snorts. By the time the seatbelt light goes off, he's asleep.

◆

Paul's mom greets them at the baggage claim. Alex hangs back, shy and unsure of his place, as she gathers Paul up in a hug.

Beth lets go of Paul and folds Alex into a hug, too. "It's good to see you."

"Good to see you too."

She pulls back and tweaks the beanie straight on his head. "How was your flight?"

Paul and his mom chat as they make their way to the exit. Alex stays quiet, content to let them catch up. Beth came out to L.A. last Christmas, when an avalanche of scheduling disasters made it impossible for them to get out of the city for the holiday. Alex likes her. But he's never been to South Carolina with Paul. He's glad to help get the suitcases into the trunk and then slide into the back seat to rest with his own thoughts.

Alex dozes through most of the two-hour drive, putting an occasional word into the conversation when Beth asks him something. He finally jerks out of a nap when they pull off the main road into the driveway.

Paul turns around in his seat, his smile gentle. "Hey there. You awake?"

"Mmm. Yeah." Alex rubs his eyes.

"Welcome to the family seat."

The driveway is long and winds up through a lawn somewhat in need of mowing to an old farm house. Weathered siding and faded shutters speak of old grandeur and care, but not much wealth. The verandah is the stuff of picture books, complete with ancient climbing roses. When the car pulls round the side to the garage, Alex can see a large vegetable garden in the back and rows of old fruit trees stretching down to woods.

When they get out of the car, the silence of the country evening is deep and peaceful. Alex takes a deep breath. The air here smells of earth and grass, and is deeply relaxing.

"So this is why you like it here so much," he says to Paul as Beth leads the way into the house.

Paul hesitates, just for an instant, before following. "I like it better with you here."

◆

Alex offers to help with dinner – strange places are always easier to manage if he can be busy – but Beth shoos them into chairs at the kitchen table and gets them iced tea. There's more chatting and catching up between Beth and Paul, and there's even more when Paul's sister Sarah and her son Jake arrive for the meal. Alex sits back and enjoys watching everyone else interact. One of his favorite things about this family is that they never treat him like a celebrity or indeed like anyone other than just Alex, Paul's boyfriend. Seeing them on their home turf is even more enjoyable. Everyone is relaxed and at ease. Even Paul, who Alex thinks of as pure L.A. in so many ways, softens somehow in this environment. Around his mother and sister his accent, which only comes through rarely at home, gets stronger.

"You boys sleep well," Beth says once Sarah and Jake have left for the evening. Night has settled outside, warm and filled with the soft hum of insects.

Paul leads the way upstairs to the guest room, which bears no particular personality of any resident, current or former. They could be at an inn as easily as at Paul's mother's house.

"Is this your old room?" Alex looks around the space and tries to imagine a teenage Paul living here. What sorts of trophies and decorations did he have? What books or magazines did he have on the shelves?

Paul, though, shakes his head slowly. "No. This was Sarah's. Mine's a craft room now."

There's something uncomfortable and weighty in Paul's voice that Alex can't figure out. Does Paul miss this house the way it was? Does he feel displaced?

"It's been a long time," Alex says.

Paul shakes his head. Alex isn't sure whether that's a no to his assumptions or a dismissal of the topic.

◆

The bed's narrower than what they have at home, and in the dark they're unavoidably pressed up against each other. In the southern spring night it's warm enough to be uncomfortable. Alex is just drifting off to sleep, finally, when Paul wanders a hand up his bare leg.

"Seriously?" Alex asks. He's hot and tired, and even if he weren't, they'd still be in Paul's mother's house. These walls aren't thick at all.

Paul hesitates but only a little. "Too long a day?"

"Too shared a roof."

"You can be quiet."

"Paul."

"Tell me no," Paul says.

"No." Alex is already getting hard. He's never been able to resist Paul. Or ever wanted to.

"Gonna be a long week," Paul points out.

Trust Paul to misunderstand. "I meant *no*, I'm not going to tell you no."

"Oh thank God." Paul has his hand around Alex's dick before he even finishes the phrase.

Despite his own objections about noise, Alex mewls as Paul starts to jerk him off. Embarrassed, he bites at the heel of his hand to stay quiet.

"No," Paul says gently. His free hand pulls Alex's away from his mouth and presses it up to the old wrought iron headboard. "Hold on, don't move, both hands."

Alex slides his other hand up his body to grab onto the headboard. He wants to tell Paul that he's being absurd, but Paul's hand on him – too steady, too slow – feels too amazing for him to be able to find any words. Whatever it is that he and Paul bring out in each other always seems to work exactly as it should.

He whimpers again. Paul shushes him.

"This isn't for you. This is for me," he reminds Alex. "And I want you to be quiet so I can hear you struggle."

The idea should piss Alex off, but it just turns him on more. He presses his eyes shut, panting and whispering "*Please*," over and over again. Paul admonishes him with shushing noises and the occasional slowing of the hand on his cock. Whatever this started as, it's rapidly getting edgier than what they usually do. Alex doesn't want it to stop. He arches and squirms on the bed.

"So fucking needy," Paul tells him. Alex is distantly aware that the bed creaks. Why did he think a handjob would be quieter than anything else?

"What if I just stopped?" Paul asks.

The thought is terrible. If Paul stops, he might actually explode. So Alex begs even harder.

♦

Alex comes abruptly and with little warning. He rides the orgasm out in Paul's slick hand, and the second he's done he's on his knees, rubbing Paul's dick across his face before sucking it into his mouth.

Paul's never been with anyone who stays down in the moment of sex quite the way Alex does. For most people, an orgasm breaks the spell, but Alex just doesn't seem to be wired like that. He goes somewhere small and obedient and doesn't always want to come back. Sometimes it's glorious. Sometimes it's concerning. Usually, it's a little bit of both.

"Holy shit," Paul says, not quiet at all. The words break the madness of what they're doing a little, and Alex laughs with his mouth full. Paul joins him until he's too overwhelmed by sensation to do anything other than grip Alex's hair too tightly and pant as he fucks up into his mouth.

When Paul comes – it doesn't take him long at all – Alex flops back onto the bed, his temple pressed to Paul's hip bone.

"So, I'm thinking we really need to practice this quiet thing," he says.

3

They sleep so late Beth has left for work by the time they make it downstairs for breakfast. As much as Alex likes her, he's relieved. After the sex last night with Paul, he wants time alone just for the two of them. Also, they were loud, and he wants to pretend Beth didn't hear them.

Paul asks if he wants the grand tour as they work their way through coffee and toast. Alex agrees eagerly.

His body clock is off, thanks to the time difference, and the sun is higher than he expects when they step outside. It's still morning, but won't be for much longer. The whole outdoors is like a fairytale compared to the Indiana of Alex's childhood. Yes, there were fields and sky there too, but the land always seemed tired and worn out. Here things are fresh and green. There's an energy to the plants and birdsong Alex can feel as they make their way down a path that leads into the woods. He scuffs happily through the layer of pine needles and leaves carpeting the path and tries to name the flowers growing up shyly under the ferns.

Eventually he becomes aware of a sound rising through the trees he can't identify. It might be a stream chattering through the woods, but he doesn't think so.

"What's that noise?" he asks as they hike up a little rise.

"That," Paul says. "Is the cricket barn." His voice is a little strained.

"Excuse me?"

"The cricket barn," Paul repeats. He nods toward what was probably a rather nice outbuilding in much better days when the farm was fully functional. "Do you want to go in?"

"No." He neither wants to ask, or know, why crickets need a barn. Is it a very small barn, or are they very large crickets? Either way, the answer isn't appealing.

"Come on." Paul tugs his hand to get Alex to follow. "You can't conceive of the profound fucked-upness of this place until you see what we're willing to do to hang on to what we've got."

"What do crickets have to do with anything?" The question is better than reminding Paul that he's from Indiana, and has plenty of experience doing fucked up things to survive.

Paul lets go of him to unlatch the door and push it open for them. Alex shoves his hand into his pocket, so he won't accidentally touch anything he really doesn't want to.

"We've got seven hundred acres," Paul says as he steps inside. "We can't farm it ourselves so we rent out most of it. The money from that covers most of the taxes, but there's never enough to keep the place up, *hence*," Paul sweeps a hand dramatically across the warm, unlit interior of the barn. "Crickets. We raise them and sell them for bait. It's not a bad enterprise."

Paul's standing inside the door, but Alex hovers on the threshold, looking into the ratcheting darkness and feeling any number of crawly things shiver up his spine. The smell is disturbing.

"This is insect hell."

"Actually, they're quite comfortable."

"Paul." Alex wants to have his back to a wall, but he also doesn't know what is *on* the wall, so he shifts uneasily from foot to foot.

"Told you it was fucked up."

"*Crickets?*"

"Why? What was your job as a kid?"

"Farm work is nothing like raising demons in the family barn." Objectively, the jobs Alex had in high school and even middle school were worse than working with crickets. But he doesn't want to talk about that. Also, that was then and the crickets are now.

Paul grins and ushers Alex back outside so he can, to Alex's relief, close and latch the door again.

"I didn't know your family was having trouble hanging on to the land," Alex says when they're far enough down the path that he doesn't keep looking over his shoulder for a following mass of tiny, too many-legged creatures. It's awkward, as always, to talk about wealth, or the lack thereof. But Paul had never mentioned anything about his family struggling.

Paul reaches for Alex's hand again. Alex takes it out of his pocket to let him have it. Out here with no one around, there's no reason not to, and Paul seems uneasy without the contact.

"It's not terrible. Just the way it's always been."

His fingers tighten around Alex's. Alex looks sideways at him. "What?"

"Speaking of things that are the way they've always been, I've got lunch today with my father."

"This is the father who wanted to disown you and from whom you're now estranged?" Alex should probably be more supportive than sarcastic, but, really?

"I've only got the one." Paul tries to joke.

"More than I have," Alex points out. "Seriously, though. Why?"

"It's what we do," Paul says. "For Mom's sake. Things aren't good between them, and I hate that I make that worse."

"That's not on you." Alex doesn't say *because your father is a homophobic asshole*, even if he is, because he doesn't know anything about the bonds between fathers and sons. Fucked up as this family situation is, he's working on trying to be more understanding.

Sometimes.

Paul shrugs. "I need to know that I can."

"Okay?" Alex says when Paul doesn't elaborate.

"Just to prove to myself that I can still be sane."

"Am I going with you?" Alex isn't sure if he should be freaked out by Paul's tone. He also doesn't know what being a good partner demands in this situation.

"Do you want to?" Paul asks.

"Is there a way I don't make that situation worse?"

"My beautiful, sharp, Hollywood boyfriend in the same room as my father?" Paul shakes his head. "Probably not."

"I would go," Alex says. He may be uneasy, but he's not afraid. He's faced worse than Paul's father, surely, in Indiana and in Hollywood.

"I know."

Alex squeezes his hand, and Paul squeezes back.

"He gave me a gun for my fifteenth birthday," Paul says abruptly.

"Yeah?"

"I wasn't very good at it. I'm not really into the whole shooting animals thing."

"So shoot cans." Alex shrugs. "It's a great way to deal with shit like your dad."

Paul shakes his head. "Yeah. Destroying things because I'm angry is not good choices for me."

"It's just blowing off steam."

"Maybe for you," Paul says darkly.

Alex looks over at him. Paul is occasionally cagey about things in his past but this is something different. "What's going on with you?"

Paul shrugs, looking helpless.

"Do you still have it?" Alex asks. It's been years since he's been near a gun. He's curious.

Paul nods. "One of the barns."

Maybe if Alex can touch it he can show Paul how not to be so uneasy around something he doesn't need to be. Maybe he can show himself, too. "Oh God, please tell me this is just a normal barn and not a demon insect barn," he tries to joke.

"Not more crickets, I swear."

Alex laughs. "Show me."

◆

"How do you know how to do this?" Paul asks. He had no idea Alex knew anything about guns. Above them in a tree, a mockingbird trills through its repertoire.

Alex has brought the gun out of the barn and is now sitting on the ground, examining it carefully. The sun glints in his hair, making the threads of gold in the red stand out. A morning outside has brought out even more of Alex's freckles. Paul marvels again at just how unspeakably lovely his boyfriend is.

"Indiana, Paul."

"Yeah, but –"

"My mom taught me," Alex says, his voice distracted but his hands on the gun sure like they are over his climbing equipment. "I had a lot of shit to get out of my system. It's relaxing."

"Okay," Paul says dubiously.

Alex asks if they have any earmuffs.

◆

When Paul gets back from the lunch, he can't find Alex anywhere in the house.

"Do you know where Alex went?" he asks his mom when he walks into the kitchen. She looks up from a recipe book spread out on the counter.

"Out back. With your old Winchester. I didn't think you'd mind."

She doesn't ask how Paul is, or how lunch went. She never does, even though Paul knows that she's glad he goes. Paul wonders if she's afraid of invoking the ghosts of all the things that have happened in this house if she speaks of them out loud.

"I'm going to go find him."

"Okay, dear."

She returns to her recipes, but Paul knows she's watching him leave and not without relief.

◆

Paul follows the measured sound of gunshots, disturbing only in their potential. Alex is on the old range that's been set up for generations, beer cans he must have raided from the recycle bin perched on an old stump. He doesn't hear Paul approach – he's got earmuffs clamped over his ears – but when he sees Paul out of his peripheral vision, he stops and pulls them off.

He doesn't ask anything, either, just looks at Paul.

"Keep going," Paul says. He picks a spot on the ground a safe way back to sit and watch.

Alex shrugs and re-positions the earmuffs before picking up the gun again.

It is profoundly strange, seeing his boyfriend use an instrument of destruction and use it well: Alex is very good at this. But it's not any stranger – and is far less awful – than lunch had been. So Paul lets himself relax watching Alex's movements and delighting in the fact that Alex never does stop surprising him.

He takes a few pictures, just to catch the moment – Alex's skill, and his profound *stillness* as he takes aim. Paul is aware that spending a week at his family's house is a prime opportunity to finally tell Alex things about his own history he probably should have shared years ago. But Alex, often ill at ease in other people's spaces, seems relaxed and happy. Paul doesn't want to risk ruining that just yet to tell him something he doesn't want to confess anyway.

♦

Eventually, Alex runs out of targets and decides that Paul has been sitting alone long enough. He packs the things up carefully, then flops down next to Paul on the grass and looks up at the sky.

"I had no idea you could do that," Paul tells him.

"Mmm. Not a thing to bring up in polite conversation. Especially not in Hollywood hippie society. But here?" he shrugs.

"You're really good."

Alex grins. "I am. I should be, even if I'm out of practice. I spent enough time shooting in high school."

"I got pictures," Paul holds the phone up so Alex can see. "Mind if I post one?"

"Knock yourself out," Alex says. He shuts his eyes.

Paul's not saying anything about lunch, which means either that Alex is supposed to ask or that Paul doesn't want to talk about it. Alex isn't going to press. If posting a random picture of him to Twitter is going to make Paul feel better about his day, he doesn't really mind.

He nods when Paul asks for his okay on a caption (*Look what Alex can do!*) and is glad when Paul slips his phone back into his pocket and then lies down next to him in the grass.

"Done," Paul says.

"Cool."

Paul's phone chimes insistently as people retweet it until he thumbs the setting over to turn off notifications. Alex rolls his eyes. Paul always forgets that things tend to get out of hand when he tweets anything that mentions him.

For a long while they drift, not saying anything and watching the clouds sail by overhead. There's so much quiet to enjoy.

"It's really beautiful out here," Alex says apropos of nothing.

"Yeah?"

"Yeah. Makes me wonder. Is Indiana beautiful, but I just can't see it?"

"Probably."

"It's not beautiful to you here, is it?" Alex asks, turning his head to look at him.

"Mmmm, no. It is. Just horror coexists. Like the crickets. And I worked hard to get out of here. Nearly didn't."

Alex hums slightly, leaving space for the conversation that he thinks is coming.

"I almost drowned in the lake when I was a kid," Paul offers.

"Didn't you know how to swim?" Alex asks.

"No, I dunno. Something grabbed my leg."

"What do you mean *something*?"

"I don't know... I mean, weeds or something. It was dumb. My sister pulled me out. I'm a better swimmer now, although you couldn't pay me to go back in there."

Paul chuckles a little, and it makes Alex fond. They're of a type to be amused by the really dumb shit that's happened to them, even if a lot of it isn't supposed to be for laughing.

"I know you want me to tell you what happened," Paul says. "And I will. I'm just – working up to it."

Alex wants to say something, but at that moment his phone chooses to ring. It's Liam. Alex frowns at it before ignoring it. He's on vacation, and that includes from colleagues he sees way too much of, no matter how close their friendship has become. If it's important, Liam will call back. Over and over again until he answers, because Liam, Alex's friend, kind-of ex, and co-star on *The Fourth Estate* is annoying that way.

"What does he want?" Paul asks.

"Didn't answer it, so don't know," Alex says. He chooses to not comment on what now seems to be an immovable bit of edginess from Paul around the way Liam is unavoidably enmeshed in their lives.

"Could be secret early renewal news," Paul offers.

Alex shrugs. Paul's not wrong. Liam is likely to hear things off-the-record from Victor long before there's official news, but Alex is fairly sure he'd only share if the word were bad. It's too nice a day – despite everything – to interrupt it with that. And if it were news about Paul's show, it wouldn't be coming from Liam anyway.

Paul takes a deep breath. "So, I didn't exactly try to kill myself," he says.

Alex feels dizzy. Of course Paul tells him he's not telling him something right now and then manages to wait only five minutes after effectively waiting years. If it weren't so strange and horrifying, the whole situation would be hilarious.

"What were you trying to do?" Alex asks, keeping his voice neutral.

"I was having a fight with my father. One of those free-ranging arguments where you want to run away but you're not fast enough and the fight goes from room to room."

Alex wants to say he has no idea what Paul means. His house growing up was so small, and he hasn't had a fight like that as an adult. But that's not true. Because that's exactly what the fight when they broke up was like, until Paul had said how angry he was instead of actually being angry.

"What was it about?"

"Nothing. Everything. Girls. The lack of girls. My grades. The thing with the pot. My best friend. My clothes. Church. I mean, anything and everything. My attitude, and Lord knows, he wasn't wrong about that." Paul gives a strange little chuckle.

"I feel like the next question is 'What did he do?'" Alex says carefully.

Paul shakes his head against the grass. "No. Valid assumption, but I was so angry, and I remember wanting to hurt him, except that didn't feel like enough? It wasn't good enough? So what if he hurt? People hurt all the time without knowing they're wrong, without having to live with the consequences of it."

Alex reaches for his hand, but Paul pulls away, folding his hands on his chest and breathing evenly.

"No. Let me get this out. We wound up in the kitchen, and I just kept asking, I mean screaming, really, at him about what he wanted from me. Like, there was this list of everything that was wrong with me, but there weren't any answers."

Alex snorts. "I love those fights," he says quietly. He knows what Paul means, even if he feels increasingly non-resident in his body as the story goes on.

"I pulled a knife out of the block in the kitchen and cut my own wrists," Paul says. "I didn't know how else to show him that I hated myself enough that he could stop talking. There was blood fucking everywhere."

Paul pauses for a long moment. Alex feels himself shrink in sheer horror. He struggles to breathe.

"So," Paul turns onto his side to look at Alex, "that's why I don't tell that story. It's a lot easier to let people think the obvious thing that's not exactly true. Also, can't recommend psychiatric inpatient treatment as an exciting summer vacation, but so it goes."

"*Paul.*" Alex feels small, and numb, and very far away. He wants to grab for Paul again to anchor him – or himself – but he's afraid to touch him. He isn't sure his hand won't go right through him, here in this beautiful, terrible place.

"I love you," he says instead, desperately, like the words can call Paul back from the past and have made this have not-happened. In what world is suicide not the worst option? His voice is shaky. The small bit of his brain that isn't obsessed with the horror of what Paul's just told him is shocked and unsettled by that. He didn't tell it to be shaky.

Paul tries to smile and doesn't quite manage. "Love you too."

Alex's phone goes off. Again.

"Are you fucking kidding me?" Alex mumbles.

"You should at least see who it is," Paul says. He's not wrong. They're both waiting on too much incredibly important news.

"Victor." Alex drops the phone between them. Dealing with his boss, let alone his casual menace, is the last thing he wants right now. But he's not going to pretend he doesn't want to know about the renewal.

"You should answer it," Paul says.

Alex feels sick. Because there's no world where this call – whatever it is – should be more important than what Paul's just told him. But this is *now* and therefore, it sort of is. With the unanswered call from Liam earlier, he does not have a good feeling about this.

"WHAT THE HELL DO YOU THINK YOU'RE DOING?" Victor yells into Alex's ear before he can even say hello.

"Being on vacation?" Alex says. He's confused and whatever delayed reaction he's having to Paul's story is just starting to kick in. He is not okay to deal with whatever this is.

"Do you have any idea how crazy you and a gun have made the internet?" Victor says, the decibel level only barely reduced.

"Everything I do makes the internet crazy."

"My God, Alex. I am in the middle of some terrible fucking negotiations AND YOU'VE JUST SINGLE-HANDEDLY REIGNITED AMERICA'S GUN CONTROL DEBATE."

"I sort of doubt that." Alex is still trying to catch up. "And Paul tweeted it."

"You two are *IDIOTS.*"

"Victor," Alex snaps to get his attention. "Your timing is not great. What can either of us do right now, and then we can all touch base later?" Alex reaches for Paul, who's looking at him with a ridiculous amount of pride in the middle of all this bullshit and misery.

Victor, of course, doesn't have an answer other than a list of things Alex and Paul shouldn't do next. The whole thing is, frankly, a little crazy. Alex feels bad for him – a little. Victor views himself as responsible for every one of the hundreds of people that work on *Fourth* and with its fate up in the air, that has to be hard.

"Is there anything else I can do?" he says once Victor has run out of steam.

"Yes. Call Liam back. Like a good little New York liberal, he's completely freaked out."

"You're fucking kidding me," Alex blurts before he can help himself.

"I am not. We will touch base later," Victor says threateningly before the line clicks closed.

Alex stares at the phone in his hand.

"Not good news?" Paul hazards.

"Apparently America doesn't like its darling little gay to have a gun."

"Technically, it's my gun."

"I think that makes it worse," Alex rolls his eyes as he scrolls to Liam's number.

Liam picks up immediately. "Alex? What are you doing?"

It's an odd repetition of Victor's initial reaction, except much quieter and less angry.

"I'm hanging out with Paul. How are you?"

"The internet says you have a gun." Liam sounds aggrieved.

"The internet is incensed about things that are not its business."

"Why do you have a gun?"

Alex rolls his eyes. "Liam. The internet being inappropriate is nothing new. This doesn't actually affect you. What the hell is your problem?"

Liam babbles his way through a paragraph of a response that is, at best, incoherent. Whatever has him upset, it's more than a principled, political objection to firearms. Yet it provides Alex no information he can use to soothe whatever inexplicable anxieties have cropped up in Liam's head.

"Okay, I don't really know what to say to that," Alex says when Liam finally winds down. "What do you need from me?"

"Can we hang out when you're back in town?" Liam sounds wary, of what, God knows.

"Sure," Alex says. "Now, I know Victor doesn't care, but I really am on vacation with Paul, so can I get back to that?"

"Yeah. Okay," Liam says. He sounds meek now. "Bye."

"*Goodbye.*" Alex hangs up and drops the phone on the grass.

Paul just stares at him. He looks like he doesn't know whether to laugh or cry. Alex can sympathize.

"So that was an interesting fifteen minutes."

Paul chuckles weakly. "You yelled at Victor."

"He yelled at me first."

"This is why I'm impressed."

Alex tries to smile. "Just priorities."

"What did Liam want?"

"To know why I've offended all of his sensibilities by having a gun. I can't figure out if he's more afraid that I'm in danger or putting everything else in danger." He takes a breath and lies back again with his arms folded behind his head. "This place is weird. I'm not sure he's wrong to worry."

"Maybe we should go back inside," Paul suggests.

"Oh, fuck no. Not yet."

"It was a long time ago," Paul says.

"I know. And in my head it was twenty minutes ago."

"Okay."

They lapse into silence again, until Alex says, "Psychiatric in-patient?"

Paul keeps his eyes on Alex. "That was not a good summer."

"Do you want to talk about it?"

"Given that I didn't tell you for almost two years, not particularly. It wasn't terrifying or traumatic or anything like that. At least not from this vantage point. But it was not my happiest time."

"And you had lunch with your father today."

Paul nods. "Yeah."

"And *I'm* the one that doesn't talk," Alex says. He's far more baffled than angry.

◆

They do eventually go back to the house, after Alex returns the equipment to its safe, locked place in the barn. Alex's head is a mess of confusion and a strange, dark grief for a tragedy that only almost happened. He also has a simmering anger that the world cares way too much what he does, especially when he's on vacation, about things that matter not at all. The timing of everything really is too awful.

Paul runs upstairs to check in on his email, and Alex finds Beth. She's in the kitchen and looks up when he walks in.

"Hey, sweetie. How'd the shooting go?"

"Good." He frowns at the absurdity of the day. He wonders if he should tell her about everything that's going on in the wider world because her son's boyfriend took his stress and introversion out on her gun range. Maybe Paul will.

"He told me," he says. "Just so you know. He hadn't before."

She meets Alex's eyes and nods. "It's about time," she says before going back to the cooking. "We repainted the kitchen together after he got home."

Sarah, her husband Mike, and their son Jake, come over later, and dinner passes without incident. Alex keeps looking over his shoulder for something else terrible to happen, and he and Paul stay closer to each other than they normally do.

Usually it's Alex who curls into Paul's side whenever he can, at least when they're not in public, but tonight it's Paul who keeps their legs pressed together under the table. More than once, Alex sees Paul's mother watching them as they bend their heads together to talk quietly, but Alex has no impulse to pull away or remove his arm from low on Paul's back.

They're all sitting out on the verandah together, watching sunset creep across the fields, when Alex's phone makes itself known yet again. This time, it's Margaret.

The whole conversation is ridiculous on any number of levels, but at least she's not shouting. Her calm, competent crisis-management mode is somehow even more frightening than Victor's wrath, and now Alex's reception of it isn't numbed by terrible stories. The liberals are furious that their sweet Indiana farm boy has the temerity to know his way around a gun. The right suddenly has to deal with the fact that their new, if inadvertent, poster boy is Hollywood's pet twink. No one is happy. Even beyond the fans who feel betrayed that J. Alex Cook would do something so terrible as shoot beer cans (he'd made Paul show him some of the choice replies), many, many people are angry.

"The NRA called," Margaret tells him.

"I'm on vacation," Alex moans.

"Have you talked to Paul's family about what happens when things like this happen?"

"Do things like this actually happen that much?" Alex asks.

"Are you planning on maintaining dangerous and politically sensitive hobbies?"

"I'm not going to defend a sport I like and I'm good at, because it makes people who say *flyover* nervous. I shoot targets, not animals, and I'm also not interested in being a spokesperson for a bunch of freaks who think the government is coming for their Jesus. Can't I just be a person who does stuff?"

"I'm taking that as a yes."

Alex swears. And then reluctantly explains that yes, he and Paul have had conversations with Paul's family about some of the realities of a relationship as public as theirs. Everyone has been gracious, but as welcoming as this family has been, Alex knows that by dating Paul he's making everyone's lives harder than they have to be.

Eventually Margaret talks him down from his pitch of righteous anger. He retreats around the corner of the verandah to keep Paul's family out of earshot as much as possible, because dumping all of this on them just seems rude. She lays out a reasonable strategy for dealing with it which amounts to much the same as Victor's: Do nothing, and do *not* do a whole lot of somethings.

"Hey, can't you just say you're trying to get me an action movie deal or something?" he jokes.

"I could," Margaret points out, "if we knew what the hell was going on with your show."

And with that, Alex finally gets why Victor was pissed. Because on top of everything else, they all live in some sort of crazy world where a tweet can be strategy and betrayal.

After he hangs up with Margaret, before he can even walk back round to the front of the house, Victor calls again. There's less yelling – and the timing is less awful – but once *that* call is over and Alex has finally slumped back into the chair next to Paul's, he's ready to never answer his phone ever again.

Which is when Paul's phone rings.

Paul looks scared. His mother looks like none of this is terribly out of the ordinary. Alex wonders if that's just because she's used to Paul's job or if her life transcended *strange* and *scary* a long time ago.

"Answer it," Alex hisses. He knows this is one of the two calls they've been waiting for and the one that will go a long way towards telling them the shape of the next year.

Paul answers it. Alex watches him closely as he nods and says *yes* and *thank you* a number of times, but he's so damn even Alex can't tell if the news is good or bad.

When he clicks off, he just stares straight ahead *breathing* for a moment. What Alex would have once taken as shock or admired as an even disposition now seems learned in the most unsettling of ways.

"Well?" he finally asks.

Everyone leans forward in their chairs on the verandah staring at Paul in the bug-filled twilight.

"Thirteen episodes," he says softly. "Option for another eight. And then we pray for season two."

The reaction from Paul's family is loud, but Alex sits there, still bent toward Paul and holding his hand, waiting for the moment to actually connect. When it does, Paul is out of his chair in a flash, hauling Alex up with him into a crushing hug.

"Oh my God, this day," Alex says in his ear.

Paul laughs in utter delight. "Will you marry me now?"

Alex laughs and shoves at his shoulder. "Staff your fucking show first."

"I have a show!"

◆

"Last bit of quiet we're going to have for a long time," Paul says once everyone else has left or gone up to bed and he and Alex have the verandah to themselves.

Alex hums, not particularly eager to break the precious silence. "I don't know, I'm still waiting for another crisis to erupt."

"So turn your phone off."

"Did after Victor called the last time. Can't control yours, though."

Paul takes the hint and digs his phone out of his pocket to silence it.

"Does this mean I have all your attention now?"

Paul smirks. He drags his eyes up Alex's body in a way that is entirely not helpful when they're outside on Paul's mother's front porch.

"Sooooo, wanna go upstairs?" Alex nudges his toes against Paul's leg.

Paul laughs, clearly delighted, and after a pause they practically chase each other into the house and up the stairs.

◆

"What do you want?" Alex shuts the door behind them and leans back against it.

Paul smiles at him. "You don't usually ask. You just do. Or let me take."

"Well, now I'm asking. What do you want?" Alex repeats.

"*Everything*," Paul breathes.

"Not helpful," Alex says. But he doesn't mind.

He winds up naked on the bed, knees tucked under him as Paul eats his ass forever, before deciding to fuck him. It's incredibly excellent. Alex is so damn glad they've done the whole testing thing and can skip the condoms and get right to the fucking. He feels amazing as Paul finally pushes his cock all the way into him, pulls back, and thrusts. Alex moans, probably louder than he should, just before the headboard slams into the wall.

"Oh shit," Paul half laughs against his back.

"Terrible choices," Alex manages. He's a little tipsy and a lot giddy. Apparently Paul is too because he goes for it, thrusting several more times and causing several more loud collisions of the bed and the wall. Laughing, Alex has to tell him to stop.

"We deserve to celebrate," Paul says even as he pulls out of Alex. He drags him into the center of the bed, turning him as he goes.

It's a decent idea – Alex sideways over the edge and Paul standing. Their momentum doesn't rock the bed into the wall this way, but the creaking is epic and the angle is bad. Eventually they wind up on the floor, laughing until Paul grabs Alex's hips hard.

Alex whines when Paul gets distracted by how quickly he can raise marks on his skin. He just wants to get fucked. Paul always, *always* wants to play first, whether it's to tease or paint him with scratches and even the faint bruises of his fingers. Alex doesn't mind – it feels amazing. He's grateful his skin is fragile enough to lead Paul into this thing and also, it seems, to stop him from ever going too far with it. Paul has never hurt him in a way he doesn't like.

But Alex has been made impatient as much or more than he's been designed to bruise, and oh, he loves Paul, but he is infuriating. Eventually, after he's begged enough, Paul grabs him by the hips as if they were grooved to his fingers and fucks into him from behind. Alex pants against the floorboards, ancient and smooth under his cheek.

When he comes, loose-limbed and messy across the floor and the edge of a knotted rag rug, it feels like an offering to the house.

"That's going to be awkward tomorrow," Alex manages once they find their way off the floor. It's dangerously tempting to drag the duvet off the bed and sleep there. Paul laughs as he cleans them up.

"I don't think I care." Paul frowns a little at the marks he's left. They both know those are more likely to deepen than fade with the day to come.

♦

After Paul hangs up from the third phone call he's gotten over lunch in the kitchen, Alex asks, "Should we talk about going home early?" He doesn't want to, but Paul's show is everything to him, and he deserves time to give it the attention it needs.

"No. Maybe. Probably," Paul says and frowns down at his phone. "We've been looking forward to this trip for a while."

"It's not a vacation if you're working the whole time."

"Does it bother you?"

Alex shrugs. "I get you no matter what."

They decide to stay. Extra time away from L.A. is worth the headache of Paul setting up shop in their room and not always being completely with his family.

The internet continues to be stupid, but Alex is happy to avoid it in favor of rambling around the property, alone when Paul's busy, with him when he's not. He loves the space and the quiet, and as spooky as so many parts of this place are – like the cricket barn and the pond that tried to drown Paul – he enjoys it.

Halfway through the week, he gets the call from his agent, Vanessa. The news isn't bad, but the call is somber. *Fourth* has been renewed, which is a relief. The terms of the renewal, however, throw everything out of whack.

"Victor only wanted another year, you know, like a normal person," Alex tells Paul, lying with his arms folded under his chin, stretched out on the bed in their room while Paul sits on the chair in the corner with his laptop propped up on his knees. "We got five more arcs."

"That's more than a year."

"But what happens after that?" Alex asks. A season and change makes no sense as a deal if it's not a clear message that the end is coming. Victor, he suspects, is furious.

"I wish I knew."

It's solving one uncertainly only by adding another. Now instead of fretting but not really worrying over the future of *The Fourth Estate*, they're facing down the prospect of it actually coming to an end one day. A world in which Victor and the studio disagree over what should happen to the show is not a stable world. Alex can feel the future starting to shift.

"I still have to go to fucking upfronts," he complains.

Paul laughs, until Alex reminds him that he has to go this year, too. And since they aren't on the same network, they won't be going together.

◆

On their last afternoon in South Carolina, blessedly uninterrupted by phone calls, Paul tells his mom about his show *Winsome, AZ* as they sit around the living room with the windows open and an ancient box fan whirring comfortingly.

She's interested in all the details of the production company he and Victor have formed to create the show: Paul has sixty percent ownership and creative control. Victor does not, but Paul gets to lean on Victor's connections and resources. Victor also gets to be sure Paul is actually out of his nest. The setup is a little unusual, but Paul is glad of it because everything is also a little terrifying. He hopes that if he works as hard as he can and has just enough luck, they can actually make his show work.

"What's it about?" his mom finally asks.

On the couch, Jake drowsing on his lap, Alex snorts.

Beth raises an eyebrow at both of them. "Yes?"

Paul says, "It's about a girl named Melissa who graduates high school –"

"This is Darcy DeRosier?" his mom asks. The name of Paul's lead actress has cropped up in phone calls.

"Yeah. She graduates high school, super smart, can't afford college, so gets a day job at a 7-11 and starts a business."

"That's a way to put it," Alex teases.

Paul smiles fondly at him. It's not like the subject of *Winsome, AZ* – named for the tiny crossroads town in the middle of nowhere it's set in – is one he's embarrassed about, since he's *running a show about it*, but this is his mom and Alex is being a shit.

"The town's on a truck route. Where there are truckers, there are prostitutes. Melissa decides she's the businesswoman to make an efficient empire out of all the inventory. Most of them are old enough to be her mother. Drama, black comedy, and strong female characters ensue." Paul loves talking about his story. He's spent more time than he cares to think about pitching various permutations of the idea to so many people.

"My son is running a show about whores," his mom says somewhere between amused and horrified.

Paul nods. Alex cackles.

She sighs and leans her cheek on her fist. "I won't say I'm not proud of you. Or that it doesn't sound fascinating. But it would be so much easier to watch if I didn't know you were running it, Paul."

By the end of the conversation Jake is asleep on Alex's lap, and Paul pulls out his phone to take a picture. It's not a conversation they're even close to having, but Alex with his nephew is just lovely.

"Going to post that one too?" Alex asks, voice quiet for the sake of the sleeping kid.

"No, this one's just for me," Paul says.

Alex smiles softly.

Paul's mom gestures him into the hallway.

"Well done, Paul," she says with a nod of her head back to Alex.

Paul smiles, so fond. "I don't know what I'd do without him."

5

As soon as they get back from South Carolina, almost before they're done unpacking, Paul starts office hunting.

The offices they used while shooting the pilot had been painfully temporary and aren't extensive enough for everyone. Not now that they're actually a real show with a real crew and cast and a full writing and production team. The list of individuals Paul is responsible for grows daily, and he starts to understand better some of Victor's neuroses when it comes to taking care of all of his people. They're here because of him, and Paul really does not want to fuck any of this up.

He feels like he's on his second chance already. The first pilot he had written – the one Victor helped him pitch more than a year ago after he and Alex had tumbled back together – had died before it had even been filmed. Now that he has other people's jobs and lives depending on *Winsome* succeeding, it's even scarier. That Alex has made clear that their mutual, yet separate, success and ambition is key to Paul getting the future he imagines for them, only ups the pressure.

At least things feel just a bit more certain when they find a space that works and start moving in.

The first time Paul visits his new office after he signs the lease, he spends five minutes standing in the middle of the empty space, spinning slowly on the spot and trying to take it all in. This is his. Paul's not sharing it with anyone else, and Victor, as a minority partner in *Winsome*'s production company, can use the admittedly shabby conference room when he visits. It's not a dream, or a bargain with Alex, or a favor handed down from Victor. This has four walls and a roof and it's real.

He feels as victorious as he did the moment he'd gotten the phone call saying this was going to happen. He takes a picture and sends it to Alex and to his mom.

♦

As Paul gets his working life in order, Alex spends his time sorting out his own next steps for the summer. He sits down with Margaret to talk about creating a brand for himself outside of *The Fourth Estate*. *Paradise Square* had been a cool thing he'd gotten to do because he was the guy from *Fourth*. If he wants to keep working, Alex needs to expand his opportunities.

Looking at life after *Fourth* means looking seriously at other projects now that have the potential to conflict with his shooting schedule, which remains in constant flux as Victor battles the season schedule out with the network.

"Victor will kill me," Alex says darkly to Margaret. It's not a happy prospect to consider. But he has to learn how to tell the world he's someone to watch regardless of *Fourth's* fate.

"You haven't made any decisions yet," she says.

Alex shrugs. He doesn't have to explain to her how much, given circumstances, it's intent not outcome that matters.

The conversation ends with a new media plan that includes more press than he'd normally do for the ramp up to the new cycle. The prospect is annoying, but it will at least keep him busy while they wait for filming to start.

◆

The interviews, once he starts them over the next few weeks, are generally business as usual, but someone always asks about the fucking gun. Alex enjoys staring down the interviewer who asks him how he'd learned to shoot without a father at home.

"My mother taught me," he says. By a supreme act of will he doesn't add, "*Asshole.*"

But then they ask about his sister and growing up in poverty with weapons. Alex is sharp with his refusal to discuss that. Guns are bad enough. There are way too many reasons he never wants to talk about knives in kitchens or criminal records right now. Or ever.

His mom sees the interview and calls him, which leads to a long, strange conversation that touches things they've never really talked about. In the end, she asks how South Carolina had been, aside from the gun.

"Good," he says. The parts that he can tell her about were, and he doesn't want to talk about the rest.

"You and Paul aren't going to visit here much, are you?"

"No," he says, and then, "I'm sorry," because he is. For her feelings, more than any regret he himself has about Indiana. Laura tried to give Alex the best chance to get out of the hell that is their hometown, but that doesn't mean she's happy he's fled so very permanently.

◆

Alex goes out to lunch with Liam a couple of weeks after he gets back from South Carolina. They go to a little restaurant that has too much quinoa on the menu for Alex's taste, but it's small and they're not any more likely to be photographed together here than anywhere else.

After they order, Liam dances around the gun thing again. He's as twitchy and uncomfortable as Alex has ever seen him about anything, but he still can't seem to articulate why he's so upset.

Alex eventually gets the conversation away from guns. When Liam mentions that Carly's been house hunting, Alex asks if that means they're finally moving in together. They've been engaged for a year, but without a date set Alex has been starting to wonder if they would even cohabitate after the wedding.

After a rambling and surprisingly knowledgeable digression into some of the more arcane aspects of real estate – Alex has no idea why he knows or cares so much about floodplains and chalks it up to yet another random Liam thing – Liam asks how Paul and Alex's trip down South went.

"There was the creepy, haunted pond," Alex says. "That sort of set the tone."

He has no interest in discussing any of the things Paul had finally confessed to him there, even with Liam. After their brief and ill-fated *thing* together – Alex still doesn't know what to call it – he trusts Liam more than anyone except Paul. Annoying as he can be, there's a bond between them now that goes beyond friendship.

But Alex suspects there's something in the dark history of the Marion farm, of which he has to acknowledge he's probably only gotten the first hints, that will appeal to Liam. After all, Liam once managed to sort of seduce Alex with trivia about *The Exorcist*.

Liam frowns. "Haunted pond?"

"Yeah. Paul said something grabbed him in it when he was a kid. I couldn't get him to go swimming," Alex opines.

"Why is it haunted? Did someone die in it?" Liam's bright blue eyes are wide, and he tugs at his too-shaggy dark curls.

Alex shrugs. "Maybe?" He'd meant this as a funny story to entertain and interest Liam, but he looks unnerved beyond what seems to Alex to be any reasonable proportion. "Why? It was just one of those things that happens to kids."

Liam shakes his head. "My grandparents passed away when I was like, thirteen. Back to back to back. It was kind of a mess and they didn't have living wills and we had to, like, decide stuff for them. Just because somebody can't talk doesn't mean they don't want things or can't feel things." Liam takes a deep breath and is briefly fascinated by his hands. "It was not a good time. I got really hung up on the details. So I don't do well with death," he says, sounding a bit exasperated with himself. "Or swimming," he adds with a rueful laugh.

6

Sunday brunches are one of the things that Paul tries to keep constant in his increasingly hectic schedule. Alex has long since stopped going regularly for a variety of reasons, including wanting more time for climbing and Gemma and way less time with Brian. But Paul still likes to put in an appearance when he can. Also, Shawna harasses him constantly via text about it. Mostly he enjoys them. This week, there's an odd sort of bittersweetness when Craig is there with Beau *and* his new boyfriend.

On his way out of the restaurant, Paul's phone chimes. It's from Alex, a picture from the top of whatever giant rock he's decided needs climbing today.

On top of the world, it says. *Wish you were here.*

Paul smiles as he types back, *If I were there you'd be only halfway up the mountain.*

He climbs with Alex occasionally, but he's not as good on the rocks and usually ends up slowing them down. It drives Alex – who always pushes for higher, faster, scarier – nuts.

I'd get to watch you from up here. Great views.

Paul chuckles. *Just come home in one piece. Then you can enjoy the views all you want.*

I always do.

◆

Alex gets home not long after Paul, happy and relaxed as he usually is after a climb. Paul decides he has plenty of time to take Alex back to bed before he has to get started on work for the day.

After, Paul gets his laptop and sits in the armchair with his feet on the bed, going through his email. Alex sits against the pillows working his way through a new set of knots he's learning for climbing. Todd, who crept in earlier when they had been distracted and now refuses to be dislodged, sits on the open book next to him, eyes fixed on the rope in Alex's hands and his tail twitching.

Paul watches them both. Quiet moments like this are always precious in their lives, and they don't get enough of them.

Eventually he asks, "Do you want to stay for the party next week?"

He hopes Alex will say yes. Thanking the pilot team and getting everyone ready for the upcoming half-season – and the hoped-for full-season order – means a get-together. This time Paul isn't acting as a proxy for Victor in keeping a team human: This is *his* team. While Paul has never had Alex's uneasiness in crowds, things are easier with him by his side. Plus, Paul wants to share this moment of triumph of bringing the *Winsome* team together in their house.

Alex considers for a moment, then looks up from his knots. "No," he says. "It's your empire, not ours."

Paul supposes the decision makes sense. Alex draws focus in any room he's in, and, aside from living with the showrunner, he has nothing to do with *Winsome*. It's just one more part of the ongoing conversation of how much they are willing to let their professional and their personal lives overlap. As much as Paul knows that this is how the business works – and how much it benefits neither of them to be seen as fucking their way to relevance – he still wishes he could have Alex next to him for everything.

But he knows – and has always known – that is never going to be the case. So he says, "All right," and stands so he can lean over and kiss him.

Alex kisses him back and goes returns his knots.

♦

The night of the party, Alex vanishes to go out with Gemma, and Paul hosts his people, crew and actors alike. Because of the nature of *Winsome* and all its drama about the desires of the aggressively average-at-best, the divide between the two is less obvious than it could be.

Victor had opted out from the party, throwing his hands up and repeating *minority partner* yet again. Then he gave Paul some good advice and reminded him that in this, Paul is his boss and not the other way around. Besides, Victor said, he has plans. From the look of his shark smile, Paul could only assume that meant Liam, or making some poor *Fourth* writer's life hell.

Paul thinks his cast is obscenely talented, completely gorgeous, and real in a way that's brave and often difficult in L.A. Looking at Ruth and Terry and Annette, it's obvious to him that they're stronger than him and all his compulsive exercise. All the charisma in the world doesn't change the deep lines and sad eyes that are just the shape of Ruth's face; Terry's beer gut is completely non-optional; and Annette may be the prettiest of them, but Paul's seen her resume. He knows the sort of roles Hollywood makes black women play. In a way, *Winsome*'s no better for her, but he's trying. At least everyone on his show is a whore.

Darcy is the room's one traditional beauty. As she bounces around the event, her blonde curls flying and her green eyes sparkling, it's obvious to Paul and probably everyone else that she knows it and thinks it a moral good. Sometimes he worries that she has a crush on him, but mostly he knows it must be hard to be eighteen in L.A. and career-oriented and successful as opposed to party-happy and insane. Paul likes her, but she makes him nervous in a way oddly not dissimilar to Liam. He assumes it's the child star thing.

When he's not playing good host and Darcy isn't trailing along in his wake, he hangs out with Ruth, whose soothing, not-unkind deadpan is decent at settling him in Alex's absence.

Ultimately, it's a long night but a good one, and at many points Paul looks around the room and remembers the first pilot party he ever went to, hosted by Victor. So many things started that night for all of them. He wonders what things are beginning now.

♦

Paul's standing at the sink rinsing out dishes, the house finally empty and quiet around him, when Paul hears Alex's key in the lock.

"Hey, you," Alex breathes in his ear as he slides his arms around Paul's waist.

"Hey." Paul leans back against him and sets the down dish he's holding. Alex is hot-skinned and a little sweaty from wherever he'd gone with Gemma. He's irresistible.

"Mhmm," Alex presses his face into Paul's shoulder, his damp hair rubbing against Paul's cheek. "Missed you."

"Missed you too," Paul says. Alex has his hands on his hips swaying them both, and it's hard to think of anything but him.

"How was your party?"

"Mm." Paul turns around into Alex's arms and rests their foreheads together. "A resounding success. Everyone has been thanked and now hopefully feels appreciated."

"I'm sure they do," Alex says.

Paul groans. Alex wrapped around him like this shorts out everything else in his brain. "I want to take you to bed."

"How traditional." Alex bites his ear.

"Fuck, you want it," Paul breathes.

"I want you," Alex breathes as he walks them towards and then up the stairs.

When they get to the door of their bedroom Paul grabs his face and kisses him. Some traditions are damn well worth keeping.

7

Now that Paul has a large and growing production team, he should be able to ease up a little and let his people take over. But *Winsome* is compelling, he is enamored of the work, and there is always some new and exciting thing he can give his attention to. Paul does his best to balance the reality of *Winsome* with his life with Alex, but it's the nature of the business that it's a losing battle. It doesn't take long before he's working six a.m. to six p.m. in his new offices before coming home for dinner and another several hours of work in the loft space that used to be Gemma's living area.

He freaks out before every table read over scripts that are done and solid and *fine*. Victor always shields his writers from so much network bullshit. Now Paul knows he must pay the debt by taking those hits for his own team.

The problem is, he's convinced he can somehow get the scripts tight enough that there won't be any hits, but it doesn't work that way. Network executives object to things to remind writers and showrunners who God really is. The battles Paul is determined to fight are largely losing ones.

As difficult as things are now – Paul is getting five hours of sleep on a good night – he knows they will become next to impossible once Alex starts filming again. There's a difference between seeing each other when only one of them is fully functional and never seeing each other conscious at all.

At least Alex has finally learned to cook something other than pasta. Which Paul finds himself enjoying for reasons that range from having one less thing to worry about to thinking that Alex looks absolutely adorable in their kitchen puttering around in a stupid apron Carly bought him as a joke. When Paul is foolish enough to tell Alex this, he gets a dry and unpleasant comment about housewives and kept boys. It screams of some sort of defensive inner narrative that Paul is hesitant to inquire about. He doesn't have time for a crisis – or a lack of indulgence – from Alex right now.

Unfortunately, that means he also doesn't have time to indulge Alex, and that's far less good. Filming on *Fourth* is still a couple of weeks from resuming, and Alex is restless and bored. Sure, he climbs as much as he can make time for between the meetings and interviews and events that pepper his days. But the act of making magic on film is what drives him. Without that center, he's clearly a little bit lost.

And Alex lost has always been, from even before it was a legitimate option, an Alex who looks to Paul. Which means he interrupts Paul's home office time constantly.

Paul knows to grit his teeth, smile, and be grateful for something in his life that is not *Winsome*. But it's hard. With every day seemingly bringing a new crisis, it approaches impossible. Paul has no idea how far Alex's patience is going to ultimately extend.

◆

Just because Victor opted out of the *Winsome* party doesn't mean he has any intention of opting out of his own yearly event for *Fourth*. The party at his house for the cast, crew, and staff is one of the rare times Victor allows anyone but his intimates into his home. It is, by necessity, much larger than the event Paul hosted.

This year, it's also considerably less happy. Were it a smaller event, Victor probably would make a speech about everyone's concerns, about his own unhappiness with the network and what they have to work with. He'd spend some time talking about how this is going to change all of their lives as they figure out how to tell the story they want to tell with a whole new set of constraints. But Victor's house is currently packed with people and all their attendant plus-ones, and Victor wants to say nothing about what he has planned – or his own anger – anywhere it might leak.

The semi-official silence on the topic doesn't stop people from talking in corners, and the whole crowd feels uneasy. Which makes Victor even more angry with the network. His people are good – no, his people are the *best* – and while Hollywood offers no one any guarantees, they deserve better than this strange situation.

◆

"Jesus, Alex, your back," Paul says into his ear as they strip out of jeans and T-shirts down to their swim trunks at Victor's house for the *Fourth* party. Alex knows he's covered in scratches from Paul. This isn't the first time the ease with which his skin marks has made things conspicuous, but it might be the most awkward.

Alex cranes his neck to look even though it's useless. He'd already caught sight of it in the mirror this morning. "It's fine," he shrugs.

Paul presses his palm against his lower back and looks worried. And guilty. "Are you okay?"

"It's *fine*," Alex repeats. He doesn't want to start this discussion. The marks aren't anything new. "But if Liam gives me shit for it, I'm blaming it all on you."

"I would hope," Paul says. Alex bumps his hip before leading the way to the pool deck. Paul doesn't seem to know whether to hover or give him his space. The third time he asks if Alex is okay or if he needs anything, Alex huffs and pushes at his shoulder.

"Oh my God, I'm fine, Paul. Believe me, I'll tell you when I need you," he adds in a whisper, and gives him a look on the right side of wicked when Paul's eyes go wide. Finding new ways to play with his boyfriend is a joy.

When Paul doesn't move from the spot Alex adds, "I see Carly – I'm going to go say hi." He kisses his cheek before he saunters to the edge of the pool, where she's floating, lazy and regal, on a bright green raft.

Across the pool from her Liam sits fully dressed on the lounger furthest back from the water. He gives Alex a wave hello.

◆

Paul stares after Alex. He has no idea what to make of any of it.

Victor appears suddenly at his elbow. "How's he doing?"

"He's good," Paul says cautiously. He's beginning to notice that Victor never asks after Alex when they are in *Winsome*-related space.

Alex jumps into the pool and disappears under the surface, kicking his way toward Carly. Paul is still wary of saying anything of great detail about his boyfriend to Victor. Especially when he's not entirely sure how, exactly, Alex is, other than happy, which shouldn't throw him as much as it does.

"And how are you, other than taking it out on him?"

Victor sounds amused enough that Paul doesn't bother to engage the insinuation. "Good. Okay. You know how busy. I don't know how you manage to sleep."

"I don't." Victor shrugs. Paul wishes that felt more like a joke; he's exhausted. "It's not going to get easier for you two once *Fourth* ends."

Paul has heard plenty about the uncertain fate of the show from Alex. He's felt superstitious about asking Victor about it, however. He doesn't work on the show anymore, but hearing it stated that directly makes him feel like some beloved relative is terminally ill. He wonders if Victor is beside himself and tamping it down in their twice-weekly calls as he tries to keep Paul's sanity afloat.

"His job, not mine," Paul says.

"Mhmmm. And what do you think he's going to do once he's done with that?"

"Victor, the first time you offered me advice about Alex, it didn't exactly go as planned. The Chinese walls you and I have going on right now? Work really well. Let's not tempt that. And how do you even know what's going to happen?"

"He's thinking about it," Victor says.

Paul has no idea what *it* is and isn't sure he particularly wants to find out.

"Nothing is certain," Victor muses. "And Alex is very good at making his own way through uncertainty."

"I've noticed," Paul says, looking for some sort of foothold in the conversation.

"Notice better," Victor says before heading off toward the corner where Liam is.

Paul sighs and goes to look for a drink. Victor is exhausting.

♦

Alex hauls himself up onto Carly's raft while she laughs and curses and threatens dire retribution if he dunks her. He doesn't, though, just stretches out next to her while she complains about him dripping everywhere.

"It's a pool, Carly," he snarks. She pushes wet hair out of his face so he can tuck his head into her shoulder without getting her too cold and damp. "There's supposed to be water."

"Yes. In the pool. Not on me."

"Diva."

"Yup. Baby boy, what happened to your back?" she asks, feigned concern all over her face. She wraps an arm around his shoulders and cranes her neck to get a better look.

Alex smirks.

Carly runs a thumbnail along a scratch that ends in a bruise on Alex's shoulder. Some of the marks are fresh, while others look older. It's quite a patchwork. "Jesus. How'd you talk him into that?"

Alex shrugs, looking smug. "It's what we do."

"Well, that's hot," Carly says, tracing another scratch. "And mildly surprising. You gonna give me any good details?" Certainly, it's not a thing Paul ever did with her.

Alex snorts. "Unlikely."

"Well, that's a shame."

♦

It takes less than two hours for the party to go from nervous and falsely discreet business chatter to people happy to cut loose out of the public eye. Some get drunk fast, while others entertain themselves by ambushing colleagues and throwing them into the water. There's not a lot of overlap between the two groups thanks to the party two seasons ago when Victor made good on his threat to publicly humiliate anyone who attempted to drown in his pool.

The more fun people have, the less polite they get. As a cast and crew they already know way too much about each other even as they don't always like each other. Which is how Alex winds up, ridiculously, having to explain the state of his flesh to someone he neither knows well nor likes.

"Climbing mishap," Alex shouts across the pool area when one of the crew guys shouts something more than a bit obscene about the state of Alex's back.

"Didn't know rocks could fuck," Dan hollers back.

"Fuck off," Alex calls, his head still resting on Carly from where he's been zoning out from the rest of the party for as long as possible. There's an edge to his voice now that makes the words half question and half threat.

"Daniel, if you don't shut up I will not stop Alex from laying you out, and if you think he can't, you are far too stupid to work for me," Victor drawls, loudly, from the corner where he's still holding court with Liam. It shuts Dan – and everyone else – up.

Conversation quickly rushes back in, too fast and too loud, in an apparent collective attempt to forget Victor's rather relaxed, but perfectly sincere, threats.

"Thank you," Alex says crisply from the pool, the words for Victor only.

Victor shrugs. Inexplicably, Liam offers Alex a thumbs up.

"I don't understand anyone," Alex whines into Carly's neck.

◆

"Paul, come here," Victor says as Paul idles with a drink in his general vicinity, watching Carly experimentally pinch Alex in various places to see how easily he does or does not bruise.

As much as he's not in the mood for another unsettling conversation with Victor, Paul is happy to go. As a former colleague and potential source of work at a time of significant upheaval, most people here are being weird around him in a way he doesn't yet know how to navigate. For all the challenge of his presence, Victor is a known quantity and something of a refuge.

Victor shoos away the people he's been talking to at his approach. Paul fistbumps with Liam before he takes a seat on the edge of the lounger he's spread out on.

"We need to look at our teams and make some moves," Victor says without preamble.

Liam ignores them in favor of spinning a disc-shaped charm hanging from his latest ridiculous hipster necklace. This far into the party, he and Victor are the only ones not in swimsuits. Victor may be ordinary looking, with tan skin, plain black hair, and fine wrinkles around his mouth and eyes, but even in street clothes and surrounded by this much poolside Hollywood fabulousness, he radiates charisma.

"Like what?" Paul knows better than to agree to Victor's pronouncements without gathering additional information.

"We're not going head-to-head, and my fate may be sealed. Even if it's not, everyone thinks it is, so I need to consolidate. *Winsome* should staff up more. My problems are going to solve your problems."

"Did they cut your budget?"

"No, but I need to keep people from jumping ship."

"By gifting them to me in what seems like a creepy power grab?"

Victor shakes his head. "I recommend – and you hire – people I don't use all the time. You get a crack team. I get left with a team that assumes they are all my very special favorites. Everyone thinks our allied empires have done them a massive favor."

"And I owe you for life."

"You think you don't already?"

"I can't tell when you're joking," Paul says cautiously.

"At least I tell you what my intentions are."

"Fair."

"So what do you need that you haven't had the sense to tell me about yet?" Victor asks.

Paul has a list, and he and Victor work through it for about thirty minutes, Victor making occasional notes into his smart phone.

"I'll send you this later," he says, waggling the phone and then setting it down. "We'll get it done."

◆

After Carly loses Alex to a gaggle of people he can't ignore as much as he probably wants to, she wanders over to Liam's corner.

"Why so quiet?" she asks. It's one thing for Liam to hang back from the edge of the pool, but he's hardly talked to anyone all day, even Victor.

"Hard afternoon. Hard crowd." Liam frowns.

Carly scootches over to sit next to him on the lounger. "Everybody's pissy," she agrees.

"Yeah. Going back to work is not going to be fun."

"They'll be fine once they have a routine again." Carly combs her fingers back through his dark curls.

Liam's shoulders sag as he relaxes into the touch. "Maybe."

"Are you staying tonight?"

"Yeah. I think so." He shrugs. "Too many people for everybody."

"The worst is almost over."

"Shhhh, you'll jinx it," Liam admonishes. He catches her hand to kiss it obnoxiously.

"We'll live. Did you see Alex's back?" she asks. Despite the smiles, Liam is still tense and a subject change is clearly necessary.

Liam laughs and wraps his arms around her. "*Everybody's* seen Alex's back."

♦

Ellen, one of Victor's prized directors, laughs when Alex whines to her about being bored and wanting to go back to work. "Speak for yourself. The rest of us are going to miss being able to take a goddamned vacation."

"Our last vacation involved crickets. I'll be okay."

Ellen raises an eyebrow, but doesn't ask. "You think that now. See how you feel when you've shot two arcs back-to-back and there's still no end in sight. Insects will start to look good."

Alex laughs. He likes Ellen. She can be as sharp as he is and has none of Victor's more manipulative tendencies.

"We'll see," he says. Everyone else seems to know what the new deal means for them, but Alex is still deciding.

♦

Much later, when the crowd is starting to thin out, Carly drops heavily into the lounger next to Paul's. "Alex is a fucking beauty."

"Don't let him hear you say that," he says wryly. He looks across the pool to where Alex is standing in a little cluster of people, including Natalie and Raphael, two of his other co-stars. Paying his respects, probably. While there are a handful of people on the crew and in the cast Alex is genuinely friendly with, including Raph, Natalie is not one of them. Then again, Natalie isn't genuinely friendly with anyone as far as Paul has ever been able to tell.

"I already told him," Carly says.

"And he didn't shove you into the pool?" Paul asks.

Carly raises her eyebrows at Paul over the rim of her glass. "We have an understanding."

"You certainly looked like you were enjoying yourselves out there."

"Are you jealous?" Carly purrs and leans against Paul's shoulder.

"Of my ex-girlfriend and my current boyfriend?"

"Stranger things have happened. Actually...." Carly presses a finger to her lips in exaggerated thoughtfulness. Paul wonders how drunk she is. "That one isn't that strange."

"Maybe not in *your* life."

"He's very cute. And warm. And cuddly," she says. "I never see him stick close to you, I didn't think he had it in him."

"Should I be jealous?"

She lifts a shoulder. "I don't know. You can't say it's not a pretty picture."

"Picture, yes," he concedes, because as much as it is in the past, there really is something about Carly that had attracted him, and Alex is Alex. "Somehow I don't think he's really interested. Hell, I don't think it would even occur to him."

"Are you sure?"

There's both an offer and a tease in her voice. The conversation has officially become drunk and absurd, because there is nothing about the idea Carly is oh-so-coyly presenting that isn't working for him.

"Did he say something?" Paul doubts it. Alex does chase the new and the unknown, but this is a whole different place they're talking about.

"Alex never says anything."

"He does sometimes." Paul is extraordinarily pleased with himself for all the ways he's able to get Alex to speak.

"Oh, really?" Carly drawls.

"Maybe I should ask him," he says.

"I think you should." Carly rolls onto her side on her lounger and gives him a long look from under her eyelashes.

"This is ridiculous," Paul says with a disbelieving laugh.

"But it's hot," Carly counters.

Paul laughs loudly enough for Alex to catch the sound. He turns around from whatever conversation he's having to raise an eyebrow at him.

"Really fucking hot," Paul muses.

"Merely some food for thought, *darling*," Carly says in imitation of Victor's most condescending cadences.

Paul chuckles and lifts a hand to wave Alex over.

◆

"What?" Alex asks, amused and indulgent when he walks over and Paul grabs his hand.

"Carly and I were just talking about you," Paul tips his head toward Carly before he pulls Alex into his lap.

"Were you?" Alex leans lazily back against Paul's chest.

"Mhmmm. We had an idea."

"Do you want to hear it?" a giddy Carly asks.

Paul shoots her a look.

"Do I?" Alex watches as Paul slides a hand over his knee, intrigued just enough not to cut this off.

"I think so," Paul breathes.

Then, as Carly watches them both, he leans closer to whisper in Alex's ear. About Carly and how Alex would look with her, about what the three of them would look like together, and about how hot it would be if Alex were ever curious.

"You're not serious," Alex says.

Paul slides his hand higher on his leg. "Aren't I?"

Paul's tendency to tease has always frustrated and delighted Alex, but he has never offered anything he wasn't interested in. As insane as this idea is, it's on the table if Alex wants it to be.

"Think about it," Paul tells him.

The conversation is both compelling and a little unsettling, but Paul's hands are on Alex's thighs and his mouth is brushing his ear. Carly watches them with interest.

It's weird, but the weirdest thing is that he's not laughing off the idea. He's as eager as ever to play along with Paul's ideas to see how far they can explore together. But Alex is in a swimsuit, and he needs to get out of here before his humiliation escalates way beyond a scratched back.

"Bathroom," he says and bolts.

♦

"Alex," Victor says when the pool area is almost empty.

Alex looks up from where he's sitting next to Paul on the pool deck, both of them dangling their feet in the water and sitting in companionable silence while the sky fades from gold to black in the west. Liam, Alex notices, is up now, talking quietly to Carly by the door to the house.

Alex leaves Paul with a squeeze to his shoulder and joins Victor by the gate in the side yard, where Victor has one eye on the driveway as people leave. "What?"

"What have Paul and Carly been conspiring at?"

Alex squints evaluatively. "Nothing to do with you."

"Does it have something to do with you?"

"Yes."

"Okay," Victor drawls, stretching out the word 'til it snaps.

"I'm not going to tell you what it is," Alex says. Victor should know better than to expect him to.

"Have you told Paul what *you're* planning?"

Alex blinks at the sudden change in subject, but he's more than happy to move away from Victor inquiring after the drunken fantasies of his boyfriend. "How do you know what I'm planning?"

"You never get tired of testing." Victor turns away from Alex to shake hands with a pair on their way out. Alex smiles at them. Once they're out of earshot Victor turns back to him. "I told him to keep an eye on you."

"Victor," Alex says sharply, frowning. "I don't know what your deal with Liam and Carly is, and I don't care. But don't tell me what to do about Paul."

"I didn't," Victor says mildly.

"Or tell him what to do about me."

"I don't think he's going to make that mistake twice. I'm telling you this so you know what's going on."

"Am I supposed to thank you?"

Victor smiles dangerously. "It wouldn't be amiss. But no."

As much as Victor infuriates him, not even Alex is immune to the lure of that smile. "Then what is the point of this conversation, except to remind me of all the ways things tend to go wrong around here?"

Victor shrugs. "Make it big, Alex."

Alex doesn't respond verbally, just tips his head and smiles. Victor smiles back.

8

By the time everyone leaves, it's late and Victor's kitchen is a mess. In the morning, long before Liam has any intention of being awake, professionals will come and clean it, taking away the rental glassware and everything else. By the time Carly shows up for brunch, because Victor likes to putter around and make them omelets in the mornings after Liam stays, it will be as if the whole thing never happened. Until then Victor is, Liam knows, likely to be his usual slightly irritated and insomniac self. And for now it's just the two of them.

"I don't understand why you have these things at your house if you hate the invasion so much," Liam says, settling himself on Victor's couch. Victor pulls the blinds closed on the big sliding glass doors, shutting out the night.

They have been having this conversation for years, in part because it's one Liam knows how to have and in part because he's never gotten a satisfactory answer. Victor can say it's the done thing 'til he's blue in the face, but Liam thinks it's guilt and some sort of strange check-in with the universe: *Am I like other people now?*

"Because it would annoy me more to do it somewhere else, and my neighbors have the good sense to call the cops on the paps."

Liam nods. He's never met Victor's neighbors. On the odd terraced hills that are part of any celebrity-worthy neighborhood in L.A. that's not uncommon. He likes them all the more for their mix of invisibility and benevolence.

Liam scrolls through movie options on the flat screen as Victor drops onto the sofa, head resting on Liam's thigh. It's always movies and never TV because TV is work. Movies – too short to be anything but ephemeral, too outside of day-to-day life to define people's decades and desires – never are. They hold no professional interest for Victor and, generally, little personal interest. They're background noise and flickering lights while they make out until Victor gets too bored or Liam gets too desperate.

"You do realize this is just a very well-telegraphed cancellation notice," Victor says after twenty minutes of ignoring *Bladerunner* and not making out with Liam.

"Yes." Liam's voice is clipped because sometimes when Victor's upset he forgets it's a tuning issue with Liam and not an intelligence issue.

"You don't have to worry, though."

Liam huffs. "I've been on TV since I was a kid and still get checks from stuff I shot when I was eleven. I only work because I like it. Yay, another syndication deal." There are ways that Victor fusses over him that are essential to his being. This is not one of them.

"I will always hire you, you know."

"I know. You shouldn't tell me that when you have your head in my lap. People will think things."

"Terrible habit," Victor drawls. "They should stop."

Liam raises his eyebrows. "Do you need to be irritable and pretend I'm lost without you –"

"You would be lost without me," Victor deadpans. "And Carly."

"Or are you just bored?" Liam continues, as if he's not been interrupted by Victor's finely honed and mostly joking cattiness.

Victor crosses his arms over his chest and drums his fingers against his lips. "I don't know what's next. I don't know how to exact vengeance. I don't know how to take care of you all. And I definitely have yet to figure out how to blow this up in the network's face."

"Give it an hour," Liam says.

Victor finally deigns to sit up and kiss him.

♦

Liam leads them to the guest room he's come to think of as his, although he keeps nothing of his there and there is nothing in it to indicate it has any particular owner. It's just white. White walls, rustic white-painted bedframe, fluffiest white comforter on earth. Victor used to frown over it, saying he'd always meant to do something with the room and then stopped, fascinated at the accidental cross between minimalist modernism and princess fantasy.

To Liam's knowledge, no one else ever stays there. There's another guest room for visitors that aren't him. As far as he has ever been informed, Victor has no other lovers. Liam isn't sure if he's technically supposed to consider himself Victor's lover at all, because he just doesn't…they just don't.

Victor does *to*, not *with*. Liam has never found it odd so much as interesting. Which is, he supposes, why they are six years into this and going nowhere. Liam fell in love with Carly when she thought it was lovely, and they are now some ever more tangled snake of a family. He's not sure where Alex fits in, although he knows that he does. Paul either comes with Alex or was already here; he's not sure about that either.

They start the way they usually do. Victor kneels beside the bed in which Liam lies naked and jerks him off, while Liam begs for kisses and Victor reminds him how much he likes to watch and how little he likes most everything else. It's not voyeurism, Victor's told him –

not sexual voyeurism, anyway. It's just Liam's face, apparently, his liquid blue eyes, and the way that in sex he loses the language through which he has taught himself to interact with the world. Hearing Victor talk about it is frightening sometimes, but that doesn't make it less true. Liam knows his mimicry falls away when he is in bed with anyone. Perhaps it happens so acutely with Victor because of the degree to which they are not, in this act, in the same place at the same time.

Tonight, though, Liam wants more. He's feeling things and doesn't have the words for them, so he needs his hands. When he tries to sit up and puts a hand on Victor's shoulder to kiss him harder, Victor pushes him gently back.

Liam frowns, but Victor shakes his head. Liam wants to obey more than he wants to push, at least for now, so he lets himself fall back on the pillow. Victor runs a hand over Liam's forehead, and nods before kissing him again.

After Liam comes, Victor kisses him until his mouth goes drowsy. Occasionally Victor's breath even hitches when Liam isn't interested in being tired at all, but he pulls away and smiles as if everything in this world is a trick of the light.

◆

Victor excuses himself when Liam is halfway to unconsciousness and returns carrying too many things: His laptop bag slung on his shoulder, a damp towel to clean them up, a glass of water to leave on the night table by Liam's bed, his metronome, and coffee in a travel mug for himself – he's learned the hard way about spilling things in this ever so white room.

He has no interest in what other people consider sexual activity for himself, but he's happy to provide experiences like this for Liam so long as he never has to be subject to the sensations of sex. It is a thing that is true and that is complicated only because the rest of the world – and the way Liam is wired to do love and relationships – make it that way. But Liam is beautiful always and most beautiful when he wants. He's never asked for anything Victor couldn't give him. Yet.

Victor has no idea how long that can last. But once he is sure Liam is settled – clean and unconscious, duvet pulled up around his shoulders and face half buried in it – Victor sits on the floor, back to the wall, laptop open on his legs stretched out in front of him, and writes to the soft tick of the metronome and the sound Liam's breath and his often fussy sleep.

Sometime late in the night, Liam wakes enough to ask what he's working on. Victor shrugs in the dark glow of his words, smiles, and says, "Whatever's next."

9

Because nothing about scheduling is ever easy, Alex's upfronts obligations are at the beginning of the last week of May, and Paul's are at the end. Neither of them can afford to take a full week away from L.A., and Paul is generally surly about the entire thing. With the ongoing death of pilot season, the sanctity of upfronts increasingly seems nonsensical to him.

Paul watches dolefully as Alex packs and promises they'll figure something out in the middle. Although they both know there's a damn good chance they'll be together for little more than a couple hours between when Alex returns and when Paul has to leave.

Alex shrugs it off. When he has to travel for work he tends to go quiet. Paul worries sometimes that's as much about what happened when they were still trying to get their shit together and Alex had to be out of town for two months, as it is about Alex needing to protect himself from the onslaught of his life.

Paul doesn't even have time to take him to the airport. It's just as well. It's not like they can kiss goodbye there without being documented, and Paul knows Alex hates that. Some days, every fan is a thief.

♦

Alex texts Paul briefly when he lands to let him know he's safe. He follows up an hour later with *I'm on a bus*. It takes Paul a full ten minutes to realize Alex isn't taking public transit. He's being weirded out by New York being covered in ads promoting upfronts, some of them with his face on them, as if they weren't an industry thing civilians shouldn't give a shit about.

I wish I were on a bus, Paul texts back.

No you don't.

On a bus to you.

It takes five days. You really don't.

♦

New York is, as ever, bracing. Alex is scheduled hour by hour – and in some cases, minute by minute – for his three days in town. Media; meetings; upfronts for fans; upfronts proper; an after-party that's still an official party he's contractually obligated to be at; dinner with Victor, Liam, Natalie, Raphael, and the rest of the people doing the roadshow that someone will surely call the paparazzi about; and then six whole hours to sleep before he has to get up and do it all again. Liam loves it, Victor devours it, and Natalie measures it in obsessing over her gains in social media followers. Alex endures it. He does his best to never look ungrateful, because he isn't, but he's pretty sure he's more offended by the process than anyone else involved.

The first night, when they've already been up for way too long, they all have dinner together, public and intentional. The paparazzi are outside the restaurant. Alex assumes that's Natalie's doing until Victor gives him a sharp look as he holds the door to usher his ducklings in. Victor seats Liam on his right, as he always does – Alex makes a point to notice these things now – and Natalie gets pride of place on his left. That leaves Alex either having to make conversation with her throughout the meal or sit next to Liam, which would be fine except for the fact that the internet exists.

Alex lets Raphael take one for the team and situates himself between him and Liam with a grimace. Raphael gives him a look back, clearly amused at the proceedings he doesn't particularly want to be part of either. Raphael may play Zach's chief rival on *Fourth*, but he's easily the mellowest of the cast present, and Alex is glad for his buffer of sanity.

Throughout the meal that follows, everyone avoids eye contact in favor of looking over their conversation partners' shoulders to see who might be listening to or documenting them. It's a strangely false performance of intimacy considering the many very genuine connections between them. Nearly three years into all of this, Alex still feels out of place at these occasions.

"Stop looking at your cutlery like it's going to stab you," Liam teases, kicking him under the table.

Alex has to force himself not to startle. Sometimes Liam is uncanny. "I'm trying to remember which fork to use," he snaps back.

"Hey," Liam says softly.

Alex sighs. "I'd be more comfortable being stared at while doing normal things if it were more explicit," he says by way of apology. He still hates when people gawk to his face, but at least it's better than this strange theater.

Liam shrugs. "If people were capable of being more explicit, they would be."

◆

"I would like to inform you that former child stars are very, very hard to deal with," Paul says when Alex calls him late that night. He's upstairs in his office, going over notes and scripts for tomorrow's filming.

"Did you have dinner with Liam too?" Alex asks dryly.

"You had dinner with Liam?" Paul tries to keep the alarm out of his voice. Alex will likely be pissed if he expresses displeasure at the idea, and Paul doesn't particularly want to have that argument right now.

"With everyone," Alex corrects. "I'm sure the pics are on the internet by now if you care."

"Do you look cute? Then I care."

"I always look cute. And slightly surly. What did Darcy do, and do you want me to talk to her?" Alex asks.

When he had initially cast the Broadway starlet as an eighteen-year-old girl determined to make an empire out of a truck-stop prostitution ring in Nowhere, America, Paul had despaired of how to give Darcy all of the background information she'd need to play the part. Eventually, he'd asked Alex to talk to her. They connected fiercely enough that they have kept up a semi-regular email correspondence since. Paul is pretty sure Alex likes her because neither of their lives make any sense.

"She sent her parents a script," Paul says. "Which she now knows is a thing she should not do."

"Shit. Seriously?" Alex, reasonably, sounds incredulous.

"Yeah. She does even better puppy eyes than Liam when she's getting yelled at, by the way. It's unnerving. But apparently darling Darcy also never told her folks what *Winsome* was about."

"Oh God."

"Yeah. They are now distraught at her and pissed at me because how could there be *hookers, Paul,* and how will Darcy's baby sister ever get to play little Cosette now?" Paul sighs heavily. "They're fucking nightmares and don't understand that she's eighteen and that they are not her managers or agents."

Alex laughs. "Are you going to have to change your phone number? And will you remember to give me the new one?"

"I love you," Paul says, amused and deeply sincere. "Come home."

"Soon as I can. Although we're gonna be ships passing in the night."

"Don't remind me."

◆

Victor thinks about hiring a car, but there's a certain mercy to dealing with Penn Station and taking the train. It's ordinary and grounding. How people live and move who are of not Los Angeles remains of fundamental importance to him, even if he exposes himself to it not nearly enough.

Besides, anything but the train, and Nigel will mock him. This isn't a new condition, but as fond as Victor is – Nigel is family as much as anyone – there have always been times he's wanted to strangle him for insisting on acting like a big brother. Just because Victor ultimately has little physical interest in Nigel – and Nigel is stunning enough, well-built and with luminously dark skin, that if Victor doesn't want to fuck him he doesn't want to fuck *anyone* – doesn't mean he thinks of him as a brother. It annoys him that Nigel thinks he's the wiser of the pair.

Mainly because, on some level, it's not untrue. Victor goes to Nigel for advice, and Nigel rarely returns the favor. They may have wrestled through Victor's asexuality together, but Nigel's interest in men, greater interest in women, and ridiculously perfect marriage to a wife far prettier than Victor thinks he deserves were all met with a shrug from both of them. Nigel's not the only person Victor's ever been lost in front of, but he's the only one who knows it. Mostly, Victor thinks the power differential is hilarious. The alternative would most likely be damaging to their friendship and many of the carefully constructed architectures of their lives.

So Victor takes the damn train, lest Nigel let it all go to his head.

◆

After dinner and once the kids have been put to bed, Priscilla sits in the living room with Victor and chitchats while Nigel fusses with tea in the kitchen. It's such an absurd thing to Victor and irrelevant to the worlds both of them have come from. Beyond their shared personal history, his bond with Nigel has absolutely been predicated on the fact that they are both men of color from working-class families that never understood their passions or had much kindness for their empires of lies. Nigel is in advertising, which is exactly like making TV shows but with much shorter episodes.

Victor smiles and hopes he doesn't look uncomfortable. He's known Priscilla for years; he likes her. She is as aware of his various personal and professional aggravations as anyone, but all of that is, and has always been, because she is Nigel's wife. Victor doesn't keep secrets from Nigel because he can't and never could. During their failed hookup the first time he'd been in New York for upfronts, he'd tumbled out everything he'd been struggling with for years.

But Priscilla, who Nigel didn't even meet until a year later, knows everything only because she's there and lovely. So Victor can stall her, even if just for a little while. With everything roiling in his head, he's happy to do it for as long as he can.

"He knows he doesn't have to do that, right?" Victor asks Pris at one point.

She laughs. "It makes him happy."

"Allow a man his pleasures," Nigel says, entering with a tray and cups, everything arranged to precision. It's the attention to details of the sort that no one else thinks to care about that is one of the things that makes he and Victor friends.

"So, how are all of your charges?" Nigel asks now that they're not at a dinner table populated by impressionable young minds. "No more fucking in the trailers?"

"More or less," Victor says half-heartedly. "No one's making any headlines they shouldn't."

"How's Liam?"

"Fine," Victor says.

"That's a remarkably few number of words for your favorite," Nigel says.

"Upfronts is an ordeal. Everyone's worn out."

"Bullshit. You never sleep. Is he not handling it well?" Nigel asks, conspicuously leading.

Priscilla uncrosses and recrosses her legs in the corner of the couch, the rustling of her dress commentary on Nigel's benign query that's anything but.

"He's handling it beautifully," Victor says. Liam's conduct – in public, at least – is as much a concern as it ever is, which is usually not much. The world finds him charming, and he has remained, somehow, impervious to scandal through being a very good judge of people.

"Is it Alex again?"

Victor laughs. "No. Thank God. Not that the two of them did not make my life very interesting for a month, but no. You know Liam's engaged."

"It was in *People*," Nigel nods, waiting for Victor to get to the point.

"You don't read *People*."

Pris props her temple on her fingers, a smile tugging at the corner of her mouth. "He thumbs through it at the grocery store."

♦

Victor had called Nigel in the whirl of media attention that had followed Liam's surprise announcements over a year ago that he was, one, bi, and two, engaged to Carly. Nigel may not approve of the way Victor sometimes conducts his relationships, in public or in private, but the pride in Victor's voice when he'd spoken of Liam's bravery had been exasperated and very real.

Now, Victor doesn't say anything. He just looks distracted.

"I can't imagine that changing the way he does things," Nigel suggests.

"I don't *know*," Victor bites back.

Nigel blinks. Priscilla laughs.

"Surely you've talked about it," Nigel says.

"He's not my boyfriend," Victor snaps.

"You are a ridiculous human being," Priscilla says while Nigel stares at his friend. "You've been dating him for *years*."

"Human beings are baffling, irritating, and, rarely – and only if I'm very lucky – somewhat interesting," Victor says.

"I've heard this all before," Nigel says. Liam is one of Victor's favorite conversation topics. "And I can't imagine what you have to worry about now if he's been content for years not to go to bed with you."

Victor shifts in his seat and coughs.

"Wait. Are you actually fucking him?" Nigel asks.

Victor briefly passes a hand over his face. "That's a complex philosophical and logistical question to which I can easily say no and he should probably say yes."

"Should I ask what you're doing exactly?" Nigel asks, more out of a desire to be irritating than anything else. Certainly, Victor deserves to be judged for whatever this outburst is.

"No, you should not," Victor snaps.

"But?"

"I may be feeling increasingly generous towards him," he says.

"Victor," Nigel chides.

"What?"

"That doesn't seem very fair to either of you."

"I so appreciate your need to defend a man you've never even met," Victor says snidely.

"He's in your life," Nigel says simply. "So I imagine someone has to. And if it bothers you so much, perhaps you should introduce us, if you've decided he's staying."

"Liam is in my life because he does not do or expect what every other person I have let into my life does or expects. And now the great worm of romanticism that has found its way into my heart means our arrangement may need to come to an end, because I am two decades well past trying to figure out how my sexuality is relevant to anybody else's needs," Victor says sharply, before finally looking away from Nigel. "I know how this goes. I discuss my feelings with him and he starts asking for things I have no interest in providing. So how's Liam? Fine, until I damage the fuck out of his already precarious little world."

10

Alex finally curls up in the armchair in his room at the end of his second night in New York, and he calls Paul. "I thought I'd continue the tradition of ill-advised late night phone calls," he says without preamble when Paul picks up.

"Hey there. How's it going?" Alex can hear the smile in Paul's voice.

"Only one person blatantly suggested I have sex with them today."

"Are you relieved or disappointed?"

"Am I Natalie?" Alex snarks before feeling guilty about it. It's not really her fault she knows how to play the very shitty game Hollywood lays out for women. It is her fault she's mean, but that's a different and not necessarily unrelated issue.

"No. You have different styles. Why aren't you out with everyone?"

"Officially off duty until morning media."

"Surely there are adventures?" Paul leads.

"Victor muttered something about social obligations in New Jersey, and I assume Liam is harassing friends or family. Don't know what anyone else is up to. Thought I'd be a good boy and stay in."

"Mmmmm, which is why you're calling me?"

Alex barks a laugh. "You know you don't have to actually be subtle about the phone sex, right?"

"I do now."

"Get your dick out," Alex says, laughing.

Paul chuckles. "Let me go be not here."

"Are you still working?" Alex asks, a little disbelieving.

"I'm home, but it's barely after nine."

"Ugh. What are you doing?" Even with the time difference, Paul's being overly dedicated.

"Storyboarding," Paul says.

"Well, don't come all over those."

"Hence moving to the bedroom, impatient one."

Alex hears Paul thump down the loft stairs and jog up the other flight to their bedroom. The door creaks open and closed – Todd is banned for all sorts of reasons, including shedding and a fascination with swinging objects, including those attached to their bodies. That had been a particularly unfortunate evening, although at least Alex now understands why Craig only took the dog.

As much as it's Alex who starts them off, phone sex still isn't something he really thinks of as his thing so much as an almost in-joke (a very pleasurable, filthy in-joke), thanks to the time Paul had

251

gotten Alex off on the phone when Craig was back in Paul's bed and Alex was being crazy.

Paul, though, loves it, would love it with anyone, that much is entirely clear. Alex is grateful for that, because it means he doesn't have to do most of the talking. The sex that works the best for him leaves him distinctly non-verbal. Masturbation and too much distance aren't really an exception. And right now what he wants, more than getting off, is Paul's voice and the way it makes him go quiet and his heart stand at attention.

Paul is happy to oblige, and Alex isn't even startled when he mentions Carly. Because the biggest problem with that incredibly weird moment sitting in Paul's lap by Victor's pool was that Paul whispering to him was hot and the timing was terrible.

It's ridiculously arousing when Paul tells him he's going to hold his head down between Carly's legs and make him lick until she gets off twice. Alex can almost feel the pressure of his wide palm across the back of his neck. The only thing he can hear other than Paul's breath and voice is the slick, wet sound of his own hand on his cock and a distant siren on the street below.

After they both come, they chuckle, but they don't talk about it at all. Alex isn't sure if that's the natural end of the topic or if there's a discussion to be had. Either way, it's something they need to talk about. It raises some questions about How They Do Things which they've never really talked about before, because *not like Liam* has always sufficed.

◆

Alex barely makes his flight back to L.A. He lets out a relieved breath only once he shoves his carryon in the overhead bin and slumps into his seat. As much as there are planes after that may even have seats, it's bad enough that he's landing at nine at night. Paul has to be at the airport at four in the morning. Between waiting for luggage and driving, that's maybe five hours they'll be in the same house, and five minutes after that they'll both be unconscious.

But before Alex can even text *landed* to Paul as his plane wanders LAX looking for a gate, his phone chimes.

Airport Westin. 2132.

???

Get your bag, get a cab, get here. Leave your bag if you want.

Alex laughs with delight, and then looks around sheepishly as he tugs his hat lower on his head. *Okay...*, he texts back, still marginally puzzled.

He's a lot less puzzled when he gets to the hotel and bangs on the door. Paul, hilariously, grabs him by the front of his shirt and yanks him inside.

"What –?" Alex blinks, startled, as he adjusts to this sudden and very welcome change in circumstance.

"I know you're exhausted –" Paul starts.

"Slept on the plane," Alex interrupts.

"*I know you're exhausted,*" Paul repeats, "and I know I should sleep, but this buys us a couple of hours and –"

"This is the most awesome thing you have ever done," Alex says when Paul trails off with a look of uncertainty.

"I'm sorry I didn't discuss it with you first?" Paul says meekly.

Alex cackles, even as it stabs at his heart a little. After everything in this absurd life they live together, he doesn't want Paul being afraid.

"Oh my God, just fuck me so we can order room service," Alex says. "Wait, how late does room service go?"

"All night," Paul says as they both start shucking clothes.

The sex follows the same pattern it has been between them lately. Alex isn't sure of the word for it. *Violent* seems wrong. As does *aggressive,* because sometimes Paul hurts him slowly, twisting bruising pinches into his thighs as he blows him. It's certainly a natural progression of what has always worked for them – Paul pushing Alex until he feels so much it hurts in the best way possible. It's just a little bit more explicit than it used to be.

That is, Alex supposes, a feature of growing up, or intimacy. Either that, or they're the perfect stereotype of *young, bored, and famous.* But they're too fucking good – and everything in their charmed lives has been too hard won – for Alex to write it off like that.

◆

Paul marks him everywhere, with mouth and nails, sucking and pinching. He bats Alex's hands away over and over again, wanting to watch what he does to him. The bruises bloom – red to white to the first flush of purple – and he refuses to let Alex pleasure him until he is wrung out and gone. It makes Paul smug to have Alex distant-present with desire. In these moments he could make Alex do anything, and that matters in the worlds of what they do.

Alex is so fair and so easy and eager to certain types of pain. That Paul gets to keep something of the history of those moments – it's amazing. But he keeps wondering when he's going to finally hit Alex's wall and find a *no.* He keeps wondering how bad of a conversation that's going to be.

"I should document these," Alex says after they've fucked and eaten, turning this way and that in the mirror on the bathroom door to see the marks. "Every time," he continues on, fascinated with himself in the way Paul supposes all actors are. "I really should."

"Isn't that dangerous in our lives?" Paul asks.

"I don't know if I care," Alex says, but the fact that he hasn't pulled out his phone to take a picture certainly makes it clear that he does.

"Com'ere," Paul says, shoving the room service tray a little bit more to the edge of the bed. He grabs Alex's hips when he stops in front of him. "Let me document it," Paul says.

"How?" Alex is wary.

"With my hands."

11

At work the next day Alex gets the tentative shooting schedule for the first block and his pages for the first week of filming. "Oh my God, no," Alex blurts.

It's bad enough that he's come to the lot straight from seeing Paul off at the airport. But that the first sequence back that's going to be filmed is a love scene with Zach and James is just *no*.

Standing next to him, having just got his own pages, Liam chuckles. "It's not going to be that bad."

Alex moans.

◆

"I don't care about the nudity," Alex snaps, when Victor attempts to mollify him. Actually, he's fairly sure the nudity is going to be the most awkward thing ever. Even if there isn't full-frontal, precedent says Victor can get away with a hell of a lot on their network in their timeslot.

Victor folds his arms. "Then what's the problem?"

"You controlling what I do and how I look."

"That's not anything new, and you're hardly being singled out."

"*This* is new," Alex says.

"You're beautiful, Alex. Why are you upset about this?" Victor asks, obviously curious.

"Stop saying that," Alex says sharply.

"Why?"

"I have one condition," Alex says instead of answering. He has no words to explain to Victor, or anyone, how dangerous being *beautiful* can be.

"What's that?" Victor asks.

"Zach isn't the one getting fucked."

Victor's eyebrows go up. Alex knows he's being judged and doesn't care.

"That's not particularly going to change how I make you look. Or what I make you do."

"No" Alex's smile is small and absolutely evil. He's not Zach, and he's still angry about Victor missing the point entirely, but if the narrative theme here is going to be gross anyway, at least it can be gross in his favor. America can seriously go fuck itself.

◆

"Hey, man, why'd you ask Victor if Zach could fuck James?"

Liam slides in across the table from Alex at lunch. Alex stares at him. Why does Liam know about that? "Excuse me?"

Liam shrugs. "I mean, it's not your thing. What does Zach fucking James get you?" He inexplicably takes a knife and fork to a slice of pizza. Alex has no idea why he does that, but he has bigger concerns than Liam's cutlery habits.

"The most awkward day at work with you ever?" he offers.

"Alex," Liam says reproachfully.

"It's going to be awkward." Alex pokes at his pasta with his fork.

"You're not answering the question."

"The question is weird." Also they're in the cafeteria, and Alex has no desire to discuss this where they might be overheard.

"I ask lots of weird questions," Liam says as if this line of discussion is entirely reasonable. "And you're the first person I've ever done a love scene with who I've actually fucked, so like, I'm trying to figure out how this all works."

"What about Natalie?" Alex asks.

Liam looks confused. "What about Natalie?"

"You had a thing and your characters had a thing."

"Oh. That was different. Marjani and James had their thing first. Actually, that's kind of how Natalie and I happened."

Alex stares. "What the fuck?"

"Not, like, on set," Liam explains patiently. "We went out for drinks after. Sort of like you and I did, although not in my hotel room. And you're way more fun."

"Liam!" Alex hisses.

"What?"

"Could you not? With the outloud voice?" Alex pleads.

"Oh," Liam looks around a little sheepishly. "Sorry."

"Whatever. Just...be quiet, oh my God."

"You still haven't answered," Liam says.

Alex sighs and pushes his plate away. "I don't want to expose myself for this any more than I have to, okay? You and me, fine. Me being gay, fine. Discovering, with you, how much I like to get fucked? Something I'd prefer not to share with the viewing public, thanks."

"You're a really good actor. And this is all just bullshit choreography in a cold studio. Nobody could mistake it for real. Even you. Promise."

Alex ignores Liam's pep talk and moans. "It's still going to be so fucking awkward."

"Worse than the pancakes?"

Liam cracks up when Alex glares at him.

♦

The sex choreography meeting is awkward as hell. The fact that there's such a thing as a sex choreography meeting at all is mind boggling to Alex.

Ellen is directing this episode. If he's going to be miserable in this particular way, at least it's with her at the helm. Although when she starts talking about how many seconds of thrusting the Department of Standards will allow, Alex puts his head down on the table and groans. Liam rubs his back soothingly, but he's laughing too hard to really mean it.

Zach and James have gotten hot and heavy on screen before, but they were always wearing clothes. The stripping and Zach shoving James down onto his back on the bed is orders of magnitude more awkward than the making out they've become accustomed to. Not to mention the goddamned hair pulling. Alex is fairly sure Victor put that there out of spite.

"You boarded the love scene, too?" Alex complains when Ellen brings out the storyboards. Bad enough the fans are going to be compulsively rewatching this frame-by-frame and in slow motion. He doesn't need to know the official planning material will live in the network's archives forever too.

She raises an eyebrow. "Did you want me to draw curtains blowing in the wind like a fucking Sirk film?"

Alex frowns. "What's a Sirk film?"

Ellen and Liam exchange disbelieving looks. Alex then gets a five-minute, digressive history lesson into German cinema and melodrama that does nothing to make this day less absurd.

"Alex," Ellen says as they're wrapping everything up. "A word with you on behalf of Makeup. There's a lot of skin here –"

"I hadn't noticed," Alex says drily.

"We can cover bruises. But if we cover bruises on you we cover freckles, and if we cover freckles then we have to cover *all* the freckles because putting freckles back on you is a pain in the ass we don't have time for. No climbing 'til after we shoot this, and tell your boyfriend to play more nicely, 'kay?"

Alex gapes. Liam covers his mouth to hide a grin.

"Just say 'Yes, Ellen,'" Ellen prompts.

Alex closes his mouth and settles for glaring at her. The state of his flesh should be no concern to the show, and he hates all of the ways that it is.

On the phone that night with Paul, he doesn't mention any of it. Bad enough that he has to battle Victor for his body and what it means. He doesn't need Paul's irrational Liam-jealousy on top of it all. Paul doesn't need the distraction anyway.

◆

Paul isn't the talent or even a well-known brand and personality the way Victor is. Unfortunately and unpleasantly for him, he still has to be at upfronts to convince people that he can be – and convince them to spend money with *Winsome*. Initial ad buys, as much as whatever the early viewing figures prove to be, are essential to a full season and the show's survival. Paul's not convinced he's charismatic enough for the job.

Thankfully he has Darcy and enough enthusiasm from the network that she's doing some of the stage show hosting; her theater career means there's no question she can handle the live audience. It's all bullshit, even if he's a little jealous of the actors and their crisp, preternatural ability to turn joyfully toward any camera. It'll be nice to commiserate with Alex later.

He's fairly certain, however, that for all the hell that Alex has had to deal with at upfronts over the years, he's never been faced with a crisis quite like Darcy's parents. Paul is sure they're perfectly nice people and appreciates, in principle, that they're supportive of their daughter. But constantly calling Darcy to spend time with the while she's in New York and camping out on the sidewalk outside of the fan-oriented part of upfronts, is really way too much. He wonders at what point they're going to become a liability as well as a nuisance. Also, how he should conduct the intervention at the point it becomes inevitably necessary?

Victor, when Paul calls him about it during the dead space between the stage presentation and the first round of parties, tells him sternly not to do anything, because they are the type of people looking for purchase to make a scene.

Paul asks him repeatedly if he's sure. Victor's answers get shorter each time until Paul eventually says, "You're giving me the eyebrow, aren't you?"

All of that is nothing, though, to seeing the three-minute *Winsome* trailer played onscreen at The Beacon for a live audience. Even though Paul spends most of his waking hours bogged down in the most mundane minutia of production, the final product is still magic. It's amazing.

Despite having clearly been raised by crazy people she now finds mildly embarrassing, at the parties Darcy is charming, bubbly, and way too chatty with the stars of some of the other shows. They are not there to party with their peers, but to flatter their way to economic viability. Ruth watches her, dryly amused, and Annette laughs when Paul sighs and goes to have what feels like a very necessary chat about where her attentions need to be focused.

Darcy may be a pro, but she's a theater kid pro. Which means she can't even begin to imagine the level of attention that's already started to come her way and the consequences of even the most normal of slightly ill-advised choices.

"Look, it's awesome you're making friends, but don't annoy anybody, and please, I'm begging you, don't sleep with anyone." Paul feels way too weary for this already.

Darcy frowns prettily. "You're not my big brother, Paul. Even though it's sweet, so thank you. I'm networking for you, go away."

"Make friends with the ad guys," he hisses.

"Do you think if I barter my virginity we can get a full-season pickup *and* a renewal?" she asks like she's not being appalling and inappropriate.

"I did not need to know that," Paul says, pointing at her wanting very much to back away and rejoin Annette.

Darcy frowns at her rum and Coke, which Paul probably should have also yelled at her for.

"No, you probably did," Darcy tells the drink, before putting her game face back on and bouncing over to the nearest cluster of ordinary, boring people to convince them that a show about an eighteen-year-old girl-pimp who has a day job at a convenience shop in the barren wastes that are most of America is the perfect platform for selling...well, anything. But probably particularly cleaning supplies, erectile dysfunction drugs, and cat food.

♦

"I never appreciated just how good you are at navigating this shit before," Paul tells Alex that night. It's incredible to him that Alex was only two years older than Darcy is now when he was doing all of this for the first time and with far less preparation. "Thank you for being well-adjusted."

Alex laughs.

The rest of the week isn't easy. The media is constant, the schedule is exhausting, and Darcy's parents remain obnoxious. But nothing turns into a crisis, and by the time he gets to the airport Paul is profoundly grateful that he's gotten through his first upfronts with his people and his show intact.

He wants to sleep on the flight. He's getting his hands on Alex once he's finally home, and he'd like to be awake enough for that to be worth both their whiles, but Darcy wants to post-mortem everything. While dealing with the newness was part of why they'd agreed to book seats together Paul largely wants to pretend the whole thing never happened.

Darcy puts her socked feet up on the empty seat between them and recounts every completely insane thing she said to someone older than her parents. Which doesn't change his mind. When he blanches at the pussy joke she apparently told everyone after he'd scolded her for her excessive flirting, she reminds him that their show is about whores.

She blinks owlishly at him. "Was I supposed to pretend it's not about whores?"

◆

By the time Paul gets his luggage and gets home, he's shrugged off most of the in-flight exhaustion. He struggles with his keys at the door, unable after all this time to tell the ones for the top and bottom locks apart.

When he finally fumbles the door open, Alex is leaning against the wall with his arms crossed over his chest.

"Problems?" he asks.

"Not anymore." Paul drops his luggage to reach for him. He unfolds Alex's arms and runs his hands up and down them.

"Was the flight terrible?"

Paul opens his mouth to tell him that working in Hollywood should be banned as unhealthy for any man, woman, or child, but then he shrugs and shakes his head. "It's over now."

Alex smiles one of his crinkly smiles that almost closes his eyes. "Upstairs?" he asks.

Paul doesn't have to be told twice. He's halfway undressed by the time they get up to their bedroom.

◆

Alex wants it just as much as Paul does, but he always marvels at Paul's need to write out his day on Alex's flesh. It's not something that goes both ways, even if Alex adores it in sensation and emotional weight.

"Let me ride you." He pulls Paul away from his neck by his hair and pushes him over.

Paul gasps, tilts his head back, and mumbles a thousand yeses. Alex grins smugly because he knows every time they do this, Paul is remembering the first time they were apart, and, more importantly, the first time they came back together. It will also, hopefully, keep Paul from marking the hell out of him without ever needing to have a discussion as to why.

Unfortunately, Alex is wrong. He can sit up straight and keep his neck tragically out of range of Paul's mouth as he fucks himself on his cock. But there's nothing he can do about Paul's nails raking deliciously over his chest and back but ask him to stop. And he does, eventually, because he has to.

"Don't." He grabs for Paul's hands.

Paul freezes, but that unfortunately includes his hips.

Alex whines. "Not that too," he pants, lifting up and sinking down aggressively to make his point.

"But?"

"The nails, not the nails," Alex says.

"Sorry. I never –"

"Shhhh. Makeup's pissed. I like. Show doesn't."

"You sure?" Paul grabs Alex's hips to still them.

"Yes," he says insistently. "I said yes. Now stop being scared and fuck me."

◆

The relief of upfronts being over lasts only until the next morning, when Paul is up at five while Alex grumbles under the covers because he doesn't have to be at work 'til eight. Alex knows that this is the life they signed up for – and has his own schedule keeping him busy – but he wishes Paul would take at least a morning off before they don't see each other awake for a week. Plus, he has to shoot the love scene today and wants to ignore the impending awkward of that for as long as possible.

Alex grabs at Paul when he walks by the bed on his way to the wardrobe. "Five more minutes?" He kneels up and tugs Paul toward him by the hand.

Paul looks like he's going to say no, but Alex smiles coyly at him and leans closer for a kiss.

He gets ten minutes.

◆

It's a supreme irony – and an inevitable outcome of one of the many misunderstandings *Fourth* fans have about reality – that Alex and Liam have actually fucked. That said, acting their characters fucking is absolutely not sexy at all. Thanks to the bathrobes between takes and the socks on dicks and the fact that set is for some reason fucking freezing, it's a long way from Alex's favorite day in front of the camera.

At one point Ellen yells at Alex for clenching his ass, because heaven forbid anyone have cellulite that shows. When Alex snarls back, because this day is just terrible, Liam collapses into laughter.

"Shut up," Alex snaps at him.

"Oh my God, your face."

"Lee," Alex pleads.

"Hey. Be glad it's your face I'm looking at."

As awkward as the day is, only some of that has to do with their history. A lot of it is simply the nature of the job and how much Alex hates some of the things it demands of him.

But it could be worse. If Alex has to trust his body to someone else in this ridiculous and somewhat humiliating way, he's glad it's Liam. Who has always been nothing but kind and peculiar and so matter-of-fact about all the vagaries of desire.

♦

Back on the lot, despite the grogginess from the too-short night with Alex, Paul is beginning to feel anxious. They've survived upfronts, but now that he and his people have done their part to ensure the economic viability of *Winsome*, the work feels way more high-stakes. In order to keep surviving, they have to make sure that the craft is the best it can be.

That means a full day on the lot, both on set and in the offices, the first day back. As much as he wishes he and Alex could both stay home, something akin to panic is setting in. From now on, every day is important, and he can't afford to fuck any of them up.

As late as Paul stays, because he wants to make sure everything goes perfectly, he still beats Alex home. He's relieved for the few quiet hours to get a few last things done and make sure his head is even more in the game.

♦

When Alex finally does get in, he yells from the front door that he's home. The day has been exhausting and he doesn't want to expend any more effort looking for Paul than he absolutely has to.

"I'm up here!" His boyfriend's voice comes from the loft after a delay that might have been him getting his headphones off but is probably just a lag in processing.

Alex pulls on the railing as he climbs up the stairs to Paul's office. When he gets there, he drapes himself over Paul's back and buries his face in Paul's shoulder. After a day spent way too tangled up with Liam, he wants Paul's body and his attention and to not have to talk at all.

"How was work?" Paul asks but doesn't stop typing.

Alex shrugs and loops his arms around Paul's neck. "Fine. What are you working on?'

"Script edits."

"Want a break?" Alex teases, running his thumb along the collar of Paul's sweater.

"Once I get this done," Paul says.

"Oh my God, you just got back yesterday, there is no way you are behind," Alex says, more disbelieving than annoyed.

Paul shrugs. "Don't you have anything else to do?"

"Who are you and what did you do with my boyfriend?" Alex is taken aback by the dismissiveness in Paul's voice. "We were apart for a week. Then we were at work. Now we are home from work. Come fuck me and then we'll make dinner."

"You go ahead, I've got to finish this first."

Alex makes an annoyed noise. Paul's tendency to get lost in his work is nothing new, but this is mildly ridiculous. *And they were apart for a week.* Alex wants, and he knows the buttons to press to get it.

"Fine," he says mildly. "I desperately need a shower, I smell like Liam. Sure you don't want to come?"

Paul's shoulders go tense in Alex's arms. "Why do you smell like Liam?" he asks tightly.

"Zach and James scene," Alex says.

"Love scene?" Paul asks. He sounds horrified.

"Yes." Alex sighs, pushing himself off of Paul and straightening up. If he'd wanted a reaction out of Paul he's certainly succeeded, but now it looks like this is going to turn into a thing and that makes him want space.

Paul spins around in his chair to face him. "You didn't tell me you were filming a love scene."

Alex folds his arms over his chest defiantly. "Does it matter?"

Paul is frowning darkly in a way he hardly ever does. Alex would feel more sympathetic if the whole premise of the burgeoning argument wasn't so stupid.

"Of course it matters!" Paul says. "Is this why I couldn't mark you up the other day?"

"I also couldn't go climbing this week because they were afraid I'd bang myself up. This isn't just about you."

"You told me Makeup bitched to you."

"They did."

"And then you lied about why."

"Paul, it's a scene. I'm an actor. Liam's an actor."

"And your ex."

"He hardly qualifies as my ex. He dumped me when he thought I wanted him to be my boyfriend." Alex stomps toward the stairs. Paul is being ridiculous.

Paul grabs his wrist. "You did want him to be your boyfriend."

Alex stares at him but doesn't try to get away. "You weren't there. You don't know, and you are being a jealous asshole. You have been a jealous asshole about Liam for *years*, possibly even regarding him and Carly, I'm not sure, but this is a new level of stupid."

"It's not that stupid when you're lying to me."

"When did you start writing an after-school special parody? I didn't lie."

"You omitted," Paul snaps.

"Yes, I did," Alex jerks his hand out of Paul's grasp and starts downstairs again. He wants out of this whole stupid fucking argument. "And you omitted Carly and your father and your *wrists* and the goddamn crickets!"

"What do the crickets have to do with anything?" Paul sounds both angry and bewildered as he shoves away from his chair.

Alex spins around at the bottom of the staircase and glares up at where Paul is hovering three-quarters of the way up. "I didn't tell you before that we were shooting Zach and James fucking because I knew you'd flip out. Go me, I was right."

"I am pissed at you. And I want to yell at you."

"Well, are you going to yell, or are you going to come take a shower with me?" Alex is never sure if Paul's recitations of the reactions he wants to have are a substitution for Paul actually reacting, or a threat. Either way, they're unsettling.

♦

In the bathroom, Paul crowds Alex back into the shower as soon as he gets the water on. He knows Alex wants or he wouldn't have asked, and Paul is happy for a distraction from work and the argument he's fairly certain isn't over. He shoves his hands into Alex's hair and his tongue into his mouth. Alex's head falls back and away under the spray, his body tense and his mind clearly somewhere else. Paul chases him, even if he knows the way he's kissing Alex is even less of a conversation than what they'd had in the loft.

Paul slides his hand around to the back of Alex's head and drags it up. "Hey," he says, biting at his collarbone. "Stay with me here."

He half expects Alex to shove him away lest Paul bruise him, but apparently that's no longer a concern or Alex has just decided it's not. Either way, Paul is happy to push it. It's got nothing to do with Liam right now and everything to do with the fact that Alex is naked in their shower and not totally present. Paul wants his attention back, and of all the things that get good reactions out of Alex, this is one that really works for both of them.

"I am," Alex mutters in response, but his eyes are still closed and his mouth is slack, like he's trying to will himself into the moment. "Keep going," he says when Paul doesn't do anything, his voice barely audible.

Paul bites again, this time at Alex's neck, and again, until Alex grabs at his shoulders and whimpers. It will feel cruel, later, how much Paul enjoys this part of it, but all he feels right now is Alex coming back to him, drawn by something in the pain or in Paul's hands giving it to him.

"There, that's better," Paul murmurs. He slides his hand down to Alex's cock. Alex smiles with his eyes still closed and begs for more.

12

The strain of the fight lingers. Alex wishes they could clear the air, but there's never time. He's working five or six days a week. When Paul takes a day off it never overlaps with Alex's downtime. The *Fourth* renewal deal really does mean no breaks for anyone. Alex – and everyone else – are wearier right from the get-go.

A handful of people depart for *Winsome*, per Victor and Paul's agreement, which means that even as *Fourth* is entering its terrible year of shooting with no vacations that's only going to end in the death of the show, work on *Winsome* is going into full swing. Alex finds it incredibly odd that colleagues of his are leaving Victor's show for his partner's. He feels like Paul made a deal with the devil, even if he's aware Paul doesn't see it that way and deserves a good staff. Alex still finds it incredibly weird that Victor and Paul are business partners.

That's probably unfair, given how entangled their work and personal lives are. One night Alex manages to pry Paul away from his desk long enough to get him into bed. They spend the afterglow wrapped around each other, and Paul mentions that Darcy's character on *Winsome* is getting a gun.

"Apparently it's the summer of firearms." Paul chuckles darkly.

"At least tell me someone's going to teach her to shoot properly," Alex says. No one on TV seems to ever know how and it frustrates him no end.

"Is someone volunteering?" Paul runs a hand down Alex's side. Alex stretches and then curls into him.

"If you're not going to get anybody else to, yes."

◆

Alex calls Darcy to set a date to go to the range and finds her as enthusiastic about shooting as she is about everything she does. Alex's own younger sister is unpredictable at best, and he's not sure if Darcy wants an older brother or a friend in him. But, despite her Broadway-turned-L.A. dysfunction, Alex likes her and finds her irritating only in ways that are fun to push back against.

Darcy is inquisitive as they walk into the range, not just about the mechanics of what they're about to do, but about what it all means. Alex has spent enough time telling her about what life in the ass-end of America is like that her questions are, by now, useful ones.

The media is still in love with Alex's Cinderella rise from Indiana.

But the story has become so packaged and oft-repeated that the parts of it that are important to him never get talked about. Most of the time, he's perfectly happy with that. Paragon is not a place he ever wants to return to.

But Darcy has gotten the full story, or as much of it as anyone has. Including all the awful, little details none of the interviewers ask about and no one really wants to know anyway. America prefers its poverty to be romantic. There is very little romantic about growing up in a town of seven hundred people where everyone is divorced or unmarried, people live in houses worth less than Alex's trailer on set, and at least one kid in his high school class died every year in a DUI or farm accident. It had been satisfying to watch Darcy's eyes go wide at his recital of those statistics, and it is satisfying to know that the world is going to get parts of Alex's story it doesn't want or like, even if it never knows that's what's happening.

Darcy doesn't bat an eye at the sketchiness of the area the range is in. Alex doesn't know if that's because she's very even or has no barometer for what's 'normal'. Inside the range she's curious and attentive, and by the end of the session she's doing reasonably well. Alex can't help but text Paul to tease him: *Your starlet is a way better shot than you.*

She does, however, ask a number of prying questions about him and Paul. She's being nosey, and she may be as bad a gossip as Liam. Glad to have someone removed from the situation to talk to, Alex confesses that things have been strange since Paul got back from upfronts.

"He seemed fine in New York," Darcy says.

"Paul is very good at seeming fine," Alex says darkly, remembering crickets and kitchens.

Darcy bites her lip and doesn't ask anything else.

At the end of the day, Alex takes a picture of himself and Darcy to send to Paul, but decides to tweet it instead.

"Are you sure you want to do that?" Darcy asks uncertainly as Alex futzes with his infrequently used account. "After everything in South Carolina?"

"Are you worried about your reputation?"

Darcy shakes her head. "No. Nor the show's, really. I mean, you're J. Alex Cook. Any gossip about this is gonna get you way more attention than it does me."

Alex stares at her, then grins fiercely. "I can't fuck up *Fourth's* renewal deal anymore, and I am so done being America's sweetheart." He punches send on the photo. "That's your job now."

♦

When Alex gets home from the range that night Paul isn't there, and the internet is already going on a mini rampage over Alex and guns. Again. As entertaining as that is, Paul's absence is irritating. This is Alex's one day off before another six-day block of shooting, and he wants some time. They're not going to be awake and together for more than an hour a day for at least the next ten days. Sometimes, their jobs suck.

Paul, though, is not making their lives any easier. Whatever panic he'd brought back from New York and upfronts is clearly still alive and well weeks later. His twelve-hour days at the office are getting longer.

On the rare occasions he is home, he rarely leaves his office except to go to bed. Even that he does reluctantly. To Alex, it becomes something of a game: how naked does he have to get – and how obnoxious does he have to be – before Paul loses focus and chases him.

Their days are exhausting and their schedules are punishing, but when their hands are on each other the rest of the world disappears: it's just them as they work best. Once they're in bed everything is fine. When they're done Paul always kisses Alex sweetly, if, increasingly a little distractedly, and then Alex drags them back to their room or under the covers. They still curl up in bed every time for as long as they can, but as the weeks go on that time gets shorter and shorter. Alex will rest his forehead against Paul's, and Paul will grab his hands, and they'll both try to start conversations that aren't "Wait, did *you* feed Todd today?"

For a while it works, but as they get into the middle of summer, Paul's hours get even longer, and the relentless *Fourth* schedule starts to take its toll on Alex. Everything turns into a discussion of their jobs or their friends or the future. Of course, on some level, it's all really about Liam. Meanwhile, Paul remains hurt that Alex keeps saying no marriage. Alex can't believe Paul, not when he keeps bringing up the issue when Alex is almost asleep or halfway out the door.

Eventually they give up trying, and the conversations in the dark stop happening. The time they do have together is much better spent quietly and peacefully in each other's arms, in this one room that belongs to them and nothing else in the world.

♦

"Are you coming to bed at all, or are you going to sleep at your desk?" Alex shouts up from the living room where he's putting the last touches on the pack for his climb tomorrow. He has a day off, and he would like to take advantage of the rare chance to sleep in with a late night with Paul.

"Yeah," Paul calls back down distractedly.

"Yeah, you're coming, or yeah, you're putting Victor to shame with your insomnia?"

"Can you give me thirty minutes?" Paul's voice is tight.

"You mean the thirty minutes that looks like an hour?"

"Alex –" Paul starts, sounding somewhere between guilty and warning.

"Okay," Alex closes the last buckle on his bag viciously. "Waiting up for you."

Alex falls asleep reading. When he wakes up in the morning his book is still open on his chest and the other side of the bed is empty.

He finds Paul in the bedroom that Alex still thinks of as Gemma's, asleep on top of the covers.

"Hey," Alex sits quietly on the edge of the mattress and nudges Paul's shoulder to wake him. "Didn't think you were actually going to pull a Victor."

Paul blinks blearily. "Came in here to rest my eyes."

"Hope they're rested; it's morning now."

"Ugh, not really. Do you have any idea how loud the wind is in here?"

"All the more reason to come to, you know, actual bed," Alex runs a hand over Paul's shoulder. The house backs up onto a canyon and sometimes when the wind howls down it, it sounds like voices. Alex doesn't mind much, but it's always freaked Paul out a little.

"It sounded like someone was dying. Are you leaving?" Paul squints at the faded jeans and T-shirt Alex wears for climbs.

"Yeah. Wanted to see if you were still here first."

"I am," Paul says, pushing himself upright and reaching for his glasses on the nightstand. "What time is it?"

"Almost eight."

"God, I need to –" Paul trails off, frowning and clearly scrambling to remember his to-do list for the day.

"You need to take a shower." Alex grimaces and kisses him briefly before he stands up.

"Be careful," Paul calls after him as Alex leaves with a wave. "Love you!"

Alex laughs from the stairs. "I'll be back tonight. Don't forget to eat."

♦

When Alex gets back, he's not sure Paul's left his office at all.

"Are you seriously still working?" he asks, grimy and sweaty and glad to be home. He nudges Paul's papers aside so he can sit on his desk. He's been gone all day, didn't share a bed with Paul last night, and wants nothing more right now than time with his boyfriend. "Come to bed with me."

Paul, to Alex's annoyance, rolls his eyes as he catches a stack of script pages before they can fall. "Can it wait?"

"Not asking for sex," he says with more shortness than he should. "It's past midnight. Come sleep."

"I need to get this done," Paul protests. "There's a table read tomorrow and the guys need notes on the script early enough to have time to fix it before the big guys hear it."

"You know this would be easier if you'd accept the reality of a head writer who isn't you." Alex nudges at one of the little wheels on Paul's chair with his foot.

"Since when are you an expert on show running?" Paul asks.

"Paul," Alex says. Everything about this hurts, from Paul's tone to the fact that Alex has to beg for Paul's attention. "You always have something to get done. I never see you awake anymore. Please?"

"Sorry." Paul doesn't bother to hide his impatience. "This work is important, not just for me. I don't have time to indulge you tonight."

"I am your boyfriend, not an indulgence," Alex snaps, stung. Paul may hedge and postpone and forget, but he's never outright refused. Alex levers himself off of the desk.

"Where are you going?" Paul turns around in his chair to look at him.

For a moment Alex thinks he's going to get called back for an apology. This conversation is strange and scary and not how they work at all. "I'm going to sulk."

"Sulk quietly."

Alex doesn't know if that's supposed to be a joke or not.

♦

That night, Paul doesn't go to bed at all.

The next night, he does, dragging Alex upstairs as soon as he gets home from work. Alex laughs, and Paul feels guilty at how relieved it sounds.

Paul fucks him, hard. That's a relief too, although a less guilty one. Alex throws his head back while Paul bites bruises into his neck and drags heavy fingernails down his back. Paul feels a little crazy with how much damage he wants to do. Alex doesn't stop him, whimpering instead and urging him on.

When they're done, Paul is left on his knees on the bed while Alex blinks dreamily up at him from the sheets. His skin is a riot of marks, spots of purple and wider patches of stinging red. The play is more intense than anything they've ever done together, and Alex can't seem to make words even as he's smiling.

Paul traces the edge of a cluster of bruises at Alex's collarbone carefully and flinches when Alex hisses.

"I'm so sorry," Paul breathes. Alex is beautiful and in pain; Paul is a little horrified to be responsible for it.

Alex frowns. "It's okay," he gets out. Paul doesn't know whether he should believe him.

♦

As time goes on Paul finds it easier and easier to sleep in the loft. At first he tells himself he's just napping, but when naps are all he ever has time for it starts to look different. Alex is a slippery slope of so many things: Jealousy, obsession, and the way Paul always fucks everything up either at work, because he can never stay on top of it, or at home, because these things happened with Craig too.

He wants to believe, like so much other pain in his life, that this period of time is something he – and Alex – can wait out. That this is an inevitable cost of what they have, professionally and personally. But it only takes thirty days to form a habit – Paul heard that on some talk show once – and it becomes easier not just to sleep on the other side of the house, but to have clothes and a toothbrush there. It becomes Paul's command center. Not for his work, but for his life.

♦

Alex assumes, at first, that this will blow over. That, terrible as it is, Paul is going through a patch of temporary insanity. He'll spend a few days running too much and sleeping too little but come out on the other side more or less intact, and more or less Alex's. Lonely and hurt as Alex is, the alternative, at first, doesn't even make enough sense to consider. He and Paul have been together, in one way or another, for nearly two years now. Paul's eagerness to give him attention has been a star around which Alex has revolved even longer, ever since the day Paul busted him for making out with Nick in front of the coffee maker.

But as the nights go on with no sign of thaw or explanation, Alex starts to doubt. As far as he can tell they're still together. Certainly the situation looks nothing like the one when they broke up before. But that the state of their relationship even crosses his mind as a question is jarring the first time it happens. Realizing his certainty in Paul is gone is frightening.

When Alex puts it to himself that way it seems dramatic, but then, he has never gotten a no from Paul before. Without any other relationship experience to go on, he can only assume it means something terrible. And Paul, who has always taught him how to do these things, has declared he has no time for him.

13

Paul comes home one night in June to find Alex sitting on the couch. There's nothing dire about that in and of itself, but he's sitting still with no sign of book or script or laptop near him. Paul watched Alex learn to act, wrote Alex into what he is now – and perhaps always was – so gifted at. He knows he's been practicing, composing and waiting, if not in his spot in the corner of the sofa's arm, then in his mind. Probably for days.

"Are you moving out, or have you actually moved out already and didn't bother to tell me?" Alex asks without preamble.

"I don't know what that means," Paul says hesitantly, even though he feels like he's been punched.

"Yes, you do. I've been sleeping alone for weeks."

"I certainly haven't been sleeping anywhere else," Paul says. He's tired, and he's annoyed, and he's frankly furious at Alex for having so deliberately chosen a moment. That's some sort of cryptic, additional insult that Paul can't even begin to figure out.

"Our bathroom and closet are still functional. Or should I say my bathroom and closet. Tell me what I should be reading into this, other than that the honeymoon is most definitely over?"

"The honeymoon is hardly over when you won't marry me." Paul knows it's a mistake as soon as he says it, but he can't take the words back. Alex's face twists in disgust.

"Oh my God. What the fuck?" Alex says. "I am twenty-three. Your parents are separated because your dad badgered you into slitting your wrists. I don't even know my dad, and this is how you try to convince me to change my feelings about an institution which, by the way, has been irrelevant to our people for, like, ever…until advertisers decided we had to be normal enough to market to? You are out of your fucking mind."

"When did you become a queer radical?"

"When you tweeted a picture of me with a gun," Alex says casually.

"After that bullshit, you think I care about *normal*?" Paul can't follow whatever strange thread Alex is weaving. "I care about you. And I would like to marry you, if you could wrap your fucking millennial brain around the concept."

Alex sighs. "I am not a child. Not any more than you, anyway. And is that the deal, you only want me if you own me? Sleeping in separate rooms…. Not even talking about the sex here, but this whole thing is feeling a bit medieval."

Paul snorts. "I would like more of you than I have, yes. Especially considering how much of you Liam still has."

"Oh my God. I AM RIGHT HERE. I am right here for the taking, and you have been ignoring me for a *month*. I *work* with Liam. He is my friend. And in case you haven't noticed, we have both made families out of our friends because our families are fucking broken, and I don't understand why you get to have pajama time sleepovers with Carly and then get pissed when I talk to Liam *at work!*"

"I don't fuck women," Paul says dismissively.

"You suggested we have a threesome with her."

"Because you'd be hot with her!"

Alex gapes. "Okay, can that, like, be beside the point while you stop and listen to yourself?"

Paul runs his hands back through his hair. "Our friends and their issues are not the point," he says wearily. "I'm sorry I've been busy, okay? But, fuck, Alex, you know what this life is like. You wanted me to do this. You made a big deal out of it. Don't be pissed at me because you suddenly don't like the costs."

"The other half of that deal was that we would make a go of a relationship," Alex says. "And, frankly, I'm not sure we're in one anymore. By the way, have you always had this ability to rewrite and forget events, or did you learn it on purpose? Or by accident?" His voice is oddly sharp, and Paul winces.

He has, however, no idea how to respond to any of that. "Do you know how many people depend on me?" Paul asks, frustrated.

"I depend on you!"

"You have a job and resources regardless of whether I fuck up," Paul says. "They don't. You're also probably the most resilient person I've ever met. My time is limited and I am trying to do the right thing at every fucking miserable second of this shit."

Alex looks away. "Maybe I don't want to be that resilient anymore."

14

Alex gives up and stops asking Paul to bed. It hurts far too much when he knows the only answer he's going to get is no. Paul doesn't go back into their room except when Alex is out to grab more of his clothes. Alex knows because he starts to check the closet.

Alex sleeps badly, whether from the stress of the situation or from having to sleep alone. To make it worse, Liam badgers him at work when he starts dragging in pale and exhausted. Alex is sure Liam can tell what the genre of problem must be without Alex having to confess anything, but it doesn't stop him from asking.

"Are you not talking because you don't talk, or are you not talking because of our history?" he asks one morning.

Alex wishes he could sit in the courtyard and drink his terrible coffee in peace and maybe go back to sleep.

"What are you even talking about?" Alex tries to deflect. He wishes Liam would learn to do small talk.

Liam sits down next to him on the bench, way inside Alex's preferred bubble of personal space. "Dude, I know something's up with you and Paul."

"Leave it."

"Look, I don't mean to be an asshole here, and I suppose this may be like all sorts of bonus terrible coming from me because I don't actually know how your brain works, but I kind of know how to do relationships, so you should, like, maybe talk to me?"

Alex considers telling all in an effort to make him go the fuck away. He does not care about the exact number of days Liam has been with Carly or Victor or whoever. And he doesn't want advice; he wants to focus on being someone fictional whose life sucks less than his real one.

"Things at home aren't good. No, it's not that Paul is busy. And no, it's not blowing over. We tried that theory," Alex says, clipped and terse.

"This is all just stuff you have to learn how to do." Liam worries his teeth over his lip. "It's okay that you kind of don't know how yet. Although it's sad that Paul doesn't. You should make him look at that."

Alex gives Liam a sarcastic *thank you* before going to hide in his trailer where he finds himself wondering if Craig actually took the dog because Paul didn't have time to walk him.

◆

"Is Alex going to come visit set again?" Darcy asks from her perch on top of the low bookshelf that runs the length of the wall in Paul's office. Paul has no idea why, but she's claimed it as her spot whenever she's in here for a meeting. Or to pester him.

"I don't know. Why?" Paul sighs. Alex has been disruptive enough to his work at home. He can't imagine it would be good to have him at the office as well.

Darcy shrugs. "I like him. He's fun to have around."

Paul frowns. "What has he been telling you?"

Darcy swings her foot gently against the shelf. "Nothing."

Paul suspects that's a flat-out lie – the rest of their friends' loyalties he can predict, but Darcy tries to play all sides. Sometimes, frighteningly, she even succeeds. Right now, though, he doesn't even have the energy to care what ulterior motives she may have.

After an interval where Paul clicks through work on his screen and Darcy is blessedly silent, she twirls the end of one of her braids around her finger. "Are things okay with you two?"

Paul considers lying, but the effort is too much. "No," he says shortly.

Now that the separate bedrooms aren't just a logistical shortcut but part of the ongoing fight their relationship has become, sleeping apart from Alex is awful and a constant reminder of how bad things are. Paul rubs absently at the back of his neck; his head is starting to ache. Even during their first separation, when Alex was on the opposite coast and Paul was a mess not knowing what they were, Paul woke up for weeks expecting Alex to be next to him. Nearly two years of living together doesn't make Alex's absence from his bed – or his from Alex's – any easier even if it's quite nearly by his own choice.

"What's wrong?"

He looks at her over the top of the computer screen. She looks genuinely concerned. Paul's vaguely aware that he shouldn't be telling one of his employees any of this. Especially not an eighteen-year-old virgin who has very little experience of real people in real relationships that have an arc longer than two hours and don't involve singing. But then Paul has never been in a place where work and personal lives aren't impossibly entangled, and it's not like he's been able to talk to Alex effectively about any of it.

"What isn't wrong?" he says.

"Are you guys breaking up?"

Paul chuckles darkly. "Way to be blunt."

"Are you?"

"No. Not yet."

"Why?"

Paul slumps back in his chair. Paul misses Alex desperately and resents missing him. It's just one more way Alex is taking his attention when it really needs to be elsewhere. Their terrible conversations are terrible, and he's constantly terrified that the next one may be the last one. "This show is a full-time commitment. Alex wants way more of my time than I can give him because I can't give him any of it."

Darcy raises an eyebrow; Paul wants to laugh at her judgmentalness. "Not any?"

"If the first thirteen episodes don't go well, we're finished. I've already sunk so much time into *Winsome*, if I give up on it now it's a waste. And I'll fail."

"Way to have faith in the rest of us." Darcy folds her arms over her chest.

Paul shrugs. If *Winsome* tanks, it really will be on him. He's filled this show with the best he could find. "I love him, but every day I think about how much easier my life would be if I did pack up and leave."

"Would it really be easier?"

"More painful, maybe, but yes. It might not be up to me anyway – Alex is thinking of leaving, too."

"Is he really? Did he say something?"

"He doesn't have to say anything." They may have fixed fewer of their communication issues than Paul could wish, but he still knows Alex. This, he's sure of, even if the prospect frightens him less than the idea of his own exit. Other people have never been Paul's worst enemy.

"How did this happen?" Darcy asks. "You used to be awesome."

Paul sighs. "Life happened. The show happened. Somewhere along the line I decided the story was more important."

"Idiot," Darcy says. Her voice is affectionate, but she looks hurt and worried. "Alex is your story."

◆

Paul still makes an effort to go to brunch, because having friends is an important part of being human. Paul desperately needs to still be human, even if, and especially because, he's a miserable failure of a boyfriend. Among other things, Alex is starting to look like a data point.

But sitting in the parking lot at their usual place, tapping his phone off the steering wheel, Paul frets. Alex left for a climb this morning but hasn't texted to say he got to the mountain safely, and he always texts. Paul thinks about walking inside and facing their friends. He can't do it. Brian will be snarky about Alex not coming because he's always snarky. Shawna will be worried because Paul's been avoiding her. Craig will be there with their fucking dog.

Paul starts his car again. Maybe he's driving home to wait for the end of it all, but, at the moment, that's a far better option than having to sit and smile and lie.

◆

Carly lets herself into Victor's house with her key. She feels weird about the fact that she, in addition to Liam, has keys to Victor's house. Any time she's raised the subject, though, Victor says that he resents interruptions so intensely that he'd rather trust them than have to bother with the door when they come over.

"Okay, we need to talk," Carly calls as she nudges the door closed with her foot and makes her way to the kitchen. Victor nods at her from the stove where he's making omelets.

"About?" he asks blandly. He crumbles cheese into one of the pans. Carly kisses Liam hello where he's sitting at the bar that divides the kitchen from the next room, his bare feet hooked on the crossbar of the stool.

"I just got off the phone with Paul. What the fuck is going on with him and Alex?" she says, dropping her bags down and leaning into Liam's side. He snakes an arm around her waist and frowns.

"Nothing good," Liam says.

"Obviously," Victor says. They all sit there silently for a long moment, listening to the faint gas hiss of the stove and Victor occasionally scraping the pans against the burners as he flips the omelets.

"I think it's Paul," Liam says.

"Don't take sides, Lee," Victor chides. "Alex is likely being unhelpful, stubborn, and possibly mean. But Paul is insecure, and that's dangerous."

They eat brunch at the circular black iron cafe table out by the pool. Carly helps ferry things out – utensils, napkins, a pitcher of juice – while Liam sits and fidgets, squinting into the sun.

"I assume at least one of you knows more about this than me," Victor says as he slides each of their plates – pesto and goat cheese for Liam; sun-dried tomatoes, spinach, and mushrooms for Carly; and summer squash for himself – onto the table.

Carly and Liam glance at each other without turning their heads. Victor laughs.

"Well, tell me what's happening," he says, "or start talking about the weather."

Liam goes first. Victor frowns through the not very informative story.

"Why didn't you tell me?" he asks.

"It's not your business," Liam says with a shrug.

Victor narrows his eyes. "Yes," he says with a smile. "But why didn't you tell me?"

Liam puts his utensils down as he considers what to say. He brushes the fingers of one hand across the other, almost as if sketching small figures in front of him. This is what he does whenever he finds himself looking for words.

"The story hasn't turned yet," he says eventually.

"What do you mean?" Carly asks.

"You're worried about what's happened," Victor says pointing at her. Then he points at Liam. "He's telling you that the thing to worry about hasn't happened yet."

15

Solo climbs are, as Alex's various instructors have insisted on telling him, riskier than partnered ones. Free climbs are even worse. But there's no one Alex trusts who also has time enough to meet him as a regular climbing partner, and he's hardly in the sport for the companionship.

He's not free climbing today because the weather looks iffy and, while Alex likes the physical risk and challenge, he does not actually have a death wish. He is alone, however, on one of the routes he hasn't been able to complete yet. He's grateful, as always, for the silence and the solitude. Home is way too quiet, but it's impossible to think there anymore because the silence between him and Paul is so damn loud. Alex is dreading the day when he finally comes home and finds Paul's car and everything gone. He's never regretted pulling his own version of that stunt on Paul years ago more than he has in the last few weeks.

His misery at work is, at least, solidifying into something actually useful. His work on *Fourth* is far from over – he, Liam, and some of the rest of the cast are headed to D.C. soon to do exteriors – but the show's days are still numbered. Alex can either get out now or wait to go down with the ship. Either way, he's not worried about finding work. But, now that he's had to start thinking of the future he can't unsee the opportunities either. There are new things to do and try and be, none of which can happen while he's still Zach Reagan and tied to Victor's behemoth.

Zach's due for his next big adventure anyway. He wiggles his fingers into a crevice and braces his weight carefully to dig his foot into the next toehold. Victor will be pissed, but Alex will hardly be the first star to jump ship for other things. He'll enjoy the challenge of finding Zach a good send-off. Liam probably won't like it, but losing Zach in one way or another will be good for James.

He's unbalanced, or the foothold isn't as strong as he thought it was, because Alex loses his footing, banging into the cliff face and getting rocked, yet again. He swears at the bite and sting of it and the way it's always scary, even with safety equipment. As he lets the ropes hold him for a moment as he comes down from the adrenaline spike, Alex giggles. He knows exactly what Zach's end is going to be.

He can't wait to tell Victor.

◆

Alex wants to tell Paul, too. Talking things out with him is part of how Alex has come to process the world, even if words with everyone else are often so damn hard.

But Paul's car isn't in the garage. The house is empty and quiet except for Todd, who winds around Alex's ankles looking to be fed. Alex is annoyed. Not even at Paul's general absence, which is nothing remotely new. But because he's not here when Alex actually has something to talk about that isn't one of their eight hundred fucking problems.

It's late already. Alex's call is early, and there's no point waiting up, so he doesn't.

◆

Alex waits to talk to Victor until shooting is done for the day. And then he waits longer. He has no urge to go home, and it feels right to do this when no one else is around to witness it.

He doesn't bother to knock on Victor's door, just leans into the office.

"Victor," he says.

"Yes?" The other man looks up from his desk.

"I need to talk to you."

Victor waves him into the room. Alex drops into the chair on the other side of the desk without further invitation.

On some level it's bizarre to sit across from Victor in this same office, in the exact same chair, where his whole new life began. Except that now, unlike then, he understands his job and is sure of what comes next.

"I'm out," he says.

"Really," Victor drawls.

"Yes. Don't act like you're surprised."

"Surprised, no. Curious, yes. Why now?"

"Because I know how it ends. And why you're not going to be pissed at me for quitting." Alex leans forward in his chair, wanting to be closer to Victor for possibly the first time ever. "At the end of the third arc, you're going to kill Zach, and it's going to be *awesome*."

Victor sits back in his chair and laughs. "This is why you are my other favorite."

Alex smiles, fierce and sly.

"Who else have you told?"

"Nobody."

"Not even Paul?" Victor asks. The question is leading.

"No. I will."

Victor pauses at that only slightly. "And Liam?"

"What do you think?"

Victor looks surprised. Probably because Alex asked an honest question instead of giving a sarcastic response. He has no idea what to do about Liam.

"When you're ready to," Victor says, "tell him you're quitting. I'll tell him about Zach."

Alex nods.

"This is going to make your D.C. shoot interesting."

"D.C. shoots are always interesting. And rarely good," Alex says.

Victor frowns. "D.C. is fine. It's the messes you drag after yourself that are not."

Alex shrugs, as if lying to Victor, or to himself, is no big deal. They both know what D.C. means to him and that there are only some days when he enjoys the sensation of a thumb pressed into the bruise.

♦

The night before Alex leaves for Washington, an appallingly hot night at the end of July, Paul is actually home, in the kitchen, when Alex finally comes in from work.

"Hey," Alex says softly, because Paul's *there* and not, for the moment, working. He's a little surprised and a lot grateful.

"Hey." Paul turns around and leans against the sink.

"I'm leaving tomorrow," Alex says. It's almost a question.

"Are –"

"The shoot. I just meant the shoot. But we should talk."

"Okay." Paul braces his hands on the edge of the counter.

Alex laughs, awkward and wet. "Can we not... in the kitchen?" He feels guilty for asking.

Paul nods and drops his chin onto his chest. "That is... fair and awkward," he tries.

Alex smiles, almost, and heads into the living room. Once there he doesn't know where to sit and stands a little uncomfortably by one of the big bookcases in lieu of figuring it out.

"Is this a you telling me things conversation?" Paul asks when he finally walks into the room.

"No. Yes... I have some things to tell you, but that's not what this is. I don't think," Alex says.

"Go ahead." Paul petulantly drops onto the couch.

Alex works not to grit his teeth and ball his hands into angry fists. He can't help but feel like Paul is trying to make trouble when they already have enough.

"I'm quitting," he says. "*Fourth*," he adds, before Paul can interject, again.

Of the roster of things Paul might have fairly expected Alex to come home with, Alex quitting his job was clearly nowhere near the list. He looks a little stunned. "Is this because of me?"

"No," Alex says. It's a vain and obnoxious question, but he also recognizes that it's not an unreasonable one. "I won't say I'm not thinking about shit differently because of whatever is going on with us, but I don't want to wait 'til the end. I want to have choices."

"That feels incredibly ominous." Paul's voice is more than a little snide.

Alex folds his arms over his chest. "Yeah. Well, right now, every time I come home feels a little bit ominous. Does it for you too?"

"Considering that you're avoiding me and we didn't talk about this?" Paul asks, leaning his elbows on his knees and looking up at Alex sharply. "Yeah."

Alex frowns. "You get that you're the one who moved into the other bedroom, right?"

"I thought maybe that would be clearer and less disappointing to you."

"What is going on in your head?" Alex asks. Every time they touch this mess it seems to make less sense than the time before.

"*You.* You're quitting your job. I didn't even know you were thinking about this –"

"You should have," Alex puts in, unhelpfully, but it's true. Victor knew, and Paul hasn't been home to tell.

"You don't get to ask me to be psychic," Paul says. "Everything else may be fucked, but I thought we had had that one thing cleared up thanks to the Great Thanksgiving Disaster."

"I didn't know it had a name," Alex says. "When did it get a name? When you liked me and it was funny or when you apparently started keeping score?"

"I can like you and not us, and I am always keeping score."

"What the fuck?" Alex starts pacing. He doesn't understand or really even recognize Paul right now.

"On me. Not you," Paul says.

It's no less horrible, but it at least makes slightly more sense. "You shouldn't do that," Alex says quietly.

"When's your flight?"

"Tomorrow at noon."

"I'll be at work."

"I assumed," Alex says shortly.

"When are you getting back?" Paul asks.

"I don't know. The schedule's still iffy. Will you even be here when I do?" It's the one terrible question. Alex is both glad Paul is actually here to answer it, and terrified of the answer, because he has absolutely no idea.

"I don't know either."

"Okay then," Alex says and sinks down onto the chair across from Paul. "Okay."

"I think we either need to make a decision now," Paul says carefully, "Or agree that we won't, until you're back."

Alex bites his lip and nods. "What do you want to do?"

"Frankly? I don't even have time to break up with you right now."

Alex thinks about throwing him out right then and there. It's not that the loss of the relationship hurts, although it does. It's that everything Paul is saying makes him feel so small.

"Trial separation, then?" he asks quietly.

Paul nods. "Something like that."

"Can I call you?" Alex asks. "When I'm on the road."

"You always do," Paul offers. It's not kind.

"Is that a no?" Alex says tightly.

"It's a maybe. You do what you want, no matter how ill-advised, and there's never an instant where I can even imagine saying no to you. That scares me to death, and it was there from the second I laid eyes on you. What if that cost me Craig and a normal, boring life –"

"You work in TV. Normal and boring weren't ever going to be an option."

"Yeah, and my number-one obsession has to be this show. That might have been possible with someone else, but it doesn't feel possible with you. I can't let you cost me this."

"That's a whole lot of irrational and unfair," Alex says. "I'm not going to cost you your show."

"You have no idea what it's like to be in love with you."

"Then tell me about it." Alex isn't fishing for compliments, nor is he hoping Paul remembers; he's hunting for clues.

"You overwhelm me. And I'm already on my second chance. If I fail at this because I never said no to you, you'll hate me. I'll hate myself."

Aside from offering reassurance he's fairly certain won't actually make a difference, Alex wants, very desperately, to tell Paul he is not cut out for this. That he should be the head writer and let someone else be showrunner and producer and all-around mad emperor. He also knows that, no matter how potentially accurate it may be, it's not a sentiment Paul wants or needs to hear right now. It certainly won't help their relationship.

"I know," he says. "You're also not Victor."

"If I could just be disciplined enough –"

"And what? Play with people like flies to rip the wings off of?" Alex asks.

"You think better of him than that."

"Not really. I don't make moral judgments about it, but I know what he is. I'm not sure why no one else does, but that doesn't matter. Everybody needs love, even flawed, controlling, funny, creepy

Victor. And certainly even you."

"He doesn't," Paul says. "And it makes me feel like maybe I shouldn't either."

Alex folds his arms over his chest. "You are being ridiculous. Victor hates humanity and yet has some fucked up thing with Liam. You're being a crappy boyfriend, and you both work in TV. That's it. That's the whole similarity, *your jobs*. Emulating Victor is not a good choice for you."

"I miss you," Paul says.

"Yeah? Well, I miss you too. And I've been missing you since before you left for the other side of the house. But I can't keep having conversations about your pain where mine doesn't exist." Alex gets up to head upstairs.

"That's it?" Paul asks.

"If you have anything else to say to me right now, Mr. Trial Separation, you can do it in the dark, in our bed, with your clothes off. With words or sex. I don't care which. Otherwise, I'll see you when I get back."

♦

As miserable as he is, Alex feels a little bit proud. He didn't storm out. He didn't even slam the bedroom door. It all feels final, though. He doesn't start shaking until he sits down on the bed.

The last thing Alex expects after he's turned out the lights – bags packed and a worried email composed to Carly, who is possibly the only person who understands Paul better than he does – is the door to open. He doesn't say anything at first, merely watches Paul undress in the dark. When Paul lifts the duvet and climbs into bed, Alex is shocked and a little ashamed at how automatically his body moves to tangle itself with Paul's. It feels like water to be touched by someone who isn't paid to do so. He's long since given up trying to explain to people what it feels like to be an object for hair and makeup and wardrobe, for the cameras, and for the fans. Even Liam doesn't understand, because that's also how Victor loves him.

"This is unexpected," Alex says softly. "And really good."

"I'm sorry, I know," Paul says, smoothing a hand over Alex's hair. "I thought if this is really only going to be a trial, we should make some rules, not make everything worse."

"No fucking other people," Alex says.

"Agreed. Not what this is about. That includes Liam."

"Still not the issue you think it is." Alex says. It's weird how, pressed together in the dark, even all this misery is suddenly just funny and so them.

"No decisions about living arrangements until you're back," Paul

285

says.

"You can't tell someone not to make a decision," Alex says. "That's not how decisions work."

"Okay," Paul says. Alex can hear in his voice it's not easy. "We're the first to know in any decisions about living arrangements. Don't fucking call movers without calling me first."

"Paul?"

"Yes?"

"Among other things, it's my house."

Paul cracks up and rolls onto his back, fist to his mouth as he apparently tries to figure out in which direction his hysteria is about to go.

"We have to fix that," he says, clearly without thinking. Then he sobers. "I mean, if we fix the rest of this."

"Yeah. Okay," Alex says. "That's...we can do that."

"Wait. Did you just agree to marry me?"

Alex blinks. It's the same leap Paul has been making over and over again. First, because he thought that *actually making a go* of their relationship when Paul started pursuing his own show meant getting married once he actually got it. Second, because Paul thinks them putting his name on the deed to Alex's house means the same thing. "No, Paul. I agreed to paperwork considerings if I don't leave you. Don't make this weirder."

Paul chuckles wetly. "That's probably fair."

"You think?" Alex decides he should also not also point out that Paul is talking marriage again an hour after considering, very seriously, breaking up with him. He wonders if Paul has always been this volatile, or if it's just something Alex is bringing out in him now.

"Can I kiss you?" Paul asks.

Against his better judgment, Alex nods.

The kiss isn't wet or deep or sexy, but it also doesn't feel like goodbye. It is solemn, though, and after, Paul presses his forehead to Alex's. It feels like a promise.

16

Paul isn't there in the morning when Alex wakes up, not that Alex is surprised. They are, for the first time in months, on the same page, even if it is a terrible one. As he leaves for the airport, he almost feels okay. He certainly feels older, which he doesn't mind at all. He needs all the tools and strength he can get.

He texts Paul when he lands to let him know he's gotten in safely and actually gets a reply. Once he's checked in, he texts Liam to the same effect but with clear instructions to not call, appear at, or otherwise consider the existence of his hotel room. They can hang out tomorrow, after they've seen each other on set. While Alex has no particular interest in fucking Liam again, outside of his agreement with Paul he still needs to be sure his costar isn't some sort of refuge – sexual, emotional, or logistical – for him right now.

D.C. is strange and haunted and odd, even when Alex isn't being someone else. As a bonus, this is probably his last time here as Zach. It makes Alex thoughtful and sadder than he had expected, both for Zach and for what he himself will be losing.

That they aren't doing night shoots this time is a godsend, but they're still outside all day in the terrible heat and humidity of summer in D.C. Given that they're trying to use every hour of daylight possible, that means pre-dawn calls and shooting through sunset. The days are long, exhausting, and disgustingly sticky.

Alex doesn't mind the physical work of it, but there is absolutely no magic in sweating through his costume before the sun is up. To make matters worse, people will not stop fussing over him and making sure he's drinking enough water. Which, fair, maybe, but Alex has no desire to revisit that particular ordeal and is perfectly capable of keeping himself hydrated. Not that that ever gets taken into account in a job where he is an asset but not quite an autonomous person.

The first day is less terrible than it could be, weather aside. That Raphael is there too is a relief, because that means Liam has someone other than Alex to badger in between takes. Alex doesn't feel like talking to anyone. For now he's happy to get absorbed in the work and be alternately amused at – and frustrated by – the fans and curious passers-by who stop to watch.

"Maybe we should kiss to keep them entertained," Liam muses during a long wait.

Alex smacks him on the arm and doesn't yell only because he knows Liam is not anywhere close to being serious. Liam has been very clear that he's looking forward to Victor joining them for a few days later in the week. Alex suspects that's likely to be more peculiar than he can currently anticipate.

♦

"So, we get to hang out now, right?" Liam asks once they've wrapped for the day and Alex is cursing mosquitoes.

"You've been looking forward to this, haven't you?"

Liam loops an arm through his to drag him off.

Alex grumbles.

"Oh, like you haven't."

Alex lets himself chuckle. Like everything else in his life right now, the answer is complicated, but complicated is something he knows how to do with Liam.

Alex has no patience for people or public right now, although he suspects his preferences may have to change later in the week in order to placate Victor. For now, he's more than happy to tag back to Liam's room with him. He wants somewhere quiet, without people and with air conditioning.

"Dude, do you want a shower?" Liam asks, when Alex drops into the armchair and props his feet over the AC vent.

Alex makes a face. "Between the trailer shower and yours, the trailer is actually preferable."

"Dude, ow."

"Also my room is next door."

"Okay, point." Liam hands Alex one of the bottles of water from on top of the dresser – ridiculous, the things that stay the same – and sits down on the edge of the bed. "How are you?"

Alex shrugs.

Liam swings a foot into his chair. "Alex," he says quietly.

"We're on a trial separation," Alex says, picking at the label of the water bottle. Liam will nag him until he says something and saying it out loud won't change the reality of the situation. But it does feel different – worse – to say.

Liam frowns. "That doesn't sound good."

Alex chuckles darkly. "It's actually better than it has been."

"How the hell does that work?"

"We had an actual conversation. No one yelled. No one wants this? Like, I know I'm whatever I am, but he is not okay."

"And separation is the solution?" Liam asks warily.

"I don't know, Liam," Alex says too sharply. It's not Liam's fault. "I don't know how this works. All I know is that I'm in this fucking city again, and I have no idea what happens when I get home."

He considers telling Liam the rest of it, about quitting, at least. He doesn't know how Liam's going to react to that, other than badly, and he wants at least one twenty-four-hour period in his life without a crisis to manage. "But I learned things here last time. Maybe I will this time too."

"That sounds less dire," Liam says carefully. "Even though it freaks the hell out of me to think about you and Paul not being together. But I still don't understand why this is happening."

Alex blinks at him. It's not Liam's to understand. "Join the club," he says.

Liam says nothing else, because Liam's an asshole and seems to have absolutely no circuit in his head that reminds him it's quiet and he's been staring for too long,

"A lot of it is time," Alex says to break the silence.

"Not enough time?"

"I don't know. No. I mean, it's not like anybody has enough, but – no."

"Then what is it?"

Alex tips his head back against the chair and squeezes his eyes shut. Liam is still staring and it's disconcerting. "Attention. Focus. Plans. It doesn't matter what we call it, we just *aren't*, anymore. At least we're actually naming it."

"And that feels good?"

"It feels terrible. Now, it's a terrible that might have a solution. So that's what we're going to try to focus on. If Paul ever picks up his phone."

"He will," Liam says. "Like, I can't imagine him not."

"You don't know what it's been like."

"Well, no, because you're not telling me, but I know he loves you."

Alex shrugs again. He adds Liam's optimism to the list of things he dislikes about him.

Liam frowns. "Okay, see, now you're acting like that part isn't important or grounds for a solution, which means we may both be out of our depths here."

Alex tilts his head back to laugh at the ceiling. It feels unsettling, even to him.

"We're so different," Liam says. "And I really regret that right now, because I want to help."

"You are one of the things we fight about," Alex says. "I shouldn't tell you that, but it's true."

"He jealous?" Liam says simply.

Alex shrugs again. "He thinks he is."

"What do you think?"

"I think he thinks if he's jealous of you, then he's not responsible for the fact that I feel like I've been left for a TV show. And he is jealous of you."

"Have you been left for a TV show?"

"He lives on the other side of the house."

"Okay," Liam says. He folds his legs up to sit cross-legged. "Why are you two monogamous again?"

"Lee! Not helping."

"No, no, no, that's not what I mean. Just, he met someone new, and he's really into her. Now you're feeling neglected because you don't know how to talk about it, and I'm feeling kind of Poly 101 at you, except she's a TV show about hookers, and you're both fucking dense."

Alex stares at him.

"Are you gaping at me because I'm right or because I'm wrong?" Liam asks.

"I don't know, keep talking," Alex says although he realizes he may regret that later.

"Okay, so, New Relationship Energy. One, *Winsome* is a bright, shiny object. It is something Paul's wanted for a long time. It makes him feel sexy and smart and powerful, so he is doing everything he can to make sure it sticks around. Two, he's got you, he's been really sure of your place in his life. He starts to focus on this other thing because you love him and he loves you and everyone knows that –"

"Yeah, that's called taking me for granted."

"Three, don't interrupt me."

Alex laughs.

"It's only called taking you for granted if you didn't discuss it and figure out how *Winsome* fits into your relationship."

"What's to discuss? It's work," Alex says. "You know we all sign away our lives to the dream."

"No, I don't know that. I've been doing this most of my life. I'm getting married to a wonderful woman. I've known my best friend since we were eight, and I've got a man who doesn't even like sex or want to need anyone thrilled to take me to bed because it makes me happy."

Alex wants to whine about it all being too much information, because it is, but Liam also has a point. "You're making me feel incompetent," he says instead.

"That's because hierarchies only work if they're flexible."

"Explain."

"I've been with Victor six years. I'm marrying someone I've been dating for four. Who's the winner?"

"Carly," Alex says automatically. He keeps to himself the fact that he's been half assuming Liam's thing with Victor will end with the wedding.

"No, idiot. *Me.*"

It's a lot to think about – and challenging. Following along with

Liam isn't always easy. But Alex is starting to see, if not a solution, at least the roots of his and Paul's problems a little more clearly. He and Paul *haven't* been talking. Not usefully. And that's on Alex as much as it is on Paul. Whether it's fixable at this point is a different question.

When Alex finally goes back to his room, he thinks about calling Paul, but decides he's not ready yet for whatever that will or won't be. He texts him instead, to tell him he's thinking of him.

A reply comes, but over an hour later, as Alex is falling asleep, his phone on the pillow next to him as his only company.

Thanks for this, it says. *Thinking about you too.*

◆

Alex waits until the end of shooting the next day to find Liam and say, "There's something I need to tell you."

Liam frowns. "Okay. Your room or mine?"

Alex sighs and stalks off.

They end up in Liam's room again, though Alex detours for a proper shower first. He'd be perfectly happy to put off breaking the news for longer, except that Victor is coming in tomorrow. Alex has no idea when Victor plans to tell Liam about Zach, but he does know he'll be pissed if Alex doesn't hold up his end of the deal. Besides, direct communication seems to be a thing that's working for him right now.

"Okay." This time Alex sits on the bed next to Liam. It's harder to tell Liam this than it was to tell Paul. His friendship with Liam isn't only about work. But their relationship started with, and has always involved, the people they are paid to be. Even if that's not in the ways the internet seems to think. But Liam gave him good advice last night, and he deserves to know this.

"You're scaring me a little," Liam says when Alex doesn't say anything after that. "Did you and Paul like break up since yesterday, or is this something totally else?"

Alex laughs darkly. "Something else. I'm quitting."

"Quitting what?"

"The show."

"What?"

"*Fourth Estate.*"

Liam blinks. "Okay. That I really don't understand."

"I'm going to stop working on the show," Alex says slowly.

"Don't be a dick," Liam says, a little sharply. "Also, you know that all that shit about being poly and everything doesn't mean you have to freak out and go and like quit all of your other things so you're not, right? Because we can go up to Poly 201 if we have to, but I thought you were at least not hearing the very opposite of what I was saying."

Alex chuckles. "Lee, I promise, this has nothing to do with that conversation. As much as I do appreciate it. I decided a while ago. I want to try some new things."

"Okaaay," Liam says slowly. "Is this because Paul's jealous of me?"

"No. It's got nothing to do with you. A little to do with Paul, though not how either of you think."

"How, then?"

"I told him he had to stop playing things safe to be with me, which is sort of how we got into this mess. But I also can't wait on his comfort to have my career. I'm good at this, and I loved *Paradise*. I don't want to be some kid who just got lucky any more than I want to be stuck in this year of vacation-free shooting. It was a nasty, nasty thing the network did to Victor."

"Yeah, but he's not quitting."

"No, but he's planning, and I need to be too."

"But the guy in my head is in love with the guy in your head."

Alex makes an incoherent noise and flops backwards on the bed. This is impossible on so many levels. Liam gets to his heart in the crappiest, most inconvenient ways.

"No?" Liam asks.

"I might be breaking up with Paul. Zach is not breaking up with James." Alex is immensely relieved Victor is the one who gets to tell Liam what happens with Zach. He also feels immensely shitty that he's about to, in essence, lie. Because he's pretty sure *death* ranks above *breakup* on the list of terrible reasons to no longer be in a relationship, even a fictional one.

"But your guy is gonna be gone."

"Nope." Alex taps a finger against his sternum. "My guy comes with me."

"I don't know what that means."

"It means that you and I are beautifully fucked up, Liam. And where I'm working doesn't change that."

"I'm going to miss you," Liam says. He sounds profoundly sad.

"Idiot." Alex lifts his head to look at him. "I'm still right here."

"But on the other side of the house."

"No." Alex works to keep several conflicting emotions in check. Liam can be exhausting. "That's a shitty metaphor. I'm still talking to you and we are not broken. You know that."

Liam takes a deep breath. "I'm really glad Victor's coming tomorrow."

"Yeah," Alex says, chagrined. "Me too."

◆

Back in his room Alex flops down onto his bed. He's tired and feeling a little terrible for unleashing that news on Liam. He loves Liam, in a purely platonic way, but it's still exhausting.

He texts Paul.

How is everything going?

The reply comes faster tonight, before he even gets his clothes off to go to bed.

Increasingly convinced Victor is inhuman.

Alex chuckles to himself. *I could have told you that from day one.* It's easier to complain about Victor than stop to actually think about him. If he did, Alex knows he'd have to deal with things about himself he wouldn't like.

I'm not convinced you're human, Paul replies. Alex sighs If only Paul would realize that there's nothing about him, or them, that's abnormal, Alex's life would be so much easier.

I'll take that as a compliment. Sleeping now.

Todd says hi, Paul sends. It's that, that sends Alex curling up under the covers, phone clenched in his hand and desperately homesick.

17

Things are better in the light of day. Once he gets himself out of bed, Alex looks forward to going to set and getting to work. Liam is unusually quiet. Alex is pretty sure that's less about his news than because Victor is expected later that morning. Of course, there may be overlap there, but mostly all Alex can see is someone excited about *boyfriend* and *hotel* on someone else's dime. Even if Liam has consistently refuted Alex's descriptors of the situation every time he's offered up another little of piece of it for his understanding.

Alex finds their relationship strange because it's not the sort of thing that would ever fit into his life. He can't even, really, see the appeal of it. But whatever it is, Alex gets that it tugs at them in the same way as that strange, sad night he and Liam spent together at his parents' place in New York two winters ago. He knows that Liam and Victor are lucky to be able to make a feeling like that work.

He also knows, after last night's conversation with Liam, that maybe his own deal with Liam – at least in Liam's head – isn't even that different. And as long as they never, ever have to talk about it (because direct communication only goes so far), Alex is good with that.

♦

When Victor arrives, he's all business. Not that he isn't to most people's eyes always. But sometimes there's a softness around his mouth and a weariness to his eyes that Alex recognizes as his having time for the more personal concerns of his friends and colleagues. This is not one of those times. Alex suspects Victor is trying to power through the jet lag he claims not to get. Whether or not other people see it, they all stand up straighter for him. Beside him, Liam is practically vibrating out of his set chair.

Victor spends the shoot day mostly silent, ensconced in a fortress of chairs and folding tables and too many digital screens. Alex has no idea if he's watching the rushes straight from camera thanks to the miracle of digital, or if he's working on something else entirely and being ominous for his own amusement. Ultimately, Alex is oddly grateful for his presence. Everything runs just a little bit tighter – and Liam seems just a little bit more solidly attached to this world – when he's around.

At lunch, Victor pulls Alex aside, fingers sharp in the crook of his elbow. "You tell him?"

"What, not how," Alex says.

"And how was that?" Victor asks.

Alex is surprised by the question, having assumed that Liam called Victor after Alex returned to his own room. "We're fine."

"I'm not planning on telling him the rest any time soon."

"That's a shit thing to do," Alex says.

Victor shrugs, amused. "You're an actor; you should have fewer qualms about lying."

Alex throws his hands up in the air at that, because *what the actual fuck*. Victor's only response is to stroll away laughing, which is oddly delightful. Alex spends the rest of the day tapping his tongue against the back of his teeth and wondering if he and Victor are somehow becoming friends.

◆

Back in his room, Alex only considers it briefly before he picks up his phone and dials Paul. It's been a long day and he's tired, even more so after Liam's strangeness and Victor to deal with, but it's been over two days now and a text isn't enough. Paul can beat himself up all he wants for it, but Alex knows Paul's not the only one who's obsessed in all of this.

To his surprise, relief, and not a little bit of fear, because Alex isn't even sure exactly what he wants to say, Paul actually answers.

"Alex," Paul says. He sounds tired, which Alex doesn't know how to read absent further clues. He wonders, though he does not want to ask, whether Paul is still at the office. Is he home yet? Having another sleepover with Carly?

Alex curls up under the covers and presses the phone to his ear. "You picked up."

"I did say maybe."

"It was the kind of maybe that sounded like a no".

"It didn't stop you," Paul says.

"No," Alex says. "You knew it wouldn't."

"Probably."

Alex rolls over onto his back and stares at the ceiling in the dark. "I told him," he says. If they're going to have a conversation at all, he wants to keep ripping Band-Aids off, no matter how much they end up hurting.

"Oh," Paul says. "Liam?"

"Yeah."

"You never told me how Zach leaves the show," Paul points out.

"You're changing the subject. And you're assuming I know."

"I know you. And Victor. And it seemed preferable to yelling."

"Paul, I am not naked in his room right now," Alex says a little testily. "As evidenced by me calling you. I don't even think Liam is in his room right now, although I would like not to dwell on that."

Paul snorts. "I think you're joking?"

Alex makes a face at the ceiling and wishes a little that Paul were here, so he could kick at him under the covers. "I don't know how to say this in words that you're actually going to understand, because I've been trying for years and no go, but Liam isn't the person I call in the middle of the night when everything is shit."

"Does that matter?" Paul asks. Alex is surprised at how plaintive it is.

"It actually does," he says softly.

"I watched the episode, you know," Paul tells Alex, a little sheepishly.

"Which?"

"The one with the Zach and James sex."

Alex frowns at the phone in annoyed disbelief. "Well, that was stupid."

"Yeah. Probably," Paul concedes. "The thought of you and Liam together was bad enough. The actual visual was terrible and also hot in ways I am not equipped to deal with."

"What did you do?" Alex asks.

"I think I threw something."

Alex snorts. "Did you break anything?"

"No. Bent a few script pages, but whatever."

"Paul."

"Yeah?"

"You are fucked up."

Paul laughs. "Yeah. I am."

Alex runs a hand through his hair and debates telling Paul all the ways in which he and Liam were not like Zach and James, but he doesn't owe him that, and the outcome won't be good anyway.

"I'm not setting conditions, although I can see how I might. And I'm not making decisions yet. But I think that's a thing we're going to have to talk about, when I get back, if...." he trails off.

"Yeah," Paul agrees though he sounds far from certain. "If."

"Are you making decisions?" Alex asks.

"Hundreds of them," Paul says. "Every day."

Alex isn't sure if Paul's changing the topic or not.

18

The next day, Liam is as quiet and steady as Alex has ever seen him. Alex's first thought is how obvious it is that Liam's gotten laid, or whatever it counts as when Victor doesn't do sex, until he remembers that Liam gets laid all the time. In fact, Liam probably only doesn't get laid when he and Alex are hanging out. Alex sighs and supposes he's glad Victor is a good influence on someone.

The day is long. While he doesn't have to do much heavy lifting as a performer, the hurry up and wait seems more egregious than usual. No matter how often the production assistants keep asking the pedestrians to keep moving, someone keeps winding up in the back of a shot, gawking. As much as Alex wants to hide in his trailer with the A.C. blasting, if everyone else is outside sweating their asses off, he's determined to be too. The person on set being paid the most should always suffer as much as the person being paid the least. He'd learned that on *Paradise Square* and he's tried to keep to it.

After work, Victor tells him that they're all going out tonight. Alex grits his teeth at how it's not a question. He winds up grabbing sushi with Liam, Raphael, and Natalie before she swans off to a lounge event and the rest of them are due to meet Victor.

"Some launch for some fucking artisanal booze," Liam says of Natalie's destination without any particular malice. As if an event designed to brand a random product with Washington D.C.'s power isn't an entirely ridiculous prospect.

Raphael catches Alex's eye and gives him a look. Alex has to stifle a laugh because Raphael works hard not to be as judgmental as the rest of them, but he is so totally judging. It makes Alex like him more.

"Is there anyone you don't like on some level?" Alex asks Liam. It's not the first time he's thought of it, but it is the first time he's' felt impelled to say it out loud.

"Nope." Liam snags Alex's pickled ginger which his chopsticks.

"I feel like I'm chaperoning you two," Raphael says.

"You're not that old," is Liam's quick reply.

Alex cackles as the conversation segues into Raphael's new baby and his extensive smartphone documentation of its first few months of life. As Liam passes the phone to Alex, he remembers his first brunch with Paul and how lost everyone else's seemingly adult lives had made him feel. Now there is this, as normal as anything in his life.

After they pay – Raphael muttering and throwing in for Natalie, because she forgot and it's not the money but the principle of the thing – Liam leads them to their next destination.

"Are you sure you know where you're going?" Alex asks. The

noise and the crowd and the nightlife are clearly three blocks to the left, but Liam is monologuing at them about the Masons. Of course – because Alex and the universe have a timing issue with each other – they arrive at their destination within thirty seconds of Alex's question, Liam opening the door and ushering him in just to be snide. Then he tries to figure out what the fuck he's supposed to think about Liam's or Victor's or whoever's idea this was taste in bars.

The place is a mostly empty dive with a mix of red walls and wood paneling that evoke the 1970s in an alternate hell universe. That Victor and Ellen are sitting at a narrow table in the corner sipping drinks and smirking at them only cements the picture.

"Fuck the artisanal booze," Raphael says from over Alex's shoulder. "Now I know why Natalie didn't join us."

Alex lets Liam slide in next to Victor, and then yanks a chair away from another table and sits down on that instead. Liam pouts, but Ellen laughs and nods her approval in a way that suggests that Victor has told her about their little affair. Alex wants to be annoyed, but it's not Ellen's fault. She's always been kind to him without being patronizing.

"Where's Natalie?" Victor asks.

"Artisanal booze launch party," Raph says dryly.

"She's trying to get in the *Washingtonian* again," Liam adds.

Victor smiles lazily. "And why aren't you trying to get in the *Washingtonian*, Liam?"

Liam gives a shrug and a little preening smile in response. Alex realizes, with some dim horror and an odd fondness, that Victor is actually flirting. The sight of Victor pursuing something and being coquettish about it is flat out bizarre.

Apparently Raph comes to the same conclusion. "Gentlemen, we're in public and your charm is showing," he says mildly.

Liam looks unabashed; Victor, amused.

Alex wonders exactly how terrible this night is going to be.

Raphael pulls his chair in closer to the table. "So now that we've all been summoned…."

"We drink," Victor says matter-of-factly.

Alex and Raphael exchange a glance because that cannot possibly be the entire punchline. Alex levers himself out of his chair.

"Alex, sit," Victor says. "Liam will fetch drinks."

Liam slides out of his chair like this is both perfectly reasonable and a request, when it's clearly neither. He takes two steps toward the bar before turning back to the table and squinting like he's just figured out this situation is fucked up.

"What's everyone drinking?" he asks.

Alex sinks back into his seat and almost groans at how guileless he is. As much as the thing with Victor is not his business, there are times when he feels like it should be. Liam may not need his protection, but as far as Alex can tell he sure could use it.

Liam leans, not on the back of Victor's chair, but on Victor himself, hands pressed down onto his shoulders as he waits for everyone to figure out what they're having. When they're not prompt enough Liam announces that everyone will be getting tequila shots if they don't give him a proper order right now. Alex thinks that's fair. It's not like he's volunteered a plan either.

Victor chuckles under his hands and Liam, to Alex's shock, bends down and kisses his hair.

Alex blinks theatrically. He slowly glances toward Raphael in hopes that a lack of sudden movement will prevent things from getting worse. Raph's eyes slide to him with the same nervous caution and a complete lack of stealth. A second and a half later they both burst into uncontrollable laughter.

◆

Victor ignores them because they are being children and tilts his head back to deal with Liam, for whom sweet and inappropriate are always the same word. What he expects to see is Liam, distracted, amused, and his ill-advised moment of public affection already forgotten such that Victor's required glare will be worthless.

But Liam's looking at him with a soft smile and the too-bright eyes reserved only for him, Carly, and the camera. For a moment the whole room pulls away from them; the noise recedes and the red of the bar goes just a little bit gray before everything snaps back into place.

"You shouldn't do things like that," Victor manages, but he knows he's off-balance and looks it.

Liam shrugs. "Tequila it is," he says and walks away.

Victor straightens up to see Alex and Raphael studiously ignoring him while cackling at each other. An amused Ellen snaps her fingers way too close to his face.

"Careful," he says to her. "I bite."

"Not me, you don't."

◆

If there is any actual purpose to the gathering it remains a mystery to Alex. Liam not only fetches several rounds of truly terrible tequila but manages to flit his way around their seating arrangements all night. At point he jokingly landing in Ellen's lap and at another he drapes himself over Alex's back. Sitting still seems beyond him.

Alex talks to Raph for a good part of the evening, eventually moving from platitudes about his wife and baby to perfectly serious *how do you do it?* questions. The answers would be less heartbreaking if Raphael didn't assume he and Paul were already talking kids. The advice, while good ("Sometimes it's hard and there's nothing you can do about it. You have to decide if you're okay with riding it out when it's like that") makes Alex despair more than a little. He's starting to learn that any problems they fix now, they're going to have to keep fixing over and over and over.

He drinks too much. They all do for a school night. But Victor seems relaxed as Liam kneads his thigh under the table. Ellen tips her head back, watching the room.

"We're the worst sort of interlopers," she says. "Fucking asshole fabulous hipsters who think it's cool to be slumming."

"We're a local shoot; we patronize local businesses," Victor says to her, a finger not quite pointing in her face, something resembling anger dulled by the rounds of tequila. "And you don't get to talk to me about slumming. You're too white and you're too rich."

"You have the biggest house," she points out.

"Yes, darling," he drawls. Alex wishes Paul were here to see Victor actually going in for the kill in the slow motion of alcohol. "Because I'm the best, because I've had to be."

"Burrrrrnnnn," Raph says and reaches across the table to high-five Victor, who responds lazily.

♦

They're all trashed by the time they leave, which is one of the benefits to not being in L.A. and not having to drive. With five of them, two cabs is the obvious solution. But what should either be Victor and Ellen sharing a cab since they arrived together or Victor and Liam sharing a cab because that situation is now more obvious than ever, somehow becomes Ellen and Raphael sharing a cab because Liam is insistent that he should travel with Victor *and* Alex. Everyone is sober enough to realize this plan makes no sense, but too drunk to argue about it.

Liam decides to squeeze the three of them into the backseat. Alex somehow ends up between him and Victor. He leans forward and makes small talk with their driver so Victor and Liam can talk and hold hands – literally behind his back. The situation is fucking ridiculous and only gets worse when they get to the hotel.

Alex and Liam stumble out of the cab while Victor pays. Alex does his best to dodge Liam's arm and get to the goddamn elevator before he and Victor catch up with him. All he wants to do is get up to his room without having to deal with them being low-filter about whatever they are together. He jabs at the button in the elevator bank a few times as he fishes his phone out of his pocket and calls Paul.

Of course, Paul answers, the elevator doors open, and Liam and Victor follow him in before they can close.

"I'm in the elevator," Alex says in lieu of a greeting. "Also I am very drunk."

"Why are you calling me from an elevator?" Paul asks, sounding startled and without all their usual discomfort of late.

"Because I am in an elevator with Victor and Liam and they are also very drunk."

"Alex, calm down, it's not like we're going to go fuck," Victor says probably loud enough for Paul to hear as the doors close.

Paul laughs. "What's going on?"

Liam makes a noise of protest at Victor's side.

"Shhhh, little one," Victor says to Liam. "The way you mean, yes, the way he means, no."

"I DIDN'T MEAN ANYTHING," Alex says far too loudly, before muttering "We're so drunk," into the phone. "And they're putting words in my mouth."

"We could —"

"Liam, whatever you're going to say, do not say it," Alex snaps through his laughter as the elevator finally arrives at his and Liam's floor and the doors ding open. Victor and Liam are lovely together in a way Alex doesn't know how to handle. If he looks at them too long he's not sure he'll be able to look away.

Alex bolts out ahead of them. He doesn't wait to see whether they're going to Liam's room or on to another floor for Victor's. He tries to tell himself he doesn't want to know.

"Okay, safe now," he tells Paul as he gets his door open. It takes a couple of tries with the keycard, because *drunk*. "They're awful!"

"They're in love," Paul says simply. Which makes Alex feel like an asshole. There's not enough happiness in the world to go around grudging it of the people who manage to find it. But *still*.

"Shhhhhh," Alex says. Better not to talk about any of that. "Be quiet with me. Two minutes,"

Paul laughs again. Alex closes his eyes and lets himself enjoy the sound of it and how none of their tension has crept in yet over the absurd.

"Oh, God," he says as a terrible thought occurs to him. "I bet they're talking about us."

"We're talking about them," Paul points out.

Alex moans again in lieu of finding words for his feelings on the entire subject. Then they actually do go quiet, and there's only the soft sound of Paul's breath on the other end of the line.

◆

Victor and Liam fumble their way into Liam's room loudly. Normally Victor would worry about noise or decorum, but this time he can't bring himself to. He crowds Liam against the wall, grabs his face, and makes him wait for the kiss he knows is coming. Liam won't drop his eyes unless Victor asks him, which he's always found fascinating. The sustained eye contact leaves them stuck there for a moment that is unreasonably long.

Victor steps back without giving Liam what he wants. When his hand leaves Liam's face, he brushes his fingers over Liam's lips.

"Get undressed," he says but then ignores Liam as he opens the overpriced spring water the hotel provides. He should be a lot more sober than he is for this. No matter how much he trusts himself, Liam trusts him more.

He leans against the wall watching Liam as he sips at the water. "Are you okay to do this?" he asks.

"In what world am I going to say no?" Liam says.

"In one that scares me less."

"I'm *fine*."

Victor is not impressed with Liam's petulance, but scolding him is so rarely effective. They're on the same side even if they never see the world from the same angle. Victor says nothing until Liam pulls off his jeans and kicks them to the side of the room.

"Fold your clothes. You can be a slob when I'm not here," Victor snaps, although there's not much heat to it. He wants another few seconds to clear his head. Hopefully Liam will understand.

Liam chuckles and does as he's told. Victor says thank you, because manners count.

"Are you going to come here, or do you want to watch?" Liam says, climbing onto the bed and settling back on his heels in a kneel.

"I don't think you'd be very happy if I only wanted to watch right now."

Liam shrugs. "You're here. I'm happy," he says, simple and serious.

Victor doesn't realize the breath has punched out of him until he hears himself on the inhale in response.

"How do you do this to me?" Victor murmurs. He crosses to the bed, grabs Liam by the jaw again, and leads him up onto his knees. "How do you do this to everyone?"

"I really don't," Liam says.

Victor kisses him.

◆

Alex eventually toes off his shoes and curls up with his head on the pillow, staring out the window at the lights of the city. He can feel the mood with Paul settle, and his whole body relaxes when Paul asks "How's D.C.?" in a tone that means he's interested in the answer.

"The first night was a little rough," Alex admits. "I hate the weather. But it's getting better."

"The weather?"

"No. The rest of it."

"You sound happy." Paul sounds surprised.

Alex considers that: The long days, the work, Victor and Liam, all the strangenesses and longings of this city. "I am."

"Is it because you're not with me?" Paul asks. He doesn't sound desperate, but asking clearly hurts.

"No," Alex says.

"Alex," Paul says fondly, but his voice is pleading, too. "More words?"

The mood is subdued now. "I'm not happy because you're not here. But now that I'm not worrying about us every moment of the day, I remembered how not to be miserable all the time."

"I'm sorry I make you miserable."

Alex tamps down his annoyance. Paul keeps finding the strangest and worst ways to take responsibility for this mess. Still, Alex wants to be both honest and kind. "You don't. Your choices and our collective crazy do. Which is why I know the separation is good, but, Paul, I want to be happy *with* you."

"I want to be happy with you, too."

"I know. But it's going to be harder than either of us thought."

♦

Victor refuses to get on the bed with him. That's not new, but the way he insists on standing and keeping Liam on his knees, neck stretching up to kiss him, is. Liam's still tipsy enough that Victor suspects he's only upright because he wants Victor – and to make Victor happy – more than he wants to lie down. He whimpers every time Victor pulls out of the kiss and then hovers just millimeters from his lips.

Victor makes a shushing sound, meant to soothe more than silence. It only makes Liam get louder. Victor laughs.

"Please touch me," Liam begs.

"I am touching you." Victor tightens his grip on Liam's face.

"Please –"

Victor is always tempted to say no. The things Liam wants, that they are both agreed he can have from him, aren't necessarily things that interest Victor. Liam makes him stretch, when he's not making him desperately want to retreat from a world that isn't, particularly, made for him.

The fact that Liam is very pretty when he's denied, when Victor can actually get him to cry, is another thing entirely. It amuses Victor to no end that what makes them incompatible, also provides the path for how they do work.

"What do you want, Liam? If you could have anything, what would you want?"

Liam closes his eyes, and Victor knows he's pushed a little too far and struck a little too deep. He loosens his grip on Liam's jaw, slides his hand over his cheek to cup the back of his head, and pulls him against him.

Liam sags in relief at the contact, his face pressed against the soft cotton of Victor's shirt.

"I've got you; it's okay," Victor says, just a little bit on autopilot because Liam or the alcohol or this much touch has him off balance. He frowns to himself at how unsurprised their audience on the other side of the wall would be to discover that most skin-to-skin contact makes him feel as if his nerves have turned to glass.

Liam makes the most delicious sound when Victor grabs his cock.

♦

"I can hear them," Alex moans, pulling a pillow up over his ear with the phone held to it.

"Hear who?"

"Liam's room is next to mine. Who do you think? Please talk to me to distract me."

Paul chuckles. "Do you know when you get in yet?"

Alex loosens his grip on the pillow a little. "Working on it. We'll wrap here Friday, and Margaret and Vanessa are trying to arrange some stuff for me in New York. So probably another week or so?"

"Define stuff." Paul sounds more tense than he has all night.

"I'm gonna talk to some people about some movies," Alex says enthusiastically. He doesn't like New York much more than he likes D.C., but he does like the work.

"In New York?"

"In a lot of places. The whole world doesn't shoot in our backyard, Paul."

"I just... to what extent is this about us?"

"To the extent that this is my job and these are always going to be the business conversations I am having. And if and when there is something to talk about, we'll talk about it. That means with opportunities and with us," Alex says. The statement is harsher and more practical than he wants, but it needs to be said.

Silence stretches on until Alex feels tense with it. Did he say the wrong thing and break everything tonight?

Before he can ask, Paul says, "I'm nodding at you."

"Oh. Good. Margaret's going to set up some media stuff too so...I'll let you know, as soon as I have the ticket."

"Is Liam going?"

"What?"

"Liam. New York."

"He and Victor are headed back to L.A. Saturday, and sometimes you make me want to lie to you."

"Don't do that," Paul says.

"Then believe me when I say that's never happening again."

"Were you in love with him?"

"Paul," Alex says sharply, because *what the fuck*?

"Well?"

Alex closes his eyes. This is starting to get ugly. He's drunk, and he's tired, and as unreasonable as Paul is being, Alex misses him. "You've been in love with lots of people. Why do I only get one?"

"That sounds like a yes."

"I love Lee," Alex tells him. He still doesn't know how to categorize or define what he and Liam were and gave up even trying to a long time ago. "But I'm not in love with him. Not the way you mean, even if I maybe used to think something different."

"This is why you and Liam scare me," Paul says.

"*Why*?"

"Because I don't understand it, and it seems huge."

"Maybe it is, but it's not about you," Alex still feels protective of that time in his life, terrible as most of it was. Liam is the only person he's been with besides Paul that's meant anything. Hard as it is for Paul to hear, Alex isn't willing to deny that. Liam means something to him and always will.

♦

Paul finally wanders away from his desk and sits down on his bed, across the house from Alex's empty room. Todd scratches mournfully at the closed door.

"Tell me why it's not happening again," he says even though he suspects he shouldn't. He wants an answer that makes sense to him. Alex and Liam never have.

Alex takes a breath. "He can't be what I want. I can't be what he needs. And I am tired of you taking out your guilt on me. It's doing neither of us any good, so can we please stop?"

"What do you want?" Paul asks. He knows Alex is telling him many things, some of which he thinks he may never be capable of understanding. He wishes he understood Alex and the way he uses words better. Although this time it may be the issues – and not how they're communicating them – that are causing so much grief.

"I want everything," Alex says. "I want you, when I'm yours. Even when I'm not. And even if you and I were over I wouldn't, with Liam, because we're a lot of things but we're not *that*. Neither of us can be that."

"The last time," Paul says too sharply, but only because he's scared, "things were bad with us, you went to Liam. You came back different."

"Paul," Alex says softly. "I came back to you."

"I don't even know what I want to hear," Paul admits, far too aware of their empty house, and the room upstairs he hasn't been in since the night Alex left.

"Then can we just go back to being quiet together?" Alex asks. "That was good."

"Okay. Yeah, okay."

Alex is quiet so long that Paul thinks he's fallen asleep. He wonders if he should hang up and go back upstairs to finish up what he was working on, or maybe even just crawl into bed himself, when Alex says with a rustle that must be him getting undressed, "I'm still happy."

"That's a good thing?" Paul asks.

"Yeah," Alex says. "It really is."

◆

After Liam comes, he is so desperately beautiful as Victor helps lower him to the bed that he can barely stand it. Especially because if he's going to stay – and he's definitely going to stay – he really needs to go back to his room for his laptop first. But abandoning Liam like this strikes him as both cruel and irresponsible.

"I'm going to go upstairs for a minute," he says when he's gotten Liam cleaned up and under the covers.

Of course, that makes Liam more alert, but not in a good way.

"I'll stay the night," he says, "assuming you'll have me. But I do need my computer first."

Liam huffs out a little laugh and closes his eyes again.

"I'll be right back, I promise."

Liam nods, thinking hard about it. Victor knows he doesn't make promises lightly, even in the most casual of conversations. Something – even if he has no idea what – is changing in the long, shifting thread of their relationship.

Victor thinks Liam is asleep by the time he returns. But once he sits up against that headboard, laptop open and typing, Liam turns over in his bed and asks, "Why did you do that?"

"What?" Victor asks, jarred out of his writing. It's one thing to feel his relationship with Liam shifting; it's another to address Liam's very fair questions when he's still working out the answers himself. After what happened tonight in the bar and on Liam's bed, there are far more questions than Victor is used to or comfortable with

He's relieved when Liam says, "In the elevator. With Alex."

"He was talking to Paul," Victor tells him. "I wanted him to laugh."

"Do you think it worked?"

"I think we'll find out."

19

The next day, the weather breaks in a spectacular thunderstorm that probably should shut down filming for an hour. But to Alex's surprise, Victor decides that Zach and James having a soaked and hilarious conversation is exactly what they need. Which is awesome and also uncomfortable. Alex is glad when they wrap for the day.

Liam offers to take a walk with him around the city, but Alex shakes his head. He wants to be inside, where it's dry and there aren't any other people. They go to Liam's room. Alex doesn't know where Victor is tonight – and doesn't particularly want to ask – but he does hesitate for a second as he chooses which bed to sit on. He knows he's being foolish and immature, but Liam blurs the lines around everything: Sex, intimacy, public life. Alex is irrationally worried that if he's not careful, he'll be pulled into the orbit of his affair with Victor.

"What's up with the sweater?" Liam asks when Alex curls up small on the bed with his head tipped against the headboard.

"We got drenched today. Still cold."

"Dude, it's like eighty out." Liam reaches out a hand to pet at Alex's arm.

Alex shrugs. "It's Paul's."

Liam snatches his hand back. "That's adorable."

"Don't tease."

"I'm not."

"Okay." Alex is baffled at Liam's sudden caution. Every time he thinks he's used to all of Liam's oddities, a new one crops up.

They talk for hours, first about Paul and then about Carly, before the meat of the conversation turns to Victor. About whom Liam is, apparently, as confused as everyone else, though for different reasons. Liam winds closer to an actual definition of whatever deal he and Victor have than he ever has before. What Alex gathers, eventually, is that deal is changing. Alex isn't sure how something that's been going on for six years can suddenly get more serious in the face of a marriage to someone else, but what went down in the bar last night was something new.

As Alex listens to Liam, drifting for some of it because he's exhausted and Liam is exhausting, what is clear is how desperately Liam *wants*. Alex is reminded, more than a little, of the way he was toward Liam in his room in New York that terrible winter he and Paul weren't together. Considering the object of Liam's focus is Victor, Alex can't imagine things aren't going to work out far worse. Sure, Liam and Victor have been together six years, but it's Victor. Trusting Victor with anyone's heart seems ill-advised. There's something rough to him, violent and proud like Alex's Indiana childhood. He's left with no good advice to offer and no courage to warn Liam of what he suspects are impending wounds.

◆

Eventually Alex, looking worn out and exhausted by work and life, falls asleep. Liam thinks about calling Carly but also doesn't want to disturb Alex. Tonight is not a Victor night. Even when they can, they don't spend every night together. Victor is an insomniac and is always doing something – tonight, it's dealing with script rewrites – but also, their relationship is historically structured on negative space.

While Liam's impulse is to curl up next to Alex and enjoy the company, he hasn't asked him to. Liam is happy to give Alex his default request for space. The question is how. He could wake him, or he could crash on the other bed and risk getting hollered at in the morning for staying over uninvited. Liam bites his lip at the two bad choices and decides on a third. They'll switch places! He slips Alex's wallet out of his back pocket to find his room key. On his way out the door Liam stops by the side of the bed and touches Alex's hair, brushing a loose piece back off of his forehead. His friend doesn't even stir.

◆

Gemma's at work, sorting through headshots, when the extension at her desk rings. It never rings, and she's not sure she should answer it. She may have all the power in the world sorting these faces into piles of *aspirational* and *character* – beautiful and ugly – but she's barely more than an intern. Everyone knows she's in casting because she can't get cast. There's no reason for her extension to be ringing.

She only picks it up because the actual intern – the nephew of one of the CSAs – snaps at her to. Whatever she's expecting, Carly isn't on the list. They've always gotten along, but it's not like they're in each other's cell phones. If Gemma's being honest, she's always felt a little awkward around Carly, because she's real and her fiancé is *Liam Campbell*. Gemma's mostly over it, but not entirely. After all, he's still really cute and annoyingly charming, and Alex, her best friend and former roommate who is now a TV star, fucked him.

Gemma doesn't get more comfortable when Carly starts talking. She's worried about Paul, and she wants Gemma's insight.

Which means she wants Gemma's information. Gemma has to cut her off. "Can I call you back on my cell phone? Because you are asking me for gossip about people known to this office, and I should kind of do this in the parking lot."

"Does that mean you have something to tell me?" Carly asks.

"Not really?" Gemma says. Alex is her friend, and as much as that's become Paul and Alex, it's not like Paul's confessing his deepest-darkests to her. She also doesn't want to betray Alex's confidence. "But I do care, and if this is a conversation you think we need to be having, I want to have it. But not in the middle of a casting office."

"I thought you guys just did background."

"Yeah, well," Gemma says. "Everybody wants a leg up. And if we're conspiring, you should at least be willing to give me your damn cell phone number."

"Sold." Carly laughs. They're okay.

Paul, however, is not okay. And both Carly and Gemma are concerned. When Carly suggests they stage something of an intervention, she's ashamed to admit she's a little bit excited. It sounds important, and dramatic, and maybe it can really help. She offers to bring sandwiches. Carly suggests she bring Darcy instead.

The idea is one more symptom of Gemma's life that touches, but does not intersect with, fame. She feels both proud and very small that she is a node, and possibly only a node, connecting Carly to Darcy. She agrees, even if she doesn't entirely understand how Paul's very young discovery is going to improve the situation.

◆

Somewhere in the course of the next day, the internet goes gets unduly excited. Which is not unusual, but this time it's over a blind item that's been posted on some trashy gossip website. Which states that a certain TV star was seen sneaking out of the hotel room of a certain other TV star while filming in a certain city on location.

"You snuck out of your own hotel room." Alex is baffled and darkly amused as they wait for the cameras to reset in between takes. He's a little pissed, too, that the internet tries to intrude into his private life, but this is uniquely ridiculous. "And into mine so you *wouldn't* be sharing a room with me. You spent two nights with Victor and this is what gets printed?"

Liam shrugs. "Victor wouldn't send in a blind about himself."

Alex stares at Liam. "I don't actually know if you're joking."

Liam gives Alex Victor's cryptic smile, and walks away. Alex buries his head in his hands.

When Alex talks to Paul that night he expects him to be pissed. Paul has always followed Alex's presence on the internet and Liam doesn't seem likely to become less of a sore point anytime soon.

Instead, Paul is also darkly amused. "I know I said I was afraid of you and Liam, but I didn't think things were so bad you'd actually run to him with Victor there."

Alex doesn't know how to take this shift in tone. He's unused to light and a lack of subtext.

"They're really, really, not. Believe me," Alex says. He's not sure he'd ever run to anyone in a situation where he and Paul were still together. He's starting to wonder, as his time in D.C. comes to a close, if Paul is different.

♦

The last day of shooting, they're back at the Tidal Basin with Zach and James. Everything they've been filming all week has been happy, which is good. Alex knows that Victor isn't doing foreshadowing because that's not how death works, but he is clearly not averse to full circles.

And maybe, Alex thinks, as they line up a shot for a kiss that's easy and light, that's because life comes with its own circles.

20

It's raining in New York when Alex lands. Which is a blessing, because it gives him an excuse to wear a hat despite the season. Everyone on the streets is too miserable and harried to give him a second glance. He decides to walk down Broadway and into Soho, on streets he's supposed to care about because he can afford to shop on them. He only feels any affection for them because some of the streets still have cobbles and haven't come that far from the old shadow New York that's been informing his choices since he shot *Paradise*. Alex doesn't like New York, the city. But he'll take New York the memory, and New York the ghost, and New York and all the strange witchery of everything that went down between him and Liam.

When he gets back to his room in the early evening, he calls Gemma and begs her to get on a plane. He's lonely, and who else can he call? Liam's working. So is Paul.

"I have work."

"I'll pay for the ticket."

"You're being gross, and I have work, and like, a life. It's Saturday!"

"Do you have a date?" he asks.

"That's not your business."

"Since when do you have boundaries?" Alex asks.

"Since when aren't you happy spending all your time alone?"

"I feel trapped in my room and sort of pathetic," he admits.

"You know people in New York," she offers.

"Biblically," he says dryly. "Talk to me?" The request doesn't make him feel any less pathetic, but she's his oldest friend and has stuck with him through stranger things than this.

Given all of that, she sounds strangely nervous when she says, "Okay, but you're freaking me out."

They talk for an hour about little things. Alex can't tell her that he's leaving *Fourth* yet, and if he can't entirely avoid talking about Paul, he can at least deflect most of her questions.

"Sorry I asked you to come out here," Alex says when Gemma says she has to go.

"You're not," Gemma says bluntly. "But it's okay. It was good to talk to you."

They hang up. Alex thinks about calling Paul but ends up texting instead. He's not sure it's going to make him feel any less lonely or uneasy, but he wants to keep that thread of contact open.

I still hate New York, he sends.

Paul takes a while to reply. *Tell me something I don't know*, he finally sends when he does.

312

Alex prickles a little. Though Paul may well have meant a dozen other things than that Alex is boring him and he resents the interruption.

It's raining, Alex tries. *Was a little easier to take a walk. I should have my schedule sorted by Monday afternoon.*

Okay, Paul texts back.

This is one of those trial separation days, isn't it? Alex replies when he fails at not feeling needy and pissed off.

Yup.

Alex stares at his phone for a second. *All right. Have fun with that I guess.* He's not sure if he's sincere or angry. Then he turns off his phone so he doesn't have to find out.

◆

Paul knows this evening may not be exactly pleasant, because Carly has been kicking his ass since forever. But they have enough history of enough different types that he always feels a little bit happy as he gets himself together to go over to her place. She is, after all, always happy to see him, and while he owes her everything in a broad context, day-to-day they're not responsible to each other. Right now, that's pretty close to the best feeling in the world. Plus, he doesn't have to shave for her.

His trepidation rises, however, when he parks in the lot of Carly's building and sees two familiar cars already there.

"All right, what are you pulling?" Paul asks, when Carly opens the door with a broad smile.

"You can think of it as an intervention or you can think of it as a girl's night in. Your choice."

"You are a terrible friend." This is not how Paul wanted to spend the night. With Carly it would have been one thing, but there is nothing about his mess of a life that needs witnesses.

"Nope, this is why I'm the best. And when did you decide to turn into mountain man?" She taps his cheek.

Paul's a little offended. "It's been four days."

"Well, you look hot even if this smells like more of your bad ideas." She finally pulls him properly into the house and pushes him into the living room.

Darcy and Gemma are sitting on a loveseat eating bonbons.

"I am not gay enough for this," Paul declares.

Darcy frowns at him very seriously. "You are being an asshole."

"I'm gonna be more of one in a second," he offers.

"Noooooo," she says. "Come here and have candy and talk to us about your pain."

"In case you haven't noticed," Gemma chimes in, "we're more

pathetic than you are in that we're here, so make it good."

"I see your hospitality is appreciated," Paul says to Carly.

"I will get booze, and we will make you talk," she warns.

"I don't know what to tell you. Not that any of it's your business."

Carly rolls her eyes and nudges him toward a chair. "I don't think you expect that to work."

Paul sits. "Who have you been talking to?" he asks.

"Who do you think?" Carly says. "You are both freaking Liam out. And one of the many things we will be talking about tonight is how you need to stop being an asshole about him."

"I have done everything in my power to keep that away from him," Paul says. "I'm fairly clear that it's my issue, although not unreasonably, I don't think."

"I don't care," Carly says. Her voice is calm, precise and the angriest he's heard her in years. "You are being unfair to him. You are being unfair to Alex. You're certainly being unfair to me, who has been stuck trying to keep this happy family together for *years*. I'm sorry he and Alex have complicated feelings about each other, but you know what? You and I have complicated feelings about each other, and your shitty behavior about it in someone who is not you is a real slap in the face."

Paul is torn between addressing her very engaging anger and asking why the fuck they have an audience. Especially if they're doing *this* as opposed to platitudes about how awesome he and Alex are together. "The situation is different."

"How? And I swear to God if you say the word *marriage*, I will slap you. Liam and I are not you and Alex. But we are all in each other's lives, and nobody is going anywhere. Unless you don't cut this bullshit out. Do you get that you will lose him over this?"

"Explain to me how I'm not supposed to be jealous of Liam if I could lose Alex over him?"

"'Cause Alex doesn't belong to you?" Darcy pipes up from the sofa. "And you know, like, you don't have to worry about Liam. Liam's so responsible he sucks. Like, he fucks everyone and wouldn't fuck me because I didn't know why I wanted to do it other than he's cute. Carly, your boyfriend *sucks*. And was all freaked out that I'm a virgin."

"Fiancé, Darcy," Carly says mildly as Gemma's whips her head around to stare at Darcy.

Paul says, "I didn't need to know any of that."

"Alex feels what he feels. You should respect the significance of his choices," Carly says before stalking off into her kitchen.

"So this is going to suck," Paul says.

"For you." Gemma shrugs.

Carly comes back with alcohol, and if drinks don't break the mood they at least moderates it. Paul still finds it bizarre to sit here with his best friend, Alex's best friend, and Darcy. That Carly is telling him, albeit with more words, things Alex has been telling him for months also sucks.

"He keeps saying no," he tells Carly when she finally lets him say *marriage* again.

"Why do you keep asking?"

"Because I'm in love with him and want to be with him? Jesus, Carly, why are you marrying Liam?"

"Because it's a thing we both want and we work by finding new ways to work, all the time."

"We're not working," Paul says despairingly.

"I know you're not. And one of the reasons why is that you are not listening to him and are not making choices he can understand. Hell, you're not making choices I understand."

"I just want to know why I moved out of that house so you could take over my side of it? That was not the point," Gemma asks. "Like, how did you go from not being able to take your hands off each other to this?"

"I need another drink before I talk about that," Paul says.

"Shots." Darcy bounces up off the couch and heads for the kitchen. "Definitely shots."

"Should you let her alone in there?" Paul asks.

"I think I can trust her not to run with scissors or poison you," Carly says.

"That might not be the worst thing at this point," Paul says.

Carly frowns. "You of all people should not be making jokes about that."

Paul lifts a shoulder. "Where's the gallows humor tonight?"

Gemma becomes fascinated with a throw pillow, but is obviously listening.

"You scared Alex," Carly tells him.

"When?"

"I got an email from him right before he left for D.C. After you had your 'trial separation' conversation. And nothing you've been doing this last week is making me think he's wrong to be worried. I have not kept you alive this long to lose you over this mess. Besides, Alex will kill me if I let you kill yourself, so let's be adults and talk about the options you're going to take, okay?"

"I'm not suicidal."

"You are depressed."

"Why are we discussing this in front of Darcy?" Paul asks as she reenters the room, carrying a bottle of gin and juggling shot glasses.

"Because leadership comes from the leads," she says, handing them around.

"Thank you, musical theater summer camp wisdom," Paul snipes.

"Don't be a dick," she says. "I'm trying to help. And I'm not going to, like, go tell or anything."

"Okay, so, borrowing from my boyfriend," Carly says. "One, you need to take care of yourself in a context other than whether it will it fix things with Alex. Two, to actually fix things with Alex, you need to step up and do the work, not just react to his own attempts, which, believe me, I know are a mixed bag. Three, please fucking go back to therapy because this is not my job."

"Three sort of sounds like one," Paul points out.

"Have you heard Liam make a list?"

Paul snorts.

"And don't tell me you're actually happy right now. I don't care how awesome your show is. You're not Victor. You have what you have wanted forever, and you are miserable. That's not about you or your work ethic; that is your brain lying to you. You deserve better. And now we're going to do shots, and then you're going to tell us why you and Alex stopped living together despite technically still being in the same house."

Somehow, that's even harder to talk about than the rest of it. It takes Paul several false starts and more than a few confessions that don't quite get to the heart of the matter. Which isn't just his terrible schedule and the burden of disappointing Alex, who is now more or less used to getting everything he wants from everyone.

"Wait, wait, wait," Carly says. "So you're having issues about being faintly kinky and stopped fucking Alex because you didn't trust his *yes*?"

"Yes?" Paul says meekly.

"This is very educational," Darcy tells her drink seriously.

"This is a really shitty intervention," Paul says.

Gemma kicks Darcy in response, which doesn't really resolve the issue.

"And why the hell are you here?" he asks Darcy.

"Way to be a friend, boss."

"*Anyway*," Carly says. "Alex does not say yes to things he does not want. He, in fact, is saying no to you quite a lot, which is part of why you're pissed at him. Until and unless you can trust and respect him saying yes, he is never going to be a partner to you."

"You saw what I did to his back," Paul says. "I've done worse since then."

"Yeah. And he was as proud of that as he knew how to be without being a tacky, bragging asshole. Why are you so dense?"

"I slit my wrists because it was a marginally better option than stabbing my father. What the fuck am I going to do to him, if he lets me?"

Darcy goes a little pale. Paul doesn't ever bother to cover his scars, but this is the first time he's ever talked about them in front of her.

Carly frowns. "Okay, *wow*, you are mixing up about eight different issues in your head. You are depressed and have anger issues, and you have a young, sexy boyfriend who loves you and trusts you and likes when you mark him up. Which is, let me say, not as kinky as you probably think it is. These two things are also completely separate."

"I hurt him."

"Not the way you're afraid of. Except for the part where you're breaking his heart because you're not trusting him because you've got your kink and your history confused."

"He said he's not allowed to say no," Paul protests, still baffled by it.

"Oh my God," Gemma says. "Is that what this is about?" She sits up abruptly.

"What do you mean?"

"I told him that. When Victor offered him Zach. Like, *years* ago. He didn't know if he wanted to take it, and I flipped out at him. And then he started saying it all the time, because of how much time he spends being a human doll for hair and makeup and fans and everything. That's never been about you, Paul. It's about being famous."

21

Alex emails Paul his flight information the night before he leaves New York. All he gets back is *Have a safe trip*. The trial part of their separation may be just about over and actual, permanent separation imminent. The last few days in New York have been fine and make him hopeful about what's next for his career. But he still hates photo shoots, and he has no idea what he's flying back into. Which makes it harder to leave New York than it would be under any other circumstances.

He spends the flight back to L.A. with his headphones on, staring out the window when he can't sleep, and thinking about how much he hates flying. Six hours where he's utterly helpless to do anything make him wild with impatience.

At the gate, Alex texts Paul to say he's landed. He has no idea if he'll care, and he doubts he'll be at the house by the time Alex gets there anyway. But it seems like the worst kind of luck to break that particular ritual now.

The last thing he expects, as he makes way out of the terminal through all the drivers with signs for their pickups, is to see Paul. He's holding a sign with the stupid fake name Alex uses for stuff like this, unexpectedly unshaven and looking faintly hopeful.

Alex's first response is to be annoyed, because *public* and *ambush* and *emotions in front of people* and no real idea of what the intent even is. But it's still Paul and home and a gesture that's stupid and romantic and absolutely perfect. He manages about three more steps before he drops his bags and flings himself into Paul's arms.

Paul catches him around the waist, and for a long moment it's just him and his familiar body. Alex melts into him.

"I know we're a mess," Paul eventually says quietly. "I know we don't know what's going to happen. But I wanted to do something ridiculous for you."

Alex nods. He can't speak. He isn't remotely willing to let go.

"People are looking," Paul says softly into Alex's hair.

"I don't care."

Paul holds him tighter. "I've missed you. Fixing this terrifies me. But I want to try."

Alex nods again into Paul's shoulder. "I'm scared when I let go of you it's going to go back to being awkward and messed up."

"It probably is," Paul pulls back and catches Alex's face in his hands. "But it won't be as awkward and fucked up as having the rest of this conversation in the middle of LAX."

◆

Paul sets Alex's bags down in the entryway and continues on into the living room. Todd jumps down from the couch and trots over to Alex for a pet. Alex picks him up because he wants to keep holding on to things right now, even though since Todd is a cat this particular activity won't last long.

"I think he missed you too," Paul says as Todd nuzzles into Alex's hand for an ear scratch.

"We haven't been giving him the quality time he deserves," Alex admits, as Todd jumps down again only to wind between his legs. One of the side effects of he and Paul sleeping in separate rooms has been both of them avoiding the shared areas of the house.

"Yeah." Paul takes a seat on one of the couches as Alex takes the other.

"So," Alex finally says when Paul doesn't add anything else. As strange and as happy as their reunion has been, Paul started this by being at the airport. Alex is determined to make him go first. "Conversation?"

Paul nods. "I don't like how this sounds, but I think the space, the last ten days, anyway, has been good. At least for me. And my extravagant gesture aside, I don't think we have any business sharing a bed with each other right now."

"It has been good," Alex agrees carefully. "All I want to do is crawl into bed with you and I know that's not going to solve anything, which is weird, because I feel like that's how we used to solve everything."

Paul leans forward, his expression earnest. "I think it solved less than we thought it did. Or that it stopped solving things when it started to be a problem itself."

Alex glances around the room like he's going to find an explanation for Paul's words floating somewhere in space. "When did it start to be a problem itself?" He can practically feel the conversation turning to Liam again. Which is something he's more than run out of patience for.

"While you were gone Carly, Gemma, and Darcy launched an intervention."

Alex's eyes go wide. "That sounds scary and entirely like something they would do. I also can't tell how much humor is present in that word choice." He wants it to be less potentially relevant to Paul's state of being than he's inclined to think.

"Not much," Paul admits. He looks at his hands instead of at Alex. "I think everyone initially thought it would be funnier than it was. Can you let me talk for a bit?"

Alex restrains himself from pointing out that he's been trying to get Paul to acknowledge him as something other than a burden or distraction and just talk to him for a long time now. If Paul is finally going to speak, he does not want to do things that will make him stop. He nods.

"We talked about some things. And Carly pointed out to me that I may have gotten some shit about sex messed up in my head with the shit I did when I was a kid. Stuff I still haven't really stopped doing now and that has never meant anything good for anyone. Particularly for me, but the people around me too."

"I don't know what that means."

Paul scratches the back of his neck as he looks up at the ceiling. "Why is this so hard? I'm an adult. I've fucked lots of people."

Alex smirks, not unkindly, but doesn't say anything.

"So here's the thing. As you know, I have some fucked up anger issues – "

"You've barely ever yelled at me," Alex says. "You tell me the things you want to do instead of doing them."

"Yeah," Paul says. "Because my wrists and my dad and that lost summer and yeah. Anger's really scary for me. It should be. And then you show up and are like…. God, I think about when I met you as compared to now. Did you even know this is how you'd like to fuck?"

"What?" Alex says. He's a little defensive and a lot surprised. "That I like to get fucked?"

"No. That you like when I scratch you, when I mark you. And that when I'm too fucked up about all the other shit going on in my life to give you the attention you deserve, your first line of action it to goad me into hurting you?"

Alex blinks several times as he processes that. About half of what Paul has said – as dreadful and agonizing as it is – makes sense. The other half feels like such a misread of everything, Alex doesn't know where to start.

"Is this where I can talk now?"

Paul nods.

"Okay, first of all. No, I didn't know what I liked when I started this with you. You know that. You were there. Maybe I just like what I like. I don't want to blame things in my life for that. And if you like what you like, that doesn't have to be about shit that's happened to you either. Or about the ways in which you're fucked up. I mean, I hear what you're saying, I'm glad you're saying it, but my main answer is *no*. I don't want my desires written off like that or the way we fuck written off like that."

"I do hurt you, though."

"It's not like that." Alex says.

"Then what's it like?"

"It's like being awake because I spend ninety percent of my life sleepwalking because of my schedule and the things my job forces me to ignore. It's like climbing and knowing sometimes I will tear my body apart to do something amazing. Are you trying to hurt me when we fuck?"

"No. At least – no. I'm trying to make you pay attention. And fall apart."

"Do you enjoy it?"

"Yes. That's the problem."

Alex shakes his head slowly. "This actually seems pretty perfect as far as compatibility goes? Like – whatever you're afraid of is in your head. You're not hurting me the way you're scared of. If you were, I would say no."

"I'm trying to tell you where I am right now, Alex, not fix it all in a day."

"Okay, but do you want to fix it?"

"I know I've said as much today."

"You have, but when you're telling me you aren't willing to believe me when I say yes, I don't feel listened to. And I definitely don't feel whatever magical safer I'm supposed to feel if we weren't sexually compatible this way, so...."

"So it's going to take time."

"And you're going to sort this out on your own while you don't touch me?"

"I don't know! I'm just trying to tell you what's going on."

"Okay, well, what else is going on? Because seriously, Paul, if this is the whole thing, I might strangle you."

"Don't make light."

"Someone has to," Alex mutters.

Paul chuckles. "Carly said the same thing."

"Look, I've never said you have bad taste."

"No, I really don't," Paul says fondly, gazing at Alex. "I'm sorry I've been a dick about Liam."

"You've said before."

Paul rocks back at that a little bit. "I know you chose me –"

"It's never been a competition," Alex interrupts firmly. He's trying not to sound as exasperated as he feels.

"You're here, despite how fucked up we are right now, because you want to be. And I know I should respect that – and respect your friendship with him the way you respect mine with Carly. I'm sorry. And I'm working on it."

"She threatened to never speak to you again, didn't she?"

"Actually, she threatened to slap me."

Alex laughs. Carly truly is awesome.

"And then she told me to go back to therapy, because clearly I am way more fucked up than any of you can really deal with."

"That's probably good choices." It's about fucking time.

"I haven't called anyone yet. And I still think you should go too."

"That's not unfair," Alex says. "But your well-being regarding activities you have total control over choosing to participate in shouldn't be determined by my willingness to negotiate."

"Is there a no in there somewhere?"

"I'm not saying I don't have issues." Alex doesn't get as sarcastic as he wants. That would be the opposite of helpful right now. "I'm saying your tendency towards codependence is not helping you here."

"How do you even know what that word means?"

"I live in L.A. Look at our friends."

"Go back to telling me about your issues," Paul says with a smile.

Alex smiles back at him. He's amazed that this is what passes for flirtatiousness in the current state of their lives. "I goad you into sex. That doesn't mean I don't like it," he says just to make that absolutely clear. "But I push you at least as much as you push me and not in a good way. I need to learn how to ask for things from you. I'm still learning how to talk."

"You've gotten better," Paul offers.

"Not as much as you think I have. You worry about hurting me, and I worry about all the ways in which you own me, which isn't, I get, something you necessarily signed up for."

"You own me too, you know."

Alex tips his head to the side. "Okay. That's good. I think. What do we do now other than retreat to our corners and let our jobs work us to death?"

"I think we keep having these conversations. And we think about therapy. And I kiss you good night, because not fucking is fine, but God, I've wanted to since the airport."

Alex slumps against the back of the couch. "Do you think that's all over the internet by now?" he asks, chagrined.

"I don't think I care," Paul says. "But if you wanted to go look at complete strangers telling us how in love we are while we're trying to figure out if we should split up, gotta say, I'm not going to stop you."

Alex pats the empty space next to him. "Come kiss me, then."

Paul almost trips over the corner of the coffee table in his haste to get to him. Alex laughs in delight. The kiss is chaste for only half a second before they tug at each other's hair desperately. Alex shivers at the delicious scratch of Paul's scruff; Paul groans and grabs the back of Alex's head to keep their faces pressed together. But when they go from vertical to horizontal on the couch they stop, Alex curling in on himself to press his head to Paul's chest.

"This is hard," he says. He doesn't mean the stopping; he means everything.

Paul curls a hand gently around the back of Alex's neck. "I know, but this is nice too."

◆

Going forward is complicated and both harder and easier than either of them expect. Neither of their jobs get less demanding as the summer drags on. Paul is still working too much. But they're not making their work the central item in the mess that is their relationship, which means they're not instantly at silent war the second they are both in the house at the same time.

Sleeping apart continues to be hard, even if it's less fraught now that it's part of their attempt at finding a solution and not the problem itself. On Paul's birthday, in early August, it feels cruel to just text him happy wishes in the morning. He'd rather go out together or welcome Paul home that evening with a celebratory blowjob.

Aside from the sex, Alex misses the easy connection of skin on skin in a shared bed. Some days he wonders how much of a solution separate rooms can really be.

Alex has a conversation with Margaret. Sitting down with her to talk about the pictures from LAX and why they happened is a unique kind of terrible. He tells her to come up with a plan to deal with a breakup that he hopes they'll never need. He also asks her to tell him about it once she's got it figured out. There are days he needs all the reasons he can get to stay with Paul, even if some of them are convenience.

He starts therapy, but only to passive-aggressively goad Paul into the same. When that doesn't work, they have their first shouting match since his return from the East Coast. They're both surprised when somehow they get through it without it being the end.

Margaret and Vanessa help Alex to keep looking at his options beyond *Fourth*. Alex isn't sure if the projects that would keep him away for months are the best option, given the good his trip did them, or the worst.

Talking to Paul about those projects when Alex isn't sure they're going to be together by the time any of them start is hard. What's worse is that he knows that taking one of them could be the thing that splits them up for sure.

When he goes up to Paul's office one night and taps on the wall at the top of the stairs, Paul looks annoyed when he first glances up. Then the annoyance turns to fear. Alex takes the smallest amount of vindication in that.

"Can we talk?" Alex asks.

"This doesn't sound good," Paul says.

Alex aches at how serious Paul sounds. "It's okay," Alex says. "At least, I don't think it's bad. Not unless you want it to be. But it's important. Can we?" He tips his head away from the room.

♦

They go downstairs because Alex says he wants neutral territory for this. But once they reach the living room Alex sits on the opposite end of the couch with both feet on the floor and his back carefully straight. Paul's anxiety ratchets up.

"I've been looking at some movies," Alex says.

Paul nods and braces himself.

Alex goes on. "There are a few options that might be good, but there's one I really want. When I was in New York I sat down with the director and did some chemistry reads. Nothing's set in stone yet, and nothing's going to be certain for maybe a long time, but I really want this. I think they want me. It just depends on whether they think the audience wants me too."

"Of course they do." Paul is still worried about where this conversation is going, but he lives daily with the consequences of just how much America wants Alex.

Alex looks surprised. "Sweet. But you know it's not that simple."

"No. But you're amazing."

"Do you want to flatter me, or do you want to hear what I'm trying to tell you?" Alex's tone is playful, but there's a note of warning there too.

Paul shakes his head. "Sorry. You were saying?"

Alex crosses his legs in a gesture Paul recognizes more from seeing Alex on TV than from their living room. Alex being this deliberate about things makes him even more nervous. But, given their current situation, it's probably fair.

"They've changed the name of the project like three times, but it's about street kids in Richmond – which is apparently a shitty, shitty city, by the way. What the hell is wrong with the South?"

"Researching again?"

Alex shrugs. "I have to do something when I'm home alone. Not that it really needs much background reading to figure out, Mr. Crickets."

"There were about three different things in that statement that were terrible," Paul doesn't know what to think about any of them.

"Were there?" Alex says evenly. "Anyway. Supporting role. Street kid who's a little too old to be called a kid. And a lot dangerous for it. Crime, drugs, prostitution," Alex shrugs. "Sounds like a challenge. It's definitely something new, and I want it."

"Okay," Paul says. So far none of this has been bad information. Serious, certainly, and worthy of discussion because this is Alex's career and Paul loves him, but he's sure there's another shoe waiting to drop. "What's the schedule like?"

"If everything goes as planned – that's a big if – it'll be shooting in Toronto, this winter."

"That's a long way from home," Paul says carefully.

"Closer than New York. In a way."

"For how long?"

Alex bites his lip. "Three months."

"Oh my God, Alex." Paul sits back heavily.

"I know," Alex says. "This is why I want us to talk about this."

"Is 'this' what I think it is?" Paul asks warily.

"I can't read your mind so I don't know what 'this' is. No, I'm not breaking up with you. But if we're going to talk about our futures, this – or something like it – is going to be a part of it."

"It feels like you're running away."

"This isn't about us, Paul."

"Up and leaving for three months?" Paul knows he should be calmer lest he piss Alex off again, but now that it's come to this he's scared.

"I am not *up and leaving*. I am talking about my career options with you because you are my partner and, fucked up as things are right now, this is a discussion I need you to be a part of."

"Are you coming back?"

"*Paul,*" Alex says. He sounds as weary as he does exasperated. "I don't even know if this movie is going to happen, much less if we're still going to be together when I leave for it. Don't go paranoid on me. Especially when you're the one living in your office."

Paul frowns. "I know we're still learning how to do logistics. But you travelling has always been hard. I need to be sure this isn't you giving me a limited renewal instead of a cancellation."

Alex, to Paul's surprise, laughs. "I can't believe you just turned our relationship issues into a *Fourth* joke."

"Yeah, well. You make me all sorts of crazy."

Alex smiles and tips his head against the back of the couch. "So can this be okay?"

"Frankly, you disappearing for three months scares me."

"I'm not yours to keep here." The smile is still there around Alex's eyes, but his voice is sharp. "I know you have reasons to be scared. I'm scared, too. And I know this kind of separation would be hard even if we were solid right now. But you're assuming the worst and sometimes it feels like my loyalty is one more way you're trying to own me. That's not doing either of us any good."

Paul looks away. "I know. But, Jesus, Alex. Three months."
"Believe me. I know."

22

They keep having conversations – about their relationship and their future and the shape of it all – in the rare moments they're both home and awake. Alex finally works his way around to telling Paul how Zach is leaving *Fourth*. Somehow that turns into a conversation about how long they're actually going to do this repair work and how to decide when it's time to pull the plug on the whole thing. They don't reach any conclusions, but it's another conversation they're going to need to keep having. At least until the day that Alex wakes up and decides he wants the relationship to be over much the way he randomly decided he wanted Zach to be dead.

"Please try to remember that was so I could keep him," he says, but Paul doesn't seem interested in getting it. Alex is grateful he's not interested in fighting about it either.

The prospect of shooting Zach's death is exhilarating. It's also going to be exhausting. As they start to swing into Zach's final arc Alex gets informed that Zach has decided red is far too conspicuous for another foray into Iran.

♦

"They're going to dye my hair," Alex tells Paul one night in the middle of August. Paul's sitting at the kitchen table, working, and Alex has just gotten home.

"Ah?" Paul saves the file he's working on and closes it and then his laptop. He doesn't think Alex is angry, exactly, but he's definitely not thrilled. "Why?"

"Because I decided Zach was going to die and Victor decided to fuck with me."

"Why did Victor say they're going to dye your hair?" Not that Paul would be surprised if 'Because I say so' had been Victor's reason.

"Because Zach is going to Iran and needs to blend in."

"That seems like a valid writing choice," Paul says. He tries to imagine Alex with brown hair. It's a strange picture, but not an unappealing one.

"I'm going to be spending a month as a brunet." Now Alex sounds pissed. He slumps into a chair across from Paul. "Not just Zach. *Me.* Victor decided that, and the team agreed on it, so that's what happens. I don't get a choice."

It's not the first time Alex has been annoyed about something regarding *Fourth* and the constraints Zach puts on his appearance, but it's the first time he's ever explained to Paul why. It certainly makes what Gemma told him about Alex and his *nos* make a lot more sense and be a lot easier for him to believe.

◆

They're going to use temporary color to shoot the scene where James helps Zach with his hair the night before Zach leaves for Iran. Because not only is Liam clumsy with fiddly things like combs and tubes of color, hair dye is a nightmare and is going to get *everywhere*. ("You've got enough freckles," Ellen tells Alex at the table read. "We don't need you to be blotchy, too.") After, he'll have to go to a salon to get his hair permanently dyed. And then he'll have to wait for it to grow back out before he gets to look like himself again – unless he wants to shave his head.

There may be something a little kind, though, about making Zach look less like Zach, and less like Alex, as far as Liam is concerned. The less he looks like Alex, the less losing him will hurt – hopefully. Alex doesn't know what, if anything, Victor has told him. Since he hasn't gotten a worried phone call from Liam about it yet, he assumes he hasn't told him anything. With the end approaching, it makes Alex nervous. If Victor's waiting to tell Liam, the reason can't be good.

A home hair-coloring session involves messy dye and a bathtub which also involves being shirtless, another reason Alex chooses to be annoyed at this whole thing. The day of the hair shoot, someone from makeup walks them through the process. Ellen obnoxiously thanks Alex for not getting himself marked up. He snaps back; it's mostly good fun but she has no way of knowing the issue bruises are in his life right now. Aside from the occasional kiss, Paul isn't touching him. In his more pessimistic moments, Alex is afraid that's as much an excuse for Paul not to hurt him as it is a part of their agreements.

The set is closed to reduce the chance of leaks. Victor is there, not directing, just observing. Alex tries not to feel like his eyes are always boring into the back of his head.

Right before they're about to start shooting, Victor crooks his fingers to Liam. Liam leans half out of the frame to him, and he cups a hand at Liam's ear and whispers something. Alex can't hear what, but he watches as Liam preens from the intimacy before going ashen. Victor has to push Liam back onto both of his feet and into the scene.

After the second take, with James being falsely cheerful, Liam won't look him in the eye. Alex realizes Victor didn't say, "We're killing off Zach" but more likely, "Zach's going to die."

◆

When Alex bangs through the door that night, he's furious. He's sure the scene turned out fantastically, but that doesn't matter. Liam had spent the rest the day not looking at Alex, and, more disconcertingly, not speaking to him. He'd dropped things, more than once, and his hands shook the whole time he'd had them in Alex's hair.

"Victor is a manipulative asshole!" Alex calls up the stairs at Paul's loft. Thank God he's home.

Paul takes his headphones off and leans his arms on the railing. "I thought you got okay with the dye thing? Oh. Hey. Brown hair."

"*Yes,*" Alex snaps. "Are you busy?"

"I was starting to think about dinner," Paul offers.

"Come down here and think."

They sit together on the couch in the living room. Alex tells him about the day and how Victor had chosen to spring the news on Liam in the most cruel way possible. Based on what Alex is hearing from Liam, Liam and Victor's relationship continues to shift. Still, Alex doesn't think something this terrible should be part of that.

Paul settles himself more comfortably into the couch. "You don't know what he said," he reasons.

Alex shakes his head. "I know Lee. I've never seen him like that. All I hear from you is about how it's your job to take care of your people – sometimes to the very detriment of you and I – and Victor did *that*."

"You sound afraid," Paul says.

"He's his lover!" Alex exclaims. Even Victor, who doesn't do human relationships the way anyone else does, surely should take better care of Liam than *that*.

"Then they'll sort it out between them."

Alex opens his mouth and then closes it. "Really?" he says, suddenly blackly amused. After all, he and Paul are lovers. Which has not meant they're capable of working out anything between them.

When Paul meets his eyes, they both crack up. The reasons are terrible, but it feels good, and they keep setting each other off.

"I'm going to kiss you now," Paul says right before he does. He pulls back, wrinkles his nose, and informs Alex he smells like hair dye.

23

The next day, Alex gets his hair properly, permanently done. He's still pissed about it, but most of his emotions are focused elsewhere. He's more worried about what Victor is doing to Liam, and what Victor is going to do to Alex before this is over. Because it's definitely going to be over now. Zach is coming to an end, and Alex hardly recognizes himself in the mirror. He'll get used to it eventually, just like everything else in life.

A week later he and Liam have the last scene they're ever going to do together as Zach and James. Liam is quiet and small in a way he never is, tucked into his chair in a corner of the set with his feet up on the seat. Alex walks over to him and gets close enough into his bubble that Liam eventually has to look up at him.

"Hey," Alex asks. "Are you okay?"

Liam blinks. "Why are you the one asking me that? Zach's the one that's…." He trails off.

"I'm fine, Lee." Alex reaches out to rub Liam's shoulder. "I'm tough, remember? Not the twink."

Liam smiles at that.

"Nothing changes because I'm not here with you every day." Alex grabs Liam's hand and kisses his palm. There will always be a thousand secret codes between them. Alex used to hate that, but the more complicated his life gets, the more he appreciates language in any of its forms.

When Liam suddenly beams, even as he still looks like he's about to cry, Alex knows he's done the right thing.

That night when he gets home, Paul asks him how he wants to handle the *Winsome* premiere. It's a testament to how long their relationship has been seriously broken that Alex hasn't even realized it's barely more than a week away.

"What do you want to do?" Alex asks him. *Winsome* is Paul's show and he is still Paul's partner. Paul has so often played this part for him.

"I want you to be there," Paul says simply.

♦

One evening a few days before Paul's premiere, Alex calls Gemma.

"And here I thought you'd left me for another woman," Gemma teases when she picks up.

"What?"

"*Darcy*," Gemma hisses.

330

Alex doesn't know if she's joking or if he wants to find out. "Hey, I'm the one who wanted you to come to New York. You said no."

"Yeah," Gemma sighs. "I know."

Glad as Gemma seems to be to hear from him – Alex knows that things have been bad and that he's been distant – she's aghast at his suggestion that they go to the gun range.

"I taught Darcy," Alex wheedles.

"You sure know how to make a girl feel special," Gemma grouses. "Why are you so hot on the whole weapons thing anyway?"

"Because you hate climbing, and I want to aggravate America."

"You know, you can just tweet that you're going to the range. No one would know the difference. You don't have to go every time."

"Yeah, but this way I get to shoot things too. Come on, I need stress relief. It'll be awesome." Alex may be famous now, but he's not above wheedling, especially with Gemma.

"Fine."

◆

"This is marginally more boring than bowling," Gemma states flatly when they take a break. "And way more sketchy."

"That's because you're from the wrong part of America," Alex tells her mildly. As much as this activity is one he's become provocative about, he does believe there's room for it to be treated with the neutrality of any sport.

"Yes, thank God."

Alex does his best not to irritate Gemma further. All he wants is a day out of the house doing something he's good at to blow off steam. Also a chance to talk over his and Paul's precarious position with someone who has always badgered him for more information than he usually wants to give.

But when he starts telling Gemma about the Richmond movie and his fear that their relationship can't stand a three-month separation, she stops him.

"Okay, I know Paul and you are having a hard time right now. But Alex, seriously? You are famous and successful and are complaining to me that you and your also famous and successful boyfriend are having potential logistics problems because you're too fucking good at your jobs."

Alex blinks. Gemma hasn't said things like that to him in ages. And he's well aware he deserves it.

"I am the same age as you, and my career has gone nowhere. That's fine, not everybody gets the dream. *Whatever.* But sometimes it is really fucking hard."

"I thought you liked your job," Alex says carefully. He knows he behaves badly toward Gemma sometimes, largely because he's still not used to thinking about other people; so much of surviving Paragon had meant pretending other people didn't exist. But that means he doesn't know how to fix the gulf between them. Gemma hasn't talked about her jealousy in a long time, but that doesn't mean it's gone away.

"I am amazing at my job. And one day I will do very big and very amazing things. Just not on the path I thought I was going to be on. You get to say 'fuck you' to the world with a tweet." She taps Alex's hip where his phone is sticking out of his pocket. "Some of us have to do a lot more."

◆

"Would it be super weird if I invited your mom to the wedding?" Carly asks Paul. It's Saturday night, Alex is still working, and Paul is at Carly's for a movie night. If he's going to make a serious effort with Alex, Paul knows he must be a person who exists outside of work.

Paul looks up from where he's digging in her cupboards. "When was the last time you talked to my mom?"

"Last week. Don't look so scared; we weren't talking about you."

"How often do you call her?" Paul asks, surprised. His mom and Carly had gotten on well when he and Carly had been dating, but he'd had no reason to think they'd spoken in years.

"Often enough. So, is it weird?"

Paul chuckles and finally manages to find the chips at the back of the shelf. "Probably. But if this is your way of asking me if I mind, no. Even though I'm kind of freaked you guys have been talking forever and I had no idea."

"Your mom is amazing and not everything is about you." Carly crosses off an item from a list on her refrigerator titled *Wedding Shit to Do*.

"So how are the wedding plans going?"

Carly tosses the pen down on the counter. "They're pissing me off. Liam's way too busy to help, which is fine, because putting him in charge of logistical decisions is a bad idea anyway. But this shooting schedule gives us no time."

"What about a house? Are you guys still going to move in together?"

"Don't ask," Carly says. "Tell me about your problems instead."

Paul laughs as he grabs a bowl for the chips and heads into Carly's bedroom, where they've got *Shark Attack 4* set up already.

Part of being a person who exists involves keeping up his friendships. Like by having movie nights with Carly. Another part of that involves talking to his best friend about something that's not his troubled relationship. While mutated sharks wreak havoc on New York, Paul tells Carly about the effort he's making to delegate at work, because he has a good team who is brilliantly capable and it is not his job to be everywhere at once.

She nods approvingly.

"My days are still fourteen hours long," Paul tells her. "But they're starting to look different."

"And Alex?" Carly asks.

Paul shakes his head. "He's fine. I don't know if untangling my shit at work is going to make anything better for us, but I need to do it."

Carly throws a chip at him. "It's about fucking time."

24

aul has been nervous about the premiere for ages. When the big day finally arrives he can hardly eat for nerves. While he's attended big industry events with Alex and been in the spotlight with things like upfronts, the premiere is a sort of focused attention he's never had in this way before. No one's red carpet performances tonight will make or break the show, but every bit counts. Paul desperately wants things to go well.

Unsteady as things still are between them, he's incredibly glad to have Alex next to him for this. Paul grabs his hand as the car pulls up in front of the venue. Alex squeezes back, his eyes bright.

Stepping out of the car and onto the carpet is like stepping into another world. Flashes go off around them, and Paul has to keep himself from blinking too much. He's never been on this side of the camera before, not like this.

"How do you do it?" Paul asks Alex. He's passed 'nervous' and gone on to 'practically petrified.'

Alex shakes his head. "Practice."

◆

Although Alex has lots of familiarity with the stop-and-pose nonsense of the red carpet, the experience is completely different at Paul's side. They're separated often in the controlled chaos outside the theater. Alex is asked over and over again about his new hair – "that would be telling" – and whether he's proud of his man. To Alex's knowledge, Paul has never been asked if he's proud of *his* man, but then Paul has never been important enough to ask until now. If they're still together the next time Alex has a premiere, he plans on keeping score.

When he won't give away any spoilers for *Fourth*, the spare, tanned people that pass for journalists in L.A. ask him about his future plans. *Any movies coming up? Will he guest on Paul's show? Could marriage be in the works?*

Alex smiles benignly. "We're talking about our futures a lot right now." He's unsure if he's very clever or very cruel.

Any time he can get back to Paul's side, he tucks himself close in a way he's never allowed himself to in public before. Paul gives him a worried, doting glance or two and soldiers on either like Alex is a given or, possibly, like he isn't even there.

When they walk into the theatre, Paul puts his hand on Alex's back. Alex lets himself lean into it. Their eyes catch briefly. In that moment, the entire evening is a shared victory.

◆

Victor skips the carpet at the premiere because this is Paul's night, not his. But at the afterparty, he seeks Paul out as soon as he can. He does it not just because Paul craves approval in a way Victor's not even sure his business partner realizes. He does it because Paul has created a very good thing and should be aware of the quality of the work.

He finds Paul in a corner with his arm around Alex. What shocks Victor isn't the way Alex is curled into Paul's side, looking small and vulnerable. What's jarring is how happy Alex looks there.

As Victor watches, Paul smiles and says something in Alex's ear, who grins and tips his head onto Paul's shoulder. They're gorgeous, and the sight is all the more delightful to Victor because he had no idea that this is who they are when no one is watching.

Finally, he understands why Liam and Alex were beautiful and could not work, with both of them too much in love with being under someone else's sway. Alex and Paul, on the other hand, are also beautiful, but so very challenging. Alex does not go gently into any form of submission, Victor knows from work. Until this moment, Victor had never realized this was a place Alex could take pleasure in. Whether Paul knows how to handle it…. He has to assume not.

"Good work," Victor tells Paul when he can finally bring himself to interrupt them. "I'm proud of you." He expects Alex to disentangle himself from Paul, or at least lift his head from his shoulder. But he doesn't, instead looking up at Victor with a dazed blink that makes his eyelashes flutter the way they had when he'd been lying in a hospital bed. The image is more gorgeous than Victor could have hoped. "I'm proud of you both," he adds.

◆

They stay at the afterparty only long enough for Paul to graciously thank everyone. Alex is willing to tough the night out as long as Paul wants, and says so, but Paul beams and shakes his head.

"I just want to go home with you."

"Okay," Alex says. This night has been good and now it feels scary in the best possible way.

The car ride is pure, delightful torture. Neither of them says anything, but there's a charge between them. Like lightning ready to strike.

Once Paul parks the car they both scramble to get out and inside. They make it as far as the foyer before Paul pushes Alex up against the wall, kissing him hard. Alex whimpers and lets himself be pushed, fisting his hands in Paul's hair.

"I realize this is a total cliché." Paul strokes his hands up and down Alex's sides.

"I don't know, night of your greatest triumph is working out pretty well for me." Alex strains forward to keep kissing Paul. Paul hasn't touched him like this in months and he *wants*. "Upstairs?"

Paul nods but starts unbuttoning Alex's shirt instead.

"What are you doing?" Alex asks breathlessly. Paul's hands on him feel so good he can barely keep his eyes open.

"What does it look like I'm doing?"

Alex digs his fingers into Paul's jacket and pushes him away. Paul looks devastated for a moment. "*Upstairs,*" Alex repeats and saunters toward the stairs.

Paul races after him.

♦

Paul hesitates in the doorway. Alex pauses too, standing in the middle of the bedroom, his hair messy and weirdly dark from the dye, his shirt half unbuttoned. He thinks about everything he should be saying, about agreements and space and what this means for what comes after, but all he can see is Paul looking at him.

"Paul," Alex says softly.

"Yeah?"

"Take me to bed."

Paul is gentle with him at first. But Alex is impatient. This, right now, is a real thing he can have. Even if they fall apart with finality tomorrow, they love each other, and they've earned this. The problem, it seems, is earning it day in and day out.

"Can't wait," Alex breathes against Paul's ear. He has to curl around him to do it, as Paul is intent on dragging his bottom lip across Alex's ribcage and up his side.

"Shhhhhhhh."

"No shhhhhh." He yanks Paul up to him by the hair. "We haven't had this in months. Let's go."

"No bells and whistles?" Paul asks with a chuckle and a ridiculous grin.

Alex lines their cocks up and wraps his hand around them as best he can. He smiles wickedly when Paul gasps. "Not even remotely."

♦

After, they're lazy and giggly, unwilling to go to sleep and wake up remembering that this was a respite, not a resolution. Eventually Paul makes the mistake of checking the internet from his phone to see if there's any buzz from the premiere.

There surely is, but stuff about the show the network will track for him. He's more interested, with his current limited bandwidth and relative happiness, on whether the internet thinks the whole unshaven thing is working for him. He's pretty sure Alex thinks it's cute, and he is not remotely above using Alex's curiosity and love of sensation play to keep him interested while they do the real work.

The internet response is less good than it could be. Not because of the beard, but because Paul has the bad luck to stumble almost immediately on someone offering in-depth commentary on whether Alex's smile reaches his eyes in the photos and interviews. Paul knows he should laugh when someone defends their analysis with the declaration that their dad studied sociology in college and knows about body language, but it's a testament to how terrified he is of losing Alex that he's not amused at all.

"What are you looking at?" Alex mumbles from where he's draped across Paul's chest.

"You telling the world we're spending a lot of time discussing our future lately," Paul says as neutrally as he can. He's not angry, just sad.

"I didn't know what else to do."

"It was very clever."

"I thought so."

"The internet's discussing whether you seem happy."

Alex opens an eye so he can give Paul a condescending look. "The internet is discussing no such thing," he says. "Obsessive people are saying irrational things because Liam."

Paul sighs. "I know I sort of count as irrational right now, but, so you know, I don't actually think he's the love of your life and you're just slumming with me."

"Well, that's good," Alex says, amused. "Because that would be crazy above and beyond our actual mental health issues."

"As opposed to in line with our mental health issues," Paul offers.

"Yes. Please don't be more crazy, because I would like to keep you."

Paul squeezes him just a little bit tighter. "Me too. Also, God, Alex, if we can't solve this, it's going to be so public."

Alex pushes himself off Paul's chest and sits up. "Okay, no. Our relationship belongs to us, no matter what happens. And none of that," he grabs the phone out of Paul's hand, "matters. I know tomorrow you're going back to sleeping on the other side of the house, and we're going to keep trying to figure out whether or not we're doomed. If you want to consult the internet on that, that's your business, but I want to throttle you and a legion of sixteen-year-old strangers right now, and guess what? *The smile is still reaching my eyes*."

"You've talked to Margaret about it, haven't you?" Paul says.

"Having a plan we don't need is better than not having a plan we do," Alex says.

"But today was good," Paul says.

"Today was good," Alex confirms, as he settles back down. "I truly am proud of you."

25

When Paul comes home a week after the premiere to find Alex sitting in the corner of the couch again waiting for him, all signals point to this being the end. Though he realizes he thinks that every time he comes home to Alex waiting for him.

"Hi," he says carefully. He watches as Alex gets up to come stand in front of him. He looks uncertain but not solemn, and Paul tries to take that as a good sign.

"Go out to dinner with me?" Alex asks.

Paul stares at him, trying to calibrate. "What?"

Alex sighs. "Small words, Paul. I. Am. Asking. You. Out. On. A. Date."

"A date?" Paul repeats.

Alex nods. "Yes."

"You mean that thing people do where they make obligatory awkward conversation before sex happens?"

Alex laughs. "You are such an asshole, can we please go out to dinner?"

"Now?" Paul asks.

"Oh my God, it's a good thing I'm still in love with you," Alex mutters. "No. This is where you check your calendar and tell me when you might like to go out with me or ramble on about how you really need to wash your hair instead. I'm going up to my room. When you figure out how to say yes, you have a phone."

"Yes," Paul blurts before Alex can even turn for the stairs.

Alex grins. "Good."

♦

Planning a date turns out to be one of the things Alex's life has not prepared him for.

"Where did you guys used to go?" Gemma asks him when he calls asking for help choosing a place.

"We didn't," Alex says. "It needs to be something new anyway. Also, I have no idea what's appropriate."

"Yeah, because there's a book for that," Gemma says. "'I'm famous and my famous boyfriend and I are about to have a very public divorce unless I can find a super cute place to take him to dinner because I had a bright idea I didn't think through all the way.'"

"Like letting my best friend move into said boyfriend's house for almost no rent," Alex shoots back.

They bicker happily for another ten minutes. When Alex finally hangs up he has a list of recommendations that aren't about sweeping

Paul off his feet but about offering to be in the world with him. Gemma's exhortations in regards to his wardrobe choices, however, he ignores.

♦

"Hey, no hat?" Paul asks when Alex comes downstairs on their agreed-upon date night.

"Living dangerously," Alex grins. "Also, brown hair!"

Alex drives. When Paul asks where they're going Alex refuses to tell him, with a look that's both smug and shy. He's ridiculously adorable.

Santa Monica is the eventual destination. "How have we never been out here together?" Paul asks after Alex parks and they're walking the pier.

Alex shrugs. Paul finds it bizarre to see him walking out in public without his hat, even if he does still have his sunglasses on.

"We got busy," Alex finally says.

"I'm sorry," Paul offers.

Alex shakes his head. "Not what I meant. We were just doing other things. Both of us."

Paul can't tell whether Alex is trying to talk about them and their mess on neutral territory or whether he's trying very hard not to. He brings things up, offers leading statements, but then retreats again whenever Paul cautiously engages. On their first date, when Paul had made them dinner at his old house, they'd hardly been able to stop talking long enough to get to the sex. The awkward pauses and hesitations in the conversation now feel like bad signs.

They get food and Alex leads them to a bench where they can sit with their backs to the pier and look out at the ocean. They get a glance or two from passers-by, but Paul only cares about things like that to the extent that they annoy or upset Alex. And Alex seems, with regards to the rest of the world at least, unusually relaxed.

At one point, as Paul is thinking about asking Alex what the hell he is up to, Alex looks at him, intent and curious over his sunglasses.

"What?" Paul asks.

Alex doesn't say anything. Instead he reaches out and folds his fingers through Paul's where his hand is resting on his thigh. He smiles coyly and holds Paul's hand as he turns his head to look back out at the water.

Once the sun starts to go down, Paul offers to drive them home. Alex, after an evaluative look, hands him his keys.

There, Alex kisses him in the kitchen, grabbing onto his shoulders and dragging him down into it. Paul staggers for balance and catches himself with his arms around Alex's waist.

Eventually Alex pulls away, but he can't stop touching Paul's shoulders, his chest, his sides. "This really sucks," he says a little breathlessly.

Paul nods.

"I want to," Alex says. There's the hint of a whine in his voice, and every part of Paul aches to touch him.

"God, me too."

Alex shakes his head minutely. "Good night," he says with that coy smile again. This time it's a little wistful. He kisses Paul one more time, long and deep, and then he's up the stairs to his room and gone.

26

Paul is just falling asleep one night when Alex knocks on his door.

"Hey," Alex says when he opens it. He's got his hat on and his bag slung over his shoulder. He looks far too awake for the hour. "I'm going out. I promise it's not what it looks like, but I didn't want you to worry."

"Where the hell are you going?" Paul's more baffled than concerned, even if 'secret midnight tryst' does fall somewhere near the top of the likely list of explanations.

"Effects for Zach being dead."

"It's two in the morning."

Alex shrugs. "Victor's being sneaky."

Paul shoves a hand through his hair. Victor's done a lot of strange things in the time Paul has worked for and with him, but this is near the top. "Jesus. As a showrunner, I feel so sane right now."

Alex laughs. "See you," he says and heads down the stairs.

♦

Effects shoots are always fun, and there's something particularly magical about this one in the dead of night in an otherwise abandoned set on the lot. The subject matter is fairly grisly, and there are gross effects Alex will have to wash out of his hair later. Getting shot in the head is a messy way to die. But it's a challenge, and it's fun. Tonight, at least, it's the kind of acting he loves best.

Filming the scene that segues into that effects shot is another matter entirely. It's being shot, not on the lot, but at Victor's house. Alex loved dying in *Paradise Square*, but he knows when he throws his bag together a few days later to film Zach's death he is in for a much, much different sort of day.

So much of Michael's death in *Paradise* was about quiet in the midst of chaos and Alex finally understanding the very minute control *The Fourth Estate*'s reviewers keep saying he has over his body. But Zach's demise is simply about terror and regret. It's not pretty, and it's not noble. It's just a waste; not all heroes die brave. Alex knows the fans will be enraged. A rather significant part of him is happy to think that they can go fuck themselves.

Alex taught himself how to act *by accident* so something as brutal as this didn't happen to him American-style in the shitty, shitty place he grew up in. But as hard as it's going to be, and as much as he's going to have to go to what-if places that don't feel as far away as he would like, he's looking forward to playing the scenes. Margaret has hinted that this may be award territory. He knows he's not supposed to let himself consider it.

He gets in his car. All he can think about is how the fuck he's going to survive twelve hours in Victor's basement. Victor's probably threatened the families of the skeleton crew to ensure secrecy. Absolutely no one is supposed to know Zach is going to die.

♦

When he gets to Victor's house, Alex realizes this day is going to be much, much worse than he imagined. Victor's going to shoot it himself on a hand-held high-def camera. The footage that James eventually sees for the first time when he shows it on air will be as unproduced as it's possible to be and have audiences accept it.

"Look, even rebels and terrorists know how to color correct these days," Victor says with a casual wave of his hand.

When the makeup artist starts working on his makeup – bruises and cuts and worse – Alex asks if she really needs the mirror.

"You don't want to see?" she asks. Normally Alex loves this stuff. After all, this was the side of the camera, the production of illusion, he had always meant to be on.

He shakes his head. "Not this time." Zach wouldn't have a mirror in those circumstances, but he'd still know he wasn't pretty anymore and that he was breaking James' heart, as if not being clever and lucky enough were some sort of betrayal. Liam won't take it much better.

With Liam no doubt preoccupied with imagining the worst for their shadow selves, no wonder he's been peculiar. Carly had even sent an email last week asking if Alex knew anything yet about how Zach was going to die. *This,* she'd written, clearly irritated, *is what we talk about every morning. Can you make it stop?*

Alex had written back *No.*

You're a liar, Carly had replied with a smiley face Alex is sure she didn't mean.

Liam's barely been in touch since the last scene they shot together, and Alex has no idea what that's about – anger or fear or trying to stay away from the mess with Paul. Hell, maybe Victor told him not to taunt the dead. The thought is grim, but Liam's pleasure at following directions from their evil overlord has become more than obvious. Increasingly, Alex suspects Victor is completely not interested in using that power only for good.

"Does Victor not have good lighting down here or is he trying to set the mood?" Alex grumbles at the too-bright work light the makeup artist has shined on his face.

She shrugs and frowns.

"There's nothing we find unreasonable, is there?" Alex asks.

"Just our wild success," she says drily.

He smiles, but it feels wrong on his face already.

He finds it harder to not look when she does his arms, especially when she starts on the rope burns on his wrists.

"Is this really necessary?" Alex asks Victor, who's hovering with his own personal professional-grade camera already in hand. The marks aren't like Paul's, but looking at himself through Victor's eyes, they're all Alex can see. Alex is unsettled, to say the least. He feels a twinge of real fear for what's about to happen to him at Victor's hands.

Most of the basement is finished. But toward the back are bare concrete walls that have been hung with the same backdrop they used in the studio. There's a chair pushed into the corner with loops of rope knotted but left loose on each side of it. Too-bright work lights flood the space. It feels like the setup for a horror movie. Which, Alex supposes, it is.

All the safety precautions he's used to for every shoot he's been on with any physical content are notably absent. As much as they've historically annoyed him, for the first time he understands their purpose. Without them, you get this – a rogue shoot in someone's basement with no boundaries that seem any type of good or useful.

Alex laughs when he registers the complete absurdity of Victor steering him into a chair and then kneeling behind him to loop the coils of rope over his wrists before pulling them tight behind his back. But this is not any sort of funny.

Alex has been clear from the pages for this scene that this was going to be a mostly improv-based scenario that will likely be edited down to just a few moments interspersed throughout the episode. Still, he does not expect the first thing Victor says to him when he turns on the camera to be, "Tell me about Paul."

"What?" Alex is shocked and aggrieved and there are people here – lights and sound and makeup. Even the most spare crew is never tiny. Whatever fucked up exercise this is, Alex has no interest in saying anything remotely personal in front of people. And *especially* not in front of Victor.

"Tell me about Paul," Victor repeats.

"He's fine," Alex says shortly.

"Don't lie. He's not."

"It's not your business." Alex grits his teeth. He's furious at Victor for bringing his and Paul's personal shit into a performance.

"When was the last time you told him you loved him?"

"What the actual fuck?"

"There are things you really don't want me to ask," Victor says darkly. "And since I'm going to, you might as well get comfortable with the easy stuff."

"I don't remember," Alex snaps. He knows, given Zach's present circumstances, that he's supposed to feel regret that, regarding James, it's never even happened. That Alex actually does feel regret makes it worse. But Victor's actions are also a violation of him and Paul and it's awful.

Alex expects another intrusive question about his relationship, but what Victor says next is, "Tell me about Liam."

"You're scaring the shit out of him with this," Alex snaps. He's been pissed at Victor for that facet of this particular stunt for weeks, and now he's too blackly angry to care who's watching.

"I know," Victor says, inhumanly calm.

"Carly's pissed I won't tell him how Zach dies."

"She'll be okay."

"Liam might not be."

"Liam will be fine."

"*You don't know that.*"

"You're right, I don't. You two always surprise me."

Alex teeters between rage and fear. Victor pokes around his edges, looking for the thing that will knock him off the edge.

"Tell me about James."

Victor keeps asking questions, and they remain all over the place – in character, out of character, alternatingly vague and precise. Alex feels unbalanced. Acting, certainly, feels impossible. He knows that the solution to this exercise is to surrender, to say whatever he needs to get through to the end.

As soon as he does, this whole thing will be easier, but giving Victor the satisfaction is unappealing. That sensation of falling under has only ever been something good and lovely and private for him. He doesn't want to use it in these circumstances, and he certainly doesn't think Victor deserves it from him. At some point the entire thing has stops being an acting challenge and has clearly become torture.

They go for hours. At one point, the makeup artist leaves the room, probably just to make a personal call, but Alex can't help but think that this is simply no longer something she wishes to witness. Victor is cruel; Alex feels crazed and, eventually, not even there. He loses whole chunks of time to the sheer emotional exhaustion of it. He also loses track of the number of times Victor actually makes Zach die. Hanging still in the chair after the gun to his head goes off is easy; the three seconds before that moment are horrific every single time.

♦

"Okay," Victor finally says. "We're done."

Alex doesn't respond for a long moment. Victor wonders if he realizes he's still crying.

"Shhh," Victor murmurs. He kneels down next to the chair, pulling his utility knife out of his pocket to cut the ropes himself. "You're okay now."

Alex shakes his head once and otherwise stares ahead glassily. His hands are white and cold to the touch from the lost circulation. Victor holds them until the blood starts flowing again. Alex looks like he wants to pull away, but doesn't have the strength or brain to manage it. After what he's done to him – and Victor knows that he's violated more than most people's sense of personal ethics here – he damn well needs to make sure Alex is okay.

When Alex finally looks like he can stand, Victor pulls him up to his feet and hugs him until he stops shaking, or at least stops shaking so violently. Alex isn't Liam. The things that will break him are different and so are the things that can put him back together.

While the rest of the crew starts cleaning up, Victor pulls a P.A. aside and tells him quietly to go upstairs and get orange juice from the fridge. Then he walks Alex over to the makeup chair and starts taking off the makeup himself.

♦

"Victor," Alex says. His voice is scratchy, and he clears his throat. Now that his awareness is filtering back in, all he wants to do is be out of there. And to not have fucking Victor in his face. "I can do that. Or the makeup artist."

"Shhh," Victor says. "I'll be out of your space as soon as I can."

"You could be out of it right now," Alex says sharply.

"No. I know you hate being here, but this needs to come off. I can't let you drive until you're at least a little okay."

Alex acquiesces, in part because he doesn't have the bandwidth to do anything else. But at least Victor knows Alex hates him and that he's been left a mess by Victor's actions.

It takes a long time. Alex just wants to be left alone with his own thoughts, but Victor is quiet in his work and doesn't ask or say anything. So Alex breathes and gets himself back under control. The orange juice helps, too.

Eventually, Victor spins the chair around so Alex can see himself in the mirror. There's no bruises, no blood, just Alex's own too-pale face.

"See?" Victor says, squeezing Alex's shoulders. "You're fine. Now go home and let Paul take care of you."

Alex doesn't know what to say to that so he doesn't say anything.

It's early evening on a weekday and there is no way Paul is not at work for hours at least. But Victor hands him back his bag and his keys and waves him out the front door. Alex doesn't have to be told twice to leave.

The drive home is a blur, and when he finally pulls into the driveway he takes a moment to sit with his forehead resting on the steering wheel. When he lifts it again he finally registers that Paul's car is there too. That makes no sense.

He unlocks the front door to find Paul on the couch, glasses on and tapping away at his laptop. He's surprised, considering how much both of them still tend to avoid the common areas of the house.

"How was it?" Paul asks.

Alex shakes his head and drops his bag to the floor.

"What do you need?" Paul sits up and shifts his laptop to the side.

Alex sits beside him and curls in close. "Talk."

Paul stammers as he wraps his arms around Alex.

"Anything," Alex clarifies with the words he can find. "Not my job. Not Victor. Not Liam. Not Iranian politics. Not Chechen separatists. Weather. Weather would be good."

Paul chuckles and squeezes Alex just a bit tighter. Paul obviously thinks he's being a little absurd as he obeys and actually talks about the weather. But the sound of his voice is soothing enough that Alex can close his eyes and not think about terrible things. Hearing that it was sunny and the world continued to turn while Zach was dying and he wasn't is oddly helpful. When Paul starts humorously ascribing emotions and motives to the sun and the clouds and that not-quite-perfect ocean breeze, Alex feels indulged and loved in a way he hasn't in a while.

"Why are you home?" Alex asks after a while.

Paul takes a breath. "Victor called a few days ago and suggested it might be the decent thing to do."

"So you did it," Alex says sullenly.

"He also told me not to tell you. And you seem pretty glad I'm here, so…."

"Sleep with me tonight?" Alex asks.

"I want to say yes, but tell me why," Paul says carefully.

"Not for sex. Just be with me. If I wake up in the night I want to know I'm not dead."

♦

They eat dinner together. Takeout, because Alex is not in a state for the kitchen and Paul doesn't seem to want to leave his side. As Paul gets him situated on the couch with chopsticks and asks if he wants the TV on – Alex shakes his head – Alex suddenly realizes that this is the end of his terrible scheduling. At least for now.

"It's really over," he says. It seems impossible that filming for *Fourth* is well and truly done.

Paul settles down next to him, keeping their shoulders pressed together. "It is. Cashew chicken or the one with the broccoli?"

Alex cracks the first hint of a smile. Nothing about this night is normal, but it's still good to be here with Paul. "Broccoli."

Upstairs, Alex curls up on Paul as soon as they're both in bed.

"If I don't quit acting because of this, nothing will ever make me quit acting." The terror of the day, in Paul's warm arms, is hardening into a resolve.

"Why?" Paul wraps an arm around his shoulder again.

"Because it wasn't acting. Remember that when you watch it."

Paul rubs Alex's arm. "That sounds cruel."

"Victor's a sadist. This may work for Liam, but it does not work for me."

"So that's an insight into the thing with you and Liam. That I didn't have before. And that I'm still not sure I wanted." Paul sounds surprised.

"I've been trying to tell you that. You do get it, right?" Alex says.

"I'm going with no?"

"Paul." He grabs Paul's hand and holds it. He needs him to pay particular attention to this. "I give up control to you because I trust you. I *like* when you push me. I love when you mark me. None of that makes me feel anything bad. I never have to sit alone in a room staring at a wall for hours after doing things with you in order to feel human again."

"You go quiet, though."

Alex lets out an exasperated sigh. When will Paul ever believe him? "That's different. Incredibly different."

"How?"

"When you hurt me, you're taking pleasure from my pleasure. When Victor hurts me, he's taking pleasure from my pain."

Paul takes time to process that. "Victor has way too much control over all of our lives."

"Write down the date and time you said that," Alex says.

27

Without *Fourth* to keep him busy, Paul worries aloud that Alex will go back to the restless boredom of the summer shooting hiatus. But the end of shooting means that Alex gets to focus on what comes next without anything else to worry about, and that's what he's wanted all along. He spends a lot of time with Margaret, looking at different projects and talking through what he wants the shape of the next year to look like.

It would be easier to do that if he knew what shape he and Paul were going to be in next year, but Alex has always made decisions with variables unknown. This variable just hurts a little more than most.

In one of their meetings, Margaret asks what Alex thinks about paintball.

"Excuse me?" The question seems apropos of nothing.

"Your *Fourth* character is about to die violently via a gunshot wound on network TV. Meanwhile the bullshit with guns keeps cropping up, thanks to your insistence on sharing with America the one hobby that pisses all of America off –"

"I am awesome," Alex interjects.

" – And you're looking at roles that involve yet more people with guns," Margaret continues with a heavy sigh. "Considering the state of the American film industry, I can't really blame you. But to keep things under control, and fun instead of terrible, running around with play guns might take a bit of the edge off."

"There is nothing about this that is not ridiculous," Alex says.

"Yeah, but you'd get to play paintball."

♦

Carly, of all people, is the one who ends up talking Alex into it. They're on the phone one night when Alex calls her because Paul is still at work, Liam isn't picking up, and Alex is feeling lonely. She's also the one who suggests making it a date.

"I'm dubious," Alex says.

"You're the one who climbs rocks for fun. And shoots. This should be right up your alley."

"Not as a media stunt!"

"Then think of it as a bonding activity. Paul needs a hobby. And some stress relief. When was the last time you two fucked?"

"I appreciate that it's you asking me the intrusive questions about our sex life for once, but I'm not going to answer that," Alex tells her.

"I'll get a group together. You just get him there."

"Will Liam be there?" Alex asks. If this madness is going to happen, he wants to know exactly what kind of madness to expect.

Carly sighs. "Guns? Not on your life, baby boy."

◆

Alex asks Paul out for the game via text because their schedules aren't lining up at all. There's also something fun about being flirty and coy. Paul finally sends back *Alleexxxx I have to go work now*. Alex replies with *;)* and lets the question rest until Paul finally gets back around to asking for a date and time.

Carly's organizational skills are practically occult; in order to manage her and Liam's lives, they have to be. By some miracle she manages to get their friends together on a Saturday afternoon in late September. It's a big group, with people from the brunch posse, Alex's crew buddies, and a handful of Paul's work people. Alex feels a little green as he contemplates Gemma chatting with Brian like an old friend.

◆

To Paul's surprise he and Alex end up on the same team – because Alex insists on it. Paul expects to lose track of him quickly, but he sticks by Paul's side. Twenty minutes in, Paul realizes, chagrined, that's not because Alex wants to be an epic team of awesome. Alex is covering him, because Paul *sucks*. It's embarrassing, but it's also sweet.

Alex loves the whole exercise. Paul, to his own surprise, does too. He's hardly done anything but work on set or at home for months. He hasn't had time even to go running. Tearing around a field while getting to shoot friends with paint is the perfect sort of outlet.

Paul feels guilty about going after any of the girls right up until Darcy shoots him in the chest. She runs away giggling while he frantically tries to wipe the splattered paint off his goggle lenses. So much for benevolent sexism. Maybe Alex is right, and Paul needs to start taking people at their word when they say they are up for some rough and tumble. Alex certainly has no compunction about it. Looking amused, he shoots Darcy between the shoulder blades. Paul is momentarily horrified until he hears her laugh even harder.

Everyone gets hot and sweaty and covered in paint. "I like the rainbow hair," Paul tells Alex, pushing dark hair that's just starting to show red at the roots off his forehead for him.

"I have a thing for headshots."

"That's gruesome."

"Only a little." Alex shrugs. "It's weird that we're doing this while we look like other people."

At first Paul thinks he means the paint. As the day goes on it gets harder to tell people apart at a distance as they get splotched with different colors. But as they're cleaning up for the drive home – Paul wants to get the paint out of his beard because neon green is not a good look for him – Alex meets his eyes in the mirror of the shitty park bathroom and smiles in the way that makes his eyes crinkle. It's then that Paul realizes Alex means his hair, Paul's scruff, and the current messy state of their relationship.

Alex starts taking off his clothes the second he walks in the door. "I'm taking a shower. I feel disgusting," he says.

The statement and the stripping aren't flirtation or invitation, Paul realizes, just comfort and familiarity. He's still happy that they can shower simultaneously without having to do so together. He feels gross too, and they've had a good day; he has no intention of pushing his luck.

The comfort and familiarity thing must be going around, because by the time Paul pads downstairs in sweats and a T-shirt after his own shower, Alex is in the kitchen, shirtless, frowning into the fridge as he considers a snack. Alex may be a good shot, but he's also clearly a good target. His arms and torso are covered in bruises from too many shots fired at excessively close range.

"Do they hurt?" Paul asks, lightly brushing his fingers over Alex's back. He's bruised too, but not as much and not as badly. Alex's paleness makes all marks look more alarming.

"I've had worse," Alex says with a shrug, closing the refrigerator door, and turning under Paul's scrutiny.

"I hate that," Paul says.

"Whatever," Alex says amiably.

◆

touching. Alex is happy to lean back against the refrigerator and arch his back just a little. Paul isn't even really doing anything and it feels amazing. One of the side effects of the current mess their relationship is in is that Alex is touch-starved and horny all the time. Now that he isn't working fourteen-hour days five or more days a week, he's awake enough to notice.

He watches Paul's fingers. It's easier than looking at his face and being too hopeful. Or asking for things and getting told no for reasons that are, at least relatively, sound.

It takes less than thirty seconds of both of them breathing too loudly in the silent kitchen for Paul's fingers to pause at the bruise on Alex's hipbone and press his fingers into it.

Alex hisses and tips his head back against the refrigerator.

"Sorry," Paul says but makes no effort to stop touching him.

"Don't be," Alex says.

Paul's fingers are almost a tickle as they move up his side and down his arm. He edges closer, and Alex can feel the heat radiating off him. He's scared to move lest he startle Paul off.

Paul runs his hand down Alex's arm, palm curved and fitting tight to the muscle. When he gets to Alex's wrist, he grips too tight, just for a moment. Then he tickles his fingers up for a moment and pressing his thumb into another bruise.

Alex moans.

"You're so beautiful," Paul whispers.

"Keep touching me," Alex says hoarsely, the words barely formed.

Paul obeys. Everything is light and fleeting except for the way he presses into Alex's bruises, making him moan. They're both trembling from holding back.

"Upstairs?" Alex finally breathes.

Paul nods.

They don't race. It's not frantic. In the room Alex now thinks of as his own, they don't turn on the light. The room is shadowed, having lost its direct sunlight while they were still out running around the field.

"We should probably talk about this," Paul says as he slides out of his clothes.

"What?" Alex says lightly. "We've gone on a few dates, and now we're going to bed."

"We'll talk about it later, then," Paul says, unable to take his eyes off of Alex as he kicks his jeans aside.

"Yes. Exactly." Alex climbs onto the bed.

Paul follows and resumes mapping his bruises. He's not teasing, the way he so often is. He's thorough and reverent and soothing. It makes Alex's breath catch and his cock fill. At one point, Paul gets himself so turned around on the bed he winds up kissing Alex's ankle and then sucking on his toes one after the other.

Alex moans loudly. "Why the hell haven't you done this before?"

Paul laughs with his mouth full. Alex retaliates by getting his hands on to Paul's ass and dragging him back so he can pull his cock into his mouth.

"Holy shit."

Alex pulls off for a second to say, "You should probably take this as a hint."

Paul laughs and then gasps. "This is gonna be way more challenging than you think."

Alex makes an unintelligible sound around Paul's cock.

Paul's not wrong. Alex is shocked both by how good it feels to get sucked off while he has a cock in his mouth too and just how difficult it is to concentrate on anything enough to get off. It's a perfect sort of misery. So much of sex with Paul is.

"Oh my God." Alex pulls off with a gasp and starts jerking Paul with his hand; that at least he can sort of concentrate on. Paul is grateful, based on the sounds he makes and his renewed efforts with his mouth. Alex knows Paul well enough to know when he's close. He urges him on with the small sounds of his own pleasure as his balls pull up tight.

Even so, Paul's orgasm catches them both off guard. Alex follows almost immediately, the orgasm wrenching out of him as Paul's thumb remains buried in the bruise at his hip.

Alex wants to talk as they both roll onto their backs and lay there head to foot, panting at the ceiling. But he feels too wrecked and too startled to make words.

"Why is that so hot?" he eventually gasps.

Paul puts a hand on Alex's thigh and squeezes. "Sorry about that," he says as Alex wipes his fingers across his now very messy face.

"Whatever," he pants. "Just discovered a thing."

"Oh, really?" Paul says.

Alex nods vigorously. "Uh-huh."

Paul makes a smug sound.

"Oh, shut up and get us a towel." Alex shoves at him ineffectually.

"Bratty," Paul says. It's fond, though, and he squeezes Alex's ankle gently before he heads to the bathroom.

♦

Alex lets Paul clean both of them up, declaring that it's his mess anyway. Paul does it willingly. He's happy to keep touching Alex, even when he's merely running a warm washcloth over his skin. When Paul tosses aside the towel and pulls the blanket up over them, Alex rolls onto his side and presses his forehead to Paul's.

"We should probably talk," Paul says.

"I don't want to stop doing this," Alex says. His voice is quiet, and he sounds almost afraid.

Paul finds Alex's hand and holds it tightly. "No. Me neither."

"The dating is good, though."

"The dating is very good. So is the sex."

Alex snorts gently. "Understatement. We're not moving back in together, though."

"No."

It's scary to lie there with Alex in the bed that used to be theirs and work out the terms of their new arrangement. As they're clarifying when sex is okay – in terms of dates, yes; booty calls and expectations, no – Paul realizes that their trial separation is over. They're living in the same house, but not together. They're boyfriends, but Alex wanting to go on dates isn't him being cute. They're back to a phase of their relationship they never had to begin with because Paul was inappropriately obsessive and Alex was in over his head. They aren't partners anymore.

When he says as much to Alex, he nods a little shakily. "I know."

"What we do to each other is amazing," Paul says, tracing a constellation of bruises on Alex's shoulder with his free hand. "But that makes it harder for us in some ways. Not because I've got my head messed up about my kinky," he says when Alex makes a noise of protest. "We're just way too good at doing this and never talking. Case in point."

"We're talking now," Alex points out.

"Because we're being very good."

"Yeah. We should keep doing that."

"We really, really should."

As they breathe together, Alex's eyes dart over Paul's face, dark and compelling.

When Paul asks what he's looking for, Alex says, "Why does this feel so scary?"

Paul's heart aches. He's feeling it too, laying here so perfectly with Alex. It's terrifying. "We forgot how good we were."

"God, you're so much to lose." Alex tightens his hand around Paul's. His voice is rough.

Paul wraps his free arm around Alex's side, pulling him close. "You too," he says into his hair.

Alex tucks his head under Paul's chin and clings.

28

As the *Fourth* shoot for James' terrible scene – broadcasting Zach's last footage and execution live – approaches, Liam is increasingly unreliable about being in touch. Alex, meanwhile is increasingly worried. Not only about Liam's capacity for dealing with the episode as written, but about the very massive and intentional gaps that exist between what they did at the table read and what Victor has actually been shooting. Alex almost wonders if Victor is trying to get the show killed early. Certainly, he's about to piss off a lot of people, none of whom have ever liked him and all of whom control the money and the network's schedule.

Alex badgers until he finally gets Liam to agree to meet for lunch the first week of October.

Something is off right from the start. Liam isn't meeting Alex's eyes, and his usual vibrancy and energy isn't quite right. He's fidgety, easily distracted, and seems to lose the thread of the conversation every other sentence.

"Are you okay?" Alex asks after Liam manages to drop his fork a second time.

Liam nods.

"Lee...."

"I'm fine." Liam nudges Alex's foot under the table. "Happy birthday, by the way. I missed having a party for you on set. Did you and Paul do anything cool?"

"No, he had deadlines. It's fine, I climbed rocks," Alex adds when Liam frowns. Frankly he doesn't give a shit about not celebrating the day, especially compared to the rest of everything he's trying to sort out in his life. "Thank you, though."

Close as they are, neither of them is part of the other's day-in and day-out support group. Liam has Carly and Victor and whoever else makes up his strange life to take care of him; he is not Alex's to worry about like this.

But with the day of the shoot getting closer, Alex thinks about his own terrible last day of filming. At least Liam's will be on the lot and not in Victor's fucking basement. But Victor is still Victor. Alex does not understand his relationship with Liam any more than he understands how Liam's brain works. More than that, Alex knows what Victor is capable of. He's not sure whether that means Victor will hurt Liam less or much, much more.

♦

"Lee," Alex says when Liam finally picks up the phone a few days later. It's late afternoon, Paul is at work, and Alex is on the couch with Todd stretched out next to him. "I know what you're shooting. And I know you have people who will take care of you. And I don't know why you're like this, but some of this is my fault and some of it is about me. What do you need from me?"

Liam takes a breath that Alex can hear all the way down the line. And then he tells Alex what he needs. This is how they have always worked and Alex is glad they still do, despite what Liam's request turns out to be. Paul's probably going to freak out. Alex has to figure out if that's a reasonable response before he's confronted with it.

Considering the size of his contact list, Alex has remarkably few people he can call to ask. This surely qualifies as high on Margaret's Do Not Tell Me These Things list. Carly, as much as they have some sort of simpatico going on, is both too biased and too much of a hobbyist when it comes to interpersonal strategy to be a choice that isn't going to blow up in his face. While Gemma may be his best friend, mostly she just wants to see him and Liam fuck. Which, if he thinks about it objectively, he can't really blame her for, but it's not useful and is fairly horrifying.

Which narrows it down to Victor, who is both untrustworthy and, as far as Alex is concerned, entirely responsible for this impending clusterfuck, and Darcy, who probably talks to Paul more than Alex does these days. Alex sighs. He's never thought she would be the lesser of so many evils but the gossip she shares isn't likely to make any sense to anyone else. And she might be somewhat familiar with whatever's going on in Paul's head these days.

Darcy, predictably, is incredibly excited when Alex tells her he needs advice.

"Let me get this out, okay?" he says before she can derail the conversation to unhelpful places.

"Now you're kind of freaking me out," Darcy says. "You never call to ask me anything. And you sound like somebody died."

"Yeah, okay, the person giving the advice is not the one who gets to freak out. Is it weird if someone you used to date asks you to stay over at their place – not for sex! – like, 'cause they're really sad about something? Is that a thing boyfriends get to freak out about?"

"Why do you ask?" she says coyly.

"Because I need to know, Darcy. Come on, why would that be hypothetical?"

"Well. Yeah. That's definitely weird. And he's totally trying to get in your pants."

"He's not."

"Yeah…no. I thought you were smart. All the magazines say what a smart actor you are."

"Stop mocking."

"Then don't call me asking questions so you can decide my answers are bad. That's really rude. Just talk to Paul about it. Since he's your actual boyfriend."

Alex sighs. "Thank you, Darcy. For your maturity and complete lack of help. I owe you forever."

"Cool! When are we doing guns again? I miss you."

Alex pulls his phone away from his ear and stares at it.

♦

"Do you have time to talk?" Alex asks.

Paul looks up at Alex where he's standing at the top of the stairs to the loft. He has things he needs to be doing, but Alex looks serious and this is one of the things Paul is working on. Twenty minutes talking to his boyfriend is not going to kill him. Or his show.

"I talked to Liam today," Alex says.

Paul tries not to have any sort of visible reaction to that, particularly not one Alex would find egregious. "How is he?"

"We talked about the shoot coming up. I asked him what he needed from me. He's been upset, and that's on me."

"It's not your fault –"

"It is, actually." Alex shrugs. "But it's mostly Victor's, because God knows what he's going to do to Lee. He asked if I would stay over with him the night before and go into the studio with him on the day."

"I realize you're expecting me to be jealous and uncomfortable, which we'll get to in a moment, but is he five?"

"Paul. Don't be mean. Liam is a lot of things, but he doesn't exaggerate and he isn't sneaky. I asked what he needed, this is what he said, and after what Victor did to me, I believe him."

"Are you asking me for permission?" Paul says even if he doesn't for a moment think Alex actually is.

"Not really. I'd still like us to have a clear conversation about the consequences, though."

"You were a mess when you got home," Paul admits.

Alex nods.

Paul looks at Alex for a long moment. "I wish to hell there was a way for me to say no that didn't make me an asshole."

"There really isn't."

"And it has to be you," Paul says.

"Yes."

"Can we talk about boundaries?" Paul is desperate to hang on to what little control he has in the face of all the things Alex may or may not be willing to do for Liam.

"If you mean agreements, yes."

"You can't sleep with him," Paul says quickly.

"I've told you I won't," Alex says. He doesn't snap, but his voice is firm.

"If you do –"

"Paul. I will not fuck Liam. That is a thing that is true and a thing that is as much about my relationship with Lee as it is about my relationship with you. Don't assume I'm a liar, don't assume I can't control myself, and *don't* threaten me."

"Don't make out with him either," Paul says weakly. He feels like he has to keep saying something, even if none of it seems likely to help.

"I don't ask you not to make out with Carly."

"I don't make out with Carly!"

"My point," Alex says. "Or not to sleep in the same bed with her –"

"I can't think about that. Is that what he asked for?"

"Paul. Stop. I have no idea. My point is that someone I feel responsible to and have made promises to has asked me to step up. I feel responsible to and have made promises to you, too. I know I'm pretty, but I'm not so pretty I can't keep two ideas in my head at the same time."

"This makes me uncomfortable," Paul says.

"I know it does. I'm a little uncomfortable too, but can you get to okay with it?"

"What would happen if I said no?" How bad, exactly, would it be?

"Then we'd keep talking."

♦

Alex has never liked Liam's house. It's massive, ugly, and decorated in the worst sort of pretentious interior design. He's spent nights here before – he and Paul both have, crashed out together in one of the extra rooms when they've been hanging out with Liam, Carly, and a couple of bottles of wine. More often, they all get together at Carly's place, which Alex prefers anyway. Her more modest apartment is one of the most normalizing things in his life. What Alex has never figured out about Liam's place is *why*. It doesn't suit him at all.

"Have you ever actually read any of these books?" he asks as Liam ushers him into the den or the great room or *whatever*. He slumps down into one of the leather chairs.

Liam shrugs. "Some of them."

"Really?" Alex asks skeptically.

"Sometimes I get bored," Liam says blandly. "Do you want a drink?"

"I don't know. Is the point of this distraction or what?"

"I don't know," Liam echoes back at him.

"Did Victor tell you about our shoot?" Alex asks, pulling up his legs to sit cross-legged on one of Liam's ugly and excessive chairs.

"He said you were great." Alex isn't sure if the pride in his voice is Liam's own or unintentional mimicry of Victor's dark enthusiasm.

"Thanks, but did he tell you what we did?" Alex never knows how much information Liam gets from Victor and usually assumes it's a lot. This situation, however, is unique. He wants to prepare Liam for what might be coming as much as he wants to not say anything that's going to set him off right now.

Liam shakes his head. "No. I keep asking, but no. Not in detail, anyway."

"Does that feel okay for you or not?" Alex asks bluntly.

"If I needed to know, Victor would tell me."

"Okay. That's positively creepy," Alex says before realizing he's being rude.

Liam shrugs.

"It was really hard," Alex tells him. "And kind of awful. I'm here right now as much because of that as because you asked."

Liam nods. "James's stuff will be different, though."

"Okay," Alex says even though he does not at all have Liam's faith in Victor's benevolence. "Then why are you so worried about tomorrow?"

"I told you I don't really do death well." Liam's face is drawn tight, and he's staring somewhere past Alex's knees. "And Zach is going to die."

Alex thinks about pointing out that, from his own perspective, Zach is already dead. He's sure it won't be helpful.

"Hey, can I see your pages?" he asks. It might give them something to talk about that's rooted in the reality of their jobs, as well as give him half a hint of how cruel Victor's about to be.

"Is it fucked up that this feels wrong?" Liam asks as he gets up to fetch them.

"I'm done," Alex says. "I'm certainly not about to leak your details about my grand departure."

"It's not that," Liam says as he rifles through a stack of papers. "It's an actorly thing. Or, no, not even that." He flicks his hand sharply, the way he does when words aren't coming as easily as he wants and he's frustrated.

"A my-guy-and-your-thing?" Alex asks as Liam looks at the pages in his hand for a moment before he holds them out to him.

Liam nods as Alex takes them. "Yeah. Like, you're *dead*. It doesn't seem right you get to find out what happens to the rest of us after."

"Are they making you do press around this when it airs?" Alex asks, skimming over Liam's script, which has been marked up in color-coded highlighters that convey information in no way Alex understands.

Liam shrugs. "Probably."

"Okay, can I ask that you work on your specificity? Because *I'm not dead.*"

Liam nods earnestly. "Yeah. Totally. Sorry. It's just hard."

"No shit."

Eventually Liam puts the pages away, at which point he apparently rediscovers the power of locomotion. Now he won't stop walking. Or talking. Which is probably good. It's also exhausting to keep up with.

"Okay. Drink now?" Alex tips his head back in the chair to follow Liam as he paces around the room.

"Sure." Liam diverts from his path around the room to head for his obnoxious bar set-up. "Hey, how's Paul?"

"In a general relationship sense, or a me spending the night at your house sense?"

"Two."

Alex shrugs. "He wasn't thrilled. But he and Darcy went out to dinner tonight, so at least he's not sitting home and brooding."

"Dude, do you need me to talk to him? I didn't mean to cause more problems between you guys or whatever."

"It's fine, Lee," Alex says. As far as he is concerned, Liam trying to have another conversation with Paul about him is something that needs to happen never.

"Are you two going to be okay?"

"I don't know." When Liam is silent for long enough Alex feels obligated to fill the space he adds, "Things are a lot better, but…."

"But what?"

"But we've got some bad cases of crazy and love might not be enough?" Alex abruptly realizes he doesn't want to say more.

"I don't understand that," Liam says.

"I know," Alex says. "Sometimes I don't either."

♦

"Okay, sleeping arrangements," Liam says once they've worked their way through a drink and another strange conversation that jumps non-linearly between Paul and Victor and Carly.

"Yes?" Alex says cautiously.

"Sleep with me?"

"I'm going to assume you mean that in the logistical sense and not the euphemistic one."

Liam laughs. "How about in whatever way you feel comfortable with?"

Alex rolls his eyes fondly. It's pretty clear Liam doesn't actually think that's going to get him laid. Though he's leaving the option open.

"Okay." Alex pushes himself upright in the chair. "Ground rules."

Liam makes a *go on* gesture.

"One," Alex starts.

Liam looks pleased to be getting a list.

"No sex. Two, no making out. Three, PJs stay on."

Liam nods. "Is cuddling okay?"

"Cuddling, yes. Groping, no."

"I sort of feel like you're assuming the worst about me here," Liam complains. "Also, the no making out thing sucks."

Alex makes a mental note that complaining is a shitty way to respect someone's boundaries. "Liam. My relationship can't handle any gray areas right now. I am here because I have promises to both you and Paul to honor. But I am also saying these things because I have promises to both you and Paul to honor."

Liam smiles a little proudly. "You're really good at this communication thing."

"Thank you?"

Liam grabs Alex's bag for him before leading the way upstairs. The gesture is sweet, but it's also a little unnerving.

"Not actually a girl, you know," Alex says dryly.

"I know. I'm being polite. Although, by the way, you should be less snide about women."

"I'll add it to the list."

They pass a few rooms Alex has been in before. At the end of the hallway, Liam shoulders open the last door and flicks on the light switch. Alex follows him in.

"This is completely not what I expected."

On some level, however, the room is exactly what Alex expected. But the small bedroom doesn't go with the rest of the house at all. It's far more like Liam's room in his parents' house in New York.

Liam shrugs.

"No, seriously, what is the deal with your weird house?"

"I moved out here, I had some money from all the work I did as a kid, and I had to prove to the world I had actually graduated from Nickelodeon, I bought a house and hired an interior designer and did some press that was shot here and whatever. Old school, classic Hollywood bachelor. It was supposed to make me look sophisticated."

"It makes you look ridiculous," Alex says.

"The colors are soothing."

Alex waves that off as he stares at Liam's bed. "How do you have so much sex and only have a full?"

"Most people don't get to see the real bedroom," Liam says.

"There's a fake bedroom?" Alex is incredulous.

"Hookups, whores, orgies, photoshoots," Liam says casually.

"I can't tell if you're joking."

"Yeah," he says. "Neither can I."

◆

"I can't believe you have glow-in-the-dark stars here, too."

Alex can feel, if not see, Liam shrug in the dark. They're not actually tangled up with each other yet, although he knows Liam's habits and knows they will be. For now though, the proximity makes everything tense in a way that feels good and possibly a little bit dangerous.

"Carly gave them to me," Liam says. "She thinks they're cute."

"Have you guys found a house yet?"

"No, still looking."

"Sucks," Alex says. He keeps his hope that Carly will be in charge of decorating this time to himself.

"It's fine. We're both busy. The schedule doesn't offer a lot of downtime."

"I noticed."

"I get why you wanted to leave," Liam says. "Mostly because you're you and I know how you do shit even if I don't always get how your brain works. But what I don't get is why you wanted to leave like this."

"I wanted to make it big," Alex says, thoughtful. He rolls onto his side and scoots closer to Liam to have it over and done with. He misses sharing a bed most nights, and even if this is a small and dangerous pleasure, it isn't one that has been explicitly declared off-limits. On some level, he suspects it probably should have been, but Carly and Paul crawl all over each other with absurd familiarity when they have their trashy movie nights. Intellectually he can't quite see how this should be different. "Also, I wanted to keep Zach." Experimentally, he puts a hand on Liam's waist.

"That doesn't make any sense," Liam says irritably. He grabs Alex's hand and tugs so that they are well and truly cuddling.

"If Zach just leaves, he could be doing anything. Everybody would get to make up their own idea of what he's up to. This way, I know where he is. Nobody else gets to own him." If fame means Alex can't own himself, then he can damn well own the character that made his life this way.

"That's fucked up."

Alex shrugs. On the nightstand, his phone buzzes. He cranes his arm awkwardly to reach it because Liam has him in a death-grip and isn't letting go.

"Who is it?" Liam asks.

"How many people do you think I have that text me this late?"

"Is it Paul? It's totally Paul. Let me see!"

"What? No!" Alex holds the phone at arm's length to try to read the message, while Liam drops his hand to make a grab for it. "Oh my God, you're five, stop!"

Thinking of you, the text says with a smiley. Given their texts while he was in D.C., Alex doesn't know whether to be exasperated or find it adorable.

"Awwww," Liam coos. "That's so cute!"

"That is Paul feeling uncomfortable and not knowing what to say," Alex says as he shoves his shoulder into Liam to get enough space to text back. *Liam's being annoying about how cute we are.*

"I'm not annoying," Liam says.

"Yeah, no, you totally are." Alex doesn't look at him, staring at his phone instead as he waits for it to chime again.

Got back from dinner with Darcy a while ago. How's it going?

"Okay, that's slightly awkward," Liam observes over his shoulder.

"Ignoring you," Alex tells him. He texts back, *Good. How's your night?*

Little weird, little lonely, mostly bored.

Glad to hear it ;) Alex types back.

"I hope you tell him how fucking in love with him you are all the time."

"Liam," Alex chides. Everything is such a mess of tentative and redefined commitment right now.

Liam stares at him. "Oh my God, you don't."

"Lee," Alex says more sharply.

"Why *not*?" Liam gives up on the phone and sits up.

"It's just not how we communicate," Alex says.

"Text him," Liam says.

"No."

"Yes."

"*Seriously?*" Alex says, annoyed. Liam catches him completely off guard by lunging for the phone and toppling Alex, who yelps, backwards and half off the bed in the process. High school wrestling seems a painfully long way away and possibly more like the unfortunate beginning of a porn movie than ever. He sighs and tosses Liam the phone.

"Yay!" Liam catches it. "*This is Liam,*" he recites, thumbing over the screen. "*Alex loves you.*"

"You dick," Alex makes a grab for the phone, but Liam punches send first.

"What? You do! Don't give me bullshit about *how you tend to communicate*, I've heard him say it to you *tons* of times."

"Yes, well, Paul's Paul, and I'm me."

"I hope this is on the list of things you're working on," Liam says sullenly.

I'm terrified of both of you right now, Paul texts back. *But in a much better way than I could be.*

29

Alex wakes up in the morning to find Liam thoroughly wrapped around him, their legs tangled and Liam's arm hooked around Alex's side. Alex moves gently as he can to brush Liam's curls out of his own eyes. Liam's face scrunches up but then smooths, and he rolls a little closer to Alex before his breathing evens out again. Being here with Liam is lovely, but it's also a little melancholy. It feels like a terribly solemn privilege to be able to hold him like this when their relationship is so not about them being lovers.

As sweet and sad as this is, though, certain rules of human biology are always in play. Liam is a restless sleeper and if either of them moves wrong things are going to get very awkward very quickly. Given what Liam's asked of him for today, what Alex has promised Paul, and his own need for sanity, that's something Alex would rather avoid.

When he slides out of bed, Liam frowns in his sleep and rolls into his spot, pulling Alex's pillow into his arms. Liam remains nothing quite like what all of America thinks he is. But all these years on, Alex can't quite believe how truthful his beauty and sweetness actually are.

He pads around quietly, takes a shower, gets dressed, and then sits in the chair-and-a-half by the bed, one sole up on the seat. He texts Paul to let him know he made it through the night unscathed and tells him he'll see him at home later. After a day like this, Alex knows he's going to be craving Paul's presence. He hugs his knees as he goes back and forth between glancing at Liam's incomprehensibly marked-up pages and Liam himself.

Alex is glad Liam's call isn't until late morning. He's also worried about what Victor is going to spring on him once he gets to work. The whole situation is such an amazingly clear argument for why people shouldn't fuck the boss, he has to stifle a laugh.

When Liam finally opens his eyes, he looks confused and then worried until his gaze lands on Alex.

"I thought you'd left," he says, his voice rough from sleep.

"Nope, right here." Alex goes to sit on the side of the bed. When he does, Liam grabs his hand and holds on tight.

"Promise me you won't go anywhere?" Liam's face is drawn, and Alex can feel how tensely he's holding his muscles. Whatever trust in Victor he has, he's also clearly afraid for today. It makes Alex's heart ache.

"For as long as I can," he says, as horrible as it is. But things happen in the world no one can control. That, of course, is what the

365

material they're shooting right now is about. No matter how much Liam may need or want reassurance, this seems like a particularly inauspicious time to ignore that particular truth.

They drive to set separately but park next to each other. On the walk inside Alex knows, because he is familiar with the energy of Paul doing the same thing, that Liam is exerting effort not to hold his hand. He gives up on it as soon as they're inside.

Alex rubs his thumb over the back of Liam's hand. Liam's shoulders relax slightly. "Right here," he says quietly. "I'm always going to be right here."

Liam nods a little frantically.

Victor interrupts them on the way to hair and makeup. He gives their linked hands a feral smile. "And what are you doing here?" he asks Alex.

"Moral support," Alex says.

Liam swings their hands a little.

"No, I don't think so."

"What?" For all of Alex's – and Liam's – worries about today, the idea that Alex wouldn't be allowed to be present for this had not occurred to either of them. Alex really should have anticipated this, though, because Victor is Victor.

"I said no. Alex, you're not coming on set today. Liam, you're late, run along."

Liam stands there looking stunned.

"Go on," Alex says softly, squeezing his hand. "It's just work, and you're going to kill it." As angry as he is at Victor for forbidding this, yelling at him in front of Liam is not going to do any good right now.

Liam goes a little gray but nods. Another moment passes before he disentangles their hands and gives Alex a sad look.

"You know where to find me," Alex tells him.

Liam nods, stepping into Alex's space like he really can't bear to leave just yet. "Bye," he says sadly and kisses Alex dryly on the mouth.

Alex gives him as brave a smile as he can before Liam turns and walks away. As he goes, he shoves his hands in his pockets in a manner that's incredibly characteristic of James.

Victor folds his arms over his chest and watches with Alex until Liam turns a corner and disappears from sight.

"Was that really necessary?" Alex asks.

Victor shrugs. "James is going to lose Zach. Liam doesn't get a safety net."

"That's cruel."

"That's storytelling. You didn't get a safety net either."

"I'm not your lover. And I'm not as fragile as Liam."

"And you are being as unwise as you are being imprecise." Victor's voice is calm, but Alex can tell he's hit something soft.

"Liam isn't going to tell you when you push him too far," Alex says.

"That's not your concern."

Alex stares at him in disbelief. "Yes, it is."

"What makes you think that?"

"Liam has been my concern since I got shoved into a scene with him and our lives got magic."

"You're revising history. He's not your responsibility, Alex. He's mine," Victor says dangerously.

"You're not going to take care of him," Alex snaps. At this point he is past caring how Victor and Liam work. Nothing he is seeing right now aligns with anything he knows Liam actually needs.

"I always take care of my people," Victor says sharply.

"Like you did with me?"

"I pushed you. You were incredible. You are also standing in front of me right now. You are fine, so stop being dramatic and let Liam do his job."

Alex realizes he's shaking. He doesn't feel fine. Not after the ordeal in Victor's basement and certainly not standing here on the lot having what feels like a fight over Liam's soul.

Victor goes on. "Today, Liam is going to give one of the best performances of his life. After this, he's going to be able to do anything he wants."

"Because you took me away from him." Dimly, Alex is aware their raised voices have started to draw bystanders and that he is probably being unreasonable. Someone yelling at Victor is not rare, but Alex doesn't remotely care enough to reign himself in.

"Yes."

"I can't believe you."

"Why?" Victor turns so that he's even more in Alex's space. He's not as tall as Alex is, and probably not as strong, but his presence has always been bigger than the physical space he takes up. Right now, every part of that presence is radiating menace.

"You're not even human! Liam is not a thing for you to play with." Alex is far too angry to care about the danger.

"Everyone here is a thing to play with. They knew that when they signed up for this and so did you. You're just the only one who doesn't like it."

"I promised him I'd be here today. You made me a liar."

Victor sneers. "Then don't promise things you can't control, little boy."

Alex reacts without thinking about it; he is far too furious for words. He shoves at Victor. Victor doesn't react, just watches him, fascinated, like Alex is merely another toy in his box doing something new and interesting.

His weight is far too well planted for Alex to move him, which enrages Alex more. Before Alex can get his fist back to really take a swing there's an arm hooked around his chest. Raphael is holding him back.

"Hey, hey, hey, steady there," he murmurs in Alex's ear. Alex wants to fight him off because *Victor is still standing right there,* lips pursed triumphantly. But Raphael's got a good grip and Alex doesn't want to hurt him. After struggling for a few seconds he forces his body to relax.

"I'm fine, it's fine," he snaps at Raph. He'll owe him an apology later, but that can wait. When Raph lets go of him Alex thinks of punching Victor anyway, but the moment is gone. Alex shakes his head and stalks away toward the doors. "Go to hell," he shouts over his shoulder at Victor.

Victor just stands there, watching him go.

30

Alex drives to the nearest climbing route he can remember. Waiting in the studio parking lot for Liam to be done with the day is impractical and also impossible. He'd stormed off after shoving Victor (maybe he'll regret that later, though he doubts it), and he can't just sit in his car and sulk. Going back to the house to stew alone all day is likewise unbearable. He has his bag and his climbing shoes in the trunk; he'll be fine. He has hours and restless energy to burn.

While Alex is tying knots and getting his harness situated, his phone rings. He's in no mood to talk to anyone, but given all the facets of his life he can't afford to ignore it.

It's his agent, Vanessa. Alex listens in shocked disbelief as she gives him the good news: The Richmond movie wants him. Nothing is certain yet, of course, because of scheduling issues and money negotiations, but if Alex wants it to happen, it's probably going to happen and very, very quickly at that. It is, Vanessa says, time for him to figure out what his demands are so he doesn't look as damn overeager as she knows he is.

Alex is dazed and angry and tried to punch Victor two hours ago. He can barely get the words together to assure her he will get back to her with some random, arbitrary points of negotiation as soon as possible.

When he hangs up, Alex regards the cliff above him carefully. He wants this movie badly. Having it so close but not absolutely certain makes him feel restless and hungry. He also has no idea how Paul will react to the news. With this on top of everything else that's happened this morning, Alex knows he's a mess.

The route is not one of his favorites. It's hard in an ugly, complicated way that Alex doesn't enjoy. There's no elegance to it; it's simply difficult. That's the sort of challenge he wants right now, though. Something to occupy his body and enough of his mind that he doesn't keep running over all of the way that he hates Victor. Or how he's afraid for Liam, for himself, for Paul, and for everything the future threatens and promises.

He's glad he got out of *The Fourth Estate* when he did. And on his own terms.

Alex climbs recklessly for a while before he slows down and tries to take things deliberately. He tries to shove everything out of his mind that isn't his body and the rock in front of him, but it doesn't work.

When he slips, it's a little thing, a thing that's happened a hundred times before. Alex hardly reacts except to brace himself for the inevitable and slightly unpleasant snag of the harness and probable collision with the rock.

But the rope doesn't catch him. He keeps falling. After the mental fog he's been in all day, one thought is all that comes through with devastating clarity: *So this is how I'll die.*

He scrapes against the cliff face until his backup rope brings him up short thirty feet down, slamming him against the rock. His shoulder blooms with pain. It takes a moment before he can even draw in a breath or process that he's not dead yet. Once he's able to take in his situation Alex is terrified to move, lest that start him down again.

Alex makes himself breathe, fights off the instinct to panic, and checks his ropes the way he was taught. There's a knot that isn't tied right. He examines it very carefully as his stinging shoulder starts to throb. There's no way to fix the rope in the air, and he's still fifty feet above the ground. Any slip from here, physical or mental, and he's done for.

He closes his eyes and takes a deep breath. And then, very slowly and very carefully, he starts the climb back down.

◆

Paul is grateful for the text he'd gotten from Alex this morning. For the most part he feels okay with Alex and the choices he's made about the people in his strange and tangled life. It may still make Paul nuts, but he's working on that.

But as the day goes on without more word from him, Paul starts to worry. He had expected at least an update when Alex had gotten to the lot. At lunch Paul texts him with *How is it going?* He tries not to be a jealous asshole when he doesn't get a reply. Alex would react poorly to that.

Paul's on his own set watching Darcy in her gas station convenience shop preparing for a night of work, both legal and illegal. If Melissa, the high school graduate, is going to start a business wrangling prostitutes, it's going to be a full customer-service experience. She's got a gun under the counter next to the case of poppers she ordered off the internet, has stolen nearly all the condoms the store stocks, and has some joints and single-serve party bottles of truly terrible liquor too.

In a break between shots as the camera resets for a turnaround, Darcy skips over to Paul with her phone in an outstretched hand. She waggles it in his face insistently until he takes it.

"Look what we did!" she says.

"What did we do?" he asks warily. His eyes try to focus on the tiny text on the poorly designed website.

"You're my new squeeze," she coos and tries to sit on his lap.

Paul laughs and shoves her off. "Lemme read."

It's a blind item that's incredibly not vague in its insinuations and is most definitely about his and Darcy's dinner out last night. Paul suspects he should be pissed about the rumor-mongering, but really it's just funny. If nothing else, the headache of it is a welcome distraction from worrying about whatever the hell Alex is up to right now.

"Did you call this in?" Paul asks her. The description of her blonde bounciness and as a long-time pro only new to the Hollywood scene is more flattering than this particular website tends to be.

"Mmmmm, I dunno. A girl has to do something in the ladies'."

◆

Zach's death as it will be revealed on screen takes six hours of shooting. The shot isn't complex, thanks to the news studio setting. But they need that much time to get all the coverage on Liam, Natalie, and Raphael. Victor is almost sure the main take he's going to use is Liam's second one. His shock is honest on the first take, but in the second, the way he ticks over from confusion, to horror, to despairing personal control and the well-practiced cadences of TV news is *exactly* what Victor wants.

Liam isn't – can't be – always a detail-oriented actor, but when he is, he's perfection. It's also one hell of a counterbalance to the chaos of the material with Alex. In the editing room, Victor knows he will wonder why he ever yelled at Liam for sleeping with Alex. In the end, public spectacles and minor headaches aside, that's been one of the most useful choices any of his people have ever made.

Raphael and Natalie are as on as they can be. Supporting a scene like this is thankless work, especially when Liam has to ask to step off set briefly on two different occasions. He lies and says that his throat is bothering him, that he just needs some water. Victor clenches his jaw as he watches. He's spent every second he's known Liam marveling at all the things Liam reflexively lies and passes regarding. Even now that he's out, the list has barely gotten any shorter. The list isn't unwise, but it makes Victor ache. There is a difference between privacy and the way that Liam has forced himself to live in the world.

Victor says nothing to be a comfort. Once Liam cracks, he'll break. Everyone's job is just to get to the end of the day. The longer Liam thinks he has to convince everyone that he is more okay than he is, the longer he'll be able to keep it together.

When he has all the coverage he needs, he thanks Liam for his work and dismisses him with a P.A. to walk him back to his trailer.

"Stay put," he says before they go, "I'll be with you in an hour."

He wants a hair more reaction material for Raphael and Natalie, just to be sure.

Liam's still outwardly holding it together by the time Victor herds him into his car, but he's fairly non-verbal. Victor has to remind him to put on his seatbelt. His compliance is the only indication Victor gets that he's listening at all.

"Try to relax," Victor says. "We'll be home soon. I called Carly, she'll come over for brunch tomorrow."

◆

When Alex's feet finally touch the ground, he makes himself reel in his ropes, check all of his equipment, and go through the motions of putting everything away properly before he slumps to the ground next to his car and starts shaking. The adrenaline rush is terrifying. Now that he's on the ground and not actually afraid for his life, he's able think about how fucking bad that almost was. Zach seems like a terrible cautionary tale, an awful omen that pales in the face of what nearly just happened.

Alex only remembers how badly he'd hurt his shoulder when he finally climbs into the driver's seat and has to put on his seatbelt. He can't move his arm without being in unbearable pain. In the cup holder, his phone flashes with missed calls and texts. Whatever they are, Alex doesn't remotely have the bandwidth to deal with them. He ignores them and starts driving.

◆

When Liam and Victor get to Victor's house and pull into the drive, Liam fumbles with his seatbelt for a moment and then gets out of the car silently. Victor unlocks the door and watches as Liam heads for his room on autopilot.

"Not this time." He wraps a hand around Liam's bicep. "Let's get you upstairs."

Liam looks confused and doesn't look any less confused when Victor leads him into his bedroom. The first and only time Liam's ever been in here was after the pilot party for *The Fourth Estate*, years ago. He'd clumsily tried to seduce Victor and, on some level and by some definition, succeeded.

Victor has to peel Liam's bag off his shoulder. He'll obviously have to help Liam do anything beyond sit there. He's been in this place with him once or twice before. He accepts Liam's brain and the way he copes with it for what it is. But it's still terrifying when Liam loses his ability to communicate verbally. Ever since Liam explained it to him, the question always becomes whether this is the new normal, whether Liam can really dodge his nature forever.

Victor finds himself kneeling at Liam's feet and taking his shoes and socks off. "I can't take care of you the way you like if I don't know what's going on with you and can't tell if you're consenting," Victor says.

Liam squeezes his eyes shut and gestures in a way that seems to go with, or in fact be, a sentence he can't actually utter right now.

Victor rests his chin on Liam's thigh. "I can be infinitely patient with you," Victor says even if it's probably not as practically true as he would like.

"I know," Liam says after several minutes.

An hour, maybe two, passes before Liam seems present enough in his extremities and surfaces to take off his clothes and crawl into bed. Victor stays on the floor watching him as he cocoons himself in the blankets and stares at him, eyes bright and wet and saying things Victor can't be sure he can allow himself to hear.

"I need to know that you're able to consent right now," Victor says but feels like an asshole for it. Liam isn't impaired, he's just not doing communication in a way Victor can totally read. Which is only confirmed by Liam's annoyed sigh and the way he pulls at Victor's hands until one palm rests over his chest.

"I'm sorry about the story," Victor says.

Liam shrugs.

"I'm sorry we're such terribly different animals." The way Liam loves has always scared him.

Liam presses his eyes shut again and shakes his head. Victor can read *Pain* and *please don't be in pain because of me* clear enough without Liam actually using words.

There are no words in any language Victor has for the way in which he loves Liam, which in the past meant he didn't have to consider whether he loves him at all. But today, when everything in the world seems fragile because of a story he made up, that's harder than usual. It occurs to him that, with an entirely different set of capacities, Alex may very well love Liam in a terribly similar way.

Victor says as much, even though it might not mean anything to Liam right now and may not even make sense at all. Liam gives him a half smile, beatific and sad. Victor runs his palm over Liam's face, fascinated by how, at times, his body is the only language he has.

"Touch," Liam says. The word is too small for all the things they do. Still, it's enough for Victor to kiss him and feel Liam flutter open.

"Do you want me to touch you?" Victor asks. "Do you want me to hurt you?"

Liam nods to the first question and manages to croak out a yes to the second. This, Victor thinks darkly, is what Alex will never understand about them.

◆

Alex's car isn't in the garage when Paul gets home, and the house is concerningly dark. After a circuit of the downstairs Paul checks Alex's room. Maybe he had an even stranger day than anticipated and got home by some means other than his own vehicle. But the bedroom is empty.

Paul calls Carly.

"Why isn't Alex home yet?" he asks when she picks up.

"Why the hell are you home, and how should I know?"

"Because my starlet – who I am apparently fucking, by the way – told me to go home because all I was doing was annoying people. And because my boyfriend spent last night with *your* boyfriend and I haven't heard from him since seven this morning."

"Awwww. And you're not even poly. Good job there, Paul."

"Carly."

"I have no idea where Alex is, but Victor called and said they finished shooting. Maybe he's on his way home. But, Paul, when Victor calls from set to tell me about the state Liam is in and that he *will be* okay, your boyfriend is not at the top of my worry list."

"Point taken," Paul says after a shocked pause. "I have no idea what else to say."

"Thank you."

"If you hear anything, will you let me know?"

◆

Liam trembles in Victor's bed. He's on his side, because his muscles can't support him any other way right now. His hands are tied in front of him, thick cotton rope braided ornately over and between his wrists, binding them tighter than any cuffs ever could. Liam's bound hands hold the dildo he can't stop sucking on; there's another one vibrating in his ass. Victor has been bringing him right to the edge and pulling him back from it all day, just in radically different ways. Tears track down his face at the realization.

Something must show in his eyes, because Victor says "Welcome back," and then gives him a smile that's slightly evil.

Liam laughs wetly, although it's muffled by the busyness of his mouth. When he comes, it's brutal, drawn out, and overwhelming. After, Victor pulls his hands and the toy away from his mouth to kiss him.

"I absolutely cherish you," he says.

Liam hums happily and closes his eyes, glad he's no longer

expected, at least for a little while, to say anything even with them. He frowns when Victor doesn't quietly unbraid the ropes as Liam is used to. Instead he pulls out a knife and saws through each segment of the design. Eventually he pries Liam's hands from each other, links of rope falling around them.

That surgery done and the toys put aside, Victor cleans him up, gets undressed, and crawls into bed with him. Liam knows this means Victor will likely sleep poorly if he sleeps at all. Liam knows the humid scrape of flesh is one of those things Victor generally tries not to think about, but apparently Liam's well-being is far more important than Victor's own comfort right now.

Liam has never even seen him naked before. He turns in Victor's arms, presses his forehead to the man's sternum, and sobs.

◆

"Where the hell have you been?" Paul demands when Alex finally walks in the door. He's been waiting in sight of the door and front windows with steadily increasing levels of anxiety all evening

Alex gives Paul a look that's angry in a way he never is for the camera. "Victor banned me from set, so I went climbing and am very lucky not to be dead right now. I also tried to punch him. My shoulder really hurts. And I'm probably going to get that movie."

Paul is dumbstruck. "I don't know where to start with that."

"Neither do I. Um." Alex drops his climbing bag by the door and rolls his shoulder gingerly. "Can you help me with this? I think I'm bleeding, I can't see it."

"What did you do?" Paul is instantly at his side, hand carefully at his waist as Alex cranes his head to look over his shoulder. His T-shirt is torn through, and there is most definitely blood.

"I fell," Alex says. "Help, please?"

If Alex can manage this much irritability, he's probably okay. Still, Paul follows Alex into the first floor bathroom with a distinct sense of doom.

The blood has dried enough that the shirt sticks to the wound. Alex grits his teeth while Paul dabs at it with a wet paper towel until it loosens enough to peel away. Paul's trying to be gentle, but it still hurts.

"Talk to me," Paul says. Alex hisses as he pulls another bit of the torn cotton away. Paul winces sympathetically. "Oh my God, I'm sorry."

Alex shakes his head. "It's fine."

"What happened with Liam?" Paul asks. He wants answers as much as he wants to distract Alex from the pain. "And what's going on with your movie?"

While Paul works at his shoulder, Alex tells him about the strange overnight. Paul's sure he's not getting the full story, but he's also sure he's not supposed to ask. Alex will tell him what he feels safe telling him, and Paul will have to be okay with that.

There are, however, some things he can ask about. "Okay," Paul says as he tosses a bloody paper towel in the trash and rips off another. "Do I want to ask about what happened on the rocks or what happened with Victor next? Or about how you're going to leave for three months?"

"You're patching me up from a fall down a cliff and you're still acting like I'm abandoning you for a job? Nothing is set in stone, and I'm not leaving you for a movie. Ask about Victor," Alex says shortly. "He makes the rocks make sense."

"Okay, then, what happened with Victor?"

"I promised Lee I'd go to set with him today," Alex recites, staring at the wall. "When I got there, Victor told me I couldn't. We got into an argument, because he's a sadistic son of a bitch and is making life hard for Liam on purpose."

"So you tried to punch him?" Paul pauses in peeling away another bit of the shirt. He doesn't know whether to be more horrified or impressed.

"Well, I shoved him first. Which was stupid. Because by the time I took a swing other people felt prepared to step in. I should have just decked him."

"Oh my God, Alex."

"I owe Raphael an apology. Incidentally."

"Please tell me you didn't try to hit him too."

Alex shakes his head. "No. He pulled me off. If it had been someone else, I might have taken a swing at them. I don't know."

"Okay. That's good, at least."

"Maybe," Alex shrugs and then winces. "*Fuck.* Ow. Anyway, I didn't want to come home and stew, so I went climbing. Which was dumb, because I was pissed and distracted and not paying attention. Ow, shit, fuck, okay."

The last is because Paul is finally pulling Alex's shirt over his head. Once it's gone, Paul stares with horror at his shoulder and back, which are scraped almost raw. What skin isn't bloody is black and blue.

"Alex," he says hoarsely. "How bad did you fall?"

"Bad enough to give me that and leave me feeling lucky."

Paul frowns deeply. "There's gravel in here. We should be going to the emergency room. Me and a bottle of hydrogen peroxide are not going to fix this."

"I'm not going to the emergency room," Alex states flatly. "No media attention. No institutional anything."

"Yeah, we'll see. Why didn't you call me?" Paul asks.

"I didn't call you because I was halfway up the side of a cliff on a rope I tied wrong. I didn't exactly have any free hands."

"That's not what I mean," Paul snaps.

Alex takes a deep breath. "I had a good three seconds where I knew I was dead. And then I had to pull myself together when the rope actually fucking caught me and get down in one piece."

Paul has no idea how he can sound so calm.

"Then I focused on putting my gear away, getting in the car, and driving home. With my full attention on every step, because it was the only way I'd be sure I'd get here."

Paul's day waiting for Alex has been more or less terrible. Now, confronted with the reality that Alex almost didn't come home at all, he's truly frightened.

More than that, he's angry. "Nobody knew where you were," Paul says, touching the side of Alex's face to make him look at him. "And then you come home looking like this. What the hell would have happened if you had fallen all the way? How long would it have taken anyone to find you?"

Alex glares. "Today has been hard enough without your pissiness, no matter how justified you think you are. I have had to deal with Liam and Victor and the movie and the fall, and now I just fucking hurt. Also, I didn't fall all the way."

"God, Alex." Paul holds his chin still and checks his eyes for a sign of concussion and also an answer that makes any sort of sense at all. "You want me to take care of you and then you can't even take care of yourself. How the fuck do you expect me to be in this relationship with you?"

Alex's eyes narrow before he jerks away. "This from my suicidal boyfriend."

31

Liam thinks the best thing about fucking Carly in his house, other than the fact that he's fucking Carly at all, is that they can both be as loud as they want without her appalling neighbors pounding on the wall.

She's on top of him, straddling his hips, riding his cock, both hands on her clit. Liam is too dumbstruck by her beauty and how fucking good it feels to be very useful at all beyond holding her waist and helping her bounce up and down while telling her how beautiful she is.

"Fuck you," she gasps with a laugh. "Even when you compliment me it's all about your ego."

He laughs, because she's being ridiculous, but it's also totally true. "I make the best choices," he says.

"No," she manages. "You just said yes to the right girl."

"Yeah?" he says, his hands joining hers as he presses his thumb against her hard.

"Oh God." She half doubles over with the too-much of it. She's just right there and not there yet, *damn him.*

He shoves her hands out of the way. She leans back, tosses her hair out of her face and braces her hands against his thigh. He rubs her in quick little circles while fucking up into her as hard as he can.

He almost wishes her stupid neighbors were pounding on the wall, because knowing that they're jealous and pissed off is awesome. When she comes, it's long and loud. She levers herself forward so she can kiss Liam through it, her tongue fucking into his mouth while he encourages her to keep moving because he is so Goddamn close.

It's all exquisitely over when she leans up just enough to whisper in his ear, "Come already, so you can lick it out of me."

◆

"So tell me how your day was," Carly says, propping her head up on her hand. The last week has been rough. Being back in Liam's bed like this hopefully means things are starting to improve.

Liam shrugs, playing with her hair. He looks more serious now that the sex is over. "I don't know."

Carly frowns.

"Victor's off. I'm off. Alex isn't there," Liam says. Carly can tell there's more there, but he's clearly not ready to articulate it.

"Have you two talked about it any more?" Carly asks for what must be the tenth time since Liam filmed the reveal of Zach's death. Victor had been quiet at brunch the morning after, but Liam was still barely talking. A night like that would have been a lot for anyone. Since then, the little pieces she's gotten from Liam about his and Victor's night together suggests a shifting landscape, but not to what or why. Liam really, really doesn't need any more change right now. Carly's worried about him in a persistent and absolute way that may well involve her calling Victor and chewing him out if she doesn't get some satisfactory answers soon.

"No," Liam says. Carly can't tell if he's being taciturn out of ability or willingness.

"Are you worried about it?"

"Yes."

"Okay," Carly says when he's not more forthcoming. "What is it you're worried about?"

Liam rolls onto his back and gropes for her hand on top of the covers. "Victor's brain and how he's making decisions. What's happening with me and him. It's all –" Liam trails off and makes the flustered gesture he always makes when he's run out of words.

"Baby," Carly chides gently. "He needs to know what you need in order to make decisions."

Liam doesn't say anything.

◆

Days pass before Alex can sleep without waking himself up every time he rolls onto his banged-up side. Paul had stayed with him the first night; pissed as they both had been at each other, having him there had been good until morning came and Paul had insisted Alex see a doctor.

"Not going to the ER," Alex insisted flatly, as Paul dug in Alex's first aid kit for more gauze pads to tape over the wound.

"Alex," Paul had said, as if he were some particularly unreasonable, petulant child. "If this doesn't get properly cleaned it's going to go septic. It doesn't have to be the ER, but you're going somewhere."

Which is how Alex had ended up in Paul's car, hunched forward so his back didn't touch the seat while Paul drove him to urgent care.

"Don't you have work?" Alex had asked sulkily. Paul's missing work for this. Things were difficult enough between them that he didn't want to give Paul one more excuse to blame Alex for being a distraction.

"You almost died. I think I can spare the time," Paul had said way too evenly.

His tone had pissed Alex off as much as anything. "Glad I rank *somewhere* in your list of priorities."

They'd had another argument that night, because when Alex

refused to let Paul sleep in his room again Paul had taken that as an excuse to be neurotic and scared about the three-month separation for Alex's movie.

"If you think you can't be in this relationship because I'm reckless, you don't get to use my pain to make yourself feel better," Alex had snapped and stalked off to his room, while Paul had sat, visibly angry and frustrated, in their kitchen staring after him.

Alex is scared too, frankly. Even more than whatever fight they're currently having, he's as afraid as Paul is of such a long separation. Alex lies muzzily in the bed that used to be theirs while Todd scratches mournfully at the door to be let in, thinking about it. No matter what entirely legitimate grievances with each other they might latch onto, if they fall apart it won't be because they didn't love each other hard enough. It will be because the logistics of the lives they lead are simply impossible.

♦

With all of the uncertainty going on with Liam right now, Victor knows that it's particularly important to keep up their weekly date nights. The first time they do dinner and an overnight after *that* night, Liam shows up as usual and the evening also progresses, more or less, also as usual. He's is more verbal that he has been recently, but he's not yet as talkative as usual. Victor is worried.

As they make out on the couch after dinner, Liam is lovely and pliant and at ease. Victor remembers, yet again, that measuring how Liam is by his ability and willingness to speak isn't always the best plan. Sometimes Liam is fine overall but not fine for the world of other people. Even so, Victor reminds himself to be careful. He doesn't want to add to Liam's stress right now. As the evening grows later, and Liam is making the sweetest little sounds into his mouth, Victor still fears the things Liam wants that he in turn very much does not. Inevitably, Victor will make things worse for him.

He braces himself for when it's time to go to bed and Liam asks to go to Victor's room instead of his own. Victor doesn't know what the answer to that request is or should be. The uncertainty feels as alien as it does dangerous.

But when they finally do get up from the couch, Liam leads the way happily to his own room as if this destination is the same matter of course it always has been. There, Victor takes care of him as he usually does; Liam is always so aesthetically pleasing in his need.

After, however, Victor makes Liam shove over, so there's enough room for him to sit up against the headboard and write. Liam curls against him once he opens his laptop and rests his head against Victor's arm.

"I'm not going to type less because your head's there," Victor says.

"S'okay."

"Mmmm, tell me that when I've been bouncing your skull around for two hours," he says as he opens a file.

Liam moves his head back onto his pillow, kissing Victor's arm as he goes.

"I'm still recalibrating," Victor says.

Liam taps his fingers against Victor's side, his shorthand always for having heard when he doesn't otherwise want to speak.

32

I can't believe you're going back up there," Paul says, flabbergasted and more than a little afraid. Alex is laying out plans for the next route he wants to try, his tablet and a tattered book of local trails open on the kitchen island next to whatever he'd made himself for dinner. "Can you even climb, with your shoulder?" It's been a couple of weeks, but Alex's back can't possibly be better yet.

"It's better than it was. Besides, I know what not to do now. I will never go climbing after I try to punch Victor again," Alex says solemnly.

"Famous last words." Paul tries not to laugh. "At least tell me you aren't going to try this alone."

"Well, actually." Alex looks up from his planning to catch Paul's eye with a gaze that's intense enough to make Paul's breath catch. Alex wanting something is always glorious and terrifying. The recent weeks of renewed tension and anxiety haven't made that less true. "I was hoping you'd come with me."

Carefully, Paul says, "I thought I slowed you down."

"I really don't want to be up there by myself."

♦

Even aside from the horrible inherent in having to play James and his private grief, working without Alex next to him is strange. As much as Liam is friends with the rest of the cast, he misses having Alex around desperately.

He's looking for someone he can sit and be with without having to talk when he barges into Victor's office without knocking, as he usually does.

Victor is there, behind his desk. Next to him, is a man Liam's never seen before in his life. He's sitting way closer to Victor than Liam is used to seeing anyone sit. And he's insanely attractive and has his hand on Victor's thigh.

They both look up at Liam. Neither seems particularly startled to see him. But neither of them says anything, either. The guy gives Victor a look that Liam can't read at all.

Liam has no idea what's going on right now, or what he's feeling, except that someone he doesn't know is in his place next to Victor. He can't get his brain untangled enough to stammer out an apology, so he leaves. He doesn't even mind letting the door slam behind him.

♦

"So that's Hurricane Liam," Nigel says once the door has crashed closed.

Victor groans. Having a friend like Nigel he can rely on for reasonable and useful support when in the midst of a crisis is something for which he is duly grateful. However, he is not sure that the frustratingly multifaceted crisis that he is having over how he and Liam fit together has not just gotten a little bit worse. "That was not the most auspicious first meeting I could have hoped for."

"I can see why he's driving you up a wall."

"Because he's beautiful or because he's exhausting?"

Nigel considers that for a thoughtful moment. "Yes, but I wouldn't blame him if that's what's required to hold your attention."

♦

When they get to the mountain, Alex checks all of their equipment obsessively before making Paul check it too. Then he checks it all again, just to be sure. Paul refrains from saying a word about any of it and is rewarded when Alex kisses him briefly before he grabs the first handhold.

The climb is slow. Paul can tell that Alex, despite his protests to the contrary, is in pain. But if this is what Alex needs to work things out both for himself and between them, Paul is willing to be here for it. There's something to be said for team-building exercises.

When they finally get to the top, Alex teases Paul for not wanting to get too close to the edge. Paul takes a few pictures of the stunning view while Alex sits with his arms around his knees staring out at the distant hills. Paul gets one of him, too, in profile, and is thrilled when Alex suffers him to post it online.

Paul knows that none of this – the climb or the pictures or even Alex's amused smile over his shoulder at him – means they're okay. But he is absolutely going to hoard the good moments while he can. He has no idea how many they have left.

Finally, he takes a breath and says, "Victor called yesterday."

"Is this really a thing you want to tell me before I have to climb rocks again?"

Paul chuckles. "It's fine. Odd, but fine. He wants us to go to dinner with him next week."

"Okayyy." Alex is clearly thrown. "That makes me nervous."

"Yeah, I don't know what's up, but I wanted to let you know."

"So I have time to properly prepare myself?"

Paul shrugs. "More or less."

♦

They discuss the topic in the car on the way home but reach no conclusions. Once they park, Paul goes to grab their stuff out of the trunk, but Alex stops him with a hand on his arm.

"We'll clean up later. Date now."

Paul is surprised. He'd hoped, but had no idea what Alex's plans for the day entailed. He's probably making decisions based on how Paul had comported himself on their outing.

Inside, Alex leads them straight to the couch, apparently not caring today that they're both sweaty and sore and dusty with chalk. They get horizontal quickly, but clothes stay on. Paul runs his hands all over Alex's back and arms while Alex whines into his mouth.

When he gets to Alex's shoulders and tugs because he wants to be as close to Alex as he can get, Alex pulls back with a hiss. "Fuck, *oww*."

"Oh my God, sorry, I forgot." Paul tries to pull back, terrified he's accidentally just ruined the day.

Alex sits up, knees bracketing Paul's hips to keep him in place. He rolls his shoulder with a grimace. "It's okay. I did too."

He doesn't look upset, and the look of concentration on his face as he stretches his arm experimentally is appealing. Paul rubs his thumbs into the skin above Alex's waistband. "So you can say no."

Alex barks a laugh and gives his shoulder one last roll before he falls forward onto Paul again. "Give the man a prize."

33

Liam, why the fuck would I have any idea who Victor keeps around?" Alex is exasperated. He and Paul are getting ready for whatever dinner clusterfuck Victor invited them to. And now Liam has called him in a panic about somebody visiting Victor on the lot. Alex tries to keep his knowledge of Victor's private life to an absolute minimum, which is usually not difficult except when it comes to Liam's involvement therein. But he hasn't been on the lot in weeks and can't even begin to fathom why Liam sounds so very close to completely unspooling over the issue.

"Victor likes you," Liam whines.

Alex gives a little shudder. He's glad they're on the phone and Liam can't see it. "Yes, but Victor *likes* you. Also, last I checked, you don't do jealousy. What gives?"

"I'm not jealous."

"You are," Carly's voice comes over the line. Alex can hear the sound of Liam zipping up her dress.

"I don't even know what jealousy feels like," Liam says, presumably to both of them.

"Like this," Alex says darkly.

"What's going on?" Paul asks, as Alex puts the phone on speaker and sets it down on the counter so Paul can do his other cufflink.

"If I knew that," Alex says not even bothering to cover the mouthpiece, "I'd be avoiding it better."

"Alex...." Liam whines.

"Not you! It!" Alex says. He's starting to hope Victor is planning to poison them all so he doesn't have to sit through this whole meal.

♦

The restaurant has the same sort of uncomfortable, aggressively modern and understated decor as Victor's house. Alex considers the possibility that Victor doesn't mean to be a creepy unpleasant bastard but just can't help himself.

He dismisses his charitableness as wishful thinking when he and Paul arrive at Victor's table to find everyone else already seated. Alex suspects they were intentionally told a slightly later time when Carly, straight-backed, voice tight, and seated between the only two empty places at the table says, "I didn't choose the seats."

"Clearly," Alex says under his breath.

Victor points to the empty seat between Carly and the mystery man Liam had been ranting about on the phone. "Paul," he says before pointing to the other seat. "Alex can sit next to Liam."

"I've reminded Victor that a lady should always do the seating assignments," Carly says.

Alex has to stifle the urge to laugh. The impulse only gets worse when Paul pulls out his chair for him. As absurd as the gesture is, Alex appreciates it. However rage-inducing the evening may prove to be, Paul at least seems unlikely to blame Alex for it.

"Someone should also remind Victor to do introductions," Paul says good-naturedly. He steps away from Alex's chair and offers his hand to the only unknown quantity at the table.

The unknown looks placidly amused at the entire proceeding but shakes Paul's hand warmly. "Nigel. Pleasure to meet you, Paul," he says.

"Same." Paul prolongs the handshake a moment longer than is strictly necessary. Next to him, Carly looks highly entertained.

After the introductions, Nigel sits back and says, "You'll have to excuse Victor. His plans tend to not take the people involved in them into account."

"We've noticed," Alex says less sarcastically than he could. They're in public and there's a stranger in their midst. But this entire thing is still ridiculous.

"Yes," Carly says. Her tone echoes Nigel's somewhat unfriendly teasing one. "What is this even about?"

They're interrupted by a member of the wait staff placing an amuse-bouche down in front of each of them. Everyone lapses into a tense silence until he's gone again.

"Oh my God, did you order for us?" Alex asks.

"Expand your palate," Victor says dryly to him. He turns to Carly. "And who said it had to be an occasion?"

"I have known you for years. Both the group social outing and the mysterious stranger are entirely new tricks for you." Despite her tone, Carly gives Nigel a charming smile. Alex takes a moment to be impressed at her ability to so keenly focus her wrath.

Victor leans over to Liam, who looks faintly ill. "I have always liked her."

Alex looks to Paul for help interpreting any of it.

Paul gives a tiny shrug. Then he asks Nigel, in a desperate attempt to get this evening on something resembling normal footing, "How do you two know each other?"

Of course the story involves upfronts. Hell begets hell.

Liam, who has been quiet since they've walked in, finally bursts out with, "Yes, but why are you here *now*?"

Alex has never seen him so socially unfluid, not in public. He braces for an explosion, even though he hadn't known until this moment that Liam is capable of one.

Victor and Nigel look at each other and chuckle, apparently unfazed. Either Nigel is as cunning and manipulative as Victor is, or he's just very used to Victor's methods of dealing with people. Alex isn't sure which of those possibilities is less comforting.

"You are all here," Victor says with a fond, if pointed, look at Liam, "Because, whether we like it or not, our lives are a tangled mess and I was raised to believe in family dinners. Mainly, though, Nigel's been badgering me."

"We don't even know you," Liam says.

"I'm trying to rectify that." Victor sounds both apologetic and a little desperate.

"Speaking for me is not rectifying it, Victor," Nigel says softly. Alex gets the impression he's said similar many times before.

Alex looks at Paul nervously. Paul shrugs. As much as he walked into this worrying about what power play Victor might be making, he now realizes he's watching his control over all of them fall apart. The possibility is weirdly awful considering it sometimes seems as if that's more important to Victor than all his public success.

The table drifts into small talk, as if pointed and stilted chatter about things as significant as Carly and Liam's wedding count as such. Then Victor has the temerity to ask when Alex and Paul are planning to get married.

Alex takes a deep breath and then another. He doesn't want to deal with this and he can't hit Victor again. He probably shouldn't have done it the first time. He leans across Carly to Paul. "I'm leaving you to answer that," he says. "Come on, Carly." He grabs her arm. "Time for girl talk in the powder room."

"Please tell me we can go outside and smoke instead," she says as she clatters after him.

"Oh my God, anything, yes."

◆

"I appreciate your concern with our wellbeing," Paul says once Alex is out of earshot. He means it, in the twisted way he's sure Victor doesn't actually intend to be evil when he asks things like that. Alex would probably disagree on the latter point. "But our relationship, and any issues regarding it, are not your business. You're not making things any easier at the moment, either."

"Are things getting any better?" Victor asks. Paul is surprised at how simply the question is phrased.

"Yes, actually. This dinner probably aside."

Victor smiles. "He's very young, Paul."

"No one is more aware of that than us, and it would be unfair to blame our issues on that complication." Paul can't believe they're talking about this in public. "I value what I view as a real friendship between us, Victor, but your good intentions are, as I remind you nearly weekly, generally poisonous."

"Yet you keep making good things come of them. And from the obstacles I put in your way."

Paul takes a moment to process the horrible novelty of Victor admitting that so frankly. Nigel doesn't say anything but is clearly riveted. Liam, however, sullenly continues to pleat his napkin while the other men ignore him.

"I never could get Alex to do a thing he didn't want to," Victor adds. "Bear that in mind while you sort out your future."

"Do you really expect me to take advice from you about him at this point?" Paul asks, disbelieving. He considers the merit of running out after Alex and Carly. But he wants to show Victor he can stay and tough this out.

"Of all of us," Victor says, "Alex and I are most alike. You don't have to take my advice, but you should at least listen."

The thing is, Paul can see how he's right. "Why is every conversation with you so ominous?"

Victor laughs with obvious delight.

◆

Outside, Alex slumps against the wall of the restaurant while Carly fishes in her purse.

"I am going to kill Victor," he says.

"So things aren't better on the marriage question, I take it," Carly says.

"You say that like we're sure we're not breaking up."

"Are you breaking up?" She pulls out a pack of cigarettes and a lighter.

"If I knew, tonight would be a lot less awful. I mean, I'm starting to think we're not, but he's still sleeping on the other side of the house. He's jealous of Liam, afraid of everything he doesn't understand about me, and a workaholic. And that's the short list."

Carly sweeps some of her hair back out of her face. "You know, back when Paul and I were dating, he was afraid of everything he didn't understand about himself. *And* a workaholic. He's making some sort of progress. But I know exactly how infuriating he can be. I also know that he loves to be loved. If you're worried about him staying, that's easy. If you're worried about your willingness to stay, I can only sympathize."

"I just turned twenty-four and I spend all my time worrying about his issues." Alex tips his head back to look up at the sky. Thanks to light pollution, he can't see a single star. "There is so much fucking up I haven't had a chance to do. It's infuriating. I told him this when we first got together, and yet here we are."

"Well, what sort of fucking up are you missing?"

"You mean other than that shithole apartment Gemma and I had?" As terrible as that apartment had been, it was the last normal thing he'd had. He misses it sometimes. Or maybe he just misses the simplicity of his old life, the one between Indiana and stardom.

"Yes."

"He's the only boyfriend I've ever had – the only relationship, aside from Lee, and that's a mess he doesn't want to touch."

"If you need to date around, you need to tell him that."

Alex shakes his head. A poly solution to their problem isn't necessarily wrong, but it's not the one he's after. "Mostly, I want him to feel my pain and not treat us like we're already married, which, by the way, is apparently some game he wants to win so he can stop trying."

"Baby boy, Paul's been acting like you've been married since you started dating."

"Not news. And not actually making me feel better."

"Shhh, listen. Paul is messed up. But being married in his head doesn't mean the door gets shut on anything you want to do or try or be as long as you keep him involved in some way. Which, you know, I couldn't deal with because I like my space, but you're so not me."

"I'm not Victor either," Alex says.

Carly laughs. "Oh, I know."

"Among other things, I'd miss the sex," Alex says.

"You might, but it works for him," Carly says gently. "I take it you and Paul still aren't fucking?"

"*No*. Well – yes. Depending how you define it. But. No. Not how I'd like, at least."

Carly raises an eyebrow. "Informative."

"I can't believe we're having this conversation out here," Alex says, looking up and down the sidewalk, where cars and people are passing, going about their more-normal-than-his lives.

"Would you rather have it back inside?" she asks.

Alex shudders and takes a breath. Anything is better than going back to that table. "It was part of the deal where we're dating but not completely together. Sex is for fun. Not a replacement for relationship work."

"That's obnoxiously mature."

"I think it's helped."

"Good. Is he still all into that an-tici...pation thing?" she asks, leaning over to pop the syllables close to his ear.

"You're bizarre," he says laughing, "but yeah."

"Wait. Have you never seen *The Rocky Horror Picture Show*?"

"Nope."

"Ugh, I was going to suggest a threesome and now I have to take you to the movies? This night is fired."

"Could do both," Alex offers with a shrug. His life can't get any weirder right now.

"You are actually blushing. That is fucking adorable."

"Ginger. We did talk about it, sort of. After Victor's party," Alex says, although he is not sure why. By any reasonable standard he should be changing the topic as fast as possible.

"He dirty talked it, didn't he?"

"Phone sex, but yeah."

Carly laughs. "I'm guessing the verdict was favorable."

"Yeah, and then everything went to hell. Unrelatedly."

"I don't want to dare you into a thing that's going to cause more strife, but hey, adventures with Paul," she says, laughing.

"You are intensely manipulative. Maybe you're the most like Victor," Alex says like it's a prize that must be awarded somewhere.

◆

From where Paul is sitting, he's the first to see Alex and Carly approach the table again. Alex has his hand at the small of her back and a gleam of fun in his eye. He catches Paul's gaze across the table and winks as he slides back into his seat. Whatever they talked about out there, Paul, or at least the rest of the table, should clearly brace for it.

He's not wrong. Conversation resumes – this time, about the far less fraught topic of Nigel's most recent ad campaign – as if no one had stalked off in irritation. Alex and Carly are clearly at play. There's bantering and whispering and hands on each other's thighs. Alex keeps grinning at Paul every time Victor frowns over it. Paul has to look anywhere else so he doesn't burst out laughing right in the midst of it all.

◆

Liam, while unperturbed by him and Carly – he actually smiles at them a few times – remains completely perturbed by everything else. Alex increasingly doesn't blame him. Especially when he makes occasional cutting comments at Paul's reflexive need to be gracious to Nigel. Paul's deference definitely verges on flirtatiousness.

Alex watches, fascinated, when Victor gets sick of disapproving of his and Carly's overly theatrical impression of teenage heterosexuality and bored of chatting with Paul and Nigel. He turns to snap at Liam about his manners instead.

Alex puts a hand on Liam's thigh as if that will protect him. Victor's done a lot of things to Liam recently of which Alex does not approve, but snapping at him in public is a whole new bucket of not okay. Carly reacts next, with a quick, appreciative nod to Alex before leaning back in her chair to try to catch Liam's eye behind Alex's shoulder. As the table descends into awkward silence Nigel and Paul stop talking as well, unable to keep up any facade of normality.

Without saying anything, Liam tosses his creased-through napkin on the table and pushes back his chair.

"Liam, honey." Carly gets up to follow him as he heads for the exit.

"No, I'll get him," Victor says.

Carly bristles. "Victor, I appreciate it, but things have been kind of tense lately and you're not helping."

"They could be so much worse."

"And they could be so much better," Carly hisses. "We have already caused enough of a scene and the public demise of this evening is not going to come down on Liam's head."

"I'll get him," Nigel says, not waiting for anyone's approval. "You lot sort yourselves out."

Alex watches him go but wonders if *he* should be the one to go talk Liam down at this point.

Carly sits again but continues to glare at Victor. "You are seriously making his life hell right now. And mine, actually."

"I am doing my best." Victor's voice is surprisingly gentle and small.

"You're really not."

Victor sighs. "Liam is one of the greatest joys of my life. Until very recently, I knew what I was supposed to do – and feel – about that."

"And, what, that's changed and you took us out to dinner to tell us?"

"Not quite, Carly. Show, don't tell," Victor says with the air of a teacher whose students have finally caught up.

Alex and Paul look at each other, and as much as their glance should probably be about what is happening to their friends at this table, Alex is nearly certain it's not. He offers what smile he can in such strange circumstances, and it's hard to tear his attention away when Paul returns it.

"I am genuinely trying to make life better for Liam," Victor goes on. "Within the landscape of the things that I have the ability and the desire to do for him, but this is very new and very difficult territory for me. I don't want him to be mad at me, Carly. I don't want you mad at me either."

Carly gapes. "I didn't know you were capable of fucking up this badly. Or this publically. He is in so deep with you, and he is terrified of losing all of it."

"Have you ever considered that maybe I am too?" Victor asks. "I am very glad he is marrying you. You can do so much for him. Have, for years."

"Yes, well, I'm amazing," she says with a nervous twitch of her hair. "Just warn us next time about the secret best friends. And don't ever, *ever* let me see you treat him like a child again."

◆

Nigel finds Liam outside the restaurant. He's leaning against a building and fidgeting with something that looks like a keychain. He's clearly angry, which is better than any alternatives Nigel can imagine.

Liam acknowledges Nigel's presence with a nod, but doesn't say anything. Nigel is too annoyed with the course of this evening to wait him out. None of this should be his job.

"Why didn't you yell at him?"

Liam looks up, startled, and shoves the keychain back into his jacket pocket.

"You're clearly as pissed at him as everyone else, and they haven't held back," Nigel says.

Liam opens his mouth to respond but closes it again without saying anything.

Nigel isn't sure if he doesn't have an answer or if he's calculating what he says. Victor makes everyone around him political.

"We're different," Liam says eventually. "Them and me."

"I know," Nigel says gently, because he does know. Liam is the only thing Victor talks about that isn't work. Whether Liam seems different to the rest of the world, or just to Victor hardly matters. In this mess, this young man isn't like anyone else.

Liam folds his hands behind his back and looks up at Nigel while he settles back against the wall next to him. "I don't know who the fuck you are to him, and I don't know why I'm supposed to keep guessing."

"Old friends." Nigel shrugs.

"You used to fuck," Liam bites.

"You don't want what we had. It didn't work and it's not on offer. I am sorry my old friend is being an asshole tonight and I am sorry he's doing it in public. He doesn't know how to do anything else, but Liam, just so we're clear, I can see why he's angry with you." Nigel

"He's as important to me as Carly, and I don't get random surprises about her life," Liam points out.

Nigel, for all that he's known Victor for decades, is not prepared to be having this conversation, on a neon-bright L.A. sidewalk, with the man Victor is, for lack of a more precise term, dating. He wishes Pris had come out with him to L.A. this time. Then at least Nigel could vent about all of this absurdity to her in person. "Yeah, well, you did. But you don't need to take it out on me. I certainly don't take it out on you for being something to him I couldn't."

"Then you don't know what it's like to be afraid of losing someone you don't even get to have."

Nigel sighs. "For a poly guy, you really need to adjust your viewpoint on possession, and if it's all down to sex, you need to step away from this mess. Just because Victor's Machiavellian and the world is hard for you, doesn't mean you're not complicit in the not-so-fun pain you're both experiencing right now."

◆

Alex, along with everyone else, watches nervously as Nigel and Liam return to the table. Neither of them looks particularly cheerful, but Nigel looks less grim than earlier. For the rest of the evening, Liam makes an effort to actually participate. Alex and Carly exchange relieved looks more than once, and Alex smiles as Paul reaches behind Carly's chair to catch his hand.

As they're leaving, Alex can only hope that Victor and Liam have a chance to clear up whatever injury this was supposed to help fix.

When they get into Alex's car, Alex turns the key in the ignition and then stops, both hands on the steering wheel. Very cautiously he turns to look at Paul. The second their eyes meet they both start laughing, nervously at first and then with more and more enthusiasm.

They've just spent an evening watching Liam fall apart, *Victor* fall apart, and a group of famous people behave dubiously in public. He and Paul weren't even the couple with the most issues for once.

"Okay, I know that was terrible," Paul says, "but what the fuck just happened?"

◆

They're still laughing by the time they get on the road, even as it's interspersed with some serious concern about Liam and general confusion about Victor. Alex relentlessly teases Paul about how flustered he was about Nigel. Which Paul supposes is fair.

"The rest of us were like, who is this asshole? And you're, like, rolling over for the pretty," Alex says as they take the turn up into their neighborhood.

Paul realizes Alex is neither jealous nor offended, just really, really amused. "Pretty isn't the word I'd use," he says.

"I've never seen you do that before. It was interesting. And probably a less bad choice than pretty much everyone else's."

Paul shrugs. "He was very compelling. But do you want to tell me what the hell you and Carly were up to?" He looks over at Alex to see him grinning at the road.

"Among other things, we decided payback was in order for the seating arrangements."

"Yeah, it's the other things I'm asking about."

"The short answer is obvious, I hope," Alex says. "The long one is actually all sorts of serious."

"Okay," Paul says. "Are we going to talk about the long one now? Because tonight was good but now I'm nervous."

"Tonight was *terrible*," Alex corrects. "The stuff I have to say isn't, but it's work, and I don't want to do it right now. I'm enjoying your company. Everyone else sucks."

Paul smiles as Alex pulls into the driveway. "I'm enjoying yours too."

"Seems like it's been a while since that's happened," Alex says without accusation.

"I don't think that's true," Paul says just as mildly.

"We haven't done it without a date, or a plan, or some effort."

"Okay, that's true," Paul acknowledges. "It shouldn't be, though."

♦

Once they get inside, Alex stops Paul with a hand on his arm before they get into the living room.

Paul waits eagerly for whatever Alex is going to say next. From the look on his face, it's going to be good.

"I had a good time tonight," Alex says. Paul would laugh at him for being facetious, but Alex is grinning and clearly means it.

"We should do this again?" Paul offers, sliding his hands around Alex's waist.

Alex giggles. "Oh my God, no. Never. Now, shh." He kisses Paul.

Paul deepens the kiss. Alex lets him for a too-short moment, then steps back. He smiles at Paul, shy and proud all at once. For once, Paul's not afraid of having hit some invisible boundary of his.

"I'll see you in the morning," Alex says before disappearing up the stairs.

Paul's shocked at how breathless he is. He's also surprised he doesn't get an invitation up to Alex's room. If there ever was a night they've earned together, it's this one. But if this is how Alex wants to play, he's content to go along with it, even if he waits pitifully for a moment to see if Alex will change his mind.

He doesn't though. Paul eventually wanders up to his own room, nudging a disgruntled Todd out of the way before the cat can sneak in.

♦

Alex is almost asleep when the yowling starts. Todd has never been thrilled about being banned from both bedrooms. He's taken out his frustration with midnight howling and scratching at their doors before. He usually gets tired of it after a few minutes, but tonight seems to be an exception. Every time Alex thinks he's stopped he hears him thunder down the stairs and then up the stairs to Paul's loft, before the yowling begins again and the whole process repeats in reverse.

The situation is absurd – and aggravating. Alex really would like to sleep without a demon running around his house. By the sixth or seventh iteration of the cat steeplechase from hell, he has had enough. He throws off the covers and storms to the door, for his own satisfaction more than any practical effect. It's not like the fucking cat cares.

"Paul!" he yells, while Todd utters a joyous mew and shoots past Alex's feet into the room. When he doesn't get a response, he just yells louder. "PAUL!"

"What?" Paul shouts as he bangs out of his bedroom.

"Your fucking cat is driving me fucking crazy," Alex shouts.

"He's your cat too!"

"It has been a very long, very hard night, and now there is a fucking hellion getting fur on my bed."

"Shouldn't've opened the door!" Paul yells back. He's clearly trying not to laugh.

Alex turns and looks back at Todd, who is happily building himself a nest in the blankets. "Paul's door is open now too," Alex says conversationally. "You could go bother him."

Todd purrs and keeps kneading the bedding. Alex sighs.

"Paul. Marion. Keane," he yells, and clomps halfway down the stairs so he can lean over the railing and see the loft. "Come get your creature out of my bed."

"Alex," Paul says, his voice softening.

"Yes?"

"Did you want to come over?"

"To your room?" Alex asks. He feels as stunned by the unprecedented invitation as he has by a dozen different things tonight, just in a much better way.

◆

Alex hasn't been in the loft bedroom since Paul moved into it. Once he's inside, he leans against the door. "I realize enough may have happened tonight that you've forgotten about me taking that fall on the rocks –"

"I haven't forgotten."

"I'm sorry about what I said." Alex fidgets with the drawstring on his sleep pants. "About the suicide thing," he clarifies.

"Thank you," Paul says. Tonight, apparently, is for discussing all the things no one could possibly want to.

"So," Alex says. "Is this a friendly chat about your cat's bad behavior, or am I spending the night?"

Paul laughs. He shouldn't let it be this easy, but he crooks a finger at Alex anyway. "Come closer and find out."

"I'm getting the impression I should lose the pants," Alex says as he shoves them off.

Paul shrugs. "I dunno, this works pretty well too," he says before grabbing Alex's hips and mouthing at his dick.

◆

After they fuck, they end up on their sides, heads together, while Paul runs a finger over the scrapes and callouses on Alex's hands.

"Do you miss how they were?" Alex says softly. The question is strange to ask. He's never liked looking soft and wound up in this whole life of his because he couldn't stand to be called a twink. Now his hands are more battered than they were from every shit job he had in high school to earn money and get away so it wouldn't matter if someone thought he was soft.

Paul shakes his head, rolling their foreheads together. "I don't like the idea that they hurt, that any of you hurts, but no. They just interest me. You interest me. It's a condition I have."

Alex smiles. From this close he can't focus on Paul's eyes. "You too. But I don't feel like that much of me is hurting right now. I got these doing some pretty amazing things."

"I know; I remember. You scare me to death half the time." Paul strokes a thumb over the back of Alex's knuckles.

"Are you getting used to that? I feel like maybe I need you to get used to that. And I don't mean like movies and interviews and stupid, creepy photo shoots that aren't even of me but, like, whatever it is the world thinks I am. I have so many more adventures and mistakes and drama in front of me. I don't want us to get back together and feel like I can't because you're all looking at me and wondering if you see husband material."

"So I can't ask you to marry me."

"You can't ask me to be a fixed point," Alex clarifies.

"What did you and Carly talk about?" Paul asks, suddenly urgent.

"We talked about that. And about how I need to keep having adventures and fucking up. And about how you're probably more okay with that than I've been willing to realize, as long as I keep you in the loop. Also about how you're a workaholic asshole, but we can't have everything," he adds.

Paul grins. "We can talk about adventures. I didn't know you thought we couldn't."

Alex shrugs. "Not to drag out the skeletons, but the Liam thing does not bring out the best in you. So I extrapolated from the data I had. I also know you're trying, and I can be okay with the Liam thing bugging you, if you can be okay with it too. Because I'm not willing to change what that friendship is. Mostly because I don't think I can."

"Oh, let's definitely talk about adventures instead," Paul says with a self-deprecating laugh.

Alex smiles. "So Carly and I talked about that idea you two cooked up at Victor's party. Mostly because that dinner was *horrible* and we were hiding and a threesome is random and more hilarious than that trainwreck was."

"Yeah?"

"Yeah. I like her. I mean, it would never occur to me, but if that's a thing you want to do, it's not something I'd want to do with someone other than her instead."

"What about with boys?" Paul asks.

"I think that's a whole different conversation."

"Agreed," Paul says with relief.

Alex laughs. "One thing at a time, and do not assume that by adventure I mean fucking. Or only mean fucking. Or mean a lot of fucking. Or something. Oh, wow, Paul, I love you, but so awkward, our lives are so awkward, and I have no idea why we've been convincing ourselves we're the normal ones in the face of all of everything that happened tonight."

Paul lifts a hand and pushes it through Alex's hair. "I love you too. Normal is relative, but I still kind of feel like we have a lock on it anyway."

"But the *awkward*."

"Yeah, definitely awkward. So is this Carly thing something you're actually interested in, or are you just trying to be generous?"

"I'm not going to fuck someone I don't want to fuck," Alex says. Paul needs to get his head around that, and also start believing Alex when he says things. About anything.

"Well, obviously." Paul's equally spiky. "But have you been

thinking about it?"

"I just had this conversation with her," Alex points out. "Also, I am offering you a threesome, and you are being difficult."

"I'm trying to prevent us from making bad choices."

"Yeah, and that's how we got into this mess," Alex says. "Look, doing this with her feels safer while we're still a little bit fragile and not fixed. Like it's allowed to cause problems, and so that way, maybe it won't? I want a trashy dumb Hollywood experience to brag about, although I never will. I want to see things about you you'll never tell me. And I want everything we do to only involve people we actually like regardless of whether it's in bed or not. So yeah, Carly."

"And I want us to have ill-advised adventures," Paul says with a smile. "So do you want to call her, or should I?"

"I've passed my quota of brave about this," Alex says, pressing his face into Paul's shoulder. "It's all you now."

34

anging out at Gemma's house is always strange for Alex because Gemma's house is Paul's house. He's never gotten over the cognitive dissonance of seeing his best friend living in a place that holds such critical memories for him.

"Can we not?" he asks as Gemma dumps the popcorn into a bowl and starts toward the stairs to what is now her bedroom.

She gives him a judgmental look. "Roommate night, Alex, we need the popcorn."

"No, not that. The popcorn's fine."

"What is it?" Gemma props a hand on her hip and gives him a curious and concerned look. "You've been off all night, is everything okay with you?"

"I'm fine," Alex says shortly. He really does not want to have to explain his current aversion to hanging out in her bedroom. Particularly considering the topic he's certain they're going to end up discussing. As uncomfortable as it makes him, that's part of the reason he's here.

"Okay. What gives?" Gemma asks, as Alex takes the bowl off her and heads into the living room instead. It takes several rounds of badgering on Gemma's part and prevarications on Alex's before he finally starts to stammer out the story.

"I don't get famous, I don't get rich, *and* I don't get to have a threesome? This shit is getting seriously annoying," Gemma says. "I also don't know if I'm hurt or relieved you didn't choose me."

"Shut up."

"Promise that if it were you and Liam, it would have been me?"

"OH MY GOD, SHUT UP." Alex knows she's teasing. He can laugh at the suggestion in a way he wouldn't have been able to in the past, but he still feels embarrassed and vulnerable. Gemma knows he has none of the power and confidence he pretends to in this world.

She cackles and digs for more popcorn. "We would have been really hot."

"Gemma," Alex says warningly.

"Okay, okay. So, like, are you just here to confess or do you have questions about pussy?"

Alex looks around for a throw pillow to hide in. "Everything you told me about anal sex was wrong. At least make up for that and be useful now?"

"That was perfectly good information."

"It really wasn't. Just – no."

"So." Gemma's grin is evil. "What do you need to know?"

◆

Paul lifts his hand to knock at Carly's apartment. "How are you doing?" he asks.

Alex is saved from having to declare how awkward he feels when Carly answers the door with a ridiculous come-hither pose and two full shot glasses balanced in one hand. "Drinks, boys?" she says in a voice as ridiculous as her pose.

Paul laughs, and Alex grins at her. Silly isn't what he imagined for this encounter, but that might be the tone that makes it work.

"Wouldn't want to leave you without," Paul says even as he liberates them from her clutches and passes one back to Alex as they walk into the apartment. Alex is grateful for the at least momentary distraction from the business at hand.

"I think I can handle pre-gaming in my own house, thanks," she says as they knock back the drinks.

"Where's Liam?" Alex asks. He doesn't want or expects him here. He just wants everyone accounted for.

"Was he invited?" Carly raises an amused eyebrow at him.

"You know what I mean."

"He's at Victor's. Negotiating."

"What's that supposed to mean?" Alex asks.

"Depends how it goes, doesn't it? Now," she says, taking charge again. "Are you okay?"

"I get less okay every time someone asks. Otherwise, I'm fine."

"Excellent. Do I need to be a good host or can you and Paul just, like, make out and be hot? I mean, unless there are any more logistics we haven't covered?"

Alex shakes his head. She and Paul have been through all their various agreements and concerns regarding this evening pretty exhaustively. Largely because of Alex's insistence on not engaging that process and everyone's willingness to humor him.

"No, and thank you for the tequila, but this is really awkward," Alex says.

"It'll pass."

Alex gives her a look.

"What, do you want me and Paul to make out instead?"

Alex nods, a little bit frantic and a little bit nervous. He retreats into an armchair, folding his legs up under him.

Carly gives him a suit-yourself shrug and holds a hand out to Paul. He looks at Alex a little nervously.

"I'll tell you if I'm not fine," Alex says. Paul's assumption that he is going to be unable to handle the sight of Paul making out with Carly because of jealousy is annoying.

"Paul," Carly says sharply. "One of the ways you prove you can respect *no* is by respecting *yes*."

Alex has to stop himself from slapping the arm of the chair and shouting *thank you*. Finally, someone gets it.

"Are you saying yes?" Paul flirts with her.

"Actually, I think I'm saying I'm impatient, and I haven't made out with you in a really long time."

Alex finds the sight completely bizarre. He's never really thought of Paul being with someone who wasn't him. The whole debacle with Craig was something he's avoided thinking about entirely. Meanwhile, Paul's history with Carly is something he's wondered about, but has very little information on.

Paul takes up a lot more space than Carly. Alex is fascinated by how instantly they look like every heterosexual narrative in every TV show or movie he's never cared about. But it's also weird how much they don't. They're both his people in a way; no matter what they are doing with each other, renders them always and deeply queer to him.

Carly is either naturally a talker too or knows how to play Paul. Alex can't tell. As soon as his mouth drifts to her jaw and her neck, she's narrating to him what Alex looks like watching them. The whole thing is a bit *turtles all the way down*, and Alex really needs to know what to do next. Because while he can picture Paul sitting here jerking off to him and Carly making out, he's not so sure that's going to work for him in reverse.

She must be able to sense something of his uncertainty. Before long she stops Paul with a hand on his chest and crooks a finger at Alex. "If you want, baby boy. He's all yours."

Alex is saved the trouble of pointing out that that is not quite the point by Paul, who turns his head to smile at him. "C'mere, Alex. Time for something new."

Bizarre as this situation is, Paul always has pushed Alex past his comfort zone in the best of ways. And that is the point. So Alex goes.

Kissing Carly is different. Her mouth seems so small he's not even really sure how to kiss her. Also, although Alex has never noticed it before, she's short, which is just a hassle. Mostly, losing himself to a moment that is all about asking himself, over and over again, if he's feeling what he's supposed to feel, is a challenge. He finds himself grateful that he spent so much of high school hiding from everyone with work and surliness. To have had to fake this at sixteen would have been a type of misery he's committed to working hard to never imagine.

The warm weight of Paul pressed against his back, though, is another matter entirely. Things may be better between them, but they're still not sharing space or fucking as much as Alex wants, and he feels hyper-aware of everywhere Paul is. He shivers when Paul kisses the back of his neck. Paul whispering in Alex's ear about how Alex and Carly look together is the least surprising thing in the world. It's also incredibly hot.

While it's not quite like a switch has been flipped, Alex finds it impossible not to follow Paul's directions when he tells Alex to start undressing her. Carly, however, must sense whatever hesitation remains and takes a step back.

"You fumbling with my bra like any of us is in high school is decidedly not sexy," she says with a laugh. "I should get naked. And you two should make out and then join me."

She stalks off into her bedroom.

"Carly's nice," Alex says to Paul dopily.

"You're really relieved about the bra thing, aren't you?"

Alex nods vigorously.

It takes a while for the awkward to pass. What ultimately helps the most though, is Alex realizing that none of this is any more awkward than the first time he slept with Paul. He's not even as drunk. It should be weirder, and it just isn't.

Besides, once he's naked and between them, the whole idea of *threesome* feels like a misnomer, because it's all about him. Carly and Paul are absolutely focused on keeping him interested, and he is very interested indeed.

If Paul has consistently been about getting Alex close and pulling him back from the edge since the very first time they hooked up, this is a thousand times worse. Everything Alex's body wants is at a price, many of them easy to provide. If he stops kissing Carly, Paul stops touching his dick. If he wants more or faster or harder, or Paul's fingers grazing over his hole, he better be paying attention to far more than Carly's mouth.

Eventually, Alex stops asking for things with words or whines. He's painfully hard and he'll go where he's put and do as he's told because he has no sense left to think of any reason not to. Paul always gets Alex where he wants to go. Eventually.

When Paul presses Alex's head down between Carly's spread legs and tells him to lick, that he's damn well going to make her come before he even gets to beg for anything for himself, he almost comes right then and there. The only thing that stops him is Paul yanking hard on his balls and Carly's delighted laugh. For half a second the laughter and the drunken ridiculousness of it all makes Alex thinks of Liam.

Going down on a girl is unfamiliar and a little strange, but Carly is responsive and Paul is encouraging. He strokes his thumb along the back of Alex' neck and up into his hair while he keeps up the filthy litany.

After Carly comes, Paul drags Alex back up by the hair and kisses him wet and deep. Alex whimpers. He is ready to come himself right the fuck now.

"Paul, please," he manages.

◆

"What do you want?" Paul asks.

Alex just whimpers in response.

"Do you want to fuck me, baby boy?" Carly asks.

Paul cracks up and leans his forehead against Alex's shoulder. He's not surprised when Alex says *yes*. Alex never does anything halfway.

He helps Alex with the condom, both because Alex is too lost to everything to focus on anything and for the gasp Alex gives when Paul runs his fingers down Alex's dick.

"You want me to get on top?" Carly asks.

Alex shakes his head. Paul flops down next to Carly with a laugh. "He's very predictable."

"Not predictable," Carly chides. She tugs Alex closer and reaches between their legs to guide him into her. "The rest should be easy, sweetheart."

Alex swears.

◆

Easy is too small a word for it, Alex thinks. Because yes, the act is familiar, but it's also different and really at this point all that matters is that he's fucking someone. That he's fucking a girl he'll freak out about later. Right now, he's just pissed off that Paul and Carly are too busy kissing each other to kiss him while he pumps into her.

Alex doesn't realize he's said as much out loud until Carly giggles. Paul leans up on an elbow to kiss Alex. Everything is perfect then, if not as sex, than as attention.

After Alex comes, he wants nothing more than to curl up in the warmth of Carly's bed and pass out. Processing this can wait until. Carly, however, is having none of it.

"You're heavy," she says after letting him rest for a moment. She taps her fingers against his back. "We've also been neglecting Paul."

Alex lifts his head briefly and snorts.

"Mmmmm, none of that." Carly shifts Alex off of her. She gives a little gasp as Alex slips out. "You want it to be like before?" she coos at him. "You want me to tell you what to do?"

She helps Alex find his knees and guides his face down between Paul's legs. Paul makes an obscene sound.

"I know you can go deeper than that," Carly says with a wink to

Paul. She presses Alex's head down to suck Paul's dick until he chokes on it.

Alex whimpers and mewls, and Carly doesn't let up in her narration. It's exactly what gets Paul off and exactly what helps Alex disappear in the best way he knows how.

◆

After Paul comes, Alex flops down face-first into the pillows and lies there, apparently dazed with it all. Then before he curls up small and pressing his face against Carly's side as Paul rubs his back.

"He gets like this sometimes," Paul says softly after a few minutes of the puzzling intensity that sometimes rolls off Alex after sex.

"You okay there, baby boy?" Carly asks Alex. She gets little more than half a nod and a vague sound, before he presses against her tighter while fumbling for Paul's arm. He clutches it too tight around him once he has it. Paul's heart melts.

Carly looks at Paul, her face thoughtful. "He's ridiculously lovely. I'm sure you know that, though."

Of course Paul knows that. It's one of the central facts of his existence. But he still has concerns. "He worries me, sometimes, when he's like this."

Carly frowns at him. "That's because you're an idiot and trust neither your judgment nor his. You're smarter than Paul, aren't you?" She turns her attention back to Alex.

He nods against her.

"You stay down there as long as you need," she says to him. "We've got you, and I know you feel real nice right now. You were so good for us."

Paul watches her with a little bit of awe, a little bit of desire, and more discomfort than is useful. She meets his eyes briefly but says nothing. She returns her attention to Alex until he seems to relax into the bed, probably more interested in sleep than care.

"So," Carly says, pulling her hair out of her face. "You two are lovely and hot and all sorts of sexy, but, wow, could I use a cigarette."

"Go for it." Paul shrugs.

"Would if I could," Carly says.

"Did you seriously leave cigarettes off your shopping list for this adventure?"

"Pregnant!" Carly blurts.

Alex snorts comically and lifts his head out of Carly's side to gape. Paul stares but recovers faster. "Seriously?"

"No, I just wanted to see your reactions. Yes, seriously, asshole," she grins.

"Jesus Christ, Carly," Paul shakes his head. Alex still looks dumbstruck. "Congratulations." He feels no jealousy; the relationship he and Carly had was a long time ago. He pats himself on the back mentally for not being weird about the situation.

"Thank you," she says to Paul before turning her attention to Alex. "Don't worry, honey. It's not yours. You can go back to sleep."

Alex chuckles and grumbles something about not having failed high school biology before closing his eyes and snuggling against her side again.

"I feel like every single thing I want to say is going to sound really rude," Paul says.

"No, it wasn't planned; yes, my tits are bigger; yes, we are kind of freaking out. Good thing I haven't bought a wedding dress yet!" Carly supplies for him.

"Is Liam okay?" Alex mumbles from beside her.

Carly shrugs. "He's afraid the baby's gonna be like him. Otherwise, yeah."

Alex snorts. "Payback's a bitch."

Paul smiles. There is something sweet and satisfying about the idea of a frazzled Liam facing down his own peculiar offspring.

"Yeah, something like that. We're moving up the wedding, too, so there's full-on logistics battles on all fronts."

"Oh, hey, that's awesome," Paul says. "Have you got a date now?"

"Not yet. Before I might accidentally deliver from excitement. Soon."

"Well, if you need any help."

"Appreciate the thought, but you are way too fucking busy. I'm not marrying into this fucked up life not to be able to pay to make my problems go away."

"Does anyone else know yet?" Paul asks, still trying to get his head around this.

"You mean when are we putting out a press release?" The subject is obviously a touchy one.

"Victor," Alex mumbles by way of translation for Paul.

"Oh. Of course," Carly says.

"How did that go?" Paul asks. As much as he and Victor are increasingly friends, there's a part of Paul that can't help imagining Victor as a particularly petulant housecat determined to suck the breath and soul out of anything that would compete with him for his household's affection. The disaster of the late dinner party aside.

"He's worried about Liam a little, but he's more or less over the moon. God, don't look so surprised. It's a baby, not a cancellation notice. He's not actually evil."

"No, he's just the devil," Alex mutters. "What if he eats it?"

Carly pinches Alex's arm. "You were at dinner," she says. "He's family. For you too. Whether you like it or not."

"The interference is toxic," Alex says.

"It comes from a place of caring."

"Alex isn't wrong," Paul says.

"What authority does he have over you? Any toxic is your own fault in acquiescing where you're not comfortable," she says.

"Not allowed to say no," Alex mumbles. Over his back, Paul gives Carly a significant look.

Carly ignores it in favor of tapping Alex on the shoulder. "Alex," she says, fond but stern. "You have this whole life of yours because you said no at the right time. Don't you get your signals crossed, too."

"You don't understand," he says petulantly.

"I'm a girl. You're never gonna know more about yes and no than me, no matter who or what you think Victor is."

"And to think," Paul says. He wonders if he'll ever stop loving and admiring these two people. "We just came for the sex."

♦

Liam's barefoot when he finally makes himself pad out of his bedroom and into Victor's kitchen. He's drawn by the sound of pans banging around unnecessarily. Victor wants him to get up and doesn't particularly know how to start, or finish, the confrontation from last night.

"Hey. Sorry I was such an asshole last night," Liam says, leaning his hip against the kitchen island.

"I see someone has remembered how to use their words," Victor says snidely.

Liam has no idea if he means to be cruel, or if this is one of those things Victor would say to anyone but lands harder for Liam because of the realities of his life.

"Yeah, thankfully," Liam says as if the remark was merely a casual observation. Last night sucked, and he really doesn't feel like fighting anymore.

Victor opens a cupboard to fish around for some ingredient or other. "I think we're going to have to start doing things differently."

Liam frowns and picks up the metronome sitting on the counter. Victor may not be the only writer to write to a steady beat, but Liam is pretty sure he's the only one that uses an actual physical metronome to find his pacing. And not the electronic kind: The old-fashioned sort that by any measure should live on Victor's piano, not his desk. He slides the little weight up the rod to a tempo he knows Victor likes and sets it going.

Victor looks over his shoulder at him. Liam shrugs.

"In what way?" Liam asks. "That sounds ominous." His own

desire to do things differently with Victor had fueled some of last night's terrible; Victor's reluctance to discuss it in any way that had made sense to Liam had fueled the rest.

"Not ominous," Victor reassures him. "But we've both been navigating this issue poorly for months. Since I had to point out to that you getting married was going to change the way you do things with all of the people in your life."

"It doesn't *need* to change anything." Liam is getting exhausted having to point this out.

"No, perhaps not, but things are changing regardless. And now your wedding's getting moved up, you're miserable out of my bed, and I'm miserable with you in it."

Liam's frown deepens. The night he'd spent in bed with Victor after filming Zach's death had been hard, but Victor's care had been vital to him.

"Under ordinary circumstances," Victor adds. "But those facts remain, so we find an arrangement that suits both of us. So if you have a list of what you need from me, now's the time."

"Okay." Liam nods along as he processes all of that. "One. I need to be useful to you. That's hard with you because you're you, and I get that that's how you work even if I don't understand it. It's fine, but it is hard. Two, I need to be able to touch you, because that's how *I* work. You not letting me do that because you're afraid of what else I'll want doesn't make things easier for either of us." Liam frowns at the metronome in his hand, and moves the slider down to make it run faster.

"Three, I have no idea what's changing with this relationship, but something is and has been since Carly and I got engaged. We even talked about it, ages ago, or at least you started the conversation and then went into denial about what, I don't even know. So I need you to acknowledge that this is changing and be specific about what you need and want from me. Also, stop acting like whatever is changing with us is the end of the world. It's not, and you freaking out is freaking me out."

♦

Liam's litany is thorough. He doesn't seem annoyed or spooked anymore. Those are both very good things. But in this moment Victor is impressed most with Liam's capacity to want and feel without any sort of shame at all. It's beautiful, and it's frightening. His confidence – when he's not having a meltdown – in his ability to navigate a situation that's left Victor so often utterly at sea is nothing short of inspiring.

"Okay." Victor turns on a burner under the pan.

"Okay?"

"Yes, something's shifted. Yes, I haven't known what to do about it, and yes, I've made a hash of it every time I've tried to talk to you about it. I am twice your age. I didn't expect to have to reexamine all sorts of things I comfortably deemed irrelevant decades ago."

"Thank you," Liam says, sincere in a way that would be surprising from anyone else.

"I know you hate change, Liam, but that's how people are. They change more than you want or not enough. And you just have to live with it; you have to live with it in yourself and your circumstances too. I need to remember that too, but I'm also never going to be exactly who you want me to be."

"I don't –"

"You do. And I can live with that if you can. So here's the plan."

"Okay." Liam smiles. "What?"

"Take some massage classes. And then you can touch and be useful in the way you need to be, because the stress of this life is going to kill me," Victor says with a laugh.

"I'm going to assume you don't mean *massage* euphemistically," Liam says.

Victor gives him a look. "You know enough to not have to assume."

"Yeah, but I'm not sure you do? Or, like, you did, and now you don't anymore?"

"The rather large space between desiring you and desiring to make you happy hasn't gotten smaller, Liam. Just a little bit more complicated."

Liam shrugs. "Complicated is fine."

"Don't get overexcited," Victor warns. "I'm not always sure, for someone who sleeps with as many people as you do, why you're still here. I adore you, but your sudden bursts of wanting to be the exception to even more rules than you already are is a bit more than I can take."

"I said I was sorry about last night."

"I know, and I appreciate it. Now, if you don't have any other questions, would you care to tell me why I am not currently making breakfast for Carly as well?"

When Liam tells Victor where Carly is, Victor stares and then shakes his head. Yelling about it will do no good, and it's none of his business anyway, but his people never do stop surprising him. Carly will be over later, Liam says.

"She's so fucking amazing," Liam says. Victor nods, very fond, as Liam goes on. "I wish this all were less hard on her."

"The wedding, the baby, or both?"

"The wedding, mostly. She's so much better about the baby than I am."

"Have you made a decision yet?"

Victor sees Liam fold back in on himself and hopes he hasn't done any terrible damage so soon after, mostly, fixing things. "Please stop expecting me to have second thoughts. We're calling it a baby, after all," he says. "If I weren't so worried, I'd be happy. You know that. It'll get better."

◆

After they leave Carly's, Paul and Alex go out for brunch, just the two of them. Alex thinks that having some time on neutral ground is a good idea. But also, he's enjoying simply spending time with Paul. He's barely aware of anyone or anything else as they grin at each other over coffee and share a newspaper.

"So what do we do when we get home?" Paul finally asks.

"Shower. Nap," Alex says lazily. He can't think much beyond that.

"Yeah, but where?" Paul presses.

"We're not going to move back in together the day after one of our crazier joint adventures." He's not surprised that Paul is trying to broach the topic. But he's also not going to budge on the reasonable boundaries they've established.

"Why not?" Paul asks. He stirs his coffee with his straw, not looking at Alex.

"Because I want to sleep. And process. I've got too much to think about as it is without worrying about making the right choice about where you keep your toothbrush."

"I don't want to be your roommate forever," Paul says. "Even a very romantic roommate."

"I know," Alex says softly. "We'll talk about it. Just not today? Because last night I fucked a girl, and now we're having brunch. Everything is very strange and, at the moment, very good."

"I worry about us not talking about things again."

"Believe me, we are not tabling the question indefinitely." He drops his voice, and Paul grins as Alex leans forward enough to be heard. "But oh my God, Paul, you talked me into a threesome. Waiting twenty-four hours for me to deal with that before we talk about our living arrangements is the least you can do."

◆

Carly breezes into Victor's house and slides a box of Krispy Kremes onto the counter along with a fast food bag.

"Did you seriously bring donuts and a burrito into my house?" Victor asks as she gives Liam a loud smacking kiss on the mouth.

"Did you cook anything for me?" she asks, looking at their half-finished meal.

"You know I don't seat late-comers."

"Liam, do you want to surrender the rest of the fried polenta rings to me?" Carly asks.

Liam shakes his head and pulls his plate closer.

Carly cackles. "Hence burrito. We can all share the donuts, even though I need my energy."

"Is that about the baby or the threesome?" Victor drawls.

Carly smacks Liam's arm. "You told."

"You were gonna tell," he says with a shrug.

"Maybe. And now I've missed all the fun. Victor, are you judging me?"

"Always. Mostly you kids and your heartbreaking waste of your low-sleep lives confuse me," he says drily.

"Yeah, but you love us anyway," Liam grins.

Victor grunts.

Carly pulls up the stool next to Liam's. "What else did you boys talk about? Anything I should know? Or brace myself for?"

"No, I don't think so," Liam says softly. Carly thinks that the fact he smiles at Victor as he says it says a lot.

"Well," Carly says in the face of whatever Liam will likely tell her later in private. "Tell me about something." She unwraps the burrito and takes a bite.

"How's the wedding planning?" Victor says benignly.

"Oh my God, Liam, can we just go to city hall with a roll of quarters, because I am sort of over this entire thing."

"If you want. My parents – and my team – will kill me, but like, whatever."

"What's the problem?" Victor asks.

"You ever try renting a venue for a wedding not sixteen months in advance?" Carly asks.

"Remarkably, Carly, no."

"Well, it's impossible."

"You could do it here," Victor says with a shrug.

"Excuse me?"

"Outside. It's not like I don't rent tents and hire caterers for other things. When do you want to do it?"

"Whoa whoa whoa whoa, *No*," she says. "Why did I buy you donuts?"

"Because you live dangerously."

Carly snorts. "No. Because your territory, your rules. I appreciate the offer, really, but this wedding thing is complicated and difficult enough and involves a whole lot of delicate egos as it is before we bring non-neutral ground into it."

"That's fine. If you're not going to do it here, there are favors I can call in. It's just like booking a location. Network knows, I do that on short notice all the time. Did you have anything particular in mind?"

<h1 style="text-align:center">35</h1>

The viewing party for what Alex and Paul have privately been calling the Dead Zach Episode is small. Of the people involved in having shot the more grueling parts of the episode, Victor is the only one with any enthusiasm for it at all.

Alex feels uneasy about being back in Victor's house – this time with low lights, candles, and hors d'oeuvres. He and Liam make wary eye-contact as they work the room. There are barely more than thirty people present, mostly connected to the show. But there's also a journalist there who will be, as far as Alex is concerned, getting only a scoop on him and Liam refusing to watch the episode. He and Liam have already made a pact to step outside for the duration of it.

When he'd told Paul of the plan in the car on the way over, Paul had frowned thoughtfully. "That'll make great apocrypha."

Alex had refrained from saying just how much that made him sound like Victor.

At one point, Alex ends up in a corner with Carly, who's staying out of the crowd and keeping an eye on Liam. Talking with her after recent events isn't awkward at all, which both surprises and gratifies Alex. Everyone, it seems, is going to continue being an adult about that adventure. Which makes Alex feel better about future adventures. In the meantime, Alex is happy to get a hug and three minutes blessedly free of conversation from Carly before he returns to the fray.

Victor is in his element, simultaneously mingling and keeping an eye on his smartphone for whatever social media he's tracking. Alex is sure the internet is already humming in anticipation. He himself has spent a decent chunk of the last week doing media for this episode. Victor's incredibly sketchy secret filming process has been successful: There have been no leaks or spoilers. Alex has taken much delight in telling interviewers and fandom that everyone should watch tonight because huge things are happening for Zach and James and their relationship.

Paul, out of some perverse curiosity, has spent the last week trawling the hashtags for the best of the internet's irrational hopes, dreams, and demands. Alex is far more amused than annoyed. Particularly because Paul hasn't been weird or jealous or anything about Alex and Liam. According to Paul's research, fandom is torn between wanting an engagement or an *I love you*. As much as that pisses Alex off on its own – of the many regrets either James or Zach have, never saying that is not one of them — he can't help but laugh at the wariness with which Paul conveyed this information. Zach and James are fictional. Their relationship, and what the fans want it to be, have no bearing on how Alex feels about whatever mess he and Paul are almost, if not entirely, out of.

♦

"How are you two doing?" Victor asks Paul. Paul startles out of his reverie. Alex is engaged in being sharply charming with someone, and Paul gave up on making his own rounds to watch him fondly.

"I notice you're asking about both of us and not just him," Paul says.

"That's because you're both a mess, and you both still worry me."

"Victor," Paul says, amused and almost but not quite chiding. Victor seems amused. "We're hardly that bad."

"Are you living together yet?"

"Victor."

"What?"

"We share a house. We have always shared a house."

"And a bed?"

"Not your business," Paul says, taken aback. Will Victor ever stop prying? "And last I checked, not your interest."

"You're sleeping with Liam's fiancée. Terribly much my business."

"I disagree. So would Carly," Paul says. "Also, not an ongoing concern."

"Glad as I am to hear it, the question stands."

Paul tries to calculate Alex's possible reactions to anything he says to Victor on this subject ever. "We're working on it," he finally says.

"Work harder," Victor says sternly.

"Oh my God, Victor, sometimes relationships are actually difficult."

Victor looks unconvinced. "You are not telling me anything I don't already know. But you two are making things harder for yourselves than they need to be, and that is simply an absurd waste of effort and potential."

Paul rubs his temple. "Why do you care so much?"

"Because you people are what I have."

♦

At ten to the hour, the room starts to shuffle into seating arrangements in front of the TV. Paul nabs a seat on the couch, and Carly slides in between him and the arm of the couch. Alex walks behind them. He squeezes Paul's shoulder briefly and gives him a little smile. Liam's standing at the door out to the back patio, holding a plate heaped with food. Alex grabs a bottle of wine and two glasses off the sideboard, and together the two of them disappear outside.

Paul thinks he's the only one who sees them go until Carly chuckles softly.

"What?" Paul whispers as Victor takes his own seat and the noise level in the room plummets.

"Thank God those two have each other."

Paul grunts and shifts a little so Ellen can sit down on the other side of him.

"Don't be like that," Carly says, amused but sharp. "I wouldn't want to put up with Liam tonight. Or Alex."

"Speaking as his significant other," Paul starts.

Carly tilts her head to the TV, which Victor has just flicked on. "Hush until you see it. Stop being an asshole, and be glad Alex has a battle buddy."

"Why, have you seen it?"

Carly shakes her head. "Liam told me."

Paul wants to know more about that, but before he can ask anything, he's cut off by the sudden score of the episode's smash opening.

♦

"So what have you been up to?" Liam asks Alex after they get themselves situated at the cafe table out by the pool. He's clearly trying to have, or at least start, a normal conversation. Alex is both surprised and glad. He's had nothing like a normal conversation with Liam in weeks.

Alex picks at the plate Liam's carried out. "Climbing. Media. Looking for work. Trying not to freak out about the last thing any more than I generally am."

"Any good options?"

"Some. I'll know for sure soon. It's not like I can really say anything officially anyway until this is done," Alex nods back toward the house. He's so close now.

"It's cool you're doing new stuff."

"Yeah?" Alex asks.

"Yeah. Like, I love doing *Fourth* and working with Victor. I miss working with you. But like, you wanted something and you're gonna get it. Go you." Liam grins as he reaches for the bottle to uncork it.

They talk quietly for a while about how Alex's movie plans are making things hard with Paul even as other things between them are getting better. Then they talk about Liam's frightened excitement about the baby and more uncomplicated happiness for the wedding.

After about half an hour, the door to the living room slides open. Victor leans out to call to them. "Liam. Alex."

"Yeah?" Liam answers, staring at the glass in his hand.

"You're up. Come see your moment of triumph."

Absolutely not. Alex turns to look at Liam, who turns to look at him at the same time. They both say, "No."

"Was there something you missed about the hiding in your backyard part?" Alex adds. He wants to be very clear and also rub in, again, how awful that filming experience was for both him and Liam.

"You've earned this," Victor says. There's that same peculiar blend of command and pride in his voice that Alex remembers hazily from their discussion when he was in the hospital with heatstroke.

"No," Liam says. He grabs Alex's hand on the table. "We've earned *this*."

Victor disappears back inside with a shrug, sliding the door closed behind him. Alex can tell by the shift of sound that the episode's back on and that everyone is watching raptly. He can hear his own voice on the TV.

"Want to take a walk?" he asks Liam.

Liam nods rapidly.

Together, they wander over to the far side of the pool, far enough away from the door that they can't hear anything. Alex sits down by the fence and Liam flops onto his back and stares up at the sky. When Alex asks him what he's looking at, Liam starts telling him about the constellations he can see, the ones they can't because of pollution, and the various legends that go with all of them.

"How do you know all this stuff?" Alex asks eventually.

Liam shrugs. "You have books. I have people who like to tell me things."

♦

Paul has kept up with watching *Fourth* when he has time, both out of fondness for the show he's spent so much of his life working on, and for the pleasure of watching Alex do what he's so amazing at. At times, that's been awkward. Certainly, he had not handled the James and Zach love scene earlier this year well.

Tonight is a different kind of experience entirely. He's well aware, yet again, that it's all fiction; he knows that Alex shot his parts for this right downstairs in this very house. But Alex had said *remember it wasn't acting* and then had fallen apart when he had gotten home that night. So watching Zach's torture on its own would be disturbing enough, but watching it knowing that it's actually *Alex* breathless and crazed with fear is very close to unbearable.

Carly finds his hand and squeezes it wordlessly.

From his throne, Victor is bathed in the glow of too many screens, solemnly and eagerly watching as much of the reaction of the audience in real time as he can. For all that Paul's been glad to count Victor as a friend, even an often meddling one, all he can see now is someone who took the trust and faith of his people and made them do *this*.

The journalist – Jennie? Jacquie? Paul can't remember – is clearly not happy that her prime subjects aren't actually in the room for her to get a look at their faces while the episode is airing. Paul's never been more sympathetic to Alex's reticence in public than he is right now. She drifts around the edge of the room to the window, through which Alex and Liam are probably vaguely visible. It's really fucking creepy.

When the show goes to commercial, everyone sits quiet and dazed in the interval. Before Paul can say or do something stupid, Carly tugs his hand and whispers in his ear to *go get a girl a drink, already*. Paul feels bad that the best he can do for her is seltzer with a twist.

When the episode is finally over, all Paul can hear is everyone in the room breathing. The atmosphere is incredibly eerie. Even if he had been watching alone and had never known Alex, seeing Zach tortured – psychologically and physically – and then shot in the head is the type of TV that would have forced him out of the house for a run. That's not an option he has right now, unfortunately.

"How could you do that to them?" Paul says softly.

"And Paul speaks for America," Victor says, tapping away at his laptop. When Paul goes to look over his shoulder, it's open to his social media deck, where Victor is probably twisting the knife into the audience with several incredibly injudicious tweets. His username is @TheShowYouHate.

"I still can't believe that's your fucking Twitter handle," Paul says.

"I know. You'd think people would be less surprised when I do things they don't like."

"You're such an ass," Paul says. His tone is good-natured, because they're in public, but he absolutely means it.

"We're going to win all the awards for that," Victor says. "Your boy is going to win all the awards for that."

"He better," Paul says.

"He's also going to be able to do whatever work he wants."

"Less of a comfort than you think," Paul says darkly.

"Feisty," Victor says. He turns to the room at large. "Does someone want to go retrieve the men of the hour and tell them it's safe to come back?"

♦

Liam is in the middle of recounting what Alex thinks is a Greek legend about Cassiopeia when Alex's phone rings. It's Gemma, and he picks up only because she's on his very short list of people he'd remotely consider talking to tonight.

"What's up, Gem?"

"Alex?" she asks. Her voice small.

"Yeah. Are you okay?"

Liam rolls his head over to frown worriedly at Alex. Alex shrugs.

"Yeah, I'm fine. I just….Are you?" she stammers.

"Gemma, why the hell wouldn't I be okay?"

"Mhmm. I know. But I watched the episode…."

Alex has to swallow the entirely inappropriate urge to laugh, especially given his own reaction to filming the episode. "Gemma. It's a TV show," he says as gently as he can.

"I know," Gemma says again. Alex swears he can hear her sniffle. "I just wanted to hear your voice."

"Well, I'm fine." His phone beeps with another incoming call. Alex pulls it away from his ear to look at it in surprise. "Hey, I've got another call, but I'll talk to you later, okay?"

"Yeah, okay."

Alex switches over to the next call with something between amusement and trepidation. Liam plays with Alex's shoelace.

"Hi, Mom."

"Hello, Alex. How are you doing tonight?"

Alex lets his head slump back against the fence. "I didn't know you even watched *Fourth*."

◆

"I'm never, ever going to watch it, you know," Alex says when he and Paul are driving home. It's after midnight. Alex has to be up in less than five hours for morning media on the East Coast.

"You're really good," Paul says. "You probably should."

"Yeah, well, one night of disturbing phone calls from all my friends has been quite enough, thanks. Plus, Liam and I have a pact."

"What are you going to do when they run that clip all through awards season?"

"Don't."

"Don't what?"

"Start spouting Victor's shit about this being my ticket to everything or bitching about Liam or whatever it is you're going to do." He can't take any more of that. Not from Victor, and especially not from Paul.

"You *were* really good," Paul says. "And I know you have good reason to have your hackles up right now, but don't. Because God, the shit I wanted to say to Victor."

"Yeah?" Alex is a little pleased at the thought of Paul defending his honor on this particular point.

"Oh yeah," Paul says. "You're not the only one who's ever wanted to take a swing at him."

"Sure," Alex says. "But I'm still the only one who has."

36

The media stuff is hard. Some of the hardest Alex has ever done, because he has to balance his own glee at the secret having been kept successfully with the grief, shock, and anger of strangers. Morning shows read him the sort of tweets he's been trying to avoid. Female journalists talk about crying, male ones talk about their wives crying, and everyone wants to know what it was like to shoot. He can't tell the truth any more than he can say, softly, that he'd really prefer not to answer the question. When Liam comes up, he reminds people about how TV magic works. None of that was filmed concurrently. Anything anyone wants to know about Liam, they'll have to ask him.

Which they're having a hard time doing. Liam, for once, skips the limelight. Alex can hardly blame him; having those clips playing everywhere is really not fun. Alex averts his eyes when they're shown if they're on monitors in the studio with him. He and Liam have a promise, and even if it's bordering on petty, he intends to keep it. While Alex is willing to take the brunt of the media attention, Liam's absence doesn't go unnoticed or unremarked on.

The internet is flat-out awful. The fans who think Liam is avoiding everything because he can't bear to talk about his lover being tortured aren't entirely wrong. Which doesn't make the situation any easier to deal with. Liam gets accused of cowardice and of abandoning a friend in a difficult time; Alex gets accused of stealing the spotlight from Liam in his greatest hour and for the worst sort of ingratitude when he doesn't express regret at leaving *The Fourth Estate*.

When he says *Zach is mine now, I get to keep him* to a talk show host, the fandom explodes with rage. Victor sends Alex a congratulatory text. *Right now everyone hates you more than they hate me. Quite the achievement.*

Paul is considerate, soothing, and interested in all of it, often to an extent Alex has to remind himself to find charming. So much of it feels like Paul angling to declare the relationship drama of the last six months over. As much as Alex is willing to do that, he's skeptical of whether the way to do it to return to the way things were. After all, the separate lives, same house, awesome slumber party thing seems to be working out pretty well. Even if Todd objects.

◆

When Alex suggests that being partners with separate bedrooms might be the best way to go forward, Paul is calm, communicative, and having absolutely none of it.

"Lots of artists do it," Alex tells him. They got home late from work, fucked, and are now down in the kitchen, scrounging leftovers for a well-past-midnight snack. Alex is sitting at the island, shirtless in pajama pants and tapping a fork into a Tupperware container. He's absolutely adorable, but he also looks entirely serious when he says, "We're not easy people."

"How many nights have we spent together this week?" Paul asks, shutting the refrigerator door.

Alex shrugs. His shoulders are lovely and dotted with bruises – some from the rocks, but some from Paul. Paul suspects Alex neglected to put a shirt back on just to show them off. The scar from his fall is there too, shiny and pink and extensive. The reminder always makes Paul feel afraid. "Some of those were your idea."

"Yes. And some were yours. This isn't a permanent fix, Alex; we're not built to live this way. I know I don't want it, and I don't think you do either."

"I'm not suggesting an open relationship. I'm suggesting space. So I'm not pissed off when you aren't here because you're trying to work your way through insecurity and so you're not pissed off when I go make a movie."

Paul frowns. "We don't need separate rooms to make that work. I can share a bed with you and deal with you being gone."

"Yeah, but when I'm gone, we're not sharing a bed at all. And when you're here but not *here* I am unhappy."

"Well, maybe I need to get a couch for the office, instead of having an office in the house."

"No," Alex says firmly. Paul is startled.

"What just happened in your head?" Paul asks.

"Assume you get a sofa bed for your office. What happens the next time we start fighting?" He asks. "Two bedrooms, one house," he reiterates. "No sleeping in your damn office."

They're interrupted by Alex's phone ringing. "Shit," Alex says, eyes darting around the room for it.

Paul glances at the clock on the microwave; it's four in the morning. "That's not good."

"No kidding. Help me find my damn phone," Alex snaps.

He's nervous. Paul lets it go as Alex shuffles around things on the counter until he unearths his phone.

"Oh my God, who the fuck died?" Alex says as he glances at the screen. The number has way too many digits; he can't even figure out where he's being called from. "Hello?" he answers tightly.

Paul watches Alex's face nervously. He can't tell if Alex is being awesome at acting or if his brain isn't sending signals to his face properly.

Alex nods rapidly, and then seems to realize whoever he's talking to can't actually see him. "Yeah," he says. Then, "No...no, I didn't....Yes. Thank you. Absolutely. I'll look forward to it." Alex clicks off the phone and stares at Paul unblinkingly.

"I'm going to assume someone didn't die," Paul says cautiously.

Alex finally seems to focus on Paul, his face spreading into a massive grin. "The part's mine," he says, not even trying to contain his excitement.

"At four in the morning?"

"Director's in Japan. He just caught up with his TV viewing and dead, dead, *dead* fucking Zach – so yes, someone died. The lawyers are typing it up, and once I sign it, it's real. I got the paaaaaaaaaaaaaaaart." Alex does a little bounce, his eyes crinkled almost shut.

Paul has never seen Alex be over the moon like this about anything. He's delightful.

"Congratulations," he says, amused and meaning it.

"Oh my God, I got the part. I get to go to Canada." Alex tilts his head. "Is it cold in Toronto?"

Paul laughs. "Do you even have a passport?"

"Have I ever left the country before?"

Paul is struck, in a way he rarely is anymore, by just how surprising Alex's life is for him. The celebrity stuff is strange, yes. But Alex is also someone who never really expected all sorts of commonplace middle class opportunities he currently only lacks time to have.

"You should know, it's only Canada. I mean, you're not even going to the French part," Paul says. "It's kind of like here."

"Paul, don't ruin it!"

"We could go on vacation sometime," he offers softly. "Like, farther than Canada. If you wanted?"

"With what time?" Alex asks, but it's giddy, not bitter.

Paul shrugs. "Twelve weeks isn't forever. And *Winsome* has breaks coming up."

Alex looks at him keenly. Paul can almost hear the wheels turning in his head. "That's a new tune."

"Yeah, well. I'm really happy for you."

♦

Three weeks pass before Alex can tell anyone, but of course a press release featuring sentences he's never actually said goes out first. As much as the process isn't totally unfamiliar, this is a much bigger deal than *Paradise Square* in terms of the size of his role. Having to learn how to navigate the personalities behind a whole new media machine, after so many years of the dysfunctional *Fourth* family, is more than a little frustrating.

Paul, in spite of the loveliness with which he'd taken the news of Alex's offer, goes back to being difficult about the prospect of him being gone for months. Alex finds it irritating and worrying, especially when he starts talking about moving back in together. Again.

"The world is not going to end if I go to Toronto from a different bedroom from you," Alex tells him shortly.

"I was kind of hoping you'd spend the night before with me," Paul says. It's flirty.

Alex grins fiercely. "Yes. Well. We have some time before then. And I appreciate you being happy for me, I do. But that doesn't mean we get to change our living situation on your terms because you were nice about something you should always have been nice about."

"Will you at least go to Liam and Carly's wedding with me?" Paul asks, obviously a little stung but trying to recover.

Alex stares at him. And then bursts out laughing.

"What?" Paul asks.

"Like you were ever going to get out of that? I'd make you go with me even if we broke up tomorrow. Whatever that disaster is going to be, I absolutely blame you for my having to know about it."

"Hey, you know Liam from work," Paul protests.

"And you're the one who's always made that complicated."

37

I s that a turret?" Alex asks, as they roll up the long, winding driveway to the house that had finally been settled on as the venue for Carly and Liam's wedding.

"A really ugly fucking turret," Paul says.

He's not wrong. It's stone and chunky and looks like a lighthouse grafted onto a Victorian. That's what you get, Alex supposes, when you have two months to plan a celebrity wedding and you let Victor find your venue.

"This is fucked up," Alex says when they get out of the car and Paul hands the keys over to the valet. It's a beautiful December day. The sun is bright and the sky is brilliantly blue. There's a heavy floral scent in the air from the landscaping and the sheer volume of flowers the florists have brought in.

"It's just like a normal wedding with more money," Paul says as they walk around a fountain in the middle of the front lawn that's glinting blindingly in the sun.

"Never been to a wedding, Paul. Don't even know married people," Alex says with a tightness Paul recognizes as nerves. "I mean, like, Raphael, I guess."

"Huh," Paul says. "Weird."

Weird gets a lot weirder incredibly quickly. They climb the steps to the house only to find Victor exchanging enthusiastic greetings with Liam's parents in an incredibly ostentatious foyer, complete with wood paneling and stained glass. Alex feels mildly terrified by the firm handshakes and manly backslapping. For heaven's sake, Liam's dad is a history professor and Victor is gay if he's anything. While still horrifying, at least Victor giving Liam's mom, Kathleen, a kiss on the cheek makes some sort of sense.

"Oh my God, do they know?" Paul hisses way too loudly as Alex grabs his arm in case they need to make a quick getaway.

"I assume they know everything about everyone," Alex whispers back. "His mom made me breakup pancakes."

Paul frowns as Alex starts to pull him further into the house. "I thought he wasn't your ex."

"Did you hear what I just said? The fucked up thing in that is pancakes. From his *mom*."

They decide they can give their respects to Victor later, because Alex, while knowing he will have to face Liam's parents eventually, doesn't particularly want to do it in front of Paul or Victor.

The foyer leads to a hallway, and they follow a stream of people into what looks to be a dining room. Everything is high ceilings and expensive Victorian chic. People are dressed in outfits Alex associates more with awards events than actual people's lives.

He's gone as casual as he possibly could, which means a suit. There was no way he could cope with wearing a tux to Liam's wedding. Paul's doing the suit thing too, and the conversation they'd had about coordinating outfits to avoid clashing – Alex is in gray, Paul in midnight blue – had been very funny. Alex has been doing Hollywood too long to feel out of place now they're here, but it definitely feels particularly foreign to him today. He wonders what his mother would think about it all.

When they round a corner away from Victor and Liam's parents, they run almost directly into another pair of people. At Alex's side, Paul freezes.

Whoever they are, they obviously know Paul; Paul greets them by name and even gets a hug from the woman, although he looks a bit deer in the headlights about it. The man gives him a solid handshake.

When Paul gets his hand back, he puts it on Alex's back. "This is my –" he starts an introduction and then stops.

"Alex," Alex says with a glance sideways at Paul. He is being way too peculiar for Alex to figure out on the spot.

"These are Carly's parents," Paul finishes somewhat pathetically.

Alex is relieved when they eventually escape the small talk and see Raphael and his wife, Irina.

"Oh my God, this is so awkward," Alex blurts. He's relieved to have found someone in the mingling he feels remotely comfortable with other than Paul.

Raphael laughs. "What did you expect?"

"I don't know. At least thirty seconds to acclimate before we had to talk to people."

"How wacky is this for you?" Raphael asks Paul. They both worked on *Fourth* from the beginning, and Raphael must remember perfectly well when it was Paul, not Liam, Carly dropped by the lot to visit.

"It's not except for the part where people keep asking me if it's wacky," Paul grouses. "Why can't you do small talk like a normal person?"

"This is Liam's wedding, and you're asking me that?" Raph says.

Paul sighs. "I need a drink."

◆

Victor is glad that the house is large enough that he can retreat to an empty room and not have to talk to anyone during the pre-ceremony drinking. Which is the best idea Carly has ever had, as far as he's concerned. People should be drunk before they have to sit through the boring and overwrought sentimentality of most people's vows. Also, considering Liam's life and relationships, all two hundred and fifty guests are likely an opportunity for the worst sort of small world theater. Victor remains amazed and slightly cowed by how unreasonably reasonable Liam's parents are about all of it.

He knocks on the open doorframe when he gets to Liam's dressing room and leans into the space without entering. The afternoon sun is slanting in through yet another stained glass window, spilling color onto the gleaming floor and the knotty pine walls and making the whole room glow. Liam's best friend, Charles, is slouched on a couch with his feet up on a coffee table. Victor is relieved to see that he's at least had the sense to take off his suit jacket so it won't wrinkle. Liam is preening – and rambling – in front of an antique, heavy-framed mirror. The composition of the entire scene is perfect, right down to the way the sun is making a halo of Liam's curls.

"Can we have the room?" Victor asks Charles once he catches his breath from the sight.

"Yup," he says good-naturedly as he bounces up and grabs his jacket. "Have fun," he says to Liam as he swerves by him on his way out of the door, shutting it behind him.

Victor and Liam both sigh, and Victor gives a little huff of a laugh, walking over to Liam and turning him away from the mirror.

"Your tie's crooked," he says, realizing that's likely what Liam had been staring at without being quite able to figure out what was wrong.

Liam doesn't say anything, and Victor has a flash of anxiety.

"You cannot decide words are too hard right now," he says sternly. Liam has a script for the ceremony and the working a room thing after should be fine, but, God, he hopes Liam knows that.

Also, as fine – as happy, as relieved – as Victor is about all of this, Liam is looking at him the way he does when he's helpless, in pain, and too damn in love with Victor for his own good. He makes Victor ache in a way that still doesn't entirely make sense in his brain. He can't imagine Liam's wedding day is an appropriate moment for him to tell Liam he's in love with him, too.

"Saving them up," Liam eventually says, looking away.

"Okay, then." Victor unties and reties the tie in silence, tapping his fingers against the knot when he's done. "I'm incredibly proud of you, you know."

Liam merely nods.

◆

Alex has nothing to compare it to at all, but the ceremony itself seems lovely if slightly too long. Carly cries, Liam cries, and Paul holds Alex's hand and smiles. They're all outside, back behind the house, and a breeze stirs Carly's veil and the ribbons on the arbor as the officiant drones on.

Victor is seated across the aisle from them, and when Alex starts to lose interest in the readings his eyes wander to him. He's watching the proceedings with a look that's far away, even wistful, and Alex has absolutely no idea what to make of that. He feels intrusive and turns away.

Alex is still not certain what this marriage is going to mean in the context of Victor and Liam. But an engagement hadn't stopped Carly from having a threesome with Alex and Paul, and Alex knows something about the capacity of Liam's heart.

Paul picks that moment to squeeze Alex's hand. Alex looks over at him to find Paul gazing at him with an expression that's both happy and longing.

Alex mouths *What?* That look, in this context, is both unsettling and gratifying.

◆

Paul shakes his head. Asking Alex, again, to marry him – particularly here, at a public and intensely emotional day that happens to be their best friends' wedding – is a horrible idea. Not to mention terribly clichéd. He very much doesn't want to upset the balance of this day, which has gone so well for them so far.

But he can't stop thinking about a day of their own nearest and dearest, having a ring on his own finger, and getting to call Alex *husband*. He fell too fast and too hard years ago, but there's no way out of it now. Hellish as things have gotten between them this past year, but Paul wants Alex forever.

Some of that must show on his face. Alex gives him a steady look back that goes challenging and then thoughtful before he returns his attention to the ceremony.

◆

At the reception – also outside – the social awkward starts up again. The circle of Liam and Carly's friends, family, and business associates is wide and random. Paul and Alex are seated at a table of people they don't know at all, but starting from the baseline of strange and fucked up Alex is used to from anything Liam-adjacent, it could be so much worse.

Paul gets caught up in a discussion about craft from someone who's apparently a film critic. Alex winds up talking about, of all things, the history of the Safavid Dynasty with one of Liam's dad's connections. The small talk might be the most interesting he's ever made, and he's now grateful for all the background reading he did on Iran for a whole new set of reasons. His conversation partner doesn't even ask about Zach.

♦

Charles, Liam's childhood best friend, gives the toast. Paul leans over to whisper in Alex's ear, "I am so glad there was no awkward sex scene in that story."

Alex nods and mutters back, "Yeah. They've totally been fucking since high school."

"Are you knowing or guessing or do I not want to ask?" Paul says a little weakly.

Alex laughs and bumps their knees together under the table.

Candles and torches get lit as the sun starts to set. Somehow they make the whole lawn, with its white-covered tables, expensive flower arrangements, and guests that are, as Hollywood requires, all better than average looking, seem like one of Nigel's ad campaigns. It's an impression the dancing – music and laughter and swirling dresses – does nothing to lessen, even if Alex is used to his own fairytales being much darker.

♦

The first dances are traditional. But later, once the dance floor is open to everyone, Paul can see them get complicated. Liam and Carly both have a lot of people in their lives for whom this day must be strange or even difficult. Certainly, Paul isn't the only one of Carly's exes here, and he watches as they both, very deliberately, seek certain people out. He assumes himself to be low on the list simply because he and Alex just slept with her. His doesn't need reassurance or attention. As to Liam and Alex, he has no idea what will happen there. He decides to ask Alex to dance before he has to find out. At least he'll be first.

"Dance with me?"

Alex looks at Paul's outstretched hand in consternation. "I don't know how," he says. "Why couldn't they have hired a DJ like on TV weddings? I did not expect the string quartet."

Paul grins at him. "Take my hand, and dance like we usually do. Just less like we're having sex." They both still get grief occasionally for how obvious they were when they danced together at Paul's house at the party where they first hooked up.

"You started it," Alex says.

"Only the first time."

Alex's eyes crinkle up in a smile, and he lets Paul pull him to his feet.

He obviously doesn't know where his hands are supposed to go and then chides Paul for wanting him to lead.

"I *don't know how*," Alex repeats. "You're being stupid."

They laugh awkwardly before they step apart for a moment and then try again.

This time, it works, and they start moving in a little circle. After the first song, Alex squeezes at Paul's arm and leans his forehead into his. Paul gasps. The intimacy of the gesture and the intensity of the look in Alex's eyes make it feel like sex no matter how gentle. Alex smiles softly.

"You little shit," Paul whispers. This is nothing like what he expected from today, and it's absolutely wonderful.

Alex simply says, "I love you."

◆

"You're very good," Carly says, laughing as Victor leads her in a proper waltz. "Why didn't I know this?"

"You weren't paying attention," Victor says lightly. A waltz, when he had grown up with salsa, is very easy. And he'd spent far too much time in his past determined to pass and impress in the circles of rich white people who had the money to fund his projects.

"Well, I should pay more, then."

Victor shakes his head. "You're fine. I'm fine. It's all fine, Carly."

"Is it?"

He shrugs. "Of course it is. A missed date night? He'll make it up to me."

"You haven't danced with him," Carly notes.

"Do you really expect me to?" Victor asks.

"I'm sure he asked."

"He did," Victor allows. "But Liam is unpredictable, and he and I are fine. You two look radiant today. That's all I care about."

"You're a very good liar," she says.

"True," he acknowledges. "But not germane."

◆

Paul and Alex have barely managed to sit down and start chatting with some of Paul and Carly's friends from college when, to Alex's surprise, Liam appears. He doesn't say anything, just grabs Alex's hand and tugs him away from the table toward the dance floor. Alex is a little exasperated but very fond. Paul, to his relief, only looks amused as Liam drags him off.

They skip the question of who leads with a bit of fumbling to at least mimic something resembling a hold, but they also don't really move at all. Instead, they sway slowly in place. Their feet only catch up to the idea of dancing the one or two times they manage to get off balance and someone has to take a step to prevent them from falling.

Alex expects rambling from Liam, or a list, or at least words. But Liam keeps his eyes down for a while, and Alex decides that this isn't about him at all, but what Liam needs. He can wait it out. In a sea of so many guests, likely no one is paying attention anyway. He hopes Liam gets what he's looking for out of this, before someone among the endless and enthusiastic supply of his friends interrupts.

Eventually, Liam looks up, silent and eyes too bright. The beauty of the look is why he's on TV, and it's unsettling enough that it's why he's good as opposed to just pretty. Liam continues to look at him too intently for a long moment and then puts his head on Alex's shoulder.

Alex sighs, in awe at how simple things between them sometimes are, and tips the side of his head into Liam's.

"I know," he says.

Back at their table, Alex sees Paul look away and sighs in relief. Paul always has been a fundamentally decent guy.

◆

This late in the year the night is cool, but L.A. is never cold, so Paul rolls the windows down as they roll back down the driveway. He feels like they have so much to talk about, after everything that happened tonight and the emotion of the day, but yet, foolishly, talking doesn't seem necessary. It's enough that he and Alex are together.

Alex tucks his feet up and leans his head against the back of the seat. His face is mostly turned away, but the moonlight falls across him beautifully. Paul can tell he's smiling. After the last eight months, they might finally be on the same page again, and a good page at that.

The drive back is silent, peacefully so, and Paul follows Alex up the stairs to the bedroom they once shared when they get home. They kiss as they undress just as silently, and Paul doesn't even feel the need to narrate or tease when they finally go to bed. They laugh a lot. Mostly with relief.

38

The next morning, Paul moves his clothes back from the other side of the house while Alex first pretends to sleep in and then sits in bed reading. He never expected Carly and Liam's wedding, of all things, to be the catalyst for them moving back in together. He's thrilled. But this part of their mess was Paul's fault, and Alex is happy to let him move his own damn crap.

When he's finally done, Paul closes the closet door with a ridiculous amount of self-satisfaction. He turns, folds his hands behind him and leans against it.

"So," he says.

"So," Alex echoes, looking up from his book. Which is the exact moment that Todd chooses to dash into the room and jump up on the bed. Alex and Paul both look at Todd – who immediately curls up on Alex's legs, purring triumphantly – and then at each other. Paul cracks up, and Alex grins as he leans over to scratch Todd's ears.

"Someone's happy," Paul observes.

The look Alex gives him is both coy and content.

"There's a thing I need you to do," Paul says once the mood settles again.

"Yeah?"

Alex doesn't expect it to be about Victor. And when it is, he doesn't expect it to make so much sense. In six weeks he's leaving to go to Toronto for three months. While they can call and visit – and Paul assures him that will involve mutual advance planning, because they're working hard at not forgetting lessons learned – a lot of Paul's care and feeding is going to be in the hands of other people. And while that means Carly, and Darcy, and apparently even Gemma, it also means Victor.

"I know what you think of him," Paul says. "And I know you're not necessarily even wrong. Or ungrateful. But he's a part of my life that I need. And if you want him to treat you like a real person, you kind of have to treat him like one too."

Alex agrees, because it will make Paul happy and likely change nothing else in his world. But that doesn't mean Alex isn't still the clever and sharp creature Victor discovered three years ago who both America and Paul fell in love with.

So Alex invites him shooting. He considers doing it via Twitter, just to fuck with him, but ultimately decides email is the better option. Victor is, when he replies, predictably appalled. But once Alex gets him on the phone, he can hear him smiling. Some people don't back down from a challenge. He's often like that himself. But Victor seems to take challenges on as an almost delighted form of *fuck you*.

430

♦

Paul sees him off at the door with an amused, if wary, "Have fun, good luck, don't antagonize the internet."

Alex knows Paul thinks this idea is unwise for any number of reasons. But if he's going to prove he's not scared of Victor by making nice with him, he's going to do it on his own terms. If he's honest with himself, Alex knows he's doing it not just for Paul but for himself. After everything Victor's done to him, Alex has earned the right to exert his own not insignificant power.

There isn't much opportunity for talking on the range, which is fine by Alex. He's darkly delighted that Victor is a miserable shot. Victor has more of a sense of humor about it than he expects.

They finally get a chance to talk in the parking lot. Alex sits on the hood of his car as Victor stands in front of him, hands in pockets, like they're ordinary people used to being in terrible, industrial parts of L.A. He finds himself mostly repeating, word for word, what Paul had said to him.

"I know who you are, Alex," Victor says in response, smiling. "It's you who doesn't know who I am."

It feels, a little bit, like a movie.

But Alex thinks about it on the drive home. About if whether all the times he thought Victor was being malevolent and cruel, he was simply doing what Alex himself does when he's surly: putting on an act to get by in the world. Only with darker consequences.

Victor doesn't control Alex; he just elicits reactions. If Alex has chosen to fall for it, because he's needed a bad guy in his life, that doesn't absolve Victor. But it does point to Alex having chosen too many of his own obstacles. In an existence where everyone fawns over him, of course Alex has needed someone who is anything but giving.

Alex chuckles to himself. He may never forgive Victor for all of the things that he's done, but if Victor of all people doesn't control him then neither can anyone else. Smiling to himself in the car as he turns up onto the steep street to his house, Alex knows a lesson like that is a powerful gift.

♦

"Hey, are you home?" Alex shouts as he walks in the front door.

The shout turns out not to be necessary. Paul's in the kitchen cooking, and he turns, a knife in one hand and half an onion in the other. Alex has to stop himself from laughing uncontrollably, it's so very perfect.

"Me and a pot of soon-to-be vegetable soup. What's up?"

"Ask me again," Alex says breathlessly.

"What?"

"Ask me again."

"Ask you what?" Paul says, clearly puzzled.

"You're gonna ruin it if you make me say it," Alex says.

Paul stares at him, his face shifting from confusion to disbelief to the most cautious, hopeful understanding. "I'm getting the sense I should put down the onion?" he says carefully.

Alex finally lets himself laugh. "Also the knife," he suggests.

Paul complies and wipes his hands on his jeans. He can't take his eyes off Alex's face as he asks like it's the very first time, "So, are you going to marry me?"

All Alex can do is beam and silently nod. For the most important things, he and Paul have never needed words.

Phoenix

Love in Los Angeles Book 3

1

 aking movies far from home is Alex's favorite thing about his job and the hardest. In the three years he and Paul have been married, they've developed a cycle: Alex goes away for a few months to film. When he returns, they cocoon together as long as they can before emerging on their very best behavior to do awards season. Then, Alex disappears for another project.

He loves the work, and he loves the adventure but being away from Paul is really fucking hard and Australia is really fucking far away. There are two months left of the six-month shoot for The Icarus Experiment. It's the longest he's ever been gone, and Alex is increasingly sure it's not something he wants to repeat. He cannot wait to get home and return to normal, or at least, what passes as normal for them.

As far as Alex can tell, Paul deals with his absence by pining and overwork. Winsome, AZ is going into its sixth and final season. While Paul has promised to take a year off when it's done, readying himself for whatever TV creation is going to be his next big adventure, there's plenty of work to keep him busy now.

Liam, meanwhile, is currently without a demanding TV shooting schedule, doing guest roles here and there and enjoying his relationships – with his wife, with Victor, and with whomever else Alex doesn't bother to keep track of. Somehow, though, Liam has taken Alex's absence harder than anyone expected.

He hasn't stopped expressing his annoyance that while Paul visited for two weeks over Christmas, he, with Carly, a five-year-old, and his own professional obligations, couldn't make the same choice. Alex knows he's supposed to find the intensity of their friendship and emotional intimacy peculiar, but now that it's stopped bothering everyone else, he finds it difficult to care. That said, he does wish Liam could at least remember when they have a Skype date.

♦

Liam's phone vibrates in the pocket of his jeans, folded neatly along with the rest of his clothes on the floor by the side of the bed. Victor has been awake for hours but Liam is, quite reasonably, not yet ready for the world. Victor reaches for the phone to deal with the unwelcome noise.

It's a text message from Alex. Where are you? the screen reads. Waiting.

Victor silences the phone and sets it aside. Alex will try again; he always does. In the meantime, Victor pulls the white coverlet up over

Liam's bare shoulders, watching the way the down settles and molds itself to the shape of Liam's body underneath. Victor made sure he was tucked in before he went to his own bed the night before, but Liam is a more restless sleeper when he's alone and managed to kick off the covers by the time Victor came back in the morning to check on him.

Victor may not desire Liam in the way Liam wishes he did, but that doesn't stop him from having a great desire to care for his body and his heart, even if he generally does both from as large a distance as he can reasonably manage. Liam's love is a terrifying gift, and Victor often wishes he were better equipped to bring him happiness. That their relationship exists at all is a testament to how hard they work for it and how well they fit in concept if not fact.

Victor kisses Liam's forehead before moving off the bed to get his laptop.

He gets an incoming Skype call from Alex almost as soon as the computer turns on and picks it up with delight as he carries the laptop out of the room.

◆

"To what do I owe the pleasure?" Victor practically purrs when he answers, settling himself at the desk in his den.

Alex lets himself laugh, because at least he knows Victor is trying to piss him off.

"Is Liam there?"

"Yes," Victor says as he twists at a ring around his little finger. It makes him look like even more of a stereotypical villain than usual.

"Is he awake?" Alex asks. He tries to ignore the fidgeting which he suspects is an intentionally targeted affectation. He imagines Victor acquiring some sort of peculiar and menacing pet in order to take the performance further.

"No."

"Ugh. He's standing me up for our Skype date." He refrains from pointing out that Victor is also not being helpful.

"He had a rough night," Victor says.

"Do I want to inquire?"

"I'm going with no," Victor says slyly.

Alex grimaces.

"That face would be easier to believe if I hadn't watched you make out with Liam on my couch."

"Jesus, Victor," Alex gapes, not quite sure where to look on the screen. He's tempted to end the call right there, but God knows what Victor would do in retaliation then. "You make it sound so sketchy."

"No, I think sketchy was when Paul – "

"Can we not talk about this?" Alex squeaks.

Victor laughs. It doesn't make him seem any less sociopathic. The last thing Alex wants to discuss is how he, Paul, Victor, Carly, and Liam got way too fucked up one night at Victor's house. There was a lot of random making out, and Paul eventually jerked Alex off not entirely in private. It's the sort of thing that would be funny and only faintly scandalous if it happened to someone else.

"You're not nearly as embarrassed by that night as you pretend," Victor says. "Even if you and Paul have a really fucked up definition of monogamy."

"You know that thing where we don't talk about that because I don't want to know about your sex life and you don't want to know about mine?" Alex says. "That was really nice. We should go back to that."

"For an actor you're remarkably unconvincing, and for a friend, remarkably inaccurate." Victor smirks.

"I'm not above hanging up on you," Alex threatens. He doesn't want to begin to examine the word friend in the context of Victor.

"You also weren't above kissing me."

"You're a bastard." Alex laughs even though he wants to die. Victor's a damn good kisser, and Alex wants to examine that fact never.

Victor decides to be merciful. "Tell me about this date with Liam," he says as if that statement is somehow less inflammatory than everything else they've just discussed.

Alex is relieved, but rolls his eyes anyway. "Appointment."

"That sounds more absurd," Victor notes.

"Then don't be an asshole."

Victor hums in thought. "Should I ask how Australia is?" It's clearly a peace offering.

"Big," Alex says after a moment. "Catalytic. Way too fucking far from everything."

2

Alex does not wear his hat. Despite having been home from Australia for a month and knowing that people will recognize him, he's hoping for a little common decency. Besides, the club is loud, crowded, and noisy, full of hundreds of men wrapped up in each other paying absolutely no attention to him and Paul edging their way toward the dance floor. It's a long way from the first time they danced together in Paul's living room, but all the important things are still right here in front of him.

Between the stress of running his very own cable TV hit and his notorious workaholic tendencies, Paul's already going gray at thirty-eight. Everyone teases him about it, but Alex loves it. Once Paul gets his arms around him, Alex wastes no time in sliding a hand up the back of Paul's neck.

"Eager?" Paul teases. He has to talk into Alex's ear to be heard over the thudding music and even then it's debatable. Alex nods and presses his forehead against Paul's. They're both already a little drunk, and he's never been able to lose himself anywhere as easily as he can in Paul's arms.

♦

Alex's eyes flutter shut when Paul slides his hands into his back pockets and pulls him closer. They're not dancing so much as grinding together, but they're hardly alone in that regard – at least they still have their shirts on, and if Alex is willing, Paul has absolutely zero desire to stop.

Paul can't hear it, but he can feel the breath of a moan on his neck when Alex gets insistent about digging his fingers into Paul's hair. He mouths at the skin above his collar. Six months apart – with only two weeks in the middle – was a very long time. The time they've had since has barely been enough to get used to sharing space with each other again, much less fall back into their relationship with all their knowledge of each other's bodies and hearts intact.

"This is possibly a bad idea," Alex murmurs at some point.

Paul isn't sure how much time has elapsed since things crossed into slightly inappropriate but totally expected territory. "I don't think you care."

"No, not really," Alex says before slipping into a whine, "but we just got here, and I don't want to go home."

"Who says we have to go home?"

"My dick."

"What? Can you not get off like this?" Paul scoffs. They might both be older than they used to be, but Alex is still a lot younger than

440

him and the thought of making him come in his pants is both delicious and amusing.

"Paul," Alex says warningly.

His only response is to cup Alex's ass and lift him so far up onto the thigh he has between Alex's legs that his feet are barely on the ground.

"Paul!" Alex says again, and this time he's neither warning nor faking how scandalized he is.

"Come on," Paul chides. "Be impressed. You're heavier than you look."

"I'm definitely impressed," Alex says breathlessly. "But this is ridiculous."

Paul shakes his head. "The way I see it," he says, kneading at Alex's ass. "You have two options."

"Yeah?"

"You can get off right here, or you can wait until the end of tonight. Because I don't want to go home either."

Alex curls himself forward and makes a deliciously pained sound as he braces himself on Paul's shoulders. When Paul shifts one hand to the center of his back and breathes, "Yeah, that's right," in his ear, he is clearly absolutely done for. Paul groans when Alex finally smiles, sly and eager.

Paul digs his fingernails into his ass and shifts him so Alex can fuck against his thigh. He starts up a litany in Alex's ear about all the marks he'd leave on his flesh, if only Alex weren't wearing so much clothing.

"I'm not doing this alone," Alex gasps, clearly trying to hold back.

Paul laughs. "You're certainly not."

"I mean," Alex says between gasps, "that if I'm going to come on the dance floor – So. Are. You."

"What makes you think that?" Paul asks with fake disinterest.

"You don't want to go home yet," Alex pants, "And I'm not blowing you in the bathroom."

Paul laughs.

◆

Alex responds by getting a hand between them and grabbing at Paul's very interested dick through his jeans.

"Jesus," Paul gasps. If Alex is after a challenge tonight, he seems to have found it.

"Too tacky," Alex says, clearly full of pride at being able to keep up and upping the stakes.

To Paul, it's both typical of the twenty-year-old boy Alex was when they first met and a testament to the man he's become. And if he's happy to let Paul lead and push in some things, it's only because Alex knows, absolutely, how easy it is for him to turn the tables when he wants to.

Paul has to kiss him, deep and desperate. Alex lets go of Paul's cock to grab his hips instead, rutting against him as they pant into each other's mouths.

Alex comes with a sharp gasp, his mouth frozen open. He grabs Paul around the waist so he doesn't actually fall over. Paul holds him up and runs a hand down his back until he stops shaking with it.

Before either of them catch their breath, Alex takes a step back and shoves at Paul's shoulders. Paul, eager and turned on, doesn't ask or protest as Alex steers them carefully through the crowd. He is startled though, because Alex able to function after an orgasm is not a thing Paul is used to.

At the back of the dance floor Alex shoves Paul against the wall and dives a hand down the front of his pants before Paul can register what's going on. It's hot and dark and Alex's face is dazed and intent the way it is after their best sex, when the rest of the world is gone.

"Are you out of your mind?" Paul hisses.

"You started this," Alex says, an entirely different sort of breathless now. "Prove to me you can finish it."

Paul barks out half a laugh before Alex twists his wrist just so, and then he lets his head fall back as he watches the dance floor with heavy-lidded eyes and mentally pages through every backroom fantasy he's ever had.

Alex clearly knows it, and so it only takes a smirk and a bit of encouragement from him for Paul to come all over his hand.

They clean up in the bathroom, laughing together as Alex washes his hands and then helps Paul with the mess in his underwear, neither of them giving a remote shit about the person pounding on the door because he thinks they're in there together to fuck. When they're done Alex all but drags Paul back onto the dance floor, and this time the dancing is fun. It's the perfect reminder to them both that Alex is actually home, for real, to stay. At least for a little while.

◆

It's obscenely late when they finally get back to their house and crawl into their bed drunk and sweaty and happy. Alex curls up on Paul's chest as soon as they're naked and under the covers.

Paul wraps his arms around him. "I'm glad you're home," he says, and it's different than all the other times he's said it lately. Everything feels so real, Paul can't imagine that he'll need to keep saying it after tonight.

Alex smiles into Paul's shoulder. "Me fucking too.

3

Paul moans at the sound of his ringtone. Alex curses next to him, rolls over, and says, "It'll stop."

He's not wrong, until it starts again a few moments later.

"It's still dark," Paul complains.

"Someone probably wants a ride home," Alex says. They've been drunk dialed by random combinations of Liam, Carly, Gemma, Darcy, Shawna, and Brian more than once and only sometimes by accident. Once, Paul's ex Craig called, and that was super awkward. Alex doesn't understand why all their very successful friends can't manage to call cabs like normal people.

The phone stops and starts. Again.

"That's not good."

Alex laughs, because the last time they said that about a middle-of-the-night call, he got cast in a movie.

"Where the fuck is my phone?" Paul asks, finally giving in and sitting up groggily.

"In your pants," Alex says unhelpfully.

Paul curses as he leans over the edge of the bed and gropes in the direction of the ringing. He finds it as it starts up a fourth time. Alex pulls a pillow over his head, because he's still drunk and the sound is unpleasant.

"Ellen?" Paul answers, groggy, confused, and a little concerned. At least the ringing has finally stopped.

There's a pause, and Alex hears Paul say, still groggy but a lot sharper, "What?"

"What's't?" Alex mutters, taking the pillow off his face as Paul starts pulling on his clothes while juggling the phone. Alex curses, because they're totally going to wind up giving someone a ride and that's just stupid.

It's Paul asking when and how and who else have you called, that Alex finally sits up and reaches for the light.

Paul's face is ashen as he struggles to get his arm with the phone through a sleeve. Finally, as Alex tries not to jump to all sorts of terrible conclusions, Paul runs out of steam and sits on the bed half dressed as he asks Ellen, "Are you okay?"

The answer is clearly no.

♦

"Let me call," Paul protests as Alex paces their kitchen, scrolling through his own speed-dial with unsteady hands.

"I've got this. You need to call your own people and convince them it's not a terrible April Fool's joke," Alex says shortly. The timing of the universe is always terrible, but this instance just might be the worst.

"This is six types of fucked up," Paul says under his breath.

Alex gulps some more water and finally dials Carly's number. He thinks he's relieved when she picks up on the first ring, but then she says, before Alex can get a word out, "I haven't told Liam, yet."

"Jesus Christ, Carly...."

"If you were me, how would you do that, exactly?"

"Quickly," Alex says curtly. "Before someone calls his phone."

"I have his phone."

"Carly!" Alex knows that managing Liam's relationship with the universe is sort of Carly's job, but the ethics of her choices here are making him more than a little uncomfortable.

"It can wait 'til morning. Then at least he'll get some sleep." Carly sounds angry, although with Alex or the universe at large, he's not sure.

"He's gonna be pissed at you," Alex says because he can't say anything else. Liam isn't his husband.

"Yeah, well," she snaps back, "he's gonna be a lot more pissed at Victor for being dead."

◆

Alex makes coffee while Paul starts calling people at the studio. Ellen promised to call the people at M.A.R.S., but Victor is – was – half the production company for Winsome, AZ, and that means Paul, as the other half, now has a lot of duty he can't shirk. He wishes he had any idea what the protocol is when an executive producer drops dead of a heart attack.

"Why don't we have a phone tree?" he asks as he waits for the executive at the network to pick up.

"Because no one thought Victor was a toddler in danger of having a snow day," Alex says without pause.

Paul lets it pass.

Alex pushes a cup of coffee across the table at him. Paul runs a hand through his hair and recites to a VP in network operations, whom he's always tried to avoid, everything Ellen told him about Victor's death. After the entirely necessary pause for shock – and as much grief as anyone in the business is likely to muster for someone who made a career out of being infuriating – they discuss how early they can schedule a phone meeting with the production team to figure out what the hell their plan is.

"I need to go see Liam," Alex says when Paul hangs up.

"In what world is that good choices?" Paul says wearily. "Carly's got him."

"I know, but I should be there."

"He'll call you if he needs you," Paul reasons. He does not have the bandwidth at the moment for Alex and Liam's now-platonic romance.

"I don't think you understand how bad it's going to be." Alex pauses. "I don't think I understand."

◆

There's already a thing on Variety.com that's clinical enough to not make any of this feel any more real. Alex wonders who the asshole was who called them from the ER because they overheard Ellen on the phone. No one else is reporting it yet, but that's only a matter of time. As soon as an associated actor cries in public or crashes their car, preferably at the same time, everyone will care. He gives it twenty-four hours.

When Paul hangs up from what he hopes is the last call for at least a couple of hours, Alex spins the pad Paul's been jotting notes on toward himself. As a to-do list it's wide-ranging, but hardly complete.

"When's the funeral?" Alex asks.

Paul stares at him in shock. "Shit. I don't even know if Victor has family."

"He didn't spring out of Zeus's head," Alex notes.

"Have you ever heard him mention anyone? Because I know I haven't. And I haven't from Carly. Liam?"

Alex shakes his head. "I try not to ask."

"Well, it's Jackson's problem now," Paul says, exasperated.

"Didn't he just hire that guy?"

"He's Victor's personal assistant. He'll know where the will is and how to find Victor's personal lawyer. God knows, this is not actually our problem."

Alex thinks it's the most sensible thing he's heard in hours. Unfortunately, he's unconvinced. "Pretend you're Victor and play that sentence back."

◆

By mid-afternoon, their phones are both ringing non-stop. They've yet to make a public statement – that's waiting on final decisions about what the hell is going on with Winsome and M.A.R.S. – but everyone from press to people at the studio to friends are calling. Eventually Paul silences his briefly so he can at least take a shower without interruption.

Finally there's a phone meeting with the Winsome production team, where it's decided that filming will go on tomorrow as planned. There will be a couple of days off whenever the funeral is, not that anyone knows what's going on with that anyway. Easter apparently complicates everything.

There's also another round of "Did Victor have any family?" that is immediately followed by one concerned murmur about Liam and a lot of jokes about Victor being hatched from an egg. A reptile egg, to be precise, because in times like this shitty jokes must be as sharp as fucking possible. Paul's pissed off, but he suspects Victor would be delighted.

Ellen, meanwhile, has not been in any of the M.A.R.S. meetings, but is in touch with someone who has, and keeps Paul updated with increasingly frantic emails about those talks.

The network isn't going to kill the show mid-season, but Paul knows she's not wrong to worry about how many more episodes are going to come her directorial way when it's unclear who's in charge and if it's going to continue past the current season. Anyone who was close to Victor is in either a very good or very bad position, depending on whether sentimentality wins over what a fucking consistent pain in the ass he was to anyone who was paying the bills.

Paul can't decide if he wants in on the opportunity the entire mess of a situation presents or if he's determined to stay as far away from it as possible.

◆

The calls Alex receives are less business oriented – at least, once he stops answering anything from numbers he doesn't know, because he'll be damned if he gets bullied or startled into making a statement about supporting his husband in a time of need and how he owes everything to Victor – but they're more emotional and crazy.

There's a public announcement of Victor's death in the early afternoon, which only makes the phone calls increase in frequency. Alex keeps an eye on the internet as he and Raphael text back and forth in the sort of quiet commiseration that's marked so much of their relationship since they were on Fourth together.

Paul is on the phone with Craig of all people, who has called to see if Paul is okay – Alex doesn't know what to make of that – when their doorbell rings. It's Alex's former roommate Gemma. She's followed fifteen minutes later by Darcy, Paul's starlet, who's in tears, and then Ellen, who looks like she hasn't slept at all.

Alex has no idea how their house has become mission control for dead Victor, but ultimately he's grateful to have people around. It reduces the number of phone calls getting made and gives him someone to yell in the direction of when Carly calls Alex to give him a heads up.

Apparently, Nigel is going to be in touch.

"What the fuck?" Alex asks when Carly tells him as much.

"He was Victor's best friend," Carly reminds him sharply. "And he will be useful. Don't be an asshole."

"How's Liam?"

"Thanks for your help," she says and hangs up.

Alex stares at the phone for a moment.

"Why the hell is Carly gatekeeping Liam?" he hollers to Paul who is still in the kitchen using their breakfast table as a command center.

"Leave it alone, Alex," Paul says, deep in his own distraction with his disaster of an inbox.

Nigel calls soon after and is calm and reasonable, even if his voice is heavy with the sort of shock and sorrow Alex doesn't know how to deal with. Nigel confirms that Victor doesn't have any family but doesn't really provide any further information before talking about arrangements with the sort of precision and detail that makes Alex relieved until he realizes he has, by default, been deputized into funeral planning.

"This is not my job," he protests to Gemma after Nigel finally says goodbye. Clearly he's already underestimated how fucked up this whole thing is going to get.

"You guys are Victor's family," she says. "And it's not like anybody else has time to handle this."

"Gemma, I hated him," Alex hisses like it's some sort of secret.

"No you didn't. You were just scared of whatever he saw when he looked at you, because you saw it too."

♦

That evening, despite Alex's vociferous protests, Paul sends him along with Jackson, Victor's PA, to pick out clothes for Victor for the funeral. Victor's house is as brutally clean and uncluttered as always, and Alex follows Jackson with trepidation as he leads the way upstairs.

"I'm sorry to be tagging along," Alex says, because he feels douchey about everything from being in Victor's house to involving an assistant he barely knows. Jackson's a black kid from Chicago by way of UCLA who signed up to learn from Victor's genius, not help bury him. Alex is momentarily pissed off at Paul all over again for putting him in this situation.

Jackson shrugs. "Like you're the worst thing in my day."

447

He heads immediately for Victor's bedroom with the air of someone who knows what he's doing, is going to do it because it needs to be done, and wants to get it over with as quickly as possible. Alex can sympathize.

Alex lingers in the hallway feeling awkward and intrusive and finally ducks into Victor's office. Maybe he can find something that might be useful for Paul in all his upcoming network meetings. There's a day planner that could be helpful, but what catches Alex's eye is the chain bracelet Victor often wore, sitting in an unused ashtray along with paperclips and loose change.

"Okay, got it," Jackson says from the doorway, carrying a garment bag. "Ready to get out of here?"

Alex nods and plucks the bracelet out of the bowl. "You should bring this too."

4

One of the very few, and very fucked up, upsides to having to get to the Cathedral for the funeral early enough to oversee various logistics, including how the flowers left over from Easter are going to be arranged by the casket, is that Alex and Paul get there before the paparazzi have the place too staked out. Alex still isn't sure exactly why he got roped into helping Nigel with this other than that he was available. Mostly, he's relieved that after today this whole ordeal – which he has definitely decided to take as Victor's parting shot toward absolutely everyone – is going to be over.

Our Lady of the Angels is exactly the sort of place that Alex thinks of when he thinks of L.A. and Victor, though he avoids this part of town like the plague. Massive and brutally modernist, the Cathedral feels as disorienting as it does inescapable. The haze of smoke blowing in from the first wildfire of the season just makes everything worse.

Alex has no doubt that Victor loved this place, even if he has no idea how much, if any, time Victor actually spent here beyond deciding he wanted to be buried in its crypt. It certainly doesn't make Alex like it any better. From the puzzlement on Nigel's face – which is admittedly warring with grief and jet lag – Alex feels confident he is not alone in his assessment. That there are Easter lilies decorating the sanctuary feels like a particularly fucked up joke. Victor may have been god of many universes, but Alex is definitely counting on him to stay dead.

Nigel's presence isn't uncomfortable exactly, but he has remained at a remove from the rest of their tangled circle over the last five years. A lot of that, Alex knows, has been simple geography and logistics: Nigel's wife and children and a career in New York that mimics, but doesn't actually involve, Hollywood magic.

Alex suspects, however, that much of it has been the wary truce between him and Liam, despite the fact that they have never been at war and were never really in competition. The only two things Alex has ever seen Liam be possessive of are Victor and cities, and it's certainly never been New York, Los Angeles, or Washington, D.C. that have been the object of Liam's rare but somewhat ugly jealousy.

♦

The descent down to the memorial chapel should be a relief after the unsettlingly pagan main sanctuary and Paul's scathing look when Alex muttered something about the "erotic baptism art" along the back wall, but it's even more uncomfortable. A staircase in three segments leads down to the crypt area below the Cathedral, and while the first set of stairs is lit normally, the second is bathed in light from a wall of windows and the Los Angeles sun. Then, a descent into the underworld as all the light is yanked away. For someone, it's surely a soothing and symbolic journey, but Alex worries that Liam will find it terrifying.

The casket stands open in front of the altar of the chapel, and it draws Alex's eyes as well as the eyes of everyone who is by now beginning to filter in. Victor looks exactly the same in death as he had when he was alive: brown, sun-weathered skin and short black hair flecked with gray, fine and unremarkable lines around his mouth and eyes.

Victor's presence was always larger than life. Now, in contrast, he looks small, almost shrunken. It's an uncomfortable feeling. As much as Alex has always resented it, Victor was a titan in his life. It feels impossible that he's dead.

Paul appears at Alex's elbow, following his gaze. "How are you doing?" he asks.

"Peculiar," Alex says, not looking at him. His eyes are finally pulled away from the casket by Paul's indrawn breath and the simultaneous click of high heels.

"He looks terrible," Paul says about Liam. Apparently, Alex isn't the only one doing peculiar.

Alex hurries to meet them, but pulls up short when he goes to hug Liam and there's no sign of Liam moving in for the same. Which is weird, because Liam hugs everyone. They stare at each other for a long moment.

"I don't know what to say to you right now," Alex manages as Paul catches up to them and hugs Carly.

Liam shrugs. "It's okay."

"Do you want a hug?" Alex asks.

Liam shakes his head. "Stoic celebrity time."

"Yeah, okay," Alex says. "That's fucked up, you know?"

Liam rolls his eyes and drifts off in the direction of the coffin. Alex watches Nigel nod to Liam from a distance and get the same in return. Whatever works, but Alex exchanges a look with Carly. When she follows Liam, Alex turns helplessly to Paul, unsure of what to do. Paul meets his eyes, which is enough to ground him and force him to let the rituals of both death and social discomfort play out.

There are a few people standing near the casket who turn to greet Liam as he passes, but he doesn't acknowledge them more than he has to. When he gets there he stands for a long moment staring down at Victor. Slowly, he lowers himself to his knees on the kneeling rail that's been placed there.

Alex makes a soft, pained sound. He's fairly certain Liam isn't religious and can only view the grace and fluidity of the gesture in the context of the little – and way too much – he knows about Liam's relationship with Victor. It's absolutely gutting and seems like something that shouldn't have an audience. He has to stifle his own impulse to turn away.

Liam reaches a hand out and gently brushes the hair back from Victor's forehead. Behind him, Carly watches with eyes already gone red. Alex waits for someone to say something terrible, but all the horror comes from Liam. He grazes his fingers across Victor's and then goes to the dead man's wrist, before deftly unfastening the bracelet Alex retrieved from the ashtray. It's completely bizarre, not just because of the circumstances, but because fine motor control has never exactly been Liam's forte.

Liam clutches the bracelet in his fist and presses it to his sternum. He bows his head slightly more for a moment, before standing. Then, as everyone in the room watches – because Liam draws eyes, always, even like this, and Alex really has no power to stop them – he leans forward and kisses Victor tenderly on the forehead.

Alex has to bite at his own hand or he's going to cry or scream, and he does not know how to deal with that impulse any more than he wants to give in to it. Eventually, Liam straightens up again. When he turns around his face is wet.

Alex goes to him, because he doesn't know how not to. If anyone had bothered to talk to him – Carly hanging up on him the day Victor died was understandable but awful, and Liam's been almost entirely radio silent since except for a couple of emails about coping through as little external stimulus as possible – he'd have a much clearer idea of what he's supposed to do.

Frankly, he's a little pissed off. Because there are rules for funerals, and no one has bothered to tell him what they are when they involve actors and people with too much money and really complicated interpersonal relationships. Funerals were so much easier back home when they were for people in his high school class Alex didn't really know or like: You said sorry, and you handed someone a casserole.

"Please don't touch me," Liam says quietly and too quickly when Alex arrives at his elbow.

It stings, more than Alex would have ever thought.

"I was with him that morning," Liam adds, as if by way of explanation.

♦

When Liam walks away and Alex instinctively leans to follow, Paul grabs Alex's elbow. Alex twists away, awkward and embarrassed, as if he's been caught out.

"Don't chase him right now," Paul tells him.

"What am I supposed to do instead?" Alex asks. He looks like he's still trying to process the implications of Victor's death.

"Nothing. I get that this is probably over for you today – "

"I'm going to be asked about Victor for the rest of my fucking life," Alex says sharply under his breath. "And I'm doing my best not to think about Liam's loss so I don't suddenly freak out over mortality."

Paul considers making a joke about being older than Alex, and Alex needing to get used to the idea, but it seems like tempting fate. He watches as Liam quietly chats with the writer/director team for his new project, and can't help but think about how fragile all of their lives are. It's not only about Victor being dead, Alex's rock climbing, or his own continued ability to draw breath. For Paul, it's about their systems and how quickly the people and things that allow them to all make magic for a living can go up in smoke.

♦

Alex drifts through the psalms and hymns of the funeral. It's all way more of the Bible than he's used to for these sorts of occasions. Paul does one of the readings, and squeezes Alex's hand tightly before he stands to walk to the lectern. Alex pays attention, because it's Paul and Alex is always proud of and interested in him, but his eyes keep drifting to Liam.

They're all in the first few pews, like the fucked up family they are. Liam stares straight ahead, not at but somewhere above where the casket is resting in front of the altar. His eyes are red, and Carly, pressed beside Alex, keeps passing him tissues. In the pew behind them, Gemma catches Alex's eye and gives him a faint and watery smile when he turns around to take in the rest of the congregation.

It's Ellen who delivers the eulogy. She'd written it too late one night last week at their house, on the notepad Paul had been using for the Winsome plans.

"I got this job because no one else wanted it," she begins. "That's probably true of most of the people in this room who have worked for Victor at some point in their careers. Let's just get it out of the way, so you all don't talk smack about me later for not saying it: Sometimes, he was an absolutely terrible human being. I'm only not putting a finer point on it 'cause we're in a church. Also, we're only in a church because he liked ritual, not because he believed in anything other than himself, and his people, which are all of you.

"A lot of you aren't prizes either. Workaholics, divas, and neurotics, as ambitious as murderous kings in many cases. And he loved every single one of you for it, although odds are, he never told you, at least not in so many words. No, Victor conveyed that information by providing opportunities, assuming loyalty, and meddling often disastrously in people's personal lives. He usually only told people they were beautiful when they were in pain, and even I couldn't always figure out when he was joking.

"But he loved people. They were his science and his religion and his avocation, and he told stories instead of becoming a therapist or an advice columnist or a teacher only because his impulse was more often curiosity than healing. But in that curiosity he honored people – you all, and the people who watched (and complained) about his shows – for what they were, instead of what they could be. And that was a vote of confidence I'd venture to say few people are lucky enough to get from anyone in life.

"Victor moved mountains in this industry, usually by pissing people off. But he believed anyone he expended even a moment of his time on could do the same thing. So if you're in this room right now, you are obligated not to let him down."

5

In the passenger seat Liam's hands are nearly white with how hard he's clenching them. He made it through the service and the interment of Victor's body in the cathedral mausoleum without breaking entirely, which is a relief. Carly has no idea how much longer he can do this.

She rummages in her purse for a granola bar and puts half of it in her mouth once she manages to get it unwrapped. "Oh my god, pregnancy is so gross," she says while trying to chew.

Liam, who normally finds her pregnancy-related complaints somewhat hilarious, barely reacts. It's not unexpected, but it always freaks her out when she feels this much on her own when he's right goddamn next to her.

"Granola bar?" she offers, holding the other half out to him.

He gives her a look somewhere between withering and confused. "We have to go to the food thing now."

"It's called lunch," she says softly as she starts the car.

♦

Darcy scurries up to Paul and Alex as soon as they walk into the restaurant and hugs them both tightly even though they saw her twenty minutes ago at the funeral.

"Okay, so, I didn't want to tell you this at the church, because, you know, church, but, you should probably see this." She brushes a loose strand of hair out of her face as she digs her phone out of her clutch.

Paul and Alex exchange a look.

"What's up, Darcy?" Alex asks. By now he's used to asking her gentle questions in the hope of getting somewhat tempered answers.

"Okay, so, people are totally gross," she says, which does not make Alex feel any better, as she hesitates between them and then hands Paul the phone. "And I'm really sorry."

Paul takes it cautiously. "What did you do, Darcy?" he asks warily.

"I didn't do anything!" she protests, waving a hand at the screen. "Read it."

Paul raises an eyebrow at her and then does. "Oh, fuck."

Darcy bites her lip and nods, while Alex leans in to read over Paul's shoulder. It's a stupid gossip website, and it has a rather detailed and unflattering blind that is most definitely about the two of them and the night they'd gone out dancing.

Whoever's written it has gone to great lengths to emphasize the fact that two subjects of the blind – a well-known actor, and a well-known showrunner, both connected to Victor and in a well-known relationship – were getting down and dirty in public while Victor died.

"I think I need to sit down." Alex unsteadily sinks into a chair.

Darcy runs over to Alex and crouches down in front of him, putting her hands on his knees. "Are you freaking out about being busted for public sex or the sketchy blaming you for Victor's death?"

Alex raises his head to look at her. "Darcy."

"Yes?"

"Stop talking."

◆

Aside from the appalling nature of the internet – Alex makes Darcy swear not to show anyone else the blind – the mood of the group lightens as more people filter in from the service. The M.A.R.S. team seems to be rallying with some determination to honor the dead via ridiculous stories, and Alex is happy to leave Darcy to her socializing and stay in a corner chatting with Ruth, who has remained one of Winsome's stars and whose sly sarcasm always makes large gatherings of people more bearable. Raphael and his wife Irina also serve as an island of freakishly well-adjusted calm in a sea of crazy despite having to keep an eye on their kids who are about as unprepared for funeral etiquette as Alex feels.

Paul winds up in awkwardly jovial conversation with Mark Bevers, Victor's head writer on M.A.R.S. and one of the many people in line for the dubious honor of worst week ever.

"We're back with filming on Monday," he tells Paul. "We've got a table read Tuesday, and then we're out of script that Victor was directly involved with the week after that."

Paul's eyes go wide while Alex wonders if he can politely drift away at this point. "Was he giving you that much rope or are you guys that far behind?"

Mark scowls and says, "Yes."

Ellen isn't any happier about the situation. When Alex finally extricates himself from the conversation with Paul and Mark to ask, she throws up her hands.

"No one knows if they're keeping me around, but apparently I'm still on the hook for directing a bunch of sobbing freaks. And absolutely everyone at the studio has an opinion about how Victor wanted it shot. A fitting tribute to his memory is not out-meddling him."

Alex smirks. "Tell me how you really feel."

"Like shit," she says. "Can we start drinking?"

"I think the sun's been over the yardarm since you called," Alex says.

Ellen fixes him with a look. "Yeah, it was about five hours earlier for me, thanks."

Alex pats her shoulder. One day someone is going to ask her about that; for her sake, Alex hopes it's not someone who actually deserves an answer.

◆

While Alex chats with Ellen, Paul is approached by a young South Asian woman with a streak of fuchsia in the front of her otherwise black chin-length hair.

"Hey," she says, shaking his hand. "Olivia Mallick, we've met at a couple of Victor's parties."

Paul nods, because it's clearly not a question. "Hi. Yeah, you write on M.A.R.S.?"

"Assistant," Olivia says, brushing the unfortunate technicality aside. "Look, I know this is crass, but this is Victor's funeral and it's not like he'd mind."

Paul raises his eyebrows, intrigued at a conversation that is not tending toward annoying business or banal sympathies.

"I want to write for you. You should hire me."

Paul glances across the room to where Frank Pearson – the VP he hates but keeps winding up on the phone with – and Mark are talking with their heads together. "We only have a year left, I don't know you, and you work for Mark," he says, a little blindsided by the proposition but also impressed.

"Wrong. I worked for Victor. Who promised to staff me at the end of this season. Which is not going to happen, because Mark is not going to keep Victor's promises; and he's going to run M.A.R.S. into the ground way before your year is up anyway. So. What do you need from me to make that happen?"

Paul laughs, from surprise as much as anything. He wonders if this is a little how Victor felt when Alex marched into his office and told him to kill Zach off Fourth.

"Okay," he says. "Send me what you have. I'll give it a look." It's a platitude because he doesn't necessarily expect her to be able to deliver.

But Olivia slaps a thumb drive into his hand.

"Sent," she says with a smile. "Pleasure talking with you."

"You too."

Alex appears at Paul's elbow as Olivia is walking away. "You look pleased."

Paul chuckles and tucks the thumb drive into his breast pocket. "Someone just did the equivalent of following me into the bathroom to pitch me. And I liked it."

"Well, at least someone's having fun."

♦

Liam and Carly arrive as everyone takes their seats for the meal. Liam looks a little more present than he did at the funeral, but Carly is keeping a hand or an eye on him at all times. Alex doesn't blame her. Were their situations reversed, Alex is fairly sure he wouldn't feel safe leaving Liam alone. He can't imagine what this type of loss does to a person, especially one as defined by relationships as Liam is.

"I'm so glad you finally made it," Natalie, their former co-star on The Fourth Estate, who Alex has been happy not to spend time with since the show ended years ago, says. Liam runs a finger back and forth over the hem of his napkin. "Did you get lost?"

"I drove," Carly says flatly. "And we were trying to minimize how much small talk we'd have to make with you."

Alex turns to Paul with wide eyes. He has never, ever seen Carly do anything like that, even when he's been able to tell which of Liam's lovers and ex-lovers she's less than amused by. She's always been very clear that she never wants to give anyone a reason to think Liam's other relationship choices have any bearing on the status of their marriage. Clearly, those excessively gracious – but probably wise – rules are not in effect under these circumstances.

Paul touches Alex's hand, a silent plea not to make this into more of a scene. Alex settles for glaring at Natalie, who tosses her hair but otherwise doesn't respond. He desperately wants to know what Victor ever saw in her other than her character. He wishes they were at a different table. Darcy and Jackson are definitely better company.

It's a relief when lunch is finished. Even if this hellish day isn't over yet, at least they're done with the glaringly public parts of it. Alex ends up stuck near the door of the restaurant with Paul as everyone says their goodbyes before drifting off to whatever's next.

"Thank you for all of your work," Nigel tells him as he shakes his hand. "Victor would have appreciated it."

"You mean Victor would have been disappointed we had so many of his people in one room and nothing got broken."

Nigel gives him a sad smile. "I don't think you're entirely wrong, but the ways that you are doesn't make this easier for the people who loved him more comfortably than you did."

"I didn't – "

Nigel chuckles to himself. "Give it time," he says.

◆

The post-funeral gathering, involving alcohol and no people they don't like, is at Paul and Alex's house. As far as Alex is concerned, it's one more reason to be pissed off at Victor. All he wants is to crawl into their bed and stay there with Paul. Instead, he has to be social.

Not that he tries that hard, staying mostly off to the side of the room, barefoot and in his shirtsleeves, nursing a beer while Paul, Ellen, and Raphael tell increasingly raucous stories about Victor and the incredibly impish and occasionally malevolent force he always was in their lives. Alex isn't sure if the most malignant aspects of Victor's interference in all of their lives are something none of them are actually aware of, or are just setting aside for now.

Alex knows most of the stories probably are actually funny, and as difficult as Victor made everyone's life, most of the people in this room did have a fondness for him. And while Alex has no problem making light of death or speaking ill of the dead, it feels unsettling to laugh over Victor's exploits. He's kind of afraid too much drunken grief-processing will summon him from beyond the grave.

Besides, as far as he knows, no one else in this room ever was tied to a chair by Victor for a scene, or made out with Victor while he pulled Alex's hair and lured him closer to the small submissive place that the torture scene for their TV show hadn't been able to take him. The possibility that Alex might not be the only person Victor ever treated like that is as unsettling as the possibility that he is.

At least no one else in the room is being accused of killing Victor by fucking their partner in public. The whole thing is massively fucked up.

Eventually Alex finishes his drink and sets the empty bottle down on the end table next to Darcy's glass and the whiskey bottle someone, probably Ellen, liberated from their liquor cabinet for efficiency's sake.

Paul gives Alex a concerned look when he stands up and heads out of the room, but Alex shakes his head and slips upstairs.

◆

Paul knocks on their bedroom door before he opens it.

"You okay?" he asks.

"Not really," Alex says from where he's stretched out on their bed facing the far wall. He can feel the mattress dip when Paul sits down on the edge.

"What's up?" Paul says.

"I feel like a ghoul. Liam's clearly a mess. You're going to be. Everyone's sad, and mostly I just think this is all weird."

"Well, it is weird, if that helps."

"Yeah, tell that to the blind."

Paul clearly has no idea what to say to that.

"I just got back from Australia," Alex says.

"I know."

"I don't want to go away again. It's too fucking hard."

"You don't have to do media for Icarus until November."

Alex shrugs.

"What is this about?"

"The fact that somehow I've become the bad guy in Victor's story. Which is ludicrous."

"If it's ludicrous, why are you flipping out? And God, it's the internet. Fuck that."

"I want everything to go back to the way it was."

"How's that?"

Alex doesn't say anything, because to say he misses a life without cameras on his face and where he can be a jerk with his friends on the internet, and where he and Gemma watch shitty TV while eating bad takeout in their crappy apartment, would be to say he doesn't want this life he shares with Paul. And that's not it, not really. But he wants everything to stop being so hard.

◆

When Alex doesn't answer, Paul takes a deep breath and pushes down his anxiety, because Alex being silent is Alex trying not to upset him. Paul reaches out and rubs a hand up and down Alex's arm until Alex rolls over to face him.

Paul gives him a tight smile, but the one Alex responds with is huge. Paul feels his entire being unclench at that, just in time for Alex to sit up, grab his shoulders, and kiss him hard.

Paul actually laughs into it.

"What?" Alex asks.

"Funerals. Sex."

"It's only a cliché if we're a terrible hookup."

"Everyone's still downstairs," Paul points out.

"Apparently we don't care about that," Alex informs him. "Also, they're drunk."

Paul puts a hand to his chest to push him back into the pillows.

"We shouldn't have done that," Alex blurts.

"What?"

"Last week. At the club."

"Who'd it hurt?" Paul says, brushing it away, but then Alex's eyes twist the knife. Paul sits back on his heels. "Well fuck."

"It's stupid right?"

"It's incredibly stupid. Considering the other time we did that, we did it in front of Victor and he thought it was hilarious."

"Victor was also really fucking high for that."

"Everyone was really fucking high for that," Paul says.

"You know, Victor's the first person I've kissed who's died."

♦

The sex is more awkward than it should be, and not because there is a living room full of people downstairs or because they've been rehashing some of their strange exploits. Alex wants to be obliterated, but Paul is cautious and not in the way he is when he's trying not to mark Alex up.

Alex finally mumbles, "What do you want?" He's tired and angry and a little drunk and just wants Paul to fuck him so he can fall asleep and pretend this whole day never happened.

Paul doesn't want to run the show either – he rolls over onto his back and pulls Alex on top of him. He cranes his head up for a kiss and then drops back on the pillow when he can't hold his neck up any longer.

It's not enough of an answer, but somehow Alex gets a clue and the ability to respond. He groans softly as he crawls up Paul's body, impatient and turned on and happy to shove a hand into Paul's hair before sliding it around the back of his head. Paul sucks so eagerly at Alex's cock when he starts to feed it into his mouth that Alex's breath punches out of him, and he has to close his eyes for a moment or he's going to tip right the fuck over. Paul protests, his mouth full, by pinching his ass.

Alex chuckles breathlessly and shakes his head, grabbing both of Paul's hands and drawing them up above his head. With his wrists pinned to the bed, Paul can't do anything but take it as Alex fucks his mouth. It's nothing like what they usually do, but it's dirty and hot and Alex doesn't moan out loud only because there are still people downstairs.

Paul struggles against Alex's weight on his wrists, but Alex leans more heavily on them and fucks his mouth harder. He wants to take the fragile look in Paul's eyes to its ultimate conclusion and shatter him utterly. It's not a familiar impulse, but it's completely irresistible.

Eventually, Paul does get a hand free, and jerks himself off while Alex runs a hand through Paul's hair over and over until his muscles cramp up and he comes, hard.

Paul coughs and swallows messily and comes himself while Alex blinks vision back into his eyes. He wipes his mouth with the back of his hand as Alex collapses on top of him, whining softly and burying his head in Paul's shoulder.

"What the fuck was that?" Alex asks, his voice muffled by skin.

6

The next morning Alex hauls himself out of bed when Paul gets up. He wants a few more minutes with him before he vanishes to the office again.

Given the number of guests and the volume of alcohol involved, not to mention their own activities once they went upstairs, he's not sure what he's going to find downstairs. But when they get to the kitchen, the only sign of human life is the various glasses and bottles accumulated on the counters and a note on the table.

Everyone's been sent on their way safely. Enjoy the peace and quiet. It's signed *Claire*, and there's a little smiley face next to her name. Alex can imagine Ellen's wife leaving the note before shooing the last stragglers out the door.

"They're gone," Alex breathes in relief. He drops the note back on the table and slumps against Paul. Given that all of their friends are grownups and it was a fucking wake, he'd hoped no one would actually crash, but experience has taught him not to assume maturity amongst this group. "You're sure you have to go in today?"

"It's not like my job got easier because my business partner died," Paul points out, a little sharply.

"I didn't mean it like that," Alex says.

Paul sighs. "Believe me, if I could stay home I would."

◆

Paul could accomplish everything he needs to do today from his home office, but normalcy is a powerful drug in the face of tragedy. He wants to be back at work even if the other half of his executive production team is never going to be on the *Winsome* lot again.

Of course, acting normal is one thing, but actually feeling that way is harder. Much harder. Paul looks over his shoulder half a dozen times thinking he's heard familiar footsteps or the murmur of a voice outside the door. His mother would be less skeptical of what Paul knows is just his imagination. Certainly, if Victor chose to haunt anywhere it would be his workplace, but Paul knows he only misses him.

It's only been a week since he died and it was yesterday that they put Victor in the ground – or at least, in a crypt in the mausoleum under the Cathedral. Paul wonders if any of them will ever realize he's really gone.

He's surprised when Nigel calls.

"Not to be rude," Paul says, not bothering with small talk after all of the emotion of the last week, "but I'd assumed you were looking forward to a few days of not dealing with Victor's human blast radius. What do you need?"

Nigel chuckles. Paul knows, from comments Nigel and Victor have made, that Paul is – of all their social group – consistently the most direct and least suspicious of Nigel, and that Nigel consistently appreciates it. Carly, he is fond of and can excuse. Liam and Alex are nightmares.

"I got named executor," Nigel says, which shouldn't be news to anyone. "And he named you his creative executor."

"What the hell does – "

"With Liam."

"Oh my God," Paul says. He still has no idea what that means, but it's surely nothing good.

"Yup, the bastard stuck me with all his worldly possessions and stuck you with – "

"What Alex would call the public display of the absence of his soul."

"Your husband is creepy." Nigel laughs.

"You have no idea," Paul says. "You call Liam yet?"

"What do you think? I'm relying on you to absorb the details. The less I have to navigate Victor's exhausting, possessive, and now heartbroken boyfriend, the better for everyone."

♦

Liam folds his arms across his chest, his phone dangling from one hand.

"What did he want?" Carly asks, fully prepared to call Nigel back and bitch him out if Liam is upset.

Liam shrugs.

"Words, Liam," Carly tells him.

He gives her an annoyed look.

"Well?" she asks. Sometimes he needs prodding.

"Just a minute." He's irritated and trying to collect to himself. "Victor named Paul and me creative executors of his estate."

"What the fuck does that mean?"

"I don't know. We get to figure out what to do with his creative stuff."

"Like, what? Scripts?"

"Yeah. Whatever. Stuff."

Carly sighs. More exposure to the problem is not likely to make Liam's life better. He's had a hard enough time functioning this last week, and Victor including him in this last request is going to make the challenge of facing the world that much harder.

"How do you feel about that?"

Liam shrugs. "I don't know what I'll have to do. Or if I'll have to do anything, Paul's the one who does this stuff. Maybe I won't have time."

He says it with a vague note of hope that's as wrenching to hear as anything. It's also the first time since Victor's death he's mentioned his own job. When Liam decided a couple of years ago he wanted to branch out into movies, Victor helped him pick *The Parrot Tree*. Victor knew and trusted the people involved, and Liam's enjoyed it so far even if little has gone to film and everything has been table reads and fittings.

"If the hanging out at home not talking to anybody isn't just indulging your grief while you have the time to, you're going to have to make some decisions about your movie," Carly says. It feels slightly cruel to say, but it's true. Whatever he ultimately wants or is able to do, Liam isn't best served by a lack of clarity as to the demands on his time.

"I'm not scheduled to shoot anything for a while."

"Yes, but are you going to get another week off like this? And then you're going to be on location, for six weeks, in India. How is that going to work, if you can't always *talk*?"

"I'll have a script," Liam says.

That's not strictly true, and Carly has no idea if it's supposed to be a joke about Liam's life or a comment on his ability to get lost in the work.

◆

After Paul leaves for the day, Alex calls Margaret, his manager, to check in on the general tack he wants to take regarding Victor's death. But when she asks about the blind, he wishes he hadn't.

"I absolutely do not need to know if it's true or not, and please do not tell me if it is, but for fuck's sake don't ever do that. Again or otherwise."

Alex slouches down on the couch. "Can we talk about *Icarus* promotion?"

"Sure. We should also talk about what you're planning to do next."

"I just got back from Australia a month ago," Alex says plaintively.

"That is true, but it's not relevant and you didn't answer the question."

Alex twists his wedding ring around his finger with his thumb and stares at the wall over their bookshelves, where pictures from the various trips he and Paul have taken for work and, more rarely, for vacation together are framed and hung.

"It means I don't want to think about going anywhere far away for a while. How bad an idea is it for me to guest on *Winsome*?"

The network has been nagging Paul about when he's going to get his A-list husband on the show pretty much since *Winsome* started its run. It's alternately amusing or irritating, depending on how uncomfortable he or Paul are feeling about their careers intersecting. Paul doesn't like to think that he got the show in part because he could guarantee a star like J. Alex Cook, and Alex doesn't want to be the guy who gets parts just because he's fucking – and now married to – the showrunner.

But *Winsome* needs an antagonist for its final season, and Alex is tickled to death at the idea Paul floated at him of playing a guy with whom Darcy's character forms a strange business and sexual partnership that leaves the audience guessing as to who is using who. As a bonus, Alex gets to die again, because Darcy's character is going to shoot him.

Victor asked Alex once, when they were all over at his house for dinner and then swimming, if he intended to die in every movie or show he was ever on.

"There's no suspense if I tell you yes," Alex said. Victor had cracked up.

Mostly though, Alex is glad that Paul's definitely not going to torture him to get a good performance the way Victor had for Zach's violent exit from *Fourth*.

Margaret pulls him back to the now. "Having a recurring guest role on your husband's show is adorable. Appearing in an arc for one season is adorable. Do not be a fucking regular on your husband's show."

Alex laughs darkly at all the things that are, and are not, considered acceptable in the place where their private and public lives intersect.

◆

Back in his office, Paul fishes the thumb drive from Olivia out of his computer case and plugs it in. He eats a sandwich with one hand while he scrolls through the contents of it with the other. Her writing is tight and vivid, and she studiously avoids directing from the page. Paul decides to do her a favor, just because he can. He sets the sandwich down and opens his email.

Olivia –

Monday. Be here.

Three minutes later, his phone rings.

Olivia doesn't bother to say hello. "Okay, I know that felt all *How to Get Away with Murder* sexy and stuff, but you can't 'be here' me.

Make me an offer and we can fucking negotiate."

Paul laughs. "Writers' room. Monday. Six episode contract."

"I want more."

"We only have seven left."

"I want in on all seven."

"No you don't," Paul says gently. "The weekly pay is better on six weeks than eight, and I know you know it."

"I don't care about the cash."

"Yes you do," Paul says. The space between an assistant's salary and union rates on an hour-long drama are massive. Olivia will earn more in those six weeks than she's made in the last six months.

"You have to let me negotiate something," she says.

"You're not gonna say no, and I've got nothing else to give," Paul says. Again, he sees why Victor liked her and made her promises, but he can also see how much she would have benefitted from the guidance he never got around to giving her. At least Paul can honor Victor's choices and give her this.

"Lunch," she blurts.

"What?"

"You have to buy me lunch. Somewhere nice. Where we can look important. Because I've done a deal, and I need some recommendations on finding a rep," she says. And then, because she's not done brazening it out, "Sometime in the next two weeks."

"You're fucking crazy, you know that right?"

"Sure," she says, tough and casual again. "But, like, who isn't?"

7

Olivia's question lingers. As the spring drags on, Paul has no idea what to do with the creative executor thing – he has the sneaking suspicion Victor made it up just to fuck with him, though God knows why Liam's involved in that case.

The network *M.A.R.S.* is on is completely onboard with the idea, however. Paul gets summoned to a mid-April meeting with the studio brass. Without so much as a by-your-leave Frank, Paul's least favorite network suit, announces that *M.A.R.S.* is bringing Paul on board as a co-showrunner. Paul hasn't seen a contract, and is perhaps less keen than he should be on saying yes.

Meanwhile, Mark's already been promoted from head writer to head writer *and* co-showrunner. There is no way, given the inside baseball of Hollywood, that this won't end in a mess of professional jealousy and disaster.

Paul also knows he's not allowed to say no. The realization, after the first vague horror of it, makes him chuckle to himself; Alex will be amused. Paul at least does have the good sense to hold up his hands, remind everyone that they need this on paper and insist they talk to his rep. Because he'll deal with Victor's files in memory of his dead friend, but solving the network's problems needs to come with a paycheck.

Unfortunately, it also gives him pause about the Olivia situation. Taking advantage of Victor's passing to hire her is one thing. Stealing her off a show he's about to have a professional relationship with, on a different network than *Winsome*, is ethically and legally a lot more dubious – even if she is just a writer's assistant to them and no one is likely to care.

As daunting as the assignment is – the network isn't really any more specific about what it wants out of Paul than Victor was – Paul knows it's a vote of confidence. With *Winsome* in its final season, that's a good sign for Paul's continued viability as a showrunner. It's also a good sign that something of Victor's vision will be allowed to stick around, no matter how many people he pissed off when he was alive.Paul is relieved; Victor may have made Alex's career in a much more visible way, but Paul owes Victor everything, too.

After the meeting, Mark pulls Paul aside in the hallway. "Look," he says. "I know you're Victor's pet and he was grooming you to take over his empire, but some of us here have a job to do and aren't actually thrilled that Victor's dead."

Paul stares. "Excuse me?" Mark's tone and body language are exactly the same as in the meeting – and the funeral. Paul is wary and also fucking confused.

"*M.A.R.S.* was Victor's show, not yours, and the last thing we need is you coming in and taking over."

"Okay," Paul says firmly. This has gotten so far out of hand so quickly he hardly knows where to start. "I'm going to be co-showrunning because the network asked me to. I *have* my own show. I do not want your job. I am here if you need me. I will go through Victor's notes, and I will give you what I find. That's it."

"Bullshit. Everyone's ambitious, and this is a perfect opportunity. I know what I'd do if the situation were reversed."

"I'm not going to complain if the studio wants to pay me to do work I'd have to anyway," Paul says evenly. "I know everything's fucked up for you, but you have no idea how tangled up Victor's life has been with mine and Alex's. This is more fucked up for us."

"Yeah, everybody knows how much Victor helped you and your boy and *his* boy," Mark says.

Paul realizes that Mark is talking about Alex and *Liam*; in the same instant he realizes his hands are shaking. There's a ringing in his ears and everything in him wants to punch Mark. Paul has spent years trying to restrain his more destructive impulses, and does his best to shove this one away.

"Crazy Hollywood power-plays aside, grief makes everybody insane." he says as he takes a deep breath and makes himself walk away. He needs to call his sister.

♦

Paul checks in at the *Winsome* offices, then heads home to work. He's still jangly from the confrontation with Mark and it feels like bad luck to bring that energy around the show that is actually his – and a little bit Victor's – baby.

Alex isn't home, and Paul assumes he's gone out climbing. Even with so much of it to do in Australia, he had little time and confessed to Paul that he missed "his" rocks. It's both weird and adorable.

He debates setting up camp at the dining room table. They bought this new, bigger house so he could have a proper office, isolated from everyone else in the basement. But when he can stand mild distractions he tries not to lock himself away from Alex. It's one of their mostly unspoken coping mechanisms for Paul's tendency to overwork even by Hollywood standards.

But he doesn't want Mark's bullshit settling into his home with Alex any more than he wants it at *Winsome*, so he trudges downstairs to his office and hopes Alex will be persistent in retrieving him later.

He opens his social media dashboard mostly out of guilt. He hasn't had time to deal with any of it since Victor died, and he has a lot of messages of condolence and support. Many of them are from industry acquaintances and folks in the business he hasn't met but professionally flirts with online about hypothetical future projects. It's probably about time to say thank you.

Of course, Paul is an idiot, and he tracks way too many social media tags – about himself, about Alex, about their shows, and about the people they work with. That has always, very much, included Victor.

Paul knows he shouldn't be surprised that the Internet is animated and deeply down in the anger stage with Victor's death. After all, Mark is, and if Paul weren't so exhausted he supposes the rage would have found him by now too.

Some of the anger, though, isn't because Victor's dead, but because it took him so damn long to finally achieve that state. There's a massive number of people retweeting exclamations of joy, as if Victor had been the Wicked Witch of the West. Victor would have probably laughed. After all, his Twitter handle is – was – @TheShowYouHate, and he used it relentlessly to antagonize the viewing audience, critics, colleagues, and sometimes even his friends. Fans never knew what to make of it whenever he and Alex went at it, mostly playfully, on Twitter.

But it's still miserable to see people celebrating the death of someone who made everything from Paul's career to his marriage possible. It all feels very, very personal, and that's before a random scan of his Twitter mentions turns up way too many tweets speculating that the only person who might be happier about Victor's death than them is Paul.

He can't get his head around it – this idea fans have that people who create shows also ruin them and are to be despised. Paul discovers he also can't convince himself these people are wrong, though he knows, or at least should know, that Victor died neither alone (Ellen's phone call was a testament to that), nor unloved.

It's sad, and it's terrifying, and Paul finds himself unable to look away, reading through days and days of messages, many of them awful, many roping in him and Alex and their whole social circle. He wants Alex but needs Victor right now – he was the only person that could ever talk him down from his anxieties about the consequences of his work.

When Paul realizes he's never going to have that again and the Internet is probably happy about that too, he chokes out his first tears about Victor until he cries for real in the way men – especially men from places like Marion, South Carolina – are never supposed to. Somewhere in the middle of it all, he realizes with a wet laugh that at least now he knows what the fuck Mark was talking about.

♦

Paul takes a run and a shower and is settled back at his desk by the time Alex gets home, sweaty and chalky and content. He's grateful when Alex hauls him back upstairs to make food together. Recent tragedy only sharpens his awareness of the happiness in their admittedly strange lives. Paul listens to Alex's account of his day on the rocks while they move around the kitchen and imagines the two of them in five or ten years and the shape of the lives he desperately hopes they'll have.

Alex is unkindly amused about the network asking Paul to co-showrun on *M.A.R.S.* until he realizes it's not actually a joke. He's even less amused that Paul and Mark are already at odds.

"Is Victor going to haunt us forever?" he asks.

Paul isn't sure how careless his choice of words is. "The entirety of our professional lives are linked to his. This isn't going to go away overnight, and you should probably get used to that idea."

"I'm still not used to the idea that he's *dead*. But since he is, some distance from him would be great."

"Well, that's not going to happen particularly soon. We still have to go through all his things," Paul points out.

"Whoa, whoa whoa. *You're* the creative executor. When did that become 'we'?" Alex looks alarmed at the prospect of spending any amount of time in Victor's house ever again. Not that Paul can really blame him.

"I can play the 'have you got anything better to do,' card, the 'Liam's going to be there and will need moral support card,' or, the 'I'm asking nicely because you're my partner and my life is about to get stupid' card."

Alex laughs darkly. "Victor really is a bastard."

"You keep saying."

"It keeps being true."

"While we're on the subject of what to do with Victor's legacy – "

"I can't believe you just used that word unironically."

" – we should talk about what this next year is going to look like for us. Because you're finally back home, and we probably shouldn't put it off any more."

"Okayyy," Alex says with trepidation. "Should I be nervous that you look like you're getting ready to make a pitch?"

"Well, when *Winsome*'s done...I was thinking about us having a baby."

"Excuse me?"

Alex's face is not exactly encouraging, but Paul plows ahead anyway. "I'm going to have the year off. Whatever I do with *M.A.R.S.*, it won't be a full-time gig, so you can stop freaking out about that. And you're between major projects."

"You know, the let's-have-a-baby-because-we-have-a-year-off thing only works if we have the baby at the *beginning* of that year," Alex says with increasing speed and franticness. "Not spending nine months waiting and then getting the kid right when we have to go back to work. Why don't we wait until your next break?" he concludes almost desperately.

"Because I'd like to have a kid before I turn forty."

"It's Hollywood. Guys have babies, like, in their seventies," Alex says. He's waving his hands around now, which is not one of his usual ticks.

"Yeah and that's kind of gross. Also Victor *died,* and he wasn't even sixty."

"For the hundredth time, you are not Victor. Like, it's a battle, but you actually sleep. And this is not a reasonable response to whatever crisis of mortality is going on in your head."

"Okay, well, there's another reason time is a factor," Paul says. He takes a breath and lays out his plan.

Alex stares at him, boggled. "You want me and *your sister* to have a baby?"

"Via a surrogate," Paul says defensively. He's a little irritated that Alex is being so deliberately childish.

"Have you talked to Sarah about this?" Alex asks, switching gears in a state that might be approaching panic. "Because you have a track record."

"Yes."

"YOU TALKED TO YOUR SISTER ABOUT OUR BIOLOGICAL FUTURE WITHOUT ASKING ME FIRST? HOW LONG HAVE YOU BEEN THINKING ABOUT THIS?"

Paul crosses his arms over his chest and refuses to take the bait. "Admit you were going to yell at me if I hadn't talked to her too, just so we can move on," he suggests.

Alex maintains his glare but eventually deflates. Apparently, Paul isn't wrong.

"Besides, we've been talking about this for ages."

"We have not!"

"All the time you were in Australia?"

"I thought that was hypothetical!"

"It's *me,*" Paul says, though he's aware that's not really a legitimate defense.

"And it most definitely did not involve Sarah," Alex presses.

"Well, that was a more recent addition."

"No shit!"

"We don't have to do it this way," Paul says because that's what fairness requires. "But I want to, and you should think about it."

8

"I do not need the gory details." Gemma interrupts Alex's monologue about how America will be obsessed over whether he or Paul is the biological father of their still very hypothetical child. They're in Paul and Alex's kitchen, Alex making popcorn while Gemma perches on a bar stool.

"Well, kids kind of come with gory details. Even when you get them with science and not sex."

Alex gives a dramatic shudder mostly, but not entirely, for comedic effect.

"Why are boys so bad at coping with biology?" she teases when Alex pushes the popcorn bowl across the island to her.

"It would be less dumb if Paul weren't making plans without me again."

"No he is not, and we are not going down that road again. You did not make me drive all the way over here so you could whine at me about your hot, talented, successful husband's overeagerness to have kids with you."

"I didn't make you drive over here," Alex protests.

"Well, you get weird when my neighbors take pictures of you coming and going so yes, you did."

"I'm freaking out that 'abstract plan' became a timetable overnight."

"Which is fair. But, Alex, seriously, you're being an asshole. Not everything in your life is out to get you, and it would be nice if you called me over here for something other than for me to give you advice about really expensive babies. I am not your therapist. Ask me how my job is going."

Alex grins. He and Gemma don't hang out as much as they used to, because both of their schedules are hard, but he appreciates her ability to call him on his shit. It was grounding the year his life went crazy, and it's still reassuring. "How's your job going, Gemma?"

Gemma launches into a monologue of her own about the struggles of trying to find her way into development without a bachelor's degree to her name.

Alex tries to listen, but he drifts off into his own head, wondering with a small bit of horror what their lives would have been like if Victor hadn't plucked him out of obscurity. Would he and Gemma still be living together? Who would Alex be with, if not Paul? Or would he and Paul have crashed into each other no matter what? After all, Paul noticed him before even Victor did. Would Alex be an A.D. by now? Or would he have had to go back to Indiana, without any of his excuses – first, no money, and now, no time – not to?

Gemma flicks his shoulder. "You're not listening."

Alex startles. "I am totally listening."

"What's the last thing I said?"

"Blah blah something about development blah?"

Gemma kicks his stool, but she's laughing. "Asshole."

Alex shrugs, mostly because he doesn't know how to apologize or how to be better. Sometimes, he feels like he doesn't know how to do anything at all. Certainly, that alone should disqualify him from being a parent.

"What the hell is up with you?" Gemma asks. "If the baby stuff is freaking you out, *talk to your husband about it.* You do not need my permission to have a family."

Alex is quiet for a long moment. Then he says, "I thought you said you weren't my therapist."

9

Paul tends to keep more reasonable hours when Alex is home but he's still often one of the last ones on the lot, which is why he's surprised to see a light on in the writers' office late one night at the beginning of May.

He sticks his head in the door to see Olivia, laptop open, typing furiously and, until he knocks on the doorframe, not remotely aware that he's there.

She jumps and then glares at him. "You should wear a bell."

"Not a lot of people around on a Friday night to scare."

"Nope," she says and goes back to typing. She gives him an annoyed look when he wanders further into the room and sits down in the chair across from her.

The *Fourth Estate* offices are long gone. It's been years since Paul was on a writing staff, but rooms like this still feel like home even if he's now on the other side of the desk, dispensing guidance instead of being lectured to – kindly or otherwise – by Victor.

"What do you want?" she asks.

"Friday night writers' bonding," Paul says. "Tell me about yourself. Your hopes, your dreams, how much *M.A.R.S.* is going to suck now." He's no Victor when it comes to wrangling people and forcing them to grow. He also knows he's kinder, and if people aren't his avocation the way they were Victor's, he still cares for them all. In Victor's now eternal absence, it's even more crucial to connect.

Olivia laughs and waves a hand at him before going back to typing, again. "Don't you have work to do? Or go home, stop bugging me."

"You're here," Paul asks, and it's leading.

"I'm working on new spec."

"Why?"

"You only gave me six episodes, and your show is ending."

"The specs you gave me will get you a job anywhere," Paul points out.

"Mmm, I wish," Olivia says. "Except I am neither white nor in possession of a dick, so Hollywood is doubly gross for me. Also I don't want a job anywhere, I want my own show. Go away."

"No, talk to me," Paul says, fascinated now. Dedication is one thing and is certainly admirable, but Olivia is working like a woman possessed. It reminds him more than a little of himself and the first year he'd spent writing for Victor, spending eighteen hours a day telling stories because the rest of his life was fucked up beyond belief. Olivia certainly seems better-adjusted than Paul was at twenty-five, but he still wants her stories, and not only the ones she's putting on paper.

"Paul, *I am working*."

"Tell me what your deal is and I'll go away," Paul gives her his most charming smile.

"Okay, this is where I explain that I am not here to entertain you or explain myself to you, and shouldn't have to bargain with you to be left alone to do my work. It's also a good thing you're gay or you would be not just rude but also creepy." Olivia hits save and folds her hands in front of her keyboard.

"Sorry."

"Thank you. Now, since you've been useful in the past... I want to tell stories. Victor was a bastard and a genius, and the world is never going to appreciate how much it's going to miss him and that pisses me off. You're crazy too, and I'm not sure how that's going to blow up yet but you are and it is; but you're not an asshole like Mark and can probably be trained. Also, if you think you're going to be my mentor, just stop now and save us both the grief."

Paul stares at her. "What makes you think I'm going to be your mentor?" he asks, a little stung but mostly amused, because Olivia is sharp and delightful and completely not wrong.

"You're in here at ten o'clock on a Friday night asking me what my deal is."

♦

Alex, to Paul's weary dismay, is still incredibly irritated that, after Victor has been buried, his house still exists and Alex is getting dragged into dealing with it. He badgers Paul about it the entire ride over.

"Why can't Nigel do this?" Alex asks as soon as they get in the car.

"He's in New York."

"Jackson?"

"Not what he signed up for."

"Right, Liam?"

"That's cruel, Alex."

"I don't understand why it's us."

"You're being a brat," Paul says with a sigh. "And as charming as you are – "

"Not charming?" Alex asks.

"Nope," Paul says almost cheerfully. "Not at all."

Alex's dread makes a lot more sense when they get there. Carly is annoyed that they're late, and Liam is sitting cross-legged on the floor by a bookcase running his hand along the tops of the books on the lowest shelves.

"You're going to get paper cuts," Alex says.

Liam stops. Which actually seems to piss Carly off more.

"Can we get this over with?" she says.

"Woman after my own heart," Alex mutters.

Paul looks around the central core of the house's public spaces and sighs. "Does anyone think this isn't going to be days of work?" he asks incredulously.

"Don't feel sorry for yourself until you see what's on my to-do list," Carly says darkly.

"Why, what?"

Carly jerks her head in the direction of the kitchen. Paul follows her, mystified and already tired, while Alex crouches down next to Liam.

"Given the nature of fucking dead Victor's relationship with Liam, what's the last thing you'd want either of those two to stumble across while we're sorting through Victor's intimate effects?" she hisses once Alex and Liam are out of earshot.

Paul frowns at her, thinking. And then his jaw drops. "Oh my God."

"Yes."

"So you're going to – ?"

"Look for Victor's hidden stash of sex toys so Liam doesn't break down if he finds them and Alex doesn't blurt something idiotic if *he* finds them? *Yes.*"

In light of Carly's mission, Paul is grateful for his relatively straightforward, if herculean, task of going through Victor's office for whatever *M.A.R.S.* information he can find. The place is ruthlessly organized, but there's tons of material – desk drawers and filing cabinets and bookshelves – that he's going to have to come back for.

He assigns Alex the task of searching Victor's den for anything possibly useful to the whole creative executor thing. Paul's sure Victor didn't keep everything in his office and wants to stick his husband somewhere he's not going to come across any of the dreaded sex toys. Hopefully the den is free of them.

◆

Liam still hasn't said anything, but he drifts into the den after Alex and sits down on the floor again. Alex folds his arms and sighs, regarding the crammed bookshelves lining the wall. Victor really was a bastard.

He tries to be methodical, but there's too much here. Some of it is books, not that Alex ever once saw Victor read anything that wasn't a script page or on a screen. There are rows and rows of DVDs. One bookcase is given over to binders and notebooks, which he pokes over at random.

Alex expects Liam to say something when he starts monologuing at him about Paul and babies, but Liam lets it all wash over him. It's unexpectedly soothing, to talk into the air.

When he kneels down on the floor to deal with the bottom shelf, Liam leans against his shoulder. It makes it kind of hard to move without jostling him, but Liam doesn't seem to mind so Alex shrugs and carries on. Liam is one of the few people he's easy sharing space with. It's unusual that Liam's still so quiet, but then, they are basically ransacking his dead lover's house. Alex doesn't want to think about ever having to go through Paul's office like this.

At least, if the unspeakable happened, Alex would get to keep the house. Though between the alternatives, Alex isn't sure which one he'd prefer. Mostly, he wants not to think of the possibility ever.

"Lee, I'm gonna move over," Alex warns him before he shifts to get a better access to the shelf. Liam picks his head up to let him, then starts playing with a bracelet – Victor's, Alex sees when he looks over. Alex is glad for the company, but the soft clink of the dead man's jewelry as Liam toys with it is completely unnerving.

The next book Alex puts his hand on is heavy, black, and leather bound. When Alex opens it, he's expecting a fancy dictionary or maybe some *Readers' Digest*-like series.

When he sees not printed text but pages full of precise penmanship, Alex snaps the book closed. Liam looks up at him curiously as Alex opens the book again, slowly.

It's definitely a diary, and, going by the dates on the entries, it's at least a few years old. The thought of Victor having a diary – not to mention one written on expensive paper and not a hard drive – is so bizarre Alex can't quite process it right away.

Alex checks the shelf; sure enough, there is a whole row of the books, all identical. He starts pulling them onto the floor. The dates go back decades, though most are from the last ten or fifteen years.

"What are those?" Liam asks, once Alex has them spread around himself in a circle.

"Victor's diaries." Alex runs a hand across a cover. "Do you want them?"

Liam thinks about it and then shakes his head. "No. Books can't bring him back."

Alex has no idea how to respond to that. "Is it okay if I take them?"

♦

Alex tucks his bag close to his side as he holds the door for Paul, who's carrying a brown cardboard file box that looks like it's from 1960. He's filled it with notebooks, a laptop, and multiple external drives. Paul hopes none of it is password protected, though he knows how likely that isn't.

Carly locks the door, and Liam doesn't give Alex their usual hug on parting; he still isn't on his usual touching terms with anyone. Paul watches, box balanced on his hip while Liam and Alex look at each other for a long moment before Liam follows Carly.

"What was that about?" Paul asks once they're in the car.

"Liam and I are gonna hang out this week." Alex carefully arranges his bag at his feet.

Paul looks sideways at him, but Alex doesn't say anything else; apparently Alex and Liam are having psychic conversations again. Paul shrugs and starts the car. He's learned life is easier when he doesn't poke too hard at whatever weird thing exists between them.

♦

As soon as they get home, Paul pulls Victor's laptop out of the box and plonks it down on their kitchen table. Alex has to resist the urge to tell him that he doesn't want it near where they eat; like bare feet in a restaurant, it's not actually unhygienic, but it still feels unseemly.

For a moment, they both stare at it.

"Are you expecting it to open by itself, cast an eerie glow, and convey a terrible message?" Alex asks, still not looking at Paul.

"Are you?" Paul asks, amused and hostile that Alex is including him in his own discomfort.

"Maybe? A little? Yes?" he finally turns to Paul.

"I wasn't 'til you said it," Paul grumbles before sliding into a chair and opening the thing.

Alex tries to leave him to it, not wanting to fret about it further. Certainly the diaries can wait. He's not going to give them power like Paul has the Magic Computer of Showrunner Godliness. Also, they really need a Victor quota.

"Can we, like, have a rule?" he asks as he stares into their refrigerator. He wants something to eat, has no motivation to cook, and can't imagine what's interesting enough to order in. That's the horror of not being on a project: he has to make mundane decisions all by himself.

Paul makes an inquisitive noise.

"That laptop never, ever, *ever* comes to bed with you."

Paul actually flinches at the thought. "Yeah. God. No."

Alex chuckles darkly.

"Fuck," Paul says.

"What?" Alex says, finally pulling out a bottle of water and hipping the door closed. Paul is staring despondently at the screen.

"Password."

Alex arches an eyebrow. "Were you expecting it not to be locked?"

"Are you going to be obnoxious, or are you going to help?"

"You know I can't read Victor's mind, either. Especially now that he's dead."

Paul sighs. "Is the sense of humor about dead Victor your way of coping or just you being thoughtless?"

Alex shrugs.

"Do you think Liam would know?"

"If I can't call him to see how he's coping with Victor's death, you can't call him about Victor's *password*."

"Why not?" Paul asks.

"Because you're co-creative executors, and Victor was his lover, and you took the laptop without so much as a by your leave – "

"Liam doesn't seem interested – "

"What would you be interested in if I were gone?"

Paul shoves back from the computer likes he's been burned. "Whoa. Don't do that."

"What, put mortality issues on the table because dead Victor makes you want to have a baby?"

"Seriously, Alex. Computer password. The sooner I go through it, the sooner I can get it out of here."

"I don't know. Call Nigel."

"No."

"Why?" Alex asks.

"Because it's weird."

"It's Victor. Nigel is not unfamiliar with weird."

"I don't want to call him with the first problem we have, okay?"

Alex rolls his eyes and shakes his head. There is nothing unfamiliar about this iteration of they-both-have-issues-but-Paul-likes-to-pretend-he-doesn't. There is, however, only so much of Paul having bursts of password hacking inspiration followed by sighing petulantly at Victor's laptop that Alex can take.

"Give me that," he says, grabbing it and spinning it toward him on the table.

He leans over it, punches in four letters and triumphantly hits enter.

For a moment he stares at it blankly. "That actually worked."

"What was it?"

"*LIAM*, you idiot. That actually worked," he says again.

"That's a terrible password," Paul says.

"Foiled you long enough," Alex says, staring at the computer still. "Fuck." He picks up his water bottle and heads for the glass door onto their deck. He needs some air. And possibly a drink.

10

Cracking the password turns out to have been the easy part. Victor's notes are simple enough to find – his computer is as ruthlessly organized as his office – but they don't make much sense to Paul or, he guesses, anyone who wasn't Victor. Ultimately, after a few days of adding notes and being as useful with them as he can in between everything he has to do with *Winsome*, he makes copies of it all and brings them in to Mark.

Mark is less than thrilled to get it.

"Fuck this," he says when Paul hands over the drive. "Like I didn't have enough notes from the network already."

"Oh God," Paul says, the penny finally dropping.

"What?" Mark says, annoyed.

"I am the network." In the last six years he's often been at odds with the powers that be over *Winsome*, and the prospect of being put on the other side of that equation is horrifying. "Victor was an *asshole*."

"Fuck, you don't have to tell me," Mark says. "He died and now I have you hovering, collecting a network paycheck, and waiting for me to fuck up."

Paul sighs. "I get a network check because, if you do fuck up, I get a call at three in the morning and have to write you an entire episode by six. No matter where I am or what I'm doing."

"Or who?" Mark offers.

Paul stares at him for a moment. Then he cracks up. It's as much tension as anything, but after a shocked second Mark joins in.

The moment ends quickly, though, and Paul is left repositioning the hard drive on Mark's desk. He's more than a little concerned Mark isn't going to look at any of its contents.

"Good luck making sense of it. I made notes where I could, but you know how he was. I doubt I was able to make out anything you couldn't."

"Then why'd you bother?"

"To piss you off?"

"Better than going through the porn on his laptop?" Mark snarks.

"Don't," Paul says.

"You ask Liam to take a look?" Mark asks. Paul understands they've cycled back to Victor's notes, but the way they've gotten there is appalling. And it makes him – only somewhat to his surprise – damn fucking protective.

"He's got enough on his plate right now, don't you think?" he says sharply.

"Heyyy, no offense," Mark says, lifting his hands from the arms of his chair defensively. "Relax. I'm not going to barge in on him in his hour of grief, or whatever. But if neither of us can translate Victor into human, I need his expertise and I don't need to go through you to get it."

Paul is unimpressed with Mark's plight. "You had some pretty choice things to say about him and my husband."

"Yeah, well, you leave me notes on my show, I leave you notes on the harem you inherited from Victor. What the fuck is going on in your life, dude?"

Paul throws his head back and laughs darkly at the ceiling. "You have no fucking idea."

"Well," Mark says with a shrug, "at least you're getting laid."

◆

Paul calls Liam as soon as he turns the corner down the hall from Mark's office. He wants to do something useful and not stew on the pit of despair that *M.A.R.S.* is, but he also wants to give Liam fair warning in case Mark actually does try to get in touch with him.

Liam, though, does not pick up. After his calls ring through to voicemail twice, Paul calls Carly instead.

Carly is not amused at Paul's implication that she might still be screening Liam's calls.

"Liam's a big boy who is, by the way, currently in possession of his phone. If he's not answering, that seems pretty fair to me considering his partner fucking died."

"I didn't know you thought of it that way," Paul says softly.

"Tell me how I'm supposed to think of it."

"I thought you were cool with it."

Carly makes a noise of frustration. "The part I'm not cool with is the part where he's dead. Now, would you like me to see if Liam wants to talk to you, or shall I continue to play his secretary so that you can be arbitrarily pissed at me?"

◆

Alex closes the journal and stares at it. Victor, at nineteen, unsettles him more than the Victor he'd known. Alex knows that's less a reflection on Victor, than on his own biases. But Victor honest and Victor angry and Victor thwarted, is fucking strange. There was never, as far as Alex had ever heard, any struggle in his narrative. One day he just showed up with stories everyone wanted to tell. Alex doesn't know what to think of someone who spent most of his life pretending he was too good for anything to ever be difficult.

Considering his own role in that is more difficult to examine.

Victor was a magician who was always careful to make sure Alex – and everyone else – was looking at the wrong hand. Now that he's dead and Alex can look anywhere he wants, his gaze is starting to feel like a violation. Which, Alex supposes, is why he hasn't told Paul or anyone besides Liam he has the diaries. Eventually, he knows he's going to have to confess. He also knows it's going to be terrible.

He's also not sure why he's reading them. Grief, or a search for understanding of the very difficult man who changed his life would be reasonable – even noble. But Alex knows he's being selfish. He wants secrets or power, wants the relief that Liam's loss is not his own. Or, somehow, he wants an answer he can give Paul about babies and science and the massive space between wanting things solely because the world doesn't wish them for people like him and the relief at not having to make everyone else's choices.

Alex is almost on his way out the door to head over to Carly and Liam's when he gets a text from Liam. His phone's autocorrect has clearly had a field day with it, and while Liam isn't generally the best typist, Alex can usually make out most of what he's saying. This time, he has no idea. He hits call while he digs around in his bag for his keys.

Liam doesn't pick up, though he must be right next to his phone and Alex calls twice more before leaving a voicemail. It's enough to make him worried, and he finally just texts, *What did you say?*

Can't do lunch, he gets back after what seems like an inordinate amount of time.

Why? Alex asks, confused but also disappointed. He misses Liam and was looking forward to seeing him. It's maybe a selfish impulse considering the loss Liam's facing, but aside from the funeral and cleaning Victor's house, Alex hasn't seen him since he got back from Australia. That may have been his own choice, because he wanted to go nowhere and see no one except Paul in the first few weeks home, but it doesn't lessen his longing for Liam's company.

Can't, is all Liam replies.

Alex sighs and tosses his phone back on the counter. He could still get in his car and drive over there and make Liam talk to him, but that seems like unwise choices for any number of reasons. Liam could be in the middle of a grief-stricken breakdown or Liam could have company of the sort Alex tries really, really hard not to think about (polyamory is fine, but he *never* wants the details). Also, it would be rude, but his and Liam's relationship is such that considerations of social niceties are irrelevant. In any case, there's nothing that he can do. It's immensely frustrating.

◆

Carly is surprised when she gets home and there's no extra car in the driveway. She assumed Alex would stay through dinner as well as lunch. She already prepared a speech for Paul in case Alex ended up passing out with Liam and Paul decided to get jealous, although he doesn't really do that anymore.

Ali's still at preschool, and the house is unpleasantly silent. She finds Liam upstairs on their bed, sitting against the headboard and scrolling listlessly through his phone.

"Where's Alex?" she asks, flopping down on her side of the bed and kicking her shoes off. Barely four months in, pregnancy is already gross and annoying. Carly could do her sound editing from home most days in the blessed comfort of her pajamas, but working at the office gets her out of the house and around other people. Being attached at the hip twenty-four/seven is not part of the structure of her and Liam's life.

"I told him not to come," Liam says, still scrolling through the contact list on his phone. Carly wonders if he's actually looking for anything, or if the clicking noise the phone makes with every name he scrolls past is soothing.

"Why did you do that? You were looking forward to seeing him." It's reasonable for Liam to want to stay in familiar surroundings, but he also needs human contact other than just her and Ali.

Liam shrugs.

"Liam, I can't read your mind."

"It's complicated."

"Why is it complicated?"

"Because he's going to want to hug me."

"And that's suddenly a bad thing?

Liam frowns and finally manages to put the phone aside. "Victor's the last person who touched me."

It makes Liam-sense, but doesn't make Carly feel better. She's never been Liam's second choice, but it pisses her off that she and Ali apparently don't count as people who have touched Liam. She is right fucking here, and Liam is still looking somewhere past her.

"Words are really hard," he says, after a long pause. "And I can't tell if it's because of my brain or if I'm too sad to be alive in the world right now."

"Good thing you and Alex don't seem to need the words," Carly says lightly, but only to cover her own sense of horror. Liam's ability to function is, reasonably, crumbling in front of her, but she has no idea how much worse it's going to get, or how many of their relationships it's going to take down with it.

♦

Paul is relieved to find Alex's car there in the driveway when he pulls in at their house. Alex's presence in combination with the conversation with his sister feels like a good sign. Liam in crisis is going to be disruptive to their lives at some point, and while Paul is resigned to the fact that Alex is, sooner or later, going to fall asleep at Carly and Liam's, he's glad he's home now. Alex hasn't been back from Australia long enough for Paul to be used to the idea he's going to be in their bed every night. Dead Victor makes it feel dangerous to get used to the idea he's going to stay there. It's a terrible feeling.

Alex is asleep when Paul gets up to their room and mumbles groggily when Paul runs a hand down his back to wake him up.

"Mm, you're home. Workaholic," he says, pulling the covers back up around his shoulders.

Paul smiles. "Are you awake?"

"No."

Paul chuckles. "How was Liam?"

"Fucker bailed on me," Alex grumbles.

Paul frowns; that's unusual, but given the circumstances, perhaps, not remarkable.

Alex doesn't offer any further information. Paul finally says, "I talked to Sarah again today, and we did some research. Want to look at it?"

Alex blinks his eyes open at that. "Okay, when did I say yes to this baby?"

"This isn't going to be like the time you signed the *Fourth* contract without reading it. Research, Alex. Like, this is your *thing*." Paul pulls up his email on his phone and tries to hand it to Alex.

Alex squints his eyes and bats it away. "Paul, at what point did you decide that our hypothetical offspring had to be genetically related to both of us?" he complains sleepily. "Is this because the Internet is going to be obsessed over figuring out which of us is the biological father? Because they will, and that pisses me off, but my masculinity isn't going to be threatened if they decide it's not me."

"Okay, there was a lot going on in there, including the thing where you've been stewing over how we each feel about our masculinity."

"There is a lot going on, and you are asking me to father your sister's baby!" He doesn't sound angry, but baffled and irritated.

"It would also be nice if you would read what I'm giving you instead of talking about this like a child."

"Paul. It's *midnight*. I was *asleep*. Your phone is glowy and it hurts. I am pretty sure this is a violation of consent."

"Okay," Paul says resignedly, dropping his phone on the nightstand.

"If you're going to talk at me anyway, at least take off your clothes and get in," Alex grumbles, closing his eyes again.

Paul chuckles, and does. He really loves Alex.

"We were going to do surrogacy anyway," he says as he slides under the covers. "This way, we get to keep it in the family. As much as possible."

"Is this about you wanting a ridiculously freckled baby? Because let me tell you, freckles as a kid are not fun."

"You know, you can tell me I have masculinity issues, but I don't hear you saying no to the part about being the bio dad."

Alex rocks back a little. "So?"

"So, you don't know your father, and I want to know if this is something you want. Because I think it is, and I am *trying to have a conversation with you about it.*"

"Your timing is atrocious."

"Blaming you for that," Paul says fondly.

"Let me sleep on it?" Alex says. He sounds, for once, thoughtful and not petulant.

"Are you saying that just to make me go away?"

Alex rolls over and pulls the covers up again. Paul wraps an arm around him and chuckles when Alex snuggles back into him. Paul is so not the only one who's missed sharing a bed.

11

Carly and Liam come over for dinner with Ali in tow one evening toward the end of May. Carly is clearly still not sure how good an idea this is, but Paul has been cajoling her to get Liam to come to their house because Alex has been sulking at him about Liam's continued absence. Dragging Liam to dinner will at least get the pressure from them off of her and, hopefully, do Liam some good.

Liam is certainly still quieter than usual, although they all manage to chat about something other than Victor being dead over the course of the meal. It feels like moving forward, or at least a collective attempt to figure out what it's going to look like when they all finally do.

After dinner, Paul takes Liam downstairs to his office; it feels more appropriate to have this conversation there than over the dinner table. He surprises himself when he only narrowly resists the sudden impulse to lead him there by the hand. Whatever Carly might say about it, it has nothing to do with seeing Liam as a child. But what it has to do with instead, Paul isn't entirely sure. He bites at his lip as he considers both how to ask Liam about Victor's notes and ask Alex about everyone's desire to touch Liam.

Liam settles himself a little uncertainly on the couch, while Paul decides to keep things simple and rolls his desk chair over.

Paul says, "So there's a thing you might get asked to do for *M.A.R.S.* I wanted to talk to you about it first, so you're prepared if anyone decides to be an asshole to you."

"You mean Mark," Liam says.

Paul blinks and thinks about hedging, because he's really trying to back off from the open warfare situation, which will only come back to bite them all eventually. "Yeah."

"That's okay," Liam says. Then, "Wait, what does he want?"

Paul can't help but chuckle. "Help making sense of Victor's notes. They're a vague and confusing mess, and I'm sure they made sense to him, but I can't figure all of them out. You knew his brain and how he worked better than any of us."

"Do *you* want me to help?"

"That's... It's Victor's legacy. It's your call."

Liam nods thoughtfully. "I will. I mean this is probably why Victor put my name down," he smiles, a little watery. And then he says, "What's Mark saying?"

Paul blinks. "Um." He's not sure how much he should reveal about that, but Liam plows on anyway.

"Let me guess – you're fucking me to get ahead in the business?"

486

"Something like that."

"Don't feel special," Liam says with a smile that reminds Paul unnervingly of Victor. "He does that to everyone."

"He's infuriating."

"Victor thought he was hilarious."

"I don't know what to do with that."

Liam shrugs and smiles cryptically.

♦

"So that's new," Alex observes to Carly, staring warily at the door Paul and Liam have disappeared through. He's not sure which of them he's more nervous for.

"What, you didn't think they were going to fight over your honor for the rest of their lives? They're big boys, Alex. They grew up."

"The growing up is fine. The conspiring worries me."

"What's conspiring?" Ali asks.

"It means Alex is being paranoid. They're *working*. Let it go," Carly says irritably.

"This is ridiculous," Alex says, rinsing plates and handing them to Carly to stack in the dishwasher. "Our husbands are discussing business while we clean up the kitchen. Which makes us 1950s housewives, you know."

"Your little crusade against being treated like a girl got a lot less interesting somewhere around the thing where I got pregnant and then you and I fucked to Paul's enthusiastic narration," Carly says blandly.

"Carly!" Alex hisses, scandalized.

"What?"

Alex jerks his head toward the five-year-old who is currently attempting to lure Todd down from his regal perch on top of the refrigerator.

"She doesn't know what it means."

"It means you get in *People*," Ali pipes up.

Alex stares at her in horror.

"The *magazine?*" she says, like he's being obtuse. It doesn't make Alex feel any better.

He turns to Carly. "Your child terrifies me."

"She's not necessarily wrong."

"Why do you think I'm scared?" Alex digs the dish detergent out from under the sink. "So apropos of you to mention pregnancy."

"Ahhh yes. Paul's thinking about kids?" Carly says breezily. It only confirms Alex's suspicions that Paul's been talking to her about this, probably long before he started discussing it with Alex. Behind them, Todd jumps down, and Ali scampers off after him.

"Yes. With pamphlets." Alex is still irritated by the whole thing.

"Tell me you two discussed this before you went and got married."

"Yes, but in Paul's world 'sure, we should have kids someday' meant I agreed to a timeline and he asked his sister for her eggs."

Carly lets out a low whistle.

"Thank you."

"Oh honey, I didn't say I was on your side. I was enjoying your discomfort saying *eggs*."

"Stop."

"Eggs," Carly repeats again, clearly finding it hilarious. "*Eggs, eggs, eggs.*"

"I hate you."

"You hate everyone."

"Eggs!" Ali shouts, reappearing from the living room.

"Yes," Alex says, trying not to crack up, "I really really do."

◆

"So how are you?" Paul eventually asks.

Liam gives him a wan smile. "Not good enough that you want an honest answer to that."

"You know, if you need anything…" Paul says. He doesn't understand Liam on either of their best days, but he knows enough of his own psychology to be more than a little worried under the current circumstances. Victor's death has been hard enough on Paul, and he wasn't his lover.

"I need a lot of things. But none of that makes me dangerous to myself or anybody else. You and I are different," Liam says with a little tilt of his head and a look that is frankly unnerving.

"I can't imagine what you're going through," Paul says pathetically.

"Don't. Don't practice this. I mean, I'm pissed off because I have no idea what I'm doing, but …" Liam trails off like he's run out of words. "I'll be glad to get back to work. I think. Scripts, you know?"

Paul nods. "Alex yells at me when I try to cope by being a workaholic."

"Sometimes Alex is wrong."

Paul cracks up at how matter-of-factly Liam says it.

Liam turns the bracelet on his wrist and goes on. "I don't need the sixteen-hour days though. I just need a thing to tell me what to do."

"Have you guys started shooting yet?" Paul asks, grateful for a topic that isn't the death of partners, or the rather complicated mess Victor left them both to clean up.

He realizes, as he does, that whatever Mark thinks of Liam's potential to be useful, that's not actually why Victor named him creative executor alongside Paul. He's sure, now, from the way Liam is responding to him and even leaning slightly toward him, that Victor wanted Paul to fill his place in Liam's creative life. In a way, that's a much bigger responsibility than the safekeeping of Victor's legacy. Paul is simultaneously horrified at Victor's presumption and desperate to do right by him and Liam.

"Not really," Liam says. "A few camera tests, some reads. Apparently we're having a theatrical experience," Liam says, rolling his eyes and making air quotes. "Not that I'd know. They've been kind though, which I know is more than you're supposed to be able to ask."

Paul blinks at him, unsure of what to say.

"Principal photography begins next week," Liam says, like he's just realized that was the answer Paul was looking for in the first place.

"Do you want me to set up a meeting for you with Mark before you have to get into that?"

Liam thinks about it for a moment and then shakes his head. "No. I mean, he's fine, but can you give me copies of everything and I'll look through it on my time?"

Paul has a sudden unwelcome image of Alex sitting in a chair on the other side of a desk, being asked by someone at his own network to translate Paul's notes for them. Sometimes, he's not sure how Liam is upright.

"Of course."

♦

After the kitchen is cleaned up Alex, Carly, and Ali all go out on the deck, where Ali becomes instantly engrossed in dropping woodchips from one of their potted plants off the edge. The sky in the distance is hazy with smoke from the wildfires that are still burning; Alex has almost gotten used to the pervasive tang of burning things in the air.

"I'm twenty-eight," Alex says, petulantly enough that he knows he sounds younger. He leans over the railing to make sure the woodchips aren't ending up in the pool, then lets her at it.

"You're not as young as you used to be," Carly says with a raised eyebrow. "If you're not ready, that's one thing, not that anybody is actually ever ready for kids, but don't blame it on your age."

"What is having kids even like?" Alex asks. The idea of having little people to teach things and play with and love with Paul is appealing, but Alex's life since he left Indiana has been one long lesson in the consequences of having the things everyone thinks they want. It makes him wary.

"It's like someone burned down your house and then gave you wings," Carly says, settling herself into one of their loungers.

"What the hell?" It's the most Liam-like thing he's ever heard her say.

"Exactly."

"I think my mom was relieved when she realized I was gay," he says, after another moment of having no idea how to pursue Carly's line of conversation.

"Yeah?"

"Yeah. Kind of reduces the risk of pregnant teenage girlfriend."

"Not necessarily."

"Yeah, but I *really* hated people in high school."

Carly cackles. "So you don't want kids because you're fucked up over Indiana and think reproducing is fulfilling some hick-ass narrative destiny?"

"I'm not fucked up over Indiana," Alex protests.

"It's the only thing I've ever seen you afraid of," Carly says in a way that makes Alex wonder if she's going to point out that they've fucked again.

"Yeah, well, you would be too if your sister tried to stab you in the kitchen," Alex says like it's no big deal, even though it is.

Carly stares. "Jesus Christ, Alex."

"I mean, it could be worse. Paul could have wanted to be bio-dad, and use Delilah's eggs."

"I don't think I've ever heard you say her name," Carly says cautiously.

Alex shrugs. "Mostly I try not to think about my felonious relatives."

"So, Indiana, bad," Carly ventures.

Alex turns and stares at her for a second before he cracks up. "Indiana, bad. Now, tell me about babies?"

Before she can answer, Ali returns from her woodchip adventure and crawls up on the lounger next to her. Carly smiles and brushes Ali's hair out of her face as she snuggles into Carly's side, then proceeds like they haven't just had a very strange conversation. After all, Alex supposes, she's married to Liam.

"Being pregnant sucks but you don't have to worry about that. Oh the magic of renting a womb. Or is that going to be Paul's sister too?" Carly asks awkwardly.

"Okay, see, this is the problem. My mother's house is worth like twenty percent of what this kid is going to cost. That is fucked up, Carly."

"At least you're not doing some sketchy foreign baby buying."

"STOP TALKING. Believe me, I wish we could do this like normal people."

Carly purses her lips. "Alex, you and Paul have a lot of money. And you're going to spend it on your child whether that's private school or an adorable little rabbit fur coat, or, you know, science! So you should probably get over the fact that you're fucking rich and it's fucking weird fucking now."

"Sweet little Alicia is going to be swearing like a sailor by kindergarten," he points out. Ali makes a face at him from under Carly's arm.

"Yes, and we'll be paying enough that they still won't kick her out. Believe me, my gratitude is eternal."

"Carly, you're not helping."

"Yeah, well, neither is the fact that you don't think you and Paul are normal people."

♦

"All right, Mr. Crickets, give me science," Alex says, stretched out on top of the covers while Paul undresses for bed.

"What?"

Alex rolls his eyes. "I know you've talked to Sarah and I *know* you've talked to Carly, who is getting much better at covering up the fact you still tell her everything first. When you say 'baby' and 'sister' and 'surrogate' what are you actually talking about? Details, please."

"Are you pissed?" Paul looks prepared to be contrite, which Alex appreciates.

"Impressed. Tonight was one hell of a coup."

Paul ignores the almost-compliment and carefully sits down on the edge of the bed. "Are we having the conversation I think we're having?"

"We're having the conversation where I say, let's have a serious conversation about what it's going to look like if and when we have a kid based on the current plan you have in your head, which I haven't actually signed off on."

"I know."

"You do, huh?" Alex asks.

Paul at least has the good grace to laugh at himself. "I know you. Even if I'm never exactly sure what's going on in your head." He smiles fondly and pushes a hand through Alex's hair.

"Well, give me science, so I can figure that out too."

Alex listens without interruption while Paul lays out his plan: egg from his sister, sperm from Alex, a surrogate. All of it is expensive, and all of it feels like the involvement of dozens of people. Alex isn't sure which he's more freaked out by, and he tells Paul as much.

"I have a team for how I style my hair and, like, what breakfast cereal I can tell people I eat. I don't want a team for a baby too. It's strange and invasive and like America is watching us fuck," Alex says, lying on his back and gesticulating at the ceiling.

"It's not like if you give me a really good blowjob the ice-skating judges are going to give you three tens and then we get a baby," Paul says.

"What is that metaphor? You spent waaaaaaaaaaaaaaaay too much time with Liam tonight, clearly."

"I'm just saying it's not that invasive. It's less invasive than the whole world knowing, every time they look at Carly, that Liam fucks her."

"And that is the magical line between your four on the Kinsey scale and my six, because I have *never* had that thought."

"You're being weird about this," Paul says.

"I'd rather be weird about it than tell you I don't know if I'll ever be ready to do this. I want to, and I think kids are cool, but they were never going to be possible for me."

"Everything in your life is unlikely. Why is this the one thing you can't deal with?"

"I never had to spend time thinking about not being famous, because nobody real is ever famous," Alex says. His voice has slipped into a cadence he almost never uses, a reminder of the past he will never be able to completely erase. "Had to spend time thinking about not having kids, though. And it's hard to stay in the closet in fucking Paragon, Indiana if you don't have a baby."

"But you were never going to stay?"

Alex laughs incredulously. "You say that like nothing ever goes wrong."

"But it doesn't," Paul says with a shrug. "Not for you. Not really."

Alex doesn't have the heart to point out that Paul is tracing his fingers over the faint scarring at Alex's shoulder from the climbing accident he still blames Victor for.

12

Liam doesn't have a dedicated home office space the way Paul and Carly do, so when he gets the files from Paul, he sets himself up with his laptop in the living room. He's at the right range from Ali and her toys that he can keep an eye on her without getting sucked into the vortex of playtime. He delights in his daughter, and she's used to and easy with his periodic silences, but his understanding of Victor's notes isn't going to be improved with interruption.

Paul may have been worried that the work would be too emotionally taxing, but really it's just that – work. Liam's relationship with Victor was rarely about Victor's words or who Liam was on-screen. It was so intimate and comfortable that they didn't usually need words to express their feelings for each other. It's only now that Liam has so little tangible evidence of their time together that, that seems like a bad thing.

Which means that on some level it's soothing to have access to Victor's thoughts like this. On another, it underscores the degree to which Liam misses his voice. Among other things, Liam will have to keep living with the fact that Victor was always clearer about his stories than his relationships with real, actual people.

Victor's thoughts on *M.A.R.S.* are easy to ascertain. Victor's thoughts about Liam now seem more uncertain. There are no scripts or storyboards to reassure Liam of the things he thought he knew about his place in Victor's heart.

◆

"I think I want to talk to Ellen," Liam says when Carly gets home from work.

"You want to talk to Ellen, or you *think* you want to talk to Ellen?" Carly asks.

"I want to talk to Ellen."

"You have her number," Carly points out.

"I know."

"Are you okay to use the phone?" Carly asks uncertainly. "It's not like you need my permission."

"Yes," Liam says irritably.

"So talk to Ellen."

"I want to ask her what happened when Victor died."

"Whoa. Whoa." Carly throws her hands up in the air. "*What?*"

"I mean I know Victor was alive in the morning when I left and then ...not, that night, and I don't know what happened in between

493

and I want to. Ellen was there, and she told me to let her know if there was anything she could do for me. I think I need to know if he was scared. Or if it hurt," Liam says and looks down at his hands.

Carly is horrified. "I don't think that's good choices for either of you."

"What would good choices be?" Liam challenges.

"Not torturing yourself about how it ended," Carly says, undaunted. "That's not what you want to fixate on."

"Can you not use impersonal pronouns?" Liam snipes.

"What?"

"It ended. You mean how Victor died."

"Liam – "

"Please do not protect me from words when I can actually use them."

"If words were the only thing I had to protect you from," Carly mutters.

"I don't need protection. I am not *fragile*. Please stop deciding that's what how I interact with the world means."

"It may not feel that way to you, but as the permanent adult-on-deck in this house, I have to take your day-to-day ability to cope into consideration. So when you want to do shit that's going to put me in the position of being a single parent, when you're right here, you're goddamn right I'm going to protect you."

Liam takes a deep breath. Because this at least is a script he knows. Explain what he is. Explain what he isn't. Restate the situation. Say what he needs. He hates when he has to do it, and it's particularly upsetting when he has to do it with Carly. With Victor it was always awful, but Victor was difficult and they often existed on opposite sides of a very deep chasm; with him, it was easier to forgive. With Carly, these moments feel unfair.

"I am an adult; I am autistic; and I am grieving. While trying to keep secrets which control what I say to who when," Liam says carefully. "I do not know how to do this. There are not books about how to do this. And it would help if you could care about what is happening to me as opposed to how it inconveniences you."

◆

Alex is deciding whether he should swing by Paul's office on the lot to say hi or go straight to the terrible basement room *Winsome* uses for table reads, when he rounds a corner and runs into Darcy.

He catches a glimpse of her tear-streaked face for a split second before she wails "Alex!" and launches herself at him and buries her face in his shoulder. "I'm so glad you're here."

For an instant, his heart stops. "Darcy, is Paul okay?" he asks, hands not working right to hug her back.

Darcy sniffles and lifts her head. Her eyes are red. "Of course. He's freaking out about the read but he always does that. Why?"

Alex breathes again. "Holy shit. Given recent events, can you maybe specify your freakout before I jump to conclusions about your showrunner and my husband?"

"What? *Oh,*" Darcy says, and sniffles. "No, he's fine. Sorry."

Since Darcy still isn't letting go, Alex pats her gingerly on the back. "What's wrong then?"

"*Everything,*" she moans, thunking her head into his shoulder again.

Alex has to work not to laugh. The extremes of Darcy's emotions are not something he's ever sure how to deal with. "What happened?"

"My parents found out about Jackson and me," she says despondently.

"Found out what?" Alex asks cautiously, not sure he actually wants to know.

"That we're dating."

"You and Jackson are dating?" Alex gapes.

"Yeah. Didn't you know? It's on the internet."

"I don't go on the internet. Since *when*?"

Darcy wipes the back of her hand across her eye. "Since Victor's funeral. We hooked up. He's really cute."

"*What*?!" Alex is appalled, not by the hookup itself, but by what he can guess of the circumstances. "Darcy, did you fuck in the church?" he hisses.

"No!" Darcy looks offended. "I have propriety."

"Not that much," Alex mutters.

"We hooked up at your house."

"YOU DID WHAT?" Alex hustles her to the side of the hall.

"After the funeral. You and Paul were upstairs sad-fucking, so." Darcy shrugs.

"So you decided to fuck in my guest room?"

"Your bathroom, actually."

Alex stares at her.

"Aren't you going to ask what my parents said?" Darcy asks.

Alex throws up his hands.

"They said that if I was going to screw a black man the least I could do was find one above me."

Alex blinks at her a few times. "I'm guessing they didn't quite phrase it that way," he says carefully.

Darcy shakes her head.

"Okay, I know you know this, and that it's not my place to say, but Darcy, your parents are crazy, racist assholes."

"I know. I told them that."

"You did?" It's not that Alex doubts her, but he's continually stunned, impressed, and kind of frightened by her.

"Mhmm. Can we go downstairs now? Paul yells when I'm late."

Before Alex can get his bearings, Darcy disappears around the corner in a cloud of bouncing curls.

♦

Paul is not as horrified by Alex's reveal that Darcy hooked up in their bathroom with Victor's assistant after the funeral as Alex expects him to be. That Darcy's parents are awful, he's known for a long time.

"We've done crazier stuff than that," Paul points out after the table read, while Alex swivels back and forth in the chair on the other side of Paul's desk. "Fucking in your trailer was a particularly memorable experience."

"Unlike Darcy, we never scarred anybody," Alex mutters.

"Zoe?" Paul points out.

Alex shrugs, though he still feels guilty about the poor P.A. who accidentally caught them. "That was different."

"How?"

"I apologized for that."

Paul laughs. "I think fucking in a trailer ranks up there with hooking up at a funeral."

"They're both incredibly tacky?"

"And traditional."

Alex grins. "Liam gave me shit about that for weeks."

"Victor was furious."

There's a bittersweetness to Paul's laughter, and Alex leans his cheek on his fist. "God, I miss that."

"What, fucking in your trailer, or getting chewed out by Victor?"

It's a strange memory; Victor was, justifiably, livid at their stupidity and poor choices. But getting screamed at in front of the entire crew for having sex was not a pleasant experience. Alex was barely able to bite his tongue and not yell back that maybe Victor would be a little less pissy about other people's sex lives if he were getting any action himself.

Knowing what he knows now about Victor's struggles with his sexuality, he's glad he didn't. God knows what Victor would have done to him if he had.

Alex feels weird talking about any of that with Paul, though, so he shakes his head. "I miss being obsessed with you, instead of all the ways our lives are hard."

Paul's face goes soft. "Me too."

"We were supposed to get that, when I got back."

"I know."

"And then, dead Victor, and baby, and," Alex waves a vague hand. "That didn't happen."

"I know."

"Do you think we'll get to have that again?" They've already had the conflict over schedules, Paul's workaholic tendencies and Alex's skittishness, and they're good now, so good. But they have careers, Victor's dead, and things are different.

"Of course," Paul says. "But I miss not being able to take my hands off of you."

"Wanna go fuck in my trailer?" Alex teases, once he's able to catch his breath from Paul's words and the hungry, wistful look on his face as he says them.

"Do you even have your own trailer?"

Alex laughs and pushes himself out of the chair. "I have half a trailer on shooting days only, and it sucks. Also, you have to work."

"And you have to climb things?"

Alex leans over the desk to kiss him. "I'll see you at home."

13

"Iow's Ellen?" Carly asks Liam when she gets back from picking Ali and a crateload of end-of-the-year art projects up at preschool. He's been curled up on the couch, hugging a throw pillow and staring out the window, since he got home. He's glad to see them, but doesn't know how to respond.

Liam cranes his head up to look at her, but doesn't say anything. The polite response of *fine* is untrue, which Carly knows anyway. And without a script he has no idea how to begin conveying Ellen's state of being, especially now that he has all the details of what happened the night Victor died.

"How are you?" she asks.

He nestles his head back into the arm of the couch and returns to staring out the window. He has way too much going on in his head right now to be able to deal with Carly's questions too. She may be his partner in everything and way more used to his day-to-day life, but Victor was always better with rolling with it when all the input to Liam's brain shut down his ability to give expected output.

Carly sits down awkwardly on the couch and runs a hand through his hair. "Talk to me?"

"Why?"

"Because I need to know that you're okay."

Liam rolls his eyes. He's tired of having to explain this.

Carly sighs as she gets up and stalks into the kitchen. "I knew your talking to Ellen was a bad idea," she says, rummaging through a drawer.

Liam frowns when she plonks the pad of paper and pen onto the couch in front of him, but he picks it up anyway. Having to think about the mechanics of making letters forces him to organize his thoughts in a way he can't verbally right now. After a moment of concentration, he writes, *It wasn't a bad idea. This isn't bad. It just is.*

Carly reads the note upside down and then asks for the pen. *You're not talking. Explain to me how this isn't bad.*

Liam bites his lip, takes the pen back, and writes, *Explain what I'm supposed to do without him.*

You can't stay like this forever, Carly writes.

It's always been a possibility.

We have a child. Not an option.

Liam grabs the pen from her and slaps it down on the coffee table and turns his attention toward the window again.

Carly picks up the pen, scrawls *To Discuss: Skills Regression* across the paper, and then drops it and the pen onto Liam's lap.

♦

"Alex?" Paul pushes open the door to their bedroom. The light's on, but Alex is asleep on top of the covers with a book open on his chest. Todd looks up sleepily from where he's curled up on the chair in the corner.

"You're not supposed to be in here," Paul tells the cat. Todd blinks at him and then curls his tail more tightly around his nose.

Paul walks around to Alex's side of the bed. "At least you're staying busy," he murmurs, picking the book up off Alex's chest and checking the cover to see what obscure topic he's investigating this week.

There's no title on the cover, though, and when Paul flips it open his stomach jolts unpleasantly. He turns a few pages. There's absolutely no mistaking Victor's handwriting.

"Alex!" he says, scandalized.

Alex stirs and blinks up at him. "Oh hey. You're home," he says groggily.

"You stole Victor's diary!"

Alex rubs a hand over his eyes. "What?"

Paul tosses the journal back to him. "What the hell are you doing with that?

Alex catches it clumsily on his chest. "Ow. Careful. Why do you keep coming home in the middle of the night and waking me up with weird questions?"

"It's seven o'clock."

"Oh."

"The diary, Alex."

"I didn't steal it. Liam told me I could take them."

"*Them*?" The only thing that makes this situation worse, in Paul's opinion, is that there is more than one diary.

Alex nods. "There's like dozens. I only grabbed a handful to start."

"You're reading a dead man's diaries."

"It's not like he's going to mind."

Paul stares at him. "This is incredibly fucked up."

Alex shrugs. "Maybe. Maybe I'm finally finding where he kept his soul."

Paul points at him. "*You* are incredibly fucked up."

"Don't sound so surprised," Alex says smugly, setting the book on his nightstand and holding out his hands for Paul. When Paul doesn't move, he gestures insistently. Paul crawls onto the bed obediently, but the whole thing is still incredibly unsettling.

It doesn't get any less unsettling when Alex frowns up at him for a moment and then asks, "Do you remember when Victor and Liam got together?"

"Yes?" Paul says, not sure where this is going.

"How did it happen?"

Paul gives him a puzzled look, but goes ahead. "It was the *Fourth* pilot party. The pretty, flaky actor guy flirted, Victor didn't shut him down, and as far as I know the rest is history. I wasn't really paying that much attention, I was too busy with the sorry state of my own love life."

"Weren't you with Craig then?"

"Nooo, way before him. I spent the morning before the party at Carly's apartment moping because she wouldn't go with me and be my wingman. Like, this was years before she and Liam were together. She yelled at me not to hook up with anybody and shoved me out the door."

"Did you hook up with anybody?

Paul chuckles. "Of course I did."

"Dated for a week and then broke up when you wanted to get married and he didn't?"

"Do you want the story or did you want to make fun of me?" Paul asks.

Alex grins. "God, you really always have been a fucking mess."

"You make me less of one."

"Is that a come-on?" Alex asks, clearly a little disbelieving at Paul's choices, which is probably fair.

"Yes?"

"Oh my God," Alex laughs. But before he can make a start at getting Paul's clothes off, Paul's phone buzzes in his pocket.

"Oh fucking seriously," Alex mumbles as Paul tries to get to his phone. "Nobody else better be dead."

Paul gives him a *don't even* look, as if Alex has some sort of magical jinxing power of life and death.

It's Carly, asking if they can take Ali for the night. Which is concerning, though Paul can tell by Carly's tone that this is not the time for too many questions as to what, exactly, is going on. He agrees after a quick check with Alex, and tells Carly they'll be over in forty-five minutes. Liam and Carly's house isn't horrifically far away by L.A. standards, but it's not particularly close either.

"Are they okay?" Alex asks after Paul hangs up. Paul shrugs, then shakes his head.

Alex slumps onto his shoulder. "Ali is fine and I love our friends and want to help them – "

"But you really wanted to fuck tonight?"

Alex nods morosely.

"We can after she's asleep," Paul offers.

"Not like I wanted to fuck."

♦

Carly is clearly relieved to hand a drowsy Ali over to Paul and Alex when they come to the door. Ali is cranky over the ordeal but she gets to wear her pink fluffy robe outside, which is apparently an event.

"She'll stop fussing as soon as she loses me as an audience," Carly tells Paul. She sounds exhausted. "And I hate that I'm probably supposed to feel like a bad mother for pawning my kid off on you, but she is five and loud and cannot understand that demanding Liam pay attention to her is making him worse."

Alex hovers in the doorway, clearly wanting to ask after Liam, but Carly stares him down and he backs away. Paul thinks, apprehensively, that the last time anyone particularly tried to keep them apart was when Victor banned Alex from the *Fourth* set. He has no particular urge to relive the sequence of events of that day, even if Victor's now dead.

Ali falls asleep in the car on the drive back. Paul has to carry her into the house and upstairs to the guest bedroom they've always put her in when she's stayed before. Alex follows with her bag packed with the requisite toothbrush and doll, and waits in the hallway 'til Paul is done settling her in.

"See?" Paul says when he emerges, leaving the door open a crack. "If we had kids it wouldn't be just us. We've got friends who would help."

"You do understand it's a certain degree of fucked up to say that on a night that we have Ali because Carly and Liam are the ones who need help, right?" Alex asks in a whisper.

Paul steps away from the door and heads back to their bedroom. "Not every night is going to be like this one."

"Nooo," Alex says, following. "Our current issue seems to be that nobody knows what any given night is going to look like."

"All the more reason to have each other's backs."

Alex raises his eyebrows as he shuts their own bedroom door behind them.

"What?" Paul asks.

"Did you set this up?"

"What?"

"You and the baby."

"Are you asking me if I manufactured a crisis with Liam and Carly so we could get their kid for a night, and I could woo you with baby feelings?" Paul asks more kindly than he could.

"Well, when you put it like that, it sounds like I'm the crazy one."

14

Gemma, one leg tucked under herself on the couch in Paul and Alex's living room, listens to Alex's complaints about having to clean out Victor's house with rapidly diminishing sympathy. "You have the time to do it yourself. Or the resources to pay other people to do it. Also, isn't this kind of Jackson's job?"

"I've been informed it's not fair to add 'packing up spatulas' to the list of bullshit Jackson has to deal with as assistant to the dead. And I'm not going to let other people into Victor's creepy house." Alex picks at the corner of a book on the end table. June sunshine pours in through the windows, and Todd basks in a beam falling across the rug.

"You know, for someone who claims to have hated him, you're being immensely protective."

"Not of him. Of anyone else he might suck into that pit of eerie creative horror."

"Victor's *dead*. He loved his work, and it's a house. You're the one being creepy."

Alex shrugs and gets up to hunt through his and Paul's liquor cabinet for the tequila.

Gemma folds her arms and sits back further on the couch. "So do you not want me to help, or are you being passive aggressive about asking and want me to volunteer?"

Alex looks over his shoulder. "I'm not being passive aggressive."

"So you don't want me to help?"

Alex grabs the bottle and two shot glasses and returns to the couch, handing one of the glasses to Gemma without saying anything.

"You never even thought about asking me," she says accusatorily.

Alex shrugs.

"Alex!"

"What? You hated him too, and you escaped his clutches. Be happy about that."

"You mean be happy you found another family I'm not a part of?"

"I've had this family almost as long as I've known you!"

"Not *nearly*," Gemma protests.

She's not sure if Alex is being deliberately obtuse or just a stupid boy when he doesn't follow her argument, and it leaves her more pissed off than ever. If Alex doesn't want her in Victor's house because of whatever fucked up feelings about the man he's still dealing with, that's fine, but Gemma really would like to feel like she's not being written out of Alex's life. For all he continues to rely on her, she can't help but feel like she's been chasing him lately. It's an unattractive revelation.

"Do you want to come to the science education dinner thing Victor was making people do for *M.A.R.S.*?" Alex asks.

"What?" Gemma blinks.

"It was one of Victor's pet charities. I have to go because Paul has to. Only now there's an extra seat, because, well..."

"Are you inviting me to a dinner to fill a dead man's seat?" Gemma asks, somewhere between appalled and amused.

"Yes?"

"And *that's* not creepy."

"Well, somebody has to. Otherwise it's gonna be empty and that's just depressing. And Paul's been bitching at me about it all week."

"You are so weird."

"Do you want to go or not?"

Gemma laughs and grabs the tequila bottle from him to actually pour them shots. "Yes. But you're still on the hook for forgetting about me."

◆

Victor's funeral aside, the charity dinner is the first time Alex has been out at a public event since he's gotten back from Australia. He hasn't particularly missed carpets and photographers and all the intrusive staring.

He's particularly irritated because he's here mostly in support of Paul. Paul isn't doing anything wrong, but when Alex stands next to him at events like this he becomes the pretty arm candy of the older, mad creator. While Alex finds Paul's beard and graying hair as hot as most of the internet does, he could really do without the damned narrative.

Victor's diaries make him look at the event differently though. The entries from Victor's college years painted a picture Alex doesn't recognize, of someone who struggled with school because both because of his grand ideas and because of institutional bias. It makes Victor's support for something like science education seem like something beyond, perhaps, merely a *M.A.R.S.* tie-in.

At least there's plenty else here for people to pay attention to. All of the network brass is there, probably happy to be in the limelight and let everyone know that *M.A.R.S.* is doing fine. So is most of the *M.A.R.S.* cast, who are being charming and fittingly subdued in respect for their fallen captain. Darcy is in attendance, and has brought Jackson along as her date – Alex isn't sure if this outing is going to mitigate the way in which his life has turned entirely upside down lately. There's also a large number of people more or less associated with Victor, who only ever come out of the woodwork for events like this.

Liam and Carly are there too. Liam works the carpet and the fans with the same seemingly effortless poise and enthusiasm he always has, but Alex can see Carly keeping a closer eye on him than usual. Alex can hardly blame her; as far as he knows, it's the first time Liam's been out since the funeral. This would be a lot for anyone.

Paul and Alex are seated with Carly, Liam, and Gemma. Nigel is also there, and while Alex has no qualms about reading the diaries, it is immensely awkward to shake hands with him while knowing far more than any non-involved party should about all the times Nigel and Victor spent without clothes on before Victor sorted out his asexuality.

But Nigel is also, apparently, one of the first people who helped Victor make sense of himself. Alex is only beginning to fathom how massive an undertaking that was, and how confusing Victor was – not just to everyone else in the world – but to himself. It makes Alex respect Nigel. It also makes him wonder all the things Nigel's figured out about *him*.

At least Raphael is there, and his wife Irina, for which Alex is grateful. Rounding out the cozy little family group is Frank Pearson the VP from hell and, to Paul's very evident horror, Mark.

"Behave," Alex has to whisper in Paul's ear more than once.

Almost no one at the table is really on the same team, and everyone makes practiced small talk that hews a line between polite and calculatedly needling. Alex is charming, because he has to be; Darcy is talkative, which is always a blessing now that she's learned to be a little less of a loose cannon in front of the execs.

"How's *The Parrot Tree* going?" she eventually asks Liam.

"They've been really good about giving me time," he says softly. While it's a coherent answer, it isn't really the right one, even if everyone at the table knows at least some of the impact Victor's loss has had on him.

Darcy rolls with it, though, nodding with a sad smile. "We've missed having him around for *Winsome* too."

"Hopefully you can do something interesting with *M.A.R.S.* now," Frank chimes in.

Alex blinks and turns his head slowly toward Frank. He laughs at the man's sheer mustache-twirling ridiculousness. It's never been a secret that the guy has hated the *M.A.R.S.* concept from day one, insistent that serious drama can't involve "spaceships and laser guns" when *M.A.R.S.* isn't about either. That a guy can be that senior and be working against his own network's interests, Alex has never understood. He's glad that whatever level of open animosity that existed toward *The Fourth Estate* was only exhibited amongst other industry people and kept well out of the public eye. Apparently it's a new era.

"The body isn't cold yet," Alex says. Several people at the table give him dirty looks, and it only occurs to him belatedly that perhaps that wasn't the best way of putting things in front of Liam.

Liam toys with his fork and says nothing.

"Maybe," Mark says graciously. Alex has half a second of thinking they're going to get out of the sudden awkwardness unscathed when Mark follows it up with "It'll be hard to do anything if I keep losing writers."

"People are bound to look for other opportunities when things get uncertain," Frank says to Mark, not expending much effort to sound sympathetic.

"That, and *Winsome's* poaching my staff." Mark says it jovially. "I should sue you over Olivia."

"You're welcome to try," Paul says. "Don't think our lawyers didn't go over that bogus non-compete with a fine-tooth comb."

Mark shrugs. "Might be bogus, might not."

"Seriously, Mark, I don't even know if you're joking, but if you were that vindictive I'd put my own money behind defending Olivia, and newsflash, I have more of it than you do."

"Thanks to your husband," Mark clarifies.

"Yeah, I hear alimony is a real drag," Alex chimes in, as much to shut up Mark as to convey the depths of his displeasure to Paul. Mark's messy divorce a few years back is no secret in their overlapping Hollywood circles and Indiana made sure that Alex is never above fighting dirty when he has to. L.A. really is the smallest of towns.

Liam whistles softly, impressed. Mark shoots both him and Alex dirty looks, and Paul winces.

"Ahh, Victor's legendary family of artists," Frank says, with the air of someone watching Rome burn and loving every moment of it. "I wondered how long you'd last without him."

Liam turns to stare at him. "We," he says, and then blinks but doesn't say anything else.

Frank looks at him. Nigel and Carly exchange looks across the table.

"You?" Frank prompts, after the silence has stretched unreasonably long.

Liam looks pleadingly at Alex; Alex shakes his head. The situation is tense enough without him helping Liam egg the disaster on, but that just makes Liam look more insistent about it.

Finally Alex shrugs. It's not like tonight can get particularly more terrible than it is right now. "We know what Victor thought of you," he says.

"And what's that?"

"It doesn't matter," Alex says, with another prompting look from Liam. "Because he was better than you, and his work is still here."

"Okay. Paul," Carly leans into everyone else's space, hands on the table as she levers herself to her feet. "Will you come with me?"

Alex hides a grin behind his fist at how quickly Paul agrees. In the flurry of movement that follows, Alex thinks he hears Nigel groan.

◆

"I swear to God, not smoking is the worst part of pregnancy," Carly says as she stalks away, Paul hurrying to keep up. "Has the table gone up in flames?"

Paul looks back over his shoulder. "Not yet."

"Alex and Liam are terrible," Carly huffs. "Like, I know you two are monogamous and you are over the whole jealousy thing but thank God they are not together. They would alienate everyone."

"What was up with that?" Paul says, standing to the side in a doorway where they can keep an eye on their friends but stay safely out of range. "I've never seen Liam like that."

"Yeah, well, welcome to the hell that is my life," Carly says. "I do not know what to do with him. He's not okay at home, he's clearly not okay to be out in public although he seemed fine on the carpet. Liam's life is not one he can live from our bedroom, and I am running out of cope."

"Carly?" Paul says gently. Carly is one of the most resourceful people he knows. Her life and her relationships never have been easy, but she's always mastered all of them. The note of helplessness in her voice is disconcerting.

"Yes?"

"What's going on?"

Carly sighs. "Do you mean the shattering grief of his losing a partner or the exciting adult autistic regression? It's so hard to choose."

For half a second, Paul thinks she's joking. But he knows how Liam numbers his points in conversation and highlights his scripts in multiple colors to note not just emotion, but tone, intonation, and pitch. He remembers, also, Victor's ongoing war with *The Fourth Estate*'s wardrobe department because they kept giving Liam's character oxfords but Liam would never tie the laces. Suddenly every flaky or vain thing Liam has ever done looks remarkably different.

"I have a lot of things to say about that," Paul says carefully. "I'm not sure any of them are useful or fair."

"I shouldn't have told you," she says.

"Hey, no," Paul says. "I mean, probably not, but... wow, autism makes me like him a lot better than the whole manic pixie dream boy thing."

Carly shakes her head and laughs, tilting her head back to the heavens.

"What do you need?" Paul asks.

She brings her head back down to look at him darkly. "Anything you can give me."

♦

"Life with you people is never boring," Gemma says drily into the tense silence that follows Paul and Carly's departure from the table. Raphael and Irina exchange horrified glances, Frank looks delighted, and Liam is staring at his plate so he doesn't have to look at Mark, who is staring at him.

"At least you didn't bring a date. We'd scare him off forever," Alex says to Gemma. He means it as a tease, but Gemma glares at him.

"Can we actually not bring my dating life into this conversation? Or any conversation in public, ever?" Gemma says, sharply.

"I said *date*; you said dating life."

"Okay." Gemma tosses her napkin down and pushing her chair back. "We are not talking about this or anything here," she says, stalking away from the table.

Alex watches her go miserably. The obligations of long friendship probably require him to go after her. It's a horrifying prospect, but getting yelled at by Gemma would probably be more pleasant than staying at the table any longer.

Alex looks at Liam, who seems unaware of the entire unfolding drama, and then at Nigel.

"It's fine, I've got it," Nigel says.

"Me too," Raph says, which is more encouraging. It's not that Alex doesn't trust Nigel or his good intentions, but the history between him and Liam is anything but smooth. Liam at least likes Raphael, and he was never a rival for Victor's affections.

Alex grudgingly stands up and trudges after Gemma.

She's waiting for him by the rest rooms. As soon as Alex appears, she grabs him by the elbow and hauls him into the women's.

"Gemma, what the fuck," Alex says, pulling out of her grasp as soon as they're inside. Gemma takes a cursory look around to make sure it's empty.

"Okay, I understand that the success and the fame of your magic life comes with some shitty downsides, but can you not fucking make fun of my relationship status *in front of a network executive?*"

"I was teasing!"

"They don't know that! Jesus Christ, Alex, it is bad enough that I have to deal with not having my own dreams come true, but, you know what? I am making my life awesome even if it doesn't look like what I used to think it would. But that be much easier to do if you weren't humiliating me in public."

"I'm sorry," Alex says contritely. "I can go fix it."

Gemma rolls her eyes. "No you fucking won't. I am a big girl and I don't need you to smooth shit over for me. But this whole forgetting that I am actually a person thing is getting increasingly fucked up."

"I actually have no idea what you're talking about."

"*Darcy*?" Gemma hisses, like it's a curse. Alex almost takes a step back.

"What the hell are you talking about?"

"We have been best friends for years, through some relatively screwed up shit, except now you never call even when I can actually be fucking helpful to you. You've replaced me with some younger prettier more famous *and white* version of myself, so you can pretend that we've all actually succeeded!"

"THAT'S NOT WHAT I DID!" Alex yells when he can finally get a word in edgewise.

"YES IT FUCKING IS!" Gemma yells back. "I am not being a jealous bitch, but you need to fucking deal with whatever shit it is that makes you think a white me is necessary, because, *God*, Alex you are a fucking moron."

"You're also jealous."

"Of course I am. Jesus fuck, Alex, we ran away from home to move out here together. Like we actually have this life, whatever it is, because we spent too much time in high school emailing each other about television shows. What am I supposed to be when we never hang out anymore?"

"Pissed at me in the women's bathroom at the Beverly Wilshire during a very prestigious public charity event?"

Gemma glares at him.

Alex offers her his arm. "Truce?" Right now he can't start to unpack what Gemma laid out for him. Her criticisms aren't unfounded, but it's also the last thing in the world he wants to spend any time examining.

Gemma gives a disbelieving laugh, but she takes it. "For now. You are such a fucking asshole."

"At least I'm better than Mark."

"Not by much."

As they leave, a toilet flushes behind them. They had not been, as they thought, alone. Gemma buries her face in Alex's shoulder and moans. *This is all going to be so stupid.*

♦

"That night could not have possibly gone any worse," Alex says. He tosses his jacket over a chair and tugs open his collar before collapsing onto the couch.

"Yeah, you were a real force for calm and civility there." Paul follows him into the living room.

"Mark is a terrible human being, Frank was being horrible, and you took their bait and used me to do it. Fuck calm and civility."

"You and Liam were lighting fires," Paul points out. "And to be fair, I did steal Olivia." He taps Alex's knee. Alex lifts his feet so Paul can sit down, and then stretches his legs over his lap.

"No, Olivia quit and was smart enough to do it in such a way that got her on a better team," Alex says. *If there's anything worth rehashing in tonight's disaster it's not the petty accusations of people they don't even like. At least Paul doesn't know about the scene in the bathroom with Gemma.*

"I think I'm flattered?"

Alex snorts and rubs his hands over his face. "Your possessiveness is always charming, yes."

"And you're trying to talk your way out of your own bad behavior."

"Are you scolding me?" Alex raises his eyebrows at Paul over his own hands.

Paul gives him a look.

"Fine. I'm sorry," Alex says. "But, fuck, all of our friends are insane. And so are our enemies."

"We should get used to that one of these days."

"Mmm." Alex looks at Paul thoughtfully.

"What?" Paul asks, when he doesn't say anything else.

Alex grabs for one of Paul's hands. "So. I thought we were gonna have a nice night and then I could say this," he says, both intent and playful. "But then it was a car crash. Which given all the players involved I should have expected."

"What were you going to say?" Paul asks curiously.

"Our friends are crazy and our jobs are terrible. Coming back from being away is always hard but this reentry has been something else. I want something that's not a part of that, and I want something that's just for us."

"Yes?" Paul says carefully.

"I want to talk to Sarah and do some research on my own," he says. "But I'm sort of starting to like the idea of a family we choose as opposed to the one that keeps choosing us."

"Really?" Paul asks.

Alex nods. After all, kids were always the plan. Paul jumping the gun from hypothetical to schedule is annoying but not surprising or unprecedented. Now that Alex has recovered from the shock, the idea is actually appealing. He is beginning to understand that their lives will never be big enough to hold everything they want to do, which is all the more reason to do what they can when they can. After all, as Victor's diaries remind Alex daily, nothing lasts forever.

"Please tell me this isn't just to apologize for being a brat tonight."

Alex laughs and shakes his head. "Take the yes and be happy, Paul."

"Okay. Well. *Wow*," Paul says, adjusting.

Alex hums smugly.

"Well, okay." Paul still sounds a bit dazed. "There was something I was going to ask you, actually."

"What's that?" Alex asks.

"Liam."

"Oh God, don't – "

"How long have you known?" Paul interrupts Alex's assumptions.

"How long have I known what?"

"About the autism, and why didn't you tell me?"

"About what autism?" Alex asks, confused. "I mean, Ali's weird, but – "

Paul stares at Alex. "Not Ali. *Liam*."

"What the fuck?" Alex says.

"Oh my God," Paul says.

"Liam's autistic?" Alex asks, trying to make sense of this new – and vague – information. "Did you just out my not-boyfriend to me?" he continues incredulously.

"I assumed you knew," Paul stammers. "And I am not processing *not-boyfriend* right now. I mean, I assumed you two talk – "

"Noooo," Alex shakes his head. "*What* the fuck? And don't assume things about me and Liam."

"I don't know what to say."

"He's, like, *normal* though," Alex protests into the lack of further information. "I mean, not normal-normal, he's Liam, but – "

"It's a spectrum," Paul says.

"But don't autistic people not talk and obsess on weird shit and, like, not live alone?"

"Okay, none of that is strictly true," Paul says carefully. "But you also just described Liam. And if you keep describing him, it's not going to be less of a match."

Alex stares at Paul. Aside from Paul, Liam is the person Alex knows best in the world. Now suddenly it feels like he doesn't, not because anything has changed, but because it all means something else now.

"Why am I *still* the last one to know anything? Seriously."

"I thought you knew!"

"Well, I didn't."

"You're seriously going to be pissed about this?"

"Yes, I'm pissed about it! Jesus, Paul, this isn't some little historical nugget. This is like, a thing that's happening. Is this why Carly won't let me talk to him?"

"I think you'd have to take that up with Carly," Paul says cautiously.

"How do you even know this stuff?"

"Older mothers have a higher chance of having autistic kids. I've been researching it."

"Bullshit."

"Well, that's true, but Carly told me when she freaked out at dinner."

Alex gives a strained, disbelieving laugh and turns back to look at Paul. "I think I need a drink."

◆

Liam's phone goes off while he's standing in the living room with Carly and Carly's long-time girlfriend, Risa, who's been watching Ali. He's trying desperately to figure out when the conversation is at a point where it's socially appropriate for him to leave and go to bed. When he finally manages to fumble the phone out of his pocket, he sees that it's Charles. He gives Carly and Risa apologetic looks before slipping off to take the call.

Charles is drunk and chatty, just home from celebrating with fellow cast members from his current show. It's funny and it's shockingly normal, Liam teasing Charles about his latest fling with the latest pretty actor boy who has caught his eye. They were each other's firsts, way back when they were still in high school together. Now they date whenever Liam is in town. It's not a serious relationship in terms of time commitment, but the history is long.

While Liam has Carly – and had Victor – and still has Alex to some strange and mostly unspoken extent, as far as he knows he's Charles's only long-term lover. Charles has always seemed perfectly happy without the web of relationships that are so vital to Liam's existence. But, now, having never really had one, he's intensely curious about what the loss of such a relationship means to Liam.

Liam goes quiet when he asks, but it's not the wave of despair and panic he's felt so often lately – mostly, because Charles has actually asked, which forces Liam to actually think about it.

"Do you remember junior year when Jamie and Sam were cheating on their SOs with each other and complaining to us about how hard their lives were?"

Charles chuckles. "They were doing that senior year too."

"Yeah but, early on. And Jamie kept wishing someone would die because then everyone could use grief as an excuse to talk about their big fucked up love?"

"How the hell are you poly after all their bullshit?"

"I keep thinking about that," Liam says, ignoring him. He fidgets with the edge of his nail. "About Victor being dead, and Jamie being wrong."

"He's dead," Charles says. "You can say whatever you want. No one will blame you. And Victor can't even yell. I know there's nothing good about what's happened, but you do have the freedom to speak."

"I really don't." Liam wishes Charles were correct, but what his friend and lover doesn't understand is that anything Liam says will have consequences for everyone else in his life.

"Why not?"

"You mean other than Carly, Ali, future baby, and the press?" Liam can't shield his family from all the consequences of who he is, but he sure can try.

"Yeah."

"Because Victor didn't belong to anyone. That doesn't change now that he's dead. And with him not here to tell me, I'm not even sure I was his."

15

Now that he's committed to it, Alex throws himself into the research process about *baby science* and *baby law* and *baby contract* with the enthusiasm he has for every subject that piques his interest. Paul's grateful, even if he knows that part of why Alex is taking this on is because he doesn't trust Paul's attention to detail. Alex isn't wrong; running a show and a half doesn't leave him a lot of free time.

They find a surrogacy agency, and Paul is insistent about selecting a woman who has been a surrogate at least once already. Alex agrees. Knowing that this is something she has done before and is willing to do again makes it not actually repugnant.

The day Alex gets the call from the surrogacy agency saying they've found a candidate, Paul finds him at their kitchen table. One of Victor's diaries is sitting on the chair next to him, and he's staring blankly at his laptop screen.

"What's up?" Paul asks him.

"I'm nervous."

"About what?"

Alex gives Paul a look.

"Hey, I'm trying not to assume here. Specificity. Please."

"I don't know if I can. It's everything. Like, science and hi, I'm going to be a parent, and there's going to be a person running around in the world that has my genes and Sarah's genes and I'm kind of freaking out about all of that?"

"Do you not want to do this?"

"Okay Paul, the thing where you ask for specificity and then get defensive and decide what I mean without waiting for me to explain? You should stop with that."

"Sorry," Paul says, and then, as instructed, waits to say more. Alex's energy is jittery and strange, and Paul can't blame him. He's nervous, too. This is entirely uncharted territory for them both.

"I want a kid," Alex states slowly and clearly. "So please take that off your worry list."

"Okay."

"But I need to go out to South Carolina."

"But everyone will be out here for the procedure. The surrogate's here," Paul says, confused.

"It's not about that."

"Then what is it about?" Paul asks. Alex likes South Carolina, but they've only ever been there for vacations, and this doesn't sound like Alex looking for a holiday.

"I've been on the phone with your sister a lot but I mean – your

514

family's doing a huge thing for us. I want to do right by them, and me, and Sarah especially, and I need to spend some time out there before all this starts to happen so I can feel okay with it."

"I wish I could go with you," Paul says. Alex's sense of responsibility surprises a little, though that feels unfair to Alex whose family structures and loyalties have never quite looked like anyone else's.

"I'll be all right."

"I'm not worried about you," Paul says with a tired smile. "I could use a fucking break."

"Well *somebody* was supposed to take a year off..."

"I still will," Paul says, but it's reassuring, not defensive.

"Does it ever bother you that I don't have a degree?" Alex asks idly.

"What?" Paul is baffled by the topic and the lack of any segue, although it probably makes sense in Alex's head.

"You went to college. Carly went to college. Liam didn't, but he went to an actual school for the arts. I have a high school diploma from my shitty, *shitty* hometown."

"Is this about you not being like other people or wanting to go back to school or thinking this has something to do with how you'll parent?"

"All. None. I don't know. Victor wrote about film school a lot. It sounds interesting. And I want to be smart for our kid."

Before Paul can investigate further, Alex closes his laptop and asks what he wants to do about dinner.

◆

Alex has no idea what to expect the first time they meet with the surrogate on a hot, smoky afternoon in July. Alex is afraid they're supposed to be friends, and he's relieved when that doesn't seem to be the narrative, saving him from being the star of his own one-season sitcom.

Some days he feels like he already is; Liam has retreated from the world entirely, and Alex tries not to be pissed or hurt at being shut out. Alex hasn't heard from him at all since the terrible charity dinner.

Predictably, Alex's snarling match with Gemma in the bathroom of the Beverly Wilshire turns up on the internet. Alex just can't decide whether the best or worst thing about it is the suggestion that they're ex-lovers. But that Gemma feels the need to leave him several irate messages about it, and its potential impact on her current professional quests, is decidedly not funny.

But there's nothing Alex can do about it, and he's not going to apologize for blinds on the damn internet. Gemma made his life this way when she insisted he say yes to Victor's offer; she can live with the consequences of being his friend now.

As far as his messy friendships go, Gemma is not his biggest concern, though perhaps she deserves to be. But Alex doesn't know what he's supposed to do about Liam. He has questions and confusion. More than once Paul takes Alex's phone out of his hand while he's angry and ready to call Liam to demand answers.

"If he wants to talk to you he knows where to find you." Paul sets the phone down on his desk before resuming his typing.

"He's my friend. Why won't he talk to me?"

"Victor died, Alex. It's not a conspiracy."

He continues to protest and gripe and worry until Paul snaps that it's not all about him.

"I don't understand how you can have the bond you have with Liam and not get how deep that thing with Victor went." Disappointment evident in Paul's voice.

"I'm not questioning that," Alex says with frustration.

"Then what is your shit? I don't mind you being moody but I do mind you refusing to examine and take responsibility for your own emotions."

"I want to help," Alex says petulantly. "No one is letting me help."

"You can't fill those cracks for him for the same reasons you two aren't together," Paul says. There's no bite to it because there doesn't have to be for it to land hard.

Alex gives him a level look and then stalks off toward the door of the deck. "Fuck you for being right," he says, before wrenching it open.

◆

Paul gives him a couple of hours to cool off, but once the sun goes down and the temperature drops and Alex still hasn't budged, he joins him in staring out at the dark landscape.

"I'm not pissed at you," Alex eventually says.

Paul nods.

"I don't know who I'm pissed at."

"Victor's been working out as a plan for you," Paul's joking, but it wouldn't kill Alex to examine his persistence about that.

"Right now," Alex says, "Victor is an angry, scared, and very brilliant asshole trying to figure out how to do life when he's not like any other people. He's not the person I knew. I'm fairly sure he's not the person you or Liam knew either. Nigel did, which is just weird. Every time I'm angry at Victor, my life blows up, so mostly I'm trying not to do that. It's starting to feel unfair."

"Will it piss you off if I say I approve?"

"Probably. If we're having a kid, you can't treat me like one anymore."

"I don't."

"No withholding information."

"I told you about Liam within hours," Paul protests.

"Because you thought I knew. And if you hadn't, you wouldn't have."

"I –"

"You know how Carly didn't tell Liam 'til morning?"

Paul nods.

"Don't ever do that to me," Alex says wrathfully. When he retreats into the house, Paul doesn't let himself follow, although it is cold and lonely in the dark.

♦

Children, no matter how dramatic and demanding, are more resilient than Carly would prefer. Because it's not that Ali doesn't notice her father's moodiness, nor is it that she doesn't care. It's that she makes it a game. Who looks prettier staring out the window, who can not react to Carly the longest, who can come up with the most complicated pattern of taps the other can still echo back throughout the day.

Abstractly, it's fascinating. Practically, it's sort of annoying. And intellectually, Carly finds it faintly terrifying. She can't be entirely sure Ali is mimicking Liam as opposed to rewiring her own brain to fit more tightly into his world.

It's definitely something she and Liam are going to have to talk about. She waits until Ali's in bed, because Ali doesn't need to overhear any of this and Carly doesn't need her here being her charming and demanding self.

She pushes a notepad and a pen at Liam, and says, "We need to talk."

Liam spins the pad around and writes *About what?*

Carly holds out her hand for the pen. When Liam gives it to her, she scribbles, *About the things you have the capacity to do, and what that means for what we're going to do.*

Too tangled, Liam writes back.

She sighs and tries to simplify. No matter how hard she tries to get it right, this always where they have the most trouble. When he needs her to clarify, it's it far too easy for her to accidentally speak to him like a child instead. Actually having a child hasn't helped that.

How we try to get your skills back. What happens if we don't.

Not a switch, Liam scribbles back. *No off/on.*

I know. Can this be our job right now?

Why is talking better than this? he writes.

Faster, she scribbles.

He snorts as she drops the pen after the word, and they look at each other, smiling. They did this, passing notes back and forth, the night they first slept together. She thought he was being whimsical, and mostly he was trying to convince her that he was. But it kept that night small and close and funny, and made him trust her. She was as not like other girls as he was not like other boys. It's bittersweet now.

Fair, he scribbles back, after he thinks on it for a moment.

You also talk for work. These words she writes more slowly, having learnt long ago that there is cadence in talking this way too.

He doesn't reach for the pen when she puts it down, but he also doesn't drift. She watches as he goes to speak. While his hands move, the words won't come. He tries twice more before writing, *I don't want to write it.*

"What? Why?" she asks, even though it's an incredibly unfair question. The potential answers are too big and vague.

He sighs and averts his eyes, proving her point.

"Okay," she says, kissing his knee before getting up from the couch. If she gives him space, there's half a chance he'll come back to the conversation, and at least it's on the table now.

She spends a few hours in her office, grateful for a to-do list that needs attention and for tasks that only involve one form of communication. When she returns, he's written *The Parrot Tree* and drawn a deliberate line through it.

◆

Alex is sitting on the couch in their darkened living room when Paul finally goes back inside. His inability or his unwillingness to use words to express himself has always been frustrating to Paul. When Alex was in Australia, however, words were all they had, and as Paul regards Alex's still and silent figure he can't help but feel that they've turned back the clock, and not to anywhere useful.

"Talk to me?" he asks.

Alex flicks his eyes up to Paul but doesn't say anything.

"Other than the fact that you're pissed off, I'm not sure what's going on in your head. Can you find some words before you decide to be pissed off at me, too?"

Paul keeps his tone light, but Alex doesn't smile, looking at him with an assessing gaze. It's unsettling, and Paul is uncomfortably reminded of why Alex keeps getting cast in roles where his characters die. His eyes are not entirely of this earth.

Alex lifts a hand and beckons Paul over. When he takes it, Alex pulls him forward and tilts his face up for a kiss. When Paul bends down to give him it, Alex turns his head to whisper in Paul's ear instead.

"Come and see." His lips brush Paul's ear, and he slips out from between Paul and the couch. Before Paul can get his bearings, Alex vanishes out of the room and up the stairs.

Paul follows. Their bedroom window is open, and the room is cool and smoky-smelling from this season's perpetual wildfires. Any thought of making Alex talk has disappeared. If he wants to deal with whatever is going on in his mind by losing himself in sex, Paul is more than on board.

Alex sits on the edge of their bed, waiting. He's nearly thirty now, but he knows how to hold his body to look younger as well as older, and it feels like the most appealing of time warps when he looks up at Paul from under his lashes.

When Paul approaches he doesn't wait, but stands up and pulls him into the kiss in one fluid motion. It's all tongue and teeth, and Paul loses his breath as Alex spins them around and pushes him down on the bed.

Getting naked is a mess of tangled sleeves and limbs, but Alex is insistent about getting to skin and growls when Paul gets distracted running his hands over Alex's back. Paul lifts his hands and Alex catches them, pinning them to the bed on either side of Paul's head.

Paul gasps and lets his head fall back on the pillow, breathless. Alex hovers over him, keeping his weight on Paul's hands. He groans in anticipation.

Alex has to let go of one of Paul's hands to reach for the lube. He immediately wraps his free hand around the back of Alex's neck and pulls their foreheads together while Alex slicks himself and starts to push in.

Like in the club when Alex shoved him against the wall, and in this bed after Victor's funeral, this is not how they usually have sex. Paul can't do anything but dig his fingers into Alex's hair and pant his name while Alex fucks into him. He stares at Paul with a gaze that's far too intense.

The orgasm, when it hits, is overwhelming. Alex doesn't stop, and Paul lets his eyes fall halfway closed and drifts while Alex continues to fuck him. It's clearly fascinating to him, to have Paul this out of it under him. When he does finally come, Alex sounds as stunned as Paul feels. He stays, shoulders bowed, over Paul while they both come down from it. It's a long time before they can get their limbs coordinated enough to pull apart and get themselves cleaned up, only to collapse onto the sheets next to each other.

"What was that about?" Paul asks, reaching for Alex's hand.

Alex laces their fingers together. "I think I missed you."

♦

In the morning, Carly is unsurprised to find Liam at his laptop, hunting and pecking an email to his manager about needing to drop out of his project. It's the opposite of any sort of solution, assuming there is one, but it's movement and choice, and it at least makes her sure they're not dead too. He's interrupted by Ali running into the kitchen for breakfast chittering about the nightmare she proudly tells everyone she put herself back to sleep from. To Carly's surprise, Liam actually picks her up and uses his voice to tell her she only has to fight monsters alone if she wants to because he's always happy to help.

Despite the email, extracting himself from *The Parrot Tree* takes the better part of the week. Andrew, the director half of the writer/director team in charge of *The Parrot Tree* actually takes time out of his schedule to come over for lunch and is concerned and understanding. And then the legal and PR wrangling begins. When the announcement goes out, Carly finds herself relieved for the first time that Liam is too lost inside his ongoing grief to pay much attention to the public fallout.

<h1 style="text-align:center">16</h1>

Alex's hopes that Victor's house and the rest of his possessions will magically box themselves up are dashed when he gets an email from Nigel, reminding him that, for Nigel's own sanity and the legal process, they really do need to get everything itemized. Nigel offers to help, since he's back and forth between New York and L.A. for work so much, but that's an easy offer to decline. Nigel doesn't need the extra work and Alex doesn't want to deal with Liam and Nigel in the same room. Particularly when that room belongs to Victor.

And so another day gets sacrificed to Victor. Even with all four of them there – Carly and Liam come too – the house feels eerie and empty.

"Why did we have to do this on your one day off?" Alex grouses as he hauls boxes and his tablet into the living room. Liam trails behind him with an armload of newspaper and bubble wrap he scrounged from the basement when Alex refused to go down there.

"There's nothing stopping you from doing this alone whenever you want," Paul calls from the kitchen, where he and Carly are regarding Victor's multitude of cooking implements with something approaching despair.

"Only the ghosts," Alex shouts back, though it doesn't feel like there's anything at all here anymore. It freaks him out. He had expected Victor to linger.

♦

Alex starts a list of all the things on one of the bookshelves while Liam stands next to the piano, frowning.

"What's wrong, Lee?" Alex asks eventually.

Liam picks up the metronome that's resting on top of the piano. "This doesn't go here."

"Okay?" Alex says. "Don't metronomes go with pianos?"

"Victor didn't play." Liam shakes his head and sets the metronome down on the floor before sliding onto the bench of the piano. Alex decides not to question him further. At best, he'd probably just get more Liam-logic for his trouble. He's also not sure he wants to find out why Victor owned a piano if he couldn't personally use it.

Now that they're actually in the same room in relative privacy Alex wants to ask Liam any number of things instead, with *why the fuck didn't you tell me* right at the top of the list. But the degree to which Liam isn't acknowledging Alex's presence is spooky. Alex is afraid of asking questions and not getting responses, as if Liam's lack of engagement would mean that Alex isn't actually here.

After a while Liam starts plucking out notes on the piano. What is at first tolerable noodling becomes a hellish repetition of a single note, over and over and over again.

"Liam? Can you stop that?" Alex says irritably first and then with more aggravation when he gets no response.

It goes on until Paul appears in the doorway, Carly close behind him. "If you want to learn to play, Liam, we will find someone to teach you, but if you keep plinking the same damn random note I am not responsible for my actions."

Liam stops immediately and tucks his hands contritely in his lap. Alex stares.

Paul blinks in the sudden silence and then turns to Carly, who raises an eyebrow at him. "I didn't need that information," he says.

"Add it to the list," Carly says and turns back for the kitchen.

♦

It's almost lunchtime, Alex's stomach informs him with a rumble, as he stares down at the pile of folders and notebooks perched precariously on the arm of the sofa in Victor's den. "I found more stuff for *M.A.R.S.*, do you want it for Mark?" Alex asks, leaning out of the doorway to shout down the hall to Paul.

"Official answer or dream answer?" Paul yells back.

Alex grins. "Just tell me what to do with the fucking stuff."

"Bring it. And then Mark can shove it up his ass for all he's using it."

Alex stacks the pile carefully in his arms – this day does not need the hassle of trying to re-organize mysterious Victor paper if he drops them everywhere – and makes his way down the hall to Paul. "Why the fuck did Victor put up with him for so long?" Alex asks when he reaches the kitchen, setting the stack down on the counter.

"He's good," Paul responds.

"He's not that good," Alex snorts.

"I know. I'm better."

Alex cackles. "Yes. Yes you are."

♦

It's by chance that Paul glances into Victor's den while he's yelling down the hall to Alex about bringing more boxes next time. He stops short at the sight of Liam huddled into the corner of the couch with his arms wrapped tightly around his knees.

Liam turns his head toward him when he walks in, and his blue eyes are huge and pleading and completely magnetic. He looks so vulnerable that Paul immediately wants to help, whatever help might mean in this case, but when he approaches, Liam pulls more tightly into himself and shakes his head.

"Okay," Paul says soothingly, taking the armchair instead. With the data he has from Carly and everything he knows about the night he and Alex took Ali, he thinks he at least has some idea of how not to make anything worse.

Eventually Liam lifts his head, shuffles his shoulders and says, "Sorry."

"Hey, hey, hey, it's fine," Paul says gently. "Are you okay?"

Liam clearly thinks it through and then nods, unwinding his limbs so that he's actually sitting with his feet on the floor and his hands in his lap. "Yeah. It's hard sometimes. Embarrassing."

Paul regards Liam for a long moment.

"You know about these, right?" He raises a hand to show Liam the scars he doesn't bother to cover and also doesn't ever really talk about.

Liam nods. "Carly."

Paul isn't surprised that Carly is the vector of that particular piece of information. That Liam has some of Paul's secrets makes the balance of the universe feel a little more even.

"You've got nothing to be embarrassed about. I had to spend a summer in the loony bin over them."

"Why did you do it?" Liam asks, gesturing at Paul's wrists.

Paul has to smile at Liam's blunt inquisitiveness. "Because most people don't understand what it's like to make entirely reasonable choices in entirely unreasonable circumstances."

Liam sits up straighter and leans forward a little. "I could have ended up so many places not L.A.," he says. "And I don't mean everyone doesn't make it in the business. My parents could have been so much less patient."

"People with good intentions can make decisions about your life in ways that are really scary," Paul says carefully. He's a grade-A asshole if he guesses wrong anywhere in this conversation.

Liam nods slowly. "Carly's pissed because I'm regressing."

"Has this happened before?"

Liam nods. "Never this long."

"How did you get out of it?"

Liam shrugs. "Time. Therapy. Victor. There's too much going on. No one is more freaked than me about what happens if I can't learn to talk on command again."

"You're doing okay right now," Paul points out, not necessarily wanting to look too closely at Liam's word choices.

"I don't have any feelings for you, so it's just words. You're easier to talk to than Alex."

Paul blinks at what he thinks is Liam's consideration for the awkwardness of the situation. When he chuckles, Liam actually cracks a smile.

"Is there somewhere else you could go? Like, if things are too much for you here," Paul suggests. Certainly his own escape from South Carolina, albeit under different circumstances, had gone a long way to letting him sort out his own shit. Considering Victor was instrumental in that process too, it's hard to know how any of them are supposed to get on with their lives in his absence. "I know it feels like being close helps, but it might not," he adds.

Liam tips his head back and forth, considering it. "Maybe. Maybe New York. But like, one, the baby's due in four months, two, I don't want to leave Carly and Ali, three, it's a lot to ask of my parents, and, four, what if I don't come back?"

At that, Paul can only shrug. "One of your partners just *died,* Liam. Anyone who's telling you you're supposed to be able to think about more than the next five minutes is probably wrong. The timing sucks, but when wouldn't it?"

◆

Alex finds Liam and Paul in Victor's den, side by side on the couch. Paul looks up a little guiltily, and god knows what that is about, but Liam seems more present than he did earlier. Alex has no idea what he's interrupted and almost feels like he should back out the door again, but Paul says "Hi," while Liam blinks thoughtfully at him.

"Carly's ready to go," Alex tells both of them, and then waits while Paul unfolds himself from the couch and then turns to offer Liam a hand up. Liam twitches the corner of his mouth up but doesn't take the hand, standing up on his own and slipping out of the room.

◆

"So. You and Liam." Alex says once he and Paul are home and in bed.

"This is a strange role reversal," Paul jokes. He's glad they're talking about this, even if he's sure that significant awkwardness is about to ensue.

"I've never seen him look at you like that."

"Believe me, you are not the one most freaked out by that," Paul admits. "Although I feel like I can see now in him what you do and maybe what Victor did."

Alex pushes back from Paul slightly. "Okay, please don't compare my relationship with Liam to Victor's."

"Why not?"

"Because Liam overshares, and they're not the same thing. No. Don't ever."

"But – "

"You're about to say something terrible, aren't you?" Alex asks.

"Maybe he needs something like that."

"Like what?"

"Like where someone's willing to exert a bit of authority with him. He seems to look at me that way, and I know he trusts you that way."

"Worse than I imagined." Alex sits up. "What is wrong with you?"

"You've been whining at me for weeks about wanting to help him," Paul points out.

Alex gapes. "I want to *talk* to him."

"Really?" Paul doesn't believe him. Even when they haven't been having sex, whatever Alex and Liam are about has never seemed like just talking.

"I thought you had put the whole jealous asshole thing to rest. Don't start again now."

"I'm not!" Paul protests. "I was fine with you two making out that night at Victor's."

"How is this conversation happening?" Alex boggles. "That was a year and a half ago!"

"Alex," Paul chides. "Would it really be that unreasonable?"

"Yes!"

"Would you stop flipping out and actually listen to me?"

Alex gives Paul a long look and then tucks his feet in to sit cross-legged under the sheets. "Okay. Fine. I'm listening, but I strongly suspect this is a worse idea than having a baby."

"He told me that whenever this has happened before Victor helped fix it," Paul says a little helplessly.

Alex rolls his eyes. "Let me spell this out for you in tiny words. Liam and I fucked because we were sort of the same age and it felt like having a boyfriend. The fact that I had no idea what I was doing with him was okay in a way it wasn't with you. You are way overstepping right now."

Paul makes a sound of protest at Alex's probably fair assessment of their early relationship, but Alex holds up a hand before he can interrupt further.

"No, listen," Alex says. "Whatever power games you think will fix this – and Paul, come on, you are not Victor – I have no interest in them. That's also why Liam and I aren't together, because I don't want that responsibility. So fuck you, okay? Like I know you're trying, but just stop, all right?"

Paul pulls back. Whenever he thinks he has a handle on Alex and Liam as a unit, he gets another piece of the puzzle and has to recalibrate. "Okay," he says, willing to drop it. Alex's tone doesn't brook an argument.

"Where is this coming from?" Alex asks.

Paul considers that. "We talked about my wrists. Which makes Liam the second person I've told about them who I wasn't dating or related to."

"And how did you get from there to sex?" Alex prompts.

"Because things are changing, and I thought maybe it could help us, too."

"Whoa. What?" Alex asks. "What about us needs help?"

"I'm hardly home and we're planning for a baby, and on top of that stuff is changing with us and sex. I'm not sure what's going on with that."

"We're having a lot of it?" Alex offers hesitantly.

"Yeah, but the vibe is different. I don't know what's going on in your head about it, but if things are changing it seems like something worth discussing."

"Okay, look, Paul, if you want to address how we fuck, *talk* to me about it, don't try to bring Liam into it. This is sloppy even for you."

"I was trying to kill multiple birds with one stone?" Paul says weakly.

"And his big sad eyes were really pretty?"

"Alex – "

"I know, okay! Ugh. But still, involving Liam in any part of this is not good choices right now. Or ever. You and I can't fix every one of our issues with sex. You can't fix everyone else with sex either. Like seriously."

"I know. But – "

"But *what*?"

"But sex is this really central thing for us. It always has been. We have a lot of it. It's incredibly important in our relationship. And it's caused problems for us in the past."

"I remember," Alex says dryly.

"Something's going on with it now, with you, and I don't understand. Given everything else that's changing I thought we should maybe have a conversation about it before anything gets out of hand."

"That's reasonable, but framing this discussion as 'Let's fuck Liam!' so you can reassert your dominance or whatever is profoundly not."

"Whoa, okay, so not what was going on there, but point taken."

"Really?" Alex asks skeptically.

"Really. Whatever we do is fine so long as it's working for us. I just want to make sure it's working."

"Well, it is for me if it is for you," Alex says with fond exasperation.

"So that's a no to the threesome," Paul says in an attempt at a joke. He wants to put this topic to rest now, if only to hopefully keep Alex from bitching at him about it forever.

"You know how you get possessive of me? I get possessive of that time I had with Liam. I'm happy with it on a shelf, but please don't try to touch it," Alex says.

"So that's no to a threesome with *Liam,*" Paul clarifies, still going for levity.

"Correct," Alex says firmly. "And to the rest of it, at least for now. Focusing on the shit going on in our lives isn't the worst thing in the world."

"You mean like asking you what's going on in your head?"

Alex gives a disbelieving laugh. "Then next time just come out and fucking ask."

"Fine. What are you doing?"

Alex sits up abruptly, and swings a knee over Paul's waist to straddle him. "Trying new things. Feeling good. Making you feel good. Expanding this *big central thing* we have."

"Don't tease," Paul chides.

"I'm not. Although you're one to talk," he says, pressing his fingers to Paul's lips with a smirk. It fades into something more serious, and Paul finds himself arrested by the way Alex's eyes dart over his face and then lock with his.

"I like our adventures," Alex says quietly, like he's trying to make sure Paul hears him. "But I want them to stay that way – adventures, that we get up to, together, sometimes, when the time and place is right. I don't want an open relationship. I don't want a triad, with Liam or anybody else. I want *you.*"

Paul is too overwhelmed to be able to respond to any of that properly. Alex shifts off of him and gets him to roll over on his stomach, kneeling behind him and then hesitating, pressing his hands almost gently into Paul's waist and ass.

"Sometimes I get so nervous doing this," he confesses as he reaches for the lube, and his voice is different, again, gone somewhere Paul still doesn't quite know how to follow.

Paul groans and folds his arms under his head as Alex lines himself up and starts pressing in. "You've been doing this a lot lately." After all, that's part of what he'd been trying to get an answer on.

"Yeah, but I can never quite believe I get to."

Alex digs his fingers into Paul's hips while he pounds into him. It's aggressive in a way that, hot as it is, Paul still isn't used to. And for all they've talked about it now, Paul still isn't sure what Alex is doing, or what it means for them.

When Alex's hands creep into his hair and pull, it's glorious. It's also a little exhausting, because even after all their talking and all this feeling, Paul still isn't sure what Alex is actually chasing.

Despite the weird conversation about sex, and the conversations about the baby, and all the lingering effects of dead Victor on their lives, Alex at least tries to keep up a semblance of normalcy as the summer passes. On his day off, he takes Darcy shooting. He hasn't been to the range in ages, and she should brush up her skills before the *Winsome* finale, not that she needs the excuse to spend a day out with Alex where they might get photographed.

Paul's grateful Alex has something to occupy himself while he has to work. It makes him feel less guilty for spending time at the office when Alex is about to take off for South Carolina so soon.

He does his best to moderate the time he's at the office, but that means taking work home with him. When he and Olivia get caught up in a discussion about her latest spec script, he glances at the clock and tells her to pack up and come back to their house with him.

"If I keep talking about pilots with you here I'm playing favorites. Come over and it's off the books," he tells her. "Also our kitchen is somewhat reasonably stocked." Olivia agrees readily.

It feels like an extension of what Paul's job was like when he worked for Victor, hosting parties and keeping everyone human and healthy. Victor did it too, for his inner circle, with meals and gatherings at his house. With Victor's house soon to be gone from their social landscape, Paul and Alex's is a logical successor.

Once there, laptops and notes spread across the kitchen table, the conversation turns from Olivia's script to the network notes from the latest table read. Paul's been pissy about them and hasn't yet brought them to the writers' room at large. When Olivia asks why, he gives her a considering look before he passes his laptop over to her.

The notes are irritating, and mostly about Alex's character, and while Paul will take some of them because it's the network and he has to, he'll fight for others. Doing this work in front of Olivia is one thing, but he really does not want to discuss any of them in a room full of ten people who all work for him.

"This is appalling," Olivia says, scrolling down the page.

"Mhmm."

"How do you not go crazy with shit like this?"

"Mostly I go crazy," Paul chuckles, although it's not really a joke.

Olivia has her hand clapped over her mouth, half in horror and half because she can't stop laughing, when Alex and Darcy come in.

"What is going on?" Alex drops his bag in the doorway.

Olivia gives Paul and then him a look.

"The network sent back notes for the episode with the love scene between you two. Specifically, they sent back notes about your love scene," Paul says.

"Oooh, let me see," Darcy says, crowding around Olivia's shoulders.

"How on earth do they have notes on that? It's not like it's chock full of dialogue," Alex says.

"Yeah, well, it wasn't the dialogue they had issues with."

"'Don't put woman on top for love scene, lest audience remember actor is gay,'" Darcy reads from the screen.

"*Seriously?*" Alex says, coming around to see for himself. He sounds more incredulous than \pissed.

"Okay, both of you need to not breathe down my damn neck," Olivia protests.

"But Melissa has to be on top," Darcy protests. "She's so much better than Jason, and my tits will look better."

Everyone turns to stare at her.

"What?" When no answer is forthcoming, she can't help but dig in deeper. "They will," she says, cupping them. "Gravity. I hate that side-boob thing."

As sarcastically as possible, Olivia types, *Actress says no due to side-boob concern* in response to the note.

♦

After Alex drags Darcy out to the back deck with beer and to *discuss your top and bottom bullshit, oh my God*, Olivia can almost see Paul slide into a funk.

"What's going on with you?" Olivia folds her arms on the island when Paul fails to talk about anything constructive. She watches as he wanders in circles, complaining about *Winsome* and the fucking network, and *M.A.R.S.* and fucking Mark. She is not Paul's therapist, but he's also not being useful to anyone at the moment, which makes her more inclined to help him sort his shit out. She's starting to understand that Paul is one of those people who needs to talk out anything and everything that's bothering him.

"Our jobs are idiotic," Paul complains.

"Our jobs are actually awesome. You've been doing this way longer than I have, and you worked for Victor. This cannot be the worst you've ever see."

"Maybe not, but Victor being dead makes it a special sort of hell. The network is giving me homophobic bullshit, the ratings have been slipping which is so not where we want to be going into the end of the series, we're not even going to talk about *M.A.R.S.'* ratings, and Alex is going to be gone for two weeks now and then a month in the fall when he has to do the media junket for his movie. Also, I have no idea what he or I are going to be doing in a year."

"You should, like, get on that," Olivia says.

Paul gives a tired chuckle. "Last time I pitched a pilot I had Victor over my shoulder the whole way. And now he's gone. I don't think I can replace him."

"In terms of needing someone else over your shoulder or in terms of being him?" Olivia asks, curious. His response has the potential to impact her own strategies and tactics.

"Both. I'm not good at working alone, and God knows I can't keep everybody functional."

"Well, you can work with me, and Alex can keep you functional."

Paul side-eyes her. "Did you just appoint yourself my new creative partner?"

"You could call Mark," she says, like that's any sort of option.

"You're really fucking manipulative, you know that?" Paul's voice is good-natured, but he's reminding himself of what she is too.

Olivia shrugs. "So was Victor."

◆

Alex could probably get more of Victor's journals while everyone is at the house in their ongoing and incomplete task of putting his life into boxes, but it seems wrong. Whatever Alex is learning about Victor feels tender and private and somehow intentionally just for him. He's not ready to share it with anyone else. Or face their reasonable outrage at him rifling through desk drawers not to organize, but to steal.

Paul keeps his set of keys to Victor's house – on loan from Nigel – hanging by the door to the garage with the rest of their keys. He seems reluctant to put them on his own key ring, which Alex can hardly blame him for. This reluctance also makes it easy for Alex to take them one afternoon while Paul's at work.

He drives to Victor's house alone. He's leaving for ten days in South Carolina soon. A trip to do right by Paul's family before they start the medical part of the baby procedure seems a fitting time to read more of Victor's journals.

At this point, Alex doesn't really need the rest of them. He knows how the story ends. He was there for a lot of it. And as much as he's learned about the man who was so often his own private villain, Victor is dead. Alex can't actually do anything with his growing empathy or possible regrets.

Somehow, though, he still wants to know the story, as Victor chose to tell it to his diary, the intended audience of which Alex still can't figure out. But Alex has known there is magic in story since he left his doomed life in Indiana to come to Los Angeles with a girl he didn't even know but somehow expected to keep him safe.

Despite all the years he has worked in TV and film now, Alex is still learning how stories work, not on his heart, but on the world. They are machines of haunting beauty and houses of the heart. Victor's diaries make him care, in a way he never has before, about the technology of language, of arc and of cadence. It would be wrong for Alex to stop reading and let this particular story's task, whatever it is, go unfinished.

◆

Liam does his best to keep Carly in the loop about what he's considering doing with his life. That endeavor would be easier if he didn't feel guilty every time he thought about leaving her alone with Ali and the pregnancy while he goes back to New York to try to remember how to drive a car and use the microwave. Carly deserves a less complicated life than the one he's able to offer her. While that's always been true, it feels more unfair now than ever. There are no lists anyone can give him that will solve it.

He's still not sure if being at Victor's house makes it better or worse. Since he can't figure it out, he tags along when Carly goes to meet Paul and Alex. As distressing as it is to see Victor's belongings packed and removed, the house, like the man who once owned it, will not be there forever. Liam wants to be able to say goodbye for as long as he can.

Alex is grumbling about being tasked with boxing up Victor's den for no reason anyone can ascertain other than that he's pissed about being there again. Liam finally has to walk away from him; he doesn't have the ability to explain to Alex all the things he wishes his friend understood about Victor. What makes it worse is that Alex may never actually understand why that's such a tragedy.

"What the hell?" Paul says as Liam wanders into the kitchen. He's reacting to his phone, though, and not to Liam, so that's nothing to worry about.

Liam drifts on to where Carly is sitting with her laptop and making a list of the kitchen contents. She'll send it to Nigel, so he doesn't have to send them polite but increasingly insistent emails every week.

Paul still has his phone in hand as he walks to the front door. Liam peers at him curiously as he opens the front door and finds Darcy on the doorstep.

"What are you doing here?" Paul demands.

"I need to talk to you guys."

Alex, as if drawn by her voice, rounds the corner from the den. "What the hell is so pressing you had to come here in person?"

"Don't be sharp," Darcy retorts. "Even though there aren't going to be blinds about you and me fighting in the women's restroom."

"Oh my God, no," Alex says. Before Paul or anyone else can react, he grabs Darcy and hauls her back outside.

◆

"The blinds were really funny," Darcy protests, as Alex makes her walk the long way around to the backyard and the pool deck.

"Yeah, Gemma was especially pleased to be the subject of internet ponderings regarding my possible bisexuality, and whether I'm suddenly dating the chick I lived with for three years."

"I used to think you were a couple."

Alex stares. He doesn't want to think of Darcy as someone who was once a fan. He feels awkward enough straddling that divide himself; he doesn't want to contemplate anyone else doing the same.

"Before I met you! What?"

"What do you want, Darcy?"

"So speaking of the internet, it's being really gross about Jackson."

Alex groans. It really only was a matter of time. While Alex is aware the internet is *always* gross about something he has no desire to be pulled into Darcy's dating drama. No matter how much he likes Jackson.

"Everyone's being really racist and saying awful things," she states. "I don't understand, it's not like we're in the fifties anymore."

"It's Hollywood. It's always the fifties."

"But everybody thinks you and Paul and your awesome gay romance is awesome."

"Are you actually listening to the things coming out of your mouth?" Alex is aghast, and if it were anyone but Darcy saying these things, he'd be yelling right now.

"What? Your awesome gay romance *is* awesome."

◆

Packing is interrupted twenty minutes later by a rustle, thud, and a sharp "Fuck!" from Paul. Alex looks across the kitchen to see Paul at the table, staring disconsolately at a stack of papers he's accidentally knocked to the floor, scattering them everywhere. Alex moves to help him pick the papers up but to absolutely everyone's surprise, Liam appears behind Paul and, very gently, puts his hands on his shoulders. When Paul doesn't shrug him off – just cranes his neck around to see what the fuck Liam is doing – Liam starts massaging his shoulders.

"What the hell?" Paul says, more confused than anything.

Liam shushes him and digs his thumb in. Paul's shoulders slump with obvious relief.

Alex understands instantly what's going on even as he finds it unsettling. Liam and Victor's negotiations regarding how Liam was allowed to touch him are, after all, a recurring topic in the diaries. Victor's solution had been massage classes for Liam so he could have the touch he needed while Victor maintained the more clinical distance he needed.

Darcy looks as confused as Paul does, but Carly shoots a look at Alex and then moves to the next cupboard. Alex continues with his work too. Paul doesn't need know that Liam has decided he needs to be cared for the same way Liam used to do for Victor.

Darcy eventually goes on her way after extracting a vague commitment from Alex that he'll do drinks with her and Jackson at some point. Liam ends up on the couch in the living room, curled up small and hugging a pillow to his chest while Alex marks the boxes of books to be donated to charity.

"I'll miss you," Liam says suddenly. Paul looks up from where he's working on itemized lists for Nigel.

"Where are you going?" Alex asks, looking over at Liam.

Liam doesn't say anything, but Alex nods after a moment, and then they don't break eye contact for minutes.

"What the hell?" Paul asks softly, when Carly walks in the room again.

She waves a hand in their general direction. "Ignore them, they're being witchy."

"No but seriously." Paul is convinced someone should be discussing this. Whatever is going on, it's unnerving. It's also not coming from Liam but rather seems to be something Alex brings out in both of them.

"Is there an explanation that exists that actually makes you feel better?" Carly asks.

"Alex was right about this house. It's creepy."

"The house is not always the problem."

18

Paul hates coming home after dropping Alex off at the airport. Alex is only going to be in South Carolina for ten days, but Paul still feels like he's just gotten back from Australia even though it's July now and that was months ago. The empty house feels entirely wrong.

He puts off calling Carly to see how she's holding up until after Alex is gone. He doesn't want to start more drama about what Liam hasn't told Alex and how much of Liam's everything Alex is – or is not – entitled to.

When Paul does finally call, she sounds exhausted. "I thought breaking up with you would have reduced your dependence on the lonely late night phone call thing."

Paul doesn't know whether she's joking or not. "How are you?"

"Six months pregnant with a five-year-old who is being even more of a brat than usual because she misses her father and a full slate of work tomorrow, whether or not I get any sleep at all tonight. How are you?" she asks with a sharp sweetness that makes Paul wince.

"I can take Ali tonight if you need a break."

"If I thought she'd go, I'd walk her there myself." There's the muffled sound of Ali negotiating to sleep in her mother's bed that night. "Just a minute, Ali, I'm on the phone," Carly tells her.

"I do not know how people do this single parent thing," Carly says when she comes back.

"Not what we expected our lives to look like in college, is it?" Paul feels guilty at the question. Usually he means all the ways his life is better than he'd ever thought possible.

"Nobody ever expects their life to look like this. I still can't believe he left," Carly says angrily.

Paul winces. Her phrasing sounds so final. "I thought you wanted him to."

Carly sighs sharply. "My husband went home to his parents because he needed a quiet, safe place to learn how to do the world again. A place that was not with me because our child and my pregnancy are apparently burdens for him. That it was the right thing to do does not mean I am not pissed that I get no support system."

"Do you both want to come over? Or me to go over there?" Paul offers, though he is aware that it's, at best, a stop-gap solution.

Carly laughs darkly. "Thanks, but let's save the exploration of the family-that-almost-was for nights more dire than this."

Paul is horrified to realize such nights might actually plausibly exist. It's an unsettling thought, not because he can see it happening but because he can see it happening whether Alex and Liam are involved or not.

◆

Alex doesn't realize how accustomed he's become to the pervasive smoke from the wildfires outside LA until he steps outside at the Charleston airport. The air is heavy with the scent of oversaturated earth and vegetation as he tosses his bags in the back of the rental car. The change is dramatic but doesn't feel like relief from either the fires or the situation he left behind him in California.

He's glad to do the drive alone, and flips through radio channels as he speeds down now-familiar roads. Eventually he lands on a country radio station all but identical to the one he used to listen to on the shitty radio in his shitty car on his way to school and his terrible jobs in Indiana. He's surprised he still knows enough of the songs to sing along. Some things don't really change.

When the sun sets, Alex flips on the headlights. He feels isolated from the world in a way he almost never does on the opposite coast. In L.A., someone is always watching, and someone always knows where he is. Here, he's just a guy in a car on a highway. He feels small in a way he hasn't in a very long time.

It's almost dark by the time he gets to the house. Beth waves to him from the verandah as he pulls up the drive and hugs him tightly when he makes it up the steps. For that moment, Alex feels like he has stepped through a portal into an entirely different life.

◆

Being back in New York is hard. On some level, it's a relief. To a certain extent Liam's systems for navigating the world kick in as soon as he can see the city from the air. This is where he learned everything that has let him have the life he has. Knowing how to get home in a crisis was one of the things drilled into him from the beginning. He never thought it would look like this.

Neither of his parents meet him at the airport when he lands on a hot, humid morning. JFK is far, and Liam doesn't want to subject them to whatever attention it might attract. But Liam knows to look for the guy with the sign and follow him to a black car. As he watches Queens and then Brooklyn pass by the windows in the dark, he realizes he doesn't feel particularly sad about being in New York. At least, he's no sadder than he is about anything else. At a given point, all loss is one.

It's a nice night, and his parents are sitting on the bench in the small courtyard in front of their brownstone when the car pulls up. He lets them hug him, but it's awkward and reminds him too much of the line of condolences he had to endure at Victor's funeral. His parents hadn't been there, because he'd asked them not to come. He heads inside without comment when they say how sorry they are.

For the first few days, everything feels much worse. Therapy doesn't really feel much better, not that it should at this point. It's all so practical. There's a soul-deep horror to realizing that even if he can learn to do things again and say words he's decided on independently, Victor will still be dead. Liam will still be completely unable to talk about it in most places or times, not because of his brain, but because of the world he lives in. It's not a particularly motivating circumstance.

It takes almost a week before Liam can muster up the will to invite Charles over.

They've known each other since they were eight, since before Liam was ever on TV, and since before he became so good at seeming like other people, more or less. Which means Charles not only understands when Liam mostly isn't talking, but that he doesn't find it particularly exceptional. They've been sleeping with each other on and off for years out of what has gone from friendly boredom to an actual, serious – if long-distance and tertiary – relationship in Liam's complex web of companionship.

Charles is loud and effusive in filling in the space that Liam's silence leaves. Liam finds that a little uncomfortable. He's also bluntly curious about what it's like to have a dead lover and how Liam is navigating this. The conversation that sparks is far outside the realm of things Liam can talk about with most other people, which is a relief. Everything is still miserable – and Liam has to think too hard about the right steps to accomplish most basic tasks right now – but not having to police himself is a definite bonus.

Charles invites himself to the house for dinner, checking in only to make sure Liam isn't too tired. Some days are better than others, and exhaustion isn't exactly the problem.

Sometimes he feels like he's everything the internet said he would – and wouldn't – be when he Googled autism when he was ten. Still, being like this feels less dishonest than so many years of passing and pretending that "high functioning" is something real or even valuable.

But Liam can tolerate Charles's presence. Possibly, more importantly, Liam can tolerate Charles touching him – a hand covering his, a touch to the shoulder – because he knew Charles long before Victor. Charles erases nothing.

Liam kisses Charles, which would be completely unsurprising in any other circumstance. Liam would happily do more, but Charles wants to have a conversation about that and Liam isn't up for one. So they wind up making out. A lot.

"This is so surreal," he tells Liam.

"Why?"

"Because I feel like we're kids, and about to get caught, and like you're a regression vortex we're all getting sucked into."

Liam frowns.

"You have a whole life you're supposed to be getting home to," Charles notes.

Speculation about the Campbell family splitting up has been all over *Entertainment Tonight*, Liam knows, because he overheard his mother watching it. He's sure Charles knows about it too, but no one has had the nerve to mention it to him directly. It's a hot mess of upsetting, but so much is wrong right now Liam is not sure how to prioritize his distress.

Liam shrugs. "I know. That's what I'm doing."

"Really?" Charles asks. "Here or there?"

"Does it matter?"

♦

Sarah, as far as Alex can tell, is taking the whole baby situation in much better stride than he is.

"It's drugs, a trip to L.A., and half a day at the doctor's office. And then you and Paul get a baby," she says, while she and Alex shuck corn.

Beth has banished them to the verandah, because they were getting the corn silk everywhere in the kitchen. It's the kind of handwork that Alex never has the time or need to do any more, unless he's here. It reminds him both of the childhood he tries not to think about as well as the vacations he's taken here with Paul. He feels young in a way that's not entirely useful given the circumstances.

"There's an appeal to keeping this in the family," she says.

Alex nods, and tries to explain that he doesn't know who his father was, and that Delilah is, as far as he's ever been informed, his half-sister. "This whole genetic continuity thing was never part of my life."

"Well, lots of things were never going to be part of your life," Sarah says with a smile.

Alex gives a thoughtful far-away hum in response.

"What are you going to do about names?" She changes the subject.

Alex chuckles. "Paul is forbidden from picking up a baby name book until after the first trimester. And I told him the kid can have his last name."

"He must have been all over that."

"It's only fair, I won the bio-dad thing." Alex doesn't think it matters either way. Alex himself has his mother's last name and Paul doesn't have any contact with his father anymore. Neither Beth nor Sarah talk to the man either. Alex doesn't blame himself for that situation, though he and a great deal of drama around their wedding was largely responsible for it. But Paul's name is Paul's name, whoever else's it may be, and if it matters to him, Alex can respect that.

"Is it really a competition?" Sarah asks.

"I'm just relieved Paul didn't want to procreate with my felonious sister."

But as awkward as Alex feels at first about discussing the topic with Sarah, it's way weirder talking about it with Sarah's husband, Mike. There is absolutely no gracious way Alex can find to open the topic.

He and Mike are on the verandah steps after dinner, left alone deliberately, Alex suspects, by the women of the house, when he finally blurts "I'm sorry I'm having a baby with your wife."

Mike stares at him for half a second while Alex wishes he could crawl under the porch. Then Mike cracks up.

"It's weird!" Alex protests.

Mike claps him on the back. "Look. It's weird that my brother-in-law writes TV, and married somebody famous, and at one point I would have thought it was weird that you're a guy, but you and I both married into a family that has a creepy farm house and a cricket barn. The baby is weird too, but everything here is weird."

"Oh my God, the crickets." Alex laughs to himself in nervous relief that he's found an ally on that particular point.

"They're horrifying, aren't they?"

"Paul acted like it was normal!"

"Yeah. No. It's really not."

◆

Paul talks to Alex almost every day. Even with the calls – and the texts and pictures Alex sends throughout his day – Paul misses him desperately. It's only ten days, but travel is always hard for them. In all of the upset their life has been for the past four months, Alex's absence is a misery.

When a new batch of completely asinine notes comes through from the network, Paul groans out loud in his office and reaches for his phone. It's late enough that Alex has to be asleep. Paul could wake him, but what he actually needs is to freak out at Victor and get a dose of sanity and tolerant exasperation in return. The call rings only once before it rolls over to a stock voicemail message.

Paul jerks the phone away from his ear and drops it on his desk as he realizes what he's done.

After a moment he buries his face in his hands. The chaos Victor's death has thrown into everyone's lives into has left him no time or space to deal with his own grief. Paul really fucking misses his friend.

◆

The pace of life is different in South Carolina. While Alex still gets up early as a courtesy to Beth, there's also a pleasure in coffee over the misty sunrise of the mornings. He spends his days rambling around the house and the property, which somehow seem less forbidding without Paul's ominous stories at his side. There are no demons in the barn, no creatures in the lake looking for children to drown, and the knives in the kitchen and the guns on the range are all just tools.

In the late mornings, with everyone he's come to see at work, he gets in his car and drives. Marion and the surrounding towns shouldn't seem as different from Paragon, Indiana as they do, but the land is lush and the strip malls aren't any uglier than the ones in Los Angeles. Alex can see, certainly, how it would have been a hard place for Paul to grow up; it probably wouldn't have been kind to Alex either were their situations reversed. But it seems like a place where people at least have the right to dreams and the possibility of getting out. Paragon never did. Alex wonders if he'll ever stop feeling like it's waiting to claw him back into the dirt.

Even with long conversations out on the verandah after dinner, bed comes early in a place where work doesn't creep on toward midnight and later, and restaurants close at nine. Alex spends the nights reading Victor's diaries.

The Liam first introduced therein is a stranger. He's so young, and Alex is fascinated by Victor's clinicalness.

Liam is just a tool in the story, not of Victor's life, but of *The Fourth Estate*. Until he asks Victor out. The entry that follows is pages of confusion and frustration at a young man who is both willing to break into Victor's bedroom at a party in the hopes of seducing him and happy to talk for hours over dinner and at least wait out his asexuality, if not accept it. Both the narrative and Victor's sudden uncertainty is fucking bizarre. And that's before Alex gets to the part where Liam wants Victor to watch him jerk off.

"I don't need you to do anything, but if we're going to be together however we're going to be together — we're together, right? — I need you to see me like this."

Alex's brain breaks on the asexuality thing, not for the first time. Victor was enraptured by Liam in a way that feels distant to Alex. Yet it was clearly anything but. Just different from how Alex experiences people. Whatever it was, was some sort of uncomfortable for Victor.

The power dynamic is also unnerving.

Liam's discovery of pain is an accident, Victor gripping his wrist too tight in the kitchen to save him from the results of an ill-advised attempt at teaching him to cook. The image is strangely hot to Alex: Liam surprised and eager; Victor, after so much literary agony over what pleasure he can and can't stand to give Liam, suddenly gifted with permission to hurt.

There are so many names of desire.

Alex reads of everyone's weary amusement during Liam's disaster with Natalie. Watching Carly morph from Paul's girlfriend to Liam's partner to Victor's friend is particularly surreal. Alex learns to recognize that Victor at times lies in his own journal, omissions indicating a grief or anger he suspects he felt he had no time for. Victor was born both ambitious and resigned.

Alex's own story is shocking. Victor's first entry about him is a single line.

I ruined someone's life today.

Alex is only sure it's about him because of the date. It's not one he can forget, and it's not one that could possibly belong to anyone else.

The other entries are mostly a wall of puzzlement, which Alex is starting to understand as Victor's way of offering praise. If he couldn't understand something and it was still interesting to him, he tried to solve it by dragging it into America's light: television.

While the diaries linger in the back of Alex's mind during the day, they particularly haunt him at night after he's closed the cover on his latest readings. Attempts to convince himself it's because he's away from Paul and not getting laid don't particularly assuage the weirdness.

For all the things Victor omits from his entries, he's incredibly detail-oriented. Alex feels as if he's read about dozens of Liam's orgasms but none of Victor's own.

In some ways Victor's relative absence from the diary makes it easier for Alex to allow himself an interest in its sexual content. Some that is his history with Liam. Liam is beautiful, perhaps most especially in Victor's prose, which narrows him to a finely focused instrument. But a lot of it is the sexual content itself.

He and Paul may fuck often, fuck well, and have their adventures, but the two things that figure most prominently in the journals – bondage and sex toys – aren't things they've experimented with much. Alex's ropes are for rocks, and buying sex toys is eight kinds of complicated in their ridiculous lives. He thinks of the blind items that could result and can't help but giggle.

But Alex also can't help but think of what it would be like to do all those things to Paul. What would it be like to make Paul beg with his own mind clear enough to just watch it happen? Alex knows he wouldn't deviate from the plan or grant unearned mercy.

Alex huffs out a little laugh at the twists his mind takes in his already complicated life and shoves a hand into his pajama bottoms. After all, without Paul here, the only plan he has is the narrative in his head of Paul bound and waiting and impatient.

Paul wouldn't be good the way Liam was for Victor. For Alex, that would be even better. Alex smiles slyly as he jerks himself harder. There's an appeal in showing off, even if it's just for the people in his head. And even if one of them is dead.

19

Paul doesn't particularly want to go to Frank's birthday party and suspects that given delicate network politics and his own unhappy headspace he probably shouldn't. Mark and the entire *M.A.R.S.* team will be there, however. Paul will need to be there to defend his and Victor's territory.

At least he recognizes that's one of the more fucked up thoughts he's had in a while.

"I could go with you," Darcy offers that afternoon as they're wrapping up on set.

Paul shakes his head. "I don't need a date. Especially not my starlet. Especially not at this event. Aren't you having enough fun in the tabloids with Jackson?"

"Let's not talk about that and yes you do. Alex is out of town and, like, probably being a hermit somewhere in the mountains because he didn't tell me where he was going, but you really don't want to go by yourself, Paul."

"I'll be fine."

"You're moping."

"I'm *fine*." Paul stalks away shaking his head. He has things he needs to finish in his office before he deals with this damn party.

"Don't say I didn't warn you," Darcy calls brightly after him. It's been a bad enough day as it is, and Darcy's cheerfulness and general habit of inappropriately camping out in his office is, at this point, just grating.

♦

Frank Pearson's house is as large as Victor's but much more annoying. Victor's place may be hideously modern, but there was a sly self-awareness to the way Victor inhabited it that made the overabundance of corners and excess of white paint bearable. This place is just ugly and Frank doesn't know how to decorate.

The company doesn't particularly improve it. The room is full of people from *M.A.R.S* who didn't like Victor, or have decided they don't like Paul or, for the sake of appearances, are acting as if they don't like Paul when they're not sucking up to him. He drinks too much, because taking another sip keeps being preferable to opening his mouth and giving his honest opinion on anything.

He ends up in conversation in the corner with one of the production guys he's known vaguely for years; Eric was part of the crew Victor kept on *The Fourth Estate* when he reshuffled half of his people to Paul in *Winsome's* first season. In hushed voices, they

543

cautiously talk far too much shit about Mark and the direction he's taking *M.A.R.S.*

The whole conversation is hilarious. Also, Paul feels ridiculously vindicated to have someone else on his side. As the evening progresses and they both get drunker, Paul gets more pissed about everything being done to Victor's legacy, especially since he's the one entrusted to uphold it. When Paul realizes that they've somehow wound up pressed together nearly against the wall in the crush of people, ducking outside seems an entirely logical suggestion to make.

Paul doesn't really register when they start making out. Eventually they wind up in the backseat of Paul's car getting hot and heavy in a way he'd be aware was a bad idea, if he weren't so angry about Victor's death and confused about his own place in the world. Right now, though, he can forget that Victor is dead and his place seems simple enough.

There's not enough room to slide down on the floor between the seats but Paul manages to fold himself up small, get Eric's pants unzipped and down, and start sucking his dick while Eric swears and pants above him. Paul feels fragile and barely there, tethered to reality only by the scent and feel of sex.

After Eric comes, they shuffle around awkwardly on the seats so he can go down on Paul, both of them too drunk to care what a mess they are. Paul is digging his fingers into his hair and encouraging him on with half-formed words and moans when someone raps at the window.

"*Shit,*" Paul hisses. Between his legs Eric jolts back. The sun has set, but the light from the garage is more than bright enough to make out Mark, waggling a phone at him from the other side of the glass. Paul can make out the pictures he's taken.

Mark blows a kiss and then saunters away. It takes every ounce of self-control Paul has left – as well as the knowledge that his life is about to get very stupid and it is entirely his own fault – not to burst out of the car and deck him right there.

◆

Jackson is still mostly asleep in bed at his apartment when Darcy reaches for her phone to start scrolling through the internet and anything interesting that may have happened last night.

"Do you have to do that right now?" he mumbles, rolling over and pulling a pillow over his head. Weekends are for sleeping in, not dealing with more of the industry bullshit his life has been since Victor hired him. Jackson's still not sure if saying yes to that job offer was the best decision he ever made, or the worst. That he's still getting paid from Victor's estate to be a dead man's assistant until everything is finally taken care of is definitely strange.

"If it's bothering you, I can stop," Darcy says, snuggling closer so she can use his chest as a pillow.

"Nope, as long as I don't have to do anything about anything that's happened."

"Promise. You're off-duty."

Jackson laughs. Darcy goes back to happily scrolling through her feed of social media and gossip sites.

"OH MY GOD THERE'S A PICTURE," Darcy suddenly shrieks. She drops the phone as if it's bitten her and scoots away from it.

Jackson, startled, flails and almost falls off the bed. "Darcy, what the hell?"

"THERE'S A PICTURE!"

"Of what?"

"OF PAUL!"

"Okay...." Jackson tries to get a rein on the sudden jolt of adrenaline while simultaneously trying to figure out how to get Darcy, who is clutching the sheets with a look of abject horror, to calm the fuck down.

Darcy takes a couple of deep breaths. "There is a picture of Paul Marion Keane in a compromising position in public with a man who is not his husband," she says with what is clearly a superhuman attempt at decorum under these trying circumstances,

"Paul cheated?" Jackson asks warily, although he does actually want this piece of information. His job, and now his relationship, put him in the way of knowing more than he ever wanted about the complicated lives of various public people.

Darcy looks like she's going to cry.

"Darce, internet gossip sites are bullshit, you send in blinds once a month."

"There's a *picture*," she wails. She fishes around in the sheets until she finds her phone and shoves it at him.

"Whoaaa, okay, more of him than I ever needed to see," he says, passing the phone back as quickly as he can. Dark, blurry, and shadowed for sure, but that picture, on not an at all reputable website, doesn't leave enough to the imagination.

"What's going to happen? Are they going to get divorced? What's gonna happen to *Winsome* if they get divorced? Is this why they thought it was a bad idea for Alex to be on *Winsome?* I still have to work with both of them!" Darcy says with increasing speed and franticness.

Jackson gently tugs her back down onto the pillows. "Okay, you have no idea what happened, no idea what any of it means, and it is not any of your business. You promised I wouldn't have to deal with anything you found on the internet today."

"You don't have to deal with anything! Oh God how are we going to deal with this? I should call Alex – "

"By going back to *sleep*."

"But -"

"No. No calling anybody. No dealing."

"Fine," Darcy says sulkily, curling up next to him again. "But if they get divorced they're going to have to deal with *me*."

"I'm sure that's the biggest concern on their list right now."

♦

Alex notices the email when he's still in bed. He's been BCCed on it – it's addressed to one of the sleazier internet gossip sites – and Alex's mind immediately jumps to Darcy. But when he clicks on the attached pictures and then zooms in, squinting, his stomach sinks. Darcy can be ridiculous, sure, but this is more than a vaguely-sourced blind. And Paul is making far worse choices than Alex could ever have imagined.

Paul picks up his phone just before it goes to voicemail.

"I'm so – "

Alex cuts him off. "Are you okay?"

Paul laugh-sobs in response but doesn't form any actual words.

"I'm going to take that as a no," Alex says.

"Alex, I'm so sorry."

"Where are you right now?"

"What?"

"Where are you," Alex repeats, more slowly. If they're going to get through this, Paul needs to answer his damn questions.

"I'm home."

"Are you alone?"

"Alex – " Paul says, pleadingly.

"That wasn't an accusation. Give me data, Paul. Are you alone?"

"Well, Todd's here. But otherwise, yes."

"Okay." Alex sits down on the edge of the bed. He can hear Beth moving around downstairs. The absolutely last thing he needs is for this conversation to be overheard by Paul's mom, for everyone's sake.

"Are you angry?" Paul asks.

"I'm beyond angry. What should I be reading into this?"

Paul hesitates. "You know I've always had a tendency toward self-injury."

"I know," Alex says. It's why, on top of being pissed at his husband, he's scared. "But are you saying that so I won't yell, or because it's true?"

"Victor's dead, you're not here, and I am *fucked up*."

Alex flops backward on the bed. "I will take it as a marginal win that you're somewhat aware of how fucked up you are," he says sharply. "How much of this was because I said no to the threesome?"

"I don't care about that," Paul says. "Do you know what it means to me that you will say no to me?"

Alex reels from that a little. That's big and powerful and not something he has the bandwidth to touch more firmly right now.

"Then, I don't get it," Alex says. "Are you unhappy? Is that why you keep trying to figure out if I am?" It's such an inconceivable idea, that Alex might not be enough or quite right for him anymore, he can hardly put it to words.

"*No*," Paul makes that half-laugh, half-sob sound again. Alex's heart breaks even as he draws a relieved breath. "No. Not the way you mean."

"Okay," he says more softly. "In what way then?"

Alex has spent so much time reading about Liam through Victor's eyes, and now has a clearer sense than ever before how much Liam has always needed the world to tell him where to go, what to do, and how to feel about it. The things Alex hated about Victor were kindness to Liam nearly always, and the diaries have only served to clarify for Alex why he and Liam could never be together.

That said – and this is the part Alex hates, the part that makes him resent Victor even as Victor is dead – Alex hasn't been able to avoid seeing his own abilities in the man. That's been unsettling, and sometimes frightening, but right now with Paul silent and seemingly unable to answer him, it's really fucking useful. Paul wants to make things better, but he needs to be told how.

"I am starting to understand that this is just how you are," Alex tells Paul, his voice steely. "But when this happens, I need you to not pick up a knife or run twenty miles or go to some party. I need you to call me so I can interrupt you."

"Oh my God," Paul says. He sounds so relieved.

"Paul?" Alex asks, and it's softer and a little uncertain now. All of this is new, and even Victor made mistakes.

"How are you so calm about this?"

"Because when I climb rocks, if I get emotional, I could die. As I have learned. Right now I'm making sure no one dies."

"What do you want to do?" Paul asks after an uncomfortably long pause.

"We're going to figure out how you're going to get through the next seventy-two hours of public humiliation for getting caught getting your dick sucked by a *M.A.R.S.* production dude." Alex is often surprised by his life, but this moment is a realm of unpleasantness previously unanticipated.

"Are you coming back?" Paul asks with equal parts hope and dread.

"No. I mean, yes, I'm coming back, but on Monday like we planned. Not today. We are getting you in a place where you're not a danger to yourself but, Jesus, Paul, I need some space from this."

"Okay," Paul says.

Alex takes a deep breath. "Also, we are going to postpone the baby."

"Alex – "

"We need to take a step back and decide whether this is really something our lives can handle right now. Or ever."

"But we already decided," Paul protests.

"We did, and then you went and hooked up with a random at a party. Carly's pregnant and alone with Ali while Liam's in New York *at your suggestion* because he can't do life. Your issues are not his issues, but that's feeling like a cautionary fucking tale right now, especially considering how entangled we all are. Before you and I have a baby we need to deal with the fact that having responsibility turns you into an asshole because this is now officially a trend."

◆

By the time Alex hangs up, he and Paul have come up with a plan – or rather, Paul has gracefully submitted himself to Alex's decisions. Paul will call Alex twice a day until Alex is back in L.A.; he will not pick Alex up at the airport; and Alex will smile and wave and be friendly at the paparazzi that will inevitably be waiting. Neither of them will comment publicly, and there will be no official statement. If anyone asks Paul about it at work, and they will, he will behave as though this is part of their agreement and there is no relationship drama.

Alex has envied Liam's ability to keep secrets from the public for as long as he's had access to those secrets. As he contemplates his strategy for returning home – and for the coming weeks – Alex is horrified that this is the sort of secret he needs to hide with that same level of skill. It makes everything feel worse.

He emails Liam while Beth is at work and the house is empty. He's not used to having to convey this type of information in writing, and once again perhaps draws too strongly on his recent reading material, in the hopes that something of Victor can help him be clear in a way Liam will get.

Lee –

This email is about three things. None of them need a response from you.

1. Because Paul is terrible, Mark got a picture of him getting a blowjob from someone in his car and now it's on the internet. Yes, not me, and no, that's not in our rules.

2. Strategy is we're going to pretend it is in the rules so maybe the media drama will go away faster. Thank God it was his dick and not mine. But when that happens, which it will as soon as I land at LAX on Monday, the internet is going to go back to wondering about you and me. Be aware.

3. I'm still reading Victor's diaries. A lot of them are about you. I feel weird about that, and I'll stop if you want. But Victor puzzling through how to be with you may have just saved my marriage, which is fucked up and I'll explain if you want me to, so I wanted to say thank you, and I'm sorry I'm always such an asshole about him, even though I am not taking back the part where he was a jerk to me a lot. I'm glad you got his wisdom and his affection; it seems like it was a good thing to have.

Please surface soon. I'll be angry if New York becomes the only way I can see you.

Alex stares at the message for a long time. He hopes it's clear enough for Liam to digest right now and not insulting for it.

He also has no idea how to sign it.

Love seems like a disaster waiting to happen. The situation with Paul makes Alex superstitious, and saying something like that to Liam without clarifying it is either perfectly fine or the worst idea in the world.

Alex sighs and decides this isn't the time for gambling. He signs his name with nothing more than a dash and hits send. From there there's nothing to do but wait, and hope that everyone he has ever known, but right now most especially Beth – and her coworkers – goes nowhere near the internet. He's glad she and Sarah don't ever really go after celebrity gossip online or elsewhere. He feels guilty for not planning to bring it up with them, but *your son cheated on me* is too terrible a thing to say when he's standing under their roof.

After he emails Liam, he calls Margaret to discuss the situation and what the fuck they're going to do about it. After Margaret is Gemma, not because Alex particularly wants to talk to her, but because calling her is much preferable to waiting for her to call him, and she will.

"Are you okay?" she asks.

"I have no idea," he says. "But I'm managing."

"I'm sorry, the internet is terrible."

"Gemma, I seriously don't want to know."

"I'll leave it to your imagination then."

"Oh God, don't do that!" Alex gives a despairing sort of laugh.

"Do you want to do lunch?" she offers, more softly than she's spoken to him in a while.

"Yeah, but in a couple weeks," he says. He has so much more to do before he can brace for that.

20

Alex drives back to the airport on a clear, blindingly bright day. He fumbles his sunglasses on one-handedly as he pulls onto the highway and away from the peace of Marion in the face of Paul's poor choices.

He spends the flight with his headphones on but not listening to music. He reads one of Paul's intro-to-film textbooks he'd grabbed from the shelf in his old bedroom. Reading the diaries in public is entirely out of the question. Given the current circumstances he doesn't want to go anywhere near the internet.

Once they land Alex, waits until everyone else has gotten off the plane then tugs the hat lower on his head, not that it's going to help him. The waiting might, however, marginally shorten the time he has to spend at baggage claim.

The strategy is sound – there are paparazzi crowded just outside the door by the carousel taking pictures and shouting obnoxious questions at him almost as soon as he gets there. Being LAX, even with his own late arrival, it takes more than a few minutes for his bag to surface.

Finally, the suitcase tumbles down the chute. Alex snags it as quick as he can. He flashes a brilliant smile at them all as he strides out the door. He pauses for effect before letting himself slide into the accent of his childhood to ask, "Haven't you boys ever heard of the zip code rule?"

♦

Alex lets himself into the house. Before he has time to even lock the door, Paul appears from the living room to stand awkwardly in the foyer, hands in his pockets.

"Hi," Paul says.

"You look like shit."

Paul chuckles weakly and looks at his feet.

Alex drops his bags by the door and goes to stand in front of him. When Paul finally brings his head up, Alex kisses him dryly. "Come talk."

Paul nods, looking scared and grateful and lost. When Alex leads the way down the hall, he follows.

"Can I say I'm sorry now?" Paul hovers uncertainly by the kitchen island while Alex opens cupboards.

Alex puts a pan down on the island and smiles tightly at Paul. They've had to deal with more crises in the near-decade they've been together than Alex cares to think about.

"Apology accepted. But it would be more useful if you told me exactly what set this off. You don't do this, not like this. At least, I don't think you do. Do you?"

Paul shakes his head. "No. I don't know what it was." He slides gingerly onto one of the island stools.

Alex gives him an unimpressed look. "Bullshit. You may be a jerk, but you're a self-aware jerk. What was it?"

Paul shrugs helplessly.

"Paul." Alex says patiently.

"You know I don't do well when we're not together. And then it was a bad day. Just, ordinary shit. Network notes and crap like that. I forgot Victor's dead."

When Paul tells him about trying to call Victor, Alex pauses with his hand on the handle of the refrigerator. "What is it with you and ghosts?" he asks.

"What are you doing?" he asks instead of answering the question.

"I'm starving and I don't think you've eaten today." Alex turned the stove on, all brisk efficiency, because one way or another, they have to get to the end of this conversation, and he has no desire to drag it out. "Now tell me why you went to the party."

♦

Getting grilled like this is intensely uncomfortable for Paul. His discomfort increases when Alex gets the chili simmering on the stove and pulls up the barstool next to him. Paul has to stop himself from physically squirming when Alex turns the unrelenting gaze on him that he usually reserves for the camera.

The discomfort of it scratches whatever self-destructive itch that got Paul into this mess in the first place. It's pain, yes, but in Alex's careful hands it makes things better for him – and them. He's grateful.

Paul recounts the story, all the way through Mark tapping on the window, his awkward extrication from Eric, and the miserable drive home he barely remembers.

"Okay," Alex says. "We need to talk about fluid risk. And you need to tell me exactly what you did, and if it was just you getting your dick sucked because you were drunk and horny and have terrible judgment."

"I already told you it was," Paul says.

"Yes, on the phone. To be fair, if the situation were reversed, honesty might not have been my first choice." Alex clearly thinks the worst of him.

Paul looks at him for too long.

"Whatever you tell me right now is the final version of the story," Alex says slowly. "I will not hound you about this. So if there's something I need to know about for our safety or our relationship, this is your moment."

Paul nods, more to acknowledge having heard Alex than anything else. When he dips his head in affirmation the second time, it doesn't come back up.

Alex takes in a sharp breath.

He doesn't look at Alex as he speaks. "I went down on him and then he sucked me off."

There's an awful silence. Paul lifts his head only to see Alex draw himself up on the stool, his spine straight and his shoulders back. It's a small movement physically, but it feels like Alex has gone somewhere miles away.

◆

All Alex can hear is Paul's breathing. He feels like his own lungs have forgotten how to work.

"Are we getting divorced?" Paul finally asks. His voice is small and quiet in a way Alex has never heard before and never wants to again.

"*No,*" Alex says fiercely. And then again, "No."

Paul closes his eyes in relief.

"You are going to get tested though," Alex says, his voice distant in his own ear. Logistics are easier than how much bigger this wound feels than he expected when he was in South Carolina and just wanted to be sure Paul was all right.

Paul nods.

"Once now. Once in three months," Alex adds.

"What about the baby thing?" Paul's voice is still too small but at least there's breath behind it now.

Alex can't quite believe the segue. If there was ever a moment to lay into Paul, this is certainly it. He takes a deep breath and continues to work the conversation like it's the side of a mountain. He needs to be calm and steady and full of acceptance for the path presented, no matter how strange.

"We both need a little time and space from this particular event," he says. "The baby topic is getting tabled for the next three months. No decisions until we get your test results back."

"You were never really on board with it anyway."

"Excuse me?" Alex has no idea why Paul thinks it's a good idea to pick a fight with him right now, but it's damn annoying. He's also not interested in giving Paul the shouting match he seemingly desires.

"I just feel like this has become really convenient for you," Paul says.

Alex blinks at him. "You cheated on me. You got *caught* cheating on me. I am not threatening to leave you; I am not even making you sleep on the couch; and now you're pissed at me because I think your terrible judgment about cheating on me and lying about it is a good reason for us to reconsider kids?"

"You said you weren't going to punish me for this, and now you're punishing me for this."

"You do not want to find out what punishment from me looks like." Alex stands up, fully aware that he's channeling Victor and not giving a remote shit. "Right now I can't trust you with my life. Therefore, I'm not trusting you with a baby's."

♦

Alex ignores most of the notifications on his phone. He does the missed call from his mother after Paul retreats downstairs to his office for a couple of hours' work after they manage to eat dinner.

She makes small talk, but it's stilted. Alex's resolve to only answer questions he's asked eventually waivers. "Are you calling because of Paul?"

"I wanted to hear from you what's going on," she says.

Alex knows that means she's read every piece of gossip she can get her hands on. With dread he considers how everyone in his hometown will treat this drama; promiscuous gay Hollywood boys who deserve whatever end is coming for them, no doubt.

He hasn't been back to Indiana since he left. He has also never had any intention of letting his small town follow him here, especially not now. But trauma is often a monster with its own mind.

"We're fine," he tells his mother. If they aren't now, they will be. "But we've changed some of our plans."

Alex hadn't told his mother about the would-be baby yet. He wanted everything to be sure. Now that their plans are in turmoil though, he needs her support. The relief of talking about the whole fucking mess with someone who is not Paul is massive. But while Alex finds it soothing to speak his wariness out loud, the possible consequences of Paul's actions feel all the more awful for it.

His mom surprised. Alex understands that it's a lot to take in, especially under the circumstances, and her support is appreciated. But Alex wishes she weren't so startled at the idea of him having a kid. Alex tries not to feel guilty as they finally get off the phone.

Then he calls Sarah. That conversation is much harder, only in part because he only left her family's house that morning. Somehow, Sarah and Beth haven't seen the news yet. It's a small and terrible thing to be grateful.

He lays out the whole story for her and asks Sarah not to call Paul to yell at him. "If you're willing to tell your mom, I won't say no, but out of respect for her and your family I will call her myself. Just not tonight."

"What am I telling Mom, other than the obvious?" Sarah's measured reaction in the face of crisis reminds Alex of just how small this particular drama may be to her. God knows how many crises she's dealt with over the years, between Paul and their father and her own marriage and child, to sound this calm.

Alex explains how they're not going to make any decisions one way or the other until the three months are up.

"You get to back out too," he says at the end.

♦

When Alex pushes open the door to their room, Paul is already in bed, sitting up with glasses on and his tablet propped on his knees. He immediately sets the tablet aside and sits up straighter while Alex walks around to his own side of the bed.

Alex doesn't say anything right away. "How's your mom?" Paul asks. He's in contact with his own family far more frequently than Alex is, especially recently given the baby situation. Alex might talk to his mom once a month but whenever he does, the conversations can last hours. Paul never knows what to make of that, but it works for them.

"She's fine."

"How's Sarah?" Paul's far more worried about that.

"She's okay."

"What did she say about the baby?"

"Paul. We didn't have that conversation yet. She needs time to think no matter what."

Paul nods miserably. "How was South Carolina?"

Alex bites his lip. "I like it there. Sometimes I wish it were closer, but then it would mean something different. To both of us."

"I notice you resisted the urge to antagonize the internet with guns again," Paul notes.

Alex gets up and starts shedding clothes.

Paul's grateful that Alex isn't making him sleep on the couch, but he also has no idea what degree of intimacy he can look forward to in light of the situation. The lack of a real kiss upon his arrival home made Paul nervous – and clearly sex is not going to happen tonight – but Alex stripping down to his briefs is at least a positive sign.

"There wasn't anyone to take a picture," Alex says.

"You do the selfie thing at the range all the time."

Alex looks at Paul over his bare shoulder, the one with the faint scar from his terrible fall. "I was trying to find a nice way of saying 'I was too pissed to feel good about picking up a gun.'"

"Oh."

"Yeah." Alex tosses his clothes in the direction of the hamper and crawls into bed.

Paul rolls onto his side to face him. "How are you?" Paul asks, when the silence stretches.

"I'm glad to be home, and I'm pissed off I came home to this. I don't know what our future looks like, and I'm furious at Victor for dying and leaving us this mess."

"This isn't Victor's fault," Paul protests, though Alex venting at a dead man instead of anyone alive is useful.

"I am in this bed with you right now because of Victor. In a lot of different ways. If I have to deal with the consequences of that, he can at least take some of the blame."

"What do we do now?" Paul asks.

Alex tucks his arm under the pillow and stares at him. "I look at you and try to imagine you with someone else. And then I try to stop, because that's a very bad idea too."

Paul tries to interrupt.

It's not jealousy," Alex says, "I just don't get it."

"I've been with other people," Paul points out carefully, because historically discussions of their respective dating history – specifically, his reaction to Alex's – have not been constructive. "We've been with other people. Together."

"I know. But even when you were with Craig – and I guess I was with Liam when you and I were a fucking hot mess – me being with you was the only thing that made sense in my head."

"What does that mean for us right now?" Paul asks.

Alex doesn't answer. He puts out a hand and traces Paul's shoulder through his t-shirt, the line of his collarbone down to his chest. He's concentrating hard, like he's trying to memorize Paul. The touch seems good but the look on his face is a little terrifying.

"Alex," Paul says softly.

Alex drags his eyes up to his face and blinks at him, like he's coming back from somewhere far away.

"Where did you go?"

"Nowhere relevant."

21

Alex is surprised and relieved when Liam calls a week later. Liam explains that replying via email would be easier. Words are still hard, and Alex writing that intimately about Paul and about Victor is a lot for him to process. Ultimately, though, Liam wants to be able to call, so he did. Alex is touched and a little awed by the amount of effort Liam is putting into a reply he didn't have to make.

They don't talk for very long, and there are a lot of pauses in what they do say, but Liam is wise about fuck ups and forgiveness and the terrible decisions people in pain make. Alex knew of this, of course, but hearing it from Liam settles and reassures him.

"New York's been good for me." Liam admits. "I don't have to concentrate as hard, and it's left room for everything else."

Grief, Alex thinks he means. "I'm sorry I dragged you into my mess," he says. He didn't have to burden Liam with any of this.

Liam makes a sound that Alex thinks would be a laugh, if the last three months hadn't been so awful. "It's fine. You did what you needed to do, and that's all you gotta do. And go easy on Paul. He's a little broken, and he missed you."

"I can't even imagine him with anyone else."

"Well, lots of things happen in life you can't imagine."

Alex doesn't know how to respond to that. "When are you coming home?" he asks after a long pause. Maybe that's a dangerous question; he's not sure. Liam has always brought out a mess of conflicting emotions in him.

"Not soon, but...soon after soon?"

"Liam. Other-people timeframes, please."

Liam huffs. "Fine. A few months. Maybe more. I don't know yet. But I'm thinking about it, and that's new."

"I miss you," Alex says.

"I know."

"I should let you go." Alex wonders if he means right now or for always as he says it.

"Okay," Liam says, but doesn't hang up.

"Can I call you later?" Alex asks.

"Totally," Liam says. "Also, hey, thing."

"Yeah?"

"I love you."

Alex actually bangs his head down on the table, even though it doesn't sound like Liam is saying it with any particular intent. He wonders if this is Liam responding to the way Alex didn't say it in his email.

"Lee!" he moans.

"Don't be dumb. Why is everyone so obsessed with words?"

"I don't even know where to start with you! Fine! I. Love. You. Too. Words don't matter, and now I'm hanging up on you."

"Bye!" Liam says, almost brightly, before the line clicks off.

Alex stares at the phone in his hand as it goes black, and doesn't know whether to scream or be grateful for all the relationships in his life that make no sense.

♦

Olivia doesn't comment on or ask any questions about the debacle that is Paul's personal life – at least not verbally. She does give Paul a long, unimpressed look over the top of her laptop the next time he wanders into the writers' room late one night in August before shoving a draft for the next episode at him. Paul finds himself oddly grateful. Victor, certainly, would have had his own opinions and he mostly tries to think about how, if Victor were still alive, Paul wouldn't want to put up with hearing them.

Now that they're into the final months of *Winsome* he needs to start worrying about what comes next. Which is how Paul ends up in his office too late one night, with Olivia in the chair on the other side of the desk, both of them staring at the whiteboard on the wall and praying for inspiration for whatever their new project is going to be.

"You know, finishing the script for the next ep might actually be easier than this," Olivia says when an hour of talking around in circles yields absolutely nothing.

"Please don't say that," Paul laughs.

"I still say the idea of the blended family with all the kids has legs for our next project."

"No. Absolutely not. We're not doing a Brady Bunch reboot."

"But what if the family was like, multiracial, and doing gay quad or poly parenting or whatever?"

"Still too much like a sitcom," Paul chuckles. "If you want to do it, have at, and I will support you, but not my thing."

Olivia twirls a pen across her fingers. "You say that, but have you actually looked at your life lately?

22

Carly is unsurprised when she gets a call from Paul in the middle of August inviting her and Ali to join him and Alex for lunch. At least he's waited a suitable period of time in which, presumably, he and Alex have gotten their shit together as well as they're going to for now. Carly's also glad for an afternoon of adult conversation and more sets of eyes to watch out for Ali.

Todd, curled up in the sunlight coming in the slider door to the deck, flees when Ali tries to pet him. He's suffered more than one pulled tail at her eager and careless hands, and Carly entirely cannot blame him. Sometimes she wishes she could deal with her daughter's excess energies the same way.

After lunch, Alex offers to take Ali to the neighborhood playground. Carly's pleased and grateful that now he's had a chance to catch up with Liam, he's giving her and Paul the opportunity to do the same.

"I won't get her dirty," he promises while she gets her shoes on.

Carly snorts. "One, I don't care. Two, you do not have anything to worry about there. Good luck trying to get her in the sandbox."

"The sand is gross. It *touches* me," Ali says, aghast.

"Then we'll try the swings. Come on, you." Alex ushers her outside.

Carly turns around from closing the door to see Paul staring at it mournfully.

"Yes, he'll make a wonderful father," Carly deadpans as she lowers herself into a chair. She kicks off her shoes so she can rub her ankles. Pregnancy seriously sucks, and if nothing else. she is very glad this particular ordeal will soon be over.

"Yeah, about that," Paul says tightly.

He deals with the lunch dishes while he lays out his and Alex's plan. The first test came back negative, but there's still another test – which will also likely be negative – and a lot of uncertainty to get through.

"Alex is good for you," Carly says when he's finished, and it's almost, but not quite, a non-sequitur.

"How's Liam?" Paul asks. "Alex said he talked to him."

"Liam is still in New York," Carly says with a viciousness now that Ali isn't around. She's talking about much more than obvious geographical location.

"And?" Paul prompts, glancing over his shoulder at her as he puts the clean dishes away.

"And he says he's thinking about coming back, but the baby's due in ten weeks and he is apparently not. I keep wondering if things would be easier if he just stayed there. I can't take care of three people, Paul. Not when one of them is my husband. Not by myself."

"He'll be better when he comes back," Paul says cautiously.

"Well, what if he isn't? Or doesn't. So he's talking on the phone with Alex. Great. How the hell is he going to deal with a newborn?" She's glad she doesn't have to hide her anger from Paul. They've been close for too long and he knows her too well to have any need to put on a front.

"What are you going to do?" Paul asks. "I mean, you always have a plan."

"I don't know. I don't know if I can stay with him. This sucks now, but if it doesn't get better, that's not fair to anyone. Especially me."

"Does Liam know?"

"I think he's scared of it. I assume he's asking himself similar questions. But we haven't talked about it. The stress would only make everything worse."

"I don't know what to say."

Carly sighs. She knows this whole mess makes her look heartless. "Look, Liam can't entirely live alone. Which means whoever lives with him is, whatever else they are, his caretaker."

"Wait... what the fuck was he doing before you?"

"Victor. Various other relationships. His 'team,'" she says with vicious air quotes. "He's very clever. His family is very clever." She shrugs. "To be fair, I did know all this going in, but the thing that sucks about love is the same thing that sucks about being with someone who isn't normal or healthy or whatever we're calling it."

"Which is?" Paul prompts.

"I don't get super powers just because he's fucked up."

"Alex apparently gets super powers because I'm fucked up," Paul offers more cheerfully than is really helpful.

"Yeah, I'm still bitter about that."

◆

Ali chatters on the entire walk to the playground. Her talkativeness is how she takes after Liam the most, aside from the wild dark curls, but even those she likes to keep tamed with sparkly purple hair ties.

She's also as fascinated with fantastical stories as Liam is, so long as they involve shiny things and princesses and attention from adoring crowds. Alex is fairly sure she doesn't get that trait from Liam, that it's Ali being a five-year-old kid, but he finds it hilarious nonetheless.

When they get to the playground, he offers to take her on an adventure.

"Where to?" She folds her arms and looks up at Alex with all the seriousness she can muster.

"Wherever you want, it's your story."

"Are there dragons? And a princess?"

"There can *totally* be dragons and a princess. There can even be a dragon princess if you want."

Ali side-eyes him. "Just a normal princess, thank you."

They set off. They have to climb the mountains of the jungle gym, and ford the mighty river that is the puddle left by the sprinklers. Alex tells her that the heavy ever-present smell of smoke from the wildfires have actually been set by the evil dragons, and Ali nods very seriously. Finally, they have to balance on magic light-beams to get to the castle.

It's the kind of play Alex did by himself, in the fields and woods of Indiana when he was a kid not much older than Ali. His games involved far fewer princesses and magic towers and more outlaws and violence but then, they grew up in a very different world.

He had started thinking about doing this with his and Paul's own baby, whenever it's old enough to walk and talk and follow a narrative. Only now he might not ever have a kid of his own. Alex is stunned that in such a short span of time he's gone from struggling to adjust to the idea of having kids, to struggling to adjust to the idea of maybe never having them.

He watches Ali with delight and also a strange sadness as she gets distracted by the game, asking questions and contradicting him proudly whenever the story takes a turn she doesn't like. She is absolutely not noticing how muddy her sneakers are getting or that her hands are dirty from climbing up and down the jungle gym.

Ali – and Carly and Liam's soon-to-be-born baby – may be the only children Alex ever really has. The terrible thing about Victor's death is the lesson that things don't stop going wrong once the worst happens.

He helps Ali up on the monkey bars and then is terrified when she hooks her legs in and hangs upside down. Carly and Liam will never forgive him if he breaks their kid. But when she seems steady enough, he digs out his phone to snap a picture of her grinning face and messy pigtails.

After a moment of deliberation, he sends it to Liam. *This isn't to guilt you, but we totally wish you could be here.*

A minute later, he gets a text back. There's a picture of Liam attached, in the backyard at his parents' house. He's got his sunglasses on, and he's smiling. It feels like an image from another life, which is eerie but also comforting. *Me too!*

♦

Paul flops down next to Carly on the sofa and puts his feet up on the coffee table. She kicks him affectionately.

"You know you and I have the same shit going on as Alex and Liam, right?" he says.

"'Cept, without the creepy psychic part."

"A little bit with the creepy psychic part. We're more vocal so we hide it better."

Carly rolls her head against the back of the couch and turns to look at Paul. "Yeah, so where is this going?" she asks.

"So you know the thing where Alex and I are kind of like Ali's other dads?"

"With an emphasis on 'kind of,'" Carly says, eyebrows raised.

"What if we made it more like actual other dads. Like, kids are difficult and exhausting, everyone has those friends who offer to help who are really enthusiastic until the kid barfs all over their guest room or whatever, right?"

"Riiiiiight," Carly says slowly, watching what's clearly going to be a train wreck of a conversation unfold with great curiosity.

"So then you feel guilty asking, and it's not really help because it's help that's about borrowing a kid not actually fucking helping or having any real skin in the game, right?"

"Also right."

"Well, you don't need that type of help."

"Why does this feel like more of your bad crazy?" Carly says warily.

"The four of us are practically family anyway. Why don't we use that to make all of our lives easier?

"Paul, whatever you're working up to, spit it out."

"You've got Ali and a baby on the way. If I'm lucky, Alex and I are going to have a kid too. What if we raised our kids like siblings with traveling homes? I mean, if we help parent your kids, you'd help with ours. Why can't each of us handle three kids on the good nights? Alex would get to feel like he had a support network and a backup system that wasn't only me and our families in their shitty small towns. You'd get help with the kids and support whether Liam's here or not. Liam would get some space when he needs it. It might keep me from turning into the asshole Alex hates when I'm given responsibility. And all of us would still maybe get to have adult lives."

Carly blinks at him slowly.

"What?" he asks. "What are you thinking?"

"That you make some valid points," Carly says. "Which you

haven't discussed with Alex, are contingent upon me not leaving my husband, may not work, and are arguably you trying to con your husband into having children. Also polyamory. Kind of. Without sex. Which, fine, but just wanted to point that out." This is certainly not the train wreck she was expecting, but that doesn't mean it's not a disaster waiting to happen.

"But other than that it sounds perfect, right?"

Carly leans down to the end of the couch, grabs an accent pillow and smacks him in the face with it.

◆

"Children. Are. Exhausting," Alex says, as he pulls off his shirt that night in their room.

Paul chuckles.

"I'm serious," Alex says. "They run fast, and they're short so you have to keep bending over to tell them things or pick them up. I ache in the weirdest places."

"You're getting old," Paul teases with a level of absolute glee that Alex finds charming.

"I'm not even thirty yet."

"The Tragic Life of J. Alex Cook."

"Ugh, don't even," Alex says, as he takes off the rest of his clothes and climbs into bed.

Paul closes the screen on his laptop halfway and asks if they're sleeping, fucking, or talking.

"I don't know," Alex half moans. "But get your computer out of this bed and turn off the light."

The second they settle into each other and the dark, Paul says, "Carly is thinking of leaving Liam."

Alex doesn't sit up and slap his hands against Paul's chest in outrage, demanding answers, which is a testament to how unsurprising this is. He goes very, very still instead.

"Do you think she will?" he asks.

Paul shakes his head. "I don't know. I don't think so. I don't think it's unreasonable for her to fantasize about a normal life sometimes though."

Alex blinks in the dark. "That's a shitty thing to say."

"Not Liam, just *everything*. They're not even thirty-five and she's helping Liam grieve a partner. She's pregnant as fuck, Hollywood's horrid, and look, I didn't spend the day with Ali but – "

"She talked about dragons."

"What?"

"You were going to say something about paparazzi or *People* or her *look*. She's five. She talked non-stop, and it was mostly about dragons. She's about as normal as I think five gets when everyone isn't expecting her to be the littlest diva on the lot."

Paul smiles. "You had fun. After totally being freaked out by her for *years*."

"We both have lives that don't make a lot of sense to other people. I mean, she still freaks me out, but Victor adored her and not merely because she's Liam and Carly's kid. She's trying to get through life and actually doing it really well all things considered. I sent Liam ill-advised pictures of her hanging upside down," he adds.

"I talked to Carly about her plans for after the baby's born."

"You did what?" This time Alex does try to sit up, but Paul pulls him back down.

"Shhhh," Paul says, "Listen to me for a second. Everyone offers to help, and then doesn't when the going gets hard. Right now, the only thing Carly and Liam have had for a while is hard, and long-term they need a better support system than friends who are willing to babysit once in a while."

Alex thunks his head against Paul's shoulder. Repeatedly.

"What's that for?"

"Wherever this is going, surely," Alex says.

"Look, whether we have a baby of our own or not, we have the resources to help them out. If we do have a kid, what's an extra baby or two on nights that are kid-focused anyway?"

Alex doesn't know where to begin. "I'm pretty sure kids are exponential in terms of headaches," he says. "I'm also pretty sure you just suggested we all mutually timeshare the collective children, of which ours may not actually exist because you are a delusional fuckmuppet."

"Kind of?" Paul says.

"Did Carly yell at you, or do I need to?"

"Carly hit me in the face with a pillow," Paul says blandly.

"And then she said what, that made you suggest we should all be one big happy platonic family in response? And by the way, you did this without consulting me, Liam, Ali, a baby that hasn't been born yet and a baby who may very well never be born." Alex sighs. "Jesus. I wanted you to turn the lights out so we could relax, not do freaky confession time."

"I'm sorry?" Paul offers.

"New rule," Alex says. "When Carly shoots down one of your terrible ideas, you don't have to tell me about it."

"It's not terrible," Paul says, and Alex is surprised at the clarity and confidence in his voice. "Our lives are hard. Babies are hard. We all trust each other a lot, and our lives are all fucked up and intertwined anyway. Why can't we share some of the responsibilities so we can all maintain some semblance of individual adult life?"

Alex squirms far enough away, though Paul keeps an arm draped over his waist, to roll onto his side. He studies Paul's face until his eyes adjust enough to the dark that he can see Paul searching his in return as well.

"We took the baby off the table for discussion for three months, Paul. The time's not even close to being up yet, and while I appreciate that you're trying to figure out how to do life in a way that works for everyone, this kind of feels like manipulation more than an actual solution."

"Hey, hey, no – "

"I'm not saying it's a bad idea, even though it is inexplicable. But it's a *lot*, and it hinges on a lot of variables that we don't have the answers to or control over. What if you're positive? What if Liam never comes back to L.A.?"

"Then we come up with a different plan," Paul says. "But why can't this be a start? At least to talk about?"

"Because it's crazy."

"Our lives are crazy."

"*Yes*, but," Alex says, and then gives a despairing sort of chuckle.

"But?" Paul presses gently.

"Explain to me why this isn't you having problems with boundaries and control."

"Because it makes sense?"

Alex does manage to roll out of Paul's arms then and onto his back. He laughs when Paul inevitably reaches out for him. "Don't touch me."

Paul pulls his hand back cautiously. Alex is fascinated by the gesture. It's not cowed, merely deeply wary.

There's a silence that draws on almost too long until Alex exclaims, "Fuck!" and starts laughing again as he presses his hands over his face. Then he kicks his heels against the mattress repeatedly. "Fuck fuck fuck."

Paul makes a careful interrogative sound.

"How do you actually make things worse when you make sense?" Alex asks, peering at Paul from between his fingers.

"Because normal is overrated," Paul grins.

"Oh   shut   the   fuck   up   and   come   here."

"You just said – "

"Come *here*," Alex says reaching for Paul, who takes his hands cautiously.

Alex practically yanks him down into a kiss, and after all the hard conversations of the day it still feels strained, but it's also funny.

♦

For a while they make out and Paul assumes that's all they're going to do. What sex they've had since Alex got home has been limited in creativity and variety, but Alex's anxiety around intercourse given Paul's transgressions is understandable. Paul is just grateful he gets to touch him at all.

Eventually, Alex pulls back and blinks up at Paul from the pillows. "Do we even have condoms in the house?"

"There's sex we can have without needing those," Paul points out.

Alex rolls his eyes. "I've missed this, I want you, and I am not letting your bad choices fuck us up even more. Yes or no, Paul."

"I don't actually know?"

"Oh my God," Alex rolls his eyes and shoves at Paul's chest. "Everything in our lives is aggravating. Would you go *look*?"

Paul crawls off the bed and heads for their bathroom muttering under his breath. Alex cackles.

They do in fact have condoms, for which Paul is immensely grateful. By the time Alex gets him on his knees and starts pressing into him everything else in their too-hard, too-complex, involving too-many-other-people lives disappears. Whatever their lives are going to look like, in three months or a year or ten years from now, at least they'll be together.

Liam looks good when he picks up for his and Carly's regularly scheduled Skype call one evening at the end of August. He's been gone almost two months now. New York City has been good for him, and she tries not to resent that too much. Their lives work by the grace of all the systems they've perfected. It is simply a reality of their current situation that their systems, both individually and as a couple, demand adjusting.

"How was your weekend?" Liam asks her, curious and warm. He's got the laptop propped on his chest, and she can see the headboard behind him. The first night she spent with him there, not long after she learned the last of his secrets, they stayed up all night talking until long after the glow-in-the-dark stars faded again.

"Ali and I went over to Paul and Alex's for lunch yesterday."

"I know, Alex sent me a picture. Ali looks amazing."

"She's doing really well," Carly says. There are, after all, so many reasons why she shouldn't be, with her father gone and her mother about to have another child. "I'm not sure if she gets the resiliency from me or you," she adds. It's an easy, if cruel, opening.

Liam laughs ruefully and shakes his head. "You I think."

"I don't have to be resilient every day though. You do. And she does, right now."

Liam doesn't say anything for a long time. Which is fine. Not only has Carly gotten used to that in the current and ongoing crisis, the thing she misses about him most is being able to sit quietly while he pores over a script and she reads a book. The silence, when it's domestic and not frightened, is welcome. Right now, it's somewhere in between.

"Can you have this conversation now?" Carly eventually asks when Liam's hands, barely in the frame, turn fidgety.

"The one we're having?" he asks, but it's not guileless or unaware.

She shakes her head. "The one about us," she says instead.

He tips his head at her for her to continue, a gesture he always uses, even when he's glib and facile. It's sweet, decorous deference, and it makes her feel like she doesn't deserve him.

"You know I love you," she says.

"Love you too," he says, like the simple matter of habit and fact that it is. Carly smiles sadly.

"We have a baby coming. And we need to make some decisions about what our family is going to look like once that happens. Are you coming back here? Are you staying there?" Carly takes a breath, because she's rehearsed this line but saying it still feels impossible. "And what do our lives look like if our relationship becomes something more secondary?"

"Those questions are massive," Liam says.

"I know. But we need to talk about them, instead of being scared of the things we're not talking about."

"Mostly," Liam says, because words are not automatic for him right now. He's explained to Carly before how sometimes he has to remember that he is supposed to speak, understand what sort of thing he is supposed to say, find phrases that work, and then add to those.

Carly rests her chin in her hand and stares at him for a while. Then she just asks it. "Do you think you'll be able to get back to where you were?"

Liam shakes his head, but it's the slow one, that doesn't mean *no*, but that he's thinking about the question. He starts and stops his response three times before he can find a way for it to make sense.

"Charles was here for dinner last night, and I told him this story about Victor and it was...well, it was terrible. I did it, though. This is still going to be the worst year, but I was okay."

"That sounds good," Carly says carefully.

"It is. New York is good for me. You could come here," he says, too brightly, and Carly's stomach sinks. "I'd have more help. So would you."

"We're not leaving California," Carly says, only marginally shocked that she feels so strongly about it.

"Why?"

"Because our life is here," she says. "My friends and my lovers and my job and all of my support systems are here. I give up so much for you. Not for my job or this city, just you. Acting and fame and the hours, and you can't. You just can't. I lost someone too. He was a brother to me, and I have had no time to do anything but feel terror because he is dead."

"Can we name the baby after him?" Liam says.

Carly starts crying. "Look," she says, wiping her eyes while Liam stares at the screen, his expression heartbroken. "Victor was a massive part of our support group, and he was such a force for good in Ali's life."

"In all of our lives," Liam says.

"And I was talking to Paul today about his and Alex's plans for kids, and what our situation with Ali and the baby looks like."

"But we don't know what our situation with the kids looks like," Liam says. "Like that's what this is about." He waves a hand to encompass, Carly thinks, this whole not-quite-argument.

"I know. That's what we were talking about. And he kept coming back to this idea that is totally dubious but that is an option I think we want on the table, while you decide whether you can handle coming home."

"What is it?" Liam asks.

Carly sniffles and brushes back her hair. "He and Alex are kind of a mess, did you know?"

Liam snorts, and, to Carly's relief, smiles. "I talked to Alex."

"Well, they're looking for child support systems too. Or at least Paul is, to try to convince Alex to have kids with him. And what he suggested was the four of us raising whatever kids we all have together. Not just trading off the babysitting but like, surrogate siblings."

"Wow," Liam says.

"Good wow or bad wow?"

"A lot to process. Like that could be really good, but there are a lot of red flags."

"This isn't about being sexual partners with them," Carly adds. In their lives that's a completely reasonable thing to need to clarify. Also she knows what kind of relationship Liam and Alex would have were Alex and Paul not monogamous. "And they bring their own issues to the table. But having other adults around Ali and the baby would be good for them and for us."

Liam nods, slowly. "That's a good option," he says, and even sounds excited about it. "Until things go wrong."

Carly nods to encourage him.

"Well, one, Paul's kind of nuts, and I think he's manipulating Alex with all of this baby stuff, and I love them but their dysfunction is intense, and I don't know if I want to get that involved in it. Two, I don't understand why this is on the table at all? I'm happy that it is, but I want to talk more about it and who gets to make decisions about what, and how you all can't leave me out just because of how I am. Three," Liam says, and sighs, "We don't even know what's going on with us yet. It's not fair to make deals with anybody else until we know what ours is. Like, I want to say *yes* but the list of reasons to say *no* or even *I don't know* is really kind of long right now."

Carly wishes Liam were not on the other side of the continent. She very much wants to reach through the screen and touch his hand, or curl up with him on his old bed in the room under the glow-in-the-dark stars.

"So with that on the table. Can you tell me what you need to come home?"

"Or if I'm not."

She nods. "We will always be together Liam, but right now I need to know how. I am providing you with as many options as I can. But I need some feedback from you."

Liam nods. "I can't," he starts, but then corrects himself. "I'll need some time, to make some lists." His voice is almost a question.

Carly's heart clenches with the mix of hope and fear she feels. "I'll be here whenever you do."

◆

Paul and Alex's schedules have rarely overlapped so that they have to get ready in the morning at the same time, but Alex starts to make an effort to get up when Paul does. Seeing each other before everything that fills their days is pleasant and their relationship need all the pleasant they can get these days.

This morning, like most mornings, neither of them are fully awake as they move around each other in the bathroom after indulging in a joint shower.

Alex frowns and rubs the mirror with his fist to clear off the fog. "Okay, plan." He meets Paul's eyes in the mirror.

"Yeah?" Paul says with trepidation. He's not sure what, aside from baby and testing, Alex has been turning over in his head.

"The internet is continuing its field day with you and your terrible choices and its own fantasies about me and Liam. If we are going to consider your ridiculous co-parenting idea with Liam and Carly – and I am *not* agreeing to anything right now – we are damn well going to remind the world that we are actually a couple, that we are not breaking up, and that I am actually very happy with you. Also, that I am not pining over Liam because he's vanished from L.A."

"You are pining over Liam."

Alex rolls his eyes. "Paul." Paul knows he isn't wrong, but Alex apparently doesn't want to poke that particular wound right now.

"Sorry."

"So for the next little while, you and I are going to be as publicly adorable as we possibly can. Date nights out, holding hands in the park, whatever cute stuff you want to do on any carpet that comes our way."

"Okay," Paul says cautiously. It's been a long time since Alex has been skittish about being seen together in public, but the attention still annoys him, and he usually keeps a reasonable degree of distance between them whenever they're at events. Paul has learned to live with it – mostly because he doesn't really have a choice – but it's not his ideal and Alex knows it. "Is this a gift or a punishment? Because it's kind of feeling like both."

"Neither. It's just a thing that needs to happen," Alex says. "If it were a punishment, you'd know."

That Alex is being so clinical about it doesn't actually make Paul feel better.

♦

As the summer winds down Alex goes about being publicly cute with Paul with as much determination and grace as he pursues anything else in his strange life. He even consents to go to brunch, though that's less about the opportunity for photos and more so he can lean into Paul's side and snark back at Brian when he's an asshole about the cheating drama.

Paul is busy with the rapidly approaching end of *Winsome*, but whenever he has a free evening he and Alex go out for food or a hike. Sometimes they even go to the movies together. Paul's thirty-ninth birthday is the perfect opportunity to get caught at some hip place for dinner, even if he's kind of freaking out about being one year away from forty. Alex tries to be amused and not irritated with that particular concern.

For Alex it's the strangest sort of performance, doing the things they'd both do regularly if either of them ever had enough time. There's a lesson in here somewhere, he's sure. He just has no idea what it is yet.

Alex recruits Darcy to help in his *Mission: Public Cute* too.

"I know you read all those blinds." Alex tells her one day at work on *Winsome* while a shot is getting reset. "Put in one about us."

Darcy raises an eyebrow. "You and me? I thought the point of all this was to like, make you guys look good."

"No! Paul and me."

"That makes more sense," she concedes sadly.

Alex sighs. "Well?"

"Normally I have my people do it."

"Come on, you're like *on the pulse*, Darcy," he says, his tone mocking every shitty gossip website in existence. "Help me out here."

She considers that for a moment, then crosses her legs at the knee and clasps her hands over them. "Okay. What did you do?"

"I don't know. This is why I'm asking you."

"You can't just be cute. There has to be a scandal element!"

"Yeah, and Paul got his dick sucked in a car. No thank you."

"Like the time you two fucked in public!" Darcy says brightly, ignoring him.

"We did not!"

"You totally did. You could do that again!"

Alex rolls his eyes. "I would only go through that pain of that fallout again if I got to have the fun of it."

"So why don't you do that?" Darcy asks seriously.

Alex is saved from answering when they're called back for the shot.

◆

During one of what becomes their semi-weekly Skype calls, Alex offers to read Liam bits of Victor's diaries.

"Some of this you should read yourself, if you want. It shouldn't be in my voice," Alex says. "But seriously, the part where he's pissed at everyone because you and Natalie hooked up is *amazing*."

Paul comes home to the sound of both cracking up in the living room. Liam waves to him from the screen. And then offers them both tips if they want to get caught together in public more.

Sitting there, with his hand around Alex's waist, feels like exactly the life Paul wants. No less – and despite his previous inappropriate suggestions – no more. It's a strange unfamiliar sort of peace, especially when he now has to wait on everyone else, and only in part because of his own mistakes.

24

Paul and Olivia both look up from their laptops when Alex knocks on the doorframe of Paul's home office in the basement. Paul isn't sure how long Alex has been up; it's ten in the morning now, but he and Olivia have been at this since six. Printed pages are scattered across the floor, and the massive whiteboard that covers almost an entire wall is covered in scrawled notes in both of their handwritings.

"Sorry to interrupt. Hi, Olivia," Alex says, as Todd uncurls himself from a stack of papers on Paul's desk and jumps down to rub against his shins.

"Hey." She waves.

"Going climbing?" Paul asks.

"Yeah, I'll be back this afternoon. Brainstorming?" Alex asks, walking further into the room to examine the whiteboard and its scribbles.

"In a manner of speaking," Olivia says.

Paul chuckles when Alex leans forward to look at a line more closely and then frowns.

"Okay, this is a day I'm glad I just have to be in the damn films."

"It's harder than it looks!"

"Clearly." Alex laughs and is glad neither of them is offended. Alex leans down to pat Todd then kisses Paul briefly. "You two have fun revolutionizing the television medium. I'm going to go climb rocks."

"Be careful!" No matter how many times Alex has gone climbing in the intervening time, ever since he almost died Paul has a stab of fear every time Alex leaves.

"Always am." Alex disappears back upstairs.

Once he's gone, Olivia leans back in her chair with a sigh, regarding the whiteboard with an expression of doom. "We completely suck."

"We don't suck. We just haven't found the right idea yet," Paul protests. He's still slated to take a year off when *Winsome* is finished, which is going to be soon now, and his own imminent parental status is somewhat in limbo. But if he's going to keep making TV magic he and Olivia need at least a plan of what they're doing next, even if not a pitch.

"You wrote down *combat dolphins*," Olivia says.

"*Elite* combat dolphins. Drama, human interest, action."

"It's *Flipper* with a fucking AK-47. No."

"Also international geopolitics," Paul points out.

"Where the hell are you even going to hire *dolphins*? What do they get paid? What are the work rules? Also did you read that thing on the internet about how dolphins are *totally* rapists? This is not a good plan! Can you even get ones that know how to shoot?"

Paul looks at her like she's grown another head.

"If I don't ask these things, the network will!"

Paul hangs his head and laughs. "Victor would fire us for this shit."

"Victor would win Emmys for this shit."

"Fucking bastard."

"Yeah."

Paul flips a whiteboard marker between his fingers and regards the list of mostly-rejected ideas. Under *combat dolphins* is listed:

Demons?

Alaska - too many parkas

Barbershop dark comedy

Ski lodge but not horror ski lodge, next to which Olivia has scribbled *WTF?*

Paul's been at this point of development before with *Winsome* and the other pilot that was never shot, but he's never done it without Victor. Olivia is more than capable, and more and more Paul is coming to rely on her as his right hand, but there's always going to be the question of what could have been. Not just with *M.A.R.S.* – which is struggling regardless of the time Paul is still dedicating to it – but with all the other stories Victor had in him. Every unmade universe feels like a loss.

Paul's own work isn't going to be any different. He'll never be able to tell all of the stories he wants to. At best he, like Victor, will leave behind people with the talent and drive to keep going when he's no longer there.

♦

Alex does not go climbing.

Instead he goes to Victor's house. Why just read a script when you can visit the set?

Pulling into the driveway feels more natural than it once did, but he still needs to take a deep breath before he unlocks the door. Despite its magnetism, the house is still difficult for him. He'll stay away from the basement; he always does.

But for all of the time Alex has spent at Victor's house over the years – and in the last terrible weeks – he has never yet been upstairs. Once he's retrieved another stack of diaries, he tries several doors before he finally finds Victor's bedroom. Alex hovers in the entrance, staring. He knows, from reading so much of Victor's life in Victor's own handwriting, that Victor was actually human. But standing in his most intimate space still feels bizarre, as though Victor's been waiting all this time for him to show up.

In the bedroom, the stark modernism of the rest of the house is only slightly muted. An occasional accent of turquoise or cream interrupts the sea of gray and white. The bed is made neatly, and Alex is unable to avoid the image of Victor making it each morning, as if it that were something that mattered in his busy and expansive life.

There are built-in shelves bracketing the bed, that are less full than Alex might have expected given how crammed the bookcases are in the rest of the house. The things here are more lovely, however – small pieces of artwork, and books that aren't about the industry.

Alex is curious about the rest of the bedrooms, but the nape of his neck is prickling now and he wants to get out of the house while he's still ahead. He's careful to lock the door behind himself when he leaves, and then check the handle to make sure it's really locked.

♦

As unsettled as Alex is by the house, he can't stay away. The next time he's there is while Paul is at work thinking he went climbing again. It takes a few attempts before Alex can bring himself to open the bedroom door he can tell, just by looking through the crack, is Liam's. When he finally does, he has to lean against the wall to stay upright.

White walls, white bedding; it's all as described in the journals. There are human touches too, visible in a way they aren't in Victor's bedroom, that scream Liam: a battered paperback thriller on the nightstand, a t-shirt folded messily on a slat-backed chair in the corner, the door to the wardrobe cracked open in a manner Victor would never tolerate. What rocks Alex back the most, though, is that the bed is unmade.

He knows that bed hasn't been touched since Liam got out of it on the morning of the day Victor died. He also knows, as far as the diaries go, that Liam never spent a night in Victor's bed other than after the terrible day Liam filmed the material around the death of Alex's character, Zach, in *Fourth*.

Standing here, Alex can picture, with uncomfortable clarity, Victor sitting on the edge of this bed smoothing back Liam's hair. Liam nuzzles happily into a pillow until he decides he wants breakfast more than he wants to stay in his warm nest and be petted.

Alex remembers vividly his own last morning with Liam, in Liam's bedroom at his parents' house in New York. He wonders if it's a grace or an unkindness that they both knew it was a last morning, that they'd already said goodbye the night before to the possibility neither of them could fulfill, regardless of how much they wanted it.

He wonders if Victor knew, when he bent to kiss Liam on the forehead before admonishing him about being late to the table.

◆

Paul, with Alex's blessing, talks to Sarah about their Very Tentative Plans for co-parenting their baby – assuming they have a baby – with Carly and Liam's kids.

Sarah, to Paul's devastation, is wary about the idea.

"I know this is not going to be my baby except genetically," Sarah says, "But I don't even know Carly and Liam."

"You know Carly," Paul points out.

"From *years* ago. I'm sure they're good people, but this is all really strange."

"Why? There was always a clan around when we were growing up."

"It's just different, Paul. Maybe it's not bad, but it's different. And then you, in the middle of this all – I don't know what you've told Alex and really I don't care, but I spent a summer visiting you after you landed yourself in the psych ward. I know the places you go when things get really bad for you. With everything that's happened the last six months, I don't know if you can handle a child. And I don't know if I can help you bring one into the world if I can't be sure what kind of life it's going to have."

◆

Darcy meets Alex at his shared trailer once he's wrapped for the day. She's bouncing up and down on the balls of her feet, and Alex greets her warily.

"Hi! Your blind is up," Darcy waves her phone at him. "Wanna see?"

Alex laughs. "Sure." Whatever crazy scandal Darcy has come up with for them, it's bound to be sexier and more entertaining than his and Paul's current drama.

Then he reads the headline.

"Darcy, what is this?" Alex's voice strains.

"Gossip! Not real gossip, obviously. But like it was super hard to top the whole public-sex thing, so I thought it would be a really nice spin on the 'look how awesome a couple Paul Marion Keane and J. Alex Cook are!'"

"This says we're having a baby."

He can't even be mad at her; Darcy has absolutely no reason to know what a hot mess of a topic kids are now. The universe really is too terrible sometimes.

"Yeah! Like, what says your relationship is awesome and solid more than that?"

Alex covers his face with his hands and moans.

25

Alex doesn't know what to think when he realizes Victor's diaries have become his comfort reading. As fraught as Victor's relationship with Liam was, it's not the kind of fraught Alex's own relationship is right now. He finds curling up on the couch when he's home alone and reading about all the weekends Victor and Liam spent together at an inn somewhere outside of town strangely lovely.

Alex knew they'd gone away from time to time, but he had no idea what those weekends consisted of and mostly tried not to think about them. There certainly was plenty of sex, at least what constituted sex for them, but Victor also recorded pages of conversation between them, about religion and philosophy and all sorts of topics their jobs and lives outside of each other didn't particularly touch.

When Carly is first pregnant with Ali, there are entries about children and family and a strange longing that stuns Alex for its abstract desperation. He realizes, for the first time, that his and Paul's own child, if they ever have one, will never know Victor. While Alex might once have made a grateful crack about that, now it leaves him feeling strangely sad.

About the really important things, at least as Alex considers them, the diaries are absolutely silent. Alex flips through pages over and over, sure he's missed something, but the entry for the day of Carly and Liam's wedding is another single sentence:

Liam got married today.

As much as Victor lies and omits and conceals, Alex can't believe that he hasn't left any more record of his feelings on the day than that. The next afternoon he can steal at the house, Alex digs into closets and cupboards he hasn't opened yet, looking for anything.

That's when he finds the flat files of sketches.

At first he thinks they're storyboards for old shows long finished or for concepts that never got made, and he starts to flip through them for anything conceivably useful for Paul.

It becomes evident, very quickly, that he has found no such thing.

Alex sits back on his heels and carefully lays the sketches out on the carpet. Some of them anyway. There are hundreds of them, and that's part of the peculiarity of them – to see so many studies, mostly of Liam, carefully preserved in the bottom drawer of a filing cabinet, never perhaps looked at after the process of making them.

For Victor, *this* is – was – sex, Alex understands. And not just because of their content.

Some are of Liam, asleep, which is an image Alex knows well

enough himself that it's not shocking. In others, he's naked on top of the sheets, sometimes with his hand on himself, other times lying still on the bed with his hands up beside his head. Alex doesn't have to imagine what Victor was saying to keep him that way, because he has the diaries. Suddenly, everything makes so much more sense.

But then there are the others ones, also clearly Liam even if his face is never showing, because curly hair and Alex knows the slope of his back and his waist. They are of Liam tied up, but not in any simple hands-tied-to-bedpost way Alex has vaguely considered attempting with Paul.

Victor must have taken hours to get the lattices of rope and knots lacing Liam's arms together just right. There are multiple configurations, all of them beautiful and strange and erotic. Victor must have enjoyed the craft and care it demanded as much as Liam adored being touched and settled as he was turned into a work of art. It's visual evidence of the way they worked together that the diaries and all Victor's words alone haven't given Alex.

Alex is too staggered by the loss it represents for Liam to even worry about his own intrusiveness.

But now that he knows these sketches exist, he has no idea what to do. Eventually, like everything else in the house, they'll need to be dealt with, but he can't imagine how. Every option is a horror. They would, he knows, fetch a fortune at auction, which is high on the list of things Alex can't let happen. But he can't steal them, simply because he has no good way of getting them home without damaging them. Besides, there's weird, and then there's weird, and there are hundreds more in the lower drawers of the filing cabinet he hasn't even begun to go through.

Not all the sketches are of Liam. There's Carly, lounging by Victor's pool looking radiantly happy. There's even one of what Alex recognizes, after a shocked moment, as Paul, younger than Alex ever knew him, curled up asleep on a couch. That one, he sets aside, as a reminder to himself to demand the story from Paul at an opportune moment; there's no entry in Victor's diary that corresponds to it.

He's not surprised to find a sketch of himself, though it freaks him out. In many ways, it's less bad than it could be. Alex is not tied to a chair or naked in any physical way, just sitting on the *Fourth Estate* set, reading through a script. His head is down, and it could be any moment on any shoot in any of the hundreds of days Alex worked on that show, but Alex didn't know Victor ever watched him with an eye to draw him. It feels unsettling, and Alex feels like anyone could be watching him right now.

Packing the sketches up takes longer than he wants, considering how much he suddenly wants to get out of here. But he's careful, and sets the ones he wants to come back for on top of the pile. He slides the drawers safely shut again before he escapes back outside to his car, pulling in huge lungfuls of air now that he's safe from the land of the dead.

♦

Alex emails their assistant, Yancey, asking the best way to transport large volumes of unmounted artwork. He gets a useful if puzzled answer back and slips out of bed early one Saturday morning while Paul sleeps in, to drive to an art supply store and then to Victor's house.

He's never used anything in Victor's kitchen unsupervised before, but it's early and the coffee maker is tempting, so Alex puts on a pot to brew while he goes upstairs to deal with the sketches. He's gotten everything spread out on the floor to decide what he wants to take first – there's far too much to get home in one run – when the entire house starts to shake.

No matter how used he is to the little temblors that hit L.A. in waves that he now barely notices – many of them are indistinguishable from a truck passing by on a road it shouldn't – he knows what this one is right away because as the shake ramps up there's a brief sense of being on the water.

Rolling in these things is never good, and Alex scoots into a doorway as quickly as he can, although that's apparently bad advice everyone takes anyway. The movement is fading out by the time he gets there. Alex takes a moment to unclench all his muscles and stop willing the floor to become stationary once again. He hears car alarms up and down the block, snapped off in quick succession.

He shakily stands up to deal with his own. Nothing significant in the house seems damaged, although a few knick knacks shimmied off their shelves and onto the floor; there are no cracks in the wall, but all of Victor's pictures are now quite crooked. It's incredibly unsettling.

Alex hits the fob for his car from inside the house. All of Victor's neighbors are outside talking about the ground weather, and he has no idea what engaging that will look like. Something bad probably. He's not sure if he should straighten the house in response or not. Mostly, he wants to get the sketches and get out. The earthquake wasn't terrifying, but being in Victor's house now is.

He's just started getting them packed up when his phone rings. It's Paul, and given where Alex supposedly is this morning it's far better to answer.

"Are you okay?" Paul demands as soon as Alex picks up.

"I'm fine, I just got down," he lies.

"Oh God, thank God. I was scared you were free climbing."

"Nope, all good here," Alex says, tucking the phone between his

579

chin and shoulder to keep packing. Paul thinking of all the ways Alex might have died is not making him feel better right now. The fact that he would have still been up a mountain, very possibly free climbing, if he weren't lying to Paul makes the whole thing orders of magnitude worse.

"Good. Are you coming home?"

"Yeah, just packing up now. Is the house okay?"

"Things got knocked over, and Todd freaked the fuck out. Olivia went home to check on her place, but we're fine."

"Okay. I'll be home soon," Alex promises, eager to end the call and get out of here. When he does manage to hang up, he's thrown by the sound of a car door slamming, too close to be one of the neighbors', and then the sound of the door opening downstairs.

Alex freezes. Once he recognizes the voices he doesn't know whether to laugh or cry.

"It smells like coffee. Why does it smell like coffee?" Darcy asks from somewhere downstairs. "Is it ghost coffee?"

Alex entirely cannot blame the note of near-hysteria in her voice as he hears Jackson soothing her. Then Jackson calls "Alex?" up the stairs.

He thinks mournfully that he really should have parked farther down the hill.

"Hi, I'll be right down," he shouts, trying not to sound sheepish or suspicious about it.

"What are you doing here?" Darcy demands when Alex thumps down the stairs.

"What are *you* doing here?" he counters.

"Why did you make coffee?" she asks.

"Because I needed coffee," Alex says.

Jackson finally has to interrupt their increasingly surreal conversation. "We came by to check on the house."

"Yeah," Alex says, wondering if he can get away with pretending to do the same. "Everything's fine. I mean, nothing's broken and nothing smells like gas."

"That's good."

"Yeah."

The silence is incredibly awkward. "I was sorting through some of the stuff in Victor's office," Alex finally blurts. "I'll just, um, grab that together and get out of here."

"Okay." Jackson shrugs, apparently deciding to roll with whatever is going on. "I'm going to check the basement, make sure the pipes are okay."

"Okay," Alex nods and escapes back upstairs before Darcy can pull him back into conversation.

It feels wrong to have other people in the house. This morning has gotten more fucked up than Alex could possibly have imagined, and he works as quickly as he can.

He gets out of the house without, thankfully, having to interact with Darcy or Jackson again. He spends the drive home debating whether Jackson will tell Paul, or anyone else who would tell Paul, and if it's worth confessing first to head off the awkward of that. He's got all the sketches in his trunk, in case he can actually get away with it all.

When he gets home, Paul hugs him tightly and Alex clings a little harder than necessary given that he wasn't actually ever in danger. But, *almost* is sometimes close enough.

"Have you seen Victor's keys?" Paul asks, pulling back and frowning a little. "I should go over and check out the house."

Apparently, this day has not yet reached its peak of fucked up. Alex takes a breath, digs the keys out of his pocket, and hands them to Paul. "The house is fine."

Paul looks baffled. "What?"

"I was at the house. I ran into Jackson and Darcy who had the same idea you did. Everything's fine."

"You said you were going climbing."

"Yeah, well, I lied."

Paul's apparently too stunned and confused to be angry. Yet. "Why the hell were you at Victor's?"

"I found some things I wanted to bring home."

"*When?*"

"The last time I was there."

"Which was?"

"I've been going, okay? Shit needs to be boxed up anyway, Nigel keeps nagging us."

"Yeah, but why do I feel like that's not what you've been doing."

"Does it matter?" Alex says petulantly.

"You're creepily hanging around the home of a dead guy you didn't even like, and I'm the one whose mental health we're worried about? Yeah, I'd say it matters," Paul says, just as petulantly.

"*My* mental health is fine."

"You're being a ghoul."

"It's not like I've been curling up in his bed or anything."

"You just said *that*. That is fucked up, Alex."

It's the weirdest argument they've ever had. Although, Alex has to concede it is justified. They go from their relative mental health to cheating, to the baby, back to the cheating – which is not useful to anyone now but it's a point Alex can plant his very pissy flag on – to Paul being incredibly angry about him lying about Victor's house.

Finally, Alex stalks out to his car to get the fucking sketches, so Paul at least can be furious at him in a specific direction. He drops the stack – carefully – on the kitchen island, glaring at Paul as he does so.

Paul stares. "That's a lot of sketches."

"Look at them," Alex says, in part because they are strange enough that he hopes they will get Paul on his side and in part because he's itching for Paul to get pissed off about naked Liam so they can scream at each other some more.

Paul gives him as sullen a look as Alex has ever seen on him and starts paging through them.

"Careful," Alex snaps when Paul accidentally almost creases one.

"Okay, curator of the odd and invasive."

"You're going to explain that one," Alex says when Paul flips past the one of himself on the couch.

"Maybe some other time," Paul says testily, and then falls silent. The sketch below is one of Liam tied up in the elaborate rope. "Oh my God," he says quietly, sitting down on one of the stools.

"Tell me it's not better for me to find that than someone random going through Victor's closets."

Paul doesn't answer right away, turning a few more sketches over. He wonders aloud, not kindly, how Alex could sort through all of them. "It feels so intrusive just to do this," he says.

Alex shrugs.

"I had no idea," Paul says, finally shutting the file.

"So maybe wait to be a dick about my choices before you see why I made them."

"And you have yet to offer a compelling and sane reason for why you were skulking around a dead man's house to begin with." Paul pushes the sketches toward him. "Now put these away."

26

Because Alex is out climbing – hopefully, actually, climbing – Paul should take advantage of having the house to himself, but so far all he can do is open Skype at his desk in his office and stare at Liam's icon. He needs to make this call, and he needs to make it now. But he also needs to not screw it up, and he's nohy t convinced of his ability to do that.

Finally, Paul makes himself click. He leans his chin on his fist as it rings through, hoping, foolishly, that Liam doesn't pick up.

He does, though, and Paul can see the walls of what he assumes is Liam's bedroom. The view on his screen shifts as Liam resituates his laptop.

"Hi," Liam says, once his face comes into view.

"Hi. Can you talk?"

Liam rolls his eyes. "Question on my abilities or polite social question?"

"Um." This is going to be exactly as hard as Paul has feared. "Social question."

Liam nods and settles himself more comfortably in his chair. "Yeah. Charles wants to take me out to a show later, but I'm here now."

"That sounds cool." Paul is aware of how pathetic he sounds. Liam, on the other hand, seems well.

"Have you ever seen a Broadway show?" Liam asks curiously.

"No," Paul admits.

"You should, it's awesome."

"Yeah," Paul says. "I'll try the next time I'm in New York and have more than an hour of downtime." He doesn't say it unkindly, but New York is a different place for all of them. It's home for Liam, hard for Alex, and for himself always too much work and too little sleep.

Liam smiles – which Paul doesn't know how to read – and then doesn't say anything for so long that Paul finally realizes he's not going to.

"Okay, so, well," Paul says. "I wanted to give you a call to talk about the co-parenting idea. Carly said you guys talked about it."

"We did," Liam allows.

"And?"

"And what? Like, if you want answers I need specific questions," Liam explains.

Paul chuckles nervously. "Okay. What do you think of the idea?"

"Carly didn't tell you that?"

"She did, a little, but if this is actually a thing the four of us are doing, you and I should probably be cool talking to each other about it."

"Okay," Liam says. "I have a few things to say."

"Yeah?"

"One, I think you're using the idea of this arrangement to manipulate Alex into having a baby, which is not cool and not something I want to be a part of. Two, you outed me to Alex, which is also not cool and you need to stop assuming stuff about how his and my relationship works. And three, stop trying to make decisions for everybody. You're not Victor. Yes, he was involved in all of our lives but he didn't do stuff like *this*."

Paul rocks back a little. Liam doesn't sound angry, but he's clearly not happy. Paul feels instantly guilty, and also worried about what this means for the viability of his, apparently shitty, plans. "I'm not trying to be Victor; I'm just trying to survive."

Liam tilts his head and stares at Paul for a long time. Of the four of them, they have always been the least close. That's been changing recently, although it's been awkward.

"That's okay, you know," Liam finally says softly. "If you need things, ask for them. Just don't come up with a scheme and pretend it's about what you think I need."

"It *is* about – "

Liam holds up a hand. "Look. Paul. This might be totally good for everyone. But you need to work out how to ask for the things you need and not make things harder for everyone else. 'Cause like, if we're all gonna raise each other's kids, you need to learn how to do that first and how to respect me – and Alex – as adults in front of them."

◆

Paul hits end on the call and takes a deep breath. That had been… more tense than he had expected. He can hear footsteps moving around upstairs; Alex is home, then. The footsteps approach the door at the top of the stairs, and the stairs creak as Alex comes down them.

Alex leans in the doorway to his office as Paul swivels his chair around to face him. He has new scrapes on his arms and his shorts have white streaks on them where he wiped his chalky hands; he really had gone climbing, then.

"How were the rocks?" Paul asks.

Alex ignores the question. "You had a fight with Liam?"

"No?" Paul says, though that's pretty much exactly what happened.

Alex looks unconvinced. "I heard your voices when I was coming in. You were arguing."

"You argue with him all the time," Paul protests weakly.

"I don't, actually, but that's not the point right now. What were you two talking about?"

"The same thing I talked to Carly about." Paul sighs. He doesn't want to rehash this right now, but he knows Alex isn't going to let him off the hook. Nor should he, really. "The same thing we've been talking about – family, and how it can work for all of us."

Alex sighs heavily and begins to pace.

"I know there are words that go with that." Paul tries to sound genial. He knows Alex's reaction, when it comes, will be something other than he wants, but he still needs to move the conversation forward without borrowing grief.

Alex stops walking and drags a hand through his hair before letting it drop. "We don't even know if Liam's coming home." He sounds more frustrated and confused than angry, but that's still not great. "We also don't know if Sarah's still willing to be bio mom. Even if we do have a baby anytime soon, you're going to be on a new project by the time it's born. I can maybe be single dad to one baby but, Paul, seriously, how am I going to be single dad to three?"

Paul blinks, waiting to see if there's more.

"I hope this is what Liam yelled at you about," Alex adds.

"Not exactly. But, it was in the neighborhood if that makes you feel better."

"Please don't patronize me."

"Look, you can't yell at me because you think everything is falling apart and we'll never have a baby at the same time you're yelling at me because you think you'll be stuck taking care of our baby," Paul tries to reason.

"Yes I can! There are so many fucking variables, Paul, we don't have the answers to *any* of them and every hypothetical decision you make keeps landing on me!"

"Is this you saying no?" Paul asks quietly.

"NO, THIS IS ME YELLING BECAUSE I HAVE NO INFORMATION WITH WHICH TO MAKE A DECISION AT ALL!"

<h1 style="text-align:center">27</h1>

The final *Winsome* readthrough has been on the calendar for weeks, but it still takes Paul by surprise when the day shows up in early September. So often he feels like the show has just gotten started. The fact that the show has been running for six years is hard to fathom. Harder still is the idea that his first show is almost over.

They have weeks of shooting left, but Darcy still shows up at *Winsome* office for the readthrough nearly in tears and sniffles her way through the first half of the script. Paul smiles behind his hand when he sees Alex rub her back during one of Ruth's last scenes.

For the rest of the read, though, there isn't much smiling. Paul and Olivia wrote most of this episode themselves, and Paul is as proud of it as anything else he's done. While he may not be as sadistic as Victor, he knows rural poverty and the shape of the violence it can create. The character Alex is playing may be the antagonist, but Paul wants to make his death punch the audience as hard as he can. Antagonists, after all, are the most compelling when they are vulnerable.

♦

The script for the *Winsome* finale is intense, and Alex needs a break when they're done with the read. Paul is going to be in meetings for hours more, and Alex doesn't particularly want to go home and be all by himself. So he treks up the stairs from the basement room where they do the reads, to Paul's office.

The lights are off, and Alex flicks them on before he tosses his bag on the couch. He stands there in the middle of the room. He's not often alone here, and it's a rare moment to take stock, not only of Paul's workplace but of their lives.

On Paul's desk is a paperweight Alex recognizes from Victor's office, years ago. Alex picks it up and turns it over in his hands. The thing is profoundly ugly, and Alex has no idea if Victor gave it to Paul, or why, or if Paul obtained it from Victor's now empty desk since he died.

He sets the paperweight down and settles himself in Paul's chair. From his bag he pulls one of Victor's diaries, the one that dates to his own final shoot for *The Fourth Estate*. Given the dead Jason material he's going to be playing, Alex is morbidly curious for Victor's take on that long-ago death scene.

He finds the exact date in the diary with trepidation. After all of the excruciatingly detailed accounts of Victor's intimate moments with Liam, Alex is afraid there are going to be pages of exacting

586

description of his own agony.

But the entry, to his surprise, is only one sentence long.

J. Alex Cook doesn't have a single submissive bone in his body.

Alex laughs aloud in shock, then shuts the diary and puts it away. Victor had no idea, and it's hard to absorb the fact that Victor, who saw so much of him, never really knew him at all. It makes Alex sad, which in the midst of the terrible memory that day of shooting was, is confusing.

While Alex may have Victor's diaries and the deepest, darkest secrets he deigned to put on the page, they are a profoundly one-way line of communication. Paul is, thank god, alive and with Alex. The questions Alex wants to ask him he can, if he just takes the right approach. And while sex may have gotten them into their current mess, it – along with the things Alex has learned from Victor – may also offer them the road out of it.

♦

Paul walks into his office at the end of the day and finds Alex on the couch, reading something on his phone. Alex doesn't acknowledge him except for a vague hum.

"I thought you went home hours ago," Paul says, dropping a stack of notes on top of one of his cabinets and pulling a drawer open.

Alex turns a page, only half listening to Paul. "Are you done for the day?"

"Finally," Paul says, squinting at the labels on the folders.

"Cool, 'cause I really want to go home and fuck you," Alex says casually, still not looking up from his reading.

"Mm, good," Paul shuffles through his stack. Then Alex's words connect, and he looks up at his husband.

Alex slowly lifts his gaze to peer at him over the top of the script.

Paul drops his files back on his desk and barely remembers to grab his bag. Alex already has his slung over his shoulder by the time Paul gets to the door. They both race out of the office, Alex cackling as Paul pounds down the stairs behind him. Neither of them, apparently, wants to wait for the elevator.

They catch each other at Paul's car, and the reality of the situation hits them.

"Fuck," Alex says, still laughing. He grabs at Paul's shoulders when he tries to crowd him into the door; like he can't decide whether to push Paul away or pull him in.

"Why did we bring two cars?" Paul complains, but he's laughing too.

"Because we are terrible planners," Alex says. He sways in close enough that Paul thinks he's actually going to kiss him right here in the parking lot before he pushes back with a sly, challenging look. "See you at home!"

"No racing!" Paul shouts after him as he turns and jogs off toward his own car.

◆

Paul gets home first and waits in the open doorway until Alex pulls in with a flash of his headlights. He barely gets the car turned off before he's tearing up the walk and throwing himself into Paul's arms.

As soon as Paul kicks the door closed behind them, Alex shoves him up against it, biting and sucking at his neck until Paul digs his hand into Alex's hair and drags his head up for a kiss that's all tongue and teeth.

Alex moans into it before pushing Paul back far enough so he can look him in the eye. He holds Paul's gaze for a long moment, dark and even in the light filtering in from the street. Paul wants to film him, just like this, with all his power and intensity trained on him.

But then Alex leans in and murmurs in his ear. "Tell me what you need."

Paul lets his head tip back against the door.

Alex kisses along the line of his throat below his ear. "Paul," he says, scolding as he grinds his hips against him.

"Fuck my mouth?" Paul asks breathlessly.

"Is that what you need?" Alex asks.

Paul doesn't know whether Alex is making a highly effective attempt at dirty talk or is genuinely asking for information. Either way, it's impossible not to answer in glorious detail.

Alex buries his face in Paul's shoulder and eventually covers Paul's mouth with his hand.

"If you keep talking I'm going to come right here in the foyer. Not. The. Plan," he says breathlessly.

Paul kisses his fingers.

Alex's face goes very soft. He grabs Paul's hand to pull him upstairs.

◆

In their room, Alex strips out of his clothes before Paul can get his hands on him. When Paul tries to kiss him, Alex puts his hands on Paul's shoulders and shoves him down instead. He knows what he wants – and what Paul has asked for – and he is going to give it to him.

Paul gets the message and drops to his knees at Alex's feet. He runs his hands up the back of Alex's legs, and tips his head back to look up at Alex from under his lashes, asking for direction.

Before Alex can give him any, though, Paul pushes his hips back a little. "Hey," he says softly.

"Yeah?" Alex says, distracted and running his hands through Paul's hair.

"Condom."

Alex whines, but only because it's a delay while Paul reaches over and grabs one out of the bedside drawer and then helps Alex with it.

Paul settles back on his knees and gives Alex that same look.

Alex doesn't need to be asked twice. He grabs the back of Paul's head and feeds his cock into his mouth. They both groan with relief.

Paul keeps staring up at him as Alex starts to pump his hips. Alex couldn't look away if he wanted to.

Alex doesn't last long, and after he comes he collapses down almost into Paul's lap. There's fumbling with belt and jeans and underwear before Alex finally gets Paul's dick out. It would be funny if Alex didn't feel so victorious, and Paul weren't looking at him with that same too-much look.

Paul comes with his face buried in Alex's shoulder, Alex jerking him off, breathing encouragement in his ear.

♦

They drag themselves up onto the bed and lie side-by-side, staring at the ceiling and panting together. Alex rolls onto his side to deal with the sex trash and actually sways a little once he gets to his feet.

"Are you okay?" Paul asks. His voice is hoarse, and he rolls his head to the side to watch Alex.

"I waited for two hours in your office so I could jump you. I'm fantastic," Alex calls as he tosses out the condom, and pads into the bathroom to get a damp washcloth.

"Yeah, but why?" Paul asks when Alex crawls back onto the bed and hovers over him.

"Are you complaining about the fucking?"

Paul chuckles and pulls Alex down onto the mattress next to him. He doesn't give a damn about cleanup right now. "Most definitely not. I am questioning your motives, though."

Alex shrugs easily. "I'm into you. That hasn't changed. Even if everything else in our lives is one massive question mark." Alex tucks his head into Paul's shoulder, and Paul drapes an arm over his waist. The sweat is starting to cool on his skin, and Alex is warm.

Paul wonders whether he should mention that in their lives – and he suspects in all lives – nothing is ever resolved. It's the same struggles and misunderstandings over and over again. All you can do is learn from the last iteration and hope the knowledge makes the next one less painful.

"So in the interest of reducing future chaos," Alex says, "What should you tell me that you haven't told me yet?"

Paul practices the words in his head before he says them aloud. "You mean about the depression I've been dealing with really badly since Victor died and probably the entire time you've known me?"

"That would be it, yes."

Paul shrugs. "You've seen it in action,"

"Put it in words so we both know what the fuck is going on, before you decide everything is too crazy again and go fuck another random," Alex says. It's more gentle than it could be.

"I won't – "

Alex shushes him. "That's exactly what you would have said two months ago with just as much good intention. I do love you, and I do trust you. But I need you to do the work, not just make reassuring sounds about it."

"Apparently," Paul says. If Alex is going to initiate this conversation, he's willing to meet him halfway. "I'm not capable of being the sane adult all the time."

"Clearly." Alex grins.

Paul swats lazily at him. "We fell into a pattern," Paul says, "and it's a really good pattern, or at least, it's worked for eight years – "

" – Except for the time we almost broke up because you can't do work-life balance – "

" – I adore taking care of you. And I love the fuck out of my job. But sometimes, apparently, I need someone else to make decisions for me. In life or in bed."

"I'm not saying this defensively or with anger or to reject you, but I can take care of myself." Alex speaks slowly, listening for any signs of panic from Paul. "You focusing on yourself for a bit – your actual self not your coping mechanisms – can only benefit both of us."

"I know that. Intellectually. But...." Paul shrugs, jostling him.

Alex nods. Everything is always easier said than done. "And you want to bring a baby into this mess. And our friends."

"I thought we were doing help-Paul-figure-out-his-shit time, not lecture time."

"Shh. Related thought, not a lecture. You can't bring the self-destruction home if we have a kid. There are only so many choices I can make for you, and I can't make you be stable and okay all the time. So work out what you need to work out. Whatever that looks like, I will help, but the status quo of you wandering in and out of therapy and always saying no to the antidepressants is not working."

Paul frowns. It's an awful lot like the advice Liam gave him. "You've never asked me to do any of that."

"Actually, we fought about you doing therapy and then you passive-aggressived at me for years. I'm still not going to make these choices for you, because it's your life. But your choices do affect me and whatever offspring we have, so I am going to give you some pretty narrow parameters because everything I'm hearing from you is that it's necessary."

Alex's tone is softer than Paul expects, all things considered. He's also talking about a baby in a way that implies one actually might happen now, if Paul follows Alex's instructions for being a functional human.

This conversation is exactly what Paul needs, and so much of what he wants even if uncertainty, as always, lingers over everything. He runs his hand along Alex's side. "How did you get so capable?"

"I've always been capable. I just haven't always needed to be. At least, not since I got here."

"I'm glad you're here." Here, in L.A., in Paul's life, in his bed.

Alex smiles. "You have no idea."

<h1 style="text-align:center">28</h1>

Paul gets more stressed and more irritable the closer they get to the Emmys regardless of the fact that none of the work they're currently doing on *Winsome* or *M.A.R.S.* is up for the current awards cycle.

He's rambled at Alex about it so often Alex knows the spiel by heart. *M.A.R.S.* and *Winsome* are both up for Best Drama this year, much to Paul's dismay. Mark continues to be terrible and uncooperative. And either because of that or other reasons related to the showrunner dying, *M.A.R.S.'* ratings have been tanking. Which has not made Mark any more tractable to Paul's suggestions, much to Paul's infuriation.

Alex mostly leaves him to it; the focused anxiety is, as a rule, much better for Paul's psyche than the broad, scattered grief and insecurities he's been dealing with all summer. Still, the control and showmanship the event demands is exhausting. Paul is always charming on the carpet – more so than Alex ever would have expected years ago when he was first stepping into the public eye – but he's way more wound than usual.

Alex is worried but takes advantage of the setting – and their ongoing mission to be adorable in public – to stay closer to Paul's side than he usually does. Photographers and interviewers call out to them questions from benign to terrible. He loops his arm through Paul's as they get asked about who made their suits and how much they miss – and are grateful to – Victor.

Victor's absence is difficult, Alex feels the lack of Liam's presence too. Neither he nor Alex are up for anything this year, but Liam never misses a carpet if he can help it. Alex longs for his energy and enthusiasm. They've done this together, in one way or another, so many times.

At least Darcy is there, with Jackson as her date. She looks stunning and bounces between cameras and interviewers with a grace and energy that Alex respects even if it's exhausting to watch. Melissa is such a serious dramatic character that even after six years the audience hasn't entirely gotten used to the fact that the actress who plays her is so girlish and exuberant. Alex probably resents it more than Darcy herself does; it's one more way people choose to confuse their lives with their work to the depreciation of both.

Off the carpet, the social whirl is worse. They run into Mark in the lobby. Paul wants to hide, but Alex puts his hand on his back and smiles sharply. He dares Mark to actually say anything. Alex is perfectly willing to deck him once there aren't a ton of cameras around.

Paul hunts for something innocuous to say, but Mark greets them both as if he's done nothing untoward and then says, "You know, we're going to split the sympathy vote and both be fucked."

Alex cracks up.

Paul looks like he wants to kill both of them, but Mark doesn't give him the chance. With a crappy salute and a smirk, he wanders away.

"Alex!" he scolds, horrified, once Mark is gone.

"Paul," Alex mocks, still giggling. "Victor would think that was hilarious."

Victor lingers over much of the night. There is the obligatory *in memoriam* montage, and Alex wonders what Victor would think of it, his career boiled down to four seconds of sentimentality in a sea of other people he mostly didn't like. He suspects he'd love it, or at least love picking apart the pieces of the dying world someone else thought important enough to share.

Ellen wins Best Director for one of her *M.A.R.S.* episodes. When she gets to the microphone, she looks out at the audience, lifts her statue, and says "This one's for Victor" before exiting the stage. It's been a fuck of a year.

When the Best Drama category comes up, Alex leans over and whispers in Paul's ear about having his game face on in case *Winsome* doesn't win. Alex means it, but he's also being funny, grinning as he hisses a litany of "Smile, smile, smile."

Paul has to cover his own mouth so he won't laugh.

Winsome doesn't win. Neither does *M.A.R.S.*

"It would seem Mark was right about the sympathy vote," Paul says under his breath.

◆

The Emmys – and the consolation party Paul hosts for the *Winsome* people a week later – feels like a bigger milestone than Alex expected. Whatever is coming next, this phase of his and Paul's life is winding down. And if Alex is going to lay out parameters for Paul, he has to be as disciplined about his own life choices.

Soon he'll have to be on the road promoting *Icarus*, the movie he filmed in Australia before Victor died and the world changed. But aside from that, he doesn't actually have any other projects or obligations lined up. Alex is, for the foreseeable future, completely free.

Being able to do almost anything he wants is a strange kind of freedom. But instead of finding a new project or travelling for pleasure or climbing the ten hardest rocks in the state, Alex keeps coming back to the idea of going to school.

Paul can say he doesn't care Alex doesn't have a degree all he wants, but Alex does. With all the things Alex has in his strange and unlikely life, there are so many he lacks. Indiana lingers, and Alex has never been taught statistics or to do textual analysis or even to write a decent essay. He may have been able to learn some Farsi on his own, but self-study can only take him so far. If he and Paul do have a kid – the waiting game seems endless and, on some days, suffocating – Alex owes it to them to have enough of an education to at least be able to help them with homework.

And if they do end up in Paul's harebrained co-parenting arrangement, splitting his time between college and childcare would be a very good arrangement. Going to classes would certainly be easier than working on a project full-time while Paul is deep into a new show. And college would definitely be something new.

♦

Despite the offer of lunch, Alex has been avoiding calling Gemma since South Carolina. But if he's going to be starting something new, he also knows he has to make right with people that have come before.

He's grateful she's not too pissy when he finally does call, though she's completely entitled.

Lunch is awkward at first, which is weird. They always bicker, but they've never really been awkward. Alex hates this, and he doesn't know how to fix it.

He doesn't hate it any less when Gemma asks him again and again what's wrong. She's always been good at needling him, and today is no exception. In the face of her questioning, Alex demurs and struggles with words. He wonders if this was a terrible idea, and if she'll ever speak to him again. If this goes badly, Alex is totally blaming Victor.

Finally, he takes a deep breath and goes for it. "Look, I never was going to tell you this, okay? Not after it was obvious it wasn't ever going to happen."

"You're making me nervous. Are you okay? Do you have cancer?"

Alex tips back his head and roars with laughter.

"What?" Gemma demands, leaning across the table to swat at his arm and almost knocking over a water glass in the process. "What the fuck is so fucking funny? Alex!"

Alex presses his knuckles to his mouth and tries to control himself. Everything in his life is so fucked up. "I'm sorry, it's nothing, it's a really long story," he says.

Gemma crosses her arms over her chest. "Start talking."

"I just, no, I don't have cancer. Okay," he says, "So back when we were kids who told each other way too much about our shitty lives over the internet – "

"I remember." Gemma sounds wistful *and* annoyed. Alex wonders if she misses their terrible apartment too.

"We were going to run away and make it big in L.A. and live out all our dreams. You asked me once if I had a plan B because you had actually applied to colleges. You were worried what I was going to do if shit didn't pan out."

"I remember that too. You didn't. You're so fucking lucky shit panned out for you," Gemma says.

Alex gives her a tight smile. She really has no idea. "Well, I lied."

"Okay?" She has no idea what he's getting at.

"I did have a plan B."

"And?"

Alex shuffles his shoulders and makes himself keep looking at Gemma, not at the ceiling, because she deserves the truth from him, even if it was long ago and terrible. None of them will live forever, and now that Victor is dead, Gemma is the one he owes everything to. "You were my plan B."

Gemma narrows her eyes at him, confused. "Like, you were going to crash on my couch forever? Because that's kind of what happened anyway."

"No. No, not like that," Alex says. "Worse than that."

"Then maybe you should fucking say what you mean before I get completely freaked out." Gemma doesn't sound angry, merely puzzled.

"If L.A. hadn't worked out, and I had had to go back to Paragon it wouldn't have been safe for me to go alone."

"What do you mean?"

"Staying in the closet is one thing when you're a surly teenager no one wants to talk to anyway. But if I'd had to live my life there, without a wife or kids, people would've assumed things."

Finally, the penny drops. Gemma covers her mouth with her hand. "Oh my God."

"Yeah."

"*Alex.*"

"I'm sorry. Even if it never happened, I'm sorry."

"I don't know what to do with this! You're telling me if L.A. had been a washout we'd be living in a three-bedroom ranch right now with a dog and our 2.1 kids."

"That would have been the best possible outcome. For me at least. Yeah."

"I knew you were gay," Gemma points out.

"I fucked Carly. I could have gotten it up enough to have kids with you."

"You thought about that?" Gemma says, appalled.

"I thought about surviving."

"You couldn't have just, I don't know, moved to Ventura and worked shitty jobs to pay rent? Or like, Indianapolis? Why did you think you would have had to go back?"

"Because, sometimes, the worst thing happens. Usually, in my life. And then I got here."

"This entire fucking thing is surreal. And also screw you and your sense of entitlement. What if I had said no."

Alex stares back at her a little cruelly but says nothing.

"Yeah, fuck you too." Gemma laughs darkly. "Is that why you've been avoiding me forever? And why we went out to lunch today? So I wouldn't yell in front of people?"

"Do you want to yell at me? I mean, it's warranted. We can go back to my place, Paul's still at work." Saying Paul's name breaks the strange mood that's had him in its hold since he sat down; a reminder of the life he actually has, instead of the one he almost had.

Not for Gemma, though. "I want to know why the hell you were so fucking scared of Indiana you'd marry a woman just to stay in the closet."

"I would have married you, had kids with you, had a house – I would have been good to you. We would have had a good life."

"I'm ignoring most of that. But I do want to know why. Why this? Why this strategy?"

Alex shakes his head, relieved when she doesn't press. There's no more answer he can bear to give.

29

The shooting for *Winsome's* finale, at the end of September, takes them out to the desert. They're not going as far as Kelso; They need Arizona scrub, not Iran's rock-strewn desert. Still, Paul and Liam both spend the week before the shoot reminding him about staying hydrated, and heat stroke, and terribly timed media crises. Alex laughs and promises he'll take care of himself. Carly's due in a matter of days and joking about the way in which everything seems to happen at once among their group feels like tempting fate.

This desert shoot brings its own particular dangers. Alex can stay in the shade and drink as much water as he wants, but there are firearms in the episode and that introduces a level of risk beyond the weather. Their gun wrangler has drilled this into them, and every crew member seems to know some terrible story. People have died from being shot by blanks fired from prop guns. No one wants their set to be the next one an accident happens on.

Alex can't prep for Jason's death scene without thinking about Zach's. Alex has never told anyone the details of what went on in Victor's basement the day Zach died. At the time it was too private and awful. As much as Alex hated the process, and hated Victor, talking about it would only have made *everyone* talk about it.

Now, despite everything, Alex respects Victor – or at least his legacy – too much to have any of that known. Someone will eventually air their extended social family's dirty laundry, and Alex is determined it's not going to be him. He doesn't ever want anyone besides Paul to know Zach's tears when he was being tortured weren't pretend.

Alex grins at the effects guys and tells them he's fine after they test the exploding blood packets on his chest. It hurts less than getting hit in paintball, and he's grateful for procedure and safety and a shoot that's not in a fucking basement. Besides, having things actually impact his body makes the acting part of the job ridiculously easy. Alex asks them not to run through the whole sequence first; surprise is his friend.

◆

Paul does not, strictly speaking, have to be out on location for this. But someone has to keep a wary half-eye on an Alex who is, in his opinion, way too excited to try out the effects that will make it look like he's been shot. Ellen is directing, and while he trusts her and the rest of his team, he wants to be in the middle of everything now that it's all ending, not watching the rushes from his office a hundred miles away.

By the time they're ready to roll, Alex is jumping around and ridiculously ready to go. Paul gets it because Jason is a jangly, strung out, fuck-up of a guy. That Alex needs to keep his adrenaline up to make that work is reasonable. Even so, the degree to which Alex always seems so cheerful about death scenes – even in light of Victor being dead – freaks him out a little.

Paul's discomfort isn't helped by the fact that they're still occasionally snappish with each other since Alex's little revelation about his ongoing exploratory missions to Victor's house. On the list of shit they have to resolve in their lives – the cheating, Paul's health status, the baby, how to navigate Liam and Carly – Alex's adventures are fairly minor. But no matter how much they've agreed on that, and to table it, every conversation they have seems to come back around to it over and over. Sometimes they fight about which one of them is crazier. Sometimes they argue about Liam. And sometimes, they're blindsided by the ever-dawning realization that while Victor may have been a force of impish hostility and persistent destruction, they're all lost without him.

As the crew works, Paul tries stay out of everyone's way. He's there if they need him and for his own pleasure. But he will not unnecessarily interfere with a machine that has worked just fine without his excessive intervention since he stepped back enough to let *Winsome* find its stride at the end of its first season.

◆

Watching Alex as Jason beg for his life in front of Melissa's unsteady hand – in six seasons, Darcy's character has never actually fired her gun – is unsettling. It's also faintly hilarious, because only Jason could make begging sound like a *fuck you* that Paul hadn't known was in the script until the table read. Paul smiles as he leans his chin into his hand and watches them do the tight shots and the over-the-shoulders, knowing that their various forms of crazy serve all of them well.

During the wide shots things start to get fucked up. Without the camera right in his face, Alex is further away from himself. He is, Paul suspects, relying more on emotion and less on the uncanny physical control that initially attracted Victor to him as a performer.

Ellen doesn't let them get to the gunshots the first couple of times, which is a choice Paul agrees with. Alex will nail that. They don't need to burn time on resetting the effects part of the shot every time Ellen wants to bracket the lead-up.

Alex paces and rubs his hands over his face during their first couple of resets. Paul leans over to Ellen and suggests she give Alex and Darcy a moment, but Ellen shakes her head and Paul, not having been as quiet as he thought, gets snapped at by Alex for his trouble.

When Alex hastily pushes messy tears out of his eyes after the next take Ellen asks if he needs a minute. He growls that he's fucking fine. Because Alex is usually a sweetheart on set, no one really takes offense. A few crew members chuckle.

Paul is aware, however, that his own breathing is off watching this. Alex isn't entirely okay as far as he can tell, but Paul's not here to undermine his or, more importantly, Ellen's authority. He reminds himself that sometimes being not okay is part of the job.

Paul flinches when Darcy fires the gun and the first of the blood packets on Alex go off. The effect is startling, no matter how many times he's seen it executed in person. Alex, as Jason, is shocked that Melissa has the balls to actually pull the trigger.

Ellen eventually calls cut when the silence of Jason trying to process what has happened stretches out too long. A second and a half after that, everyone realizes the problem isn't Jason. Or acting. The problem is Alex, who still can't find his breath or his words and has gone an awful shade of shaking gray.

Paul doesn't understand how that's visible under the makeup, as the special effects technician, the first aid guy, and the gun wrangler run to him. Everything happens very quickly after that.

Darcy – despite all the training Alex and the crew have drilled into her – drops her gun and takes a step back. The look on her face is enough to make Paul realize that she thinks she's actually shot Alex.

Paul is out of his chair and trying to get to him so fast he actually knocks it over, tripping his way into where the crew guys are trying to get Alex on the ground and calm enough for them to see what's going on. That would be easier if Paul wasn't in the way, Alex wasn't fighting them off in a panic, and Ellen wasn't yelling at both of them to let the crew do their goddamn jobs. Darcy, who is progressively getting more freaked out, is louder than all of them.

"Alex!" Paul barks as he elbows one of the guys aside. "Words!"

That gets Alex's attention, but he freezes again for a moment before his eyes go wide and startled. Then he laughs, awkward and shocked and more than a little watery.

"I'm fine, I'm fine. Oh my God, I'm fine."

"Stop moving around and let them check," Paul says harshly because that seems to be what's working.

Alex acquiesces. Paul spares a second to exchange a look with Ellen. No, he has no idea what just happened.

When they finally get the all clear that Alex really is fine and Darcy didn't fucking shoot anyone, Alex staggers up and out of the frame.

"I just need five," he says, still breathless.

◆

Paul follows him back behind where the cameras are set up. "What the fuck was that?"

"Fucking terrifying," Alex answers, a hand half over his mouth. He feels like he's going to be sick.

"An answer I can understand, please."

Alex shakes his head and finally looks at Paul, who seems helpless and small. "Not now."

"WE THOUGHT DARCY SHOT YOU," Paul hollers, which sets Darcy off on another crying jag behind him. "TELL ME WHAT THE FUCK JUST HAPPENED."

"I thought she shot me too," Alex says in a small voice, still filled with that incredibly unsettling wonderment.

"Jesus Christ," Paul says in clear frustration. "I feel like I'm having a conversation with Liam."

Alex shakes his head and finally goes to Paul. He leans into him and tugs at Paul's arms to demand that he hold him in a way that has always been against the rules for them on a set – regardless of the power dynamic in play, crisis at hand, or public media image they're trying to project.

Paul, heedless of the fake blood Alex is getting all over him, squeezes him tightly around his waist. Alex props his chin on Paul's shoulder and looks out at the infrastructure of make-believe they've hauled into the desert. He is aware of it – and of what they must look like against it – in a purely cinematic way he doesn't generally consider. He blames Victor's diaries and cries.

30

When the van finally drops them off at the *Winsome* lot, Paul insists Alex ride home with him.

"Two cars," Alex says, apparently too tired to even be petulant about it.

Paul unlocks his car and opens the passenger side door for him. "We can get yours tomorrow. In."

"I'm *fine*," Alex says but slides in anyway, pulling the door shut behind him.

"You had a panic attack you still won't explain, and then you sobbed on my shoulder for ten minutes," Paul says, getting into his own seat. "I'm driving."

"It wasn't that long," Alex protests. "Right now I just want to crawl into bed and sleep forever."

Paul is happy to drive them home in silence. After Alex got himself back under control, his makeup was fixed, and the effects were reset – and Darcy had been calmed down – he went back out to the cameras and absolutely nailed the shot.

It was everything Paul could have possibly hoped for and he knows, from the look Alex gave him as they wrapped, that Alex is proud too. Jason died with a small, satisfied smile on his face. It was unwritten and completely disturbing, but only in a way that Paul appreciates as making fantastic TV.

All that remains is the question *why*. Paul waits until they're home – and Alex has dragged himself upstairs to face-plant on their bed – to ask again.

Alex rolls his face to the side so he can look at Paul and also actually breathe. "What do you want me to tell you?"

"I want you to tell me why today went to shit. What happened in your head?"

Alex shrugs.

"Why are you being so cagey about this?"

"Remember how you didn't tell me about your wrists for two years?"

"Can this not be a competition about who is fucking crazier for five minutes?" Paul snaps, exasperated.

Alex sighs and rolls over onto his back to give Paul a tired glare. "Victor's dead. We're still waiting for your test results. Sometimes when you're an actor weird shit happens. Can we just not talk about any more mortality right now?"

Paul holds his gaze for a long time. He knows Alex is lying, but he also isn't wrong. Everything today and in the last six months has been so strange and full of death and so many uncertainties. He sighs

601

and lets it go.

"Okay," Paul says, crawling onto the bed and stretching out beside him.

Alex smiles faintly and lets his eyes close when Paul starts dragging a hand from Alex's chest to his stomach.

Paul thinks he's fallen asleep and startles when Alex says, "I kept thinking about Victor."

Paul makes an encouraging noise.

"After they got me down on the ground, I kept waiting for him to come and tell me I was okay and shove me back onto my feet."

"Alex," Paul says softly.

Paul softly strokes Alex's stomach while Alex blinks at the ceiling. He doesn't look like he's going to start crying again, but his eyes are still red and bruised-looking. "Apparently, I'm finally mourning Victor. That's uncomfortable. And overwhelming in a way I don't know how to handle. I have to live with that, and with knowing that no matter how much I hated Victor, he took care of me in a way nobody else – not even you – ever could."

◆

They wake up from their unplanned nap sometime in the small hours of the morning. Alex says he's starving. Paul tells him he can get his own damn snack, Paul has no ability to get out of bed again, and Alex teases him about being old until Paul throws a pillow at him.

Alex brings back leftovers and two forks, because he is awesome. He and Paul end up passing the container back and forth while talking aimlessly about what happens next. Paul scrolls idly through his phone, checking messages he missed while they were asleep.

"Oh," he says quietly.

"What is it?" Alex asks.

"Voicemail from the doctor's office."

"Oh," Alex repeats quietly.

Alex wraps his arms around a pillow and stares at Paul as he punches in his pin and listens to the message, and doesn't move until Paul hangs up, tossing the phone to the end of the bed and turning his head to stare back at Alex.

"Good news or bad news?" Alex asks, clearly freaked out.

"That was the doctor's office. Test results came back."

"*And?*" Alex demands, sitting up. He has exactly zero patience with Paul's sense of dramatic tension right now.

"Everything's negative. No HIV. Or anything else to worry about."

"Oh my God," Alex breathes, collapsing back onto the bed and staring at the ceiling.

"Mhmm," Paul says, crawling up the mattress to hover over him. There's no intent, but he wants to be in Alex's line of sight for whatever conversation happens now.

Alex gives a strange, gasping laugh. "It had to be today."

"What's wrong with today?"

"I thought I was dead!" Alex shouts, before giving a hysterical giggle and clapping his hand over his mouth.

"Well, you're not."

"I'm really happy about that," Alex admits. "But do we have to talk about babies right now?"

"We don't have to talk about anything," Paul says because he's learning how to time things with Alex better. Also, today has been hard enough already.

"I kind of feel like I owe you the conversation. I mean, two tests, three months, baby back on the table, this was the deal. And realistically speaking I was sort of exaggerating the HIV risk anyway. Which you never called me on, so thank you."

Paul nods, because Alex is staring intently at him and is clearly working up to something. When minutes go by without Alex saying anything, though, Paul touches his cheek gently and then sits back. "Words, Alex."

"The last six months have been *terrifying*." Alex begins to tick items off on his fingers. "Victor died, Liam left, you cheated, and I'm not even going to get started on the baby drama. You are still alive and we're still together and I'm afraid to say that out loud in case I jinx it, which is probably fucked up. But you still have mental health issues. I'm still overwhelmed, and what if you can't curb the self-destruction the next time disaster hits? I can't put a kid through losing you."

Paul stretches out on the bed and rests his head on Alex's shoulder. Alex automatically wraps his arms around him.

"I am working on my bad crazy. You're working on your bad crazy. But I've had some really fucked up experiences, and I'm ten years older than you. Victor may have been the first person you kissed who died, but he's not going to be the last. The chances of both me and Liam outliving you are really, really low."

"What about Nick?"

Paul takes a second to realize who Alex is talking about. He laughs. The memory of catching Alex making out with his old intern is absurd and also precious.

Alex gives him that look he gives the camera sometimes. That always freaks the fuck out of Paul – it's so quietly indicting.

"You're telling me we can only have a kid if I'm not going to die,"

Paul says. "I can't promise you that. But I am trying to have the best, longest life I can with you."

"I thought we were done with talking about mortality for today," Alex says.

"You alluded. I'm trying to reassure. Besides, we're talking about babies now, too."

"Okay," Alex says.

"Okay what?" Paul says cautiously.

"Okay, let's have a baby. If our fucked-up family hasn't completely scared away your sister. And if it has, we can talk other options."

"You don't have to make that decision right now. Or anytime soon," Paul says. The last thing he wants is for Alex to make a decision too quickly only to reverse it later.

"Me saying yes doesn't equal automatic baby. This is just exchanging one set of unknowns for another," Alex reminds Paul.

He nods. Alex isn't wrong, but he wants this so desperately. "What's your stance on the co-parenting thing?" he asks. If everything is back on the table, he wants to have all of these conversations while Alex is willing and verbal.

"If Carly – and Liam if he ever gets back – want in, I'm in."

"Yeah?"

"Yeah. If it makes our collective lives easier, that's awesome. Clearly, we're a family anyway whatever we choose to do. But whether our friends are involved or not I want to do this."

"You know, if I knew you were going to say yes so easily I would have been a lot less stressed the last three months."

"We should go away," Paul suggests fifteen minutes later, peeling Alex's fingers away after he claps a hand over Paul's mouth to stop him from trying to discuss baby names when Alex just wants to keep making out.

Alex raises his eyebrows. "How?"

"You, me, a car, some fucking B&B somewhere. Your birthday's coming up and we should do something for that. I want some time alone with you before the rest of the world starts demanding things from us. 'Cause it's only gonna start wanting more."

Alex snorts, because *understatement.* "Can you get the time away anytime soon?"

"We have a week left of shooting. I'll take a long weekend once that's done."

"I know a place," Alex offers, too quickly.

"Please tell me this isn't where Victor took Liam," Paul says warily. Alex has told him about those entries. With the whole thing with the house and the sketches, Paul has good reason to be suspicious.

Alex shrugs.

"Alex!"

"What? I checked it out on the internet. It's pretty."

"You are so fucked up."

"L.A. Victor. *Fourth.* Famous. You. Stop sounding so surprised."

<h1 style="text-align:center">31</h1>

s soon as they get onto the 101 and the promise of L.A. falls back behind them, Alex rolls the windows down, flips on the radio to the same sort of shitty country rock he still hasn't managed to outgrow, and smiles at the still too-dry landscape whizzing by. It's the first week of October and winter is coming, but it still hasn't rained.

Paul is eager to talk. So much has been strange lately, but Alex looks more unencumbered than Paul has seen him in what feels like years. His ease is a silent admonition for Paul to let go of some of the tension in his shoulders and worry in his heart. They have four days and more than words to remind themselves that they've always known each other's secrets. Paul decides to smile and let things go.

That they are on the way to Liam and Victor's secret getaway is, at this point, only humorously weird. Alex made a compelling point regarding pre-vetted discretion. Then he sucked up making the phone call to make sure they weren't going to wind up with the same room as Victor and Liam. As if all the beds in any accommodation don't see hundreds of guests per year. But Alex played grief and apologies – not insincere, just not his style – to delicately raise the issue. Either it worked or they'll at least hopefully never know if it didn't.

They talk quietly. Not to hash out any of their many lingering issues, which seems to have been all they've talked about recently, but simply for the pleasure of the conversation. They talk about filmmaking, not in terms of the thing that dictates their lives, but in the abstract, about art and story. Alex is a font of interesting trivia and curious questions about the process of filmmaking. Alex brings up the school thing, and talks seriously about going to college. And then they talk about their friends.

"I can't believe Liam and Carly don't know what sex the baby is," Paul blurts at one point when he's taken over driving.

"Dirty hippies," Alex laughs.

"I'd want to know. Wouldn't you?"

Alex nods. "Seems odd to be able to know and not know." Then he asks, "Which do you want?"

"Don't care," Paul says.

"Liar," Alex says with a completely smug smile.

Paul chuckles. "Why, what about you?"

"Girl," Alex says easily.

Paul's face goes soft. "I didn't know that."

"Mhmm. Just not with the fucking freckles. For her sake," he adds.

"Your freckles are sexy."

"They're weird."

"*You* are sexy."

"I am also weird."

Paul laughs with delight.

They stop at a little store on the way, because wine and cheese and bread are necessities. Alex leans against their car in the parking lot, of his sunglasses in his teeth as he checks their onward directions on his phone and utterly not giving a shit about anyone else in the vicinity who is not Paul.

When Paul kisses him, a peck at the corner of his mouth, Alex grins at him, his eyes crinkling up.

◆

Late afternoon sun pours in from a window looking out over a valley that is ridiculously bucolic and totally gorgeous. The floorboards and knotty pine walls glow in the light. The furniture, rugs, and bedding are all patterned in rich reds and browns, and the whole place feels about as far from the hideous modernism of L.A. as it is possible to get.

They make out on the bed forever, lazy and playful until Paul bites hard at Alex's shoulder and Alex whimpers, his head falling back against the pillows and his limbs going loose and pliant.

"Requests or protests?" Paul asks, starting to pull off Alex's clothes.

Alex shakes his head.

Paul crawls up his body so he can be eye to eye with Alex. "You cool with no condom?" he asks.

"Point of trip," Alex says, resentful of the intrusion upon his head-space. Although the trip is really about so much more than that. It's the culmination of their coming back together and getting everything back on track that Victor's death derailed.

Paul gives him a quick kiss on the lips before sliding down Alex's body, grabbing his ankles, and shoving his knees up to his chest.

"Efficient," Alex murmurs.

"I promise you're not going to mind," Paul says.

Alex huffs. Paul has ten seconds to get on with it, or he's going to whine.

Paul doesn't tease, not really, instead pressing his face between his cheeks and licking along his hole.

"Oh my God." Alex loves this. The sensation is the perfect mix of tease and actual action for him. It makes him desperate without being agonizing. This is also one of the first things they ever did together besides kiss, and after eight years together and everything that has happened in this one, it has a place in his heart. It's not something they do enough. With their work and their schedules, so much of everything in their lives is determined by what's fast and easy.

Their lives are going to get more chaotic with far less time for just the two of them soon, but there's a lesson here, in celebrating this choice and maybe mourning all the change that it brings. They have to be, no matter how exhausted and harried, more deliberate people. Not so that they'll remain together – that deal seems well and truly done and pretending otherwise at this point, even when things go grievously wrong, is absurd – but so that they can enjoy what they can't help but have.

Alex is certainly enjoying it now. Paul makes him delirious with want. He feels like he could ride this out for hours, like a drunk. Paul moans against him, the vibrations chasing up his body.

Eventually he says it's too much, meaning *fuck me now*, but Paul waits him out. He hovers close, petting at Alex's hip until he begs for more. Paul grins ferally, obviously pleased with himself.

"If you don't fuck me soon," Alex eventually manages, "I am going to kill you."

Paul shrugs. "I have a better idea."

Alex makes a noise that's somewhere between a laugh and a moan. This whole mess is the best sort of despair. He doesn't want to go back to their real life ever… not the old one or the new one.

"Two seconds." Paul dives over the side of the bed to fish something out of their suitcase.

"We said no condoms," Alex whines.

Paul comes back with a vibrator and lube, and raises an eyebrow at Alex.

"Not psychic," Alex snarks, letting his legs drop to the bed and palming his own dick.

"This fucks you while you fuck me," Paul explains.

It seems like so much effort. But worth it, and the whole point of this weekend is effort. "Less talk, more electronics," Alex says.

Paul smiles as he lubes up the toy and presses it slowly into Alex. Cold and mostly unyielding, the intrusion feels peculiar. He's not inherently opposed to peculiar, but it's perhaps not the intimacy he's been looking for.

At least that's what he thinks until Paul turns the damn thing on. He's expecting quick vibrations and a lot of buzz, instead what he gets is a sort of twisting, rolling motion that's deep and slow. If Paul taps the base of the thing one more time, it will probably be right up against his prostate.

"If you want me to fuck you," Alex says breathlessly, "turn it off."

◆

Paul laughs again and obliges, before helping Alex up onto his knees and getting down onto his own elbows and knees for the best angle.

Alex is having none of it. He pulls and pushes at him until he's on his back. "I want to see you."

Paul smiles at Alex's sweetness. He just hopes they're not too damn clumsy and desperate for this to even work at this point.

Alex insists on getting inside before Paul is allowed to touch the toy's remote again, which is probably wise. He can see the concentration on Alex's face from trying not to come too soon and the stretch and burn of having him inside him is still, always, surprising.

He lets Alex get a rhythm going, and it's so good it would be easy to forget the plan. But then he asks Alex if he wants more, with little more than an interrogative sound. Alex understands the unspoken question, and gives Paul a nod in return.

He pushes the slider up on the remote slowly and watches Alex freeze – mouth open, eyes closed – with the pleasure of it. He pushes the heel of his foot against Alex's ass, and urges him to move. Alex does then, and it's clearly all or nothing, because he slams into him with a joyous and deliberate outrage at being made to feel so much.

He doesn't last long, but Paul doesn't care, because it's extraordinary to watch and be both part and cause of.

♦

After he comes, when his hips still and his shoulders sag, Paul has the damn decency to turn the toy off. Alex is grateful and collapses, his forehead to Paul's chest, though he knows he's been spoiled and Paul hasn't come yet.

Eventually, when Alex feels like he can make words, he asks Paul what he wants. Paul tries to have a conversation with him about it.

"No," Alex says. "Tell me what to do."

Something in his voice clearly makes Paul understand that this is what will make him feel best. They're both grateful when Alex is on his knees again. He turns around so his ass is in Paul's face. Paul slowly works the toy out of him while Alex sucks his dick.

When the toy is removed and Alex feels aching and gaping and too emotional, Paul tosses it aside. He puts a hand on the back of Alex's head, holding him still while he fucks up into his mouth until he comes.

Alex sprawls the wrong way on the bed, both of them just breathing. Being here like this feels delightful and easy and not ominous at all. Paul hates that that's a thing to note but is so glad that they have arrived here

♦

Alex is jolted out of sleep by the sound of Paul's phone ringing. Apparently, they will never get through a month without that happening again.

"You have got to be fucking kidding," Paul says groggily, rolling over in bed and into Alex's feet; he's still lying the wrong way on the bed.

Alex pulls a pillow over his face until Paul picks the damn phone up.

"It's Carly," Paul says before he answers it. Alex takes his hands off his face to stare.

Paul doesn't say much, just, "Really? And "Okay," and "Do you need anything?" and "We'll be there." He hangs up, he stares at Alex.

"Do not tell me Carly went into labor three hours after we got away on vacation," Alex says flatly.

"She's on her way to the hospital now."

"Oh my God."

"Liam's flying out from New York."

"Oh my *God*," Alex repeats.

"And we really do have to put on clothes and drive back."

Alex covers his face with his hands and moans.

32

Paul flips on the windshield wipers as they roll out of the driveway and onto the road because it has chosen tonight – of all nights, after months of drought – to finally fucking rain. Alex laughs at the absurdity and sheer luck of their lives, and plugs in Paul's iPod for the drive back. All of the abstracts and hypotheticals they've been trying to make decisions around for the last six months have gotten way less hypothetical and abstract.

The closer they get to the city, the worse the traffic gets. Alex eventually reaches over and keeps his hand on Paul's thigh, because he is white-knuckling; entirely unnecessarily given that by her own account, Carly is fine and in good hands.

"Why aren't you freaking out?" Paul finally asks Alex as they get off at the exit for the hospital.

"You and Liam. Saving my strength."

◆

Ali runs chattering up to Alex as soon as they walk into the waiting room. She holds up a drawing done in purple crayon and waves it eagerly in his face... or as close to his face as she can reach.

Alex crouches down to see it better. "What's that?"

"Dragon! It's bringing the baby," she announces proudly.

Alex looks up at Paul to find him smiling down at them expectantly.

"Don't storks bring babies?" Alex asks her.

"No. It's a good dragon."

"That is totally awesome," Alex says, standing and swinging her up in his arms as he does. Of everything he expects he'll have to deal with in the next twelve or twenty-four or however many hours, the five-year-old is going to be the easiest.

"Hi, Alex." A woman he doesn't recognize greets him with a wave. As Alex walks Ali over to where her paper and coloring supplies are laid out on a table, two women sitting there say hi as well.

Alex looks between them, both thrown off and annoyed at the unfamiliar people. "I've never met you."

"TV. Carly. Why pretend?" the first woman says drily, waving her hand in disinterest.

Alex tries to ignore that it seems like she's had this moment planned for a while. "You're all here with Carly?" he asks instead, looking between them while Ali wiggles out of his arms again back to the floor. Carly said there would be people at the hospital with

611

them, but she wasn't specific as to who or, for that matter, how many.

They nod.

Alex turns plaintively to Paul. "Nobody told me Carly has a coven."

The woman laughs. "You think you're joking."

◆

Alex spends the wait with his nose in one of Paul's film textbooks he'd brought for vacation reading. He also checks his phone at increasingly frequent intervals for any word from Liam. Both activities are better choices than berating Paul for apparently knowing these random women and, as is too often par for the course, never mentioning any of it to him.

At least Alex doesn't think Paul ever dated any of them, but his life is full of surprises and he expects an inevitable correction on the matter.

Several hours pass before another woman – another member of Carly's coven, Alex assumes – comes out and announces to the group that Carly's had the baby, it's a girl, and mother and baby are both healthy and doing fine.

Amid the whoops and hugs, Alex checks his phone again.

"It's a six hour flight," Paul says, when he sees him do it. There's no possible way for Liam to get here yet.

◆

They're sitting around deciding what to do next – no one's eaten dinner, and Ali is getting tired and cranky and insistent about seeing Mom and going home – when Liam finally arrives. He's dressed for October in New York, not L.A., and looks like he isn't completely sure how he's gotten there.

There's a raucous chorus of hellos from Carly's women, and Ali perks up and charges at him with full five-year-old speed, jumping up and down and chattering over everyone until Liam picks her up.

Alex stays put, because as much as he wants to tackle Liam himself, Ali comes first.

The hubbub finally settles down – Liam is verbally grateful to them all for being here, but is insistent that he really does need to get to Carly, and no one wants to delay him any further. He sets Ali down with a promise that he'll be back soon. Liam waves to Paul and then grabs Alex by the wrist. Liam smiles, his blue eyes sparkling, and presses a kiss to Alex's palm before vanishing through the double doors.

◆

Carly's awake and trying to ascertain if the fussy baby is hungry or still indignant about her arrival in a bright, loud world when there's a tap at the door.

Liam is hovering in the door. He smiles hesitantly. "Hi."

"You made it," Carly says cautiously. She's so glad to see him, but she's exhausted and isn't sure yet what happens from here.

"Yeah. Sorry I was late."

Carly laughs. Liam has, as far as she's ever been able to tell, never been on time for anything other than work in his life. That he's apologizing for being late because he's been in New York City for months is just one more reason their lives are strange, and wonderful, and fragile.

Liam's smile grows impossibly wider.

"Come in and see your daughter." Carly says when he doesn't move from the doorway.

He sits down gingerly on the edge of the bed and leans over to get a good look at the baby.

"She's beautiful," he says.

"Yes, well, we have good genes."

Liam runs a fingertip gently over the baby's downy head. "Hi, Victoria."

The baby squinches her face up. Liam laughs softly. He looks thoughtful, and his eyes are bright with tears Carly's not sure are happy or sad. Probably both.

"Can I stay?" he asks quietly.

"For good or for now?"

"Both."

"If you can, you may." Carly is thrilled and relieved to have Liam finally here, but she knows better than to take his presence or his functionality for granted.

"He should be here and he's not. It's always going to be hard. But I want to try."

Carly nods. "Do you want to hold her?"

◆

When Liam finally texts them to come in and say hi, Alex is unsurprised to find Liam not in one of the chairs but sitting at the head of the bed next to Carly, carefully cradling the baby. He shows absolutely no inclination to let anyone else have a turn holding Victoria.

"Sorry to interrupt your vacation," Carly tells them, more amused than apologetic.

"Wouldn't miss it," Paul tells her.

"You know this is only the beginning of the chaos," Carly says.

Paul looks across the room at Alex, who meets his eye and gives him the most private smile. "We can only hope."

"Do you want us to take Ali tonight?" Alex asks.

Carly shakes her head. "Nah. Risa's taking her back to our place, and Liam will be there. You should go back to your getaway. Rest up and all that. We'll need you when you get back."

Paul chuckles. "Yes ma'am."

◆

Finally, Liam lets everyone else have a chance to hold the baby. When it's Paul's turn, Alex steps back to dig out his phone and take a picture. Ali is curled up asleep on Carly's bed next to Liam, who's combing his fingers through her hair. Carly's smiling upon all of them.

Alex sends the picture to Sarah and then checks the time. It's already six in the morning here; on the East Coast, she'll definitely be awake.

He steps outside to make the call. The sun is just starting to come up, and there are puddles everywhere. For once, nothing smells like smoke.

When Sarah picks up, Alex says, "So if you say no at this point that is still completely fair; it's always been your decision, but I wanted to show you what our family looks like."

Sarah laughs. "The baby is adorable. Boy or girl?"

"Girl. They named her Victoria."

Sarah's quiet for a moment. "You all really are something."

"Good something or bad something?"

"*Something* something," she says fondly. "How's Paul doing?"

◆

Paul and Alex debate whether to drive back to the inn or crash at their own house. The sky is lightening with the coming day and they've not slept at all, but they're both too wired to sleep. Better to power through.

Sarah hasn't said yes or no, and in the current situation – new baby and Liam back, but who knows for how long – they're both a little wild with waiting. She asked for time to think, and Alex doesn't know if she's waiting to feel confident in her yes or doesn't want to mar everybody's new-baby happiness with a no.

Paul reaches across from the driver's seat to rub the back of Alex's neck, which at least drops the pitch of his nerves.

The room is exactly the same as when they'd left it fifteen hours before, and Paul crawls into bed while Alex is still taking his shoes and socks off.

"Please tell me your phone is off," Alex mutters, sliding under the covers and into Paul's arms.

He's asleep before Paul answers.

♦

It's early afternoon by the time they wake up again. Paul considers rolling over and going back to sleep, but lying in bed and stroking Alex's side as he slowly comes back to the world is pleasant too. They may never get enough sleep, but he also would like to be conscious and present for at least some of their holiday.

When he finally fumbles for his phone to check the time, he has a missed call and a voicemail, both from Sarah. He sets the phone on speaker and lets the message play so they can both hear it.

He's glad he does, because if Alex wasn't listening to it too, Paul would be afraid it wasn't real.

"So that's yes on baby," he breathes when the message finishes.

Alex nods mutely.

"What's that face?" Paul asks.

Alex's eyes crinkle up when he smiles. "This is the face I had on right before I said yes to Victor."

<h1 style="text-align:center">33</h1>

Bthe time they get back to Los Angeles proper three days later, Carly and Vic (Liam vetoed Vicky as a nickname almost immediately) are home from the hospital and Liam's parents have arrived in town. Alex is far less disturbed by them than Paul, who has clearly suddenly realized what he's gotten them into.

"All I could think about for that entire meal was the breakup pancakes," Paul says to Alex when they drive back from a particularly awkward brunch.

Alex tries not to look as victorious as he feels. This may be what they're doing, but Paul should still suffer a little.

That said, there's plenty of suffering to go around. No matter how much Alex whines, wheedles, and cajoles, neither Paul nor his mother are willing to make the call to Alex's high school to get his transcripts for his college application. To make matters worse, his mother suggests that it would be incredibly inappropriate for Alex to do anything but make the call himself.

"You're their most famous graduate," she says, when Alex informs her he'll just make their assistant do it.

"I'm their only famous graduate," Alex says sullenly.

"And you never visit or do anything to make these kids' lives better."

"I'll write a fucking check." Alex feels about as ugly as he ever has since fame has become a thing – and an increasingly normal thing – in his life.

"Those kids are not your enemy. Which you should probably get your head around, if you and Paul are going to have one."

"I'll like *our* kid."

"Sure," his mom says. "But how happy is anyone going to be if you're afraid of your kid's friends?"

◆

With *Winsome* days away from wrapping for good it falls to Alex to schedule all of the baby-related logistics. Their surrogate is over the moon that they're starting the process for certain this time, and Sarah is nervous but excited about flying to L.A. for a week for the procedure, a vacation, and to see Carly and Liam and meet their kids.

The schedule is a nightmare. Somehow, Alex doesn't realize that the day of the baby procedure is the same as the closing on Victor's house until he gets the email from Nigel reminding him of the date and stating that he's coming out to L.A. to finalize everything. That the *Icarus* premiere is forty-eight hours after all of this is just icing.

Alex isn't sure if he's horrified or relieved that Nigel has some common sense and suggests a final meeting of Team Victor at the house before the sale is finalized.

After he checks with Liam, Alex invites Sarah along. That will be a hell of a capstone on her whirlwind L.A. tour/medical trip, but also, if anyone deserves a glimpse into the house that made all of their lives possible, it's her.

♦

On the day, Alex is sorry Sarah doesn't get to see the house as it was when Victor was still alive. Most everything of any personal significance is long gone into storage or various people's homes. Much of what remains will simply be sold at auction. Modernist furniture may be ugly, but it's certainly valuable.

The emptiness and staging of the house doesn't make being there easier for any of them. The house is filled with ghosts, not of Victor, but of who each of them was in relation to him. Carly, with baby Vic in a sling, still seems happy in the sunlight of the kitchen. Liam is perturbed that the company that staged the house rearranged the living room, swapping the piano and the couch. Paul, his sister at his side, stares at the in-built shelves in Victor's office that used to hold his awards; those now live at the *Winsome* offices, at least until they get relocated to wherever Paul is next. Darcy and Jackson talk quietly by the dining room table. When Alex finds himself wanting to sit down on the floor by the now emptied filing cabinets, he forces himself to go down to the basement instead.

He's tempted to say *I was never afraid of you* to the echoing space, because that's what would happen in a movie. But it's not true, so he stands there, walking in a slow circle for the thirty seconds he can stand to, before he jogs back upstairs. At least he's sure it really happened now.

When he gets back upstairs, Carly's being impatient and sliding her copies of Victor's keys back and forth across the kitchen counter. The noise is intolerable to Alex, but when he looks around it's clear that no one else – not even Liam – cares. Possibly because Nigel is pouring out shots for all of them. On some level Alex is almost irritated. They've been doing this for months, and this doesn't seem like enough to have driven across town for. On the other hand, at least this is finally, *finally* going to be over.

Nigel makes a speech. His words are scaled appropriately – after all, there are only eight of them there – but it's still a speech. Everyone downs their shots with an enthusiasm that's a testament to how terrible the last six months have been. Liam still glowers briefly at Darcy when she slams her empty shot glass down on the piano.

Because Darcy is sometimes still a child, she makes an irritated face at him in response. He laughs at her before going back to fidgeting with the metronome on top of the piano.

With nothing left to do except be together, conversation turns to everything that's happened recently and is going to happen soon. Gemma should be here too, Alex thinks; she was the first member of his chosen family, and this moment feels like one for all of their clan.

After a few minutes, Liam makes a softly irritated noise.

"What are you doing?" Carly turns to ask him over her shoulder.

"The metronome's jammed," he says, frowning over the back panel of it.

"Why does Victor have a metronome? I didn't think he played," Darcy says.

"He didn't," Liam tells her. "The metronome was for writing."

Darcy is more interested in Alex complaining about Mark than in Victor's writing habits, and the conversation drifts away from Liam again.

Everyone is startled out of their grumbling about the social part of their very strange jobs by Liam fumbling the metronome as he finally manages to force the back cover off. Not only does it hit the top of the piano, causing Nigel to wince, the body of the metronome also skids out of his hands.

By the time everyone has turned toward the commotion, the dismantled timekeeper is not what any of them are staring at. A gold ring, which must have been what was jamming the device in the first place, spins like a coin on the top of the piano.

"Oh my God," Alex breathes. All he wants to do is turn and see the look on everyone else's faces, but he's afraid if he does, the ring will disappear. It doesn't seem fair to do that to Liam.

"You got anything on this?" Nigel asks Jackson, but Jackson just slowly shakes his head.

Even Darcy doesn't speak as they all wait for the ring to stop spinning. Once it does, no one moves.

"What the actual fuck?" Paul says quietly.

Sarah raises a questioning eyebrow at Alex. He shrugs at her.

"Liam?" Carly says quietly.

He shakes his head.

"Jesus Christ, it's not going to bite," she replies.

"Yeah," Alex says, "that's what you think."

Somehow that earns him a smile from Liam, who then, very politely, asks everyone if they could please stop staring. Then Liam snatches the ring up, opens the sliding glass door to the yard and pool area, and slips outside.

"So what are the chances that that was like his mom's wedding band or like something faintly sane?" Jackson finally asks.

Nigel gives him a withering look. "None," he and Alex say at the same time.

♦

"To be clear," Sarah asks, once she, Paul, and Alex are in the car, "We just witnessed a proposal from a dead man?" It's phrased as a question, but Paul knows it's not.

"Was there anything in the diaries about this?" he asks Alex. He assumes there was something, and that Alex didn't say anything at the house because Nigel and everyone else was there. Which Paul has to admit is somewhat fair, and even a touching bit of care and loyalty for Victor's privacy from a man who hated him so much when he was alive.

"Specifically, no." Alex says. "Generally, yes. Sort of. By omission."

Paul rolls his eyes over with a look that says *specify*.

Alex says, "Victor didn't write about the most important things."

"That doesn't clarify anything," Paul says.

"Then you haven't been paying attention." Alex sounds smug.

"I don't know what to think about it," Paul says. "Other than that Victor was a mysterious asshole."

"I've been telling you that for years. Why, what do you think I'm going to tell you?"

"I don't know, you were the one lying about skulking around a dead man's house for weeks," Paul shoots back.

From the backseat, Sarah makes a sound that Paul knows is her trying not to laugh. Clearly she and Alex are well suited to each other. Paul wonders how terrified he should be about their offspring.

"What?" Alex protests. "Victor never wrote 'I bought Liam a weird not-wedding ring today!' And it's not like I went through his bank statements or receipts or anything – "

"No, just his diaries and his drawings," Paul deadpans.

" – so fuck if I know anything about when or where he bought it." Paul gives him a skeptical look. "I swear!"

♦

Carly drives as Liam sits next to her in the passenger seat, staring at his hands. The rings don't match – hers with Liam is a wider band and platinum – but there's something to the symmetry that's probably pleasing to Liam beyond the obvious.

"Did you know anything about this?" Carly asks.

"No."

"Does it make any sense to you?" she asks.

"Not really," Liam says. "I keep thinking about what if we hadn't found it."

"It wouldn't have changed anything."

"Yes it would," Liam says. "It would have changed the story."

Carly smiles and shakes her head. While Liam's new ring maybe proves something, it also doesn't really prove anything at all. Love is faith. Whether you have jewelry to go with it or not.

34

The baby procedure goes routinely. They'll know if it worked or not in about a week; until then, all they can do is wait.

Liam, when Alex drops by their house to give him Victor's sketches, laughs way too hard at Alex's mortified account of his own role in the baby-making process. "In a *cup*, Lee," Alex whines.

Carly is completely unsympathetic, but Liam can't stop laughing.

Alex is afraid the sketches will ruin Liam's good mood. Liam does go quiet when he finally opens the box into which Alex has carefully packed all the ones he thinks his friend could possibly want. But then he smiles, carefully brushing his thumb over the corner of one of the sketches where a date is scribbled.

"That was the day Carly and I got married," he says so softly Alex can hardly hear him.

♦

Alex gets up early the morning of the *Icarus Experiment* premiere. Which is a questionable choice when he was up late driving Sarah to the airport and when their assistant and a stylist are coming over at two to get them ready for the premiere. But he lies to Paul one more time, and says he's going climbing, when he's really, really not.

He can no longer drive to Victor's house. Instead, he heads into Downtown, to a Los Angeles he essentially never sees, run by the people who pretend that the industry doesn't exist, and that they don't hate toiling not in its service, but its shadow. He parks in a garage a block from the Cathedral. He has no idea why he avoids its lot, but it's a creepy place, and he'd rather not be mistaken for being any part of it. He's here to visit the dead, and Victor had been sure to make it an ordeal.

He's as efficient as he can be, jogging across the street and through the courtyard with constellations etched into the concrete – a welcome to atheists or the city's stars, Alex isn't sure. He slips into the cathedral and walks along the somber hallway that wraps around the sanctuary. He tries to ignore the fact that, being Sunday, mass is on. He's grateful that Catholics seem to keep their heads bowed. The churches of his childhood were always filled with people turning their palms and faces up for blessings that, like rain, would never come.

He takes the stairs down to the mausoleum slowly, but only because he's pretty sure appearances demand it. He stifles a laugh at the thought of the gossip item – *J. Alex Cook seen running in church!* – and then wends his way to Victor's niche. It's in the back, past

621

Gregory Peck and a maze of small chapels.

When he gets there, Alex frowns. While he doesn't necessarily expect to feel Victor's presence there, he wouldn't be surprised if he did. Victor was creepy like that, and if anyone could have the force to exist through ash it would be him.

"Well, this feels stupid," Alex says.

That he knows Victor would laugh helps.

"You know, you could have saved everyone so much grief if you'd ever told anyone the stuff you wrote down. Or the stuff you didn't."

Alex stares at the name carved into the marble. "Somehow it's even more annoying to get the silent treatment from you now." He sits down against the opposite wall, his back to a nun who died in the 1960s.

Alex has a lot to say, and most of it he doesn't say aloud, in part because he can hear other people moving around the space, which echoes spectacularly. He wonders how he'll know when he's done or that he's been heard. Even if he doesn't really believe in ghosts and spirits and souls, regardless of how essential Paul is to him or how many times he has probably known Liam.

Ultimately, he decides it's a choice, just like everything else. When he gets up to leave, he presses a palm against the stone too long for a man that had hated to be touched – which is exactly why Alex does it – and says thank you. Then he leaves, smiling smugly.

◆

That evening, Alex and Paul attend *The Icarus Experiment* premiere. After everything that's happened in the past six months, it's odd to see his castmates and director again. Australia seems like a lifetime ago.

Alex also has no idea when he'll next be attending an event like this for a project of his own; for the next couple of years, he'll be playing a supporting role to Paul's appearances. The reversal is odd to contemplate, but no odder than anything else that's changed in their lives recently.

Being happily on Paul's arm after so many weeks of performing intentional cuteness in public after the cheating scandal is a relief. With Victoria in the world, Liam back, Victor's house sold, and good news about their own future family hopefully being imminent, today is anything but a performance.

Alex always gets held up more on the carpet than Paul, simply because he's an actor and Paul's not. Today, Alex pulls at his husband's arm to keep him close and snarks back at a photographer that rudely hollers at him to get out of the shot.

"I love that," Paul whispers at him. It sounds dirty.

The photographers may be ruder, but they're easier to deal with than the video stuff. Alex struggles to focus on the questions in front of him amid the din all around him. He wonders how the hell Liam has ever managed to do this. That maybe Liam's brain is an asset in this strange, shitty business isn't a thought Alex has considered before, but it makes as much sense as anything. He wishes that he and Carly were here, but Liam's still adjusting and Victoria is so young. Alex knows he's being selfish.

He prattles something about the hilarious terrors of the plane ride into Darwin from Sydney when Paul's cell phone goes off. Paul awkwardly pats his pockets, apparently having forgotten how clothes or hands work.

Alex rolls his eyes and gives him an indulgent smile.

With a mouthed apology, Paul steps out of the frame.

"The horrors of the digital age," Alex quips.

When Paul slides back into the picture, he puts an arm around Alex's waist to whisper news from the doctor in his ear.

Alex's face splits into a grin.

"Something we should know?" the interviewer asks.

Alex shakes his head. "You shouldn't know anything," he says playfully. "But if you're very, very good, and we're very, very lucky, maybe we'll tell you next year."

More by These Authors

Visit www.Avian30.com to join Erin and Racheline's mailing list and get information about new releases!

After the Gold

For over a decade, world-champion ice skaters Katie Nowacki and Brendan Reid have been partners in every way but one. But now that their electric on-ice chemistry has led them to Olympic gold, will Brendan be able to convince Katie to trust him with the off-ice intimacy that only spelled disaster in their past?

A Queen from the North

Library Journal's Best Indie Ebook 2017

Lady Amelia Brockett, known to her family as Meels, is having the Worst. Christmas. Ever. Dumped by her boyfriend and rejected from graduate school, her parents deem her the failure of the family.
But when her older brother tries to cheer her with a trip to the races, a chance meeting with Arthur, the widowed, playboy Prince of Wales, offers Amelia the opportunity to change her life – and Britain's fortunes – forever.

The Art of Three

24-year-old Jamie Conway has just moved to London, is starring in his first feature film, and hasn't yet figured out how to navigate fame, adulthood, or being bisexual in public.

When Jamie hooks up with his much older polyamorous costar Callum Griffith-Davies, he sets off a chain of delightful complications, including an unexpected affair with Callum's no-nonsense wife, Nerea.

This Rainbow Awards-winning romance features three countries, two men, one woman, and absolutely no love triangles.

The Love in Los Angeles Series

Starling, Book 1
Evergreen, Book 1.5 — A Holiday Story
Doves, Book 2
Phoenix, Book 3
Cardinal, Book 4
More coming soon!

Love in Los Angeles is a queer romance series, with elements of magical realism, set in and around the TV and movie industry.

When J. Alex Cook, a production assistant on The Fourth Estate (one of network TV's hottest shows), is accidentally catapulted to stardom, he finds himself struggling to navigate both fame and a relationship with Paul, one of Fourth's key writers. Love in Los Angeles is the story of Paul and Alex – and of their friends and family – as they navigate love, and life, both in and beyond Los Angeles.

The Love's Labours Series

Midsummer, Book 1
Twelfth Night, Book 2
More coming soon!

42-year-old John Lyonel has never been attracted to men before, but falling for 25-year-old Michael Hilliard is actually the least screwed up thing that's happened to him in years. Even if sometimes he thinks Michael's a changeling.

Short stories:

Sample and Hold
Off-Kilter
Lake Effect
Snare
The Omega's Reluctant Alpha
Alpha Bodyguard
The Hart and the Hound